1/23

DOÑA QUIXOTE
RISE OF THE KNIGHT

REY TERCIERO
art by **MONICA M. MAGAÑA**

HENRY HOLT AND COMPANY
NEW YORK

To my abuela.

Te amo. Te amo por siempre.

—Rey

For my very own abuelo, Miguel Hernandez,

who taught me to always follow my creative dreams;

and for Mom and Dad and my whole family—this is for you.

—Monica

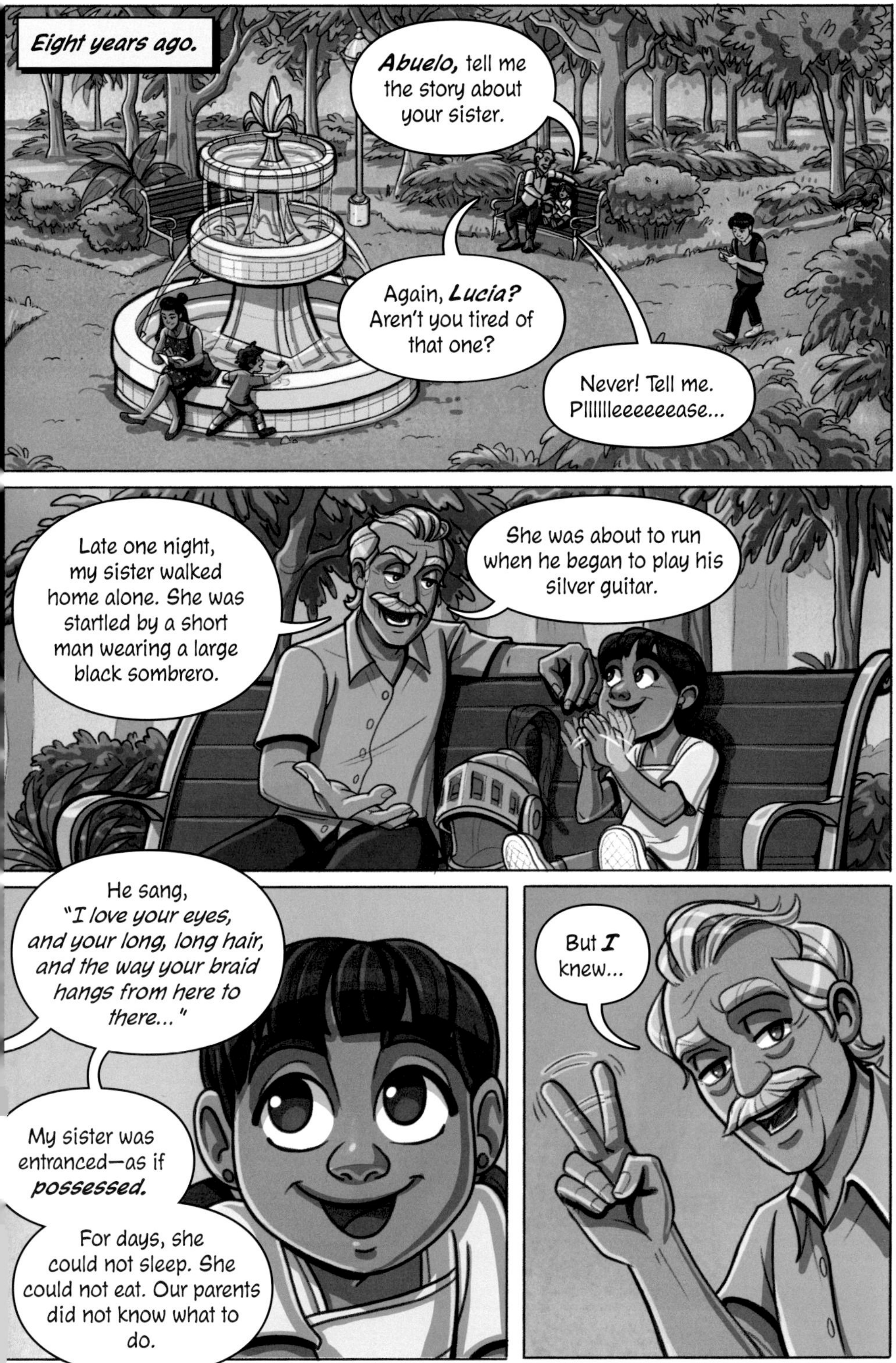

Eight years ago.
Abuelo, tell me the story about your sister.
Again, *Lucia?* Aren't you tired of that one?
Never! Tell me. Pllllleeeeeease...
Late one night, my sister walked home alone. She was startled by a short man wearing a large black sombrero.
She was about to run when he began to play his silver guitar.
He sang, *"I love your eyes, and your long, long hair, and the way your braid hangs from here to there..."*
My sister was entranced—as if ***possessed.***
For days, she could not sleep. She could not eat. Our parents did not know what to do.
But ***I*** knew...

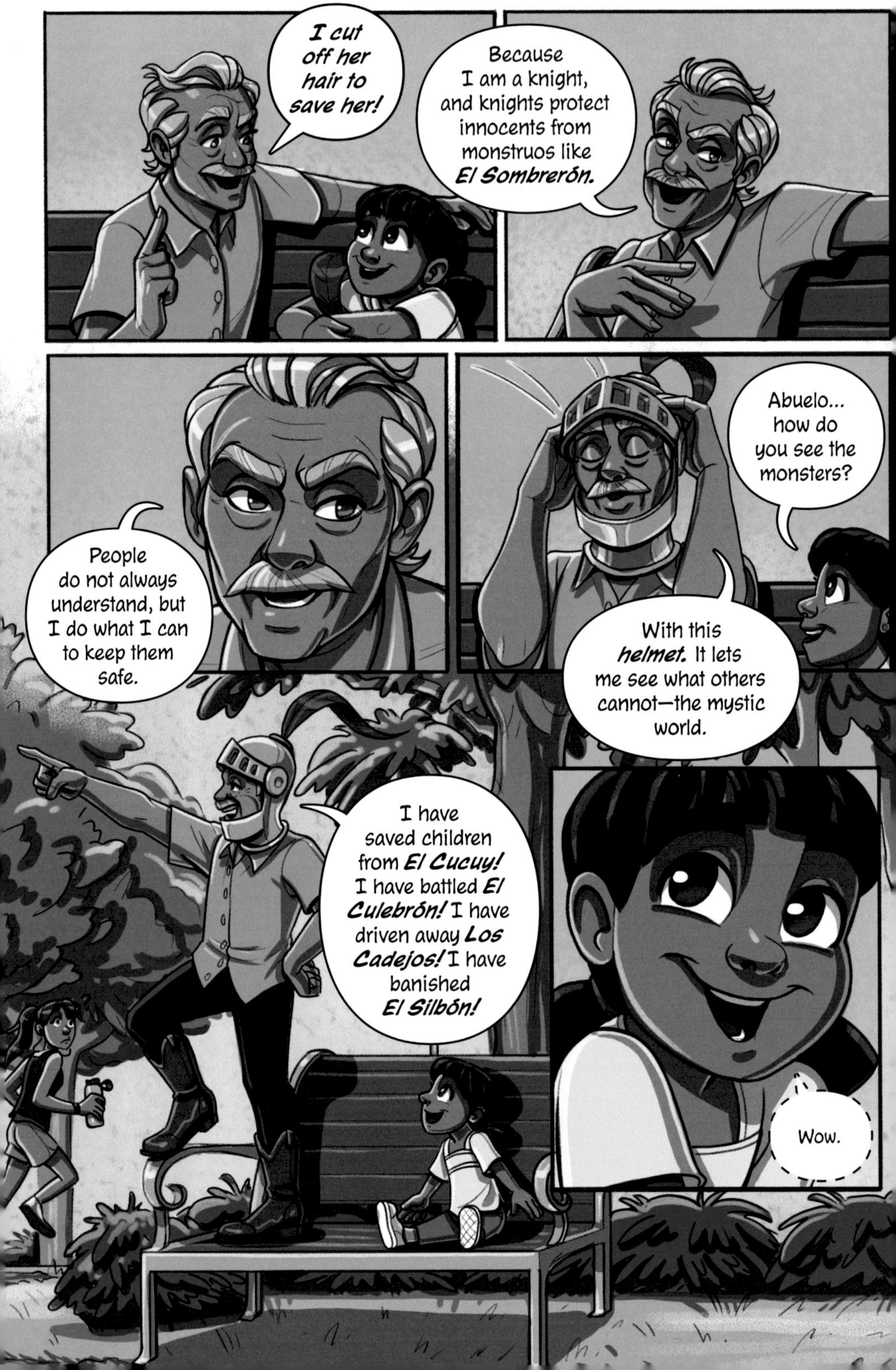
I cut off her hair to save her!
Because I am a knight, and knights protect innocents from monstruos like El Sombrerón.
People do not always understand, but I do what I can to keep them safe.
Abuelo... how do you see the monsters?
With this helmet. It lets me see what others cannot—the mystic world.
I have saved children from El Cucuy! I have battled El Culebrón! I have driven away Los Cadejos! I have banished El Silbón!
Wow.

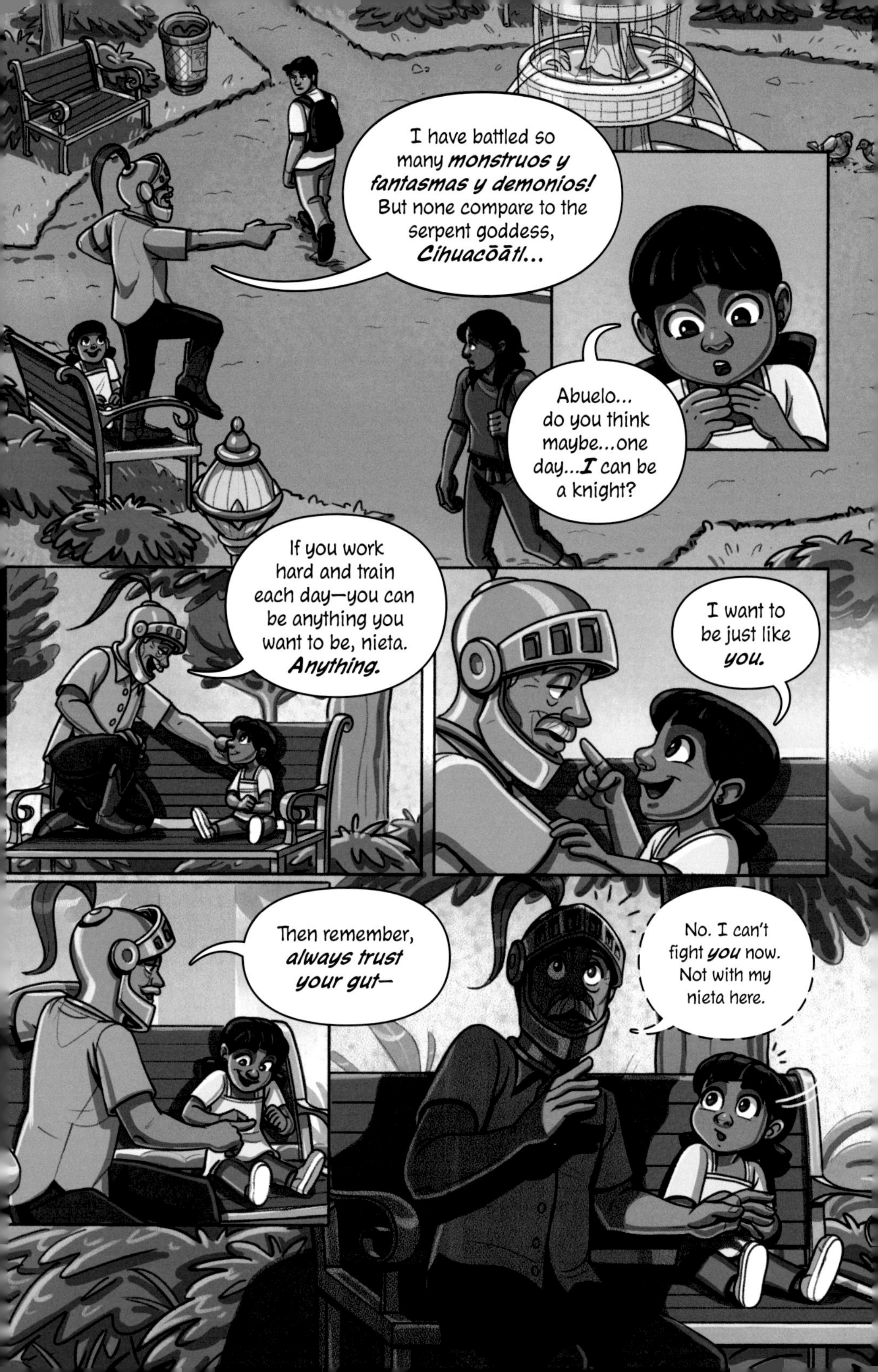
I have battled so many monstruos y fantasmas y demonios! But none compare to the serpent goddess, Cihuacōātl...
Abuelo... do you think maybe...one day...I can be a knight?
If you work hard and train each day—you can be anything you want to be, nieta. Anything.
I want to be just like you.
Then remember, always trust your gut—
No. I can't fight you now. Not with my nieta here.

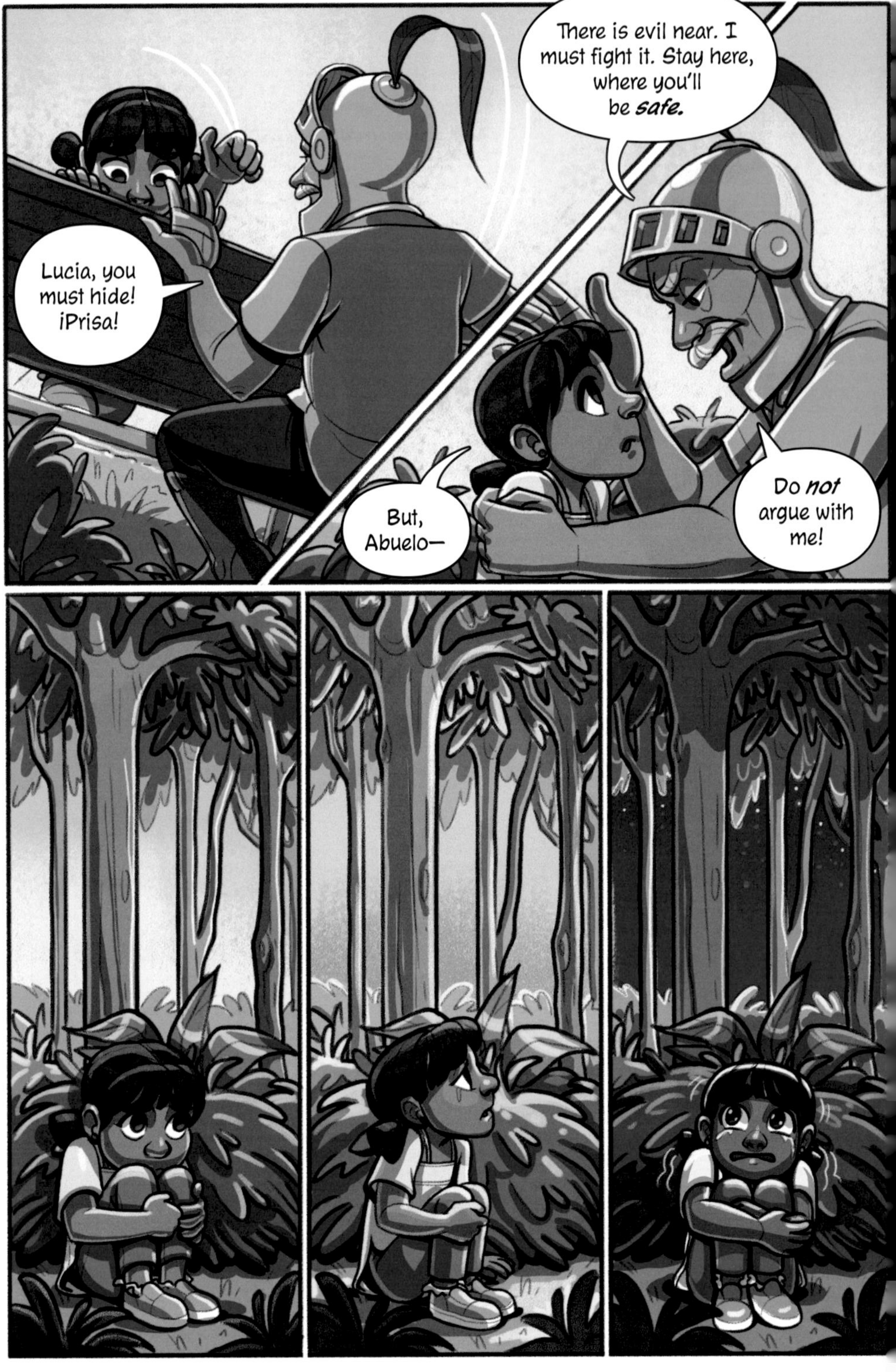
Lucia, you must hide! ¡Prisa!
There is evil near. I must fight it. Stay here, where you'll be *safe.*
But, Abuelo—
Do *not* argue with me!

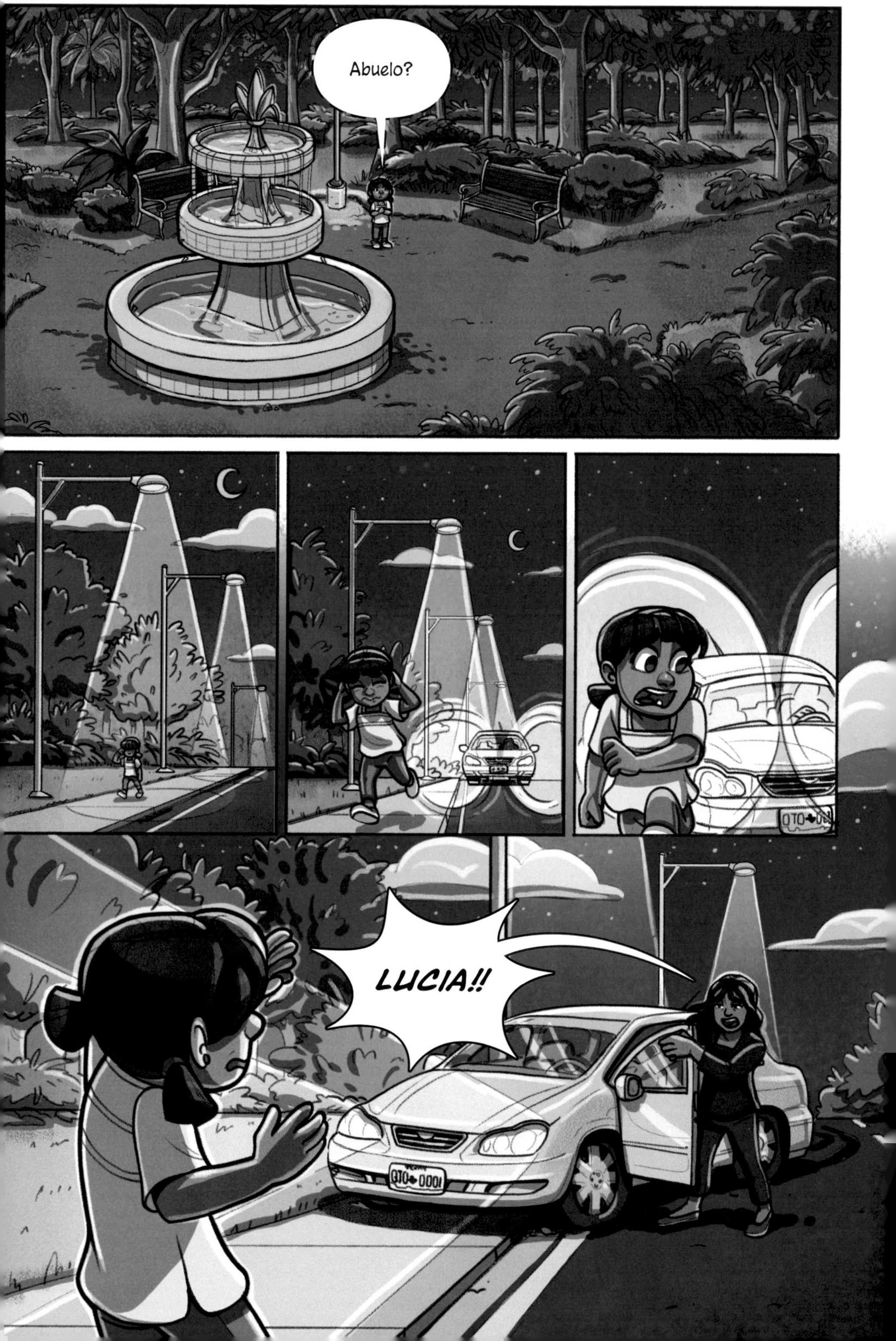
Abuelo?
LUCIA!!

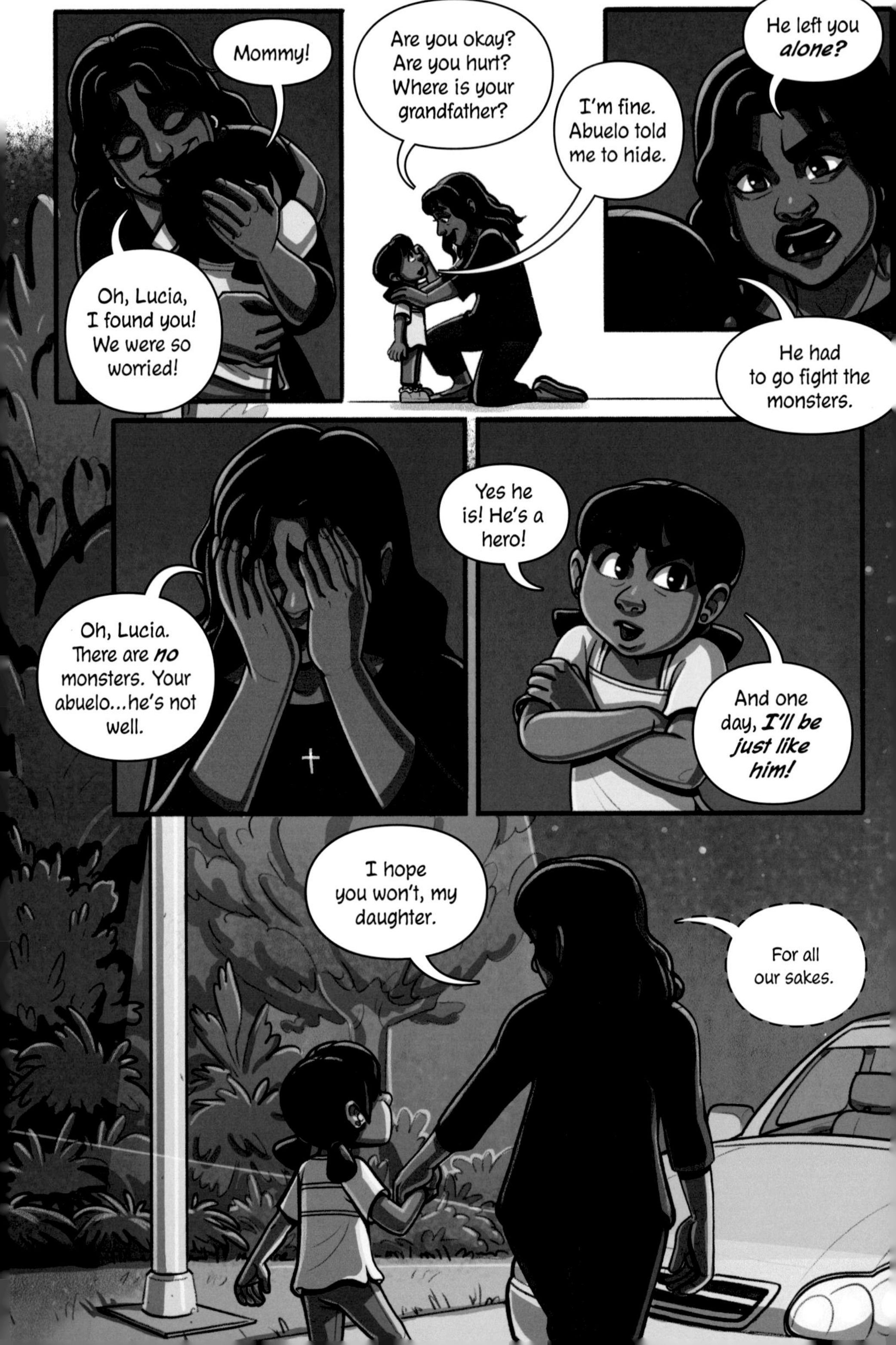
Mommy!
Oh, Lucia, I found you! We were so worried!
Are you okay? Are you hurt? Where is your grandfather?
I'm fine. Abuelo told me to hide.
He left you *alone?*
He had to go fight the monsters.
Oh, Lucia. There are *no* monsters. Your abuelo...he's not well.
Yes he is! He's a hero!
And one day, ***I'll be just like him!***
I hope you won't, my daughter.
For all our sakes.

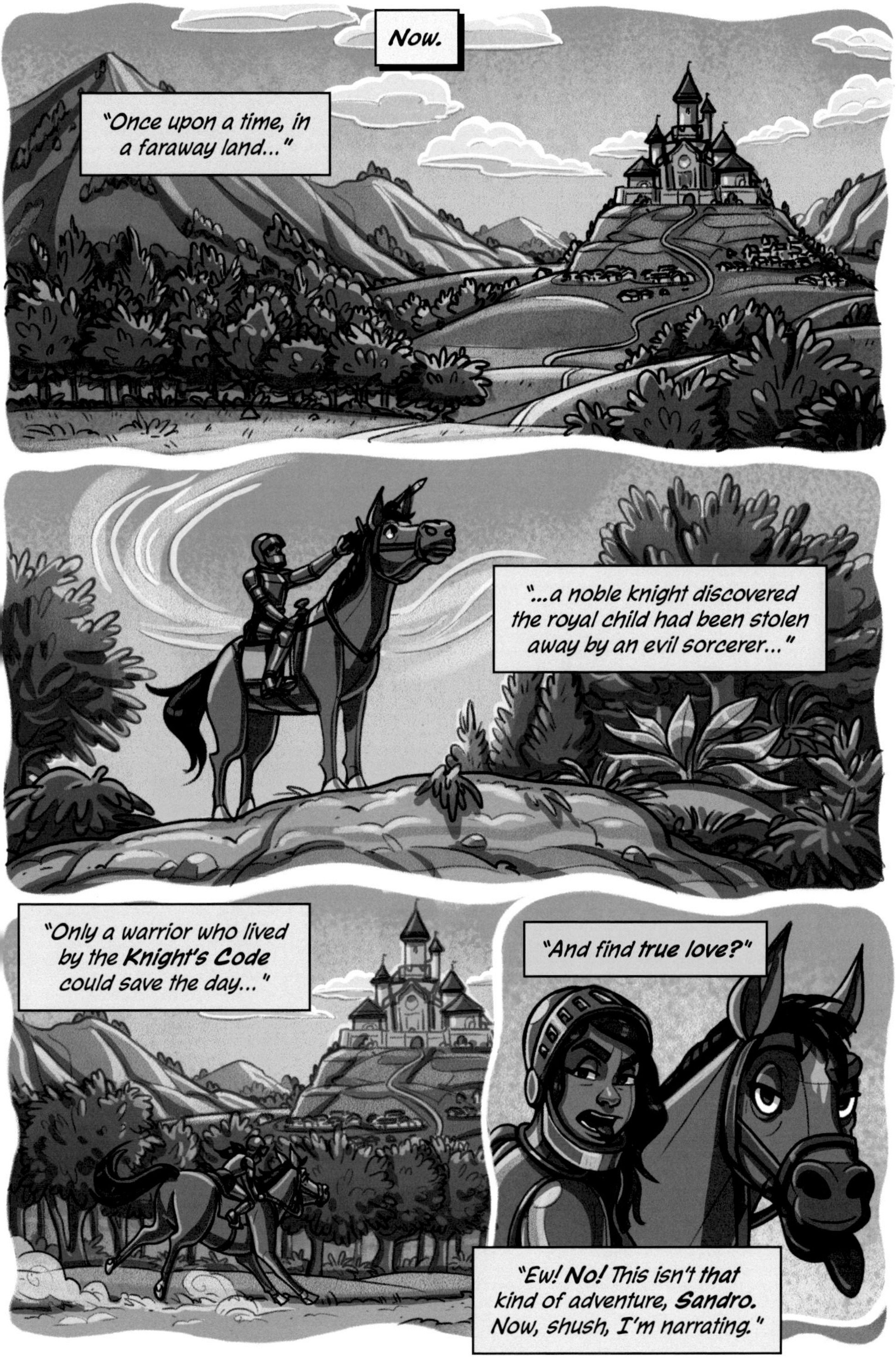
Now.
"Once upon a time, in a faraway land..."
"...a noble knight discovered the royal child had been stolen away by an evil sorcerer..."
"Only a warrior who lived by the **Knight's Code** could save the day..."
"And find true love?"
"Ew! **No!** This isn't that kind of adventure, **Sandro.** Now, shush, I'm narrating."

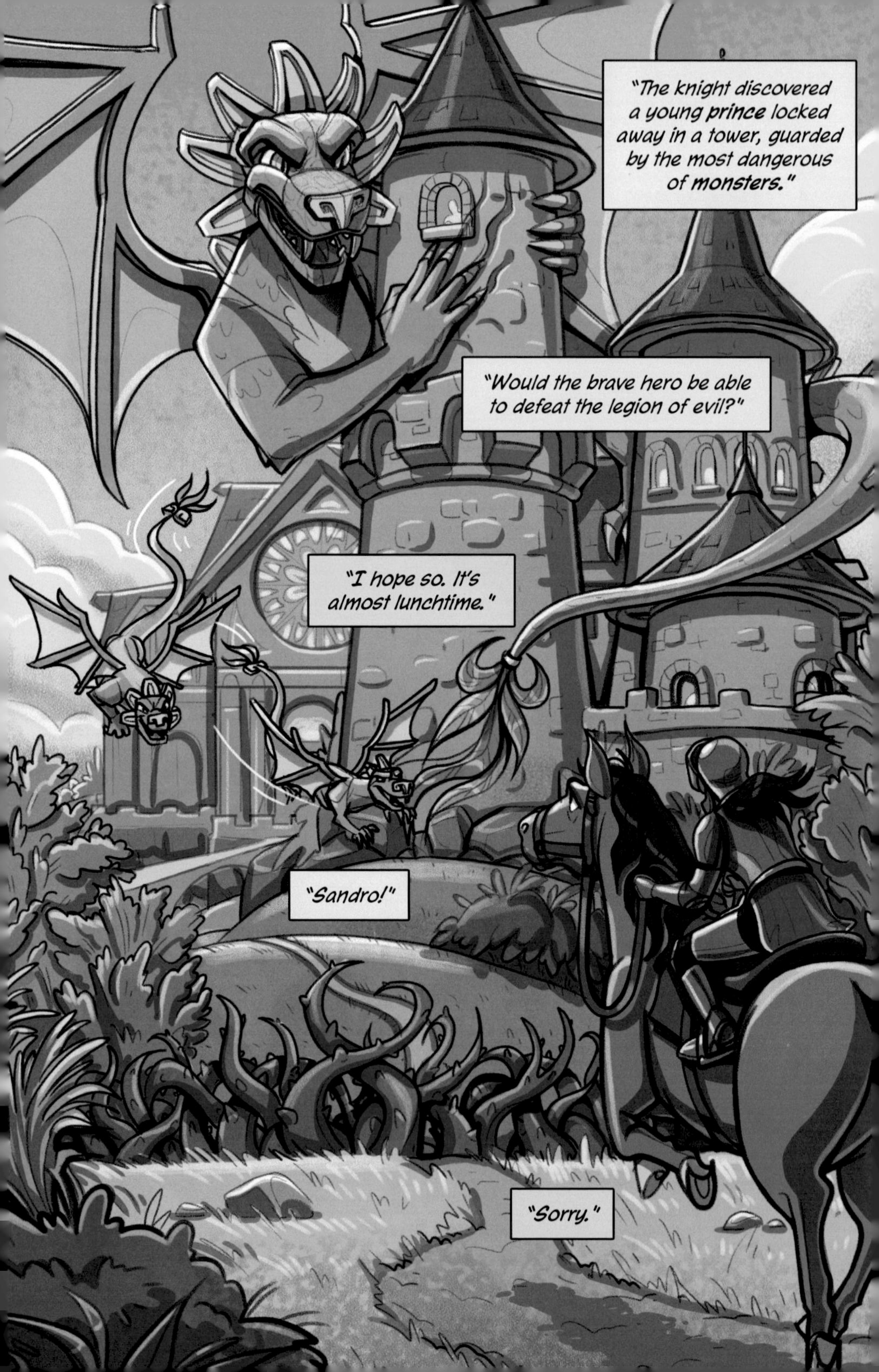
"The knight discovered a young prince locked away in a tower, guarded by the most dangerous of monsters."
"Would the brave hero be able to defeat the legion of evil?"
"I hope so. It's almost lunchtime."
"Sandro!"
"Sorry."

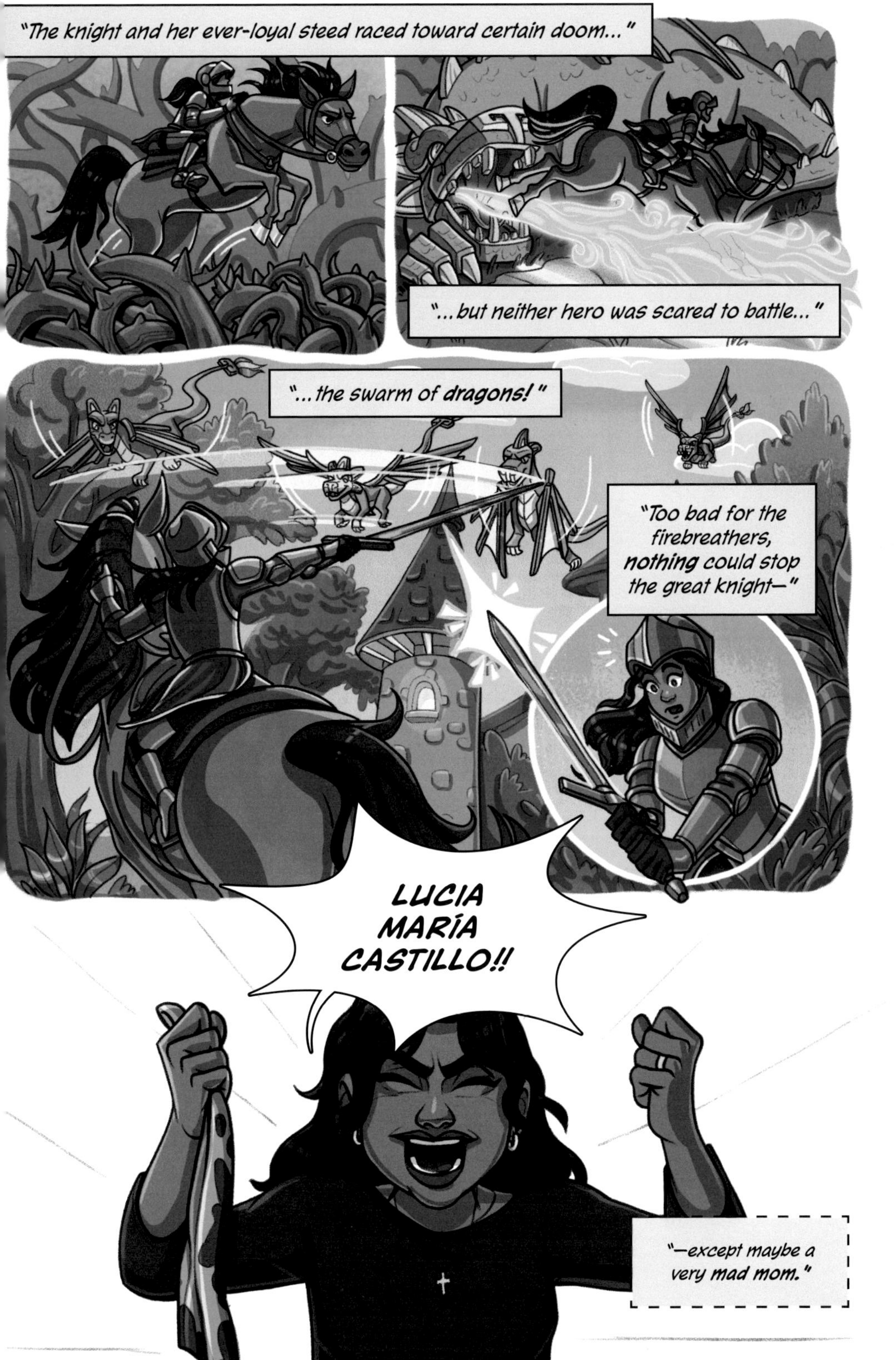
"The knight and her ever-loyal steed raced toward certain doom..."
"...but neither hero was scared to battle..."
"...the swarm of dragons!"
"Too bad for the firebreathers, nothing could stop the great knight—"
LUCIA MARÍA CASTILLO!!
"—except maybe a very mad mom."

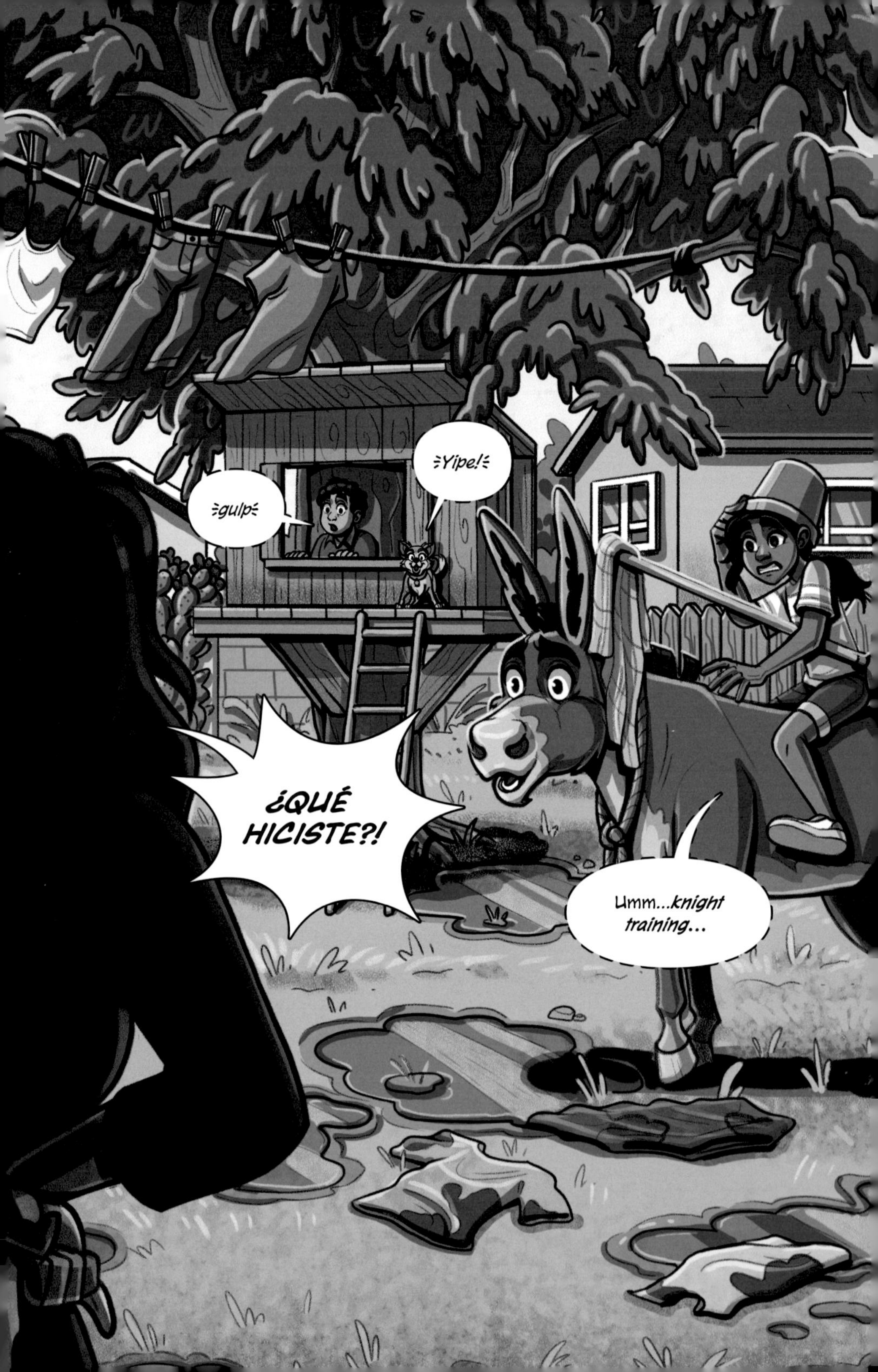
gulp
Yipe!
¿QUÉ HICISTE?!
Umm...knight training...

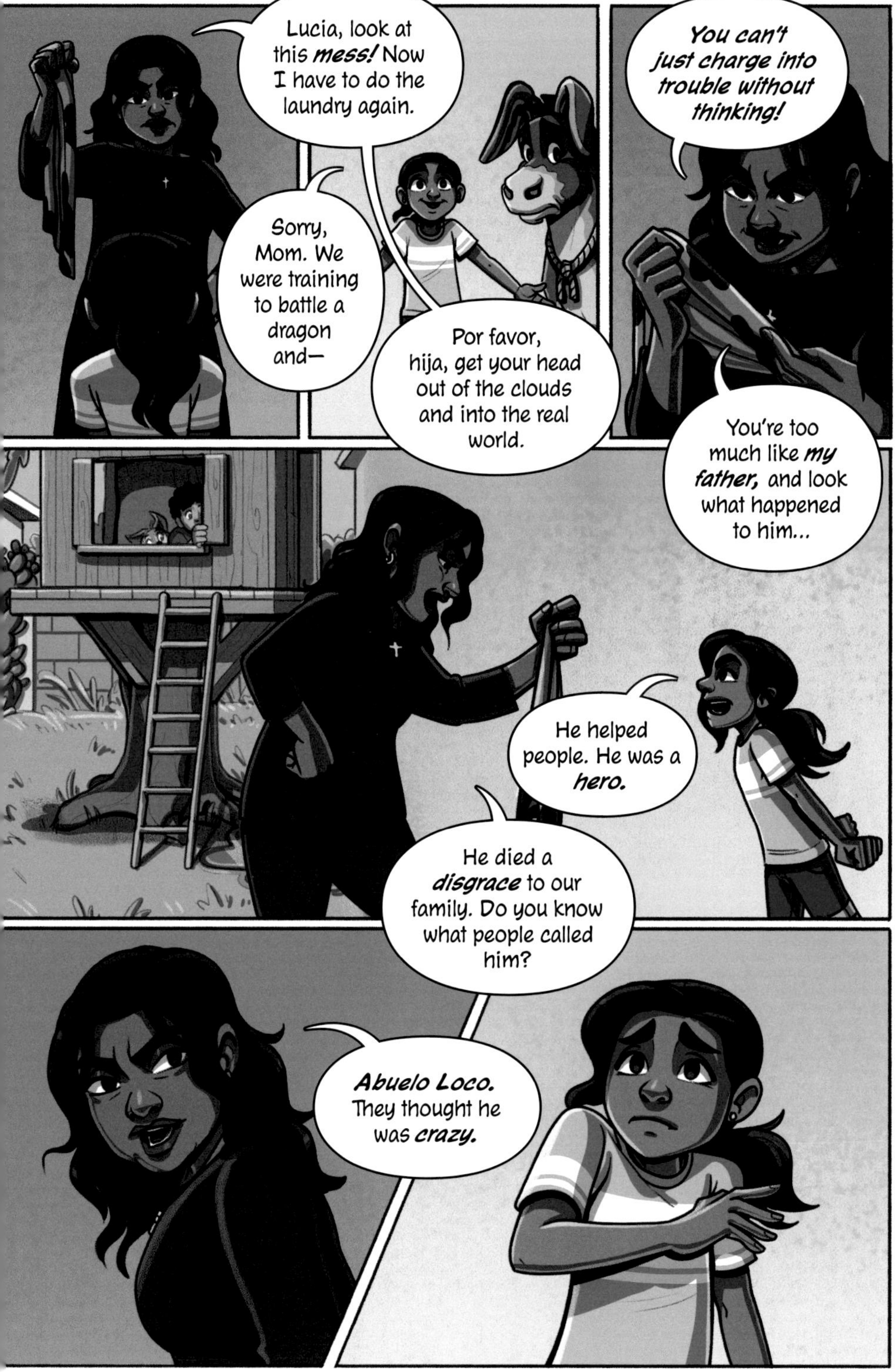

Lucia, look at this *mess!* Now I have to do the laundry again.
Sorry, Mom. We were training to battle a dragon and—
Por favor, hija, get your head out of the clouds and into the real world.
You can't just charge into trouble without thinking!
You're too much like *my father,* and look what happened to him...
He helped people. He was a *hero.*
He died a *disgrace* to our family. Do you know what people called him?
Abuelo Loco. They thought he was *crazy.*

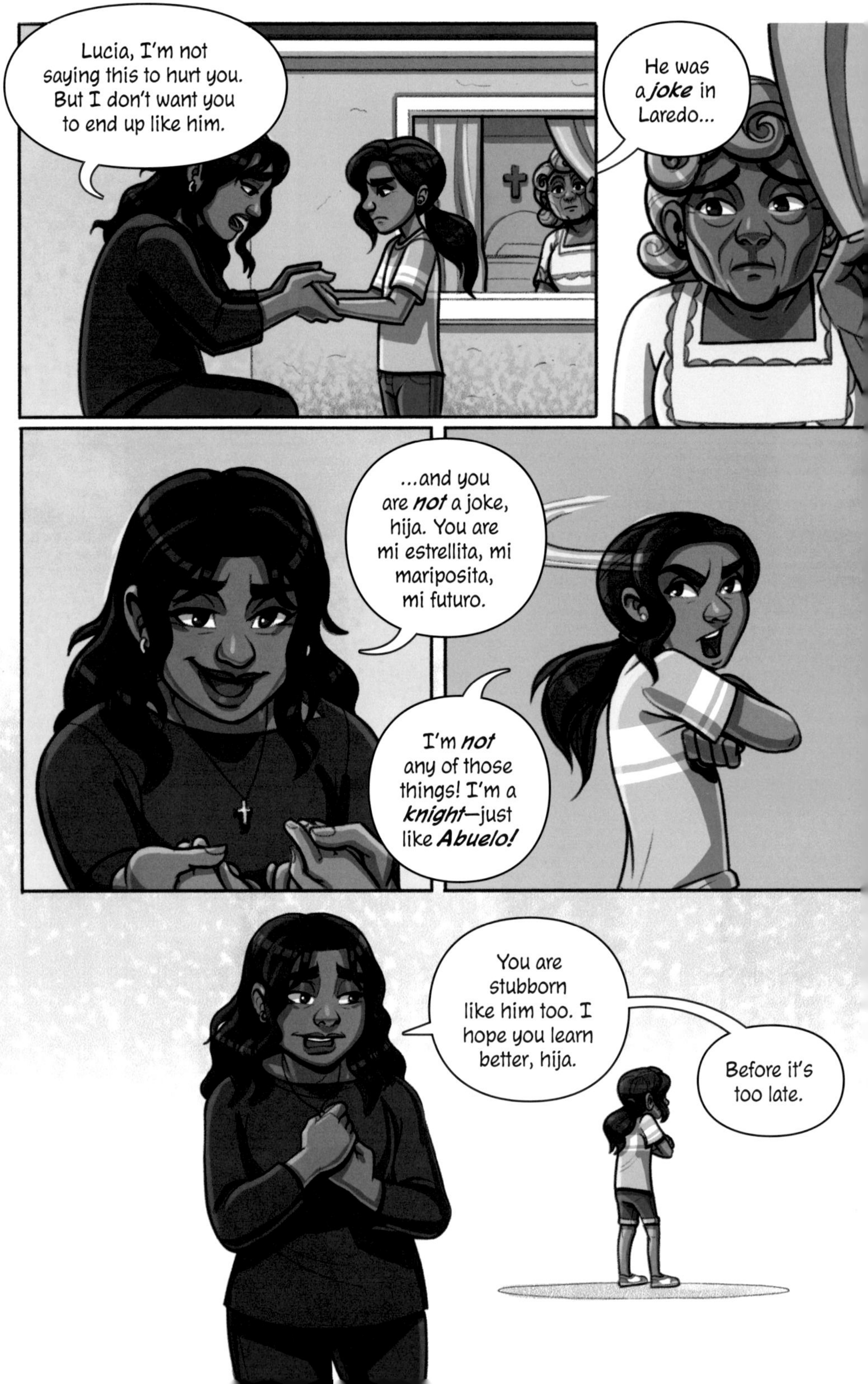
Lucia, I'm not saying this to hurt you. But I don't want you to end up like him.
He was a *joke* in Laredo...
...and you are *not* a joke, hija. You are mi estrellita, mi mariposita, mi futuro.
I'm *not* any of those things! I'm a *knight*—just like *Abuelo!*
You are stubborn like him too. I hope you learn better, hija.
Before it's too late.

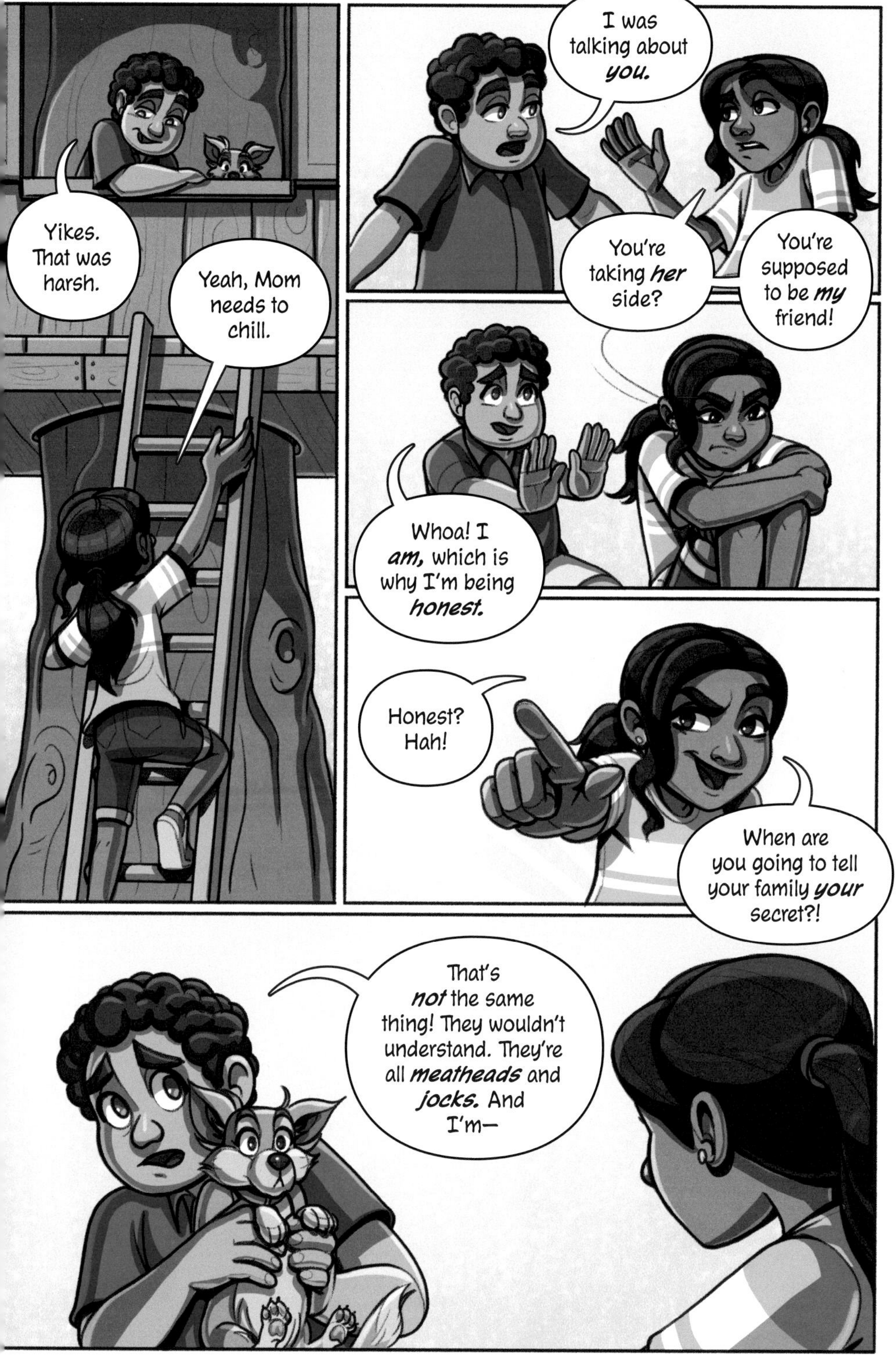
Yikes. That was harsh.
Yeah, Mom needs to chill.
I was talking about *you.*
You're taking *her* side?
You're supposed to be *my* friend!
Whoa! I *am,* which is why I'm being *honest.*
Honest? Hah!
When are you going to tell your family *your* secret?!
That's *not* the same thing! They wouldn't understand. They're all *meatheads* and *jocks.* And I'm—

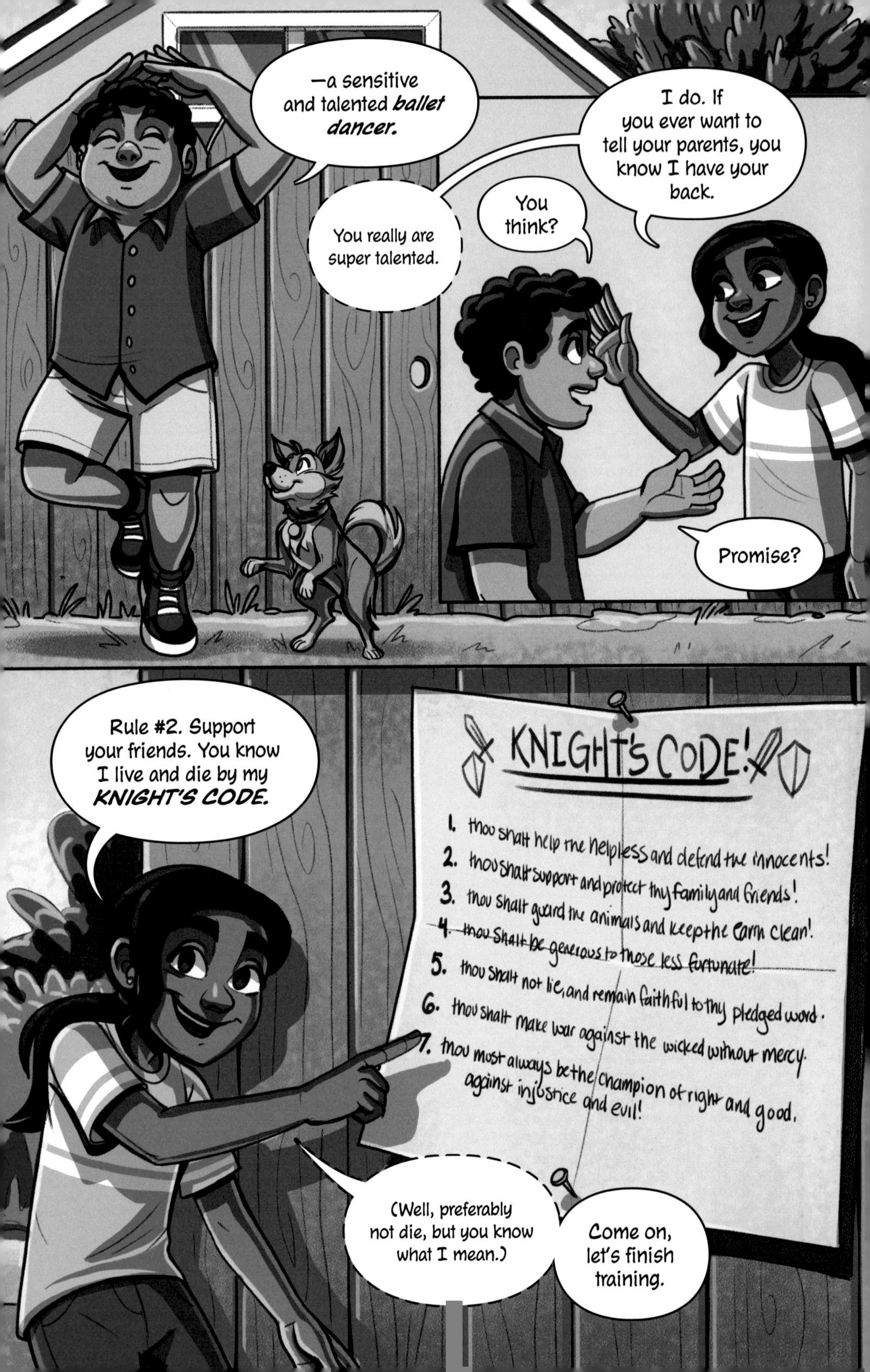
—a sensitive and talented *ballet dancer.*
I do. If you ever want to tell your parents, you know I have your back.
You really are super talented.
You think?
Promise?
Rule #2. Support your friends. You know I live and die by my *KNIGHT'S CODE.*
KNIGHT'S CODE!
1. thou shalt help the helpless and defend the innocents!
2. thou shalt support and protect thy family and friends!
3. thou shalt guard the animals and keep the earth clean!
4. thou shalt be generous to those less fortunate!
5. thou shalt not lie, and remain faithful to thy pledged word.
6. thou shalt make war against the wicked without mercy.
7. thou must always be the champion of right and good, against injustice and evil!
(Well, preferably not die, but you know what I mean.)
Come on, let's finish training.

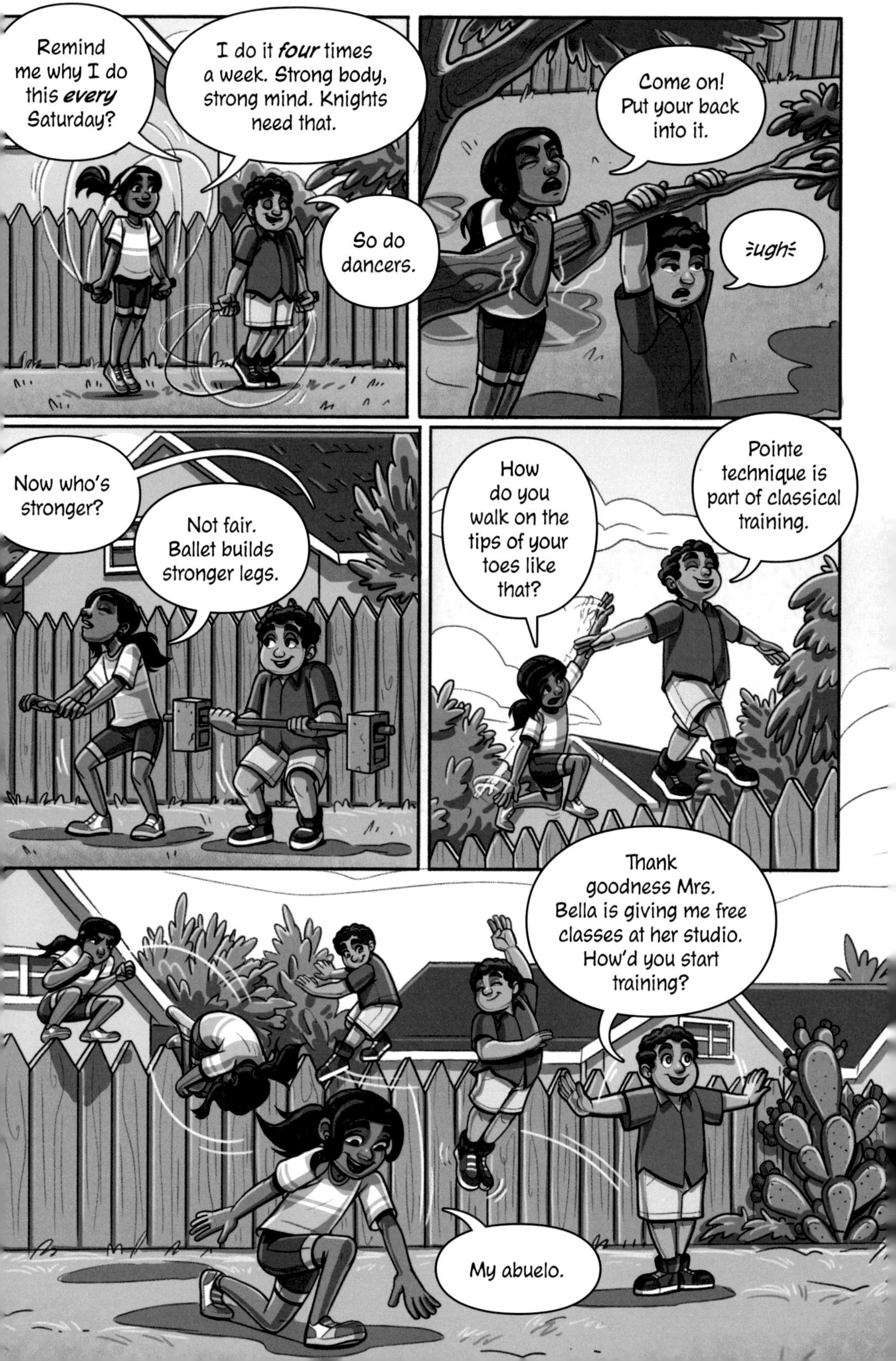
Remind me why I do this *every* Saturday?
I do it *four* times a week. Strong body, strong mind. Knights need that.
So do dancers.
Come on! Put your back into it.
ugh
Now who's stronger?
Not fair. Ballet builds stronger legs.
How do you walk on the tips of your toes like that?
Pointe technique is part of classical training.
Thank goodness Mrs. Bella is giving me free classes at her studio. How'd you start training?
My abuelo.

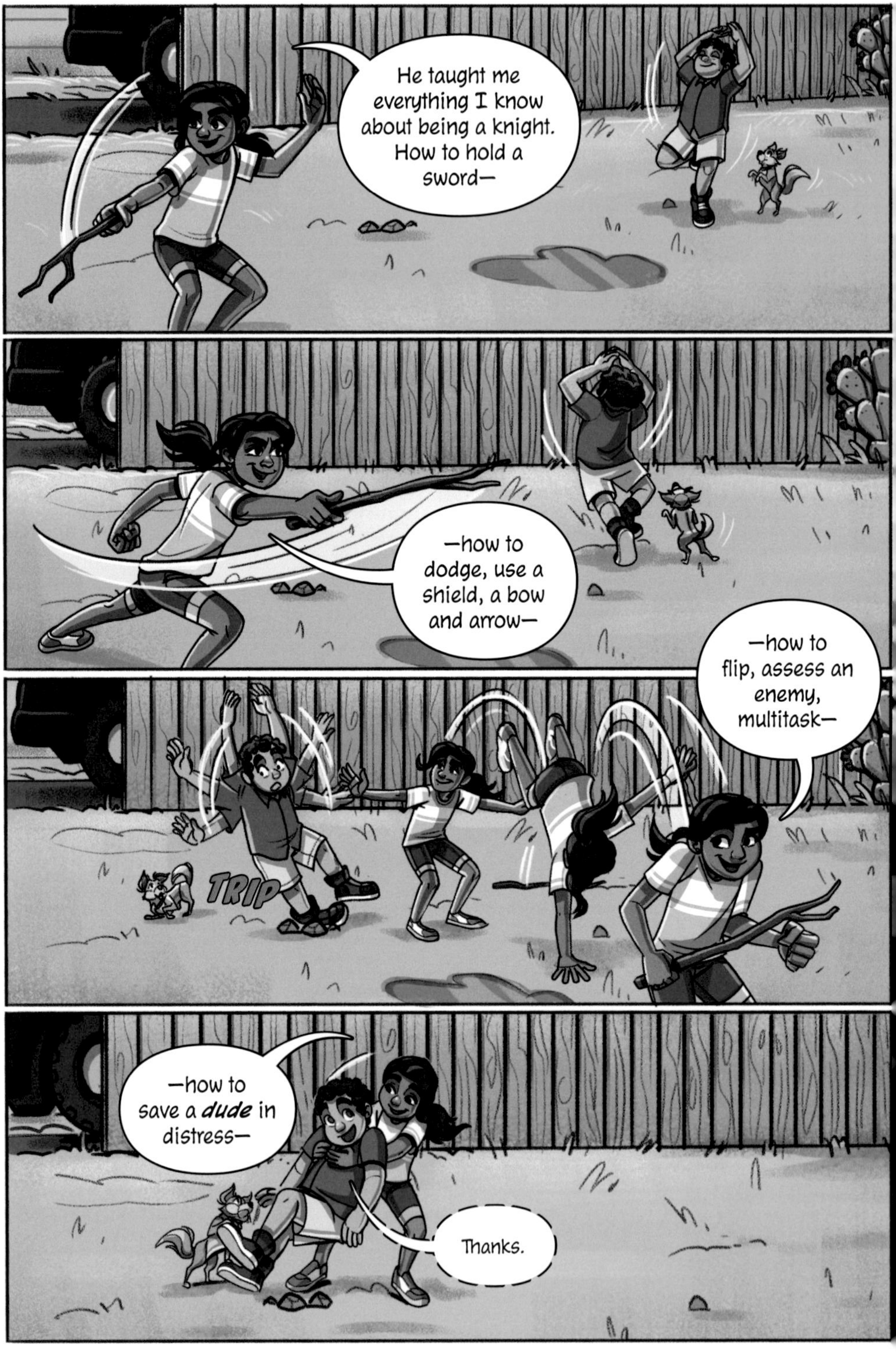
He taught me everything I know about being a knight. How to hold a sword—
—how to dodge, use a shield, a bow and arrow—
—how to flip, assess an enemy, multitask—
TRIP
—how to save a *dude* in distress—
Thanks.

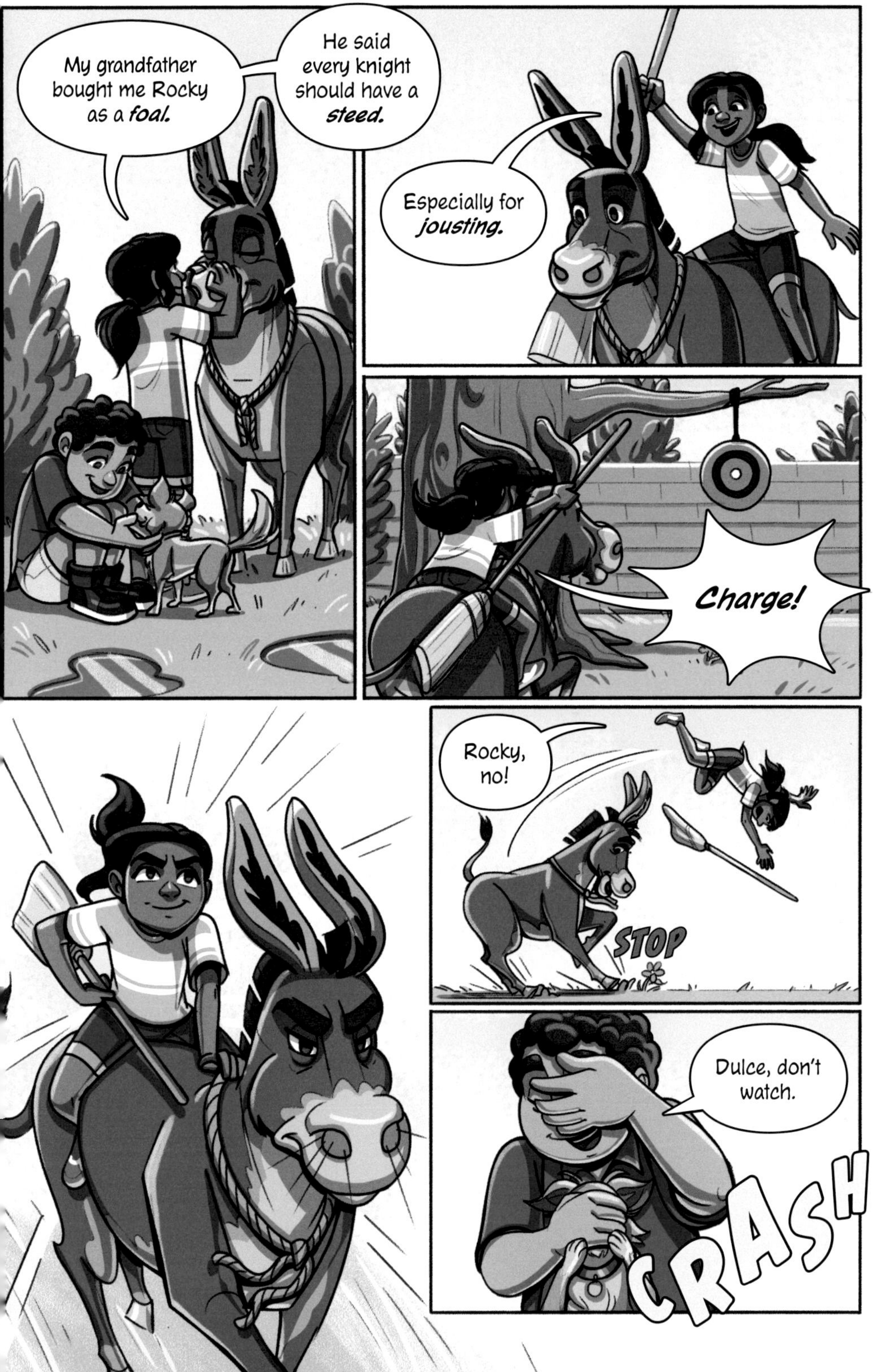

My grandfather bought me Rocky as a *foal.*
He said every knight should have a *steed.*
Especially for *jousting.*
Charge!
Rocky, no!
STOP
Dulce, don't watch.
CRASH

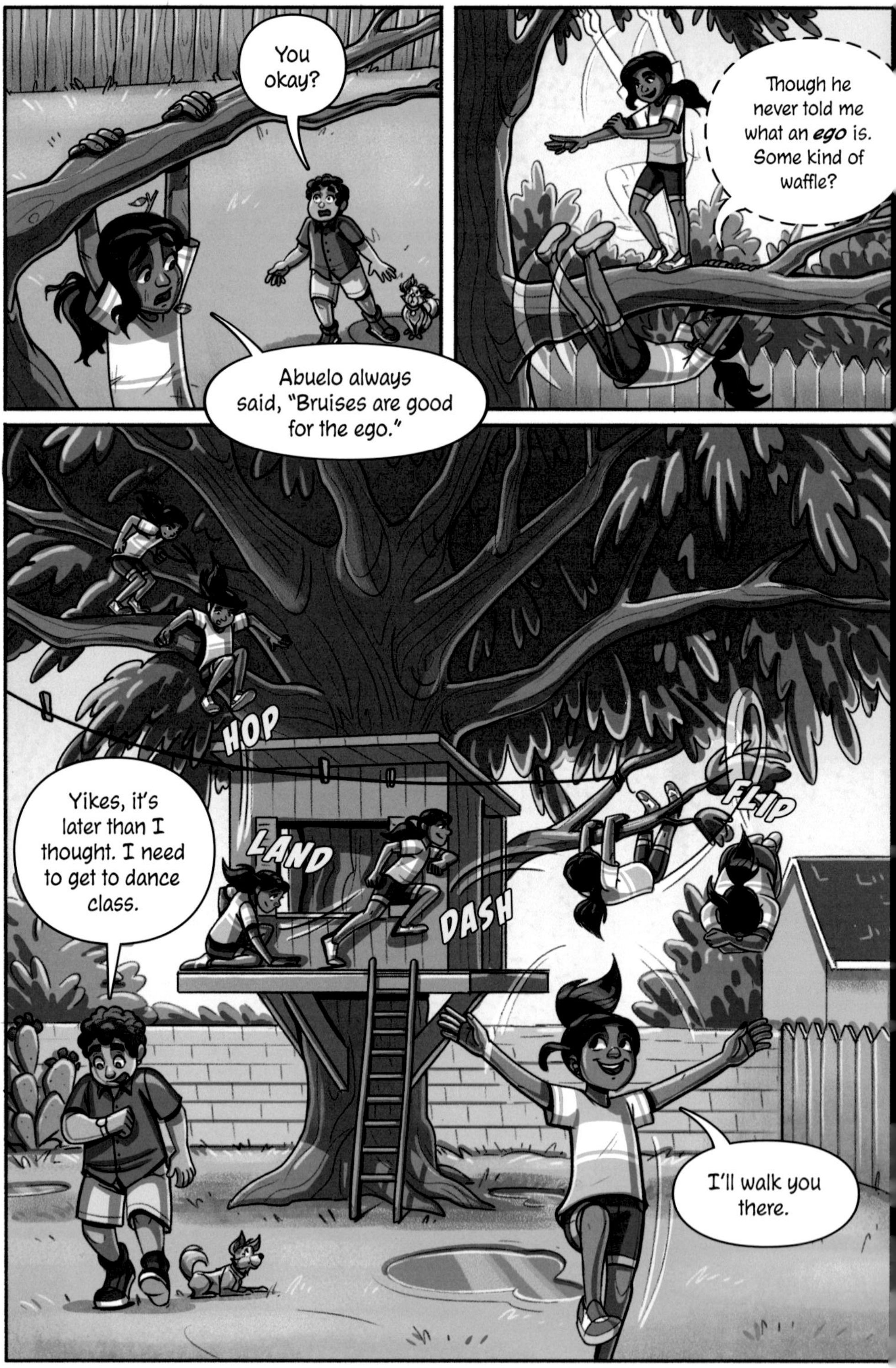
You okay?
Abuelo always said, "Bruises are good for the ego."
Though he never told me what an ***ego*** is. Some kind of waffle?
HOP
Yikes, it's later than I thought. I need to get to dance class.
LAND
DASH
FLIP
I'll walk you there.

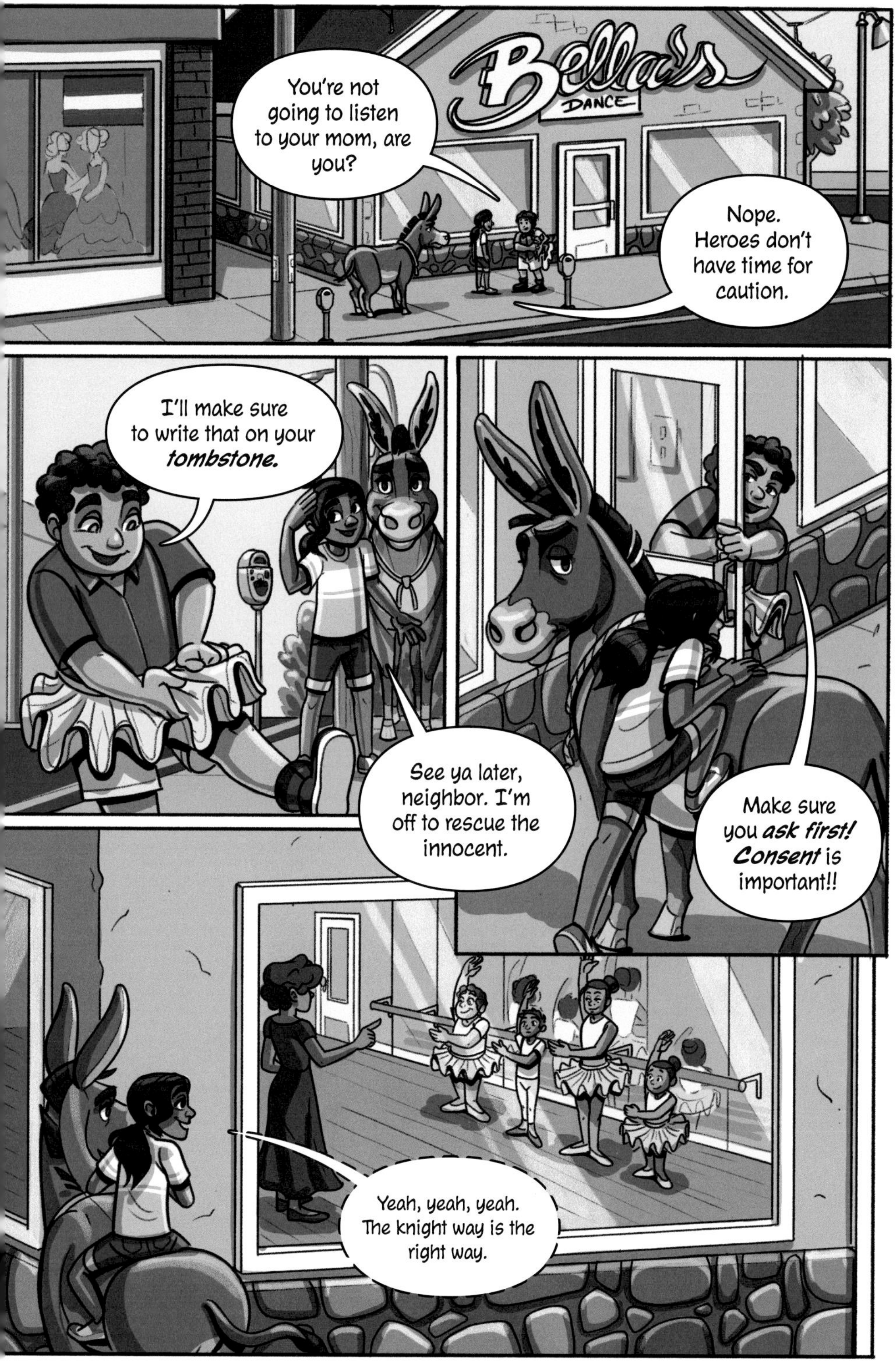

Bella's
DANCE
You're not going to listen to your mom, are you?
Nope. Heroes don't have time for caution.
I'll make sure to write that on your *tombstone.*
See ya later, neighbor. I'm off to rescue the innocent.
Make sure you ***ask first! Consent*** is important!!
Yeah, yeah, yeah. The knight way is the right way.

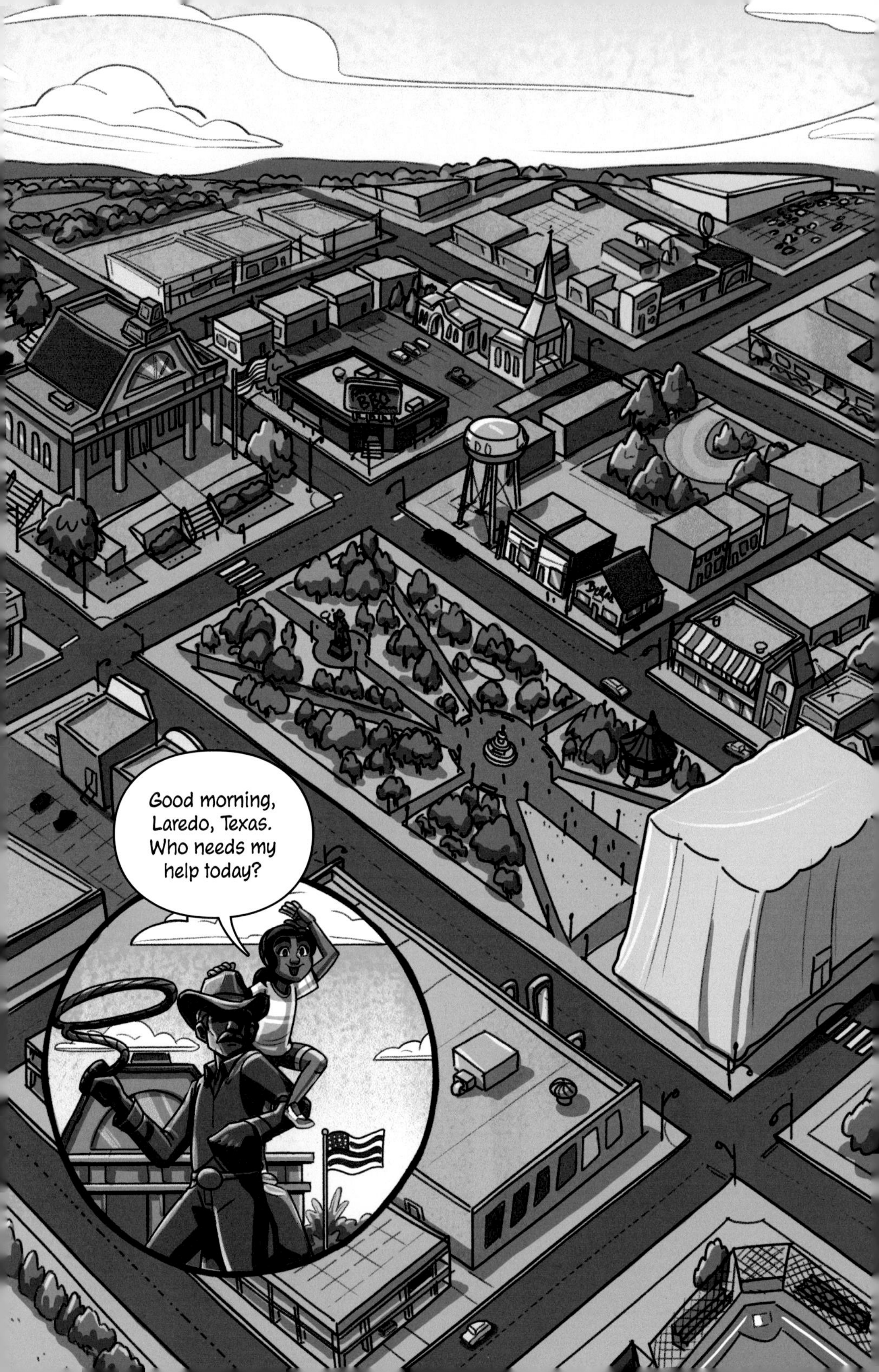
Good morning, Laredo, Texas. Who needs my help today?

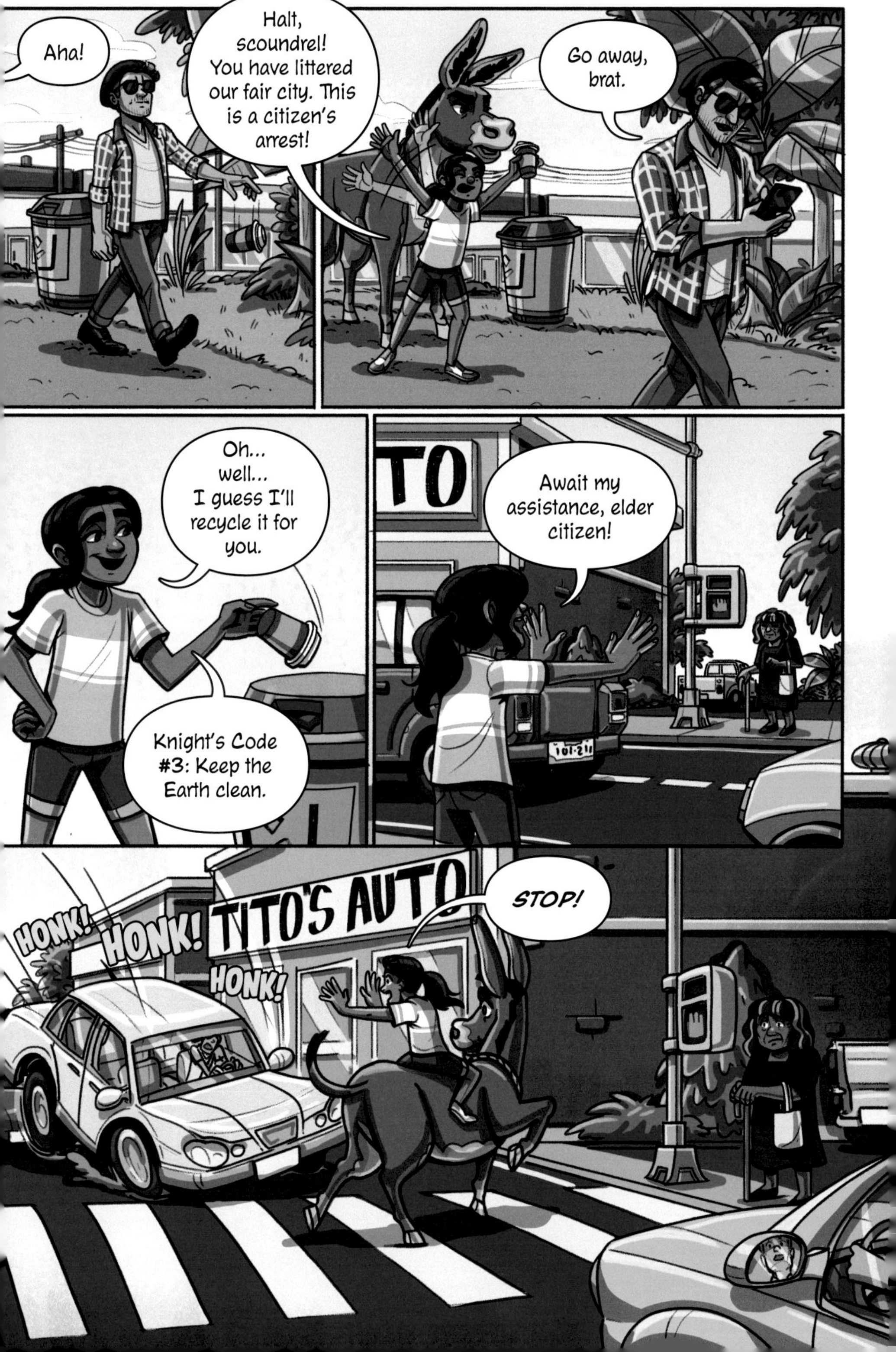
Aha!
Halt, scoundrel! You have littered our fair city. This is a citizen's arrest!
Go away, brat.
Oh... well... I guess I'll recycle it for you.
Knight's Code #3: Keep the Earth clean.
TO
Await my assistance, elder citizen!
TITO'S AUTO
HONK!
HONK!
HONK!
STOP!

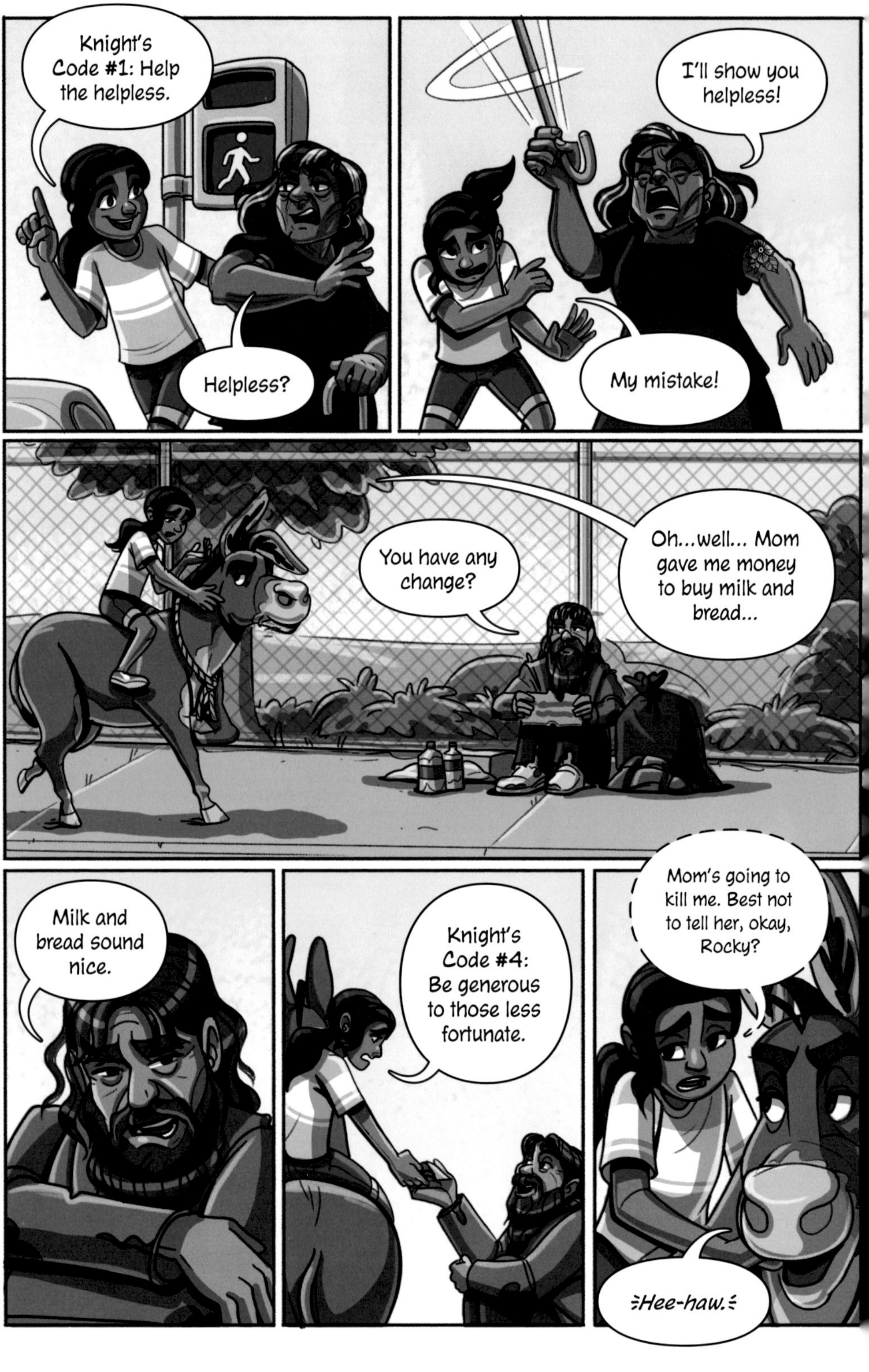
Knight's Code #1: Help the helpless.
Helpless?
I'll show you helpless!
My mistake!
You have any change?
Oh...well... Mom gave me money to buy milk and bread...
Milk and bread sound nice.
Knight's Code #4: Be generous to those less fortunate.
Mom's going to kill me. Best not to tell her, okay, Rocky?
Hee-haw.

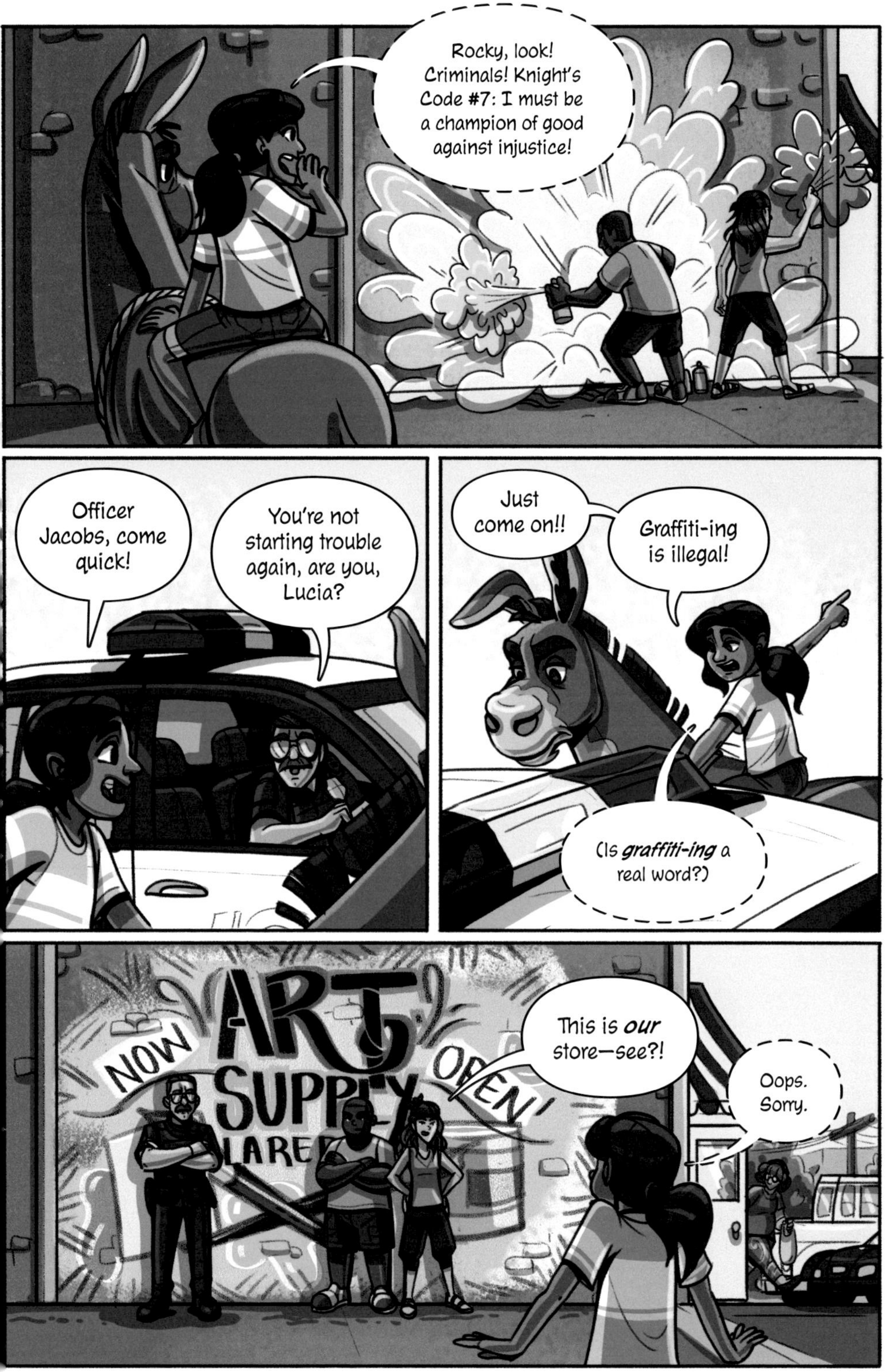
Rocky, look! Criminals! Knight's Code #7: I must be a champion of good against injustice!
Officer Jacobs, come quick!
You're not starting trouble again, are you, Lucia?
Just come on!!
Graffiti-ing is illegal!
(Is *graffiti-ing* a real word?)
NOW ART SUPPLY OPEN
This is *our* store—see?!
Oops. Sorry.

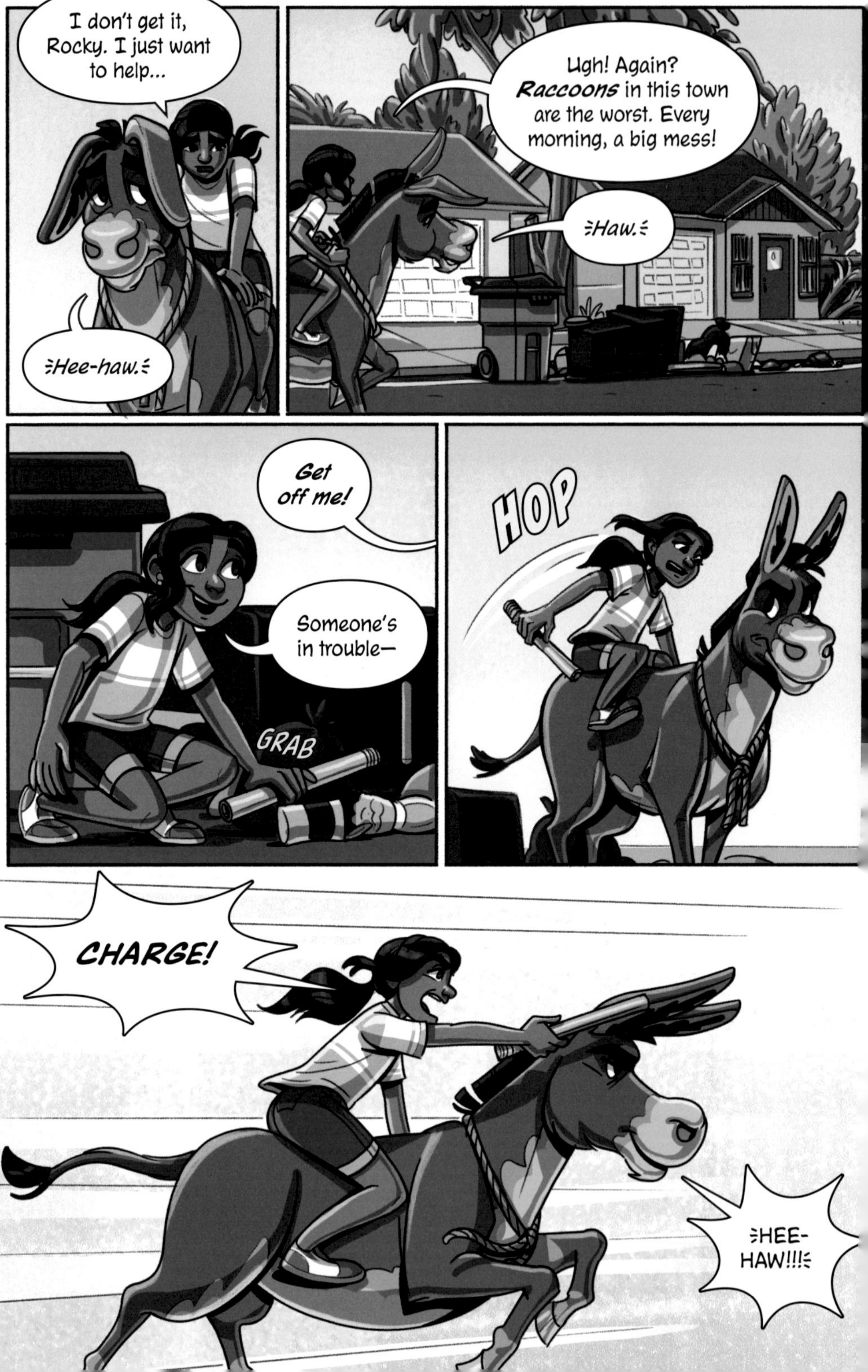
I don't get it, Rocky. I just want to help...
≒Hee-haw.≒
Ugh! Again? *Raccoons* in this town are the worst. Every morning, a big mess!
≒Haw.≒
Get off me!
Someone's in trouble—
GRAB
HOP
CHARGE!
≒HEE-HAW!!!≒

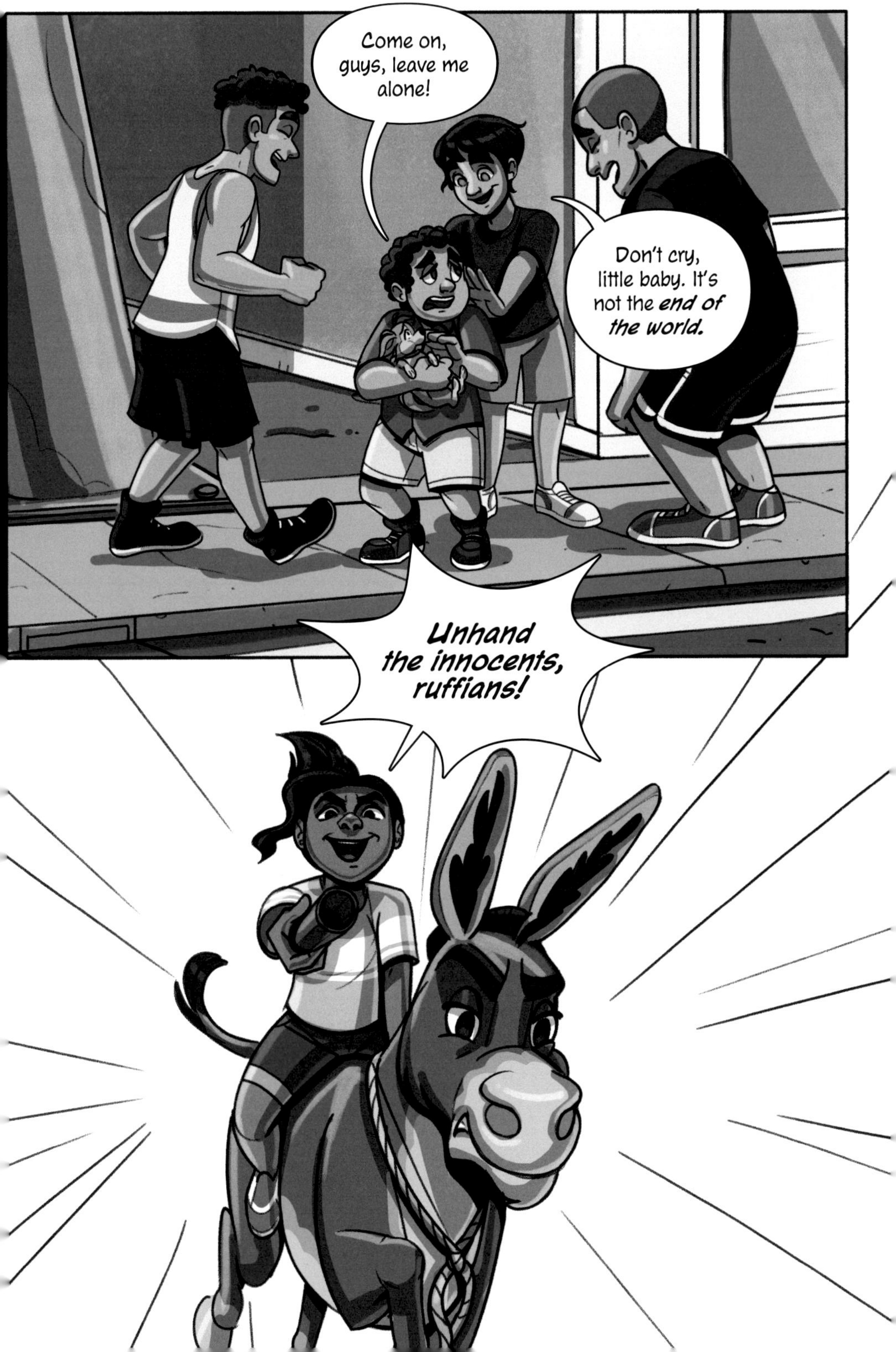
Come on, guys, leave me alone!
Don't cry, little baby. It's not the *end of the world.*
Unhand the innocents, ruffians!

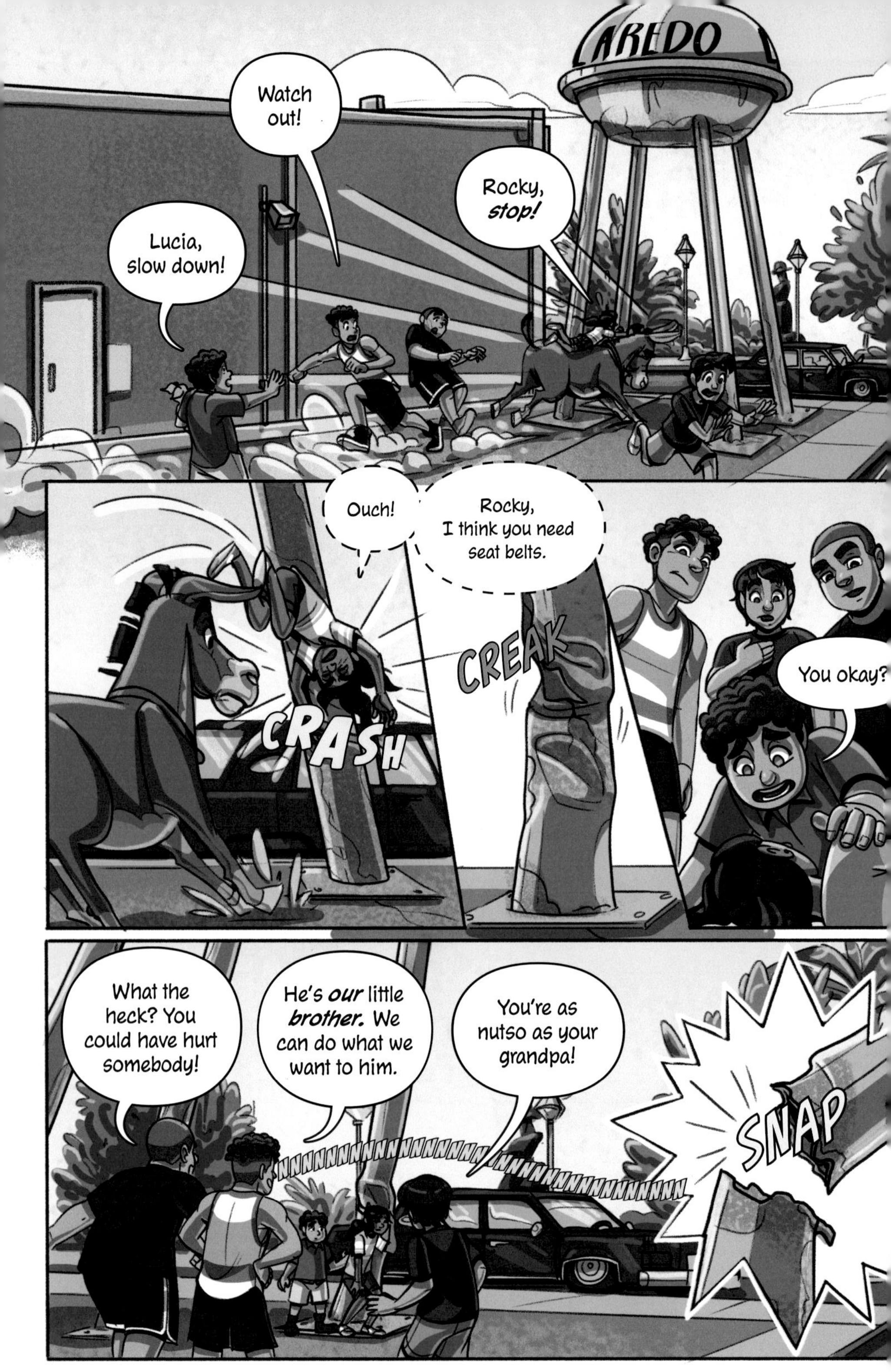
LAREDO
Watch out!
Rocky, *stop!*
Lucia, slow down!
Ouch!
Rocky, I think you need seat belts.
CRASH
CREAK
You okay?
What the heck? You could have hurt somebody!
He's ***our*** little ***brother.*** We can do what we want to him.
You're as nutso as your grandpa!
NNNNNNNNNNNNNNNNNNNNNNNNNNNNNNNNNNNNNNNNNNN
SNAP

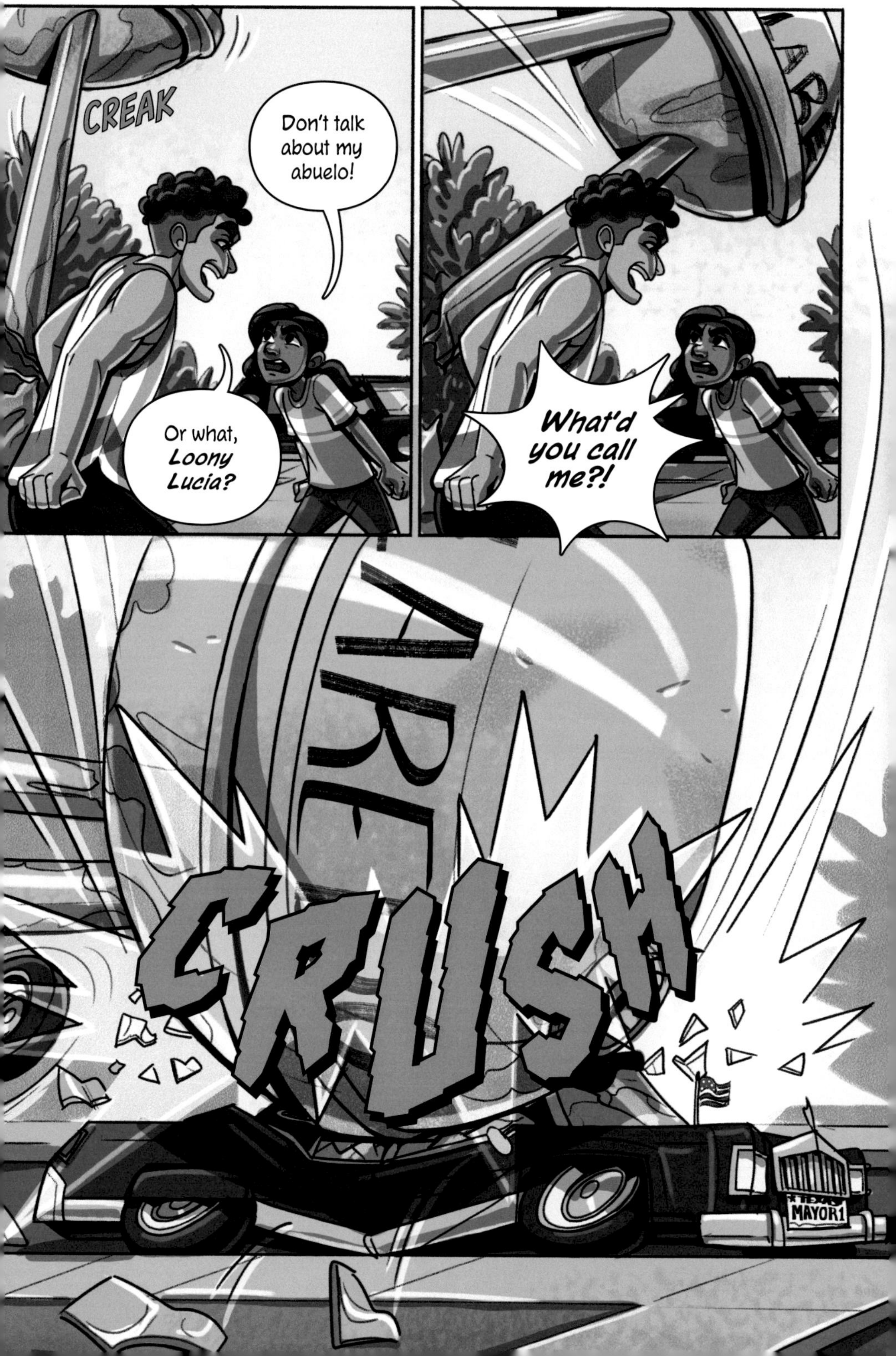
CREAK
Don't talk about my abuelo!
Or what, Loony Lucia?
What'd you call me?!
CRUSH
MAYOR1

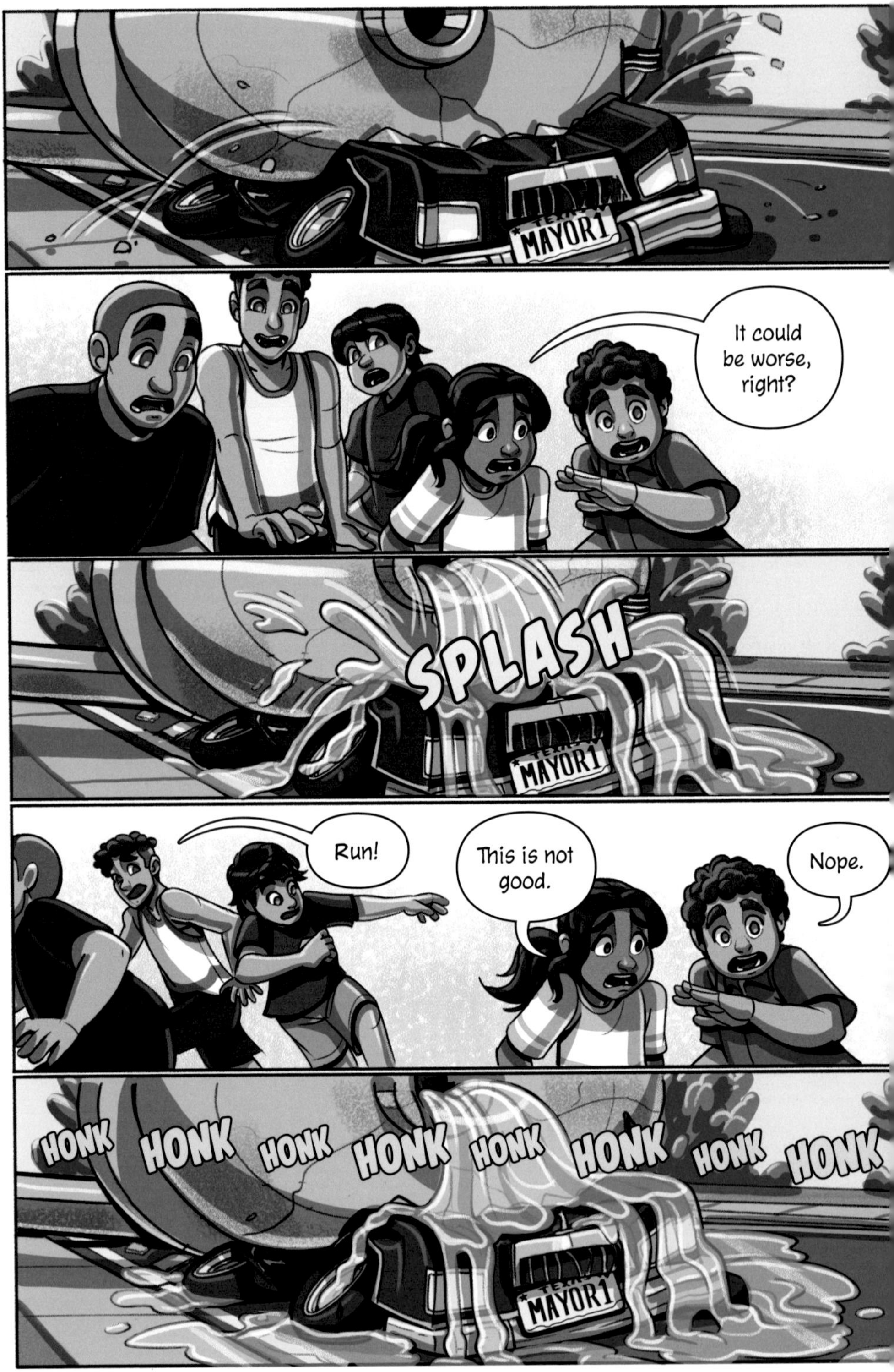
MAYOR1
It could be worse, right?
SPLASH
MAYOR1
Run!
This is not good.
Nope.
HONK HONK HONK HONK HONK HONK HONK HONK
MAYOR1

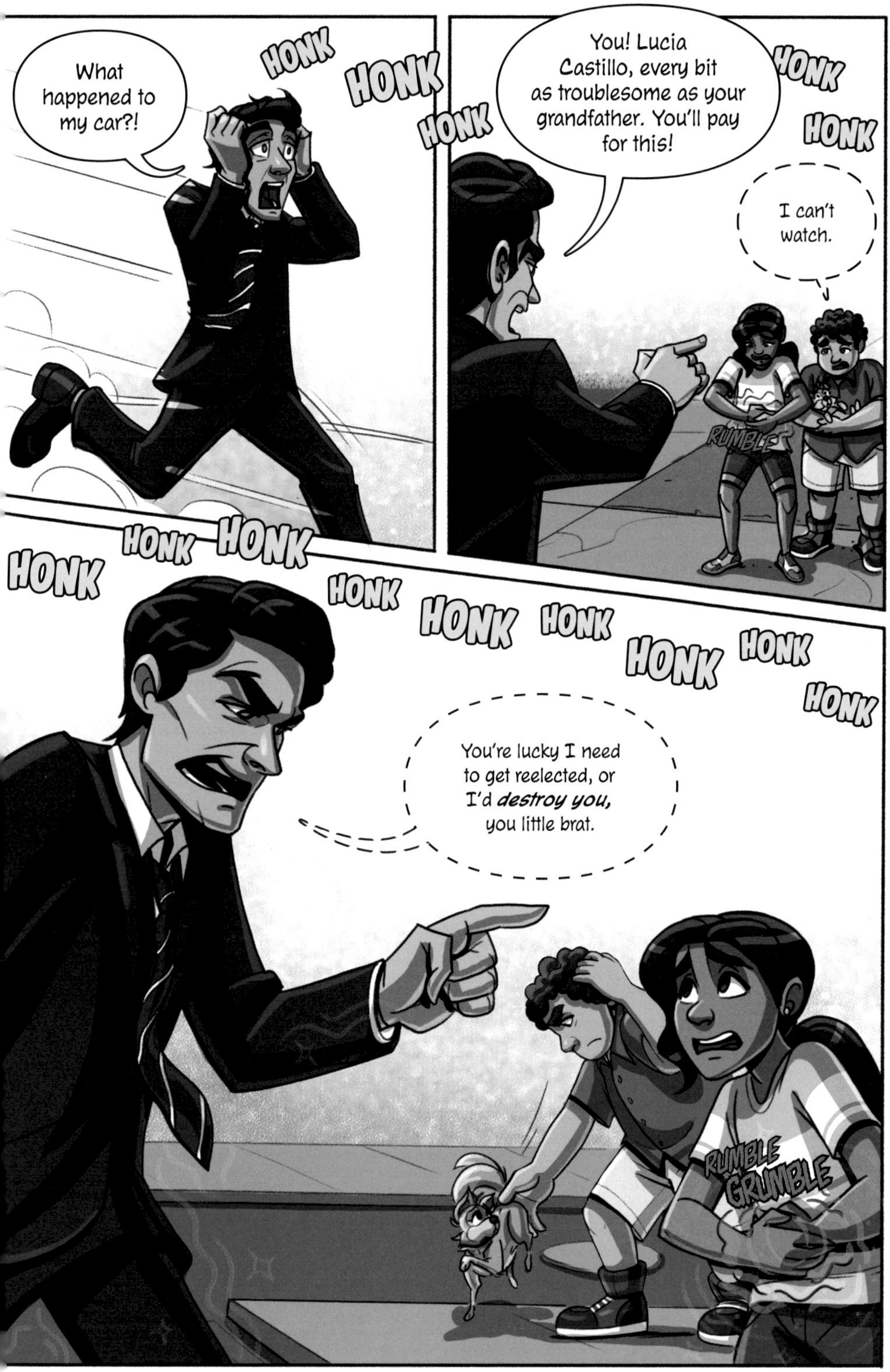
What happened to my car?!
HONK
HONK
HONK
You! Lucia Castillo, every bit as troublesome as your grandfather. You'll pay for this!
HONK
HONK
I can't watch.
RUMBLE
HONK
HONK
HONK
HONK
HONK
HONK
HONK
HONK
HONK
You're lucky I need to get reelected, or I'd ***destroy you,*** you little brat.
RUMBLE
GRUMBLE

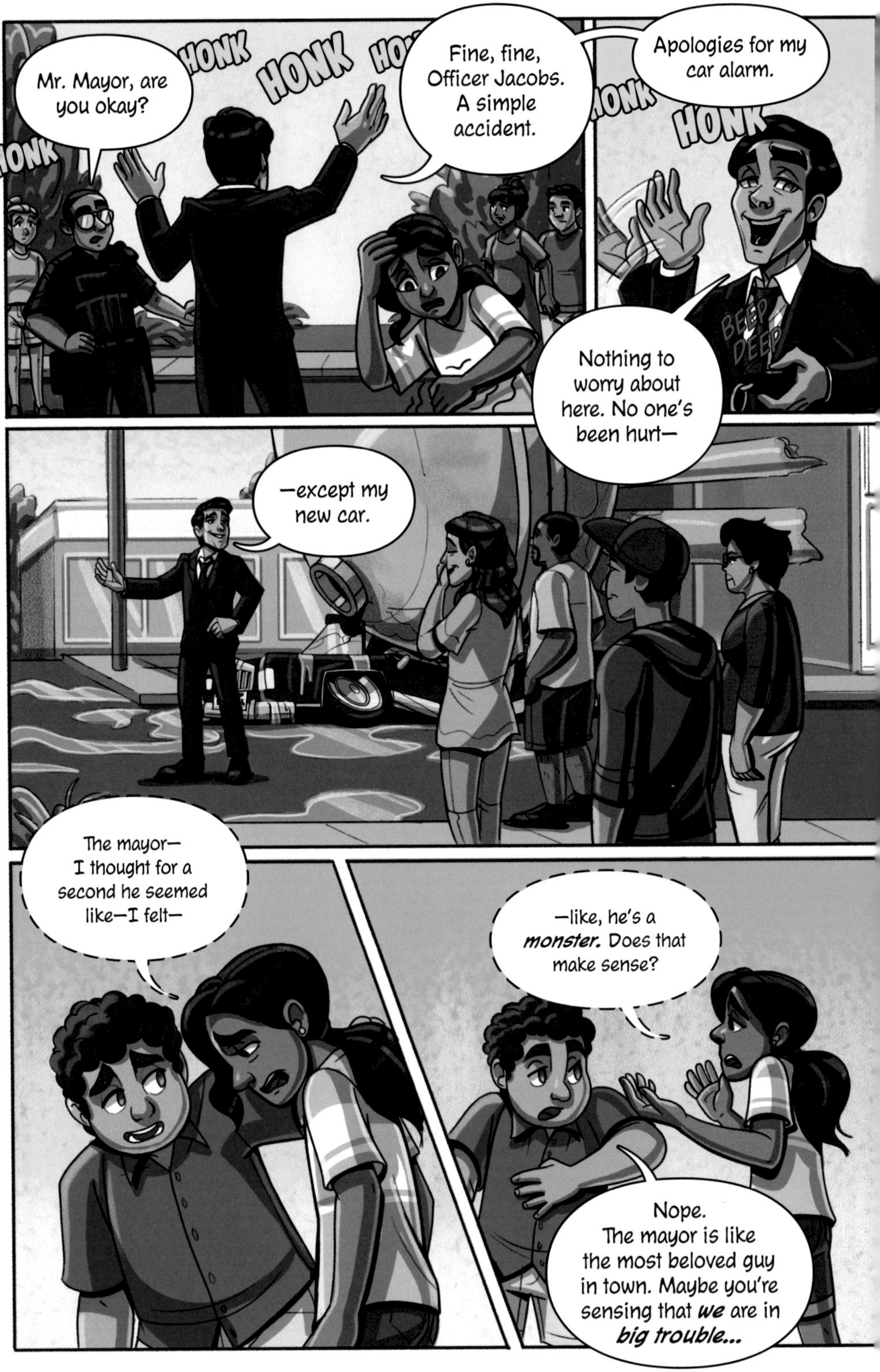

HONK
HONK
HONK
HONK
Mr. Mayor, are you okay?
Fine, fine, Officer Jacobs. A simple accident.
Apologies for my car alarm.
HONK
HONK
BEEP BEEP
Nothing to worry about here. No one's been hurt—
—except my new car.
The mayor— I thought for a second he seemed like—I felt—
—like, he's a *monster.* Does that make sense?
Nope. The mayor is like the most beloved guy in town. Maybe you're sensing that *we* are in *big trouble...*

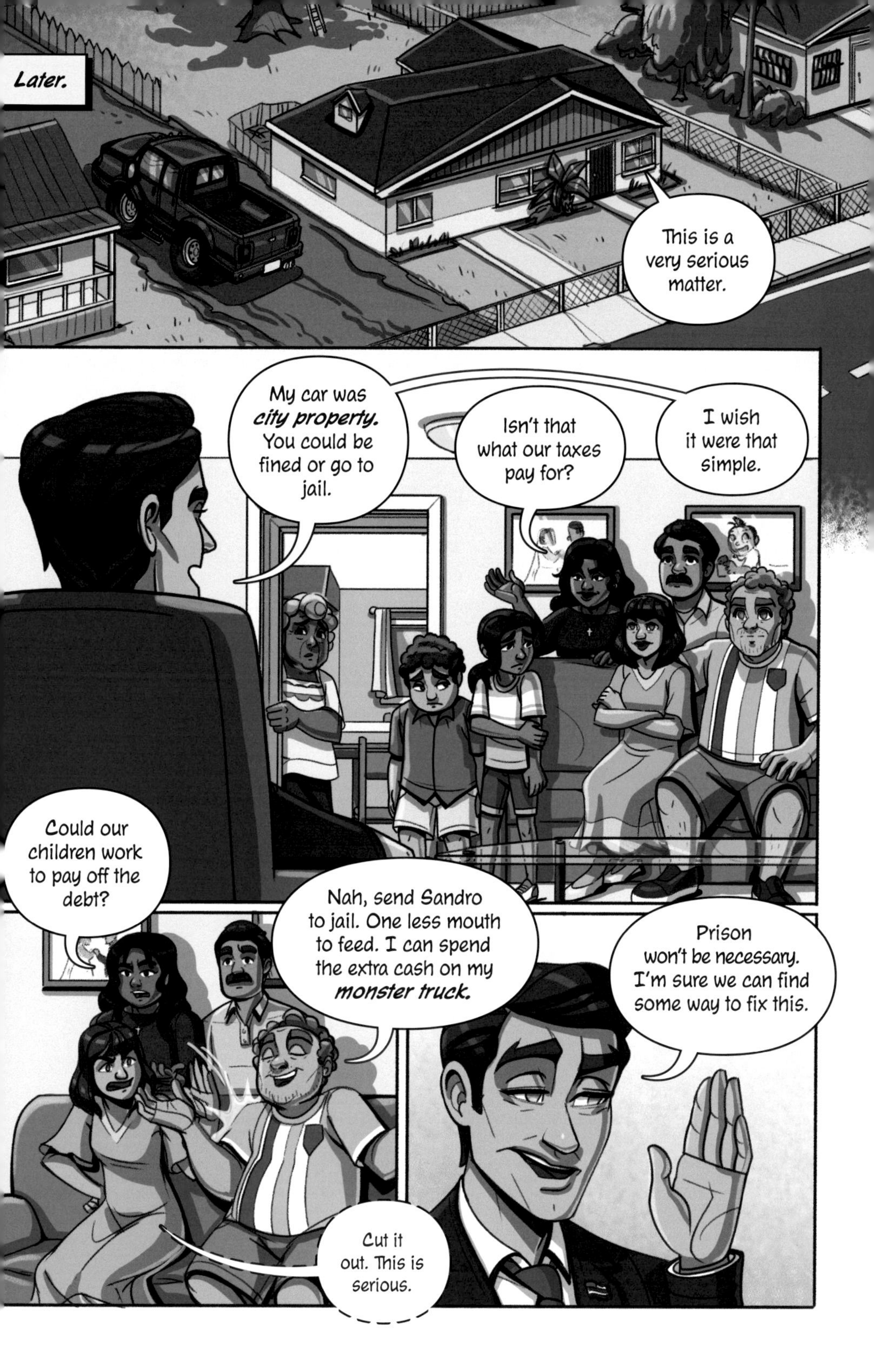
Later.
This is a very serious matter.
My car was *city property.* You could be fined or go to jail.
Isn't that what our taxes pay for?
I wish it were that simple.
Could our children work to pay off the debt?
Nah, send Sandro to jail. One less mouth to feed. I can spend the extra cash on my *monster truck.*
Prison won't be necessary. I'm sure we can find some way to fix this.
Cut it out. This is serious.

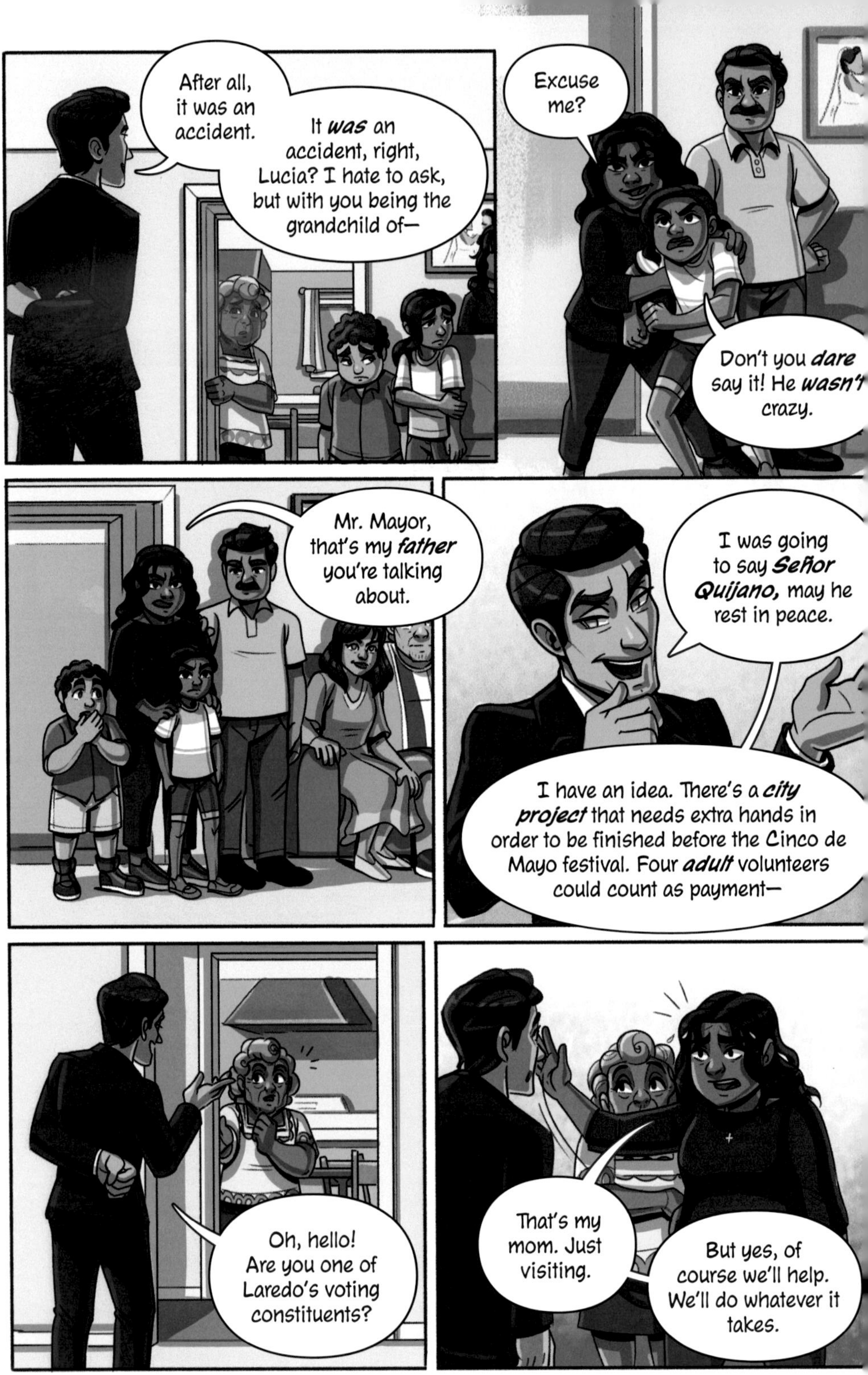
After all, it was an accident.
It *was* an accident, right, Lucia? I hate to ask, but with you being the grandchild of—
Excuse me?
Don't you *dare* say it! He *wasn't* crazy.
Mr. Mayor, that's my *father* you're talking about.
I was going to say *Señor Quijano,* may he rest in peace.
I have an idea. There's a *city project* that needs extra hands in order to be finished before the Cinco de Mayo festival. Four *adult* volunteers could count as payment—
Oh, hello! Are you one of Laredo's voting constituents?
That's my mom. Just visiting.
But yes, of course we'll help. We'll do whatever it takes.

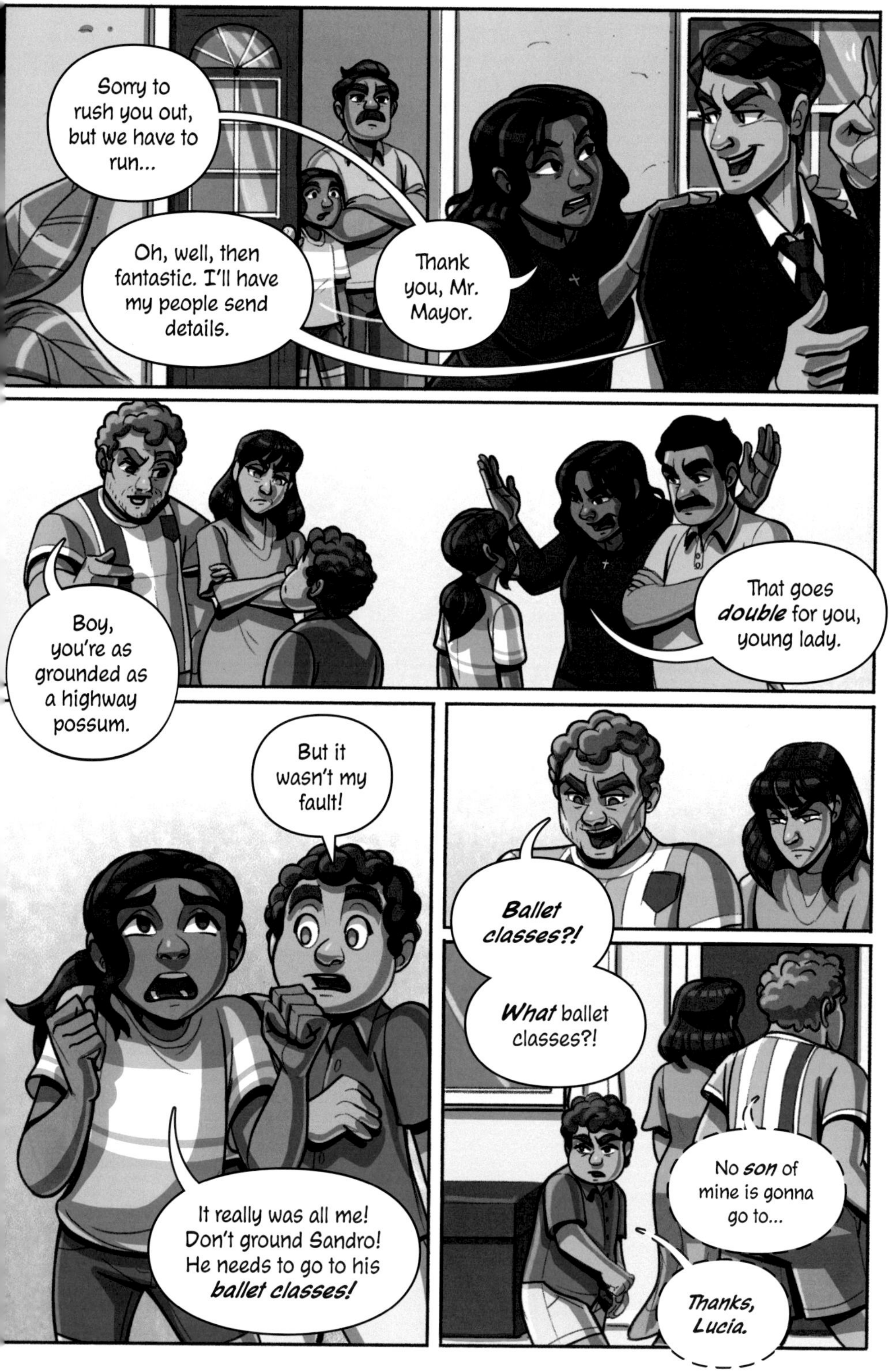
Sorry to rush you out, but we have to run...
Thank you, Mr. Mayor.
Oh, well, then fantastic. I'll have my people send details.
Boy, you're as grounded as a highway possum.
That goes *double* for you, young lady.
But it wasn't my fault!
It really was all me! Don't ground Sandro! He needs to go to his *ballet classes!*
Ballet classes?!
What ballet classes?!
No *son* of mine is gonna go to...
Thanks, Lucia.

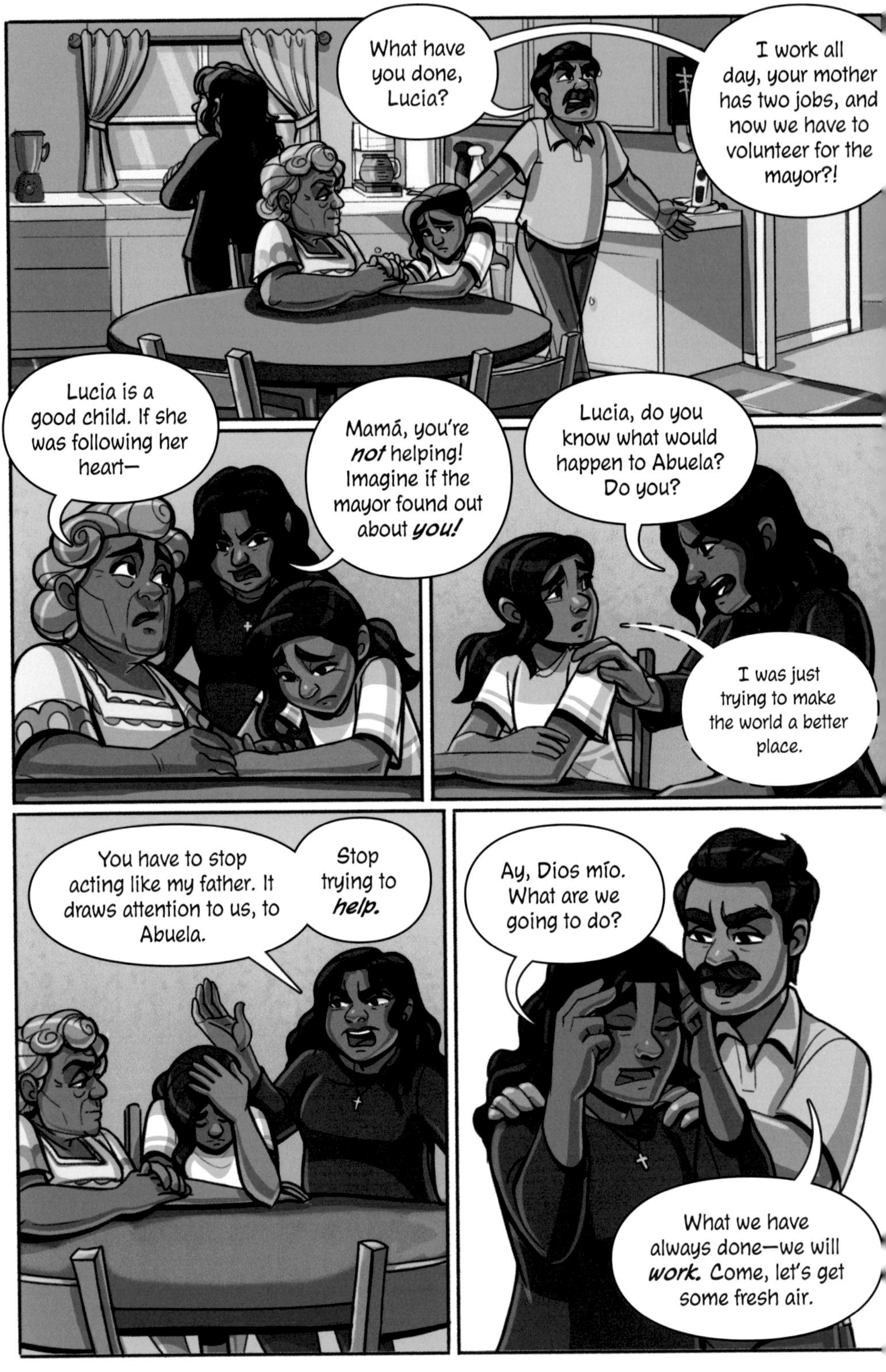
What have you done, Lucia?
I work all day, your mother has two jobs, and now we have to volunteer for the mayor?!
Lucia is a good child. If she was following her heart—
Mamá, you're ***not*** helping! Imagine if the mayor found out about ***you!***
Lucia, do you know what would happen to Abuela? Do you?
I was just trying to make the world a better place.
You have to stop acting like my father. It draws attention to us, to Abuela.
Stop trying to ***help.***
Ay, Dios mío. What are we going to do?
What we have always done—we will ***work.*** Come, let's get some fresh air.

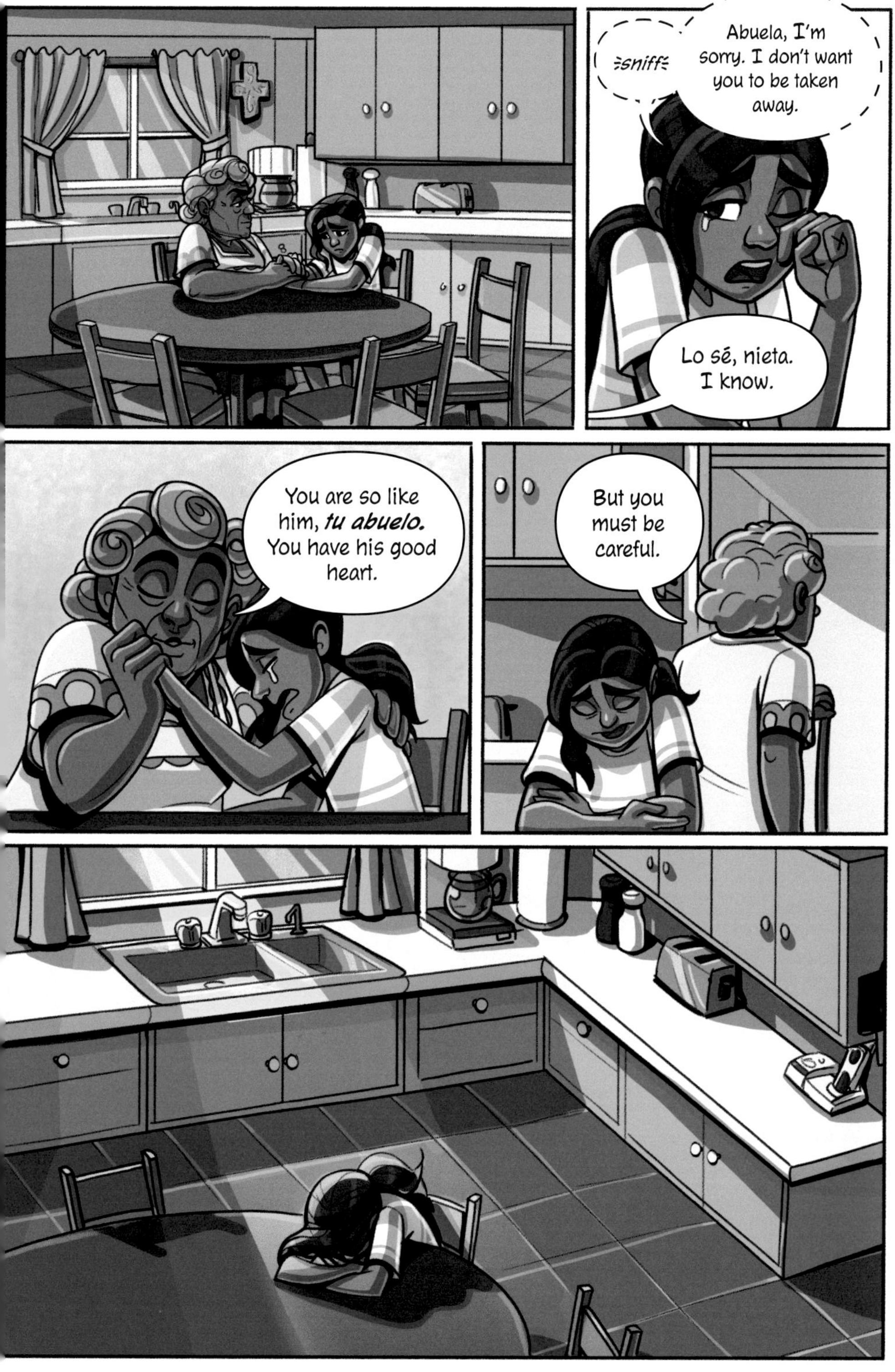

sniff
Abuela, I'm sorry. I don't want you to be taken away.
Lo sé, nieta. I know.
You are so like him, ***tu abuelo.*** You have his good heart.
But you must be careful.

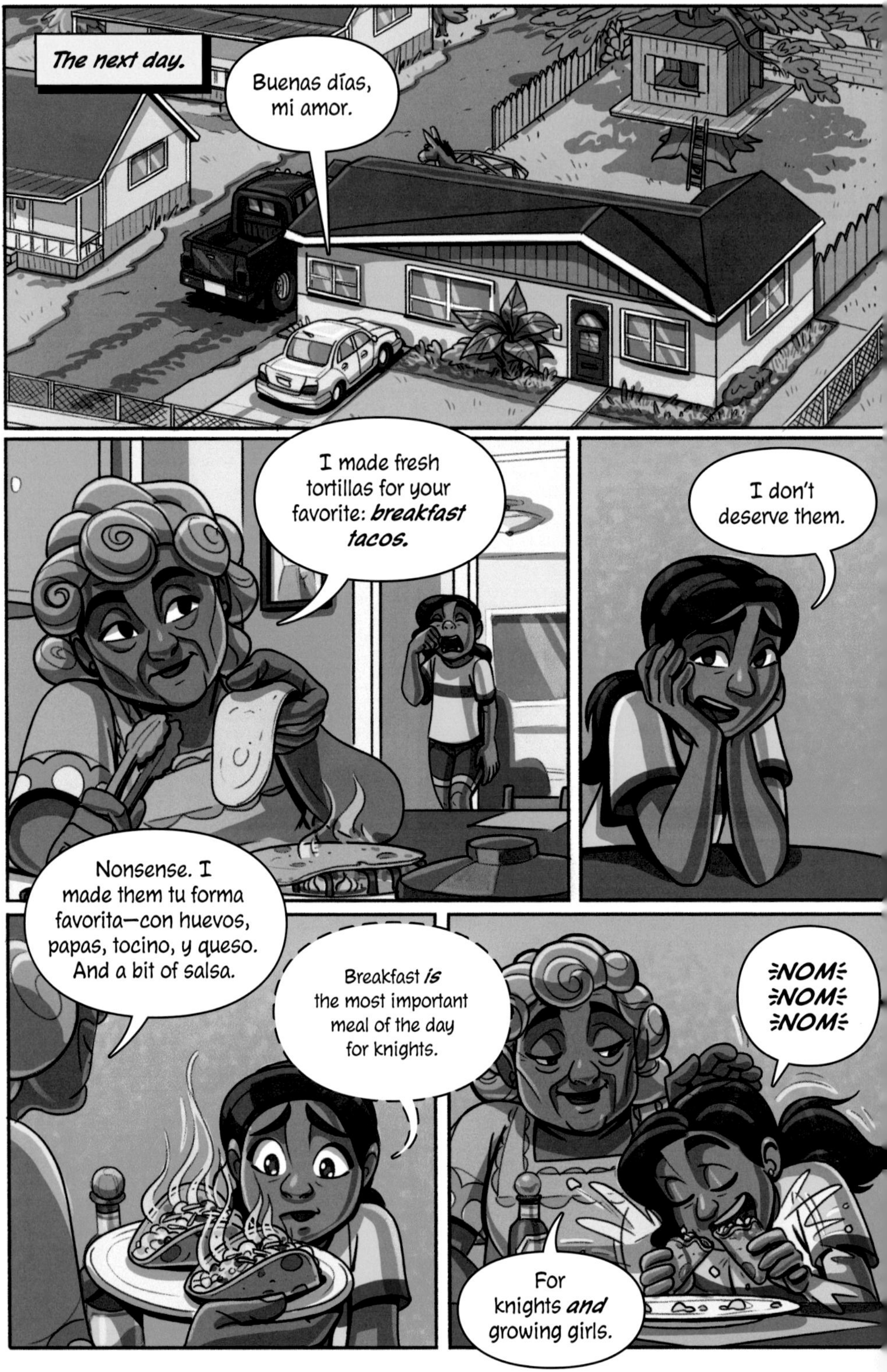
The next day.
Buenas días, mi amor.
I made fresh tortillas for your favorite: *breakfast tacos.*
I don't deserve them.
Nonsense. I made them tu forma favorita—con huevos, papas, tocino, y queso. And a bit of salsa.
Breakfast *is* the most important meal of the day for knights.
NOM NOM NOM
For knights *and* growing girls.

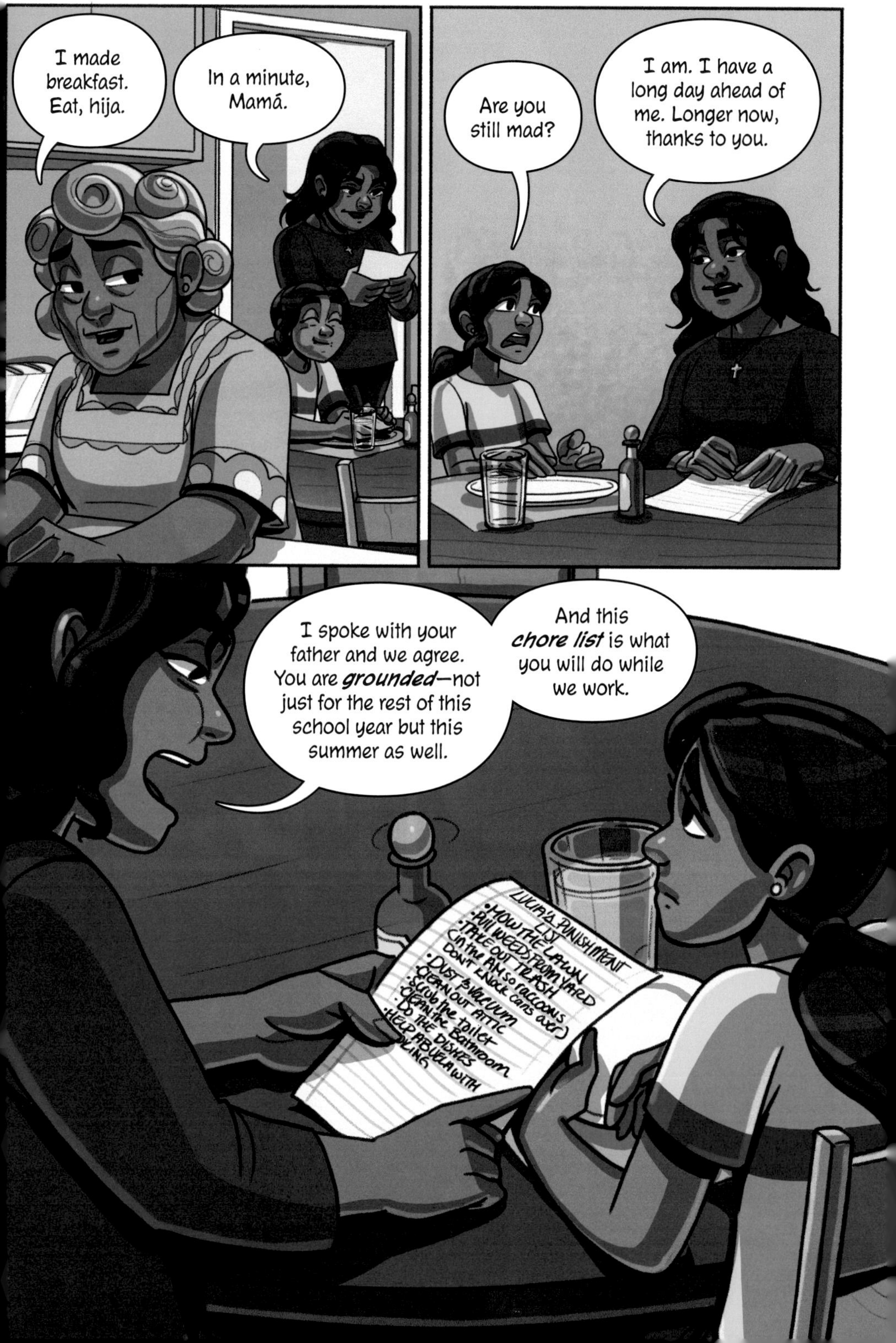
I made breakfast. Eat, hija.
In a minute, Mamá.
Are you still mad?
I am. I have a long day ahead of me. Longer now, thanks to you.
I spoke with your father and we agree. You are ***grounded***—not just for the rest of this school year but this summer as well.
And this ***chore list*** is what you will do while we work.
LUCIA'S PUNISHMENT LIST
•MOW THE LAWN
•PULL WEEDS FROM YARD
•TAKE OUT TRASH (in the AM so raccoons DON'T KNOCK cans over)
•DUST & VACUUM
•CLEAN OUT ATTIC
•Scrub the toilet
•CLEAN the Bathroom
•DO THE DISHES
•HELP ABUELA WITH ...ING

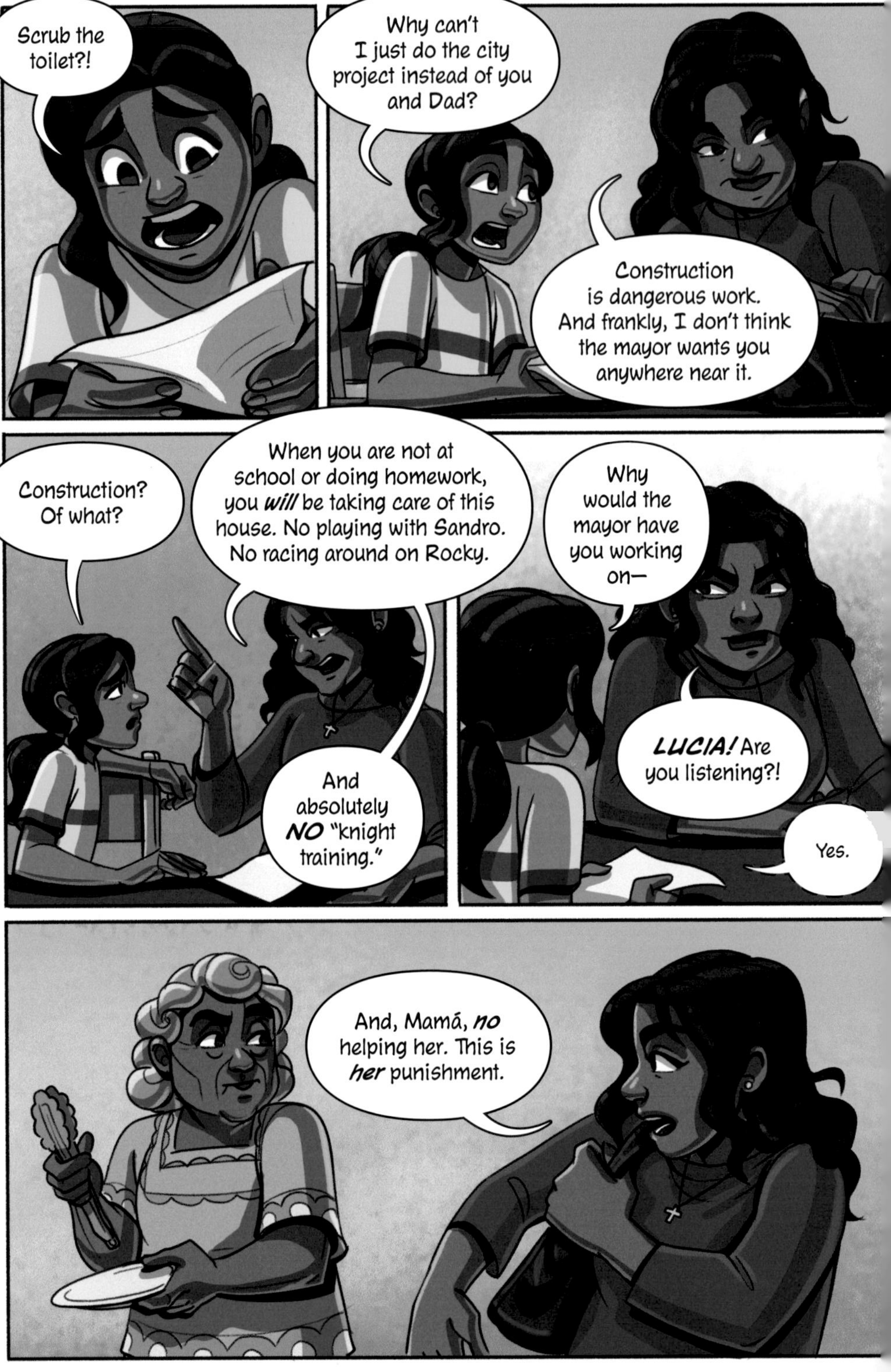
Scrub the toilet?!
Why can't I just do the city project instead of you and Dad?
Construction is dangerous work. And frankly, I don't think the mayor wants you anywhere near it.
Construction? Of what?
When you are not at school or doing homework, you *will* be taking care of this house. No playing with Sandro. No racing around on Rocky.
And absolutely ***NO*** "knight training."
Why would the mayor have you working on—
LUCIA! Are you listening?!
Yes.
And, Mamá, ***no*** helping her. This is ***her*** punishment.

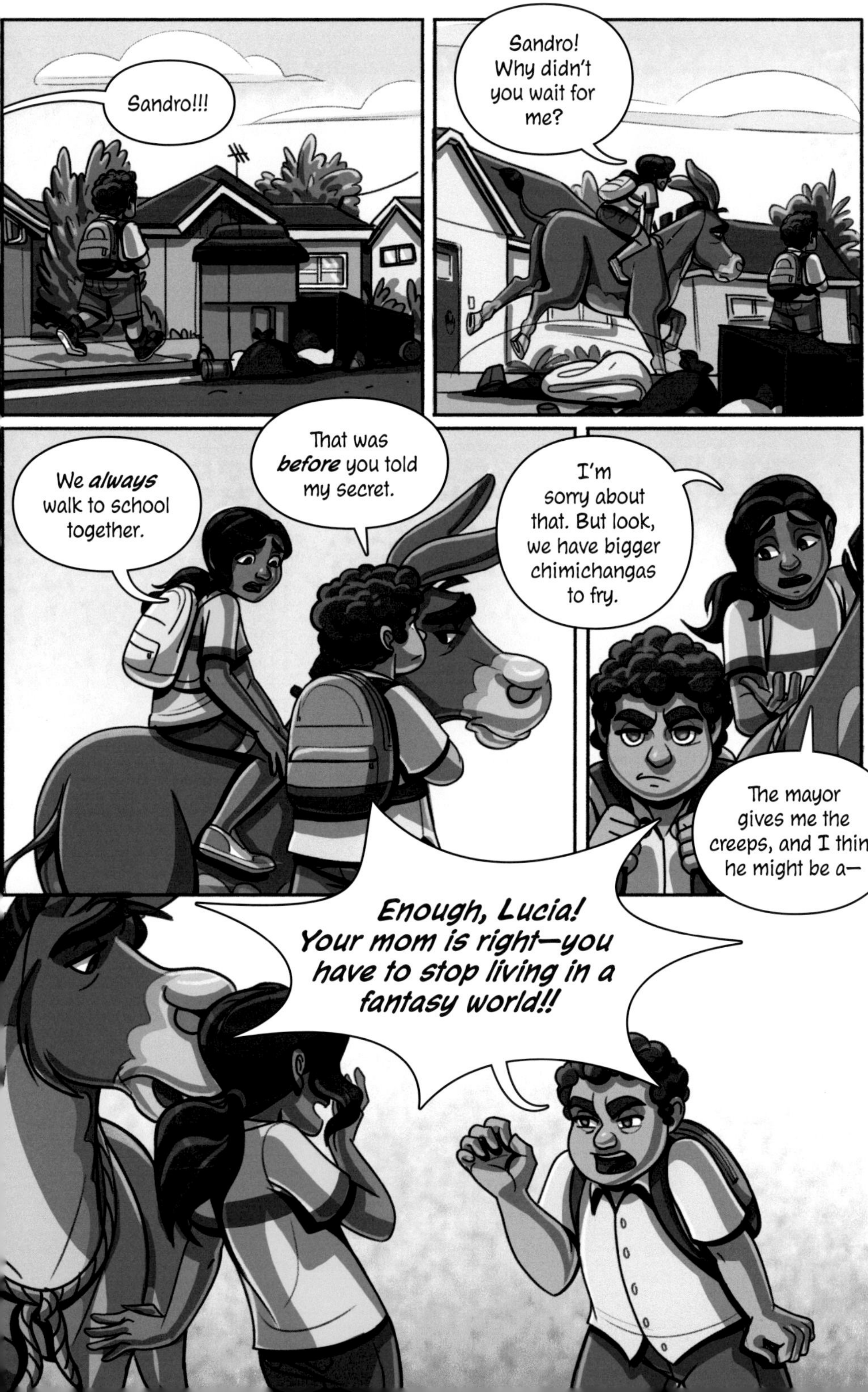
Sandro!!!
Sandro! Why didn't you wait for me?
We *always* walk to school together.
That was *before* you told my secret.
I'm sorry about that. But look, we have bigger chimichangas to fry.
The mayor gives me the creeps, and I think he might be a—
Enough, Lucia! Your mom is right—you have to stop living in a fantasy world!!

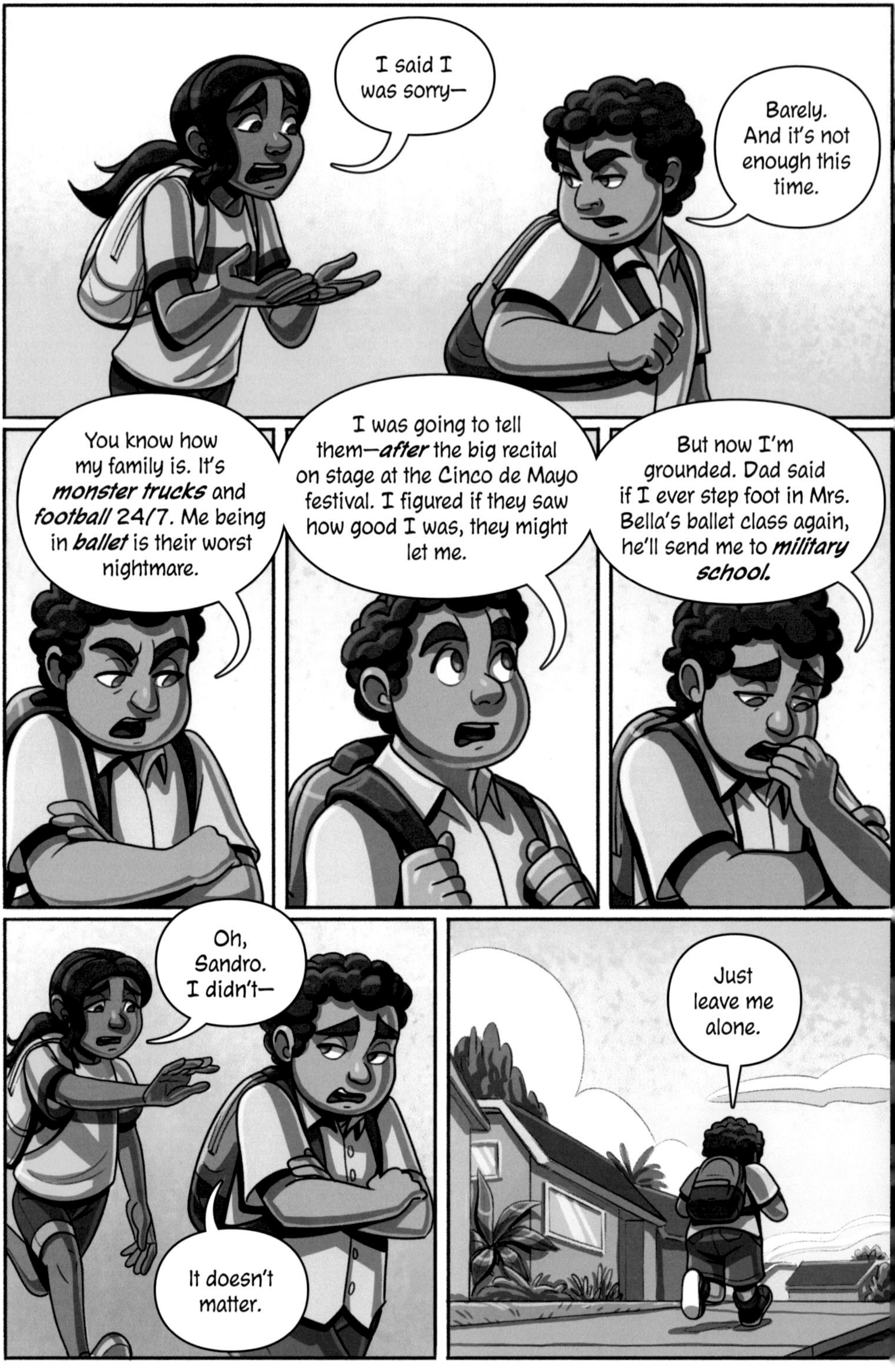
I said I was sorry—
Barely. And it's not enough this time.
You know how my family is. It's *monster trucks* and *football* 24/7. Me being in *ballet* is their worst nightmare.
I was going to tell them—*after* the big recital on stage at the Cinco de Mayo festival. I figured if they saw how good I was, they might let me.
But now I'm grounded. Dad said if I ever step foot in Mrs. Bella's ballet class again, he'll send me to ***military school.***
Oh, Sandro. I didn't—
It doesn't matter.
Just leave me alone.

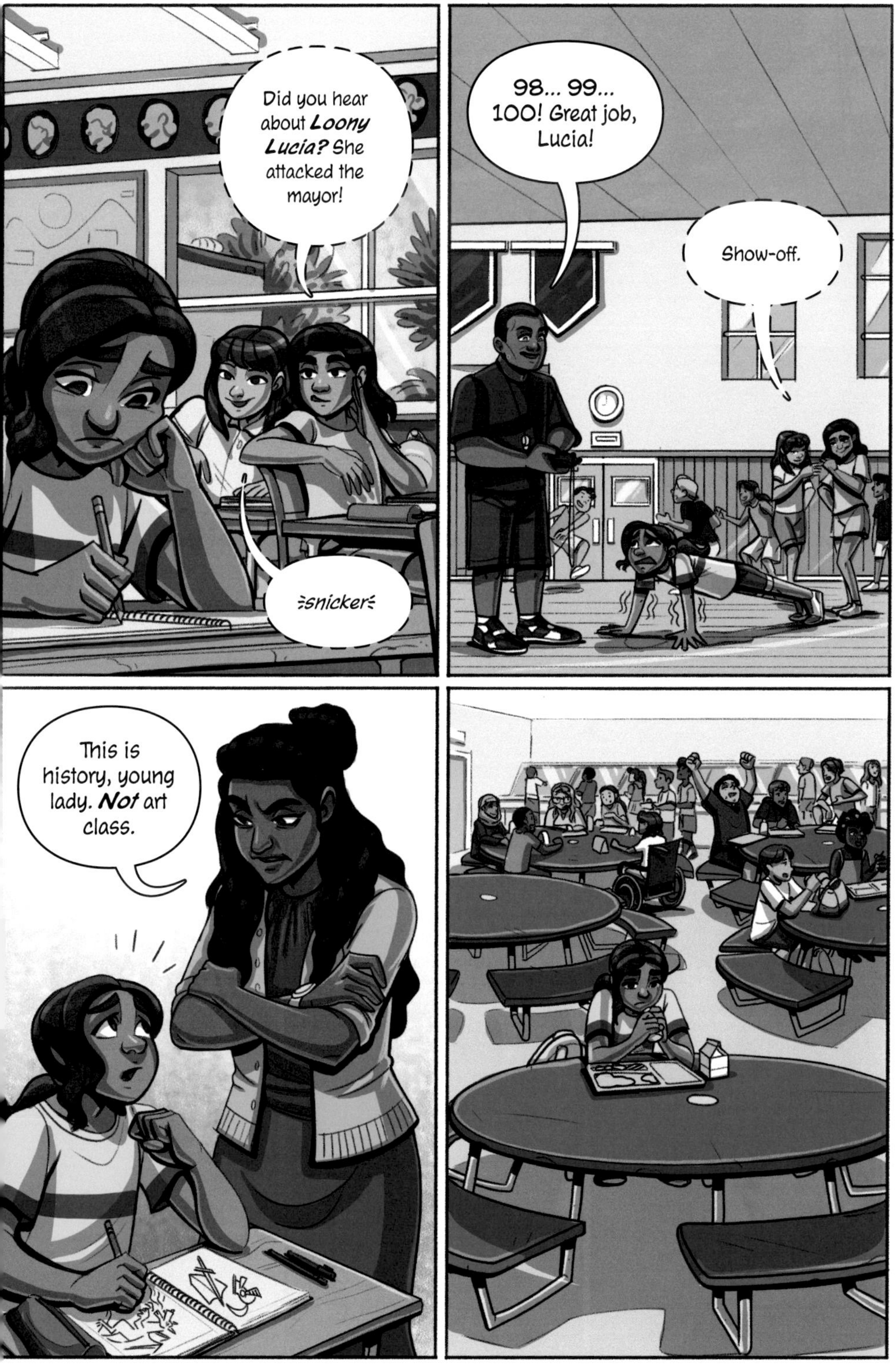
Did you hear about *Loony Lucia?* She attacked the mayor!
snicker
98... 99... 100! Great job, Lucia!
Show-off.
This is history, young lady. *Not* art class.

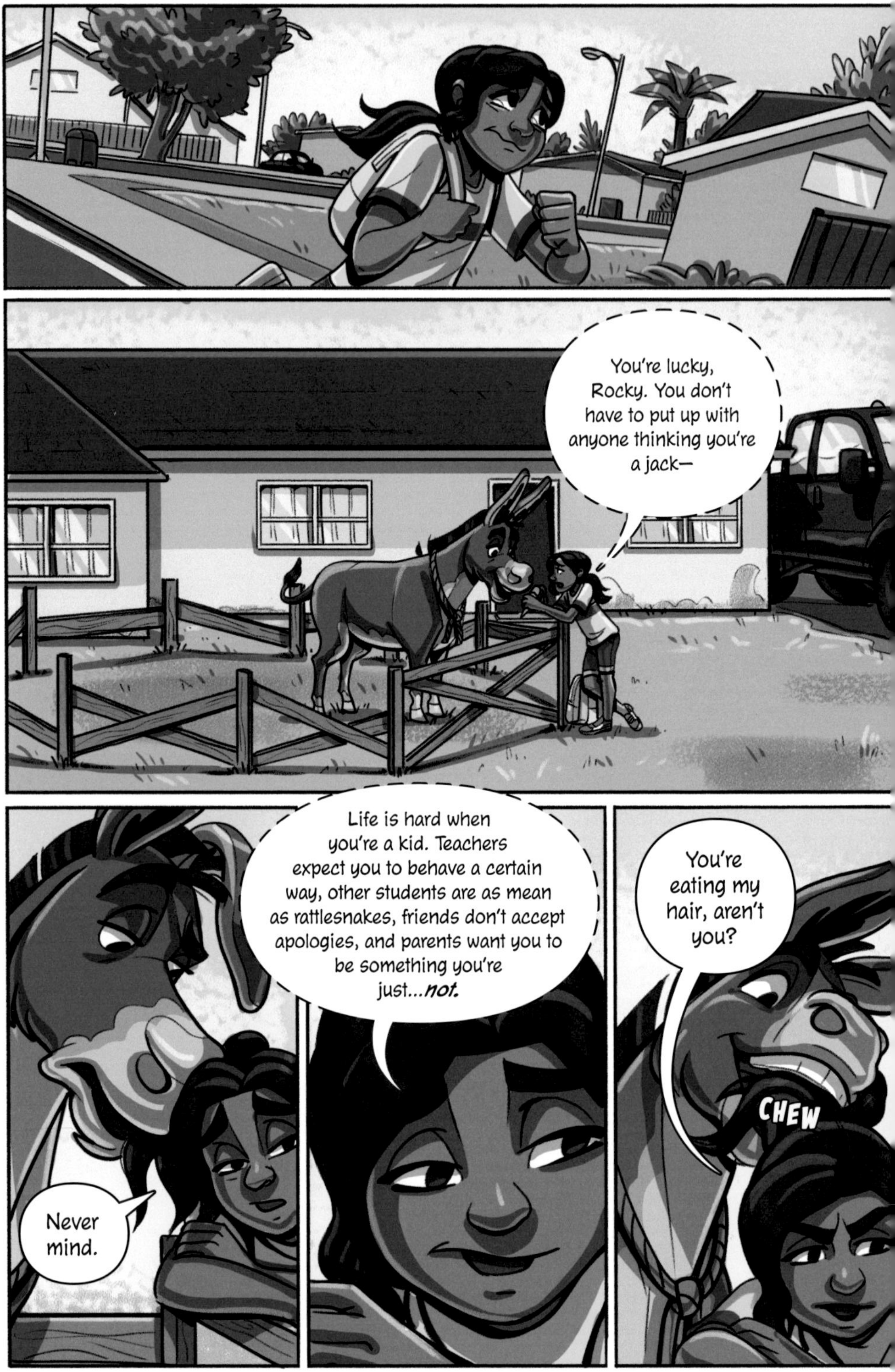
You're lucky, Rocky. You don't have to put up with anyone thinking you're a jack—
Never mind.
Life is hard when you're a kid. Teachers expect you to behave a certain way, other students are as mean as rattlesnakes, friends don't accept apologies, and parents want you to be something you're just...*not.*
You're eating my hair, aren't you?
CHEW

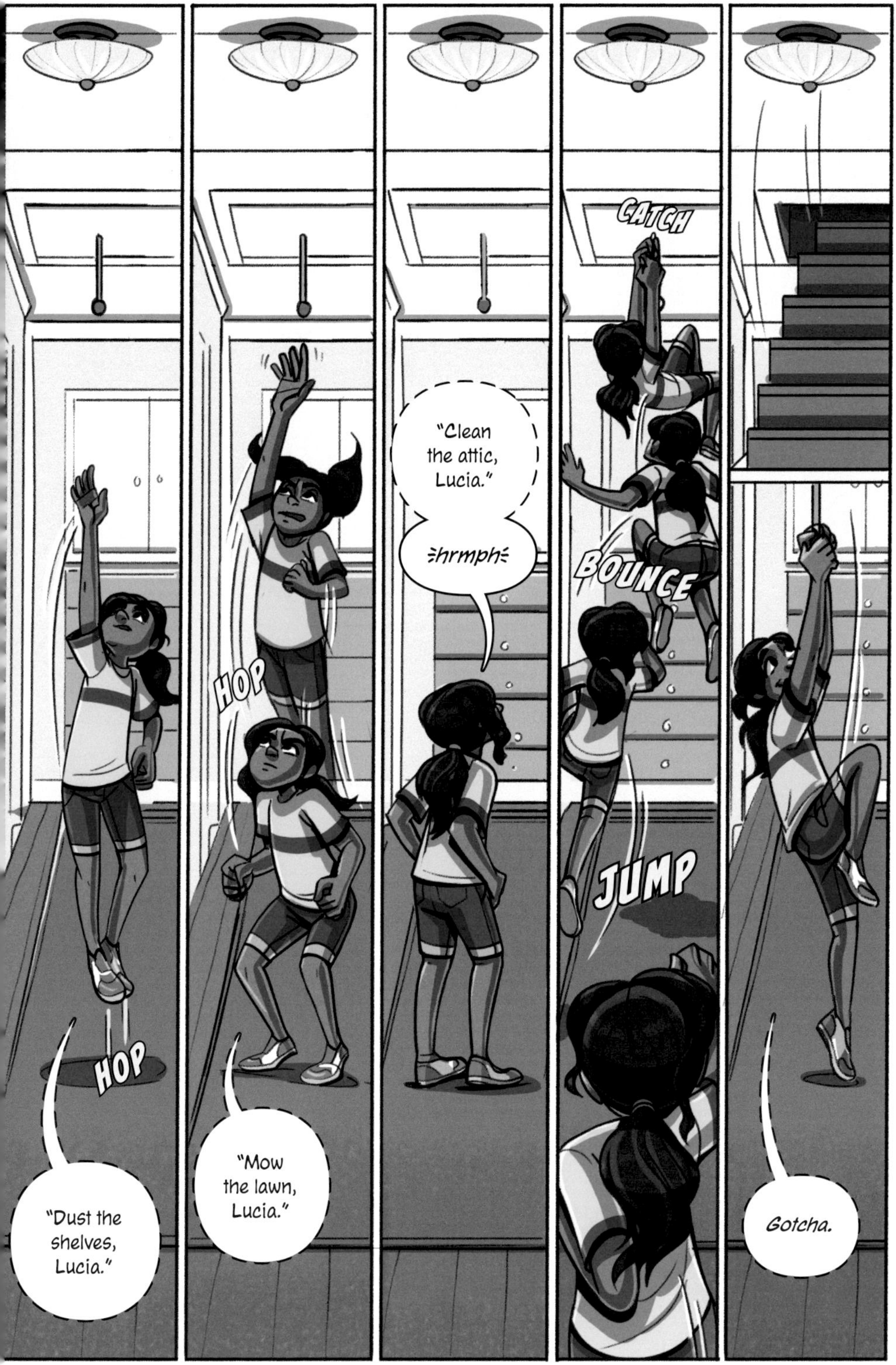
HOP
"Dust the shelves, Lucia."
HOP
"Mow the lawn, Lucia."
"Clean the attic, Lucia."
hrmph
CATCH
BOUNCE
JUMP
Gotcha.

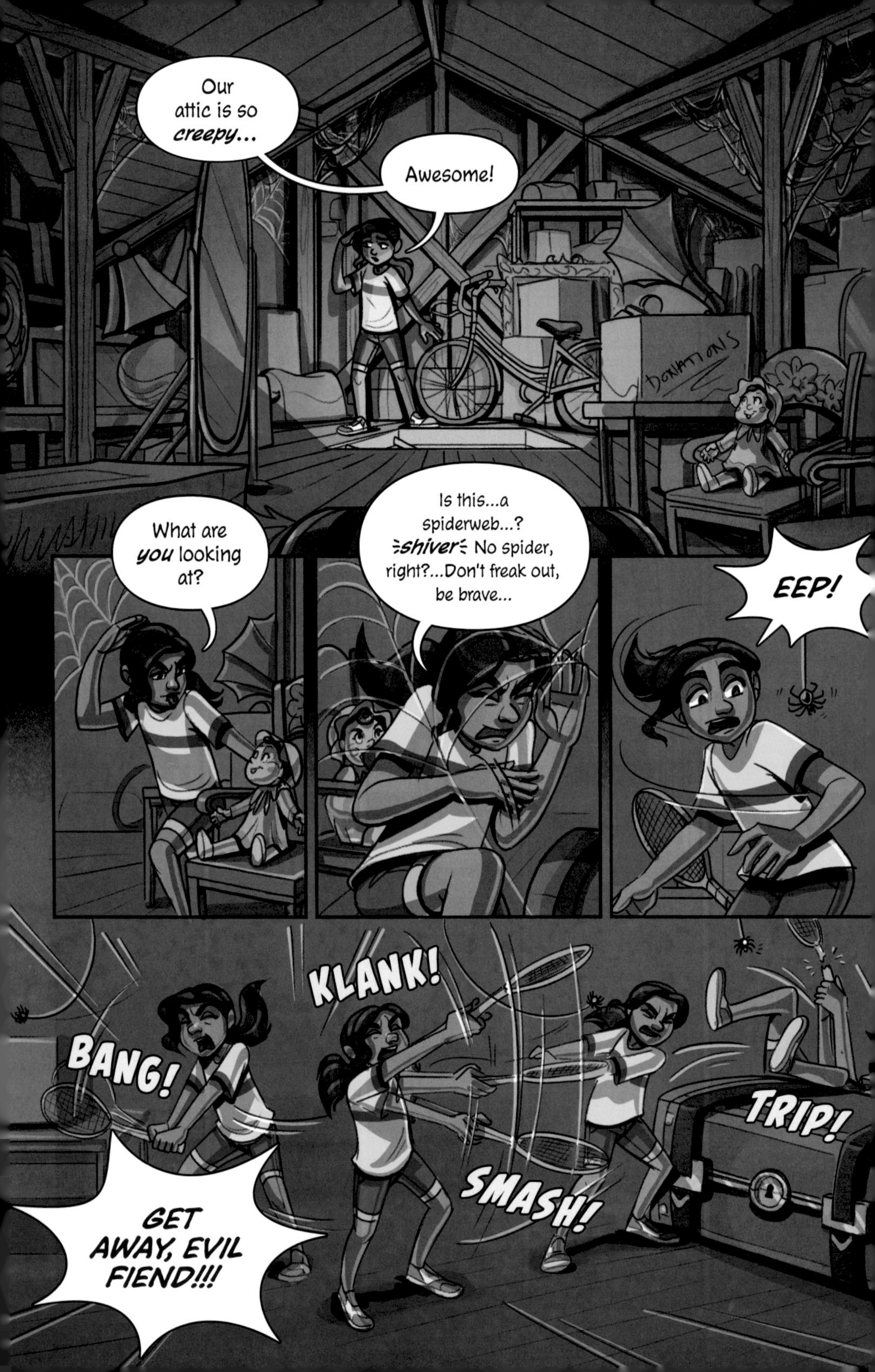
Our attic is so *creepy...*
Awesome!
What are *you* looking at?
Is this...a spiderweb...? *shiver* No spider, right?...Don't freak out, be brave...
EEP!
BANG!
KLANK!
SMASH!
TRIP!
GET AWAY, EVIL FIEND!!!
DONATIONS

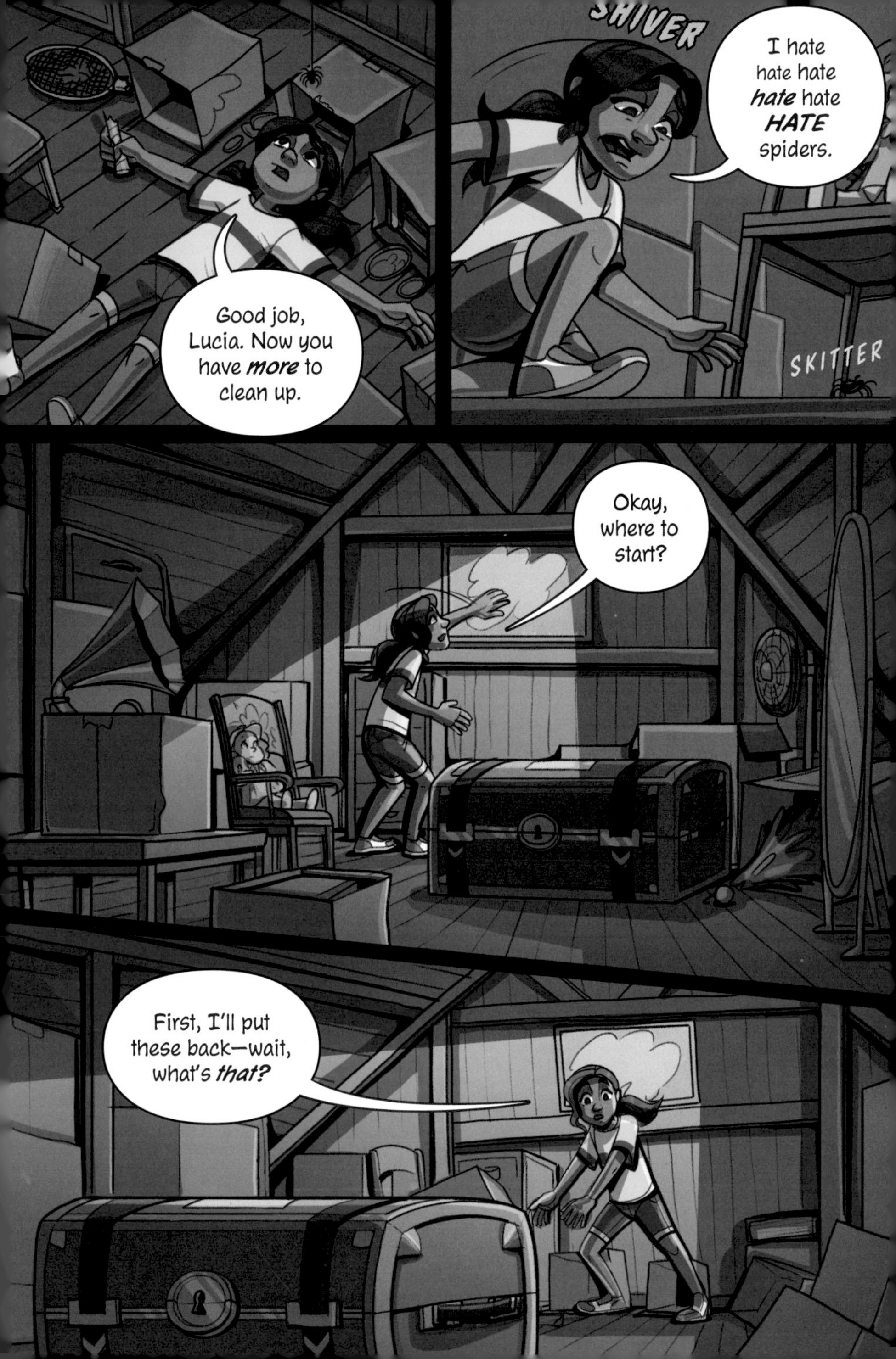
Good job, Lucia. Now you have *more* to clean up.
SHIVER
I hate hate hate *hate* hate *HATE* spiders.
SKITTER
Okay, where to start?
First, I'll put these back—wait, what's *that?*

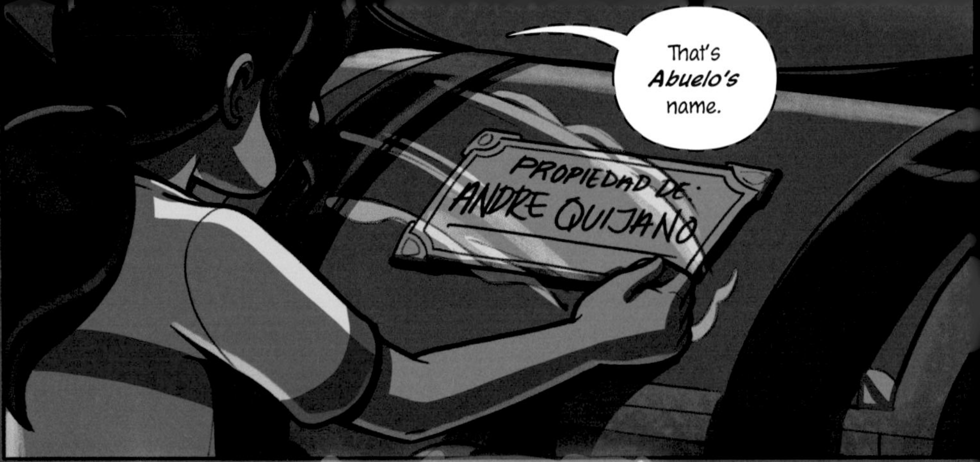
That's *Abuelo's* name.
PROPIEDAD DE:
ANDRE QUIJANO

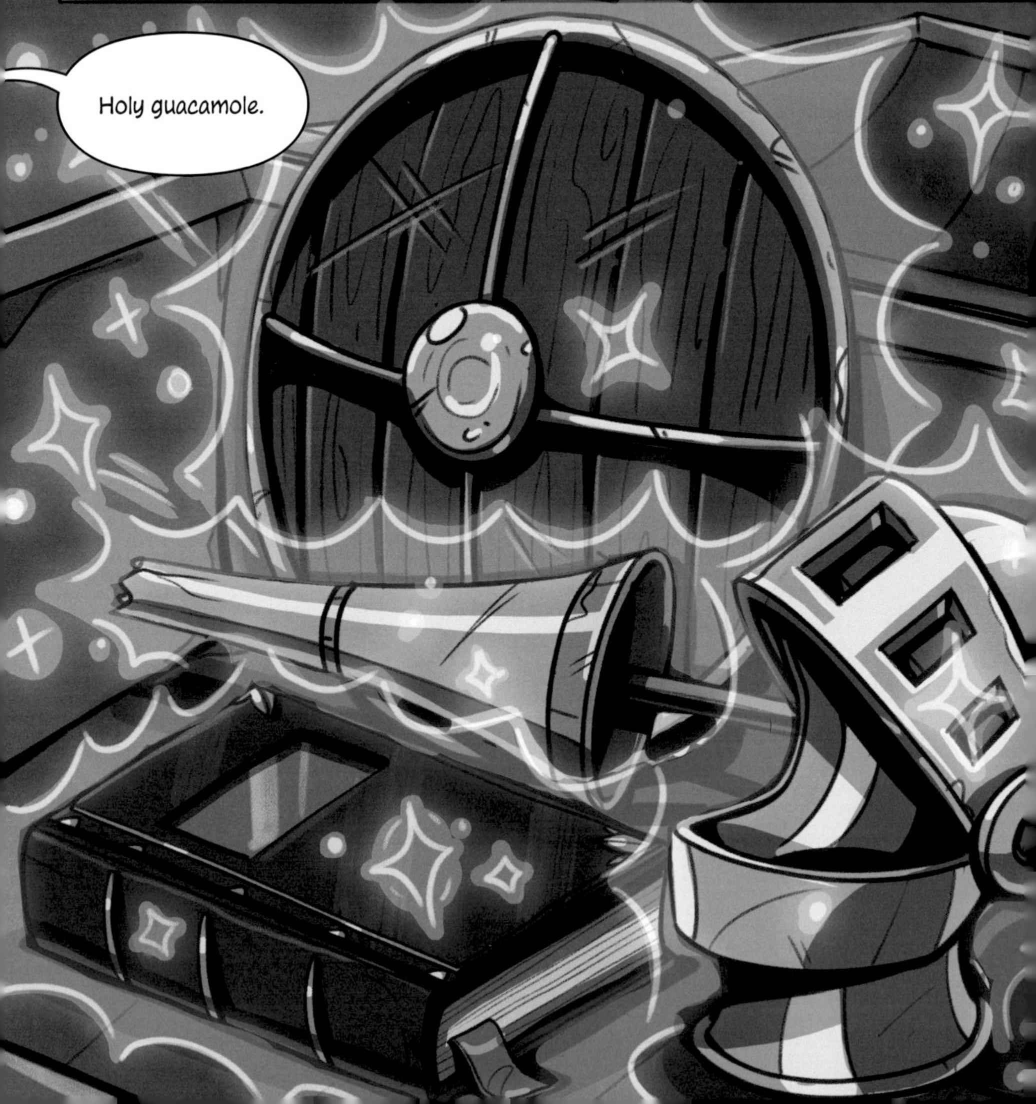
Holy guacamole.

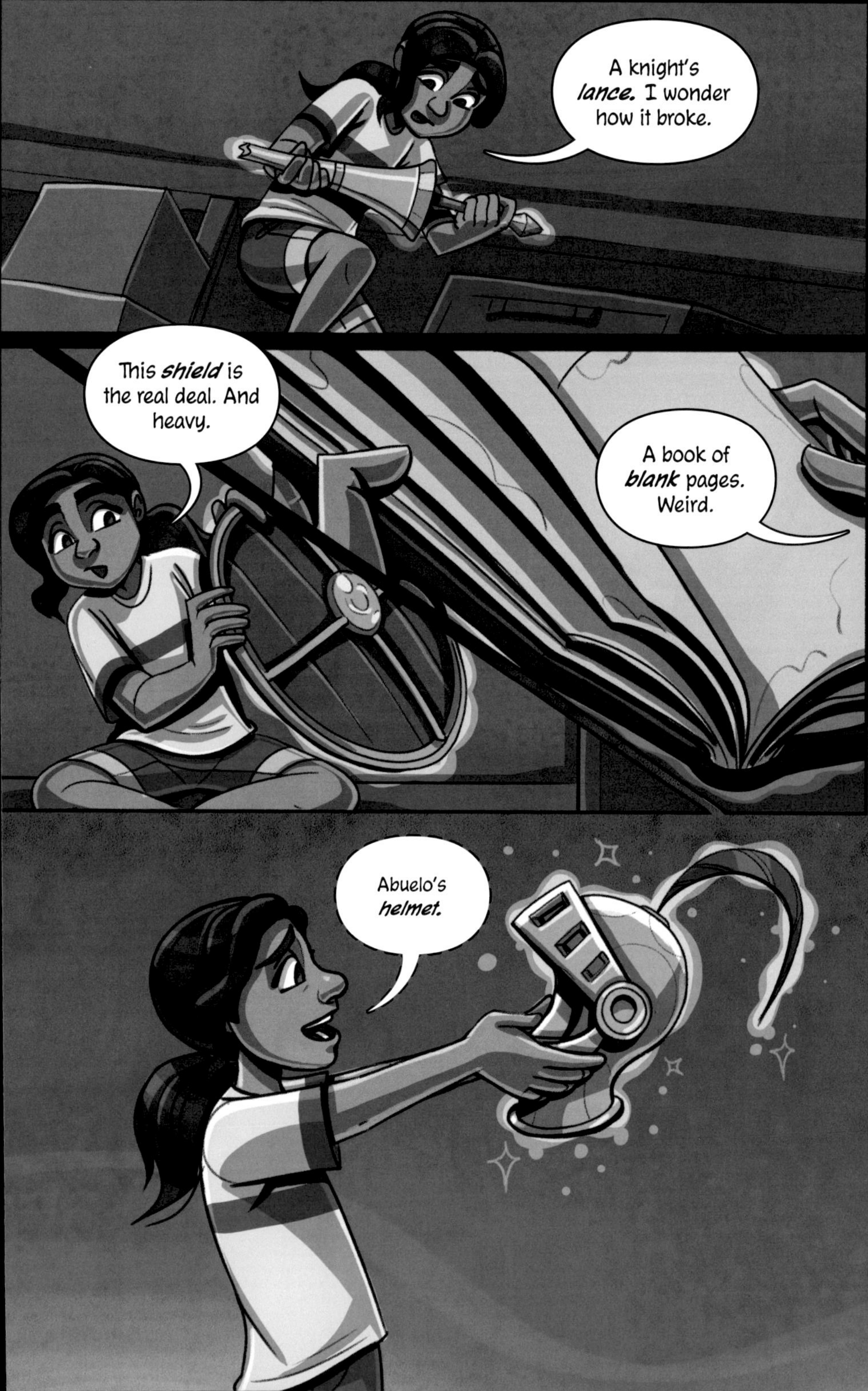
A knight's *lance.* I wonder how it broke.
This *shield* is the real deal. And heavy.
A book of *blank* pages. Weird.
Abuelo's *helmet.*

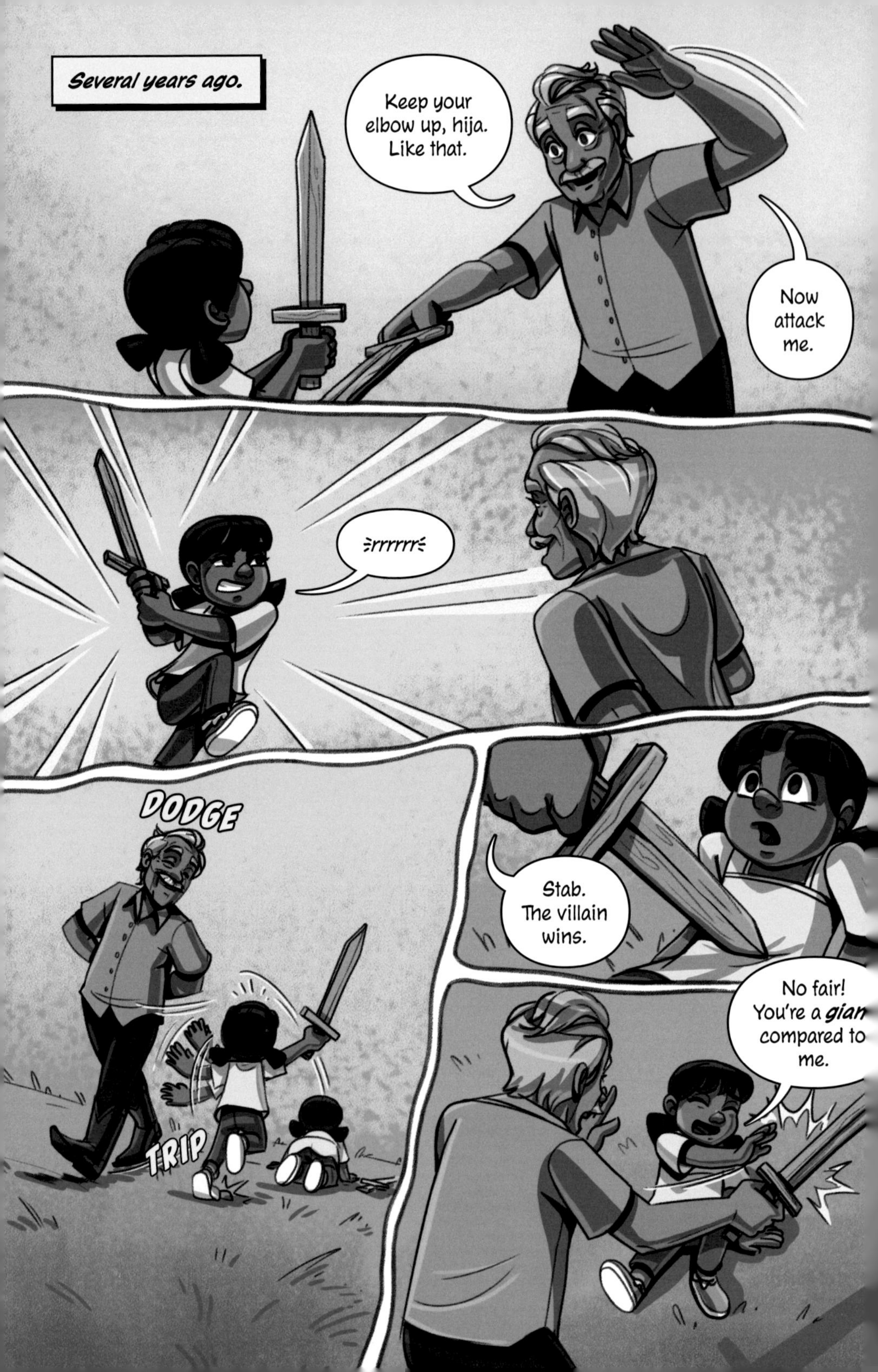

Several years ago.
Keep your elbow up, hija. Like that.
Now attack me.
rrrrrr
DODGE
TRIP
Stab. The villain wins.
No fair! You're a *gian* compared to me.

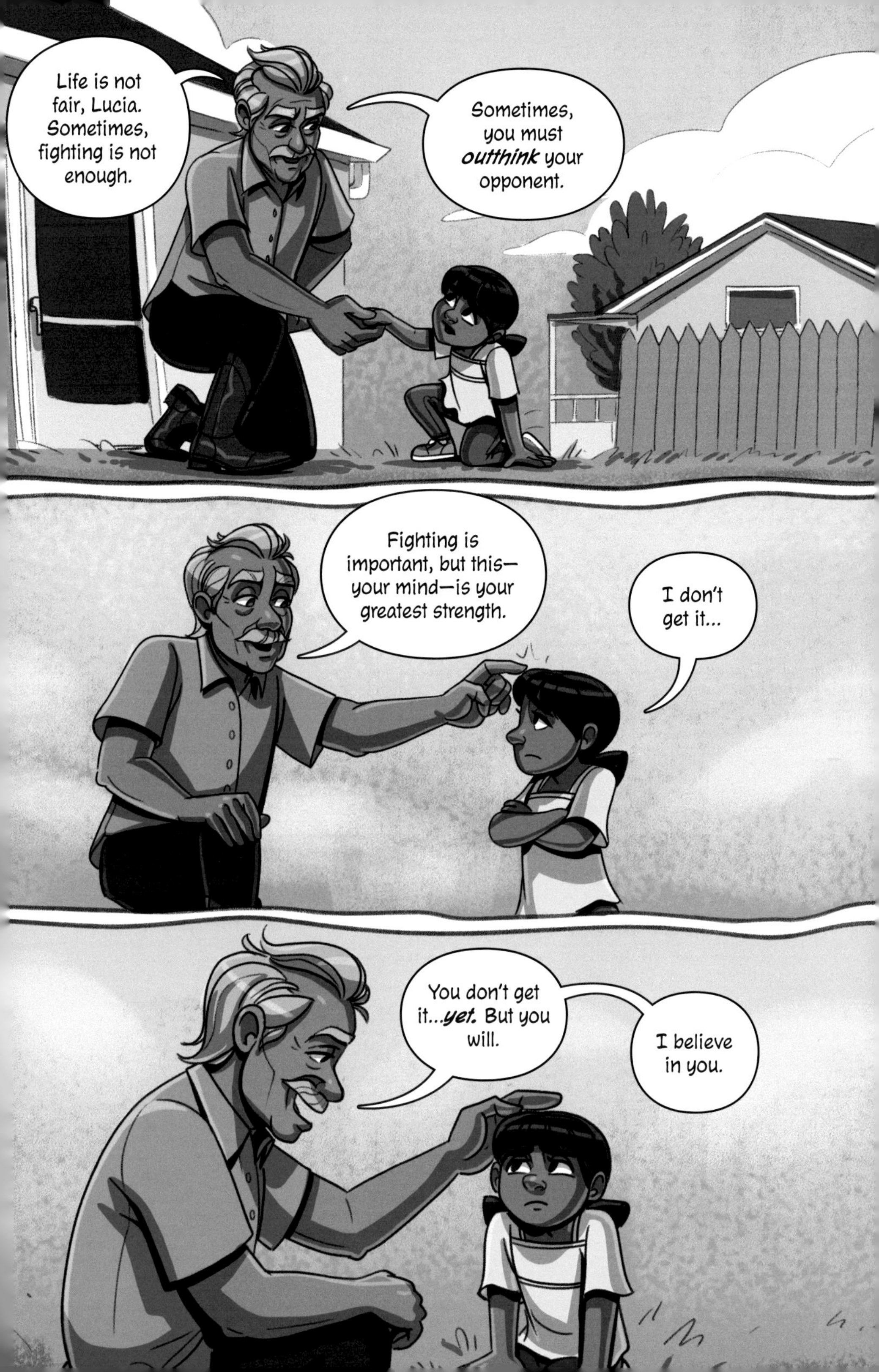
Life is not fair, Lucia. Sometimes, fighting is not enough.
Sometimes, you must *outthink* your opponent.
Fighting is important, but this—your mind—is your greatest strength.
I don't get it...
You don't get it...*yet.* But you will.
I believe in you.

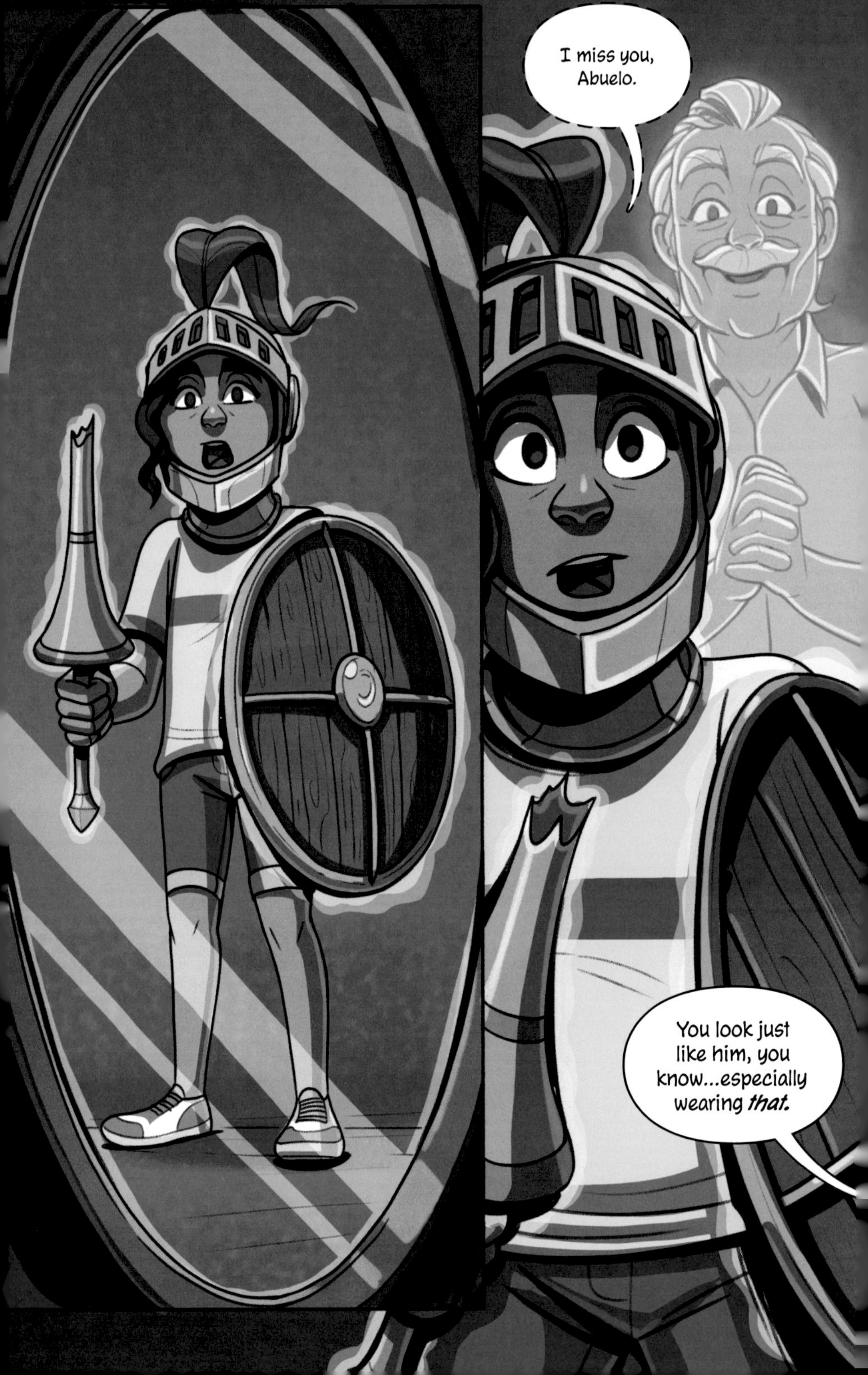
I miss you, Abuelo.
You look just like him, you know...especially wearing *that.*

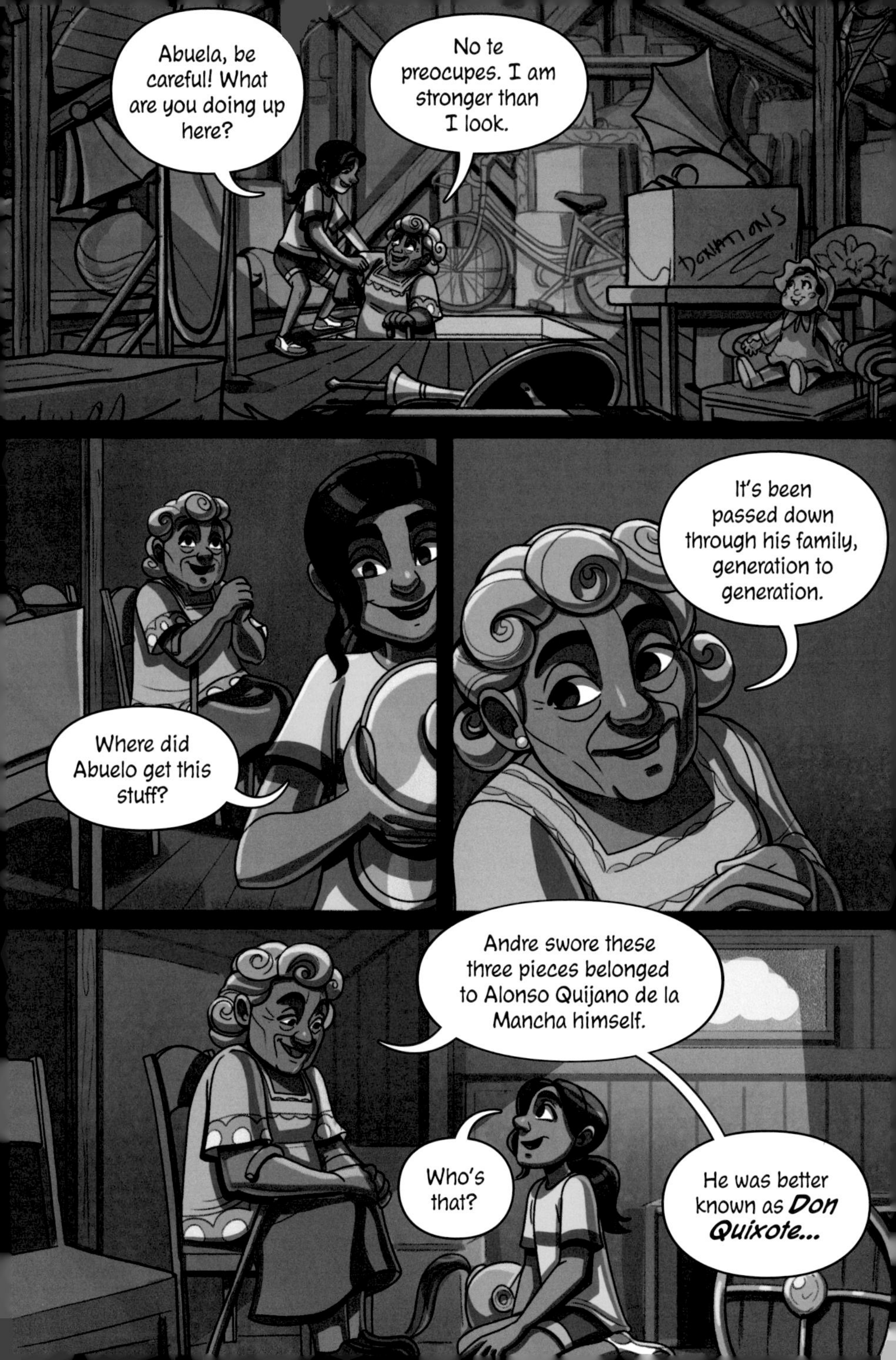
Abuela, be careful! What are you doing up here?
No te preocupes. I am stronger than I look.
DONATIONS
Where did Abuelo get this stuff?
It's been passed down through his family, generation to generation.
Andre swore these three pieces belonged to Alonso Quijano de la Mancha himself.
Who's that?
He was better known as ***Don Quixote...***

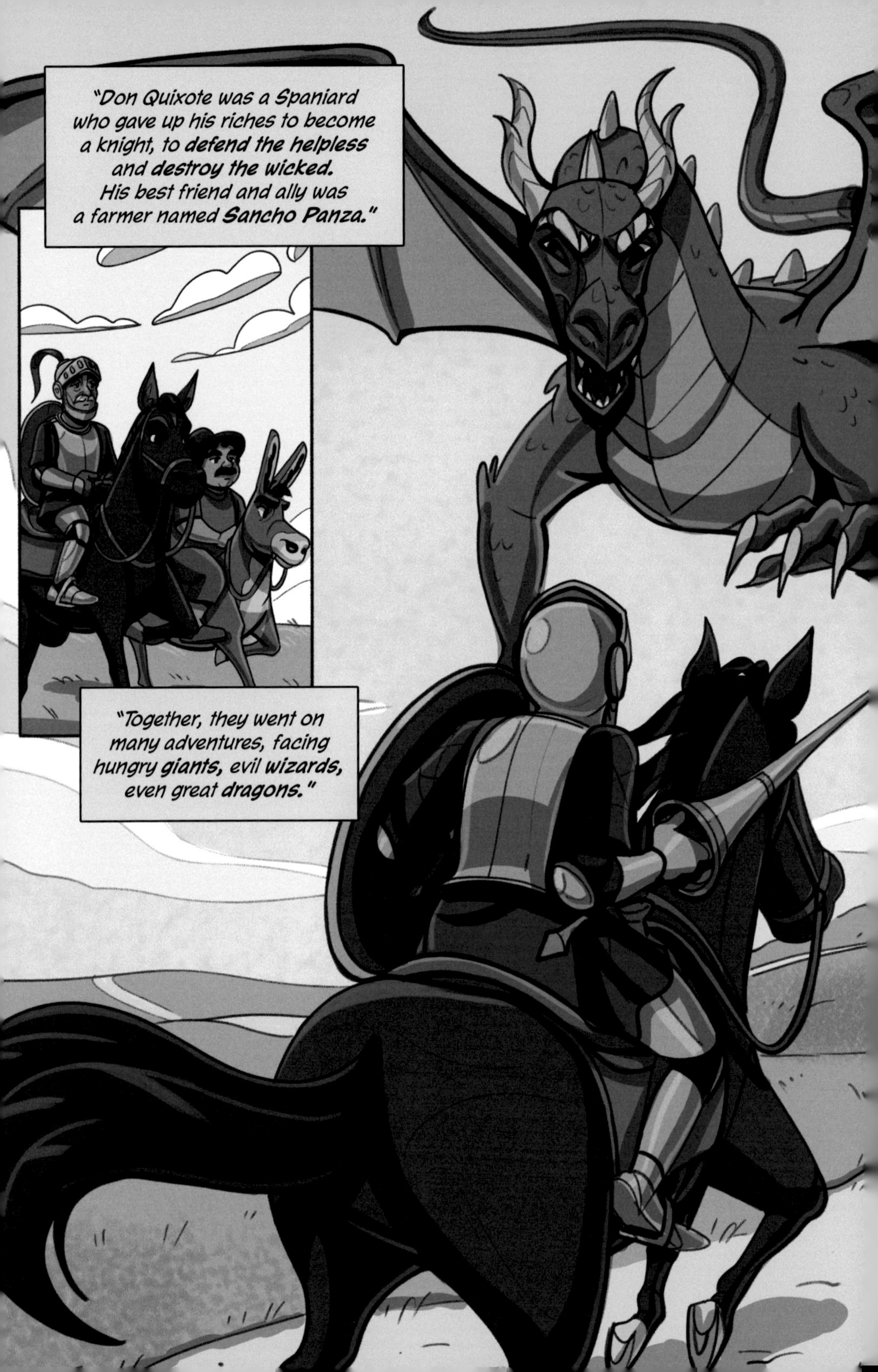
"Don Quixote was a Spaniard who gave up his riches to become a knight, to **defend the helpless** and **destroy the wicked.** His best friend and ally was a farmer named **Sancho Panza.**"
"Together, they went on many adventures, facing hungry **giants,** evil **wizards,** even great **dragons.**"

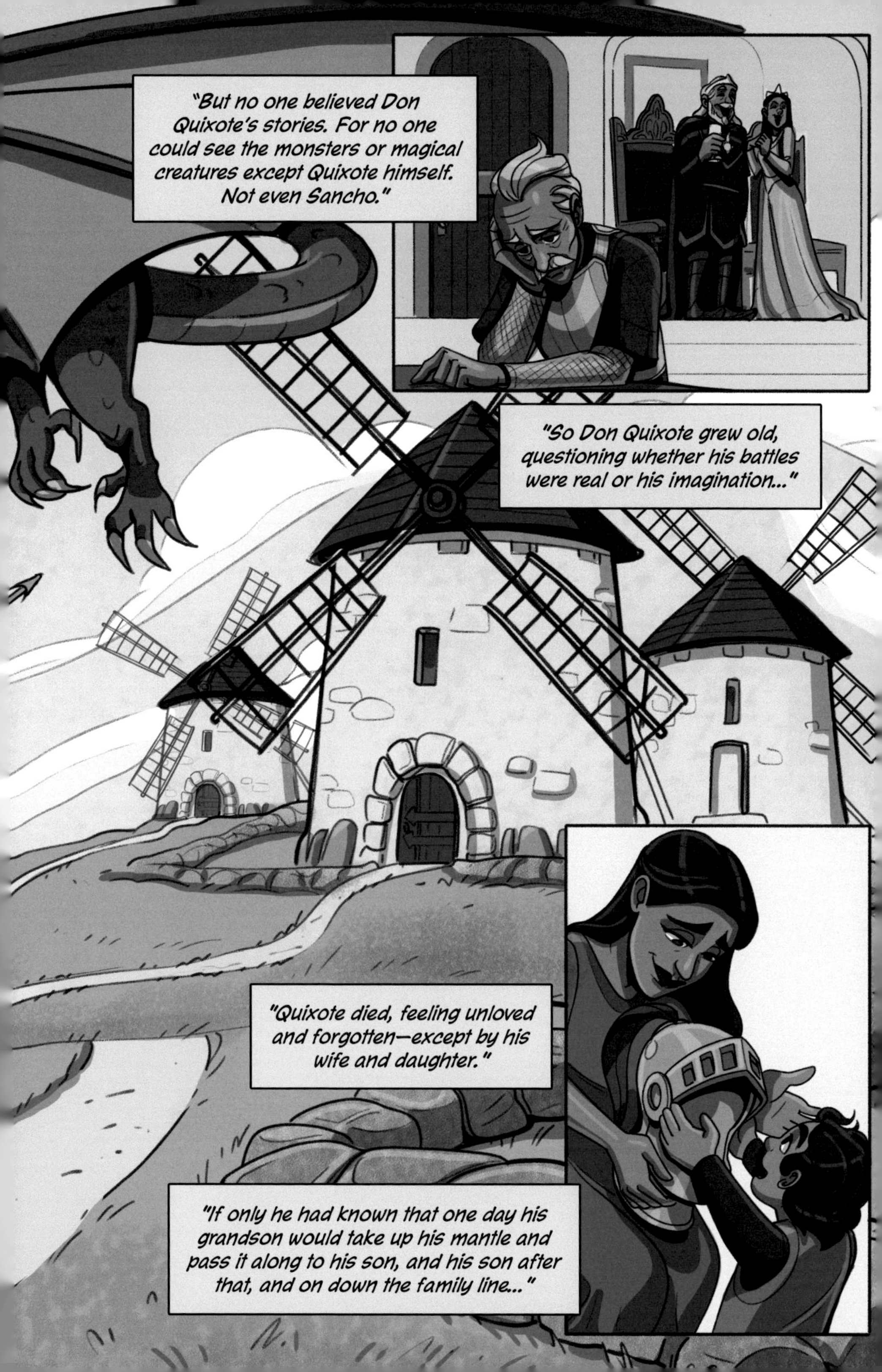
"But no one believed Don Quixote's stories. For no one could see the monsters or magical creatures except Quixote himself. Not even Sancho."
"So Don Quixote grew old, questioning whether his battles were real or his imagination..."
"Quixote died, feeling unloved and forgotten—except by his wife and daughter."
"If only he had known that one day his grandson would take up his mantle and pass it along to his son, and his son after that, and on down the family line..."

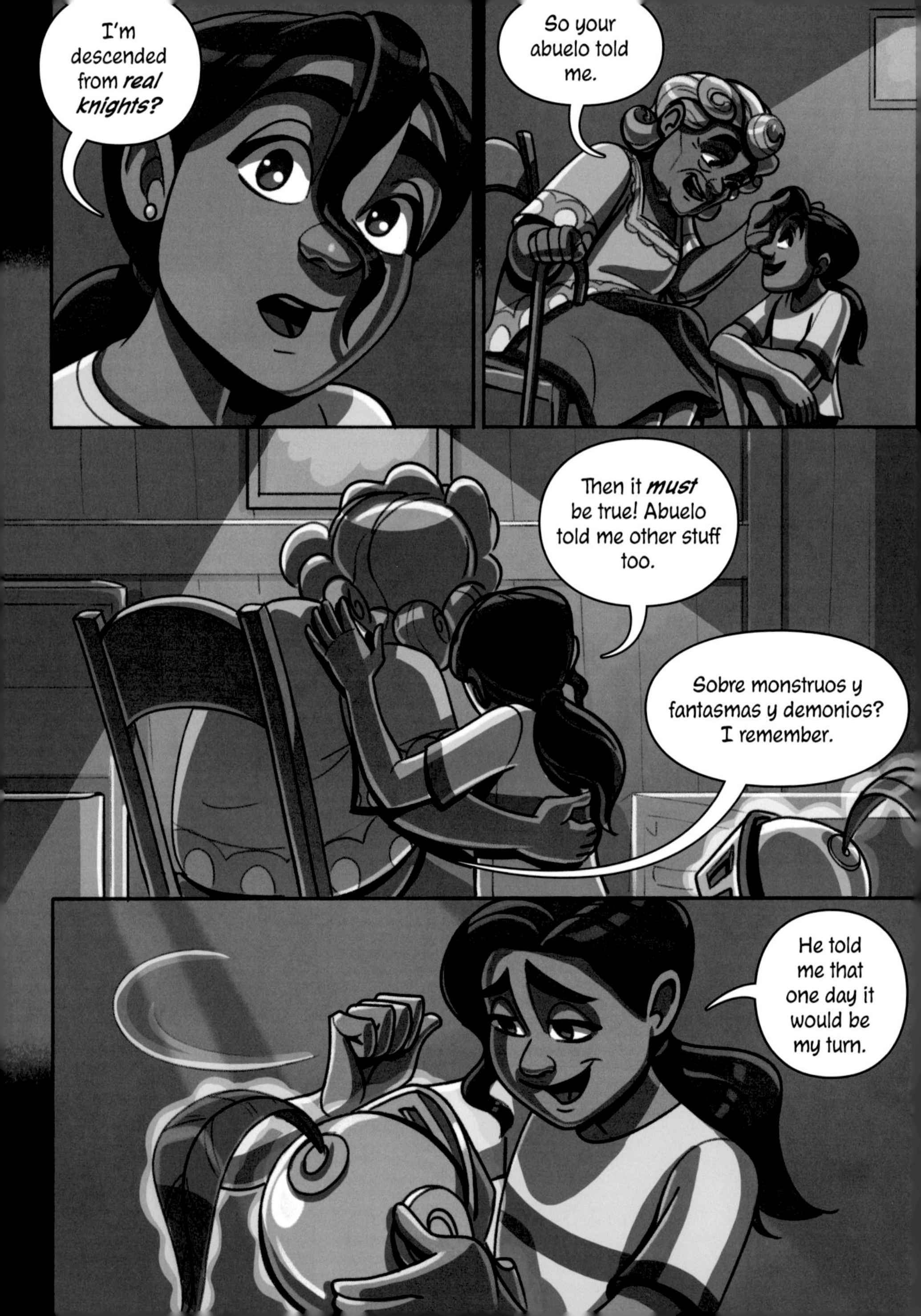
I'm descended from *real knights?*
So your abuelo told me.
Then it *must* be true! Abuelo told me other stuff too.
Sobre monstruos y fantasmas y demonios? I remember.
He told me that one day it would be my turn.

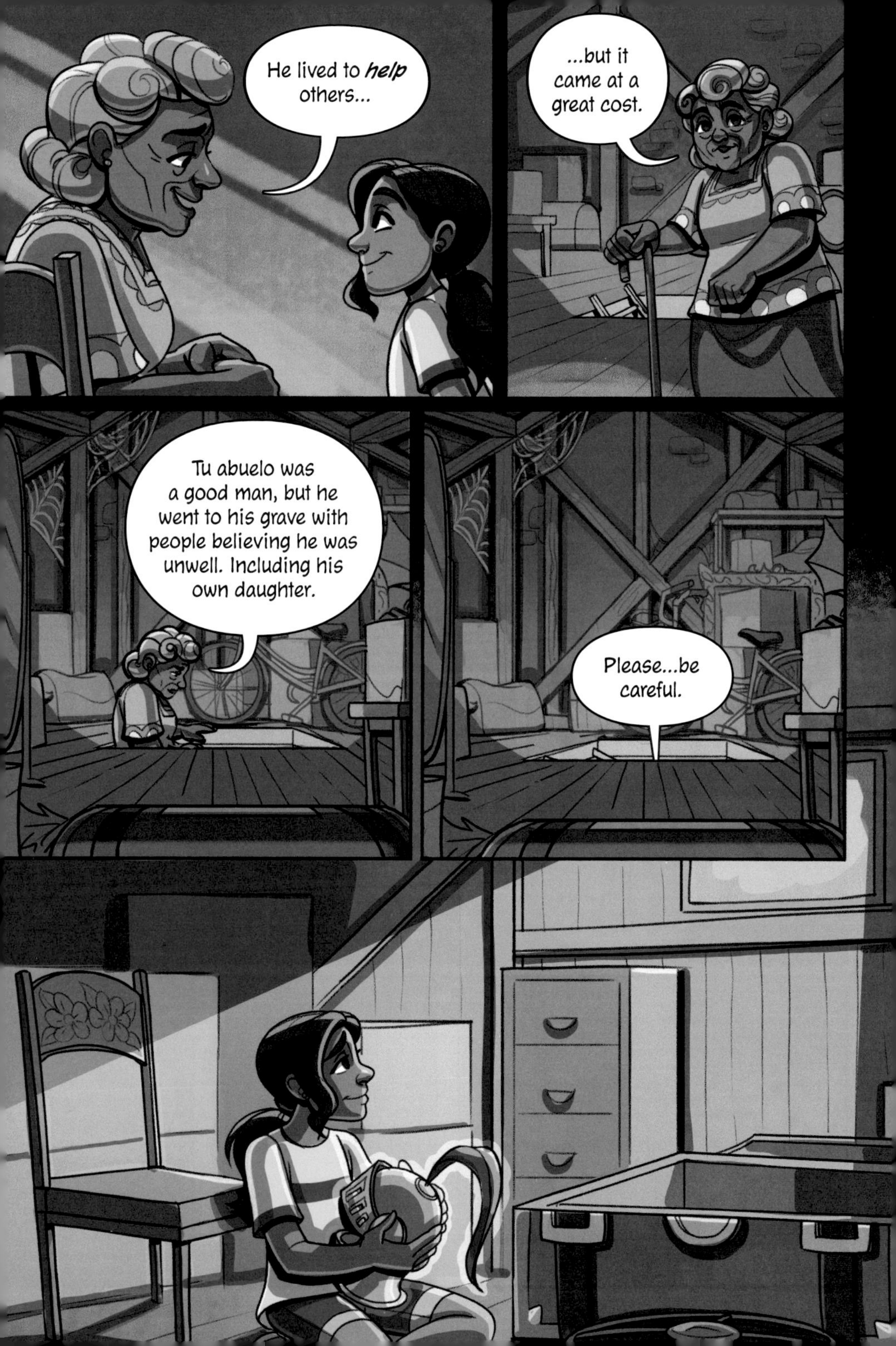
He lived to *help* others...
...but it came at a great cost.
Tu abuelo was a good man, but he went to his grave with people believing he was unwell. Including his own daughter.
Please...be careful.

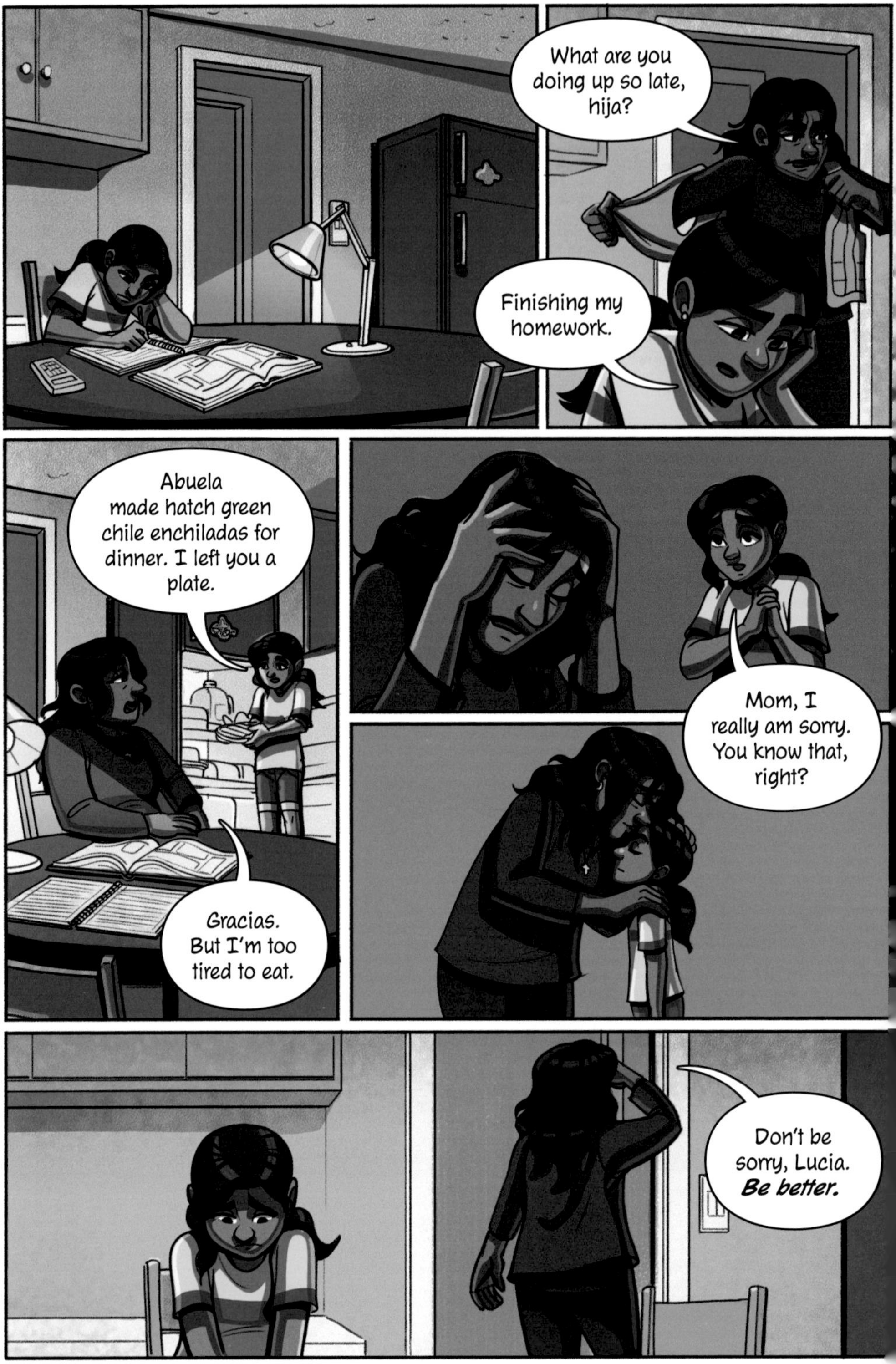
What are you doing up so late, hija?
Finishing my homework.
Abuela made hatch green chile enchiladas for dinner. I left you a plate.
Gracias. But I'm too tired to eat.
Mom, I really am sorry. You know that, right?
Don't be sorry, Lucia. ***Be better.***

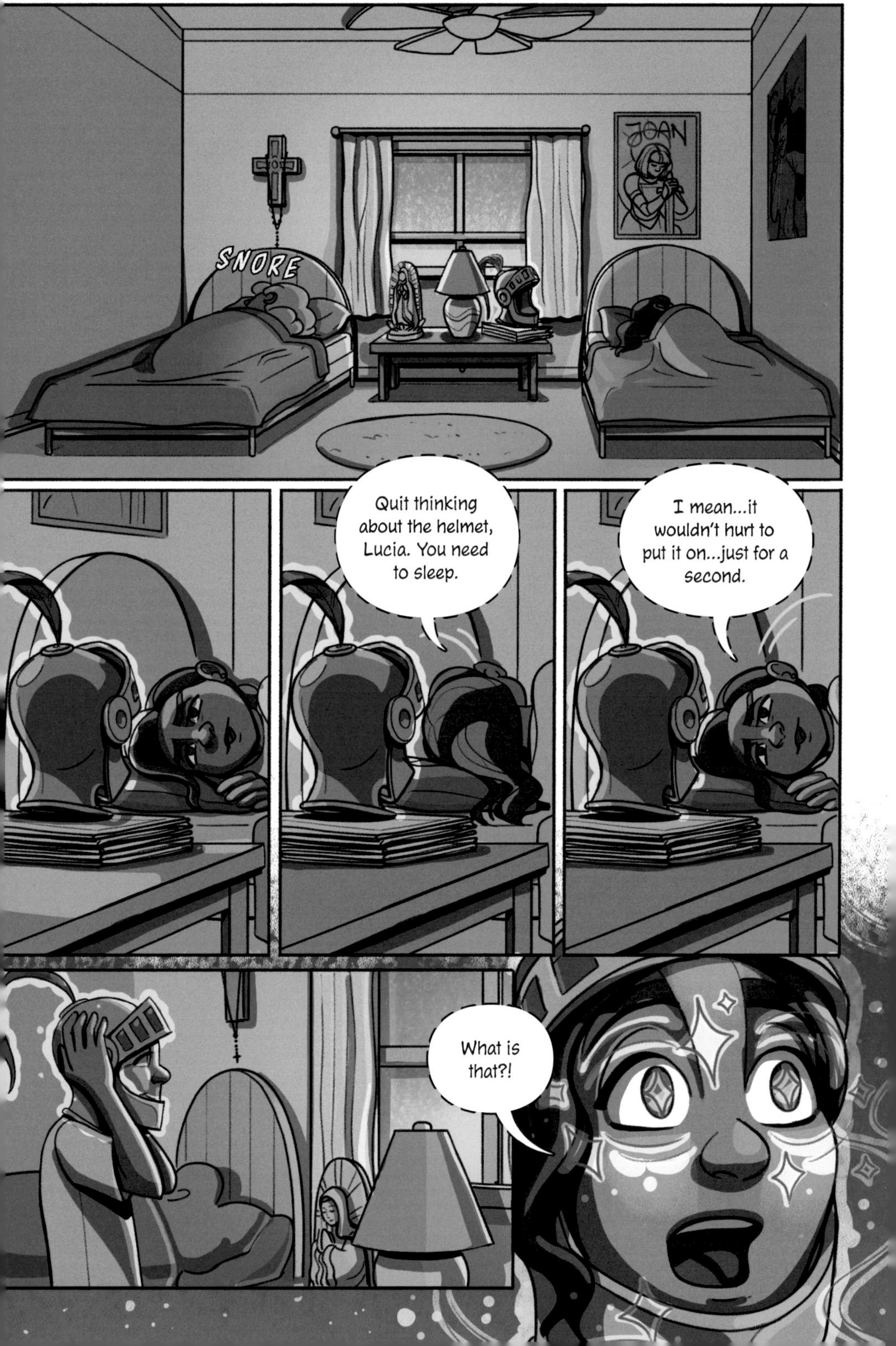

SNORE
Quit thinking about the helmet, Lucia. You need to sleep.
I mean...it wouldn't hurt to put it on...just for a second.
JOAN
What is that?!

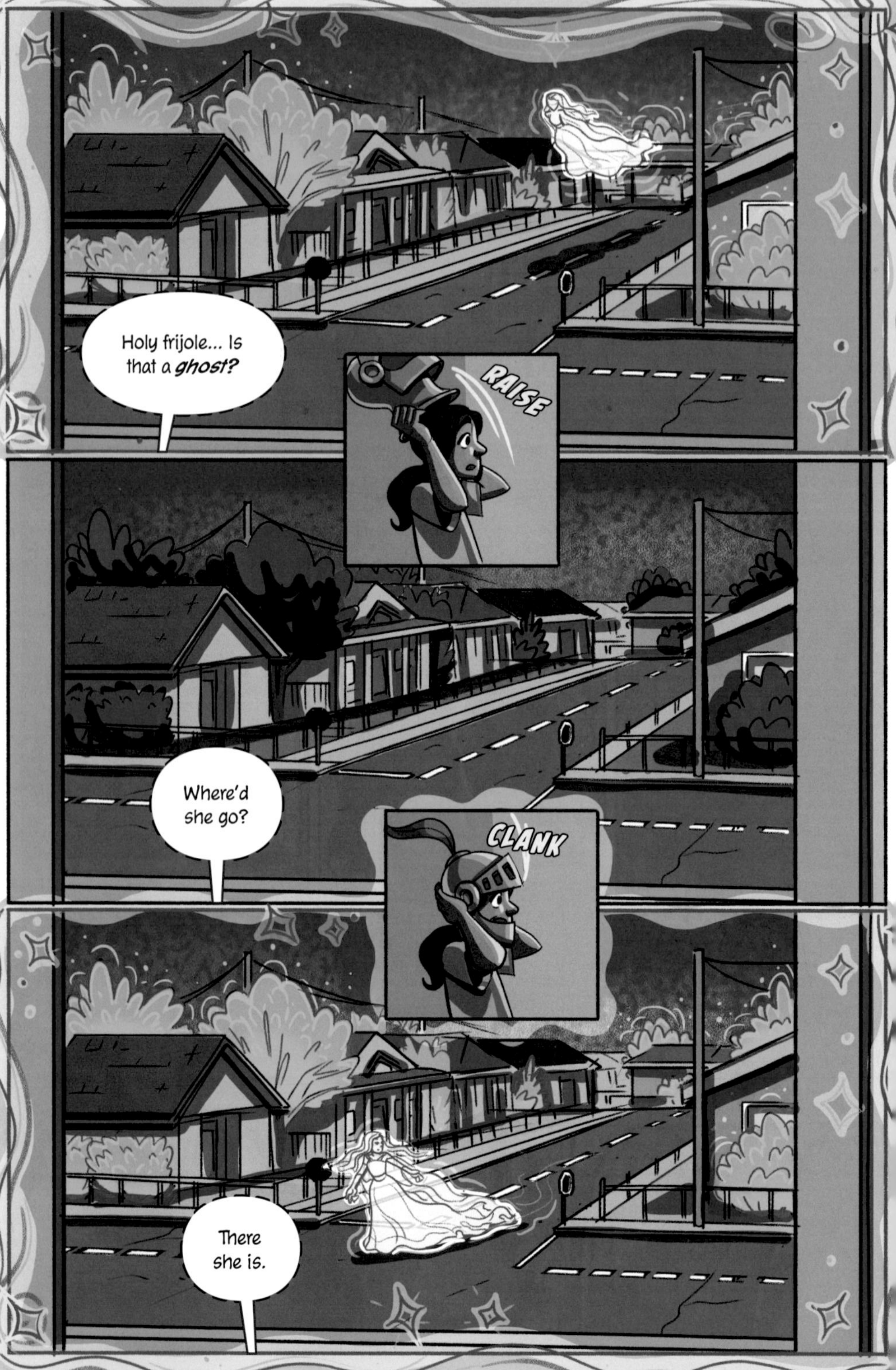
Holy frijole... Is that a ghost?
RAISE
Where'd she go?
CLANK
There she is.

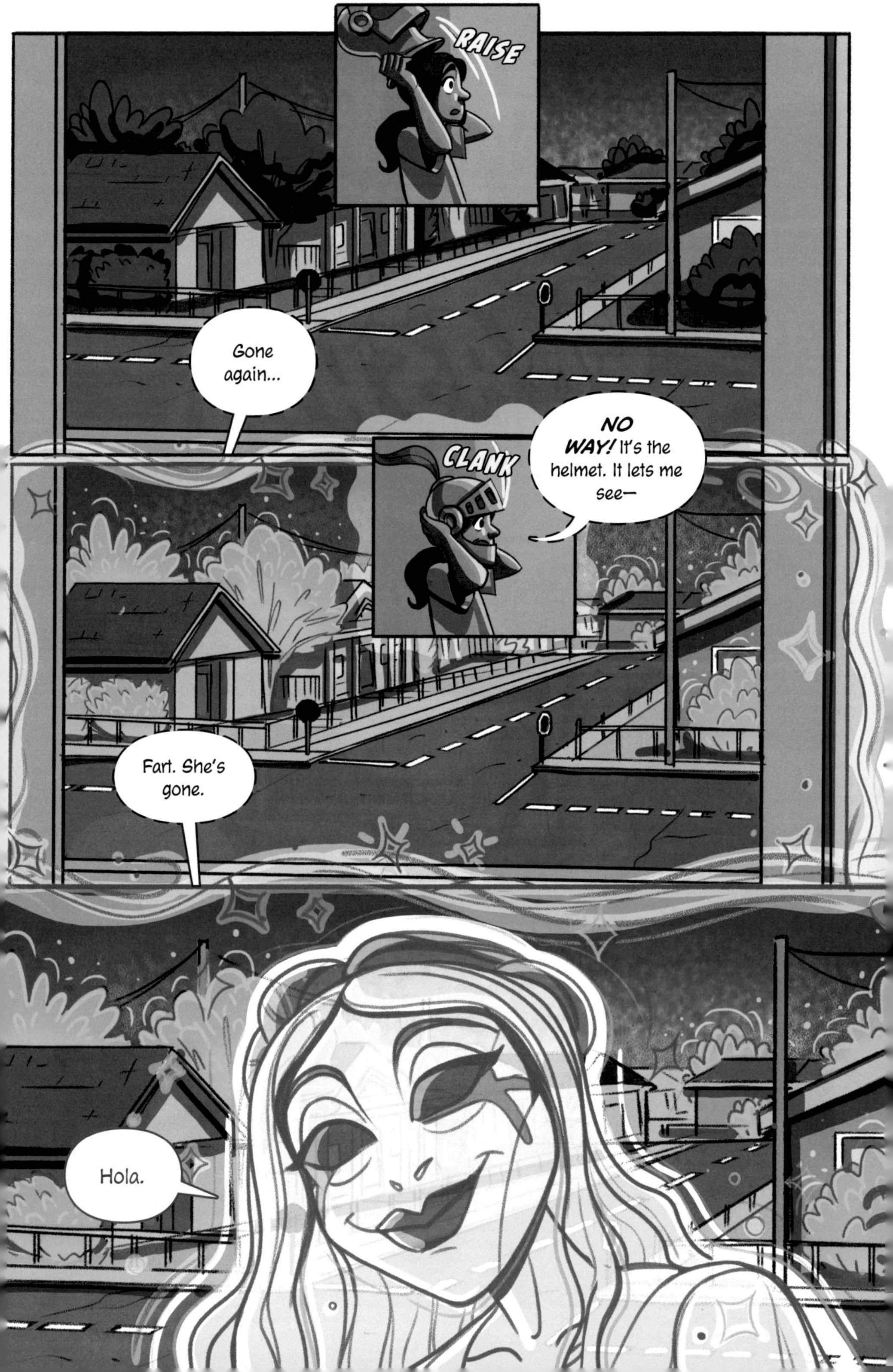
RAISE
Gone again...
CLANK
NO WAY! It's the helmet. It lets me see—
Fart. She's gone.
Hola.

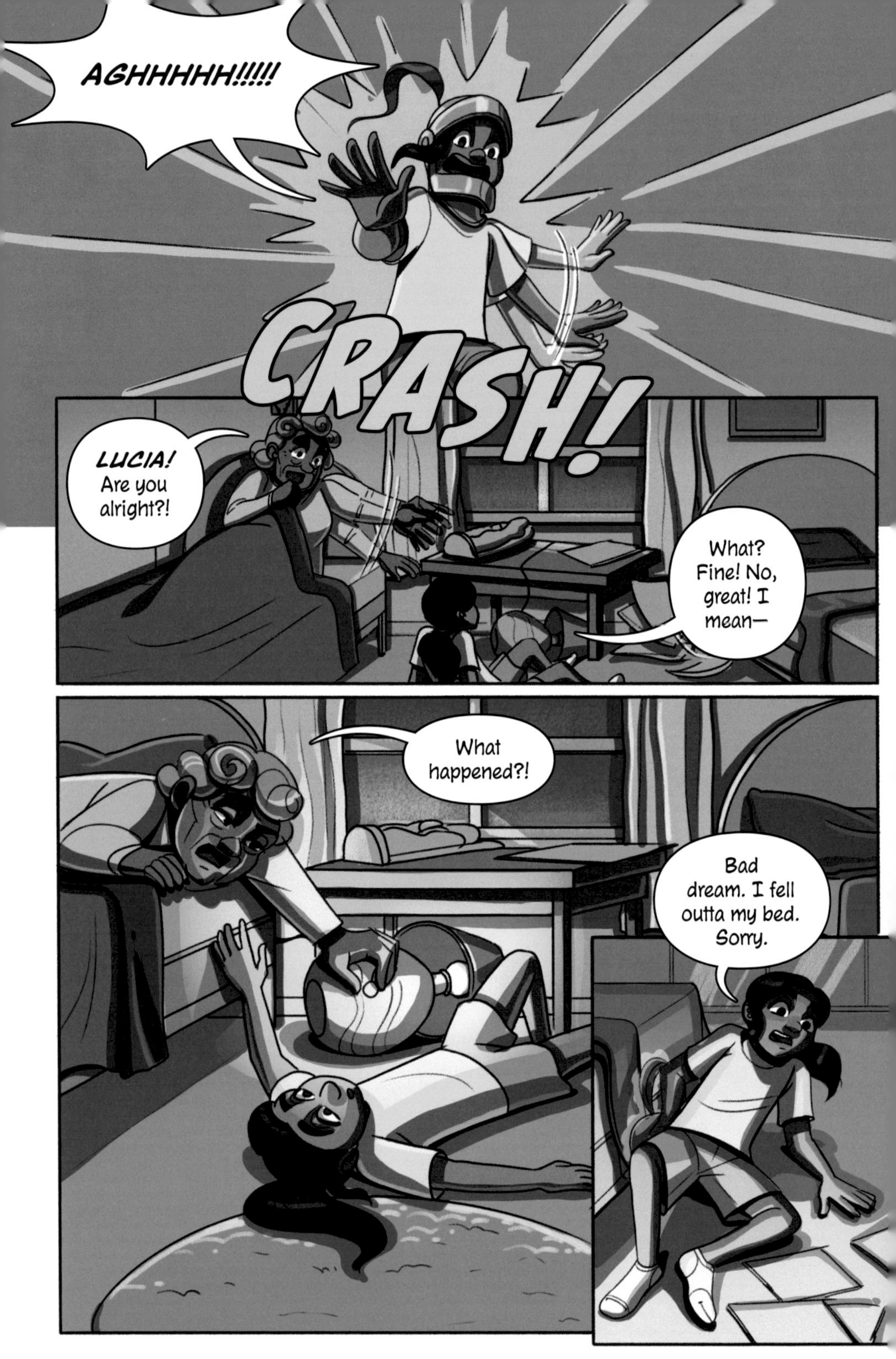
AGHHHHH!!!!!
CRASH!
LUCIA! Are you alright?!
What? Fine! No, great! I mean—
What happened?!
Bad dream. I fell outta my bed. Sorry.

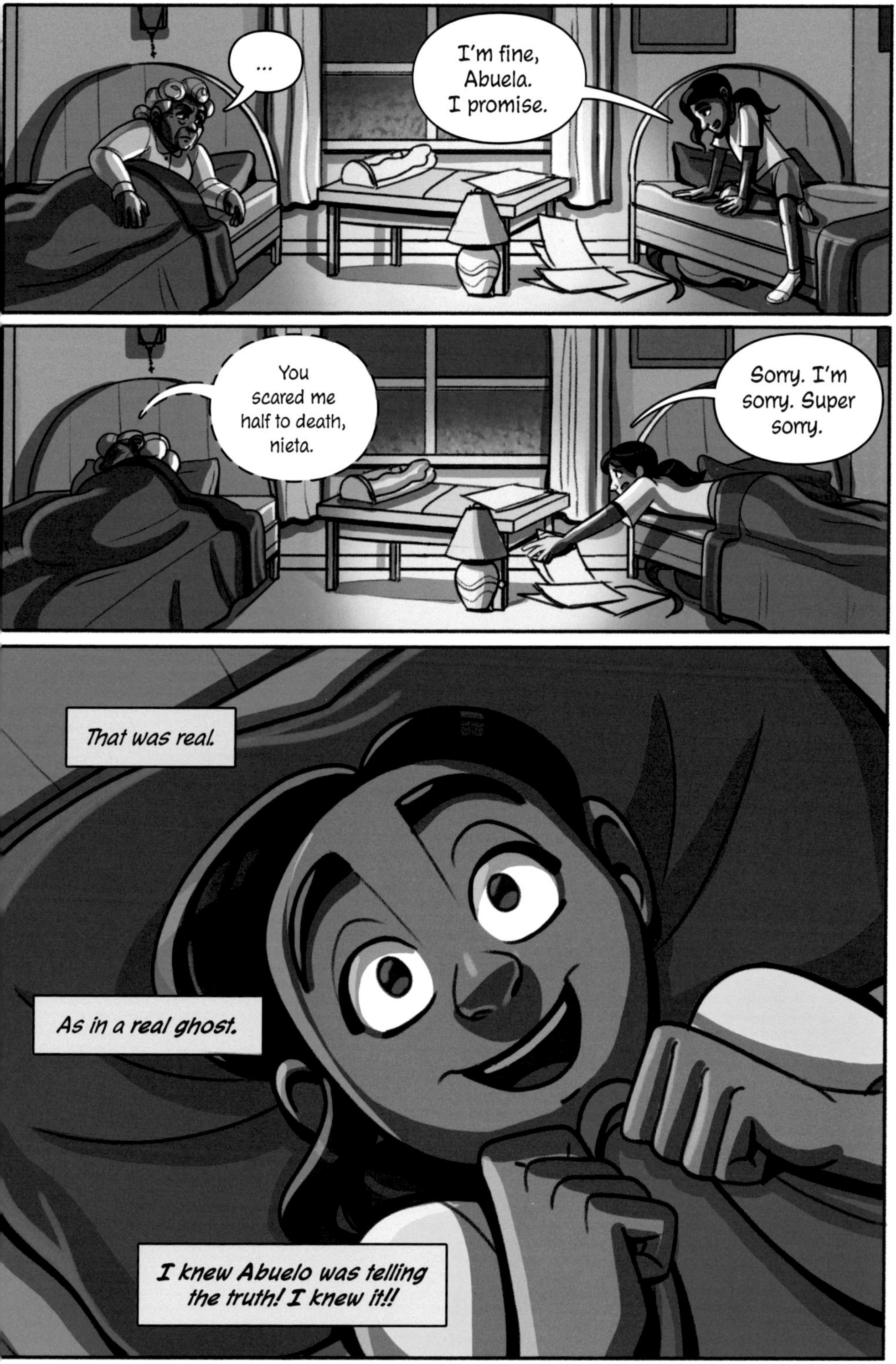
...
I'm fine, Abuela. I promise.
You scared me half to death, nieta.
Sorry. I'm sorry. Super sorry.
That was real.
As in a real ghost.
I knew Abuelo was telling the truth! I knew it!!

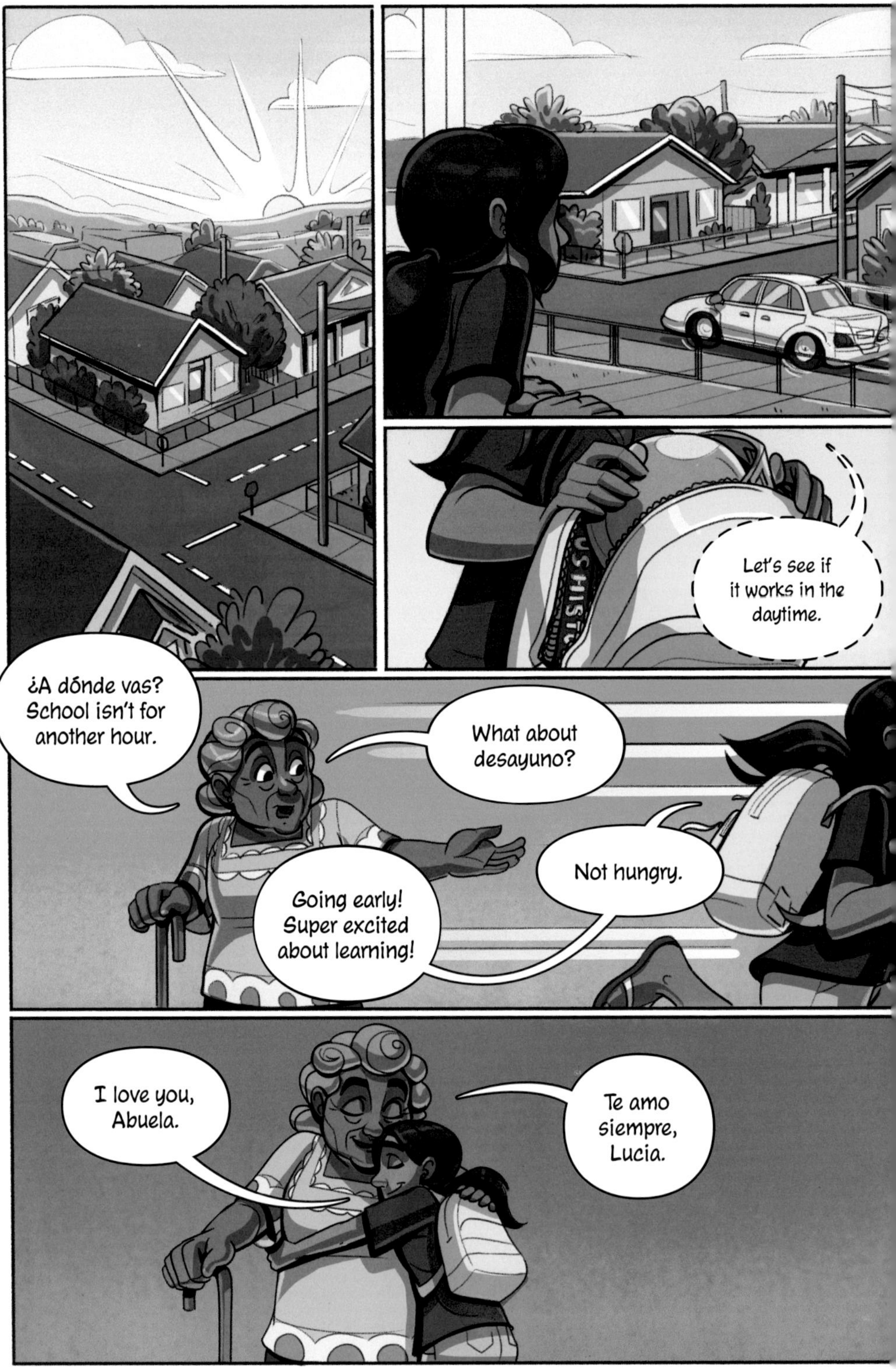
Let's see if it works in the daytime.
¿A dónde vas? School isn't for another hour.
What about desayuno?
Going early! Super excited about learning!
Not hungry.
I love you, Abuela.
Te amo siempre, Lucia.

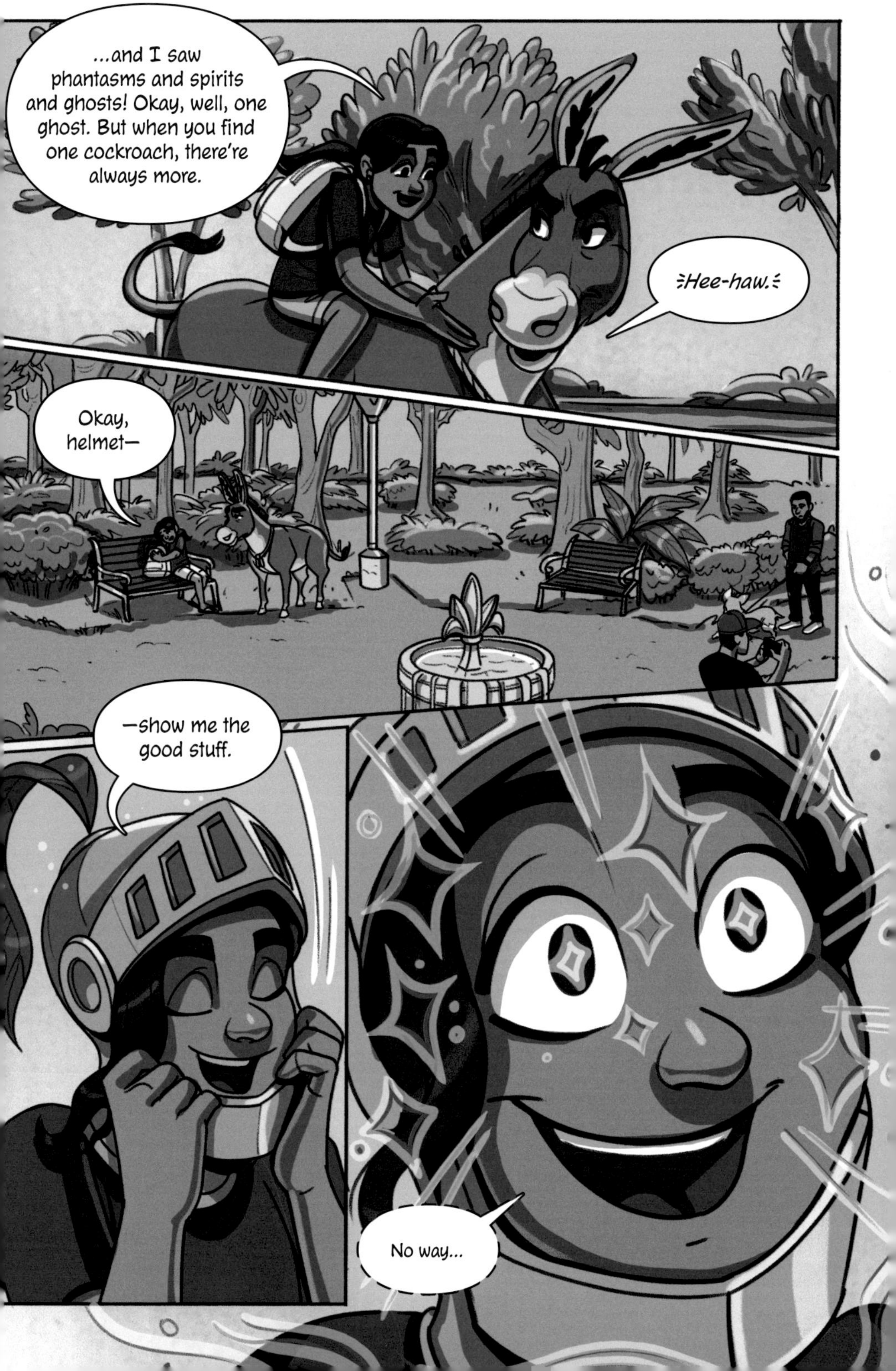
...and I saw phantasms and spirits and ghosts! Okay, well, one ghost. But when you find one cockroach, there're always more.
Hee-haw.
Okay, helmet—
—show me the good stuff.
No way...

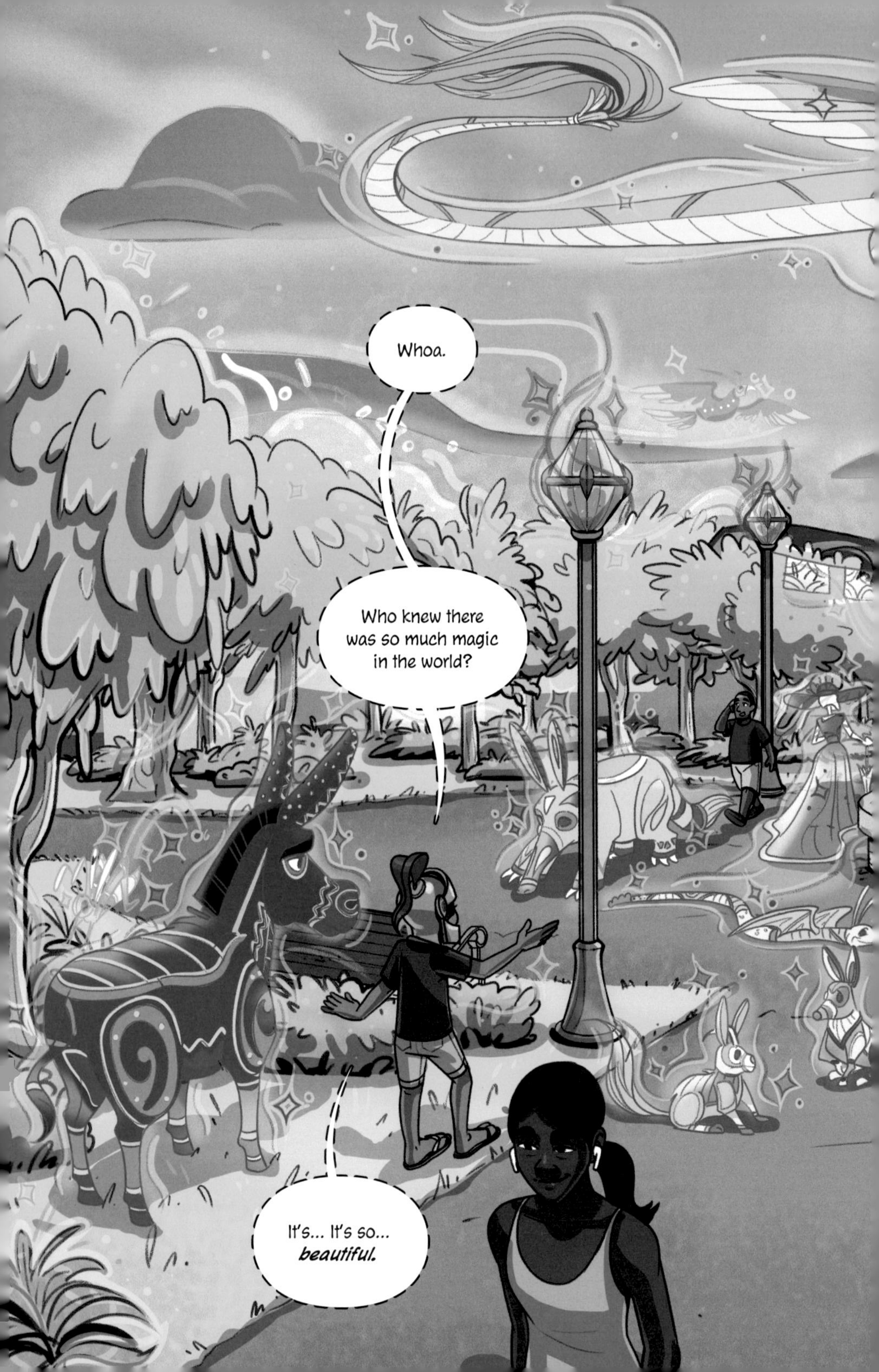
Whoa.
Who knew there was so much magic in the world?
It's... It's so... *beautiful.*

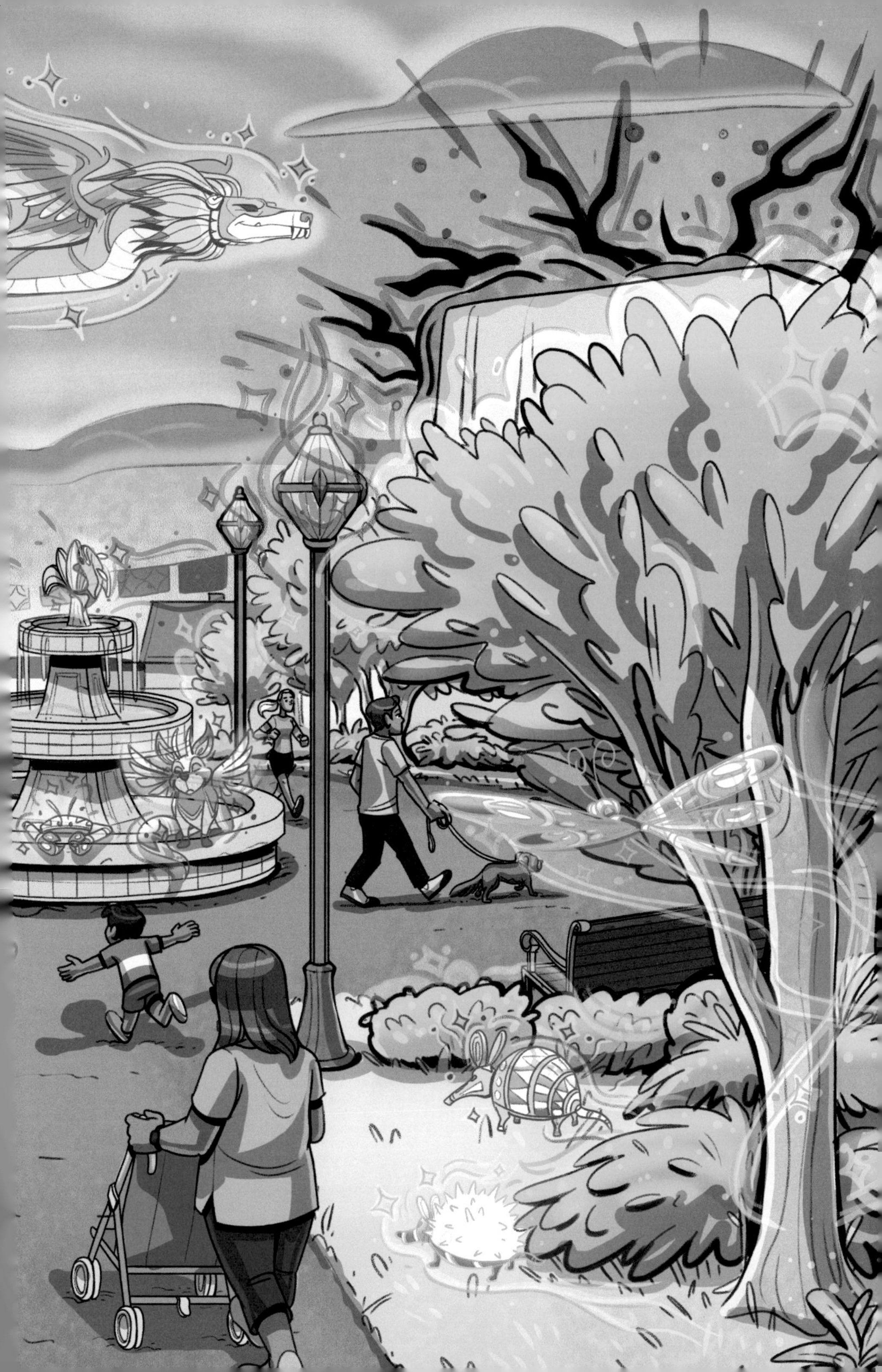

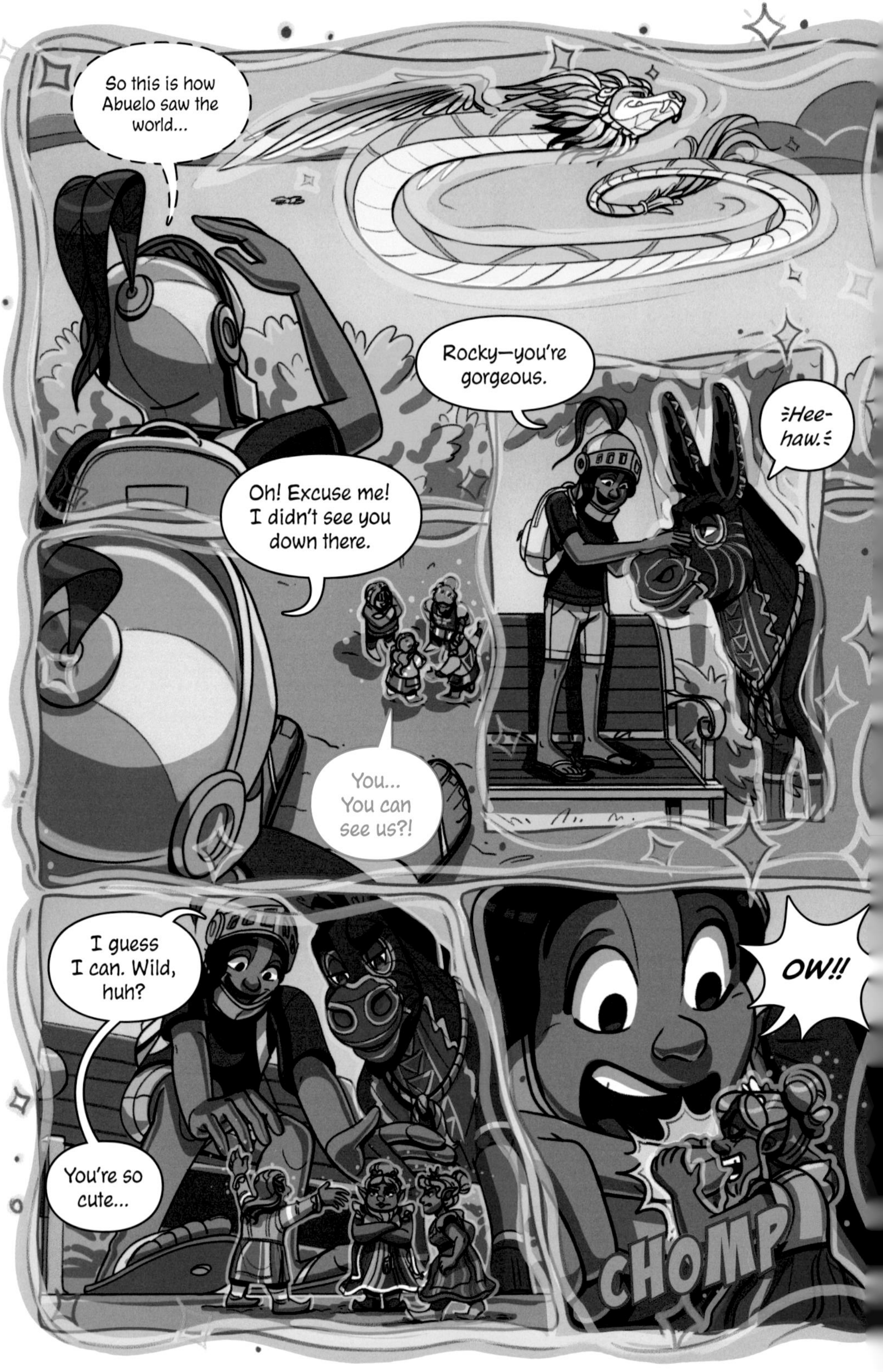
So this is how Abuelo saw the world...
Rocky—you're gorgeous.
Hee-haw.
Oh! Excuse me! I didn't see you down there.
You... You can see us?!
I guess I can. Wild, huh?
You're so cute...
OW!!
CHOMP!

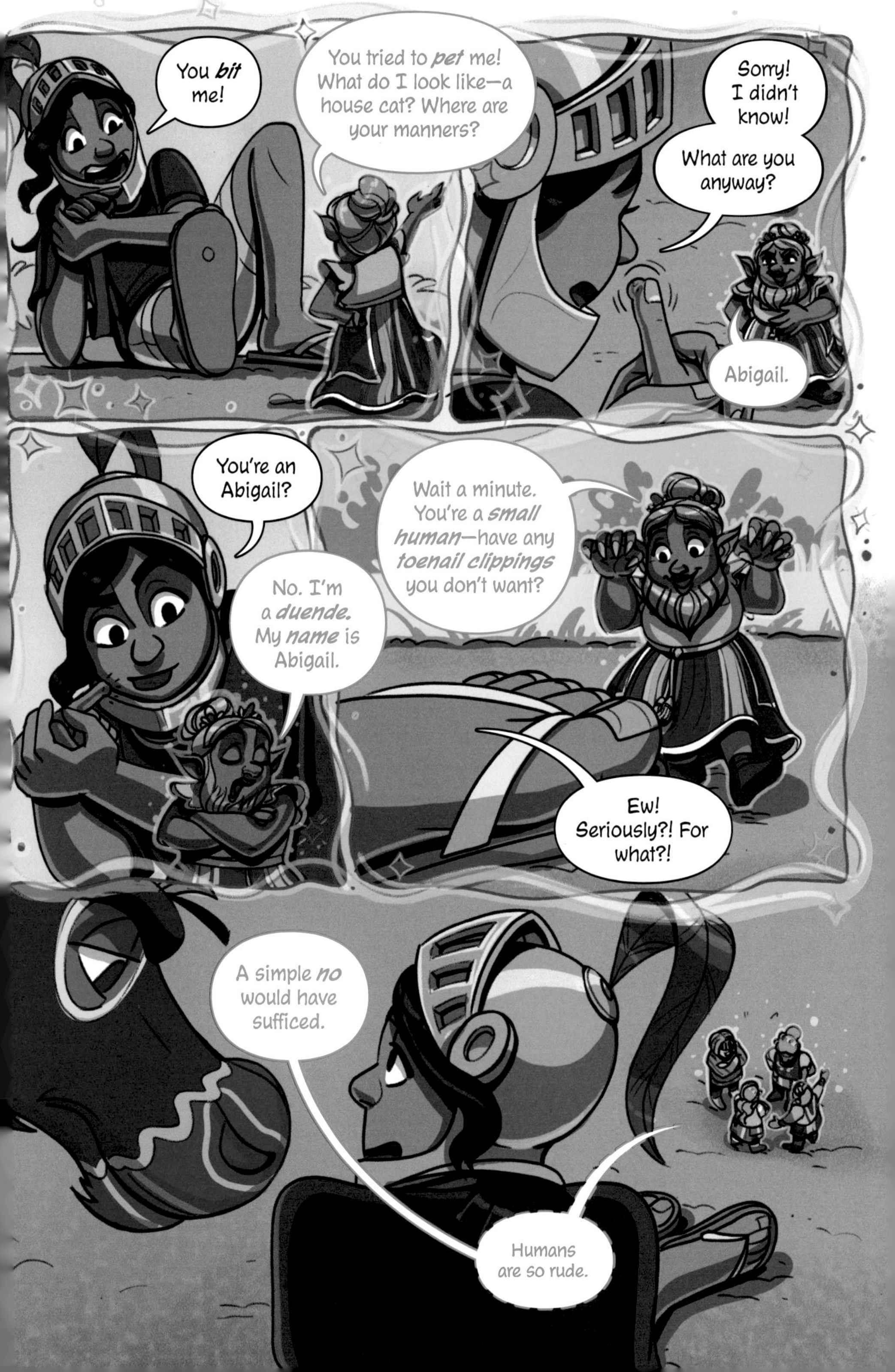
You *bit* me!
You tried to *pet* me! What do I look like—a house cat? Where are your manners?
Sorry! I didn't know!
What are you anyway?
Abigail.
You're an Abigail?
No. I'm a *duende.* My *name* is Abigail.
Wait a minute. You're a *small human*—have any *toenail clippings* you don't want?
Ew! Seriously?! For what?!
A simple *no* would have sufficed.
Humans are so rude.

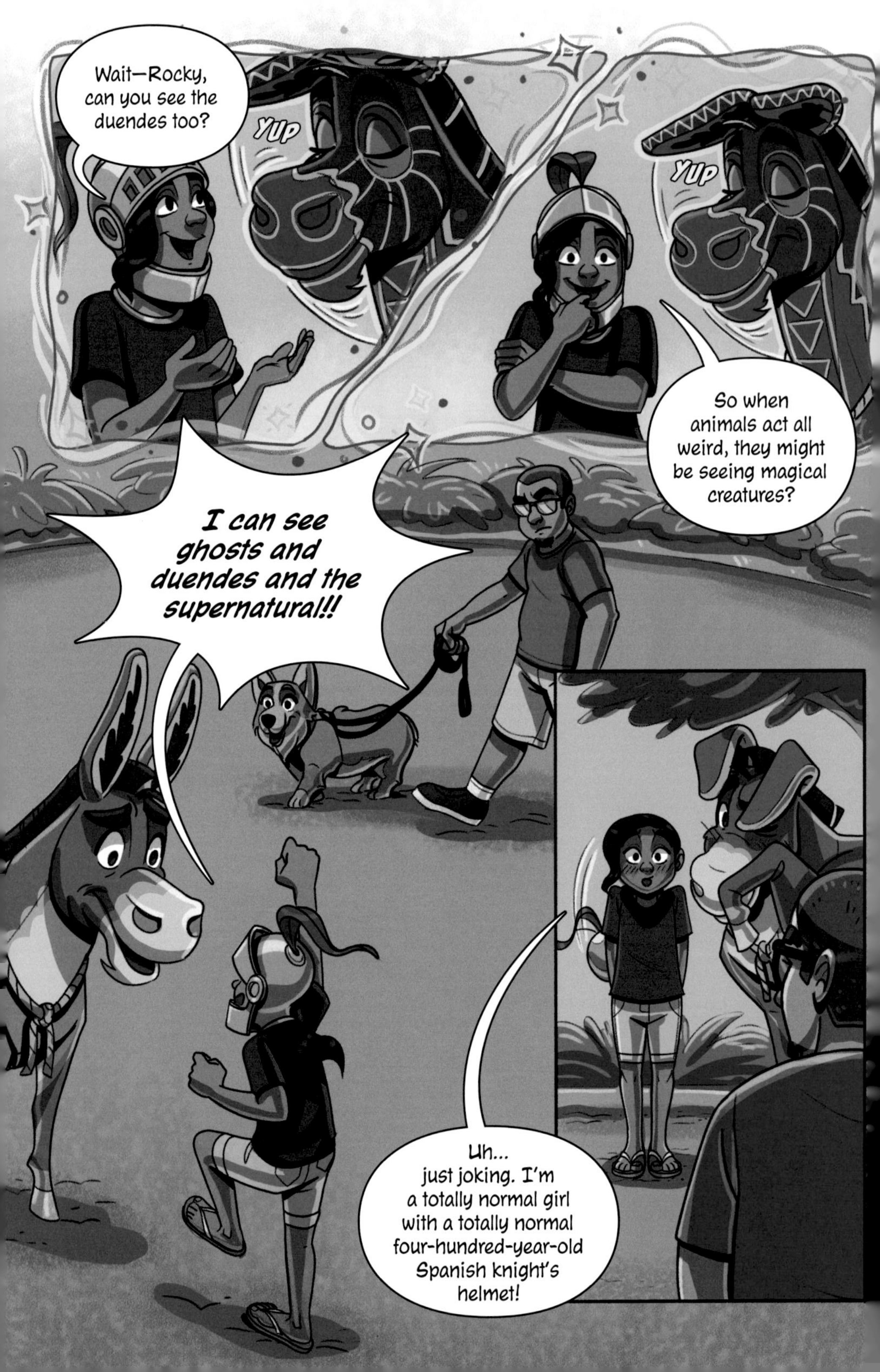
Wait—Rocky, can you see the duendes too?
YUP
YUP
So when animals act all weird, they might be seeing magical creatures?
I can see ghosts and duendes and the supernatural!!
Uh... just joking. I'm a totally normal girl with a totally normal four-hundred-year-old Spanish knight's helmet!

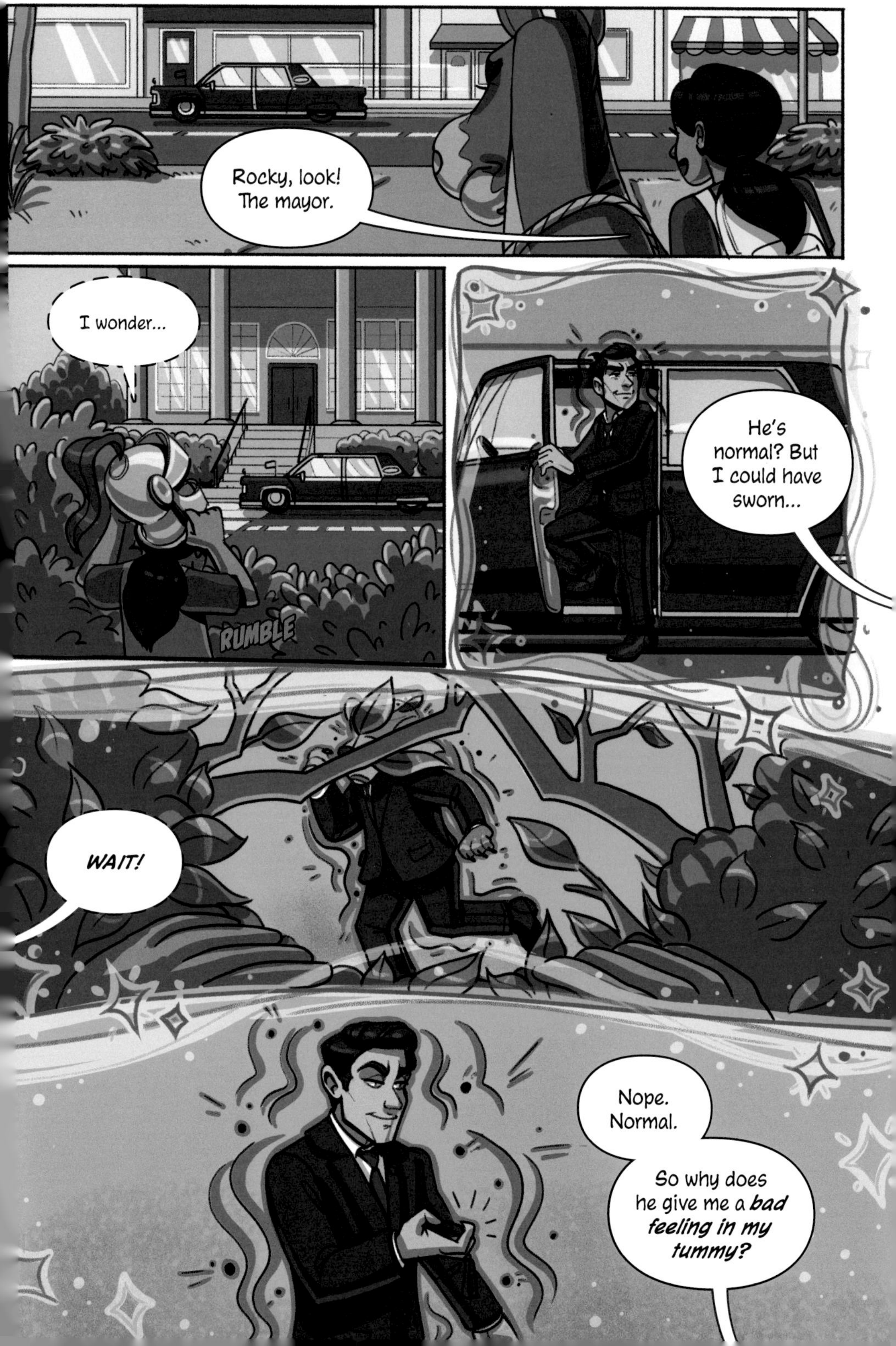
Rocky, look! The mayor.
I wonder...
RUMBLE
He's normal? But I could have sworn...
WAIT!
Nope. Normal.
So why does he give me a *bad feeling in my tummy?*

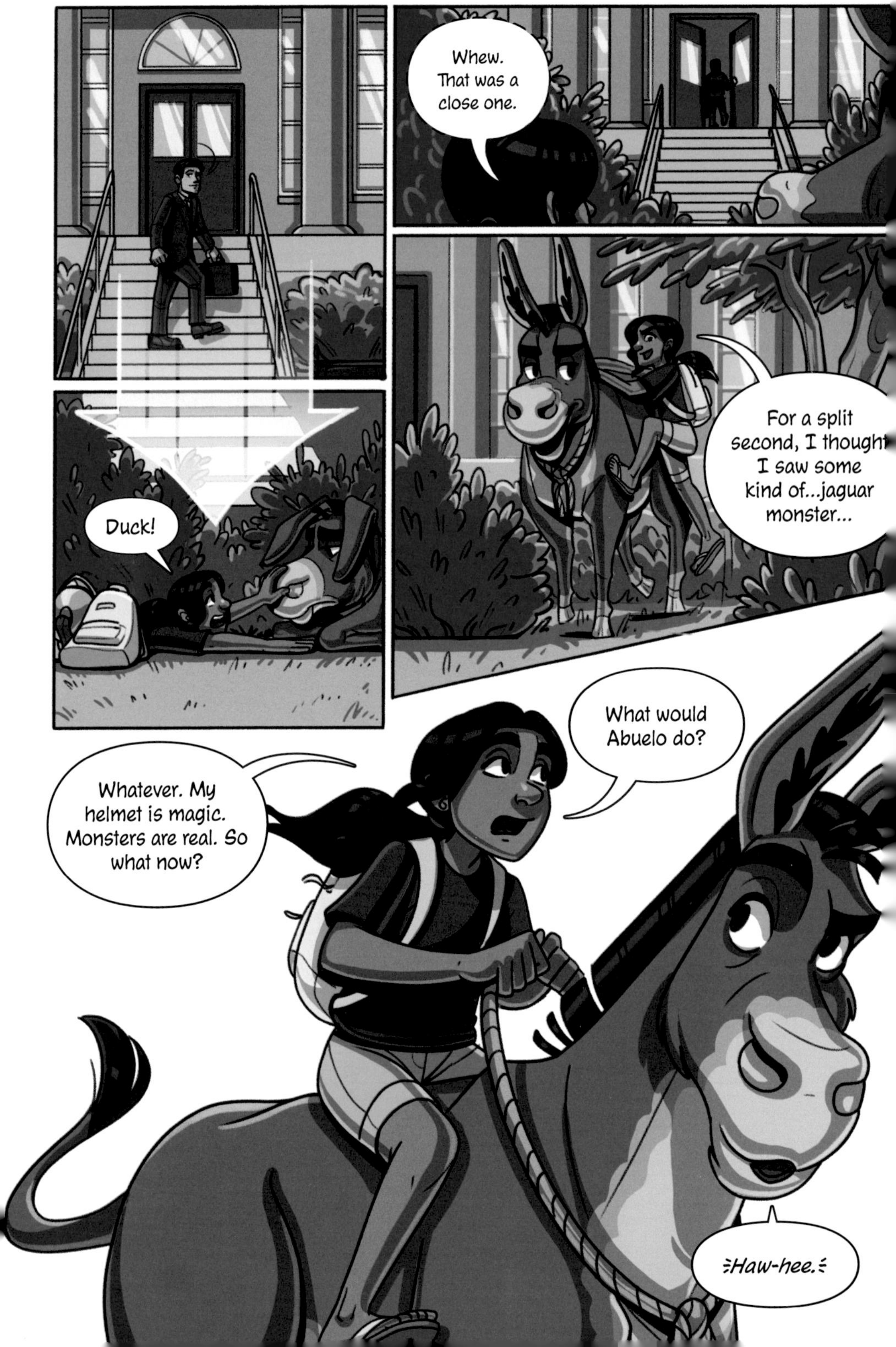
Whew. That was a close one.
Duck!
For a split second, I thought I saw some kind of...jaguar monster...
What would Abuelo do?
Whatever. My helmet is magic. Monsters are real. So what now?
Haw-hee.

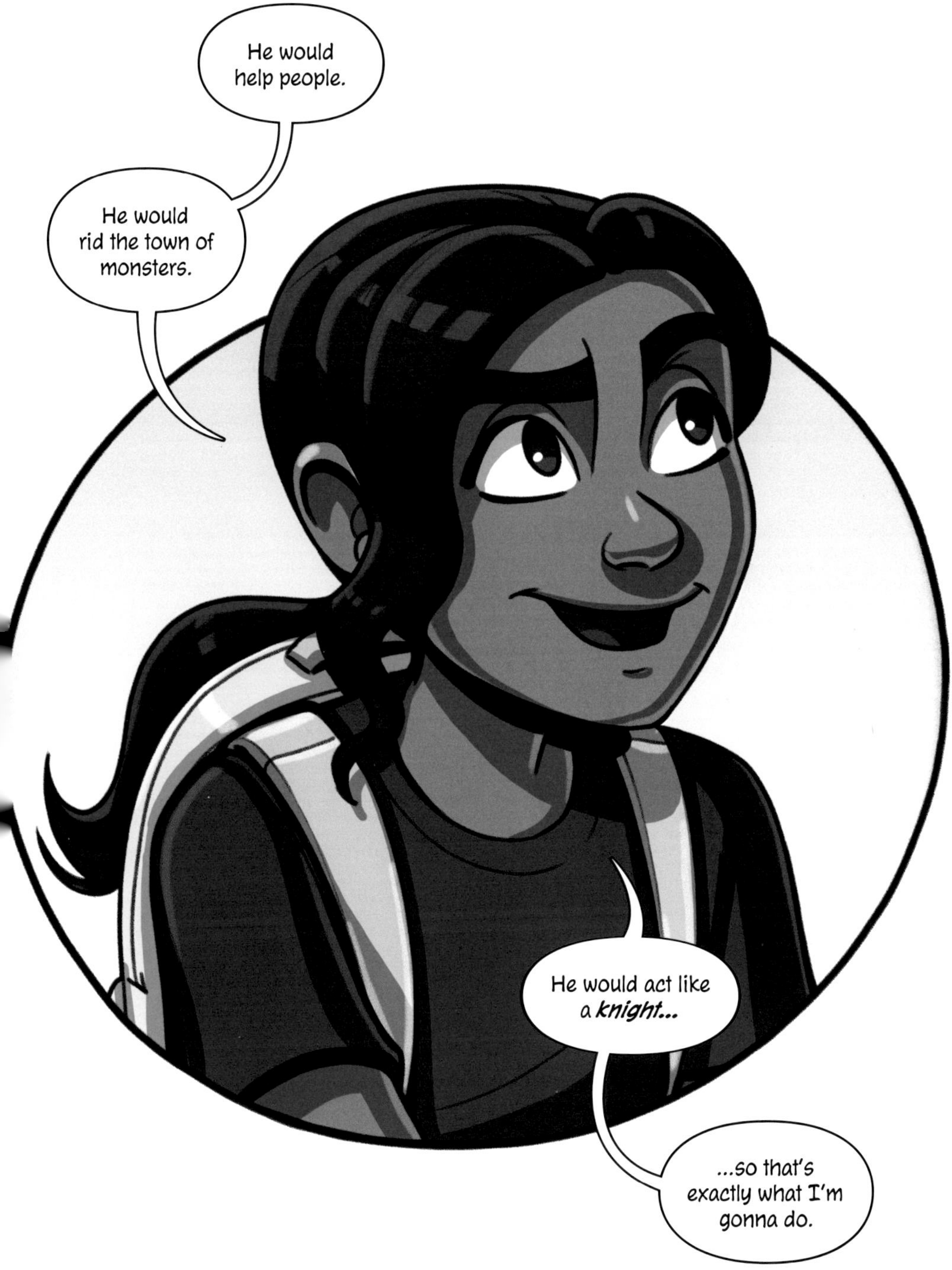
He would help people.
He would rid the town of monsters.
He would act like a ***knight...***
...so that's exactly what I'm gonna do.

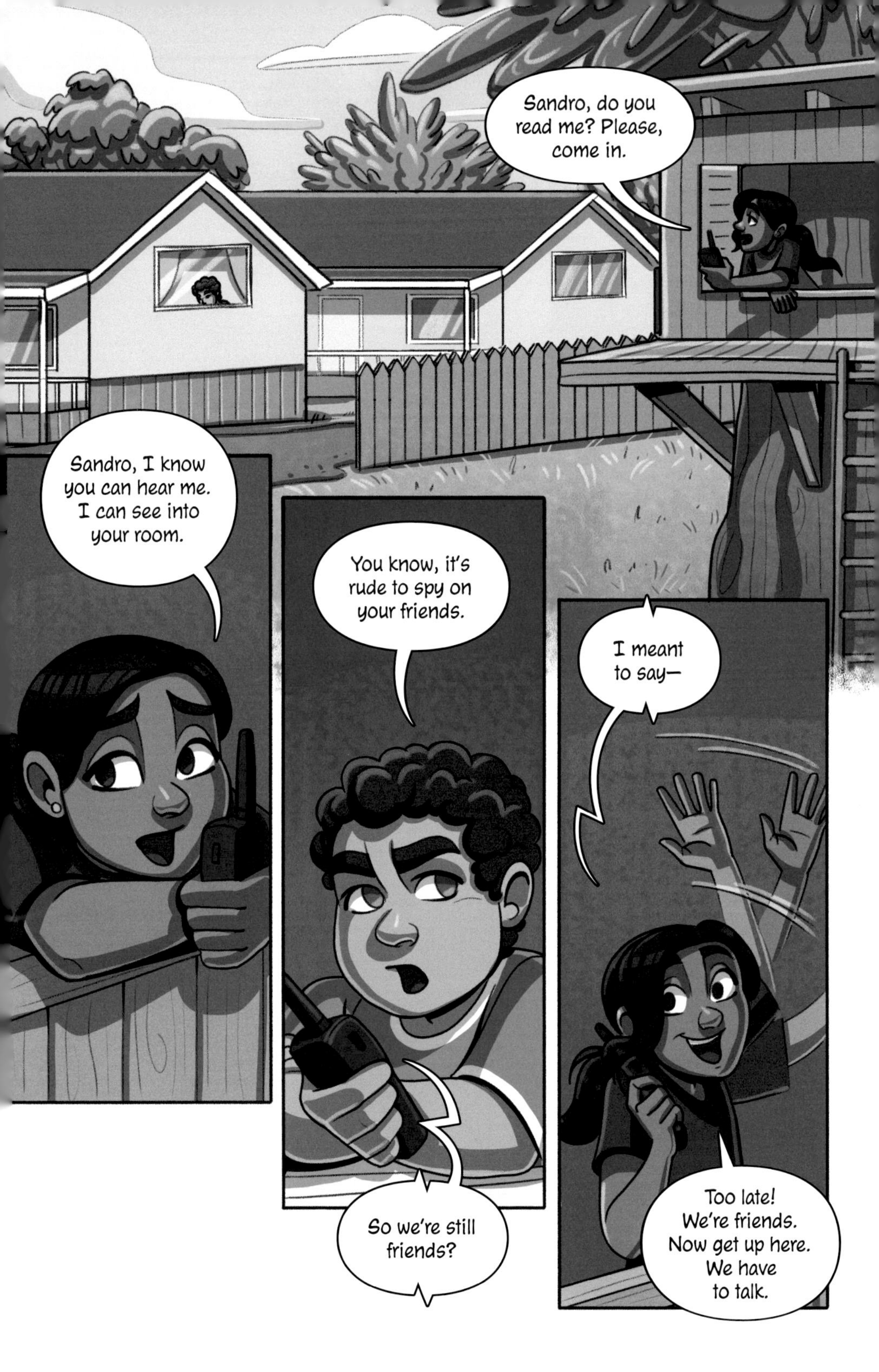
Sandro, do you read me? Please, come in.
Sandro, I know you can hear me. I can see into your room.
You know, it's rude to spy on your friends.
I meant to say—
So we're still friends?
Too late! We're friends. Now get up here. We have to talk.

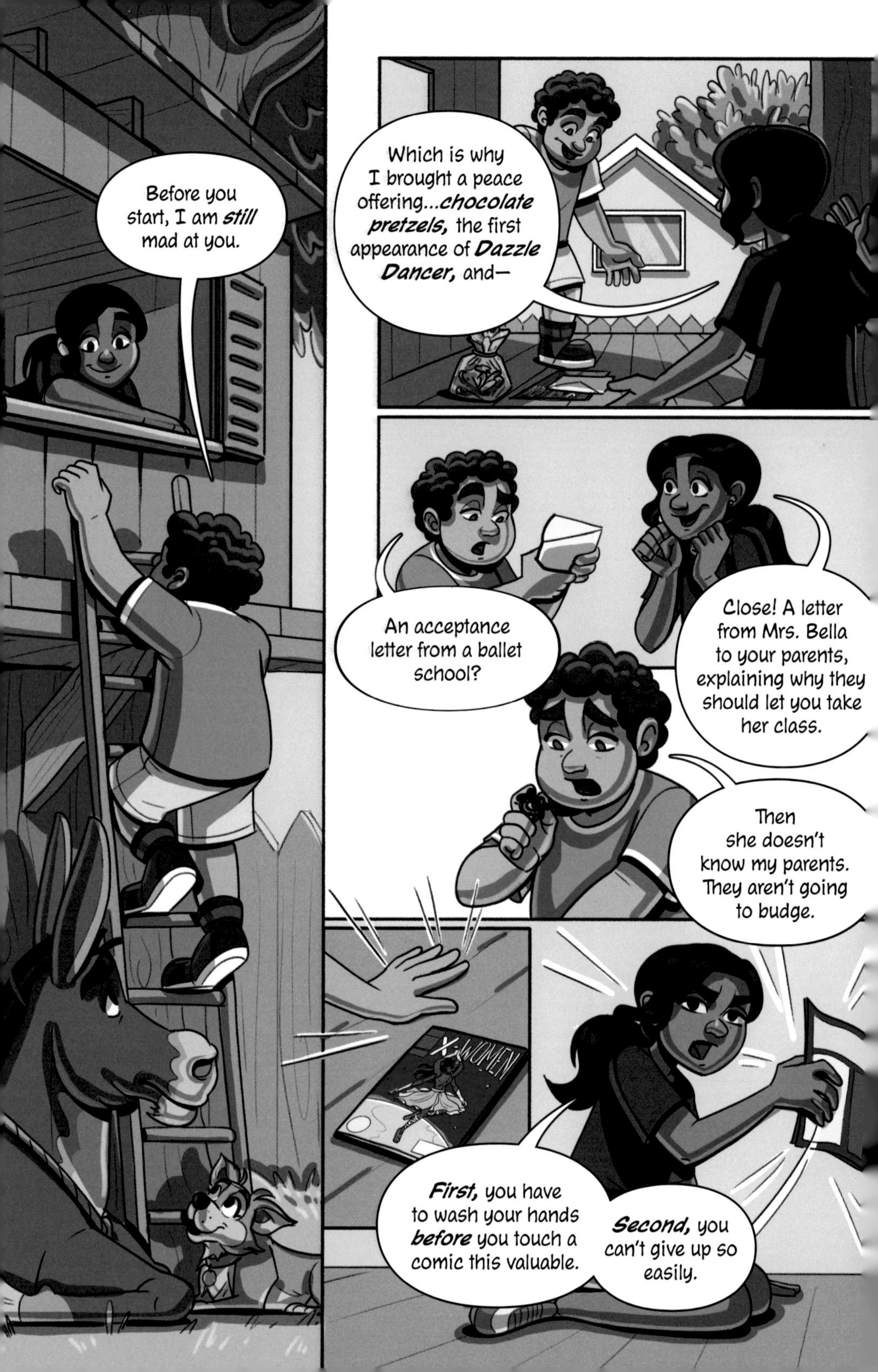
Before you start, I am *still* mad at you.
Which is why I brought a peace offering...*chocolate pretzels,* the first appearance of *Dazzle Dancer,* and—
An acceptance letter from a ballet school?
Close! A letter from Mrs. Bella to your parents, explaining why they should let you take her class.
Then she doesn't know my parents. They aren't going to budge.
X-WOMEN
First, you have to wash your hands *before* you touch a comic this valuable.
Second, you can't give up so easily.

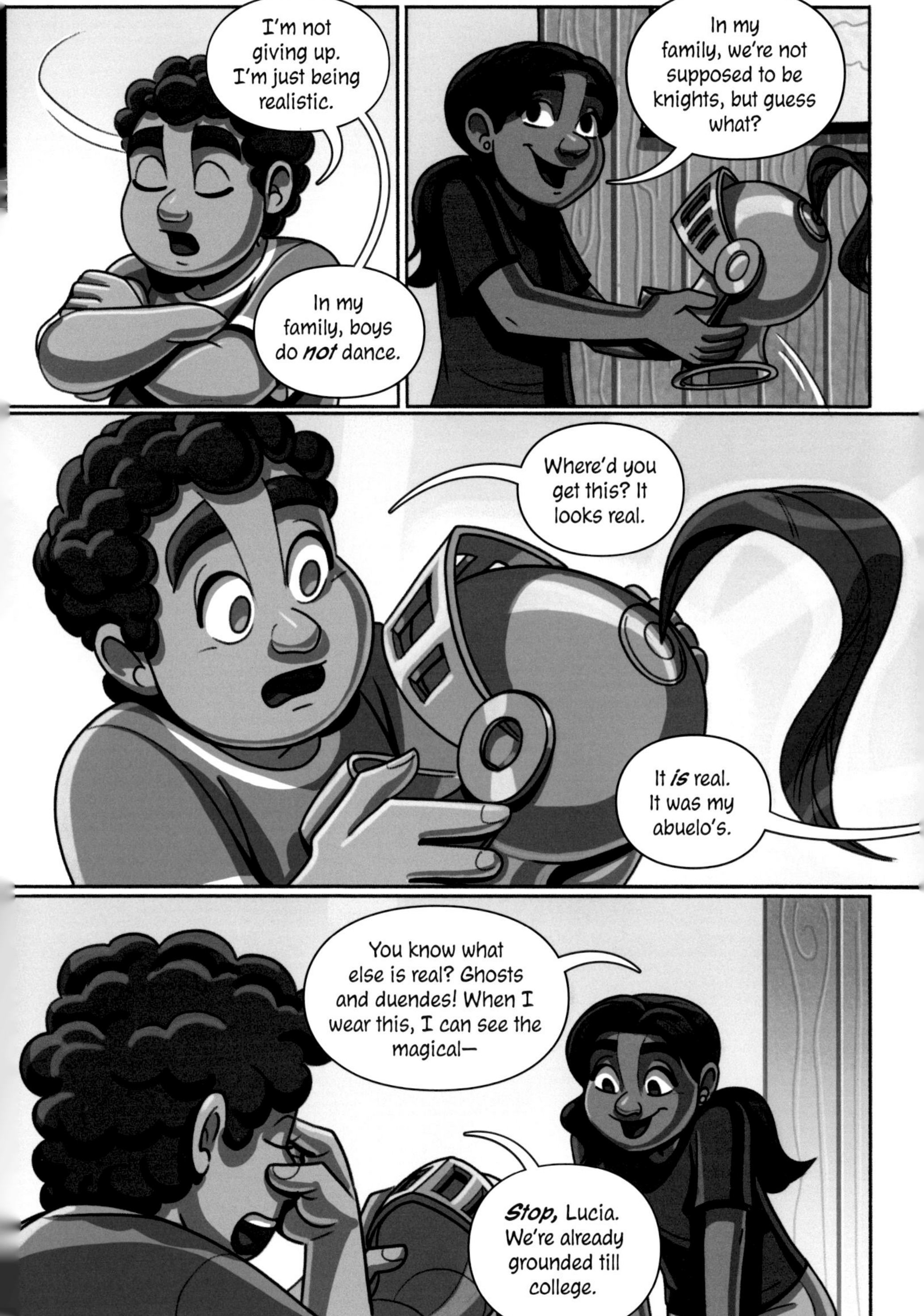
I'm not giving up. I'm just being realistic.
In my family, boys do *not* dance.
In my family, we're not supposed to be knights, but guess what?
Where'd you get this? It looks real.
It *is* real. It was my abuelo's.
You know what else is real? Ghosts and duendes! When I wear this, I can see the magical—
Stop, Lucia. We're already grounded till college.

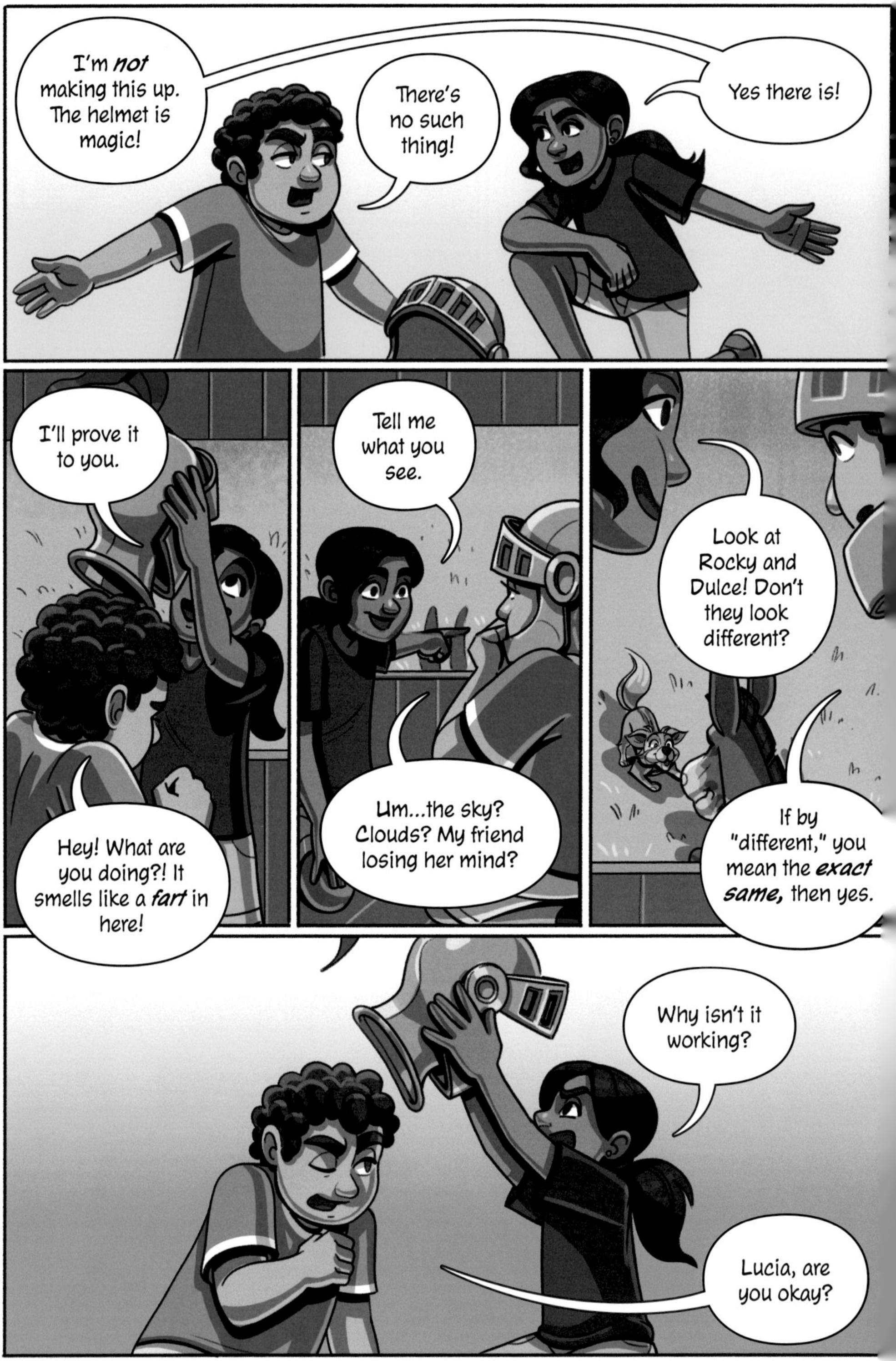
I'm *not* making this up. The helmet is magic!
There's no such thing!
Yes there is!
I'll prove it to you.
Hey! What are you doing?! It smells like a *fart* in here!
Tell me what you see.
Um...the sky? Clouds? My friend losing her mind?
Look at Rocky and Dulce! Don't they look different?
If by "different," you mean the *exact same,* then yes.
Why isn't it working?
Lucia, are you okay?

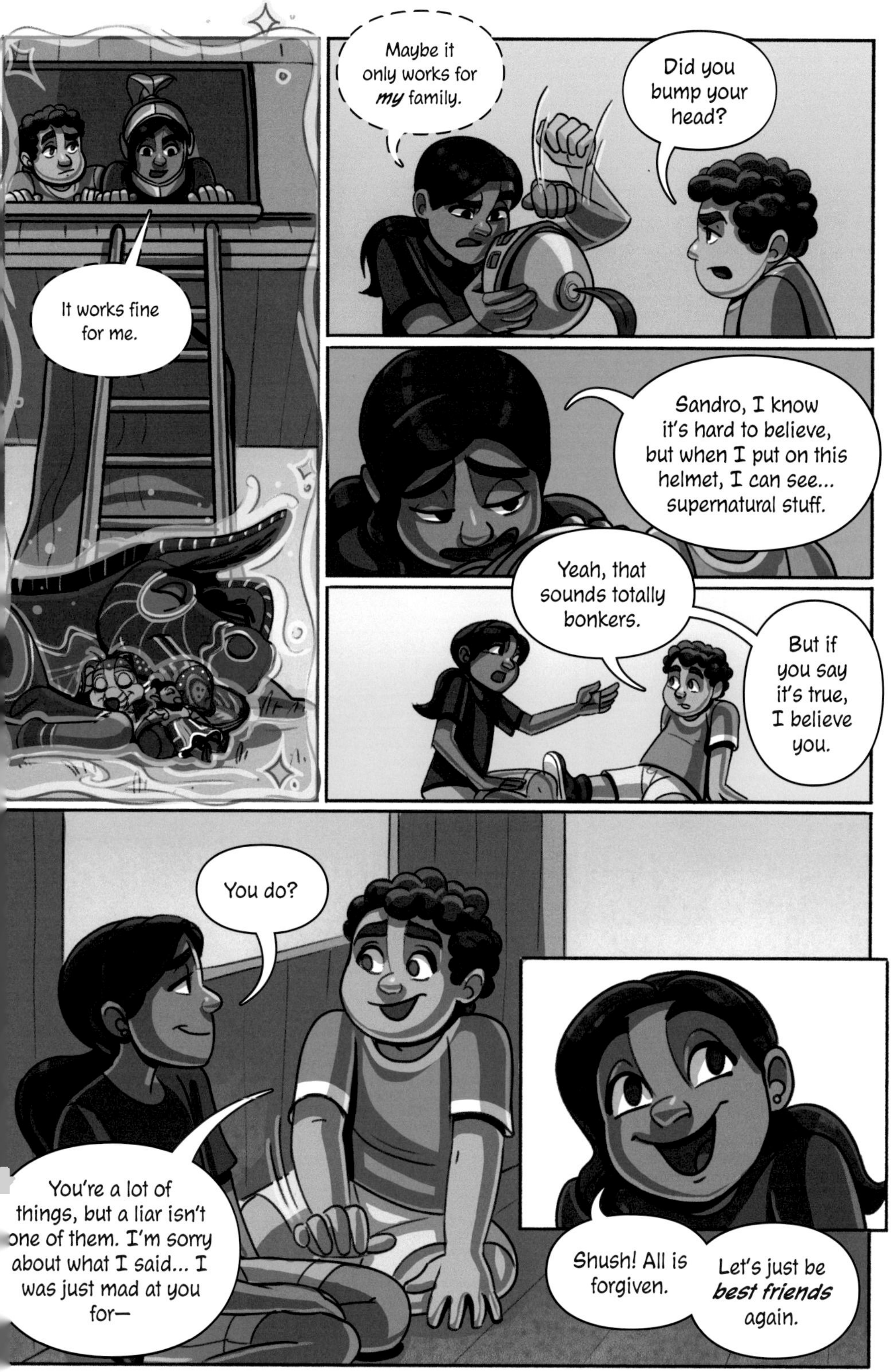
It works fine for me.
Maybe it only works for *my* family.
Did you bump your head?
Sandro, I know it's hard to believe, but when I put on this helmet, I can see... supernatural stuff.
Yeah, that sounds totally bonkers.
But if you say it's true, I believe you.
You do?
You're a lot of things, but a liar isn't one of them. I'm sorry about what I said... I was just mad at you for—
Shush! All is forgiven.
Let's just be ***best friends*** again.

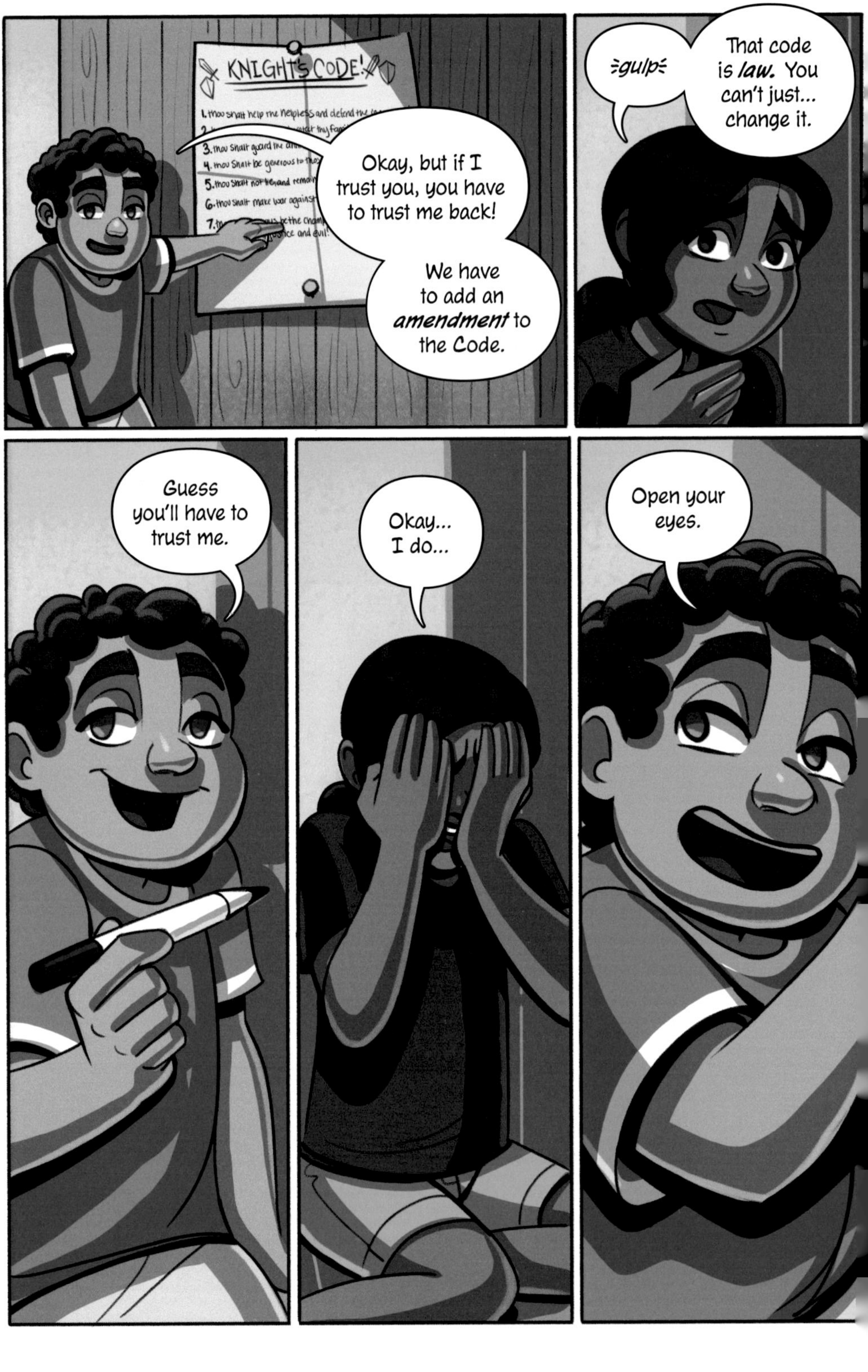

KNIGHT'S CODE!
Okay, but if I trust you, you have to trust me back!
We have to add an *amendment* to the Code.
gulp
That code is ***law.*** You can't just... change it.
Guess you'll have to trust me.
Okay... I do...
Open your eyes.

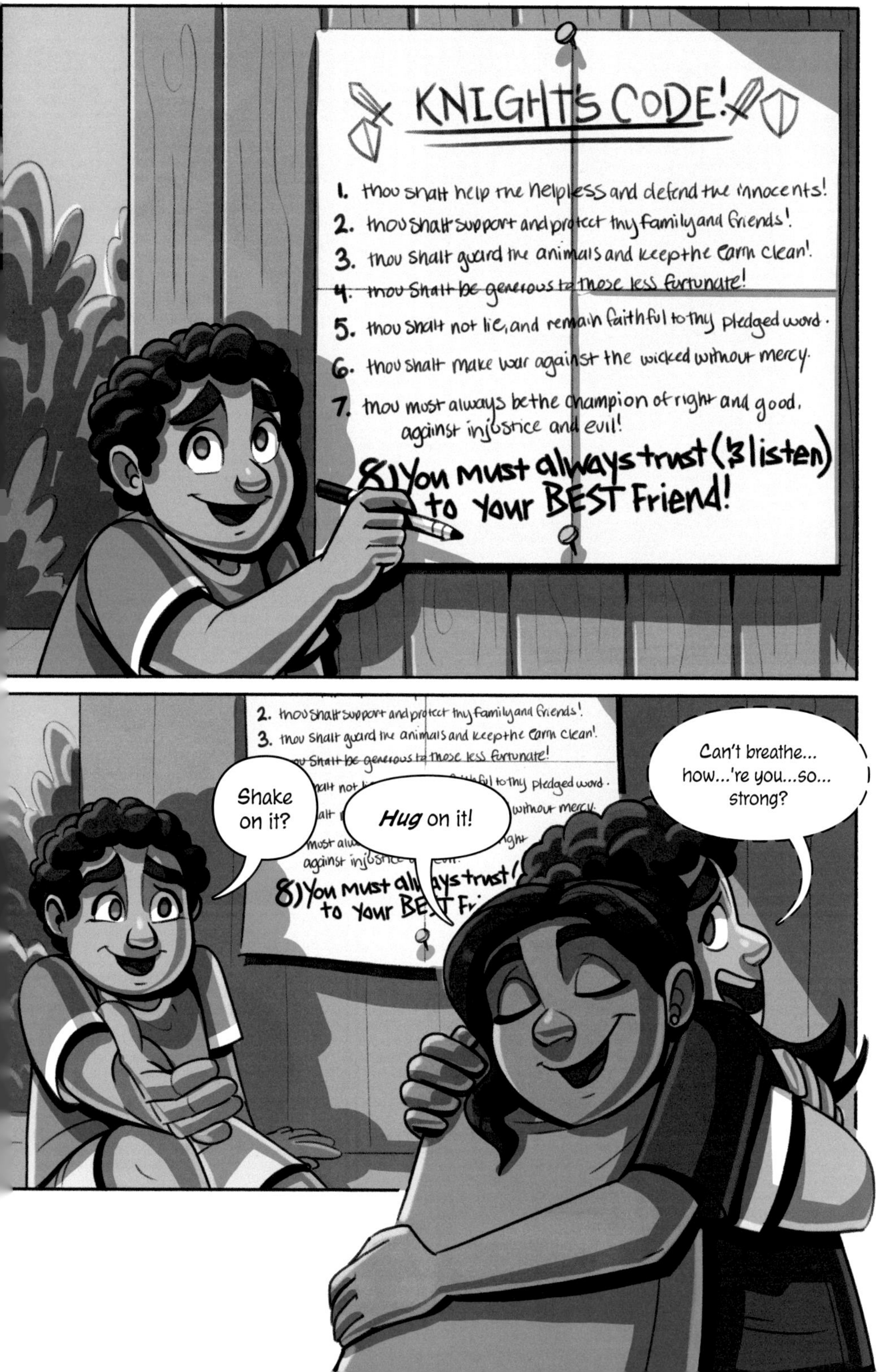
KNIGHT'S CODE!
1. thou shalt help the helpless and defend the innocents!
2. thou shalt support and protect thy family and friends!
3. thou shalt guard the animals and keep the farm clean!
4. thou shalt be generous to those less fortunate!
5. thou shalt not lie, and remain faithful to thy pledged word.
6. thou shalt make war against the wicked without mercy.
7. thou must always be the champion of right and good, against injustice and evil!
8) You must always trust (& listen) to your BEST Friend!
Shake on it?
Hug on it!
Can't breathe... how...'re you...so... strong?

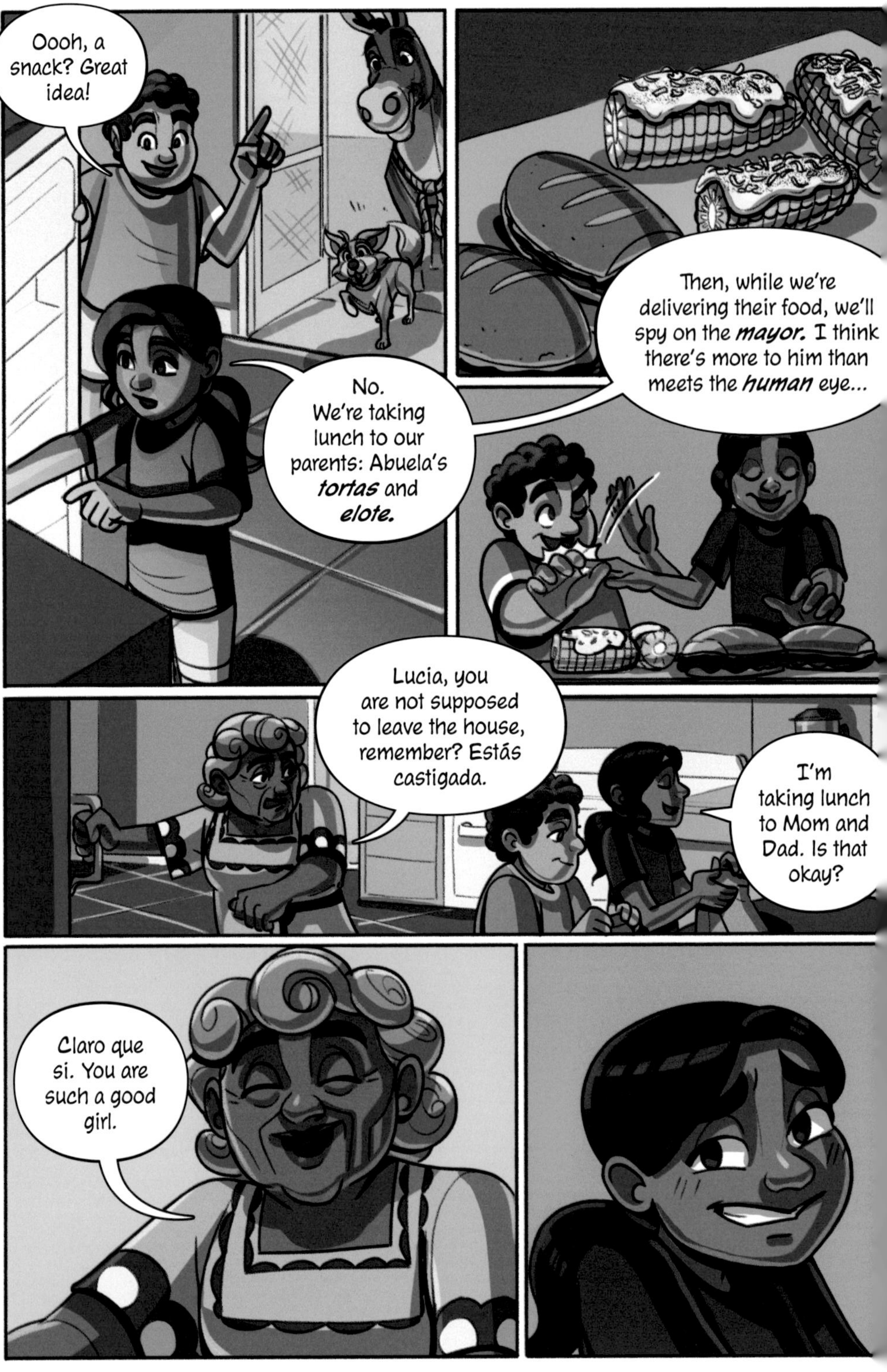
Oooh, a snack? Great idea!
No. We're taking lunch to our parents: Abuela's *tortas* and *elote.*
Then, while we're delivering their food, we'll spy on the *mayor.* I think there's more to him than meets the *human* eye...
Lucia, you are not supposed to leave the house, remember? Estás castigada.
I'm taking lunch to Mom and Dad. Is that okay?
Claro que si. You are such a good girl.

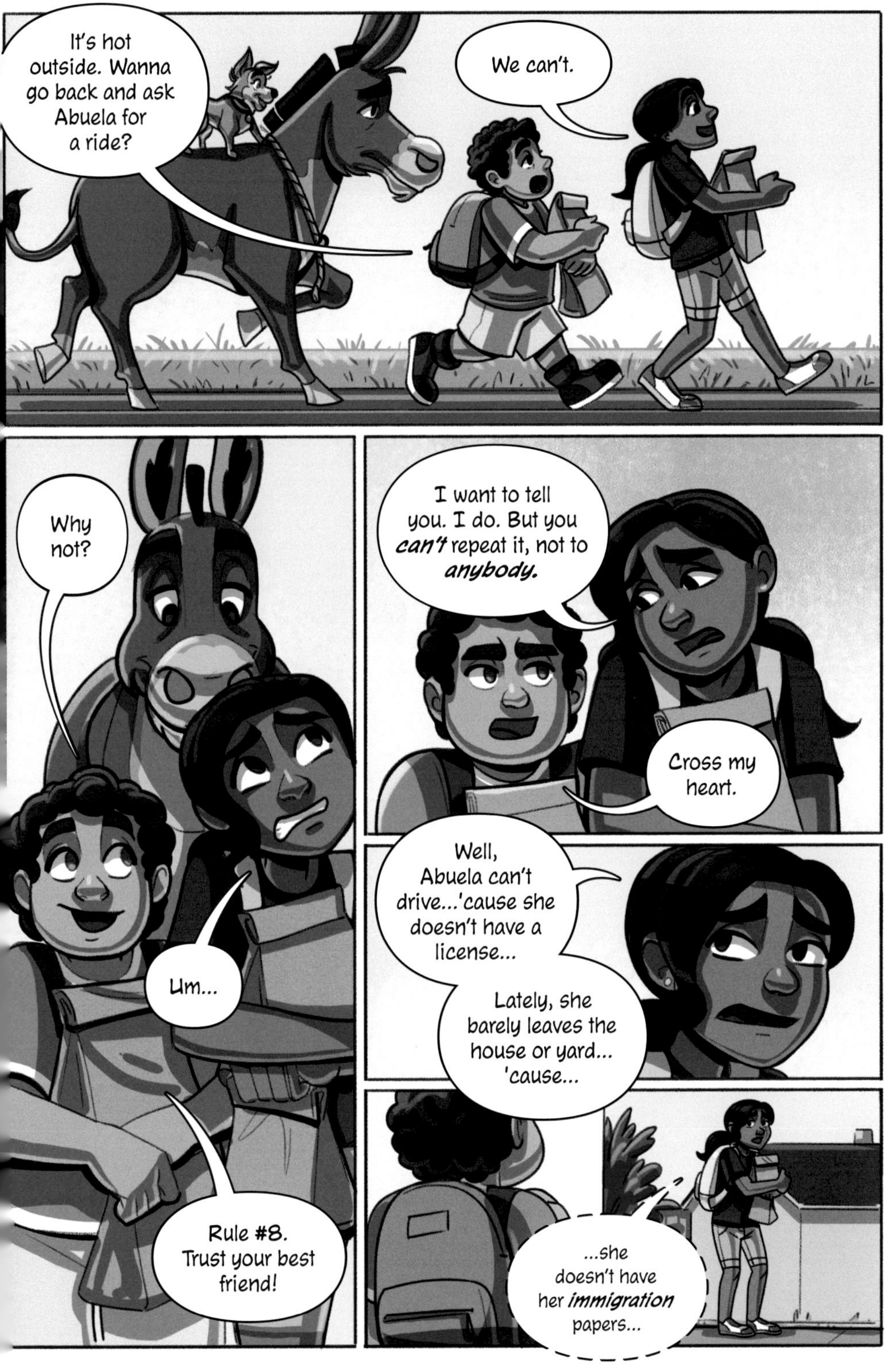
It's hot outside. Wanna go back and ask Abuela for a ride?
We can't.
Why not?
Um...
Rule #8. Trust your best friend!
I want to tell you. I do. But you *can't* repeat it, not to ***anybody.***
Cross my heart.
Well, Abuela can't drive...'cause she doesn't have a license...
Lately, she barely leaves the house or yard... 'cause...
...she doesn't have her *immigration* papers...

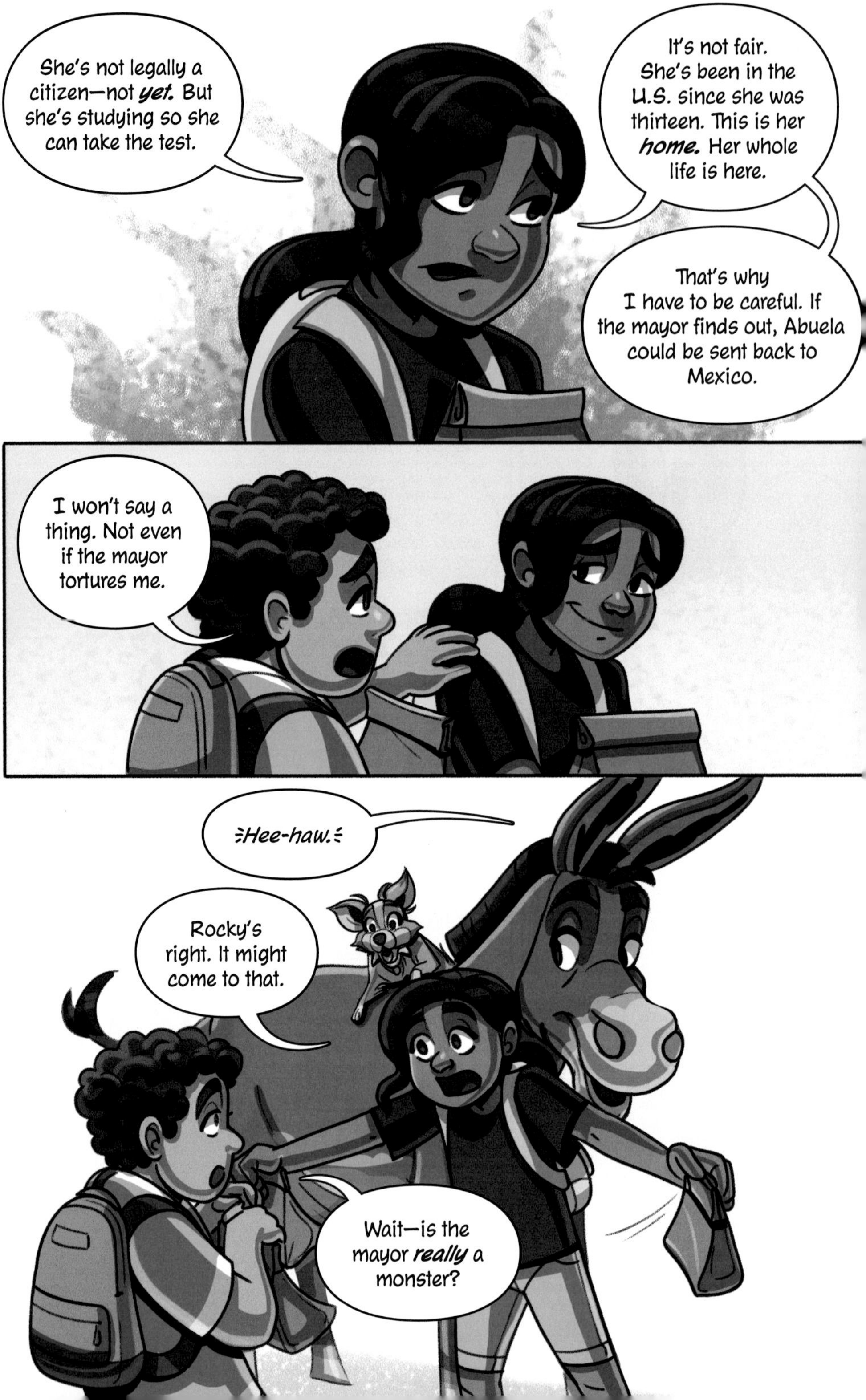

She's not legally a citizen—not *yet.* But she's studying so she can take the test.
It's not fair. She's been in the U.S. since she was thirteen. This is her *home.* Her whole life is here.
That's why I have to be careful. If the mayor finds out, Abuela could be sent back to Mexico.
I won't say a thing. Not even if the mayor tortures me.
Hee-haw.
Rocky's right. It might come to that.
Wait—is the mayor *really* a monster?

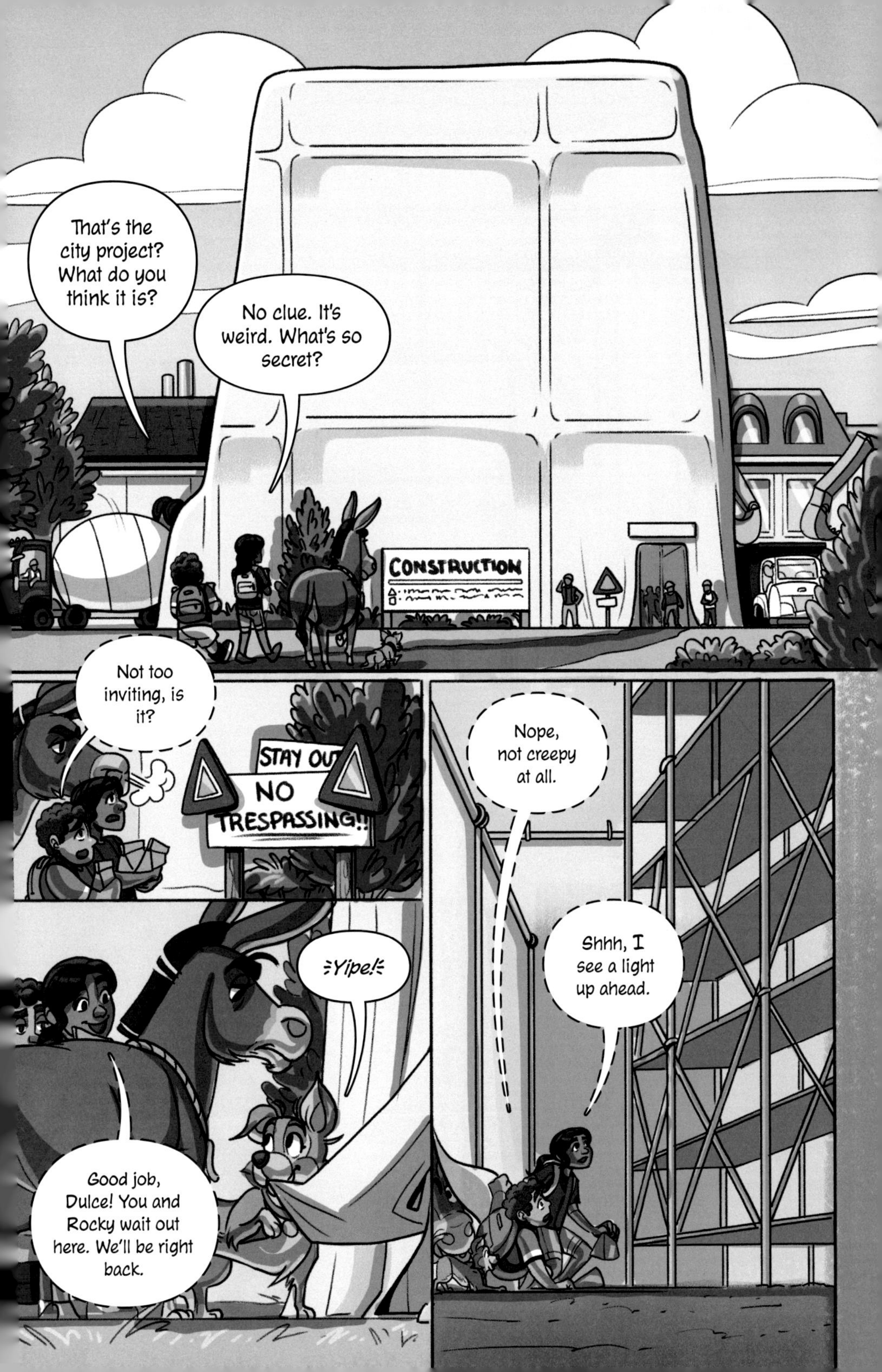
That's the city project? What do you think it is?
No clue. It's weird. What's so secret?
CONSTRUCTION
Not too inviting, is it?
STAY OUT
NO TRESPASSING!!
Yipe!
Good job, Dulce! You and Rocky wait out here. We'll be right back.
Nope, not creepy at all.
Shhh, I see a light up ahead.

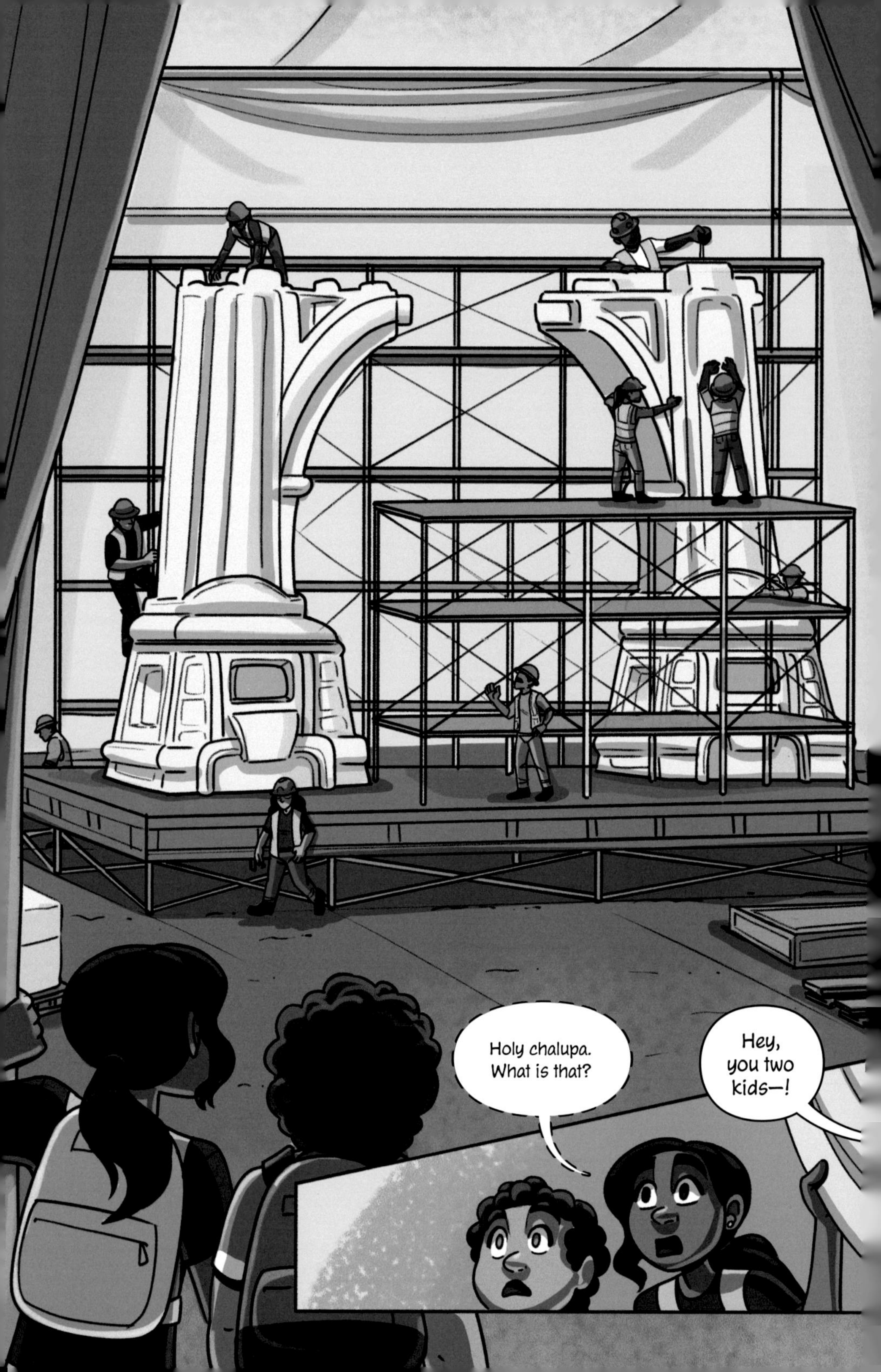
Holy chalupa. What is that?
Hey, you two kids—!

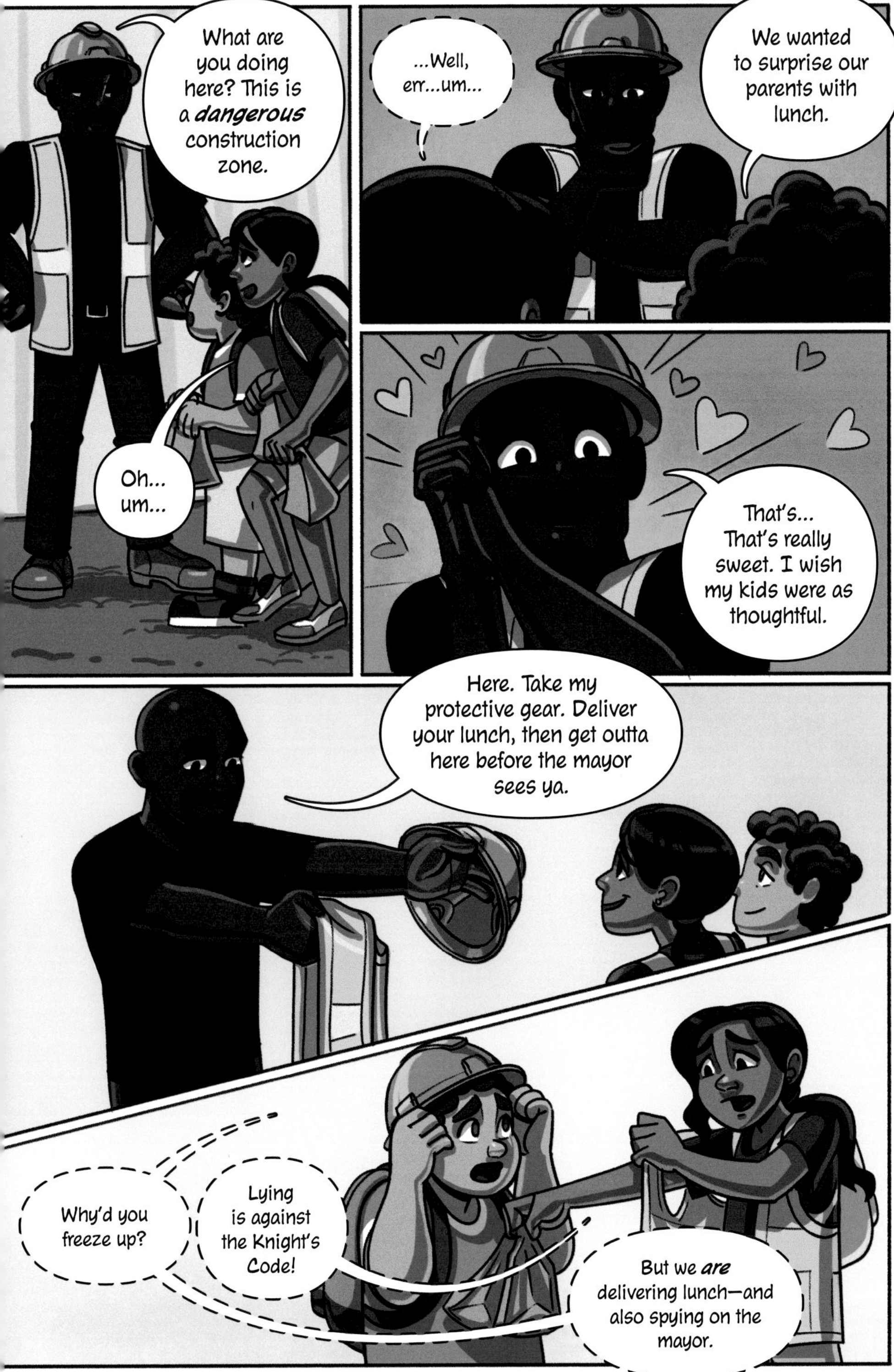

What are you doing here? This is a *dangerous* construction zone.
Oh... um...
...Well, err...um...
We wanted to surprise our parents with lunch.
That's... That's really sweet. I wish my kids were as thoughtful.
Here. Take my protective gear. Deliver your lunch, then get outta here before the mayor sees ya.
Why'd you freeze up?
Lying is against the Knight's Code!
But we *are* delivering lunch—and also spying on the mayor.

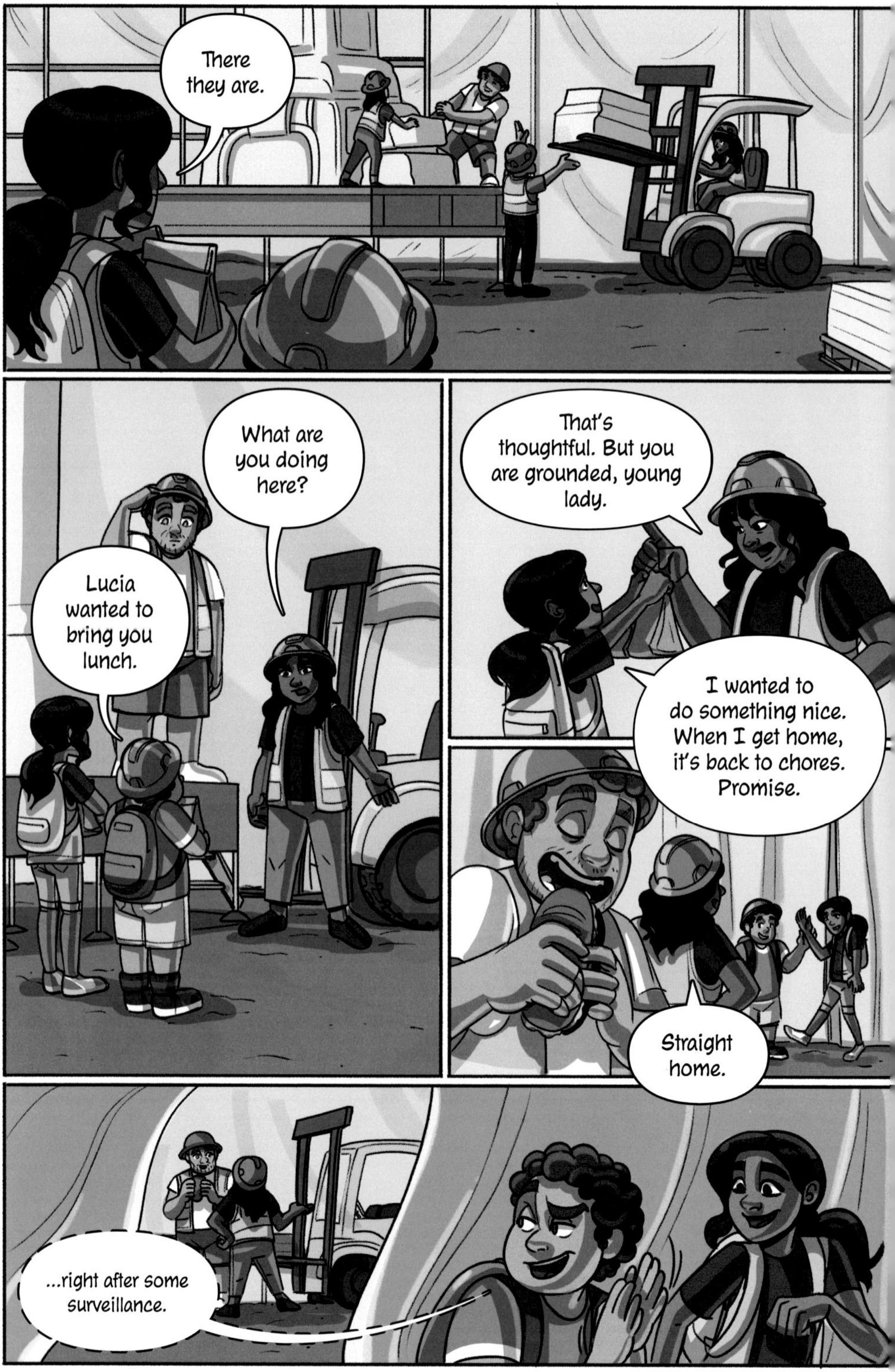
There they are.
What are you doing here?
Lucia wanted to bring you lunch.
That's thoughtful. But you are grounded, young lady.
I wanted to do something nice. When I get home, it's back to chores. Promise.
Straight home.
...right after some surveillance.

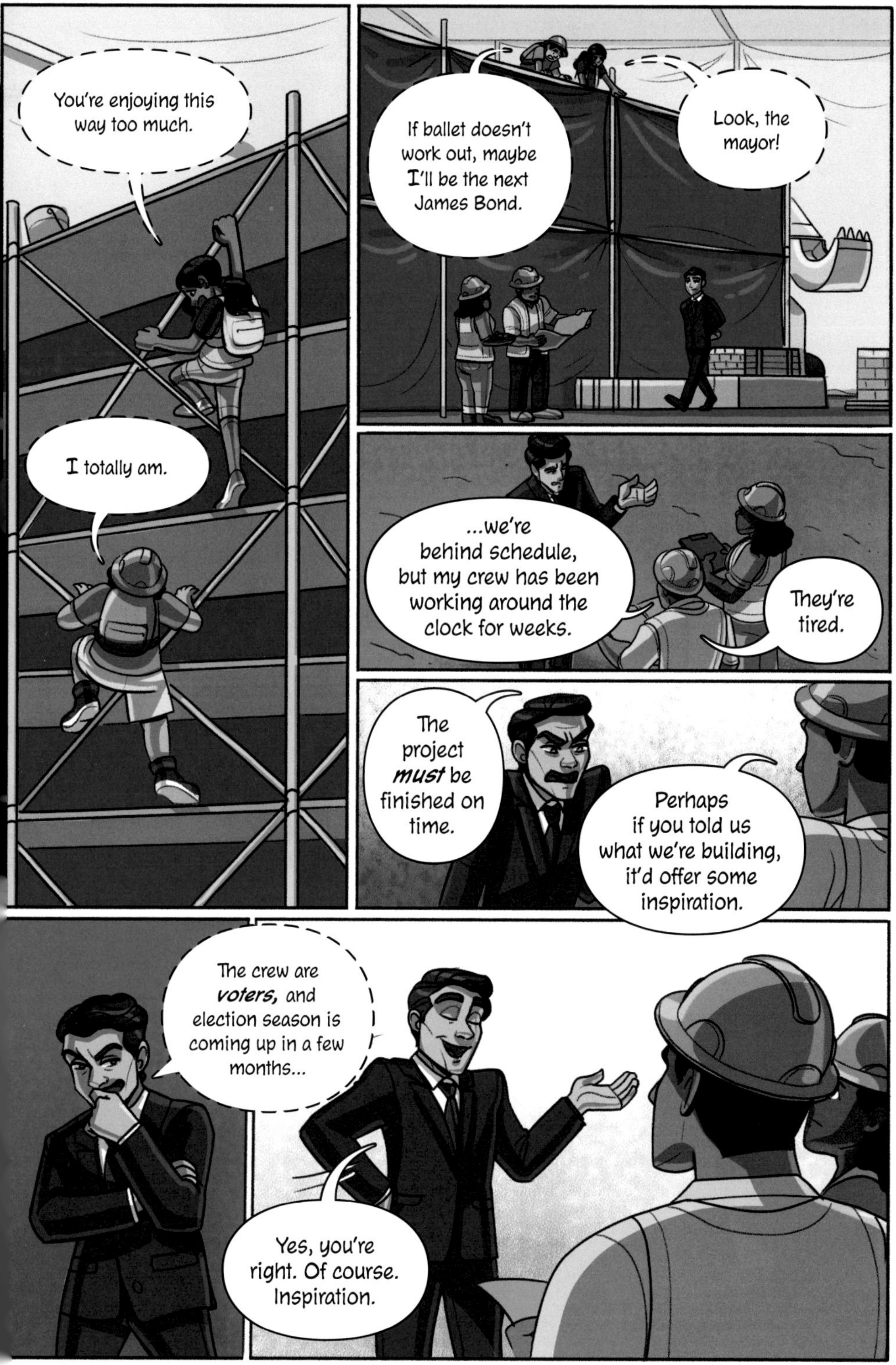

You're enjoying this way too much.
I totally am.
If ballet doesn't work out, maybe I'll be the next James Bond.
Look, the mayor!
...we're behind schedule, but my crew has been working around the clock for weeks.
They're tired.
The project *must* be finished on time.
Perhaps if you told us what we're building, it'd offer some inspiration.
The crew are *voters,* and election season is coming up in a few months...
Yes, you're right. Of course. Inspiration.

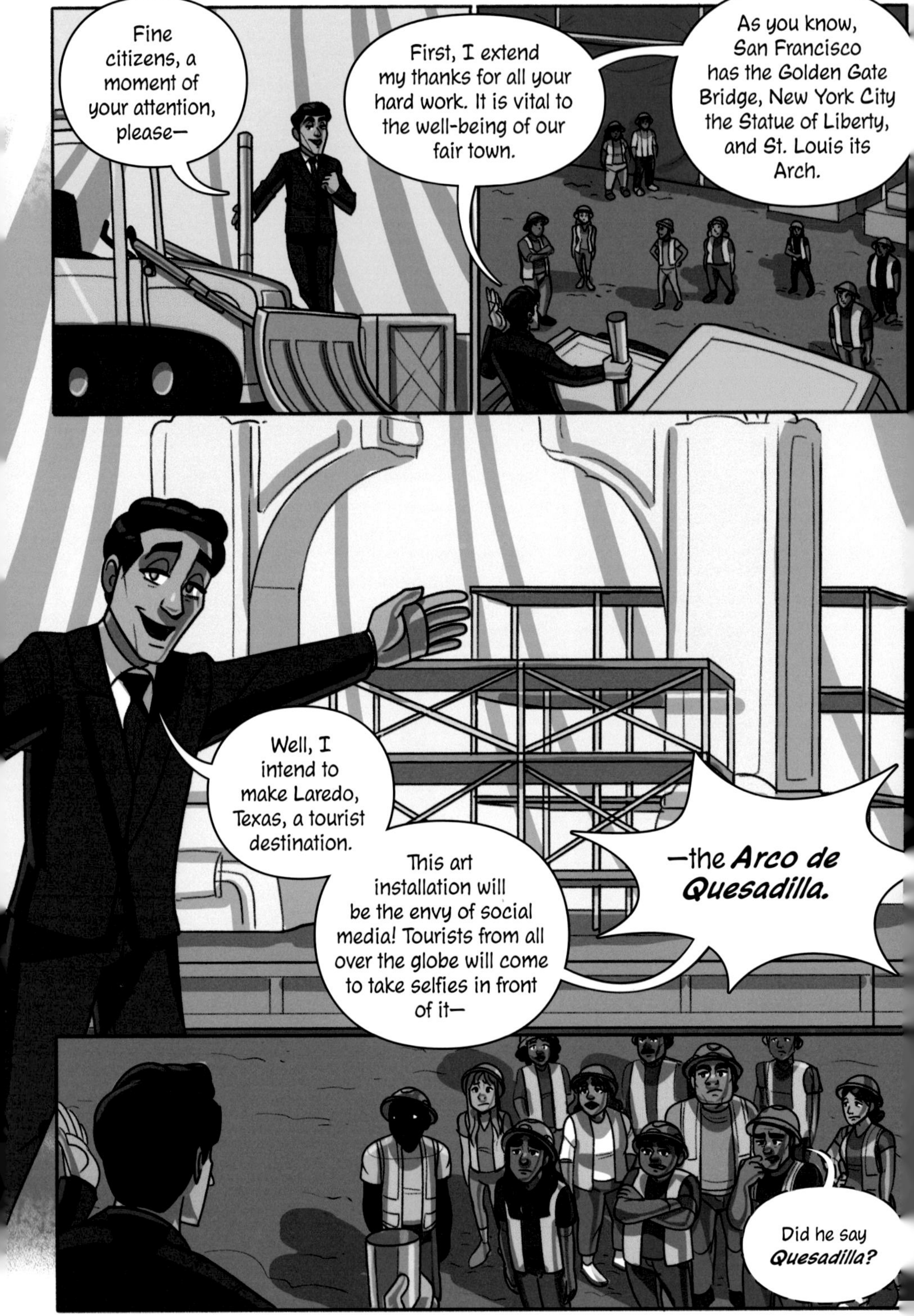
Fine citizens, a moment of your attention, please—
First, I extend my thanks for all your hard work. It is vital to the well-being of our fair town.
As you know, San Francisco has the Golden Gate Bridge, New York City the Statue of Liberty, and St. Louis its Arch.
Well, I intend to make Laredo, Texas, a tourist destination.
This art installation will be the envy of social media! Tourists from all over the globe will come to take selfies in front of it—
—the ***Arco de Quesadilla.***
Did he say *Quesadilla?*

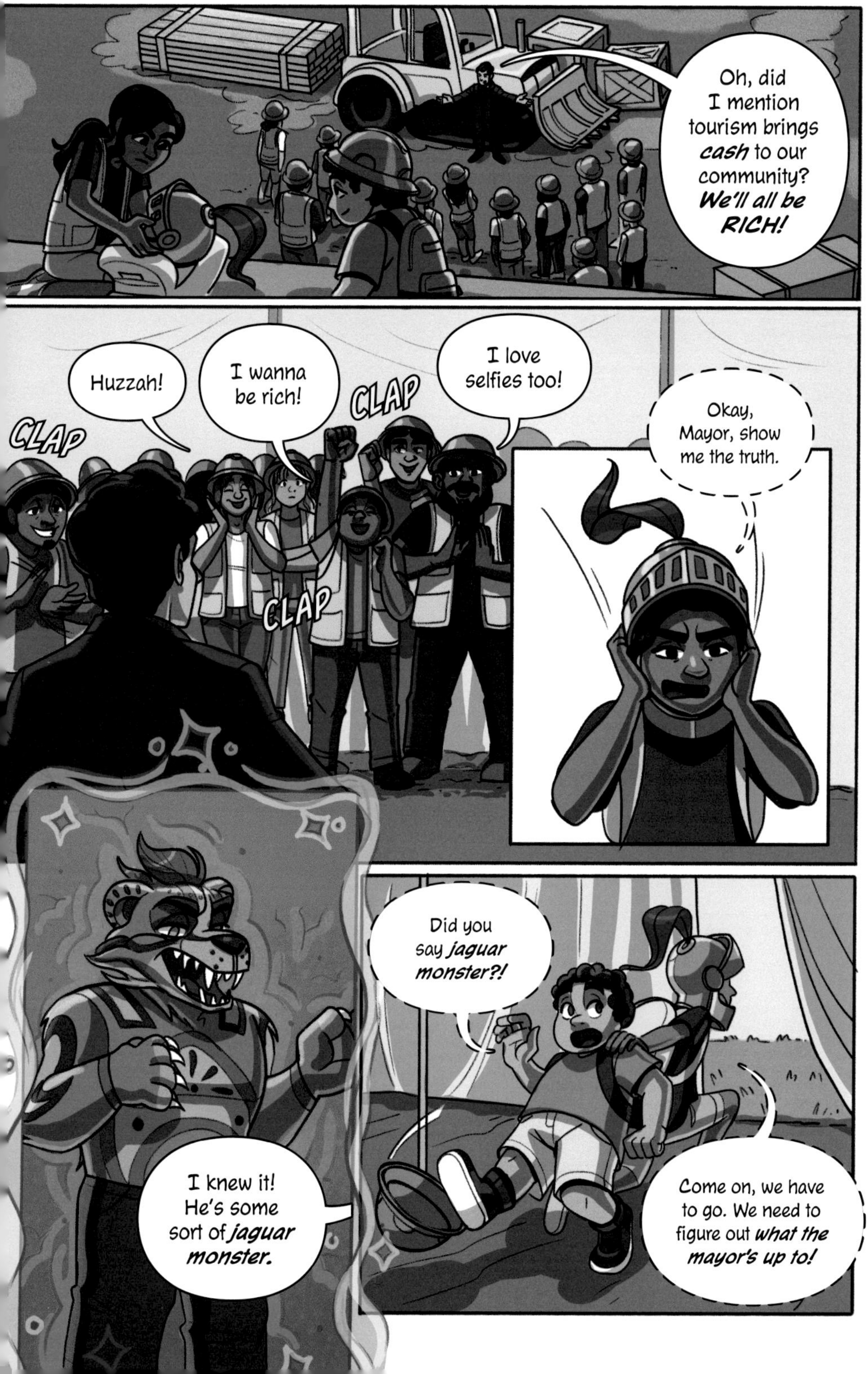
Oh, did I mention tourism brings *cash* to our community? ***We'll all be RICH!***
Huzzah!
I wanna be rich!
CLAP
I love selfies too!
CLAP
CLAP
Okay, Mayor, show me the truth.
I knew it! He's some sort of ***jaguar monster.***
Did you say ***jaguar monster?!***
Come on, we have to go. We need to figure out ***what the mayor's up to!***

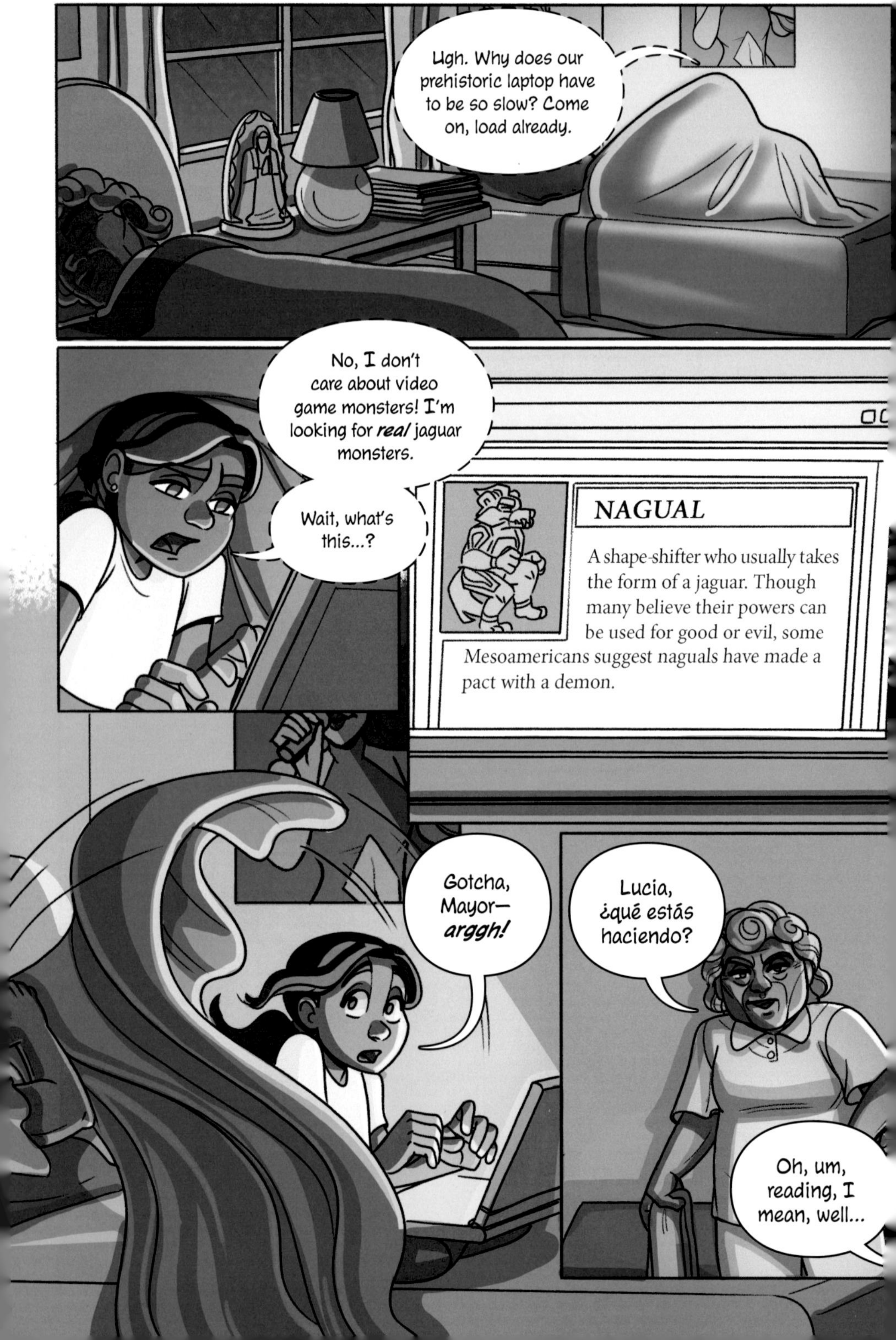
Ugh. Why does our prehistoric laptop have to be so slow? Come on, load already.
No, I don't care about video game monsters! I'm looking for *real* jaguar monsters.
Wait, what's this...?
NAGUAL
A shape-shifter who usually takes the form of a jaguar. Though many believe their powers can be used for good or evil, some Mesoamericans suggest naguals have made a pact with a demon.
Gotcha, Mayor—*arggh!*
Lucia, ¿qué estás haciendo?
Oh, um, reading, I mean, well...

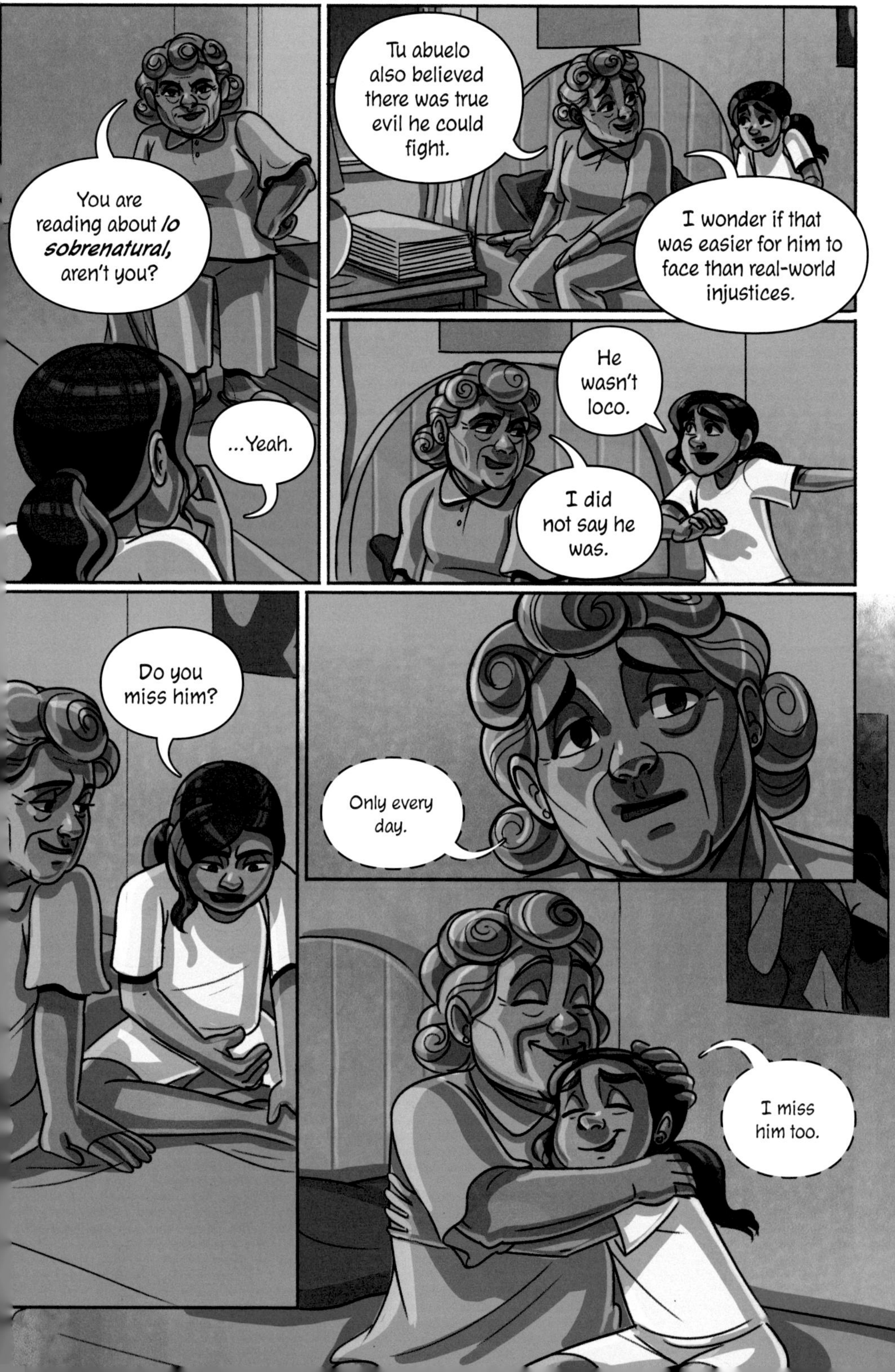
You are reading about *lo sobrenatural,* aren't you?
...Yeah.
Tu abuelo also believed there was true evil he could fight.
I wonder if that was easier for him to face than real-world injustices.
He wasn't loco.
I did not say he was.
Do you miss him?
Only every day.
I miss him too.

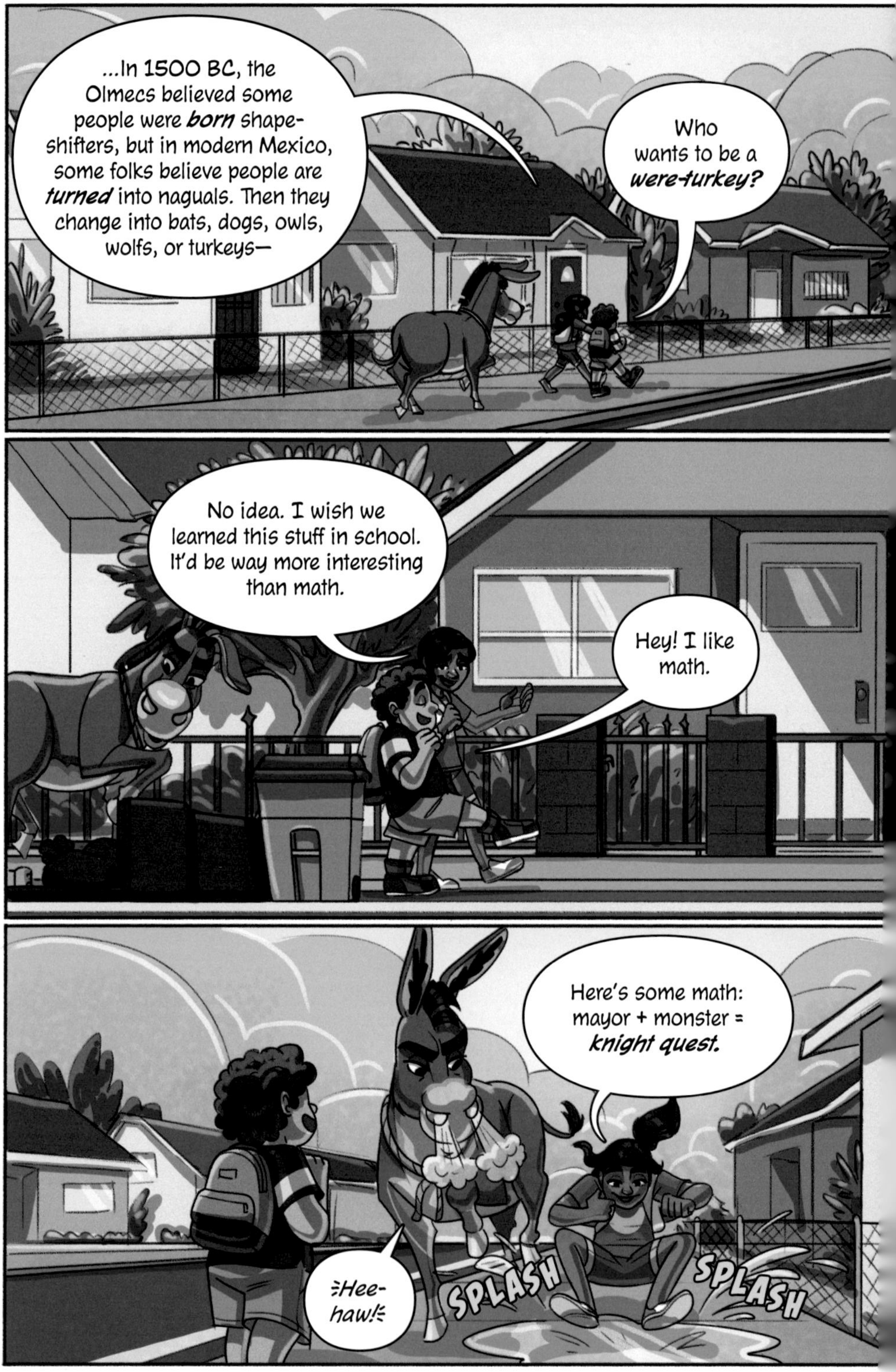
...In 1500 BC, the Olmecs believed some people were *born* shape-shifters, but in modern Mexico, some folks believe people are *turned* into naguals. Then they change into bats, dogs, owls, wolfs, or turkeys—
Who wants to be a *were-turkey?*
No idea. I wish we learned this stuff in school. It'd be way more interesting than math.
Hey! I like math.
Here's some math: mayor + monster = *knight quest.*
Hee-haw!
SPLASH
SPLASH

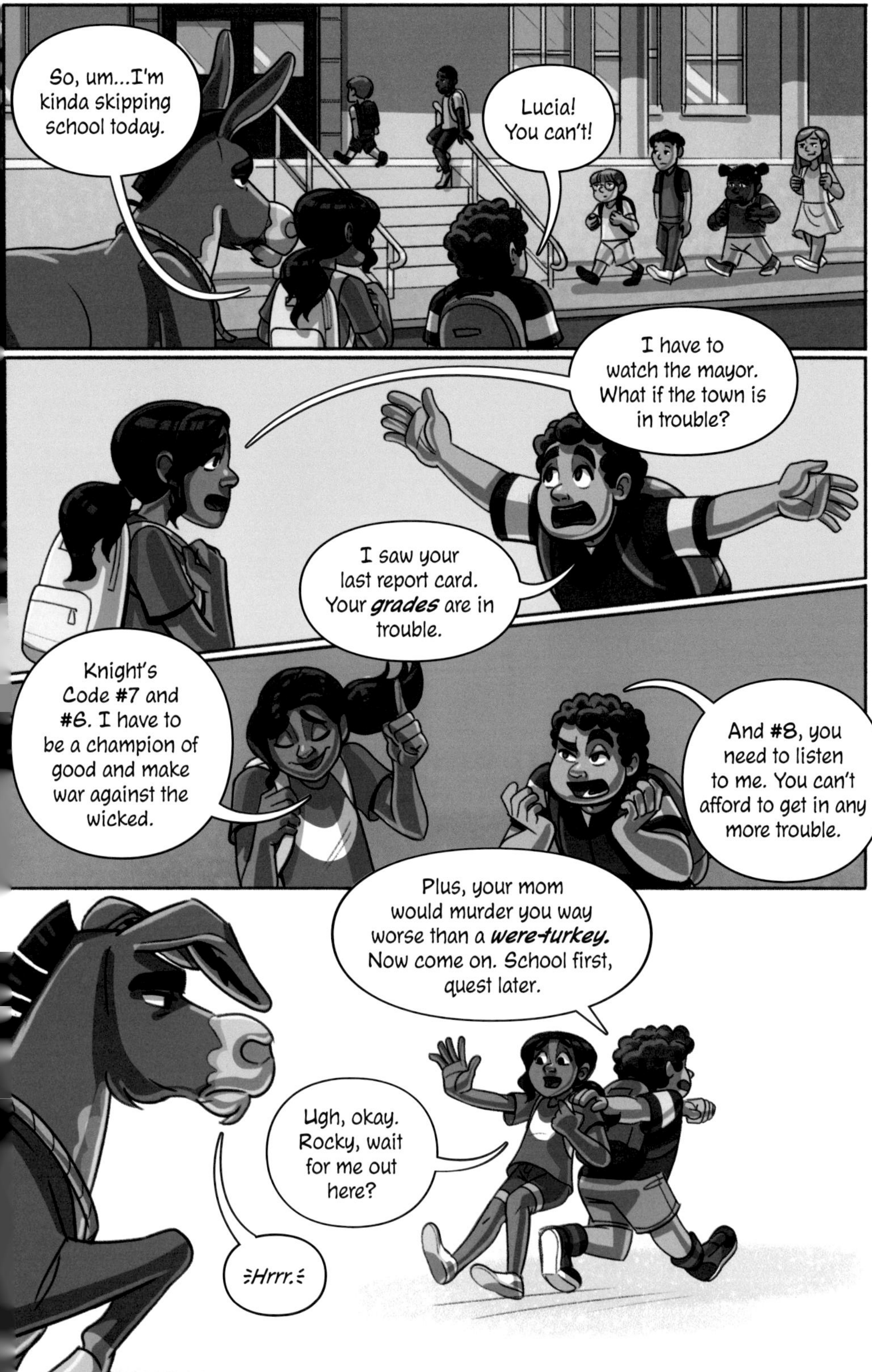
So, um...I'm kinda skipping school today.
Lucia! You can't!
I have to watch the mayor. What if the town is in trouble?
I saw your last report card. Your *grades* are in trouble.
Knight's Code #7 and #6. I have to be a champion of good and make war against the wicked.
And #8, you need to listen to me. You can't afford to get in any more trouble.
Plus, your mom would murder you way worse than a *were-turkey.* Now come on. School first, quest later.
Ugh, okay. Rocky, wait for me out here?
Hrrr.

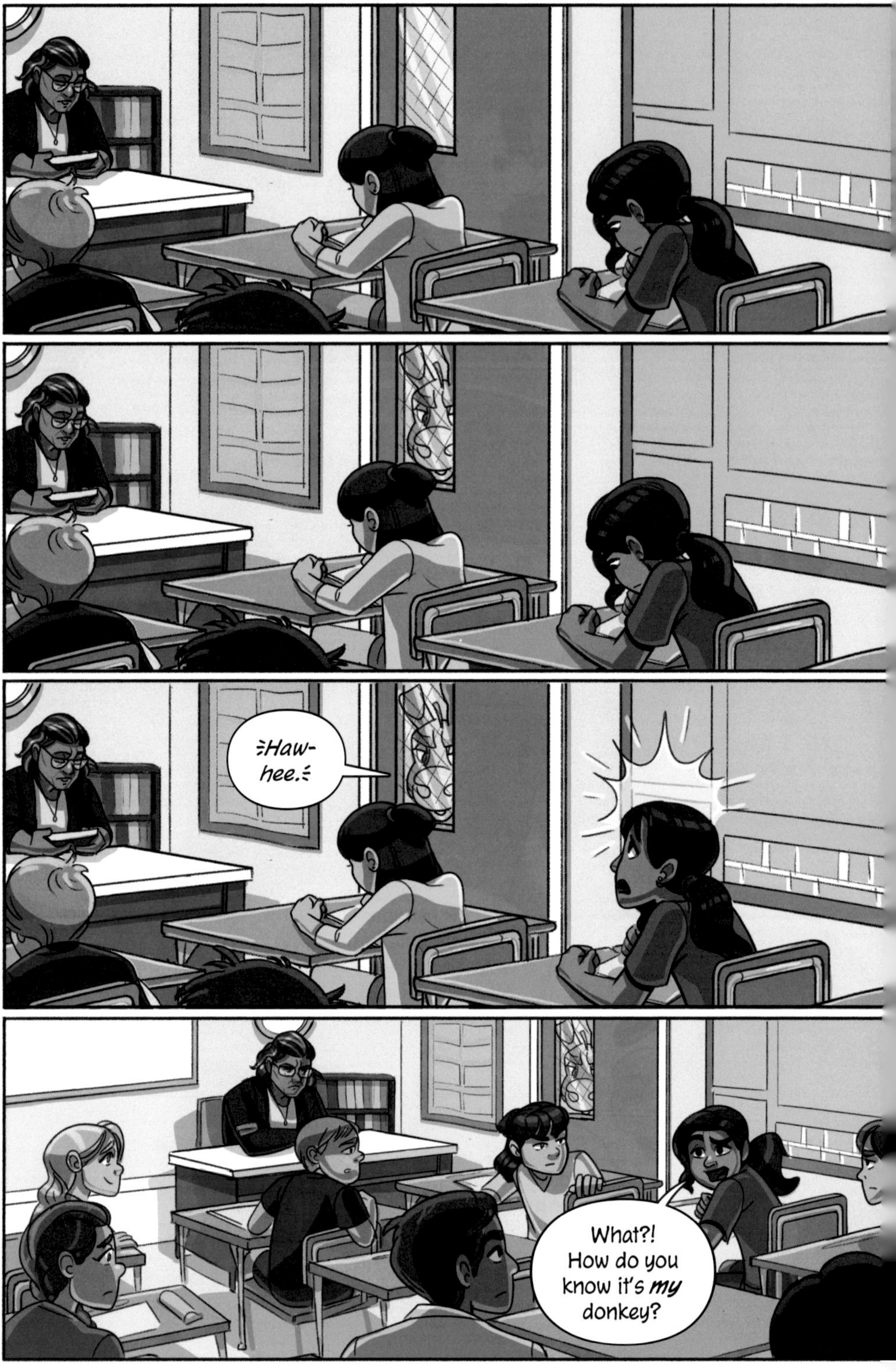
Haw-
hee.
What?! How do you know it's *my* donkey?

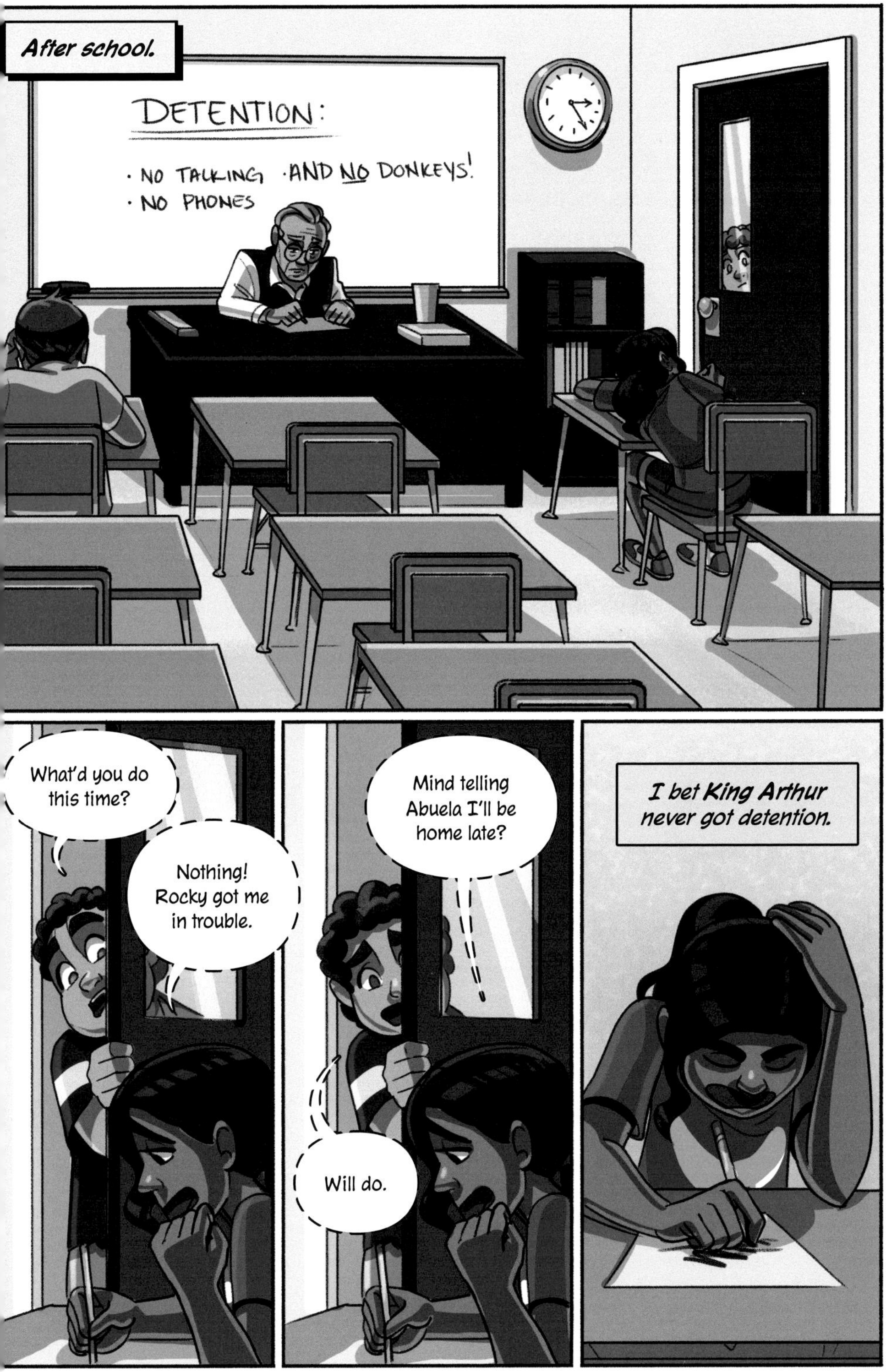
After school.
DETENTION:
· NO TALKING
· NO PHONES
· AND NO DONKEYS!
What'd you do this time?
Nothing! Rocky got me in trouble.
Mind telling Abuela I'll be home late?
Will do.
I bet King Arthur never got detention.

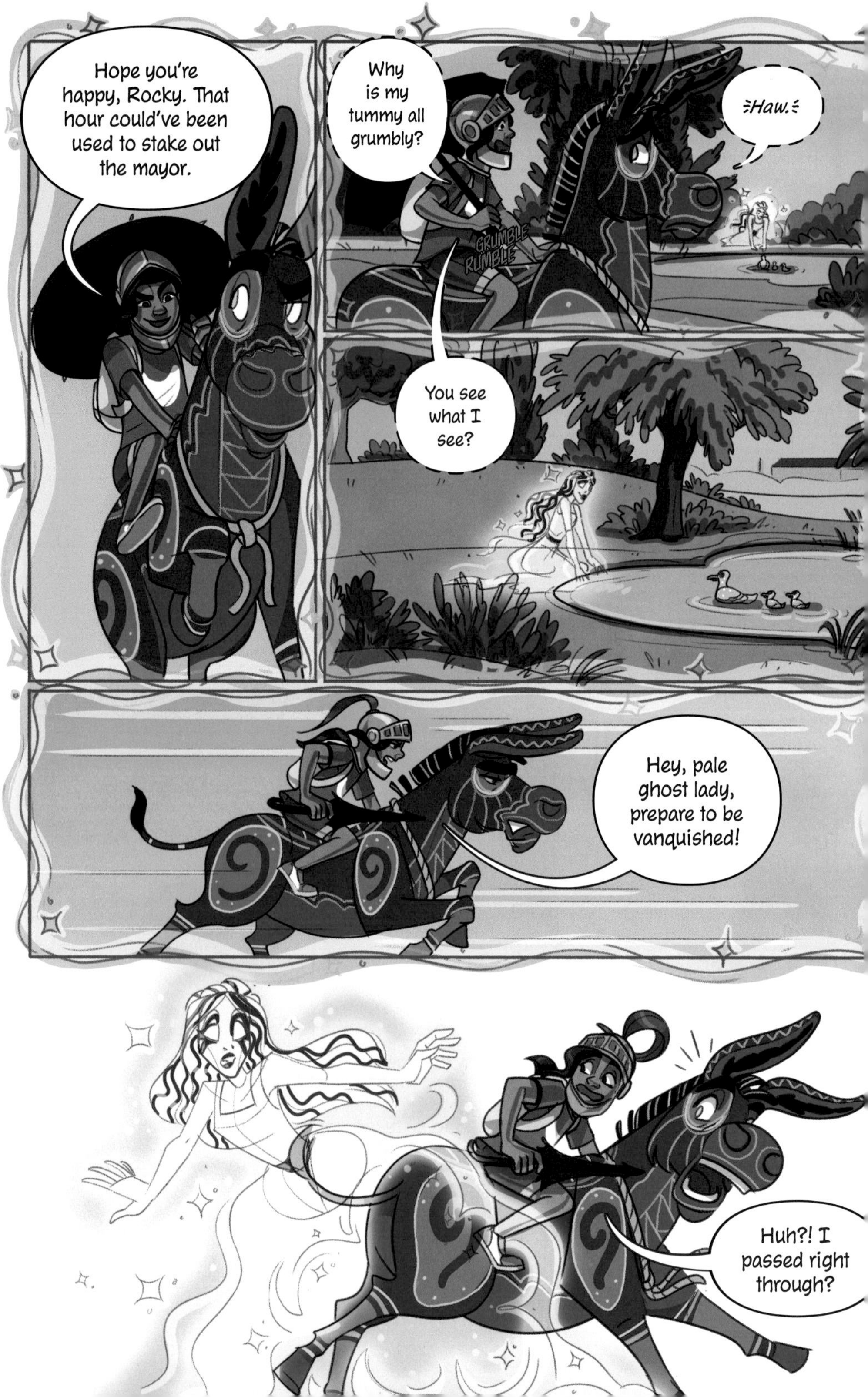

Hope you're happy, Rocky. That hour could've been used to stake out the mayor.
Why is my tummy all grumbly?
GRUMBLE RUMBLE
Haw.
You see what I see?
Hey, pale ghost lady, prepare to be vanquished!
Huh?! I passed right through?

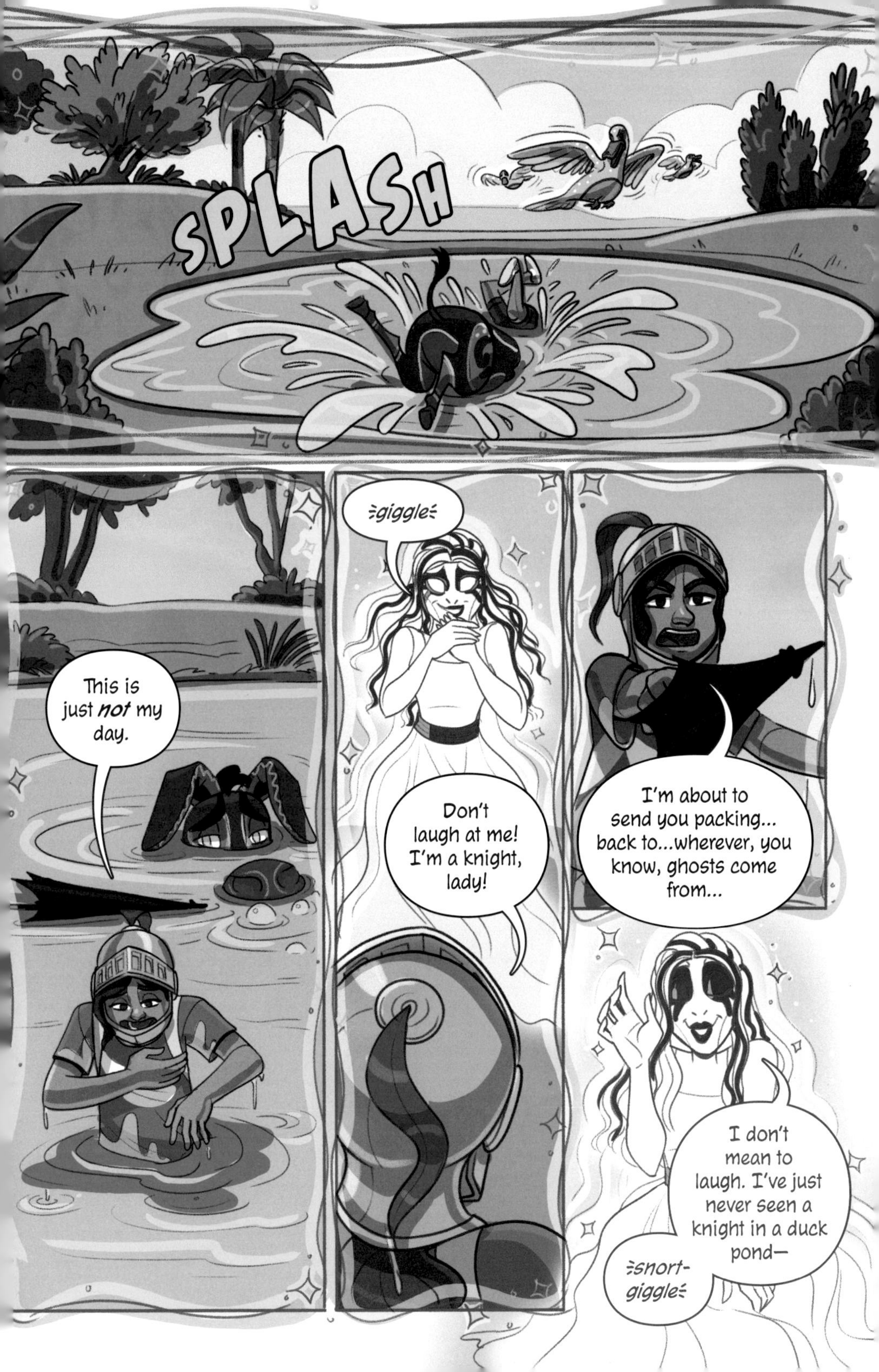
SPLASH
This is just *not* my day.
≈giggle≈
Don't laugh at me! I'm a knight, lady!
I'm about to send you packing... back to...wherever, you know, ghosts come from...
I don't mean to laugh. I've just never seen a knight in a duck pond—
≈snort-giggle≈

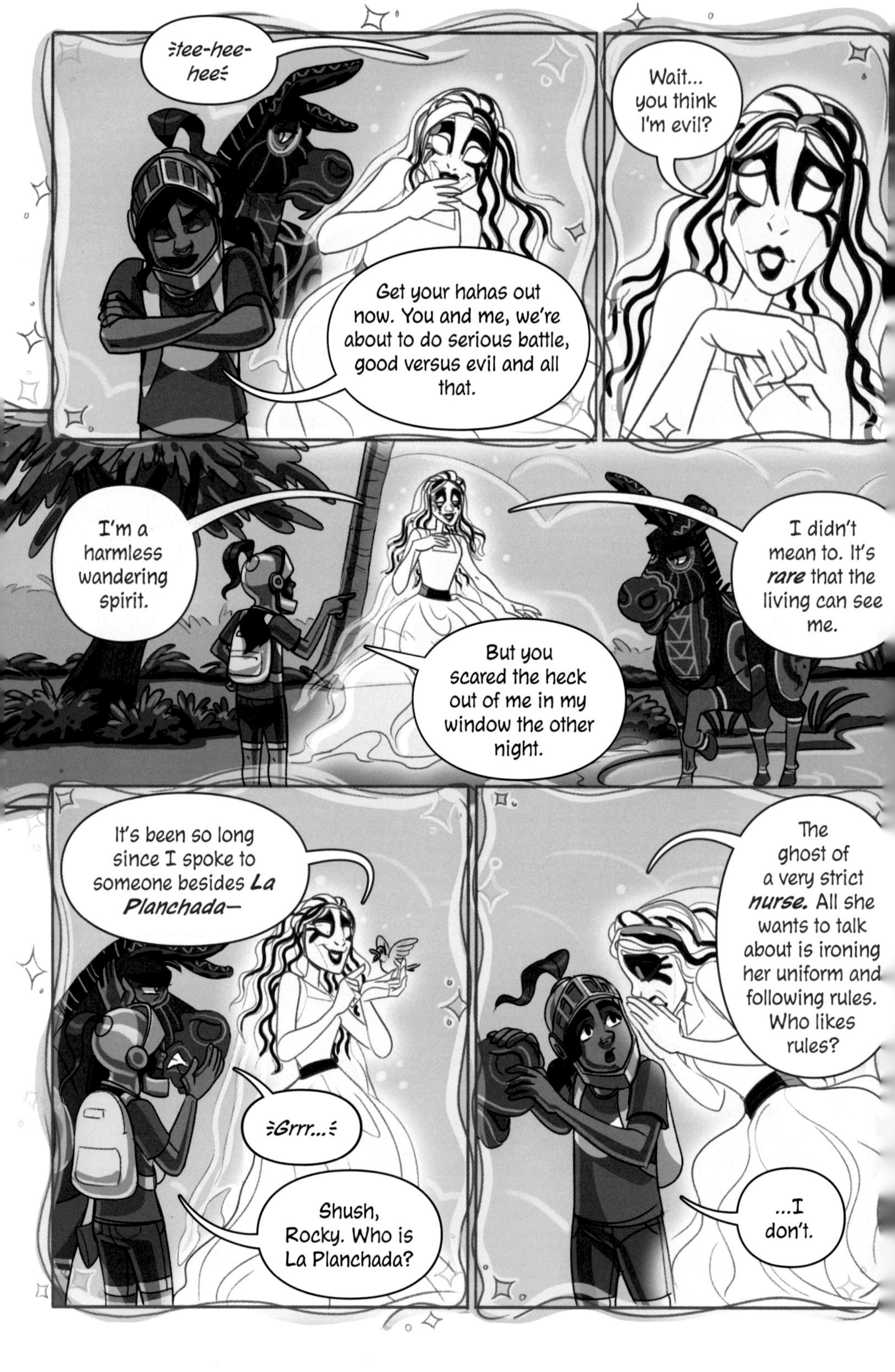

tee-hee-hee
Get your hahas out now. You and me, we're about to do serious battle, good versus evil and all that.
Wait... you think I'm evil?
I'm a harmless wandering spirit.
I didn't mean to. It's *rare* that the living can see me.
But you scared the heck out of me in my window the other night.
It's been so long since I spoke to someone besides ***La Planchada***—
Grrr...
Shush, Rocky. Who is La Planchada?
The ghost of a very strict ***nurse.*** All she wants to talk about is ironing her uniform and following rules. Who likes rules?
...I don't.

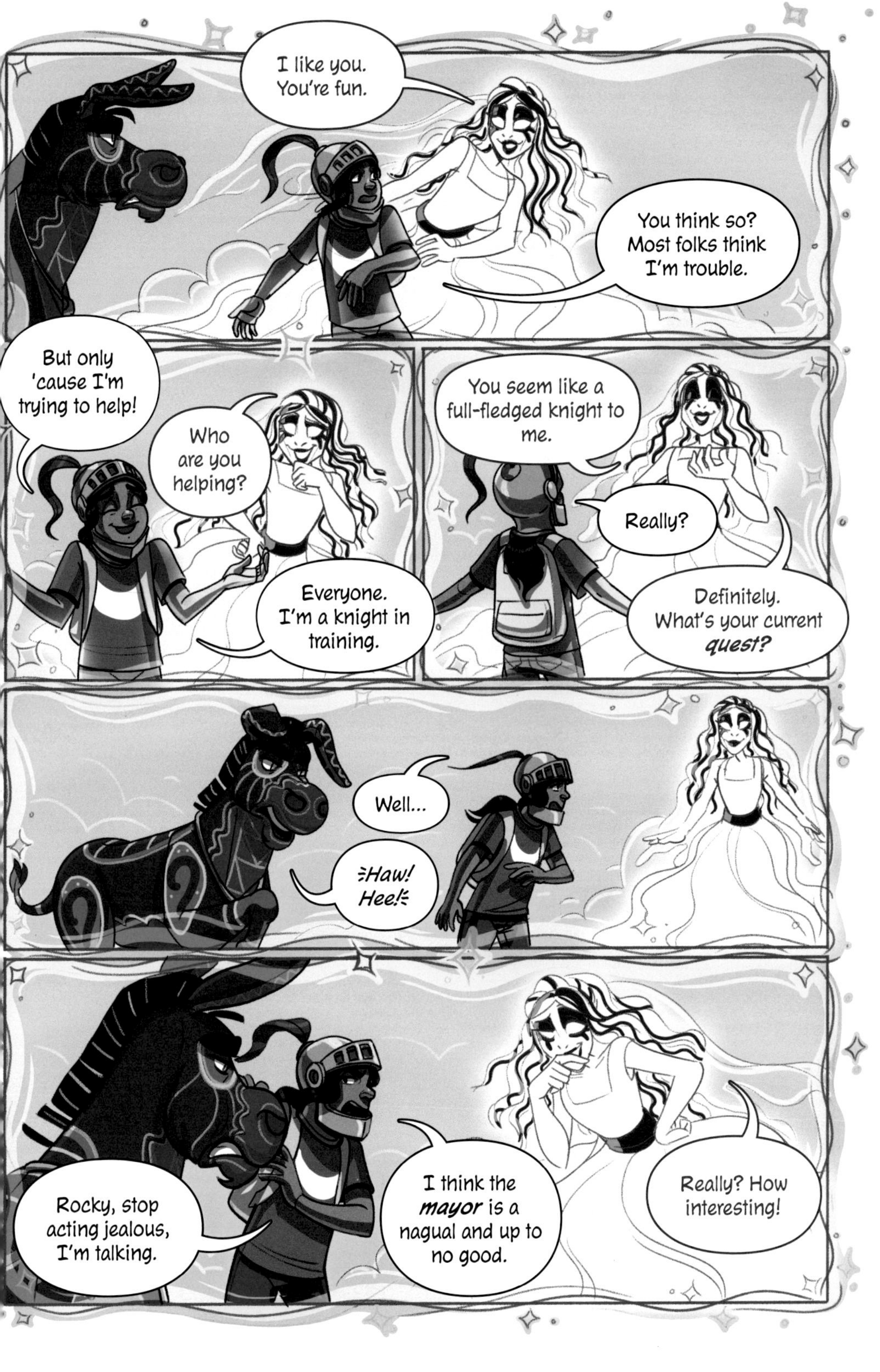

I like you. You're fun.
You think so? Most folks think I'm trouble.
But only 'cause I'm trying to help!
Who are you helping?
Everyone. I'm a knight in training.
You seem like a full-fledged knight to me.
Really?
Definitely. What's your current *quest?*
Well...
Haw! Hee!
Rocky, stop acting jealous, I'm talking.
I think the *mayor* is a nagual and up to no good.
Really? How interesting!

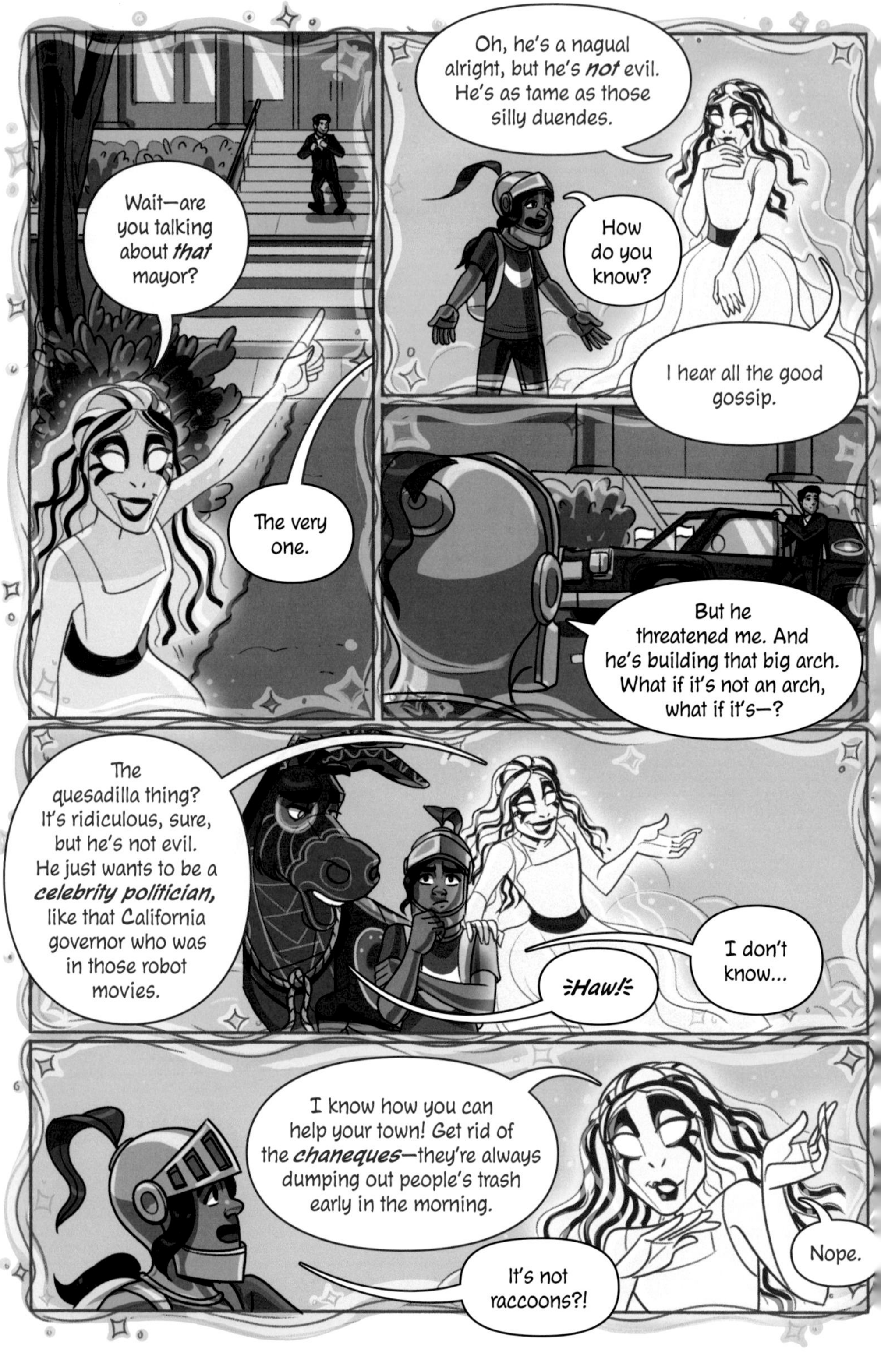
Wait—are you talking about *that* mayor?
The very one.
Oh, he's a nagual alright, but he's ***not*** evil. He's as tame as those silly duendes.
How do you know?
I hear all the good gossip.
But he threatened me. And he's building that big arch. What if it's not an arch, what if it's—?
The quesadilla thing? It's ridiculous, sure, but he's not evil. He just wants to be a ***celebrity politician,*** like that California governor who was in those robot movies.
I don't know...
Haw!
I know how you can help your town! Get rid of the ***chaneques***—they're always dumping out people's trash early in the morning.
It's not raccoons?!
Nope.

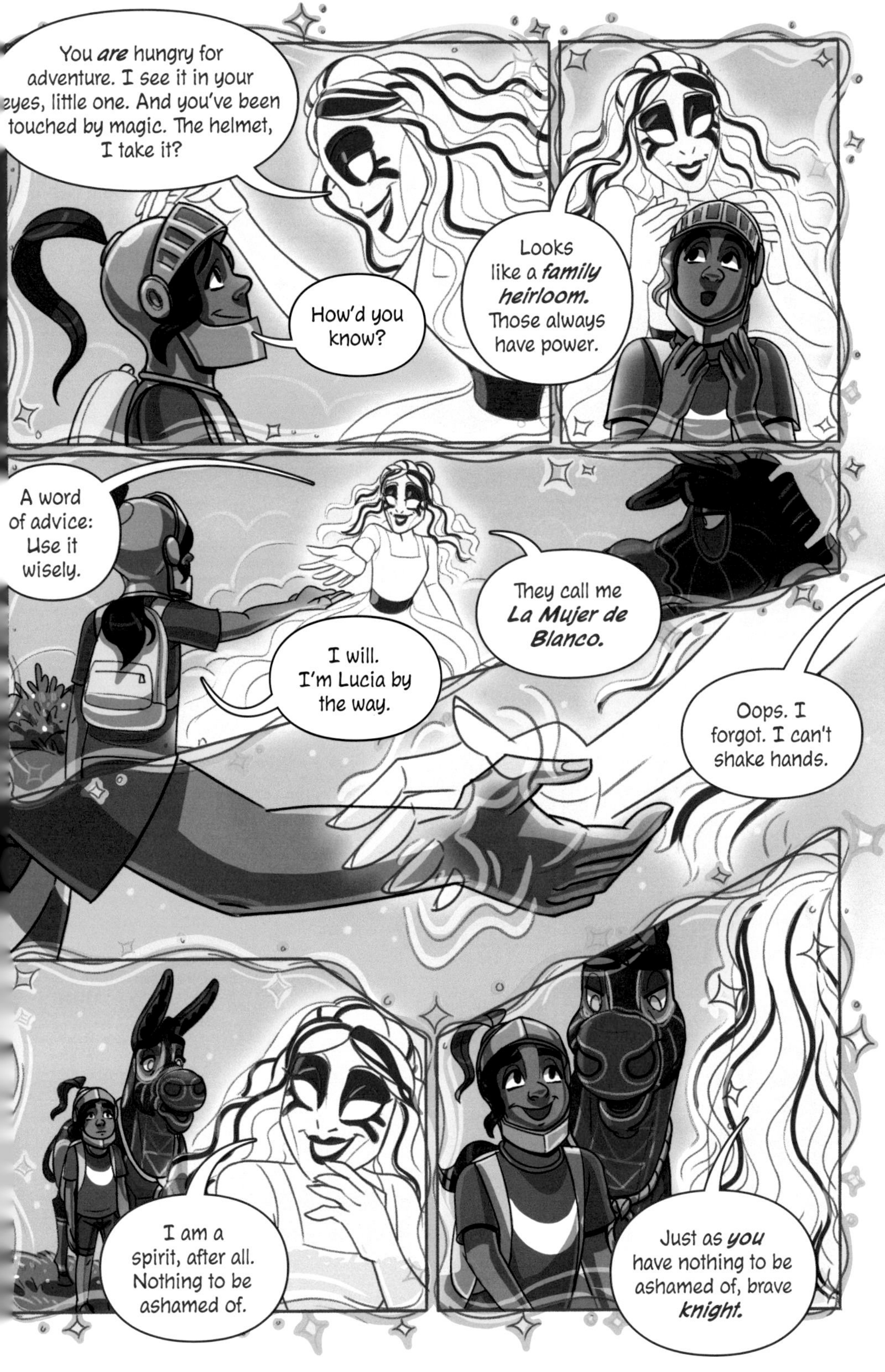
You *are* hungry for adventure. I see it in your eyes, little one. And you've been touched by magic. The helmet, I take it?
How'd you know?
Looks like a ***family heirloom.*** Those always have power.
A word of advice: Use it wisely.
I will. I'm Lucia by the way.
They call me ***La Mujer de Blanco.***
Oops. I forgot. I can't shake hands.
I am a spirit, after all. Nothing to be ashamed of.
Just as ***you*** have nothing to be ashamed of, brave ***knight.***

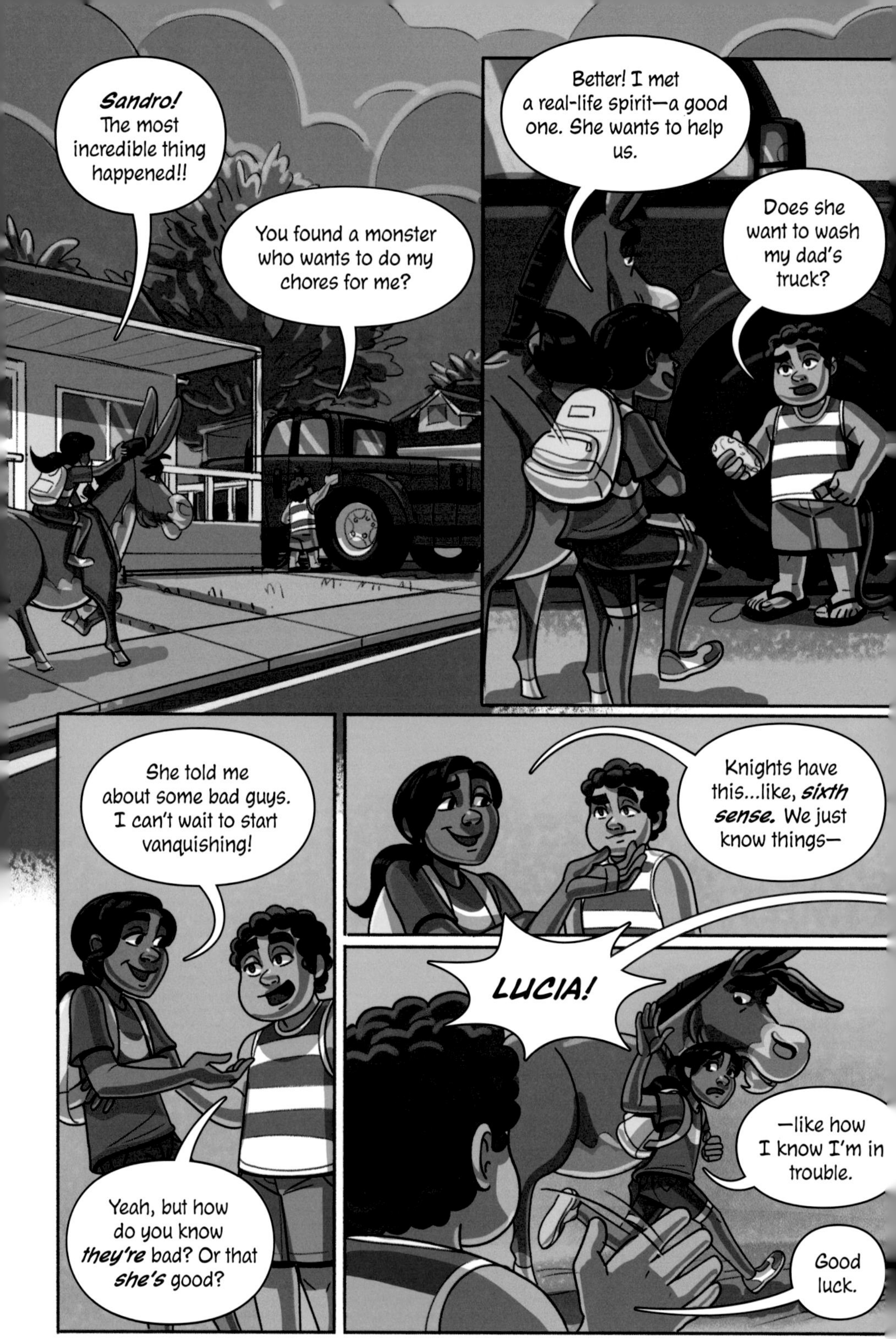
Sandro! The most incredible thing happened!!
You found a monster who wants to do my chores for me?
Better! I met a real-life spirit—a good one. She wants to help us.
Does she want to wash my dad's truck?
She told me about some bad guys. I can't wait to start vanquishing!
Yeah, but how do you know they're bad? Or that she's good?
Knights have this...like, sixth sense. We just know things—
LUCIA!
—like how I know I'm in trouble.
Good luck.

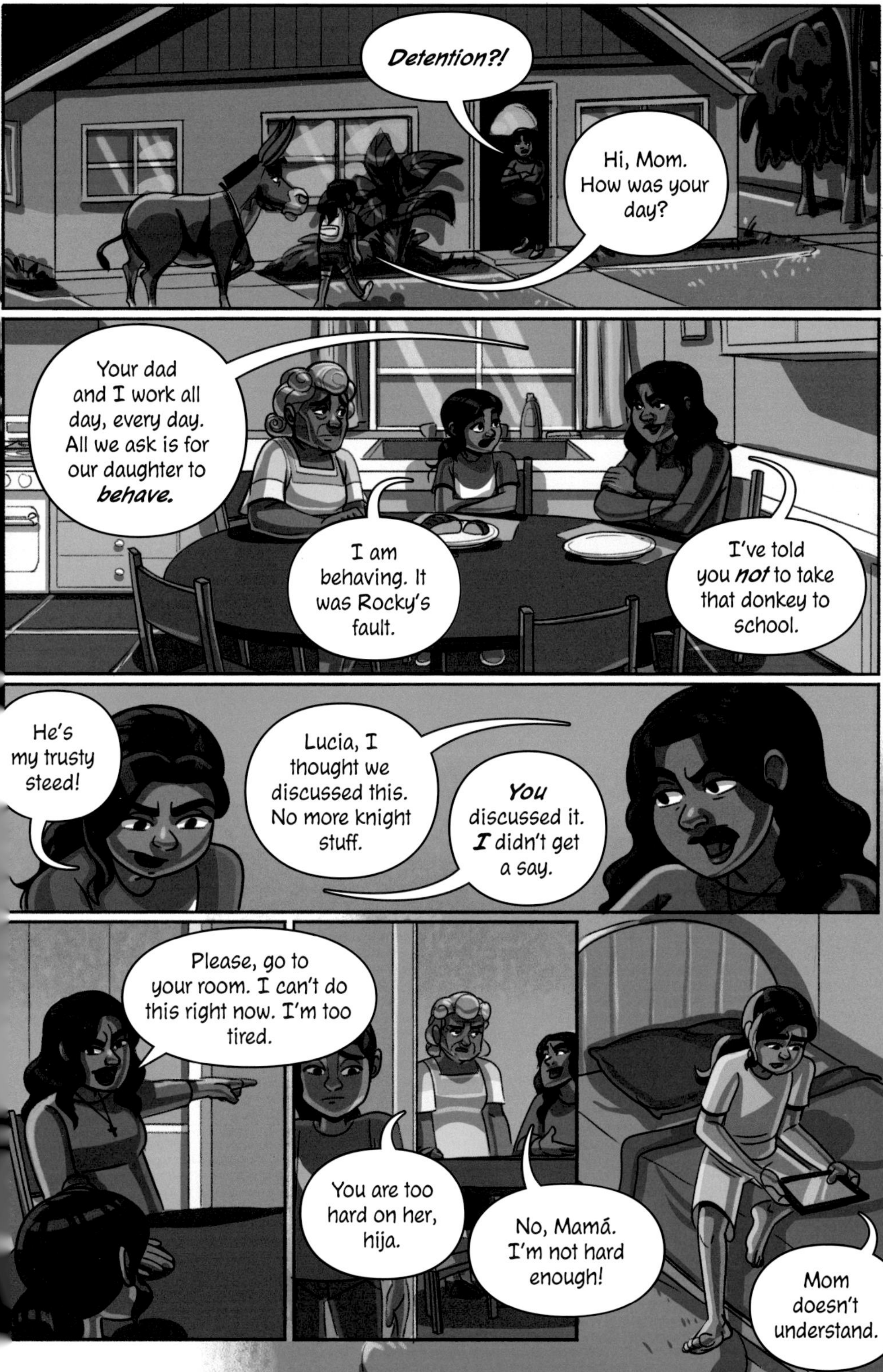
Detention?!
Hi, Mom. How was your day?
Your dad and I work all day, every day. All we ask is for our daughter to *behave.*
I am behaving. It was Rocky's fault.
I've told you *not* to take that donkey to school.
He's my trusty steed!
Lucia, I thought we discussed this. No more knight stuff.
You discussed it. *I* didn't get a say.
Please, go to your room. I can't do this right now. I'm too tired.
You are too hard on her, hija.
No, Mamá. I'm not hard enough!
Mom doesn't understand.

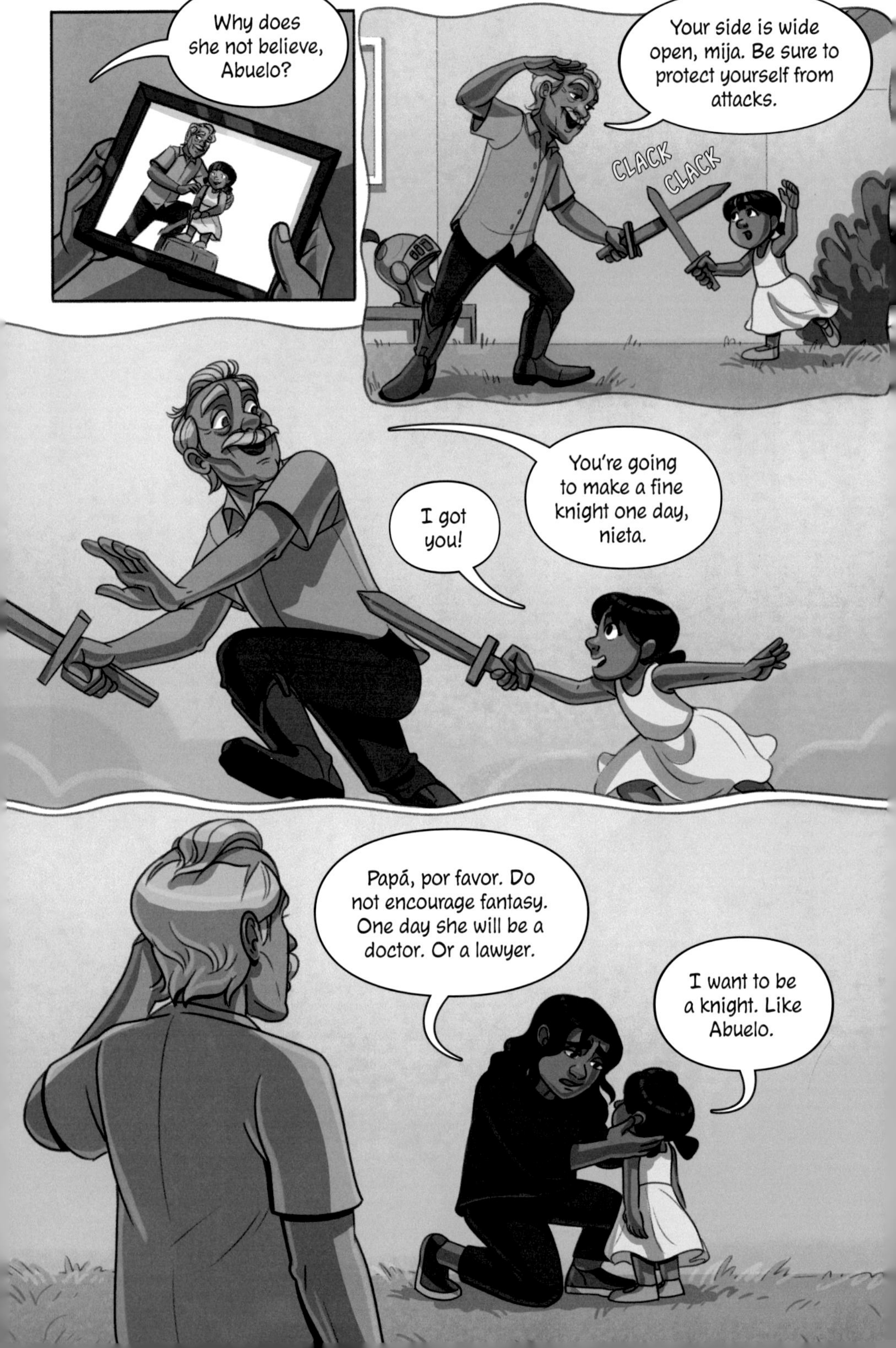
Why does she not believe, Abuelo?
Your side is wide open, mija. Be sure to protect yourself from attacks.
CLACK
CLACK
You're going to make a fine knight one day, nieta.
I got you!
Papá, por favor. Do not encourage fantasy. One day she will be a doctor. Or a lawyer.
I want to be a knight. Like Abuelo.

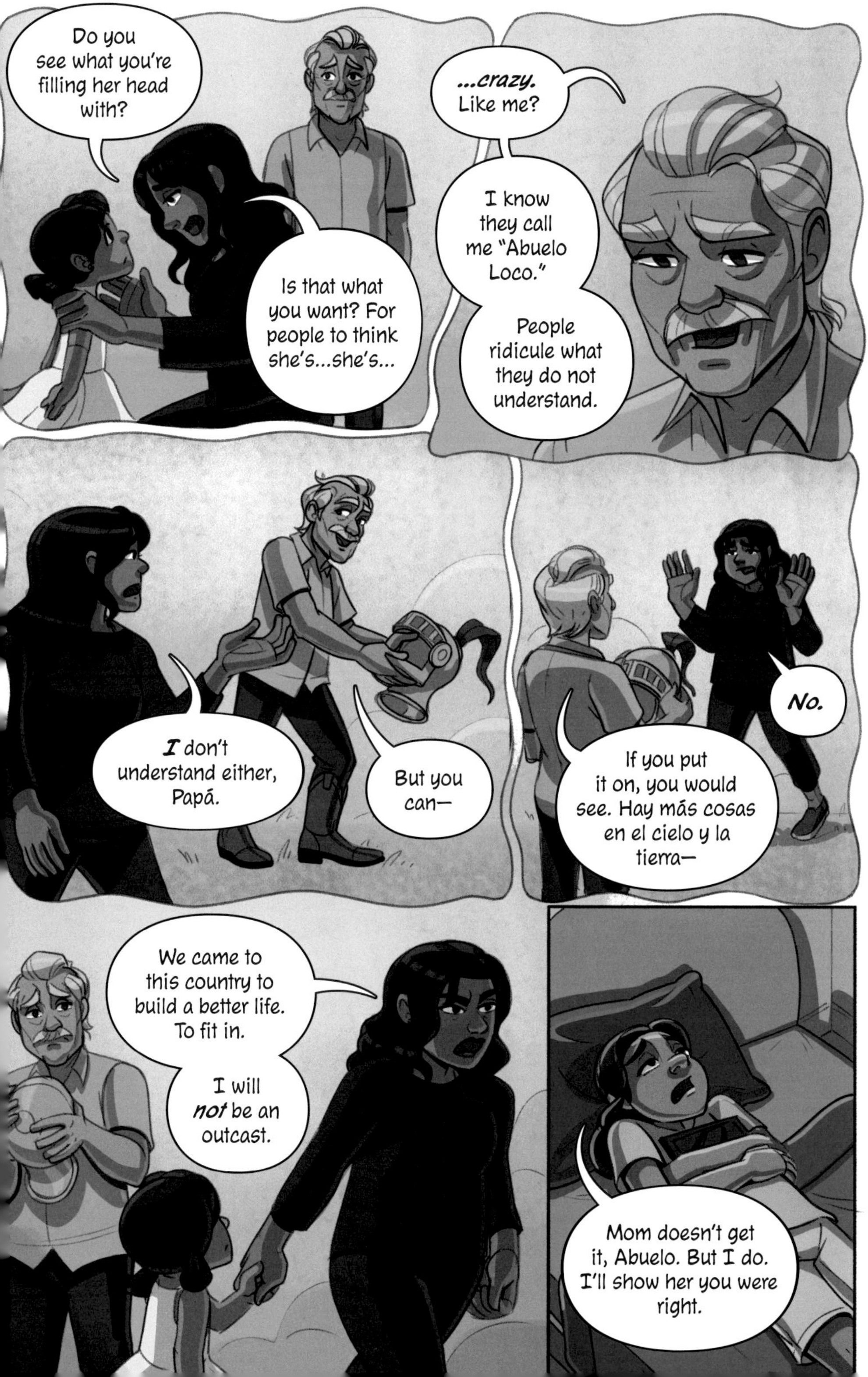
Do you see what you're filling her head with?
Is that what you want? For people to think she's...she's...
...crazy. Like me?
I know they call me "Abuelo Loco."
People ridicule what they do not understand.
I don't understand either, Papá.
But you can—
No.
If you put it on, you would see. Hay más cosas en el cielo y la tierra—
We came to this country to build a better life. To fit in.
I will not be an outcast.
Mom doesn't get it, Abuelo. But I do. I'll show her you were right.

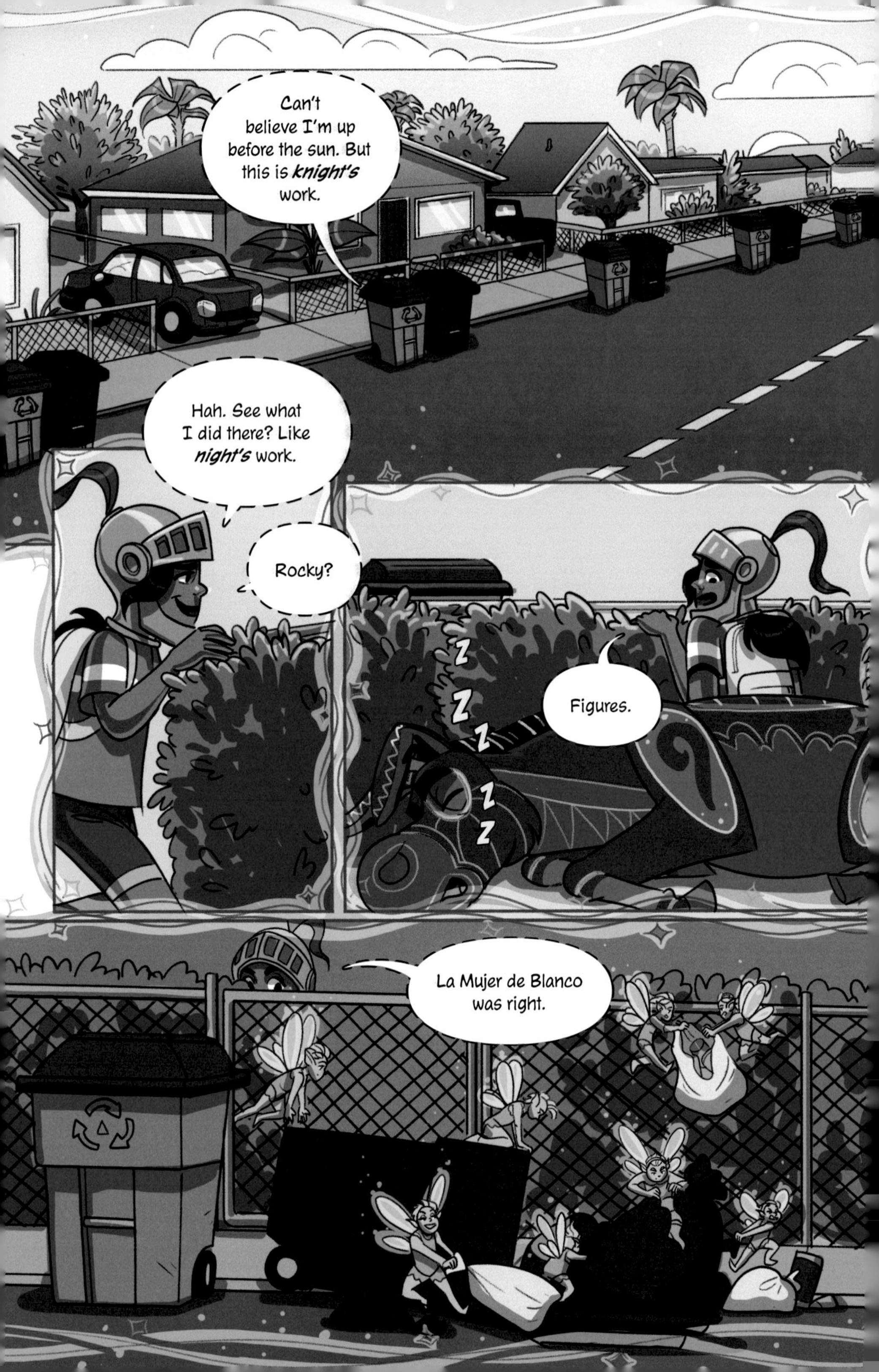
Can't believe I'm up before the sun. But this is ***knight's*** work.
Hah. See what I did there? Like ***night's*** work.
Rocky?
Z Z Z Z Z
Figures.
La Mujer de Blanco was right.

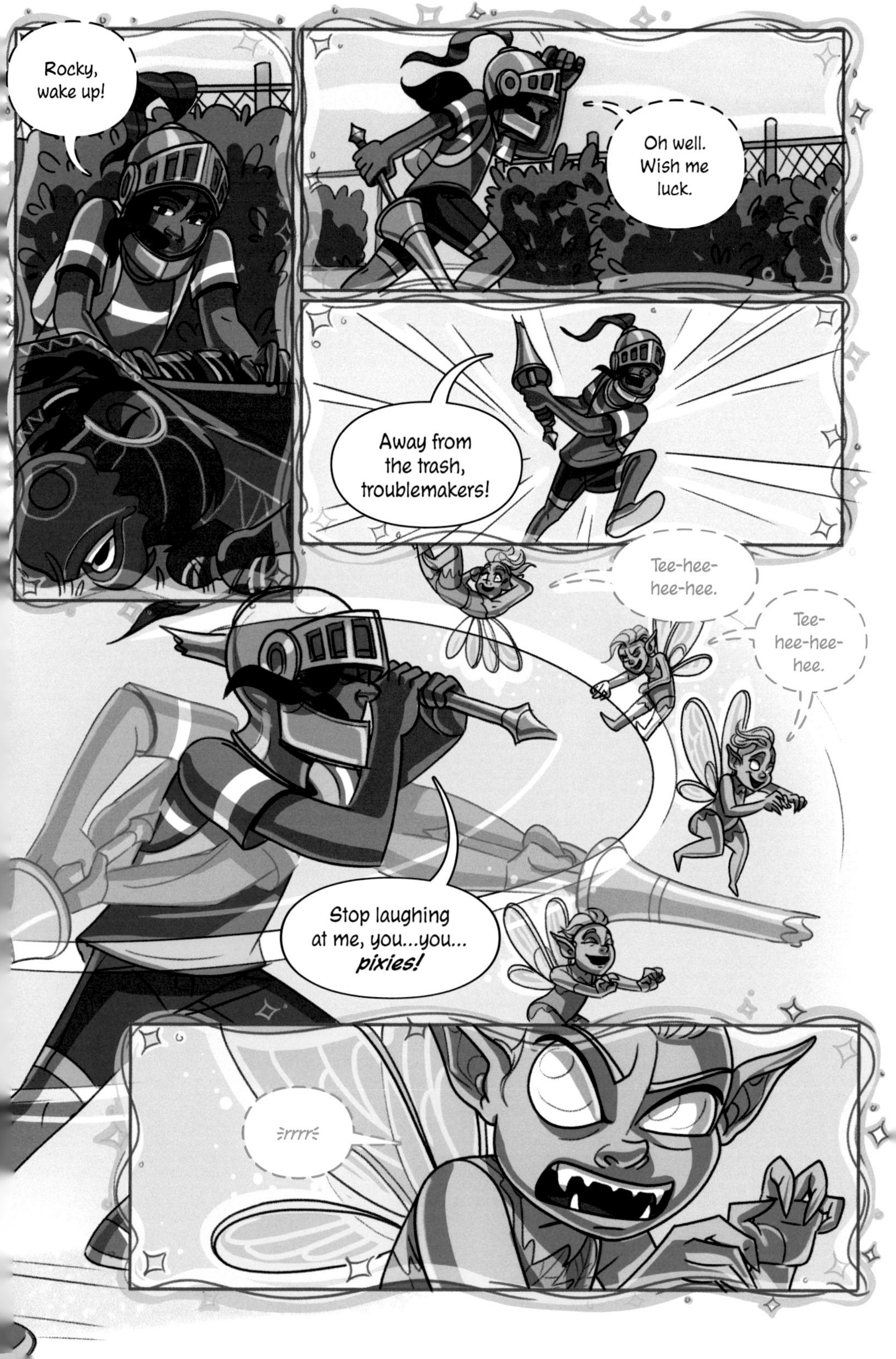
Rocky, wake up!
Oh well. Wish me luck.
Away from the trash, troublemakers!
Tee-hee-hee-hee.
Tee-hee-hee-hee.
Stop laughing at me, you...you... *pixies!*
rrrr

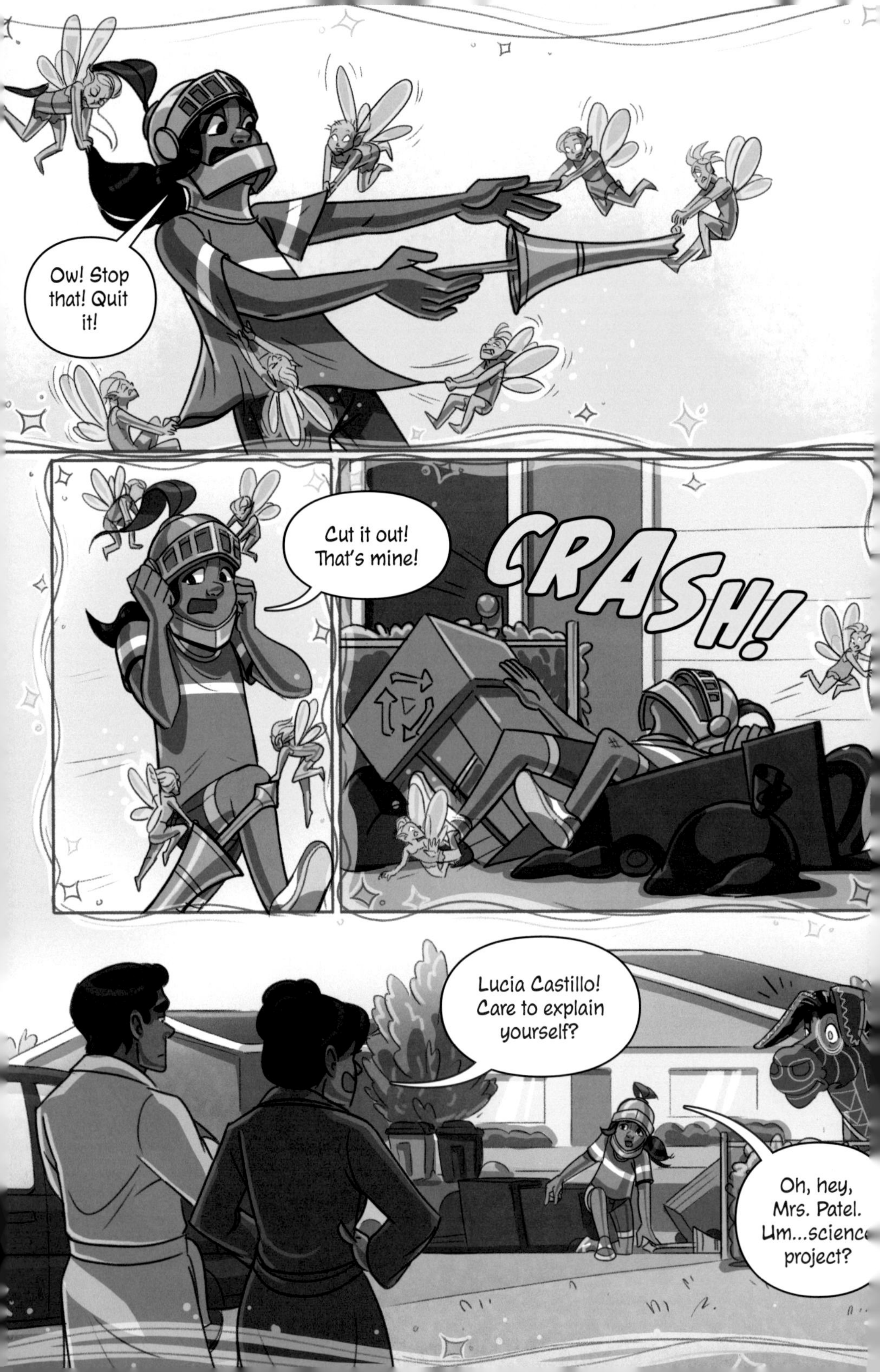
Ow! Stop that! Quit it!
Cut it out! That's mine!
CRASH!
Lucia Castillo! Care to explain yourself?
Oh, hey, Mrs. Patel. Um...science project?

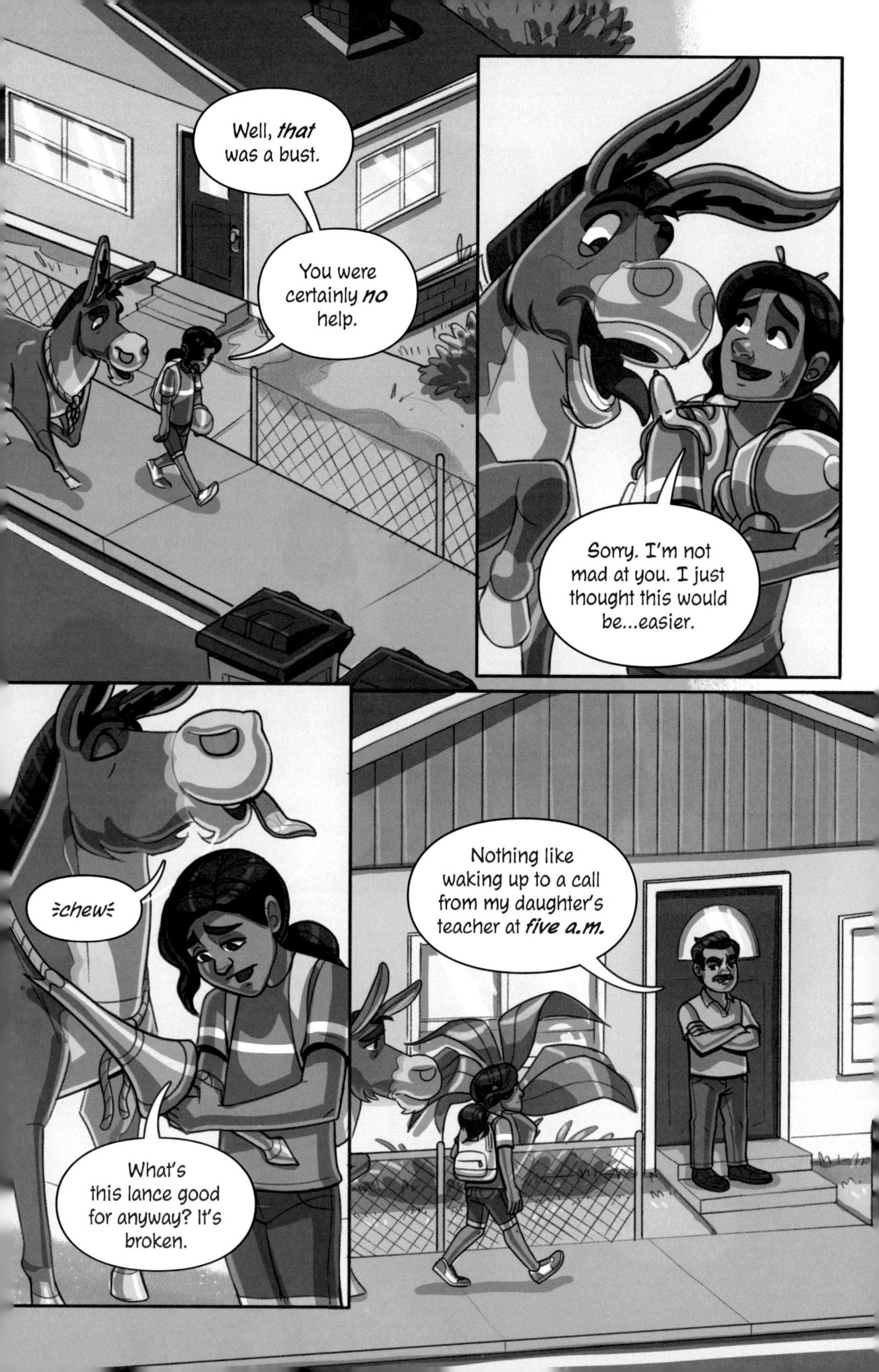
Well, *that* was a bust.
You were certainly ***no*** help.
Sorry. I'm not mad at you. I just thought this would be...easier.
chew
What's this lance good for anyway? It's broken.
Nothing like waking up to a call from my daughter's teacher at ***five a.m.***

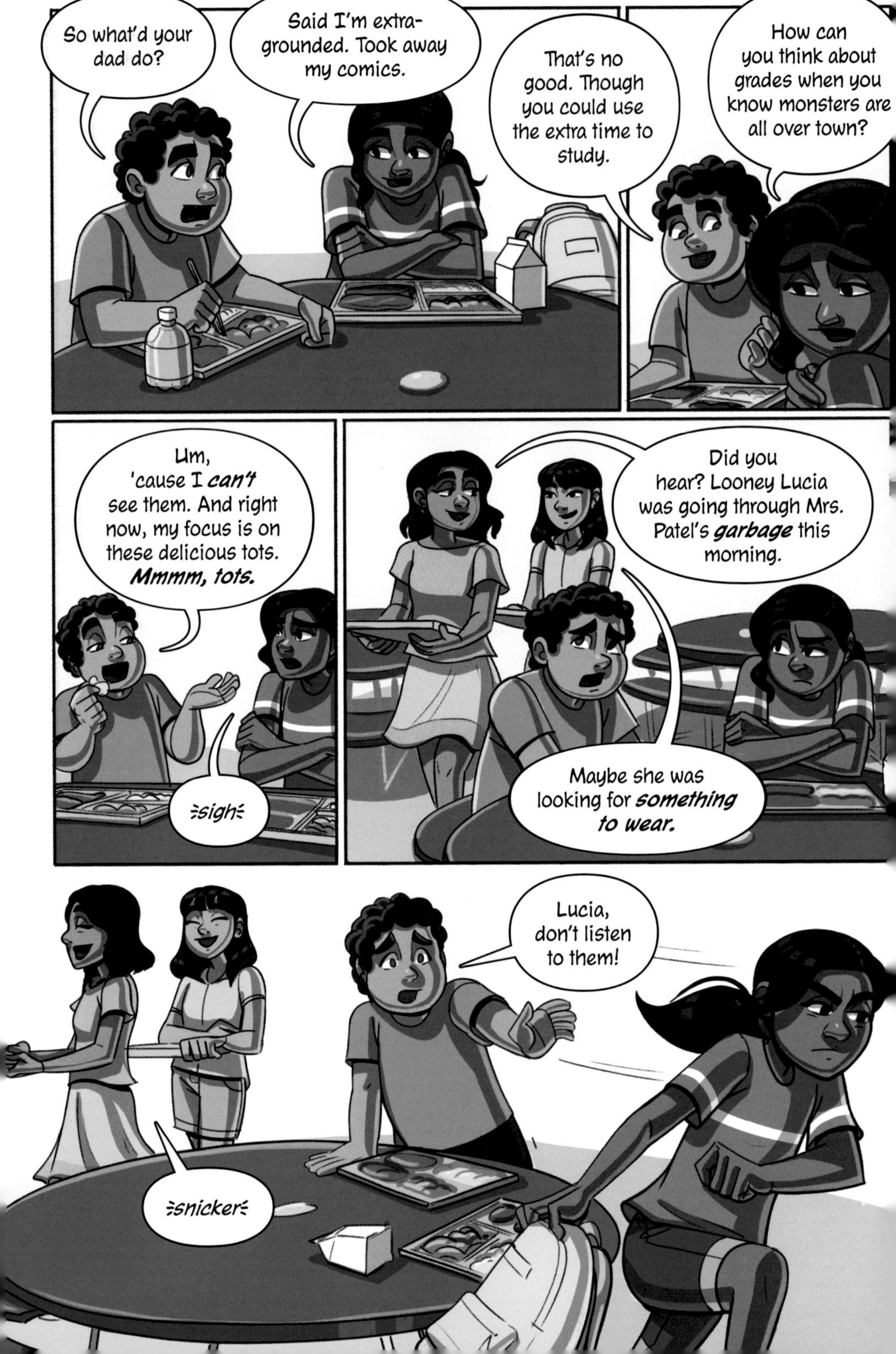
So what'd your dad do?
Said I'm extra-grounded. Took away my comics.
That's no good. Though you could use the extra time to study.
How can you think about grades when you know monsters are all over town?
Um, 'cause I *can't* see them. And right now, my focus is on these delicious tots. ***Mmmm, tots.***
sigh
Did you hear? Looney Lucia was going through Mrs. Patel's ***garbage*** this morning.
Maybe she was looking for ***something to wear.***
Lucia, don't listen to them!
snicker

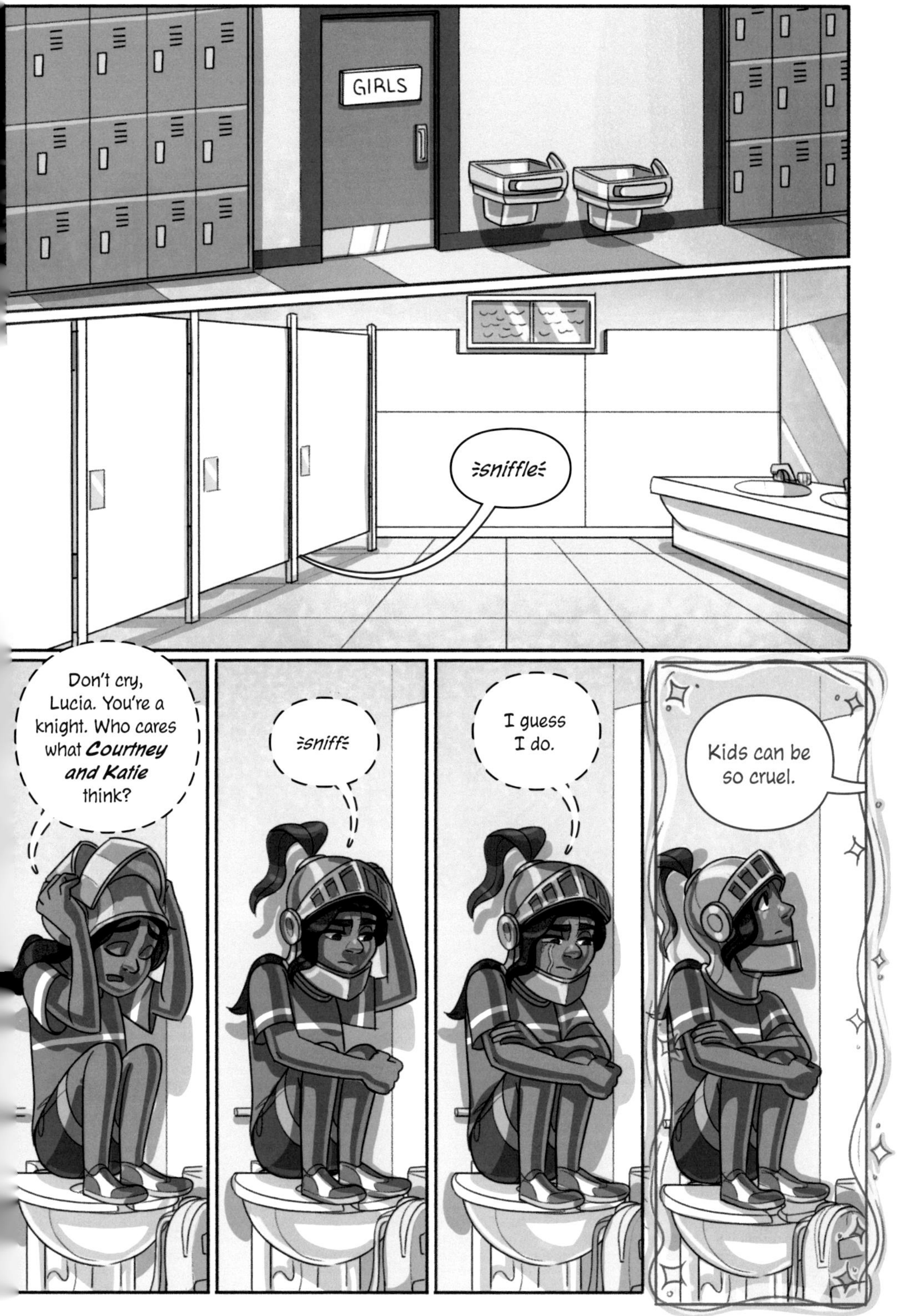
GIRLS
≈sniffle≈
Don't cry, Lucia. You're a knight. Who cares what **Courtney and Katie** think?
≈sniff≈
I guess I do.
Kids can be so cruel.

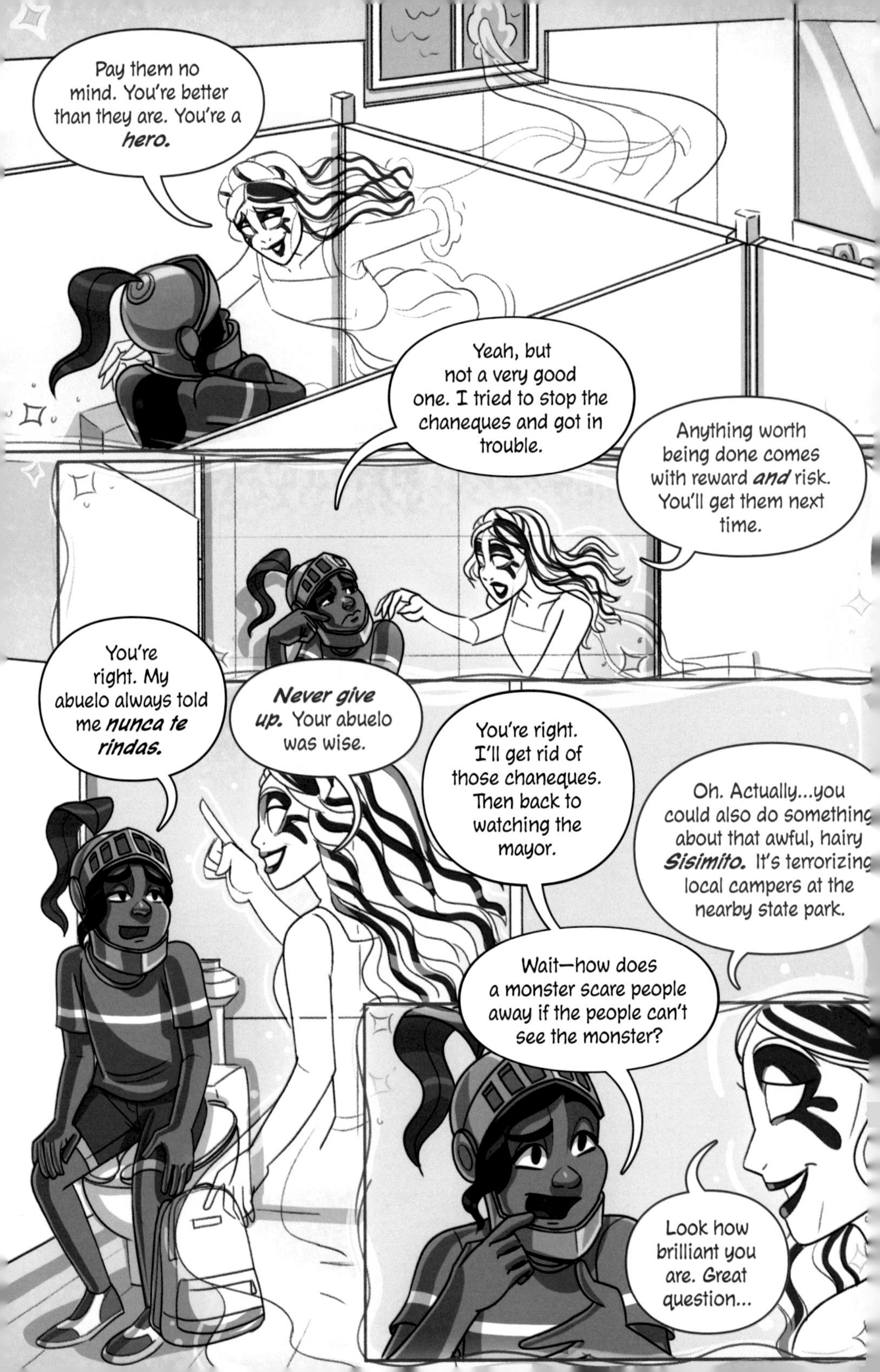

Pay them no mind. You're better than they are. You're a ***hero.***
Yeah, but not a very good one. I tried to stop the chaneques and got in trouble.
Anything worth being done comes with reward ***and*** risk. You'll get them next time.
You're right. My abuelo always told me ***nunca te rindas.***
Never give up. Your abuelo was wise.
You're right. I'll get rid of those chaneques. Then back to watching the mayor.
Oh. Actually...you could also do something about that awful, hairy ***Sisimito.*** It's terrorizing local campers at the nearby state park.
Wait—how does a monster scare people away if the people can't see the monster?
Look how brilliant you are. Great question...

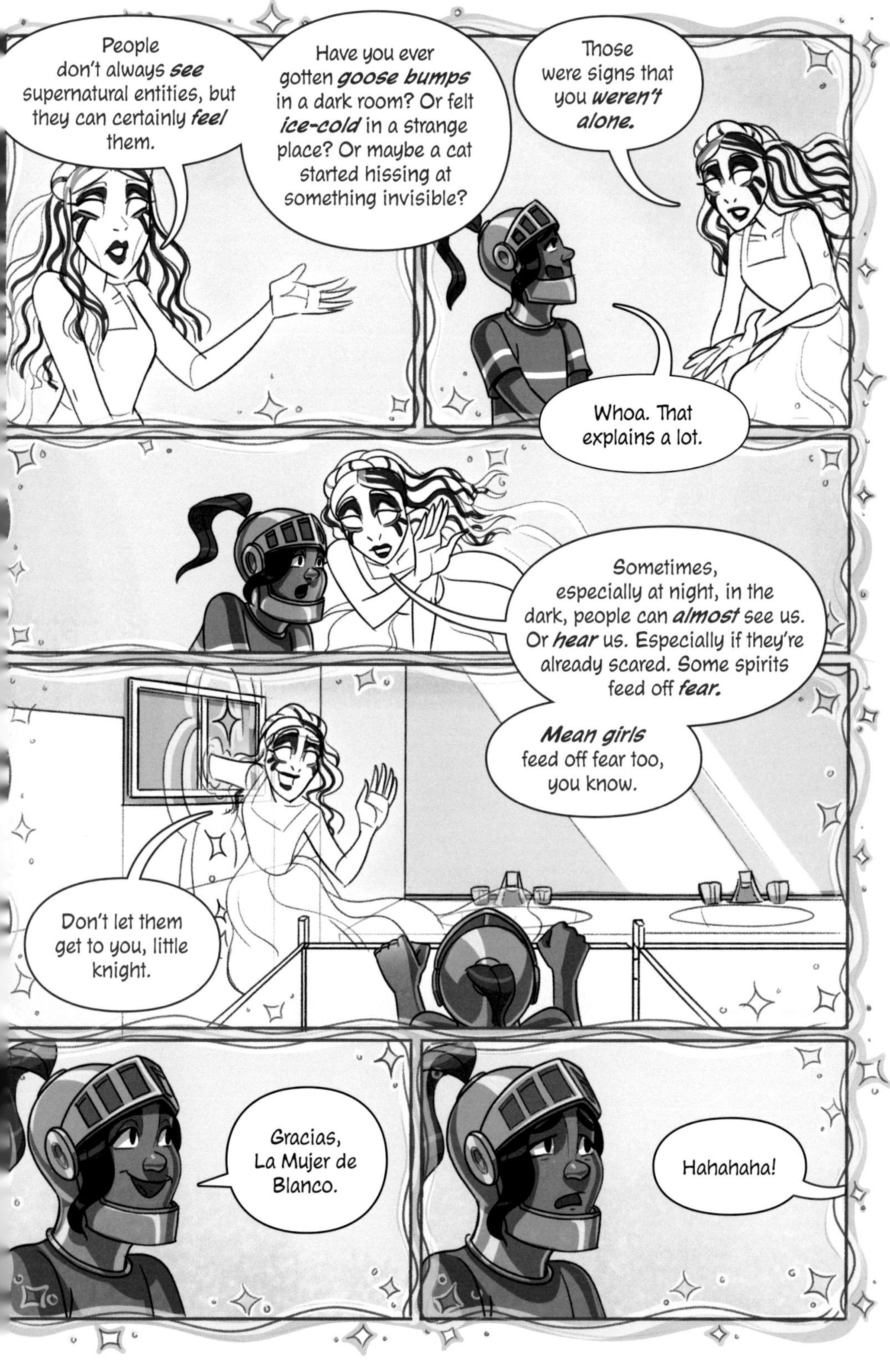
People don't always ***see*** supernatural entities, but they can certainly ***feel*** them.
Have you ever gotten ***goose bumps*** in a dark room? Or felt ***ice-cold*** in a strange place? Or maybe a cat started hissing at something invisible?
Those were signs that you ***weren't alone.***
Whoa. That explains a lot.
Sometimes, especially at night, in the dark, people can ***almost*** see us. Or ***hear*** us. Especially if they're already scared. Some spirits feed off ***fear.***
Mean girls feed off fear too, you know.
Don't let them get to you, little knight.
Gracias, La Mujer de Blanco.
Hahahaha!

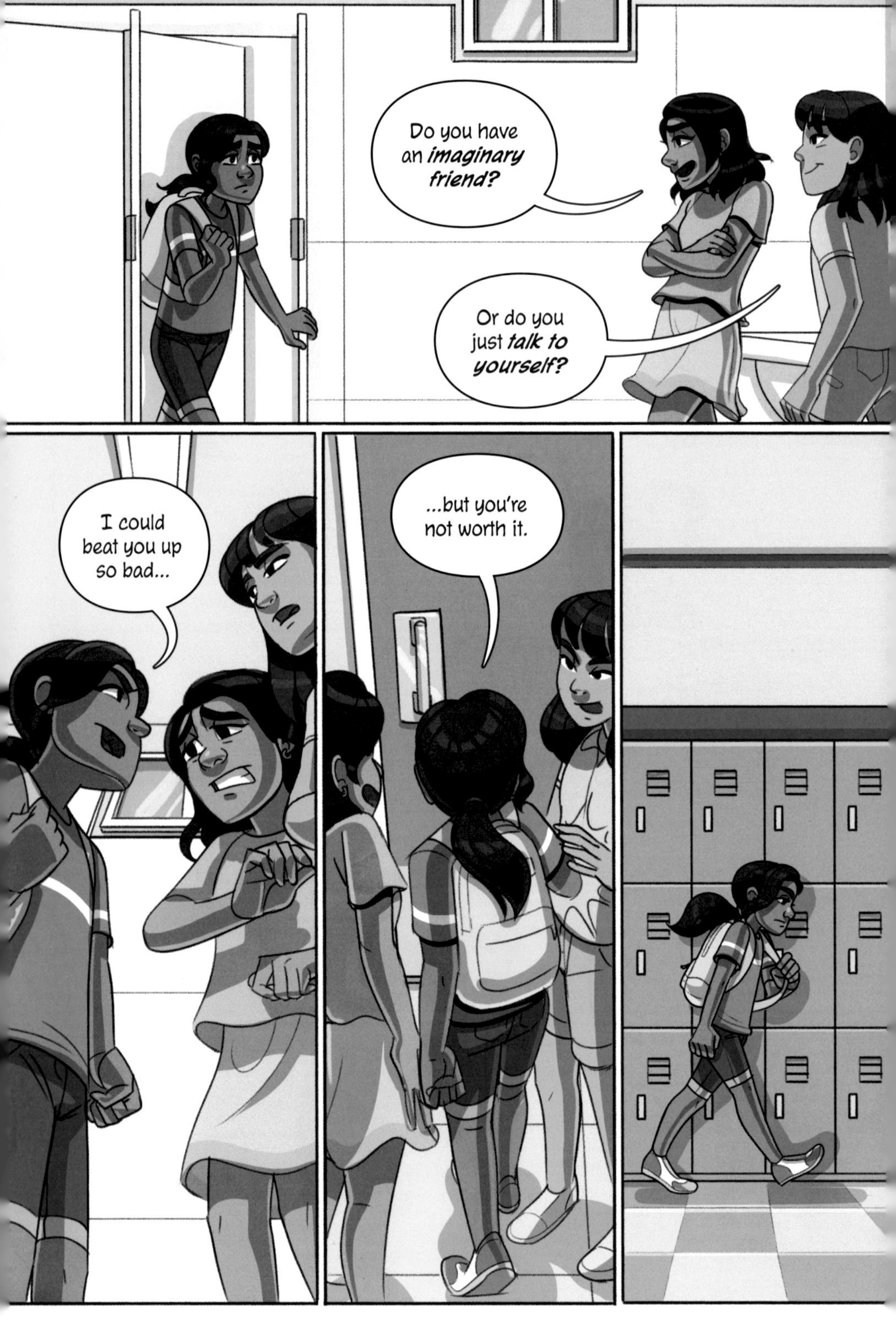
Do you have an *imaginary friend?*
Or do you just *talk to yourself?*
I could beat you up so bad...
...but you're not worth it.

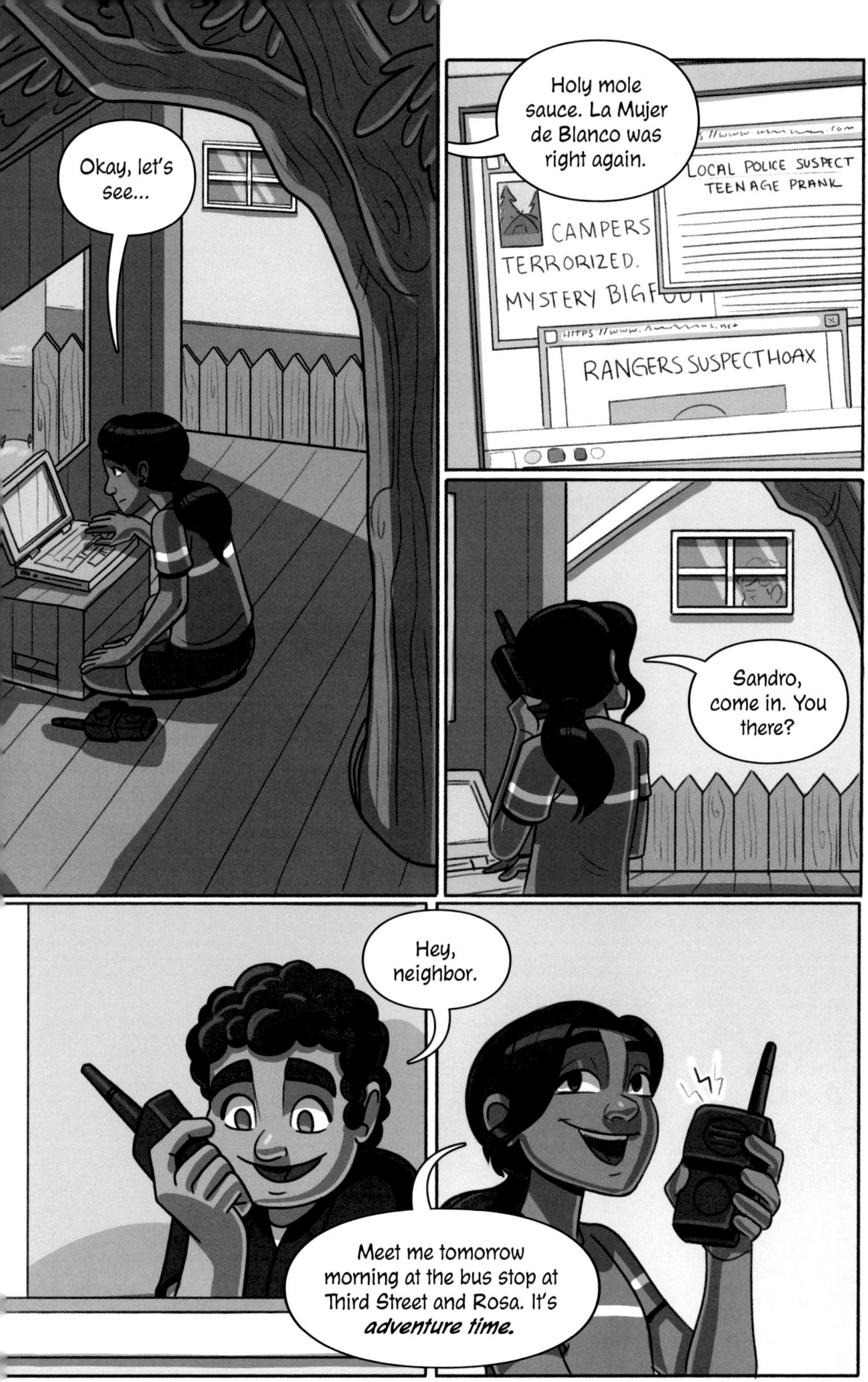

Okay, let's see...
Holy mole sauce. La Mujer de Blanco was right again.
LOCAL POLICE SUSPECT TEENAGE PRANK
CAMPERS TERRORIZED.
MYSTERY
RANGERS SUSPECT HOAX
Sandro, come in. You there?
Hey, neighbor.
Meet me tomorrow morning at the bus stop at Third Street and Rosa. It's *adventure time.*

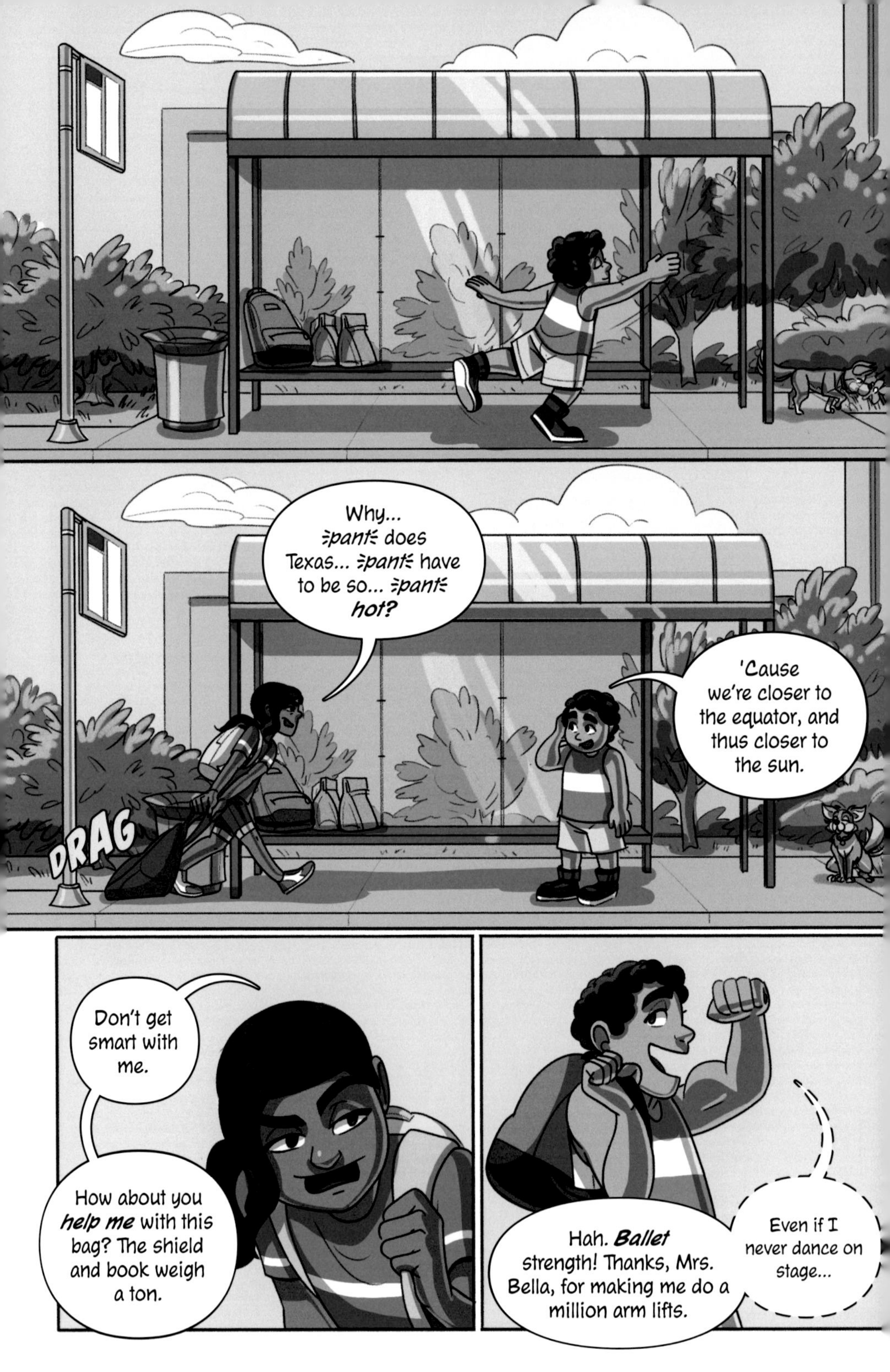

Why... ⁼pant⁼ does Texas... ⁼pant⁼ have to be so... ⁼pant⁼ *hot?*
'Cause we're closer to the equator, and thus closer to the sun.
DRAG
Don't get smart with me.
How about you ***help me*** with this bag? The shield and book weigh a ton.
Hah. ***Ballet*** strength! Thanks, Mrs. Bella, for making me do a million arm lifts.
Even if I never dance on stage...

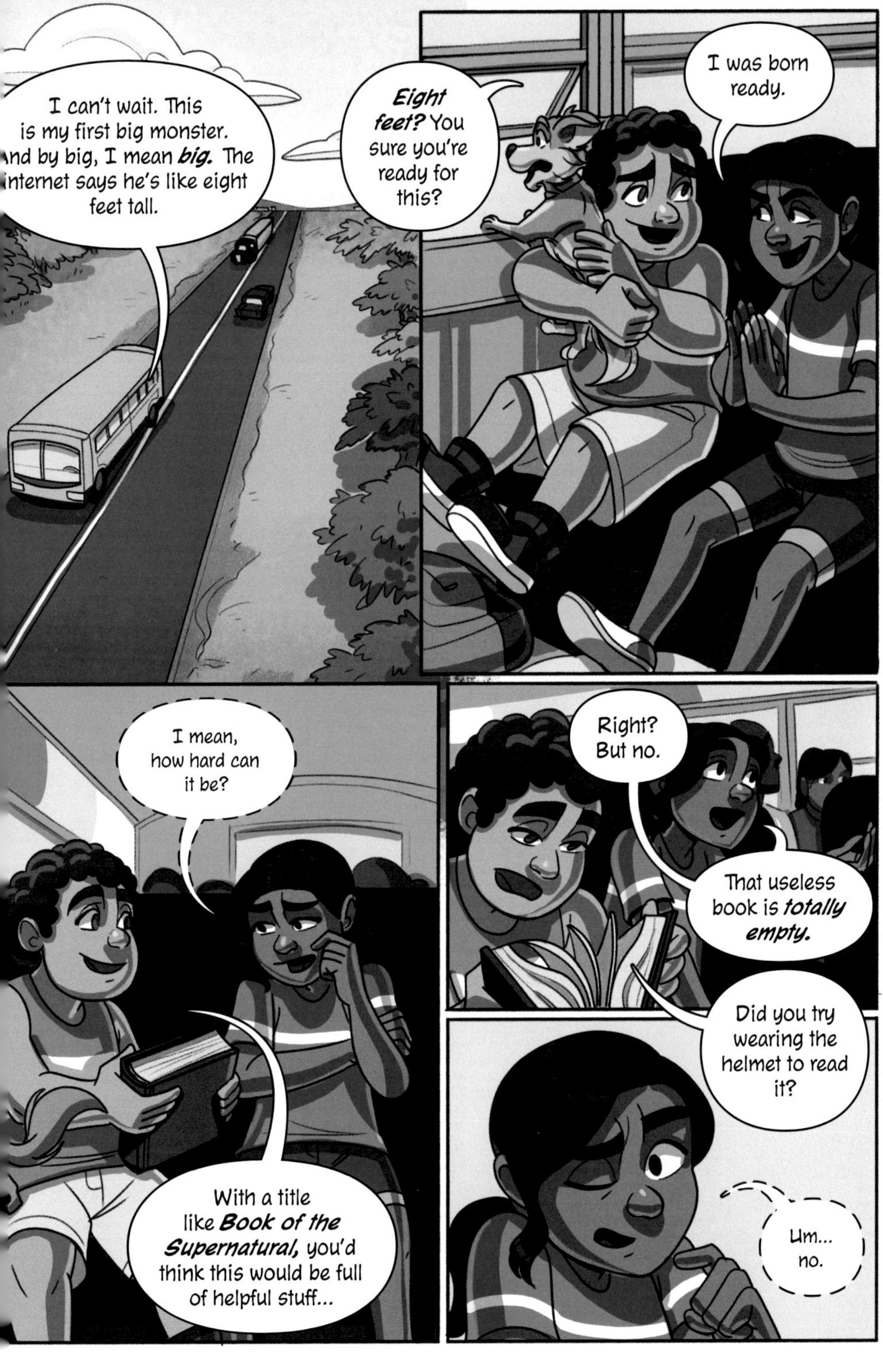

I can't wait. This is my first big monster. nd by big, I mean *big.* The internet says he's like eight feet tall.
Eight feet? You sure you're ready for this?
I was born ready.
I mean, how hard can it be?
With a title like ***Book of the Supernatural,*** you'd think this would be full of helpful stuff...
Right? But no.
That useless book is ***totally empty.***
Did you try wearing the helmet to read it?
Um... no.

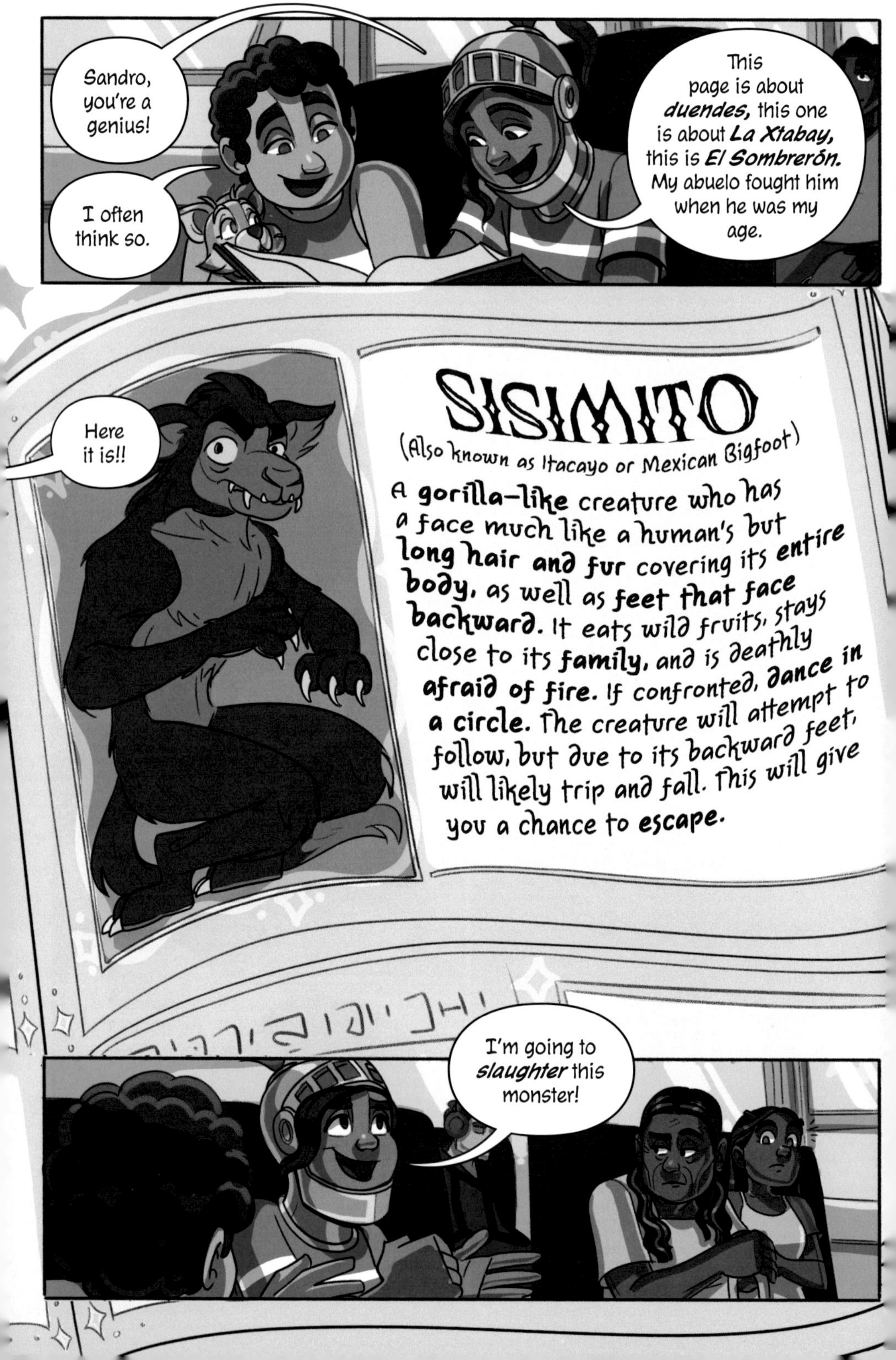
Sandro, you're a genius!
I often think so.
This page is about *duendes,* this one is about *La Xtabay,* this is *El Sombrerón.* My abuelo fought him when he was my age.
Here it is!!
SISIMITO
(Also known as Itacayo or Mexican Bigfoot)
A **gorilla-like** creature who has a face much like a human's but **long hair and fur** covering its **entire body,** as well as **feet that face backward.** It eats wild fruits, stays close to its **family,** and is deathly **afraid of fire.** If confronted, **dance in a circle.** The creature will attempt to follow, but due to its backward feet, will likely trip and fall. This will give you a chance to **escape.**
I'm going to *slaughter* this monster!

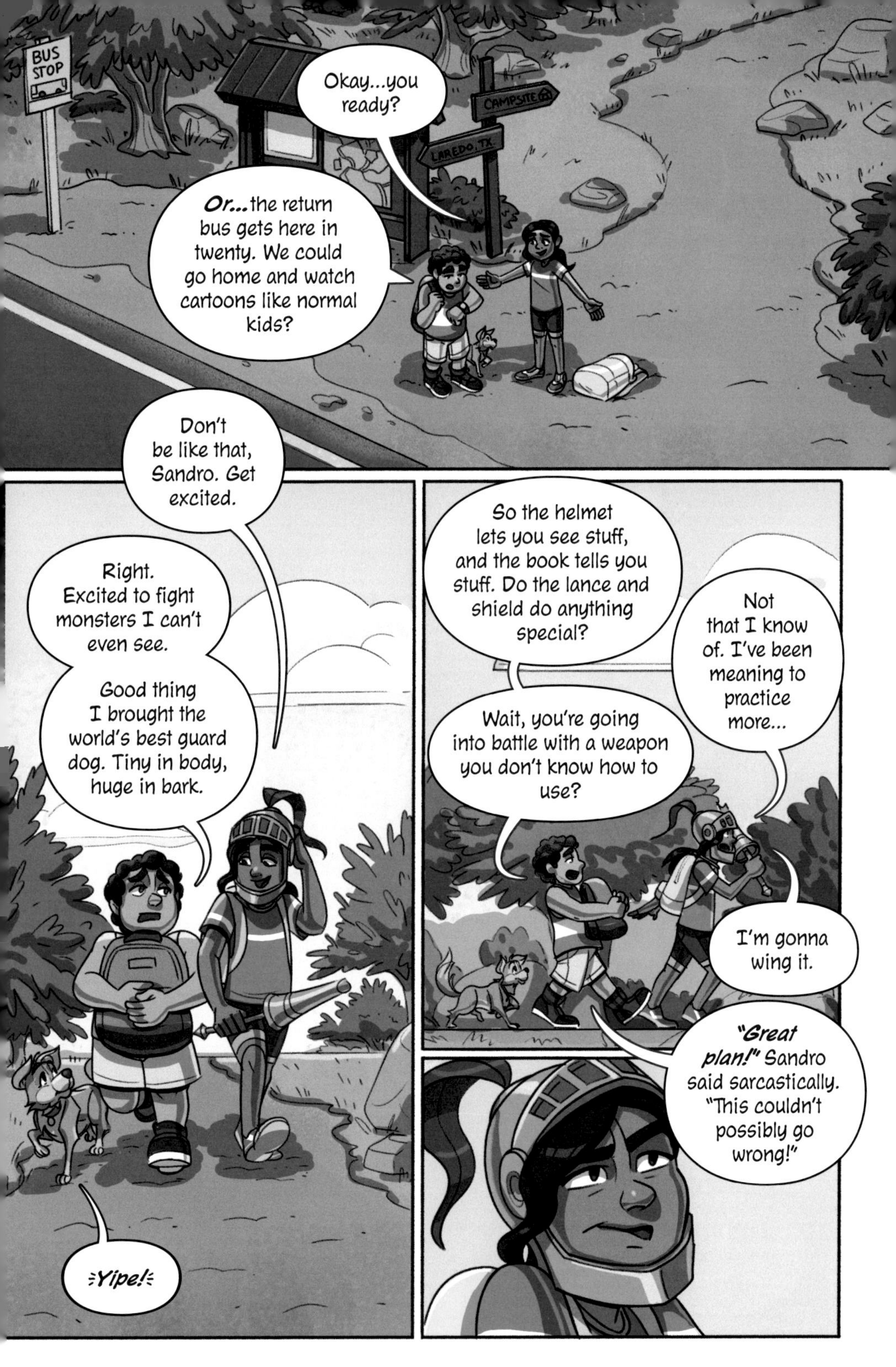
BUS STOP
CAMPSITE
LAREDO, TX
Okay...you ready?
Or... the return bus gets here in twenty. We could go home and watch cartoons like normal kids?
Don't be like that, Sandro. Get excited.
Right. Excited to fight monsters I can't even see.
Good thing I brought the world's best guard dog. Tiny in body, huge in bark.
Yipe!
So the helmet lets you see stuff, and the book tells you stuff. Do the lance and shield do anything special?
Not that I know of. I've been meaning to practice more...
Wait, you're going into battle with a weapon you don't know how to use?
I'm gonna wing it.
"Great plan!" Sandro said sarcastically. "This couldn't possibly go wrong!"

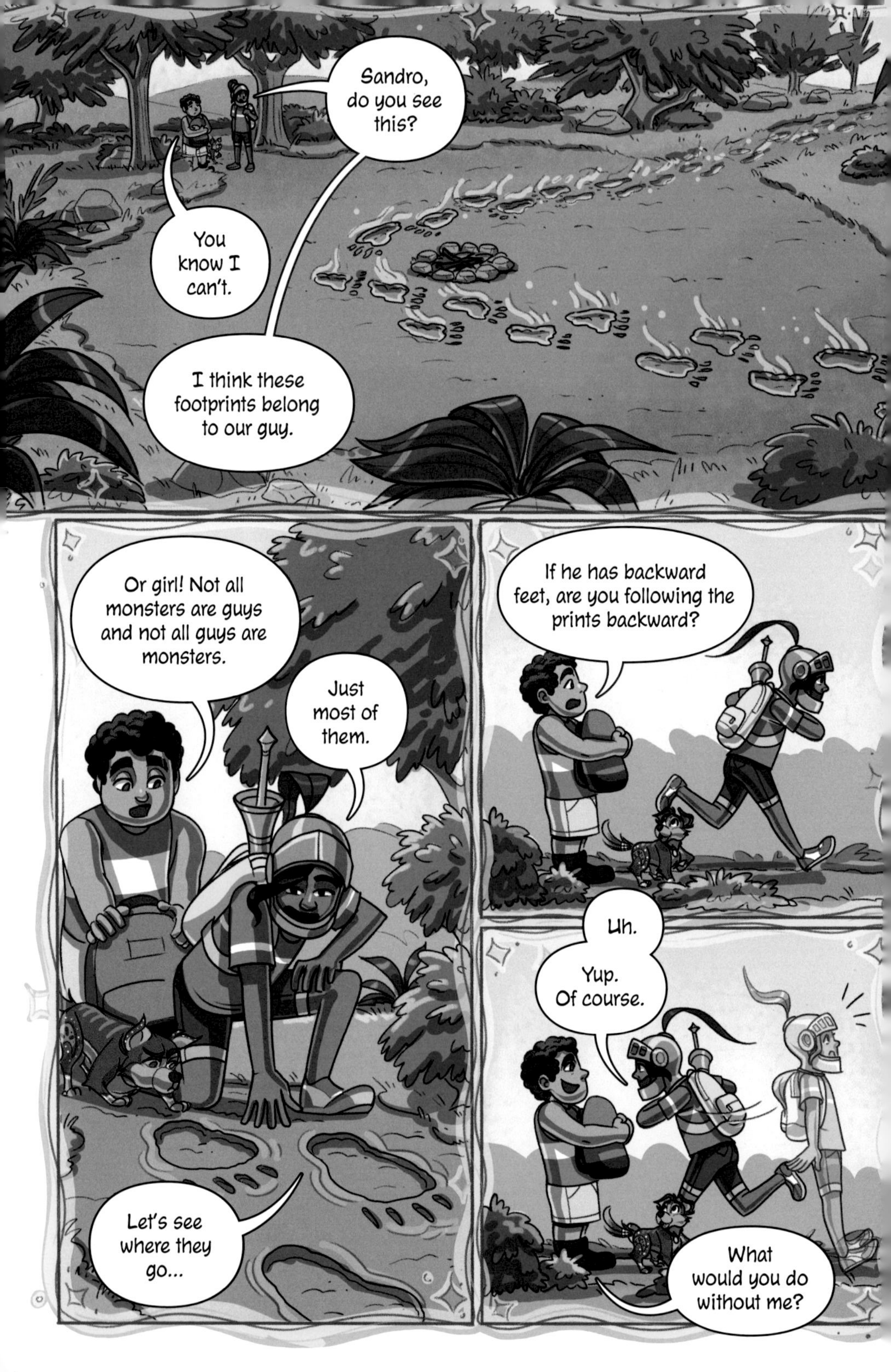
Sandro, do you see this?
You know I can't.
I think these footprints belong to our guy.
Or girl! Not all monsters are guys and not all guys are monsters.
Just most of them.
Let's see where they go...
If he has backward feet, are you following the prints backward?
Uh.
Yup. Of course.
What would you do without me?

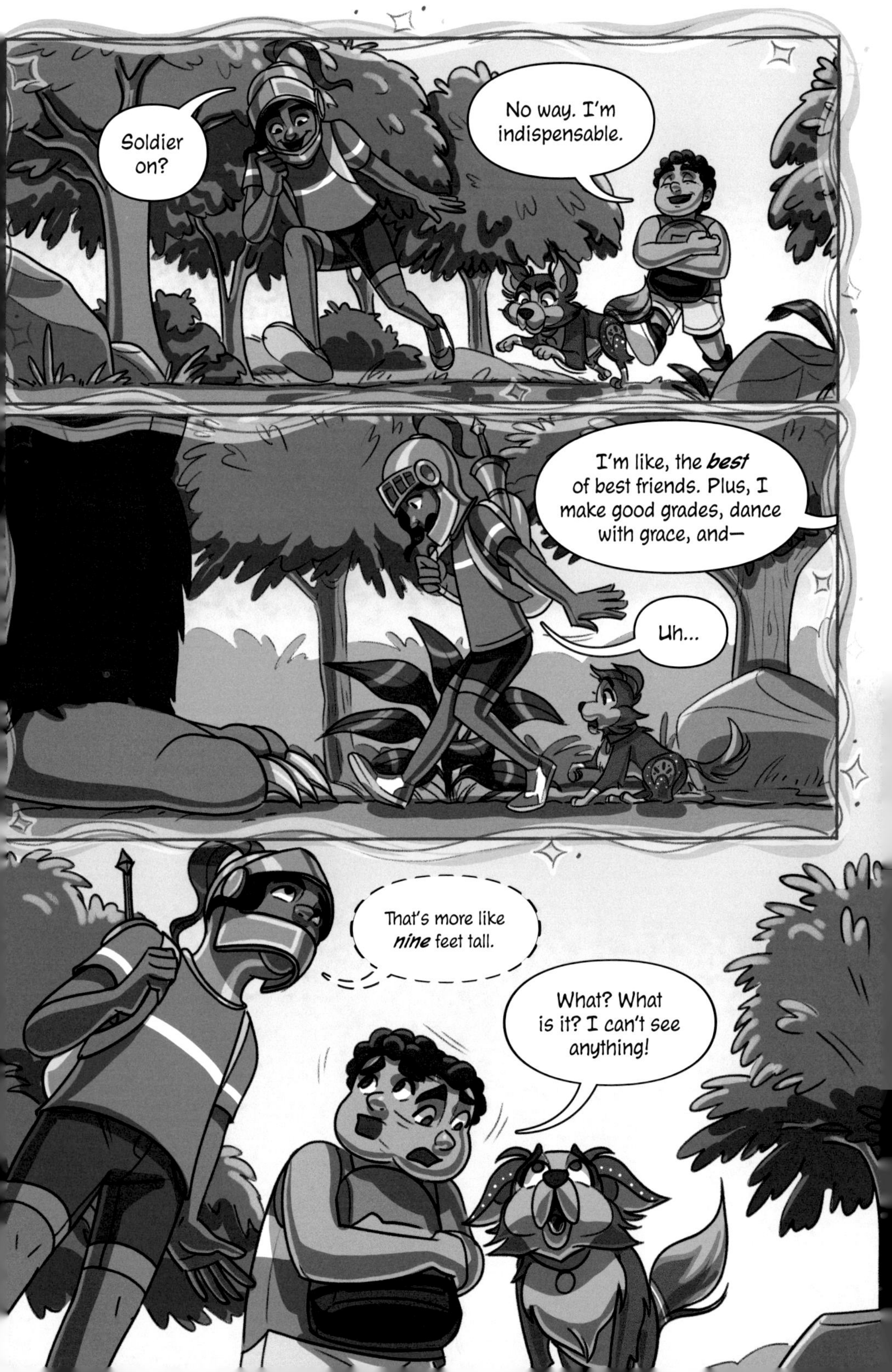
Soldier on?
No way. I'm indispensable.
I'm like, the *best* of best friends. Plus, I make good grades, dance with grace, and—
Uh...
That's more like *nine* feet tall.
What? What is it? I can't see anything!

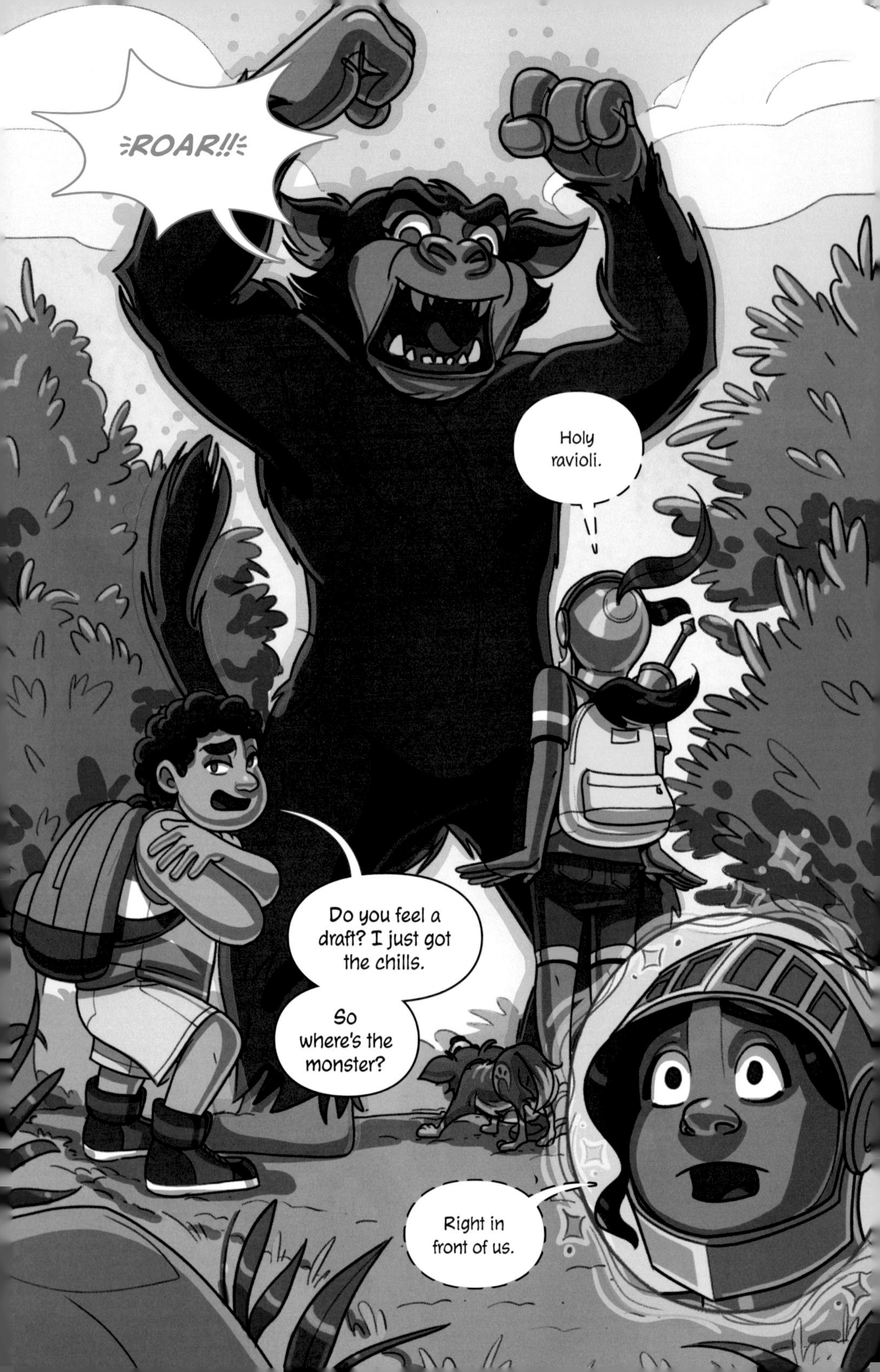
ROAR!!
Holy ravioli.
Do you feel a draft? I just got the chills.
So where's the monster?
Right in front of us.

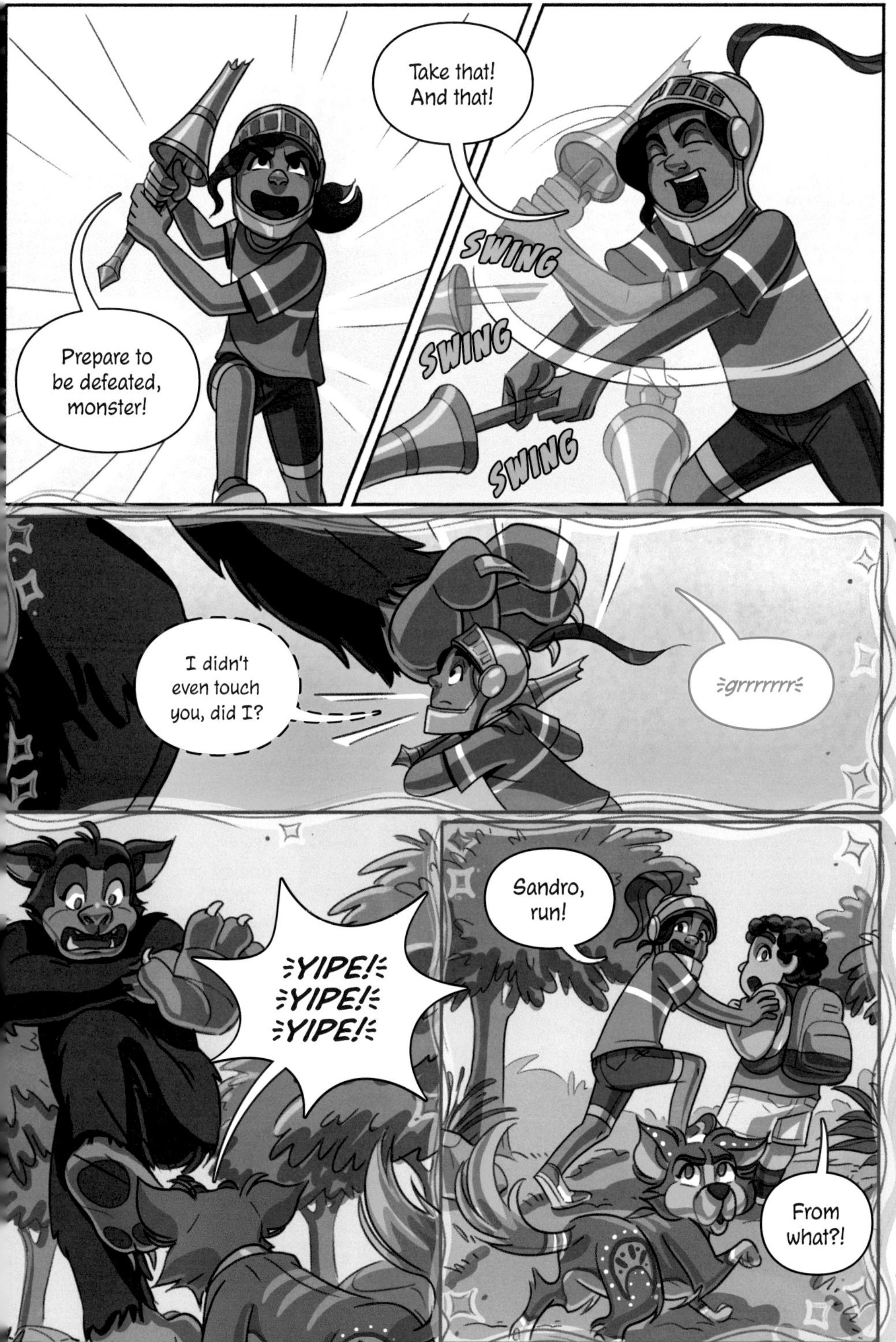
Prepare to be defeated, monster!
Take that! And that!
SWING
SWING
SWING
I didn't even touch you, did I?
grrrrrrr
YIPE! YIPE! YIPE!
Sandro, run!
From what?!

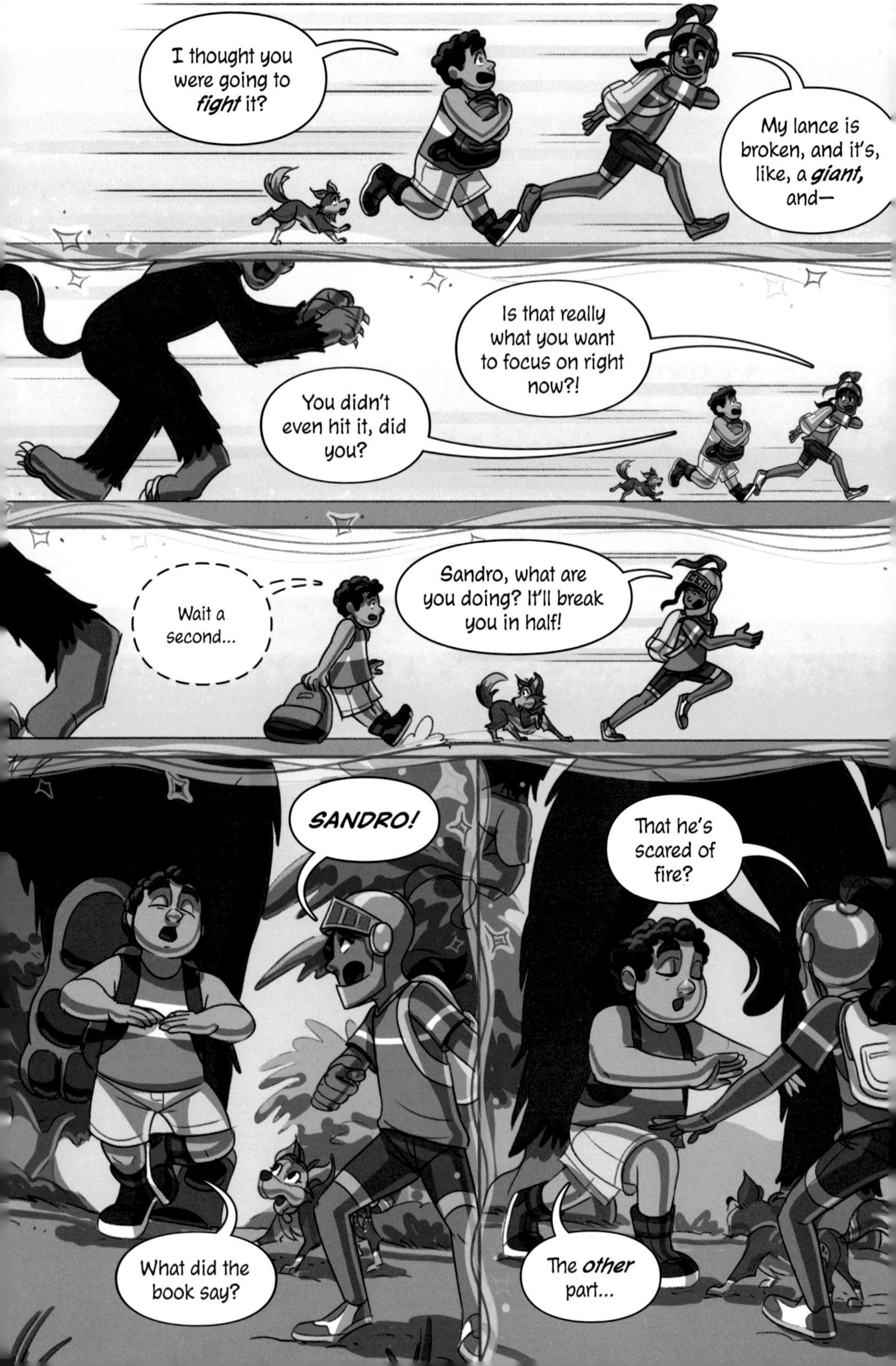
I thought you were going to *fight* it?
My lance is broken, and it's, like, a ***giant,*** and—
Is that really what you want to focus on right now?!
You didn't even hit it, did you?
Wait a second...
Sandro, what are you doing? It'll break you in half!
SANDRO!
What did the book say?
That he's scared of fire?
The *other* part...

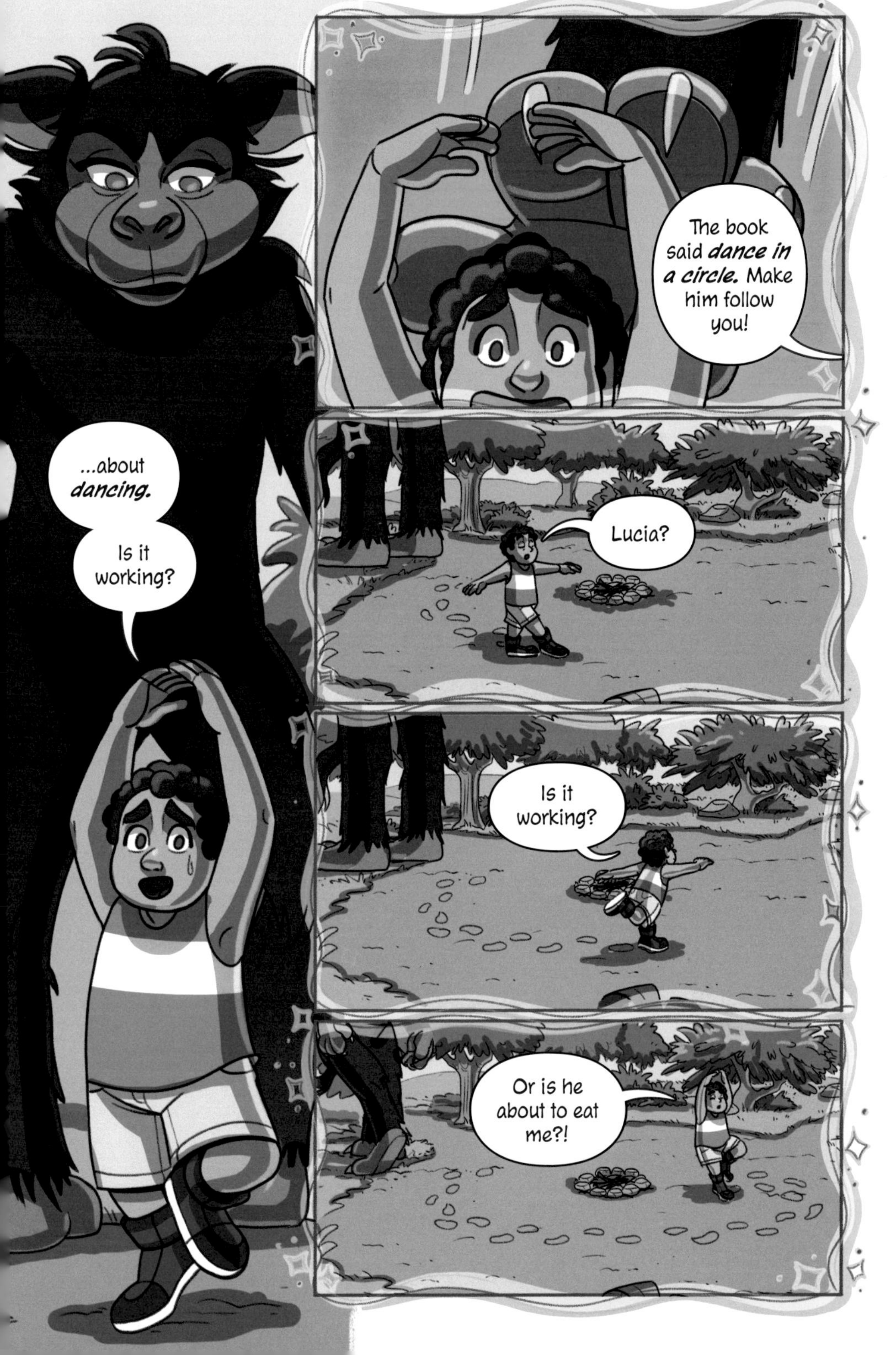
The book said *dance in a circle.* Make him follow you!
Lucia?
Is it working?
Or is he about to eat me?!
...about *dancing.*
Is it working?

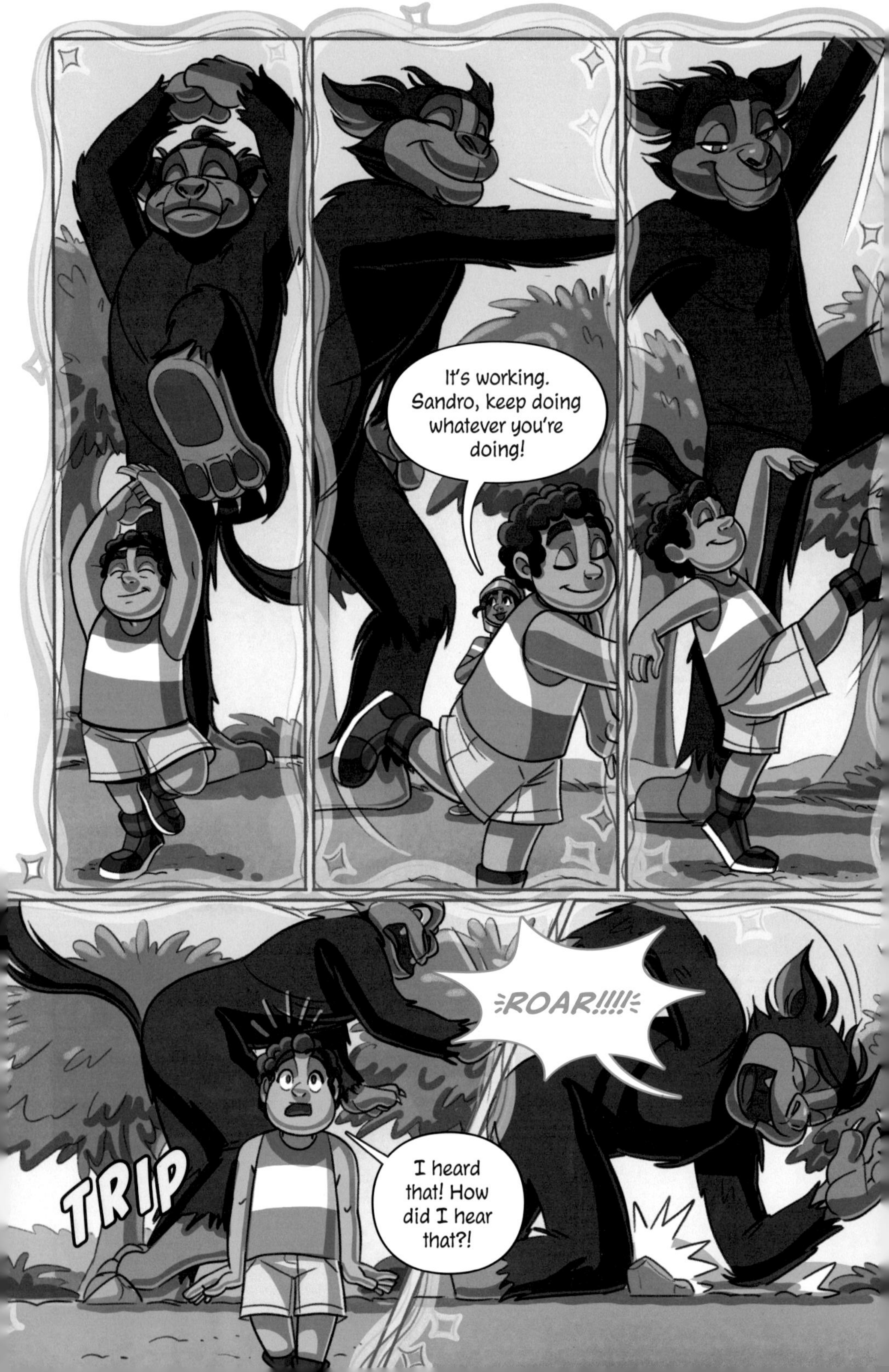
It's working. Sandro, keep doing whatever you're doing!
ROAR!!!!
TRIP
I heard that! How did I hear that?!

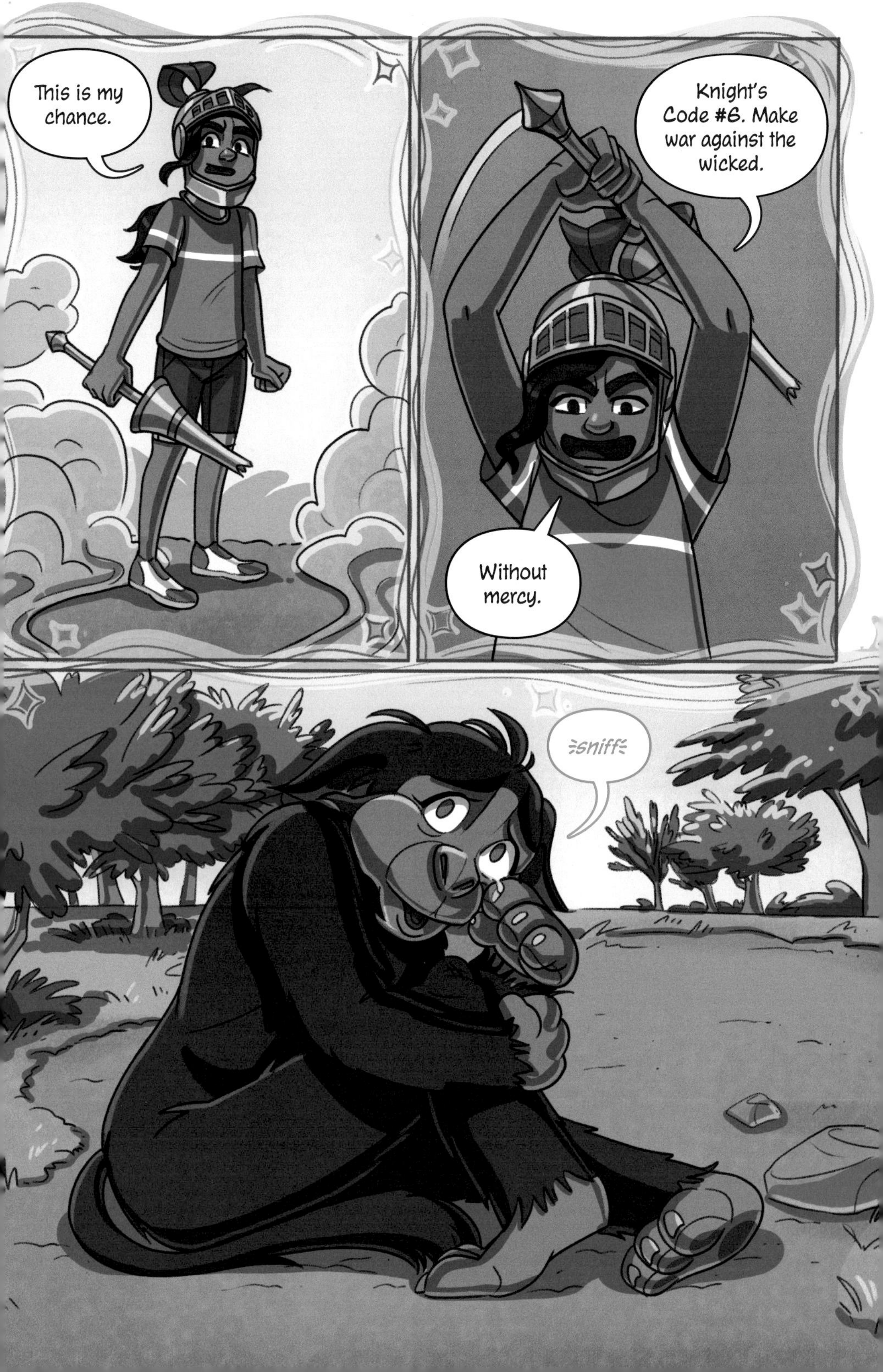
This is my chance.
Knight's Code #6. Make war against the wicked.
Without mercy.
sniff

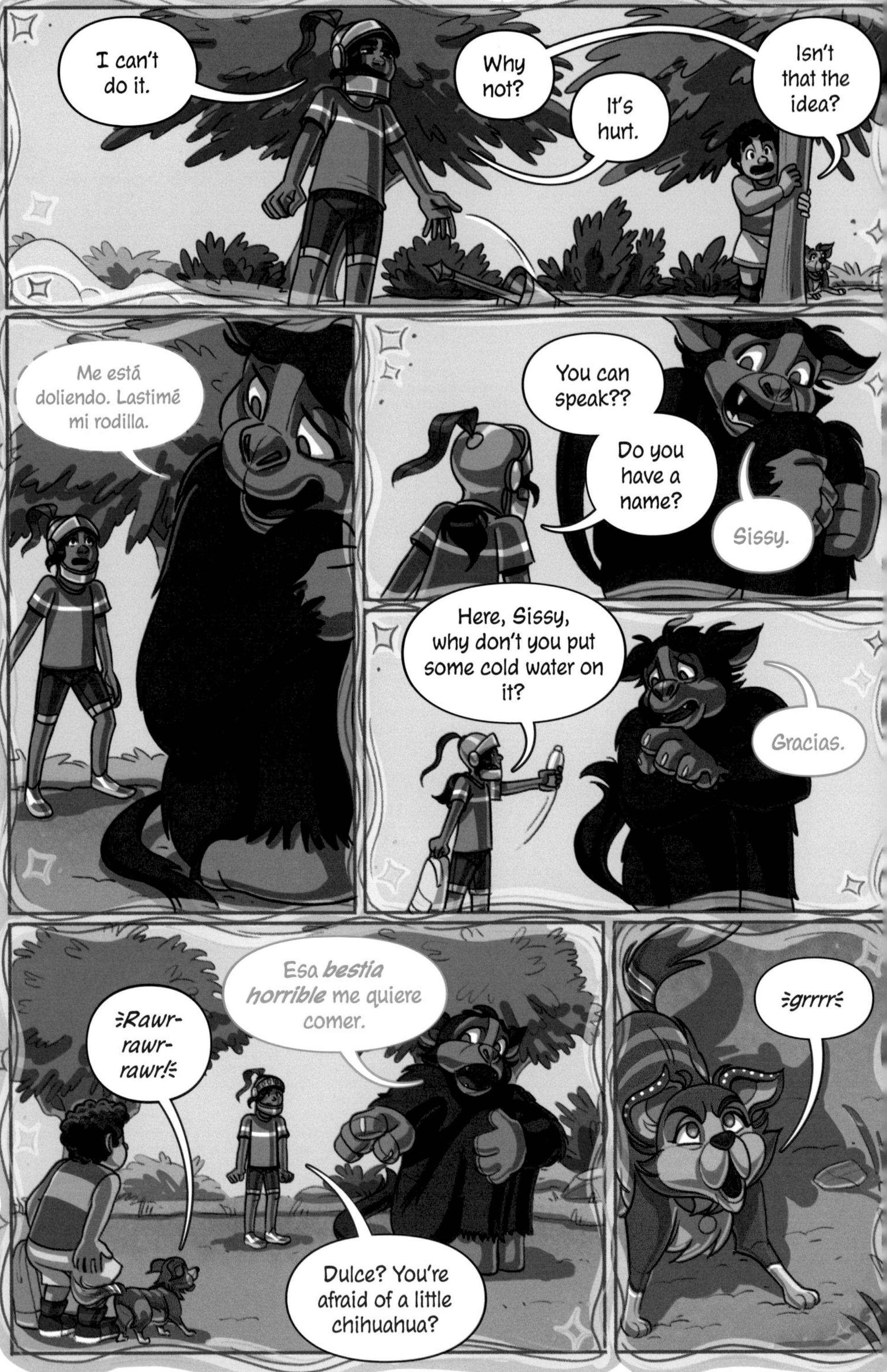
I can't do it.
Why not?
It's hurt.
Isn't that the idea?
Me está doliendo. Lastimé mi rodilla.
You can speak??
Do you have a name?
Sissy.
Here, Sissy, why don't you put some cold water on it?
Gracias.
Rawr-rawr-rawr!
Esa *bestia horrible* me quiere comer.
Dulce? You're afraid of a little chihuahua?
grrrr

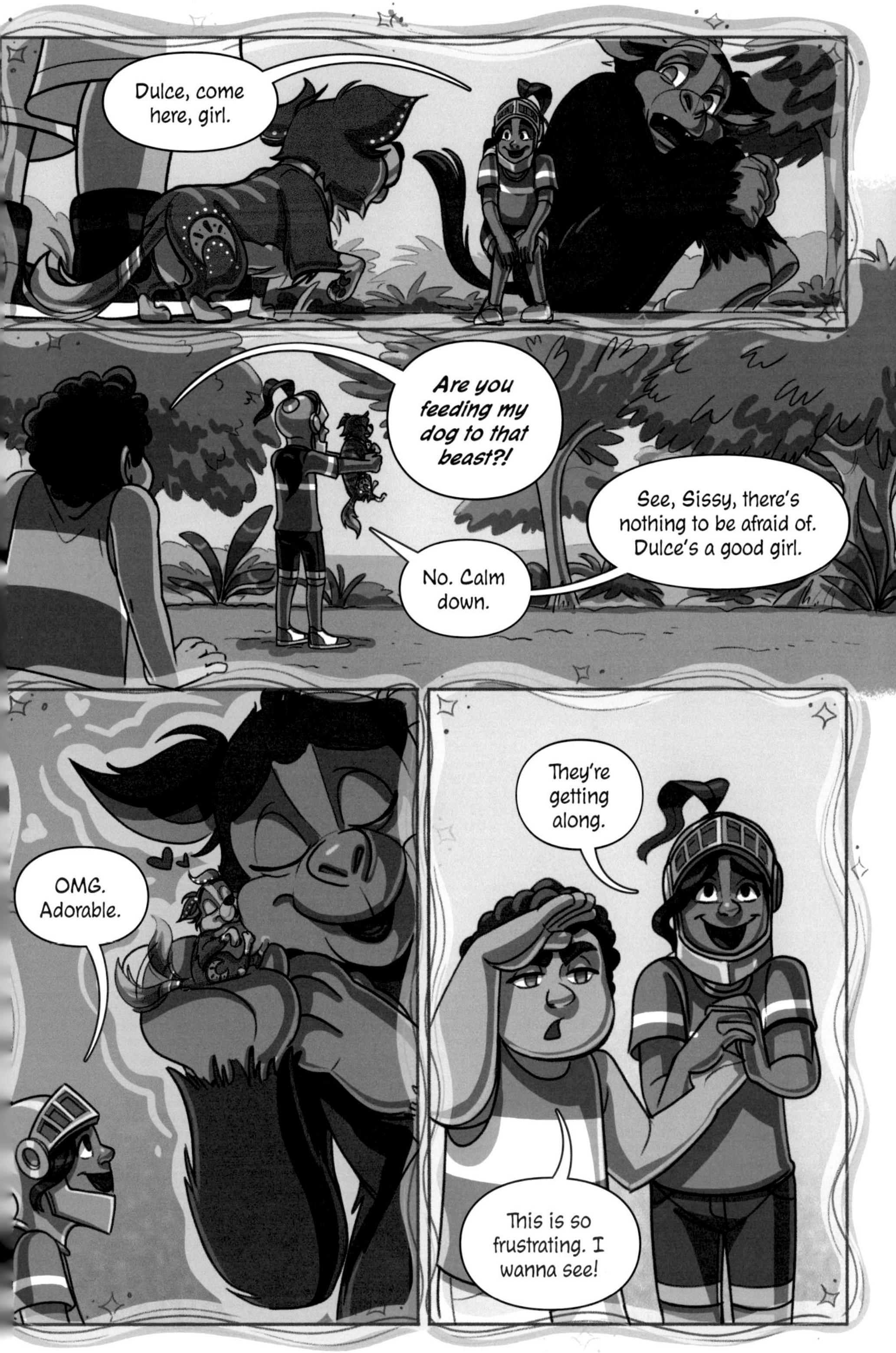
Dulce, come here, girl.
Are you feeding my dog to that beast?!
No. Calm down.
See, Sissy, there's nothing to be afraid of. Dulce's a good girl.
OMG. Adorable.
They're getting along.
This is so frustrating. I wanna see!

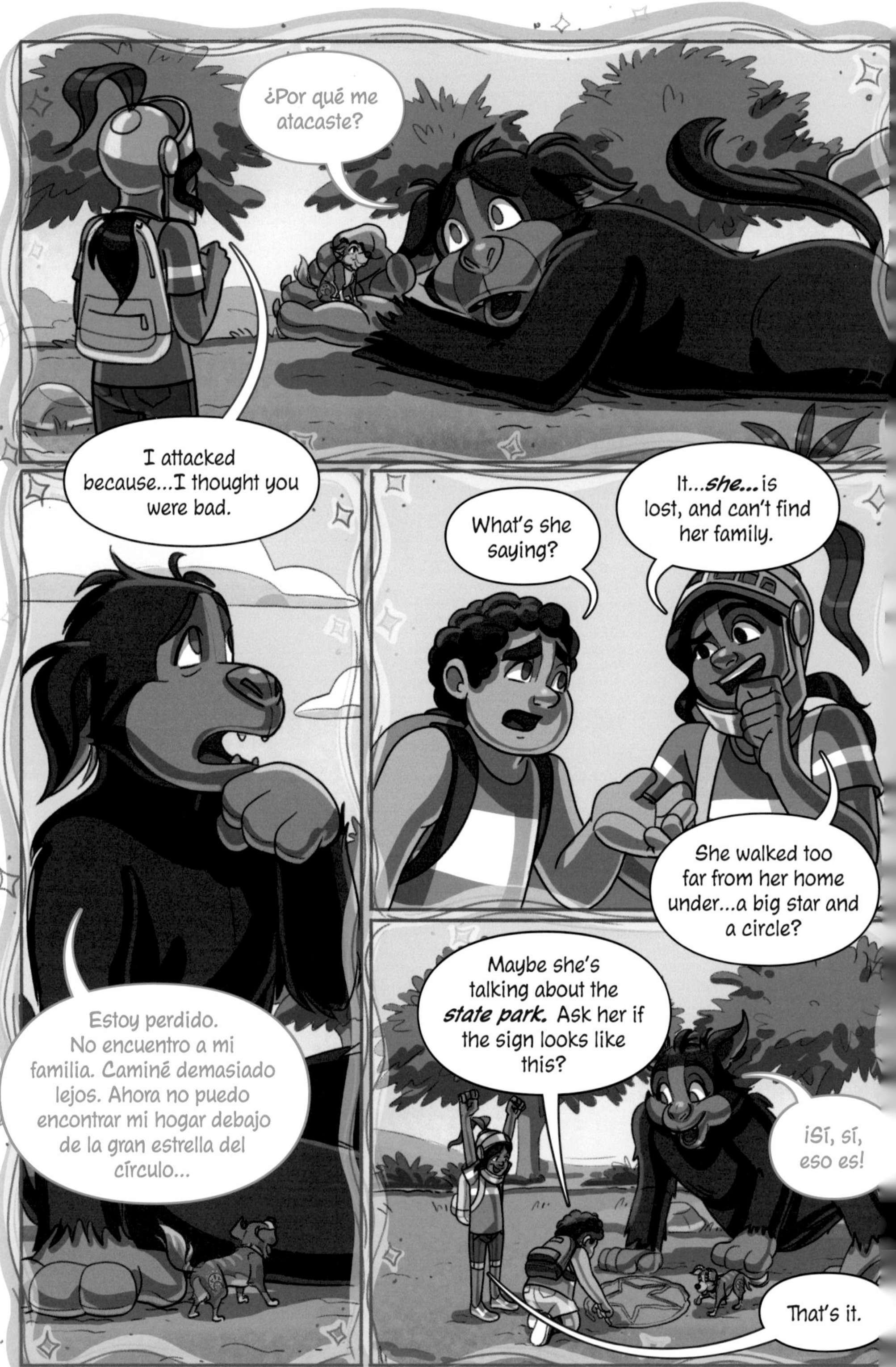
¿Por qué me atacaste?
I attacked because...I thought you were bad.
Estoy perdido. No encuentro a mi familia. Caminé demasiado lejos. Ahora no puedo encontrar mi hogar debajo de la gran estrella del círculo...
What's she saying?
It...*she...* is lost, and can't find her family.
She walked too far from her home under...a big star and a circle?
Maybe she's talking about the ***state park.*** Ask her if the sign looks like this?
¡Sí, sí, eso es!
That's it.

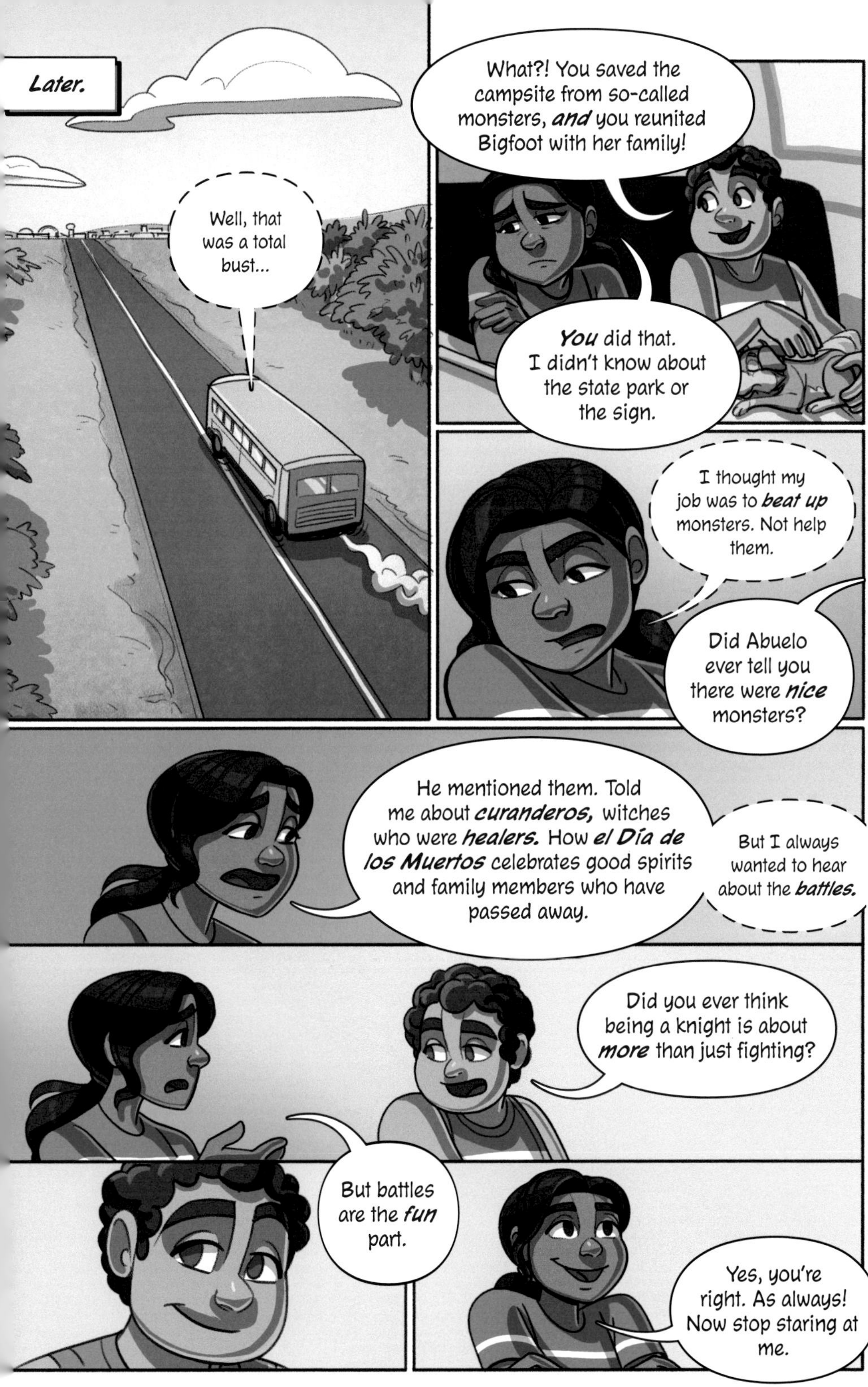
Later.
Well, that was a total bust...
What?! You saved the campsite from so-called monsters, and you reunited Bigfoot with her family!
You did that. I didn't know about the state park or the sign.
I thought my job was to beat up monsters. Not help them.
Did Abuelo ever tell you there were nice monsters?
He mentioned them. Told me about curanderos, witches who were healers. How el Día de los Muertos celebrates good spirits and family members who have passed away.
But I always wanted to hear about the battles.
Did you ever think being a knight is about more than just fighting?
But battles are the fun part.
Yes, you're right. As always! Now stop staring at me.

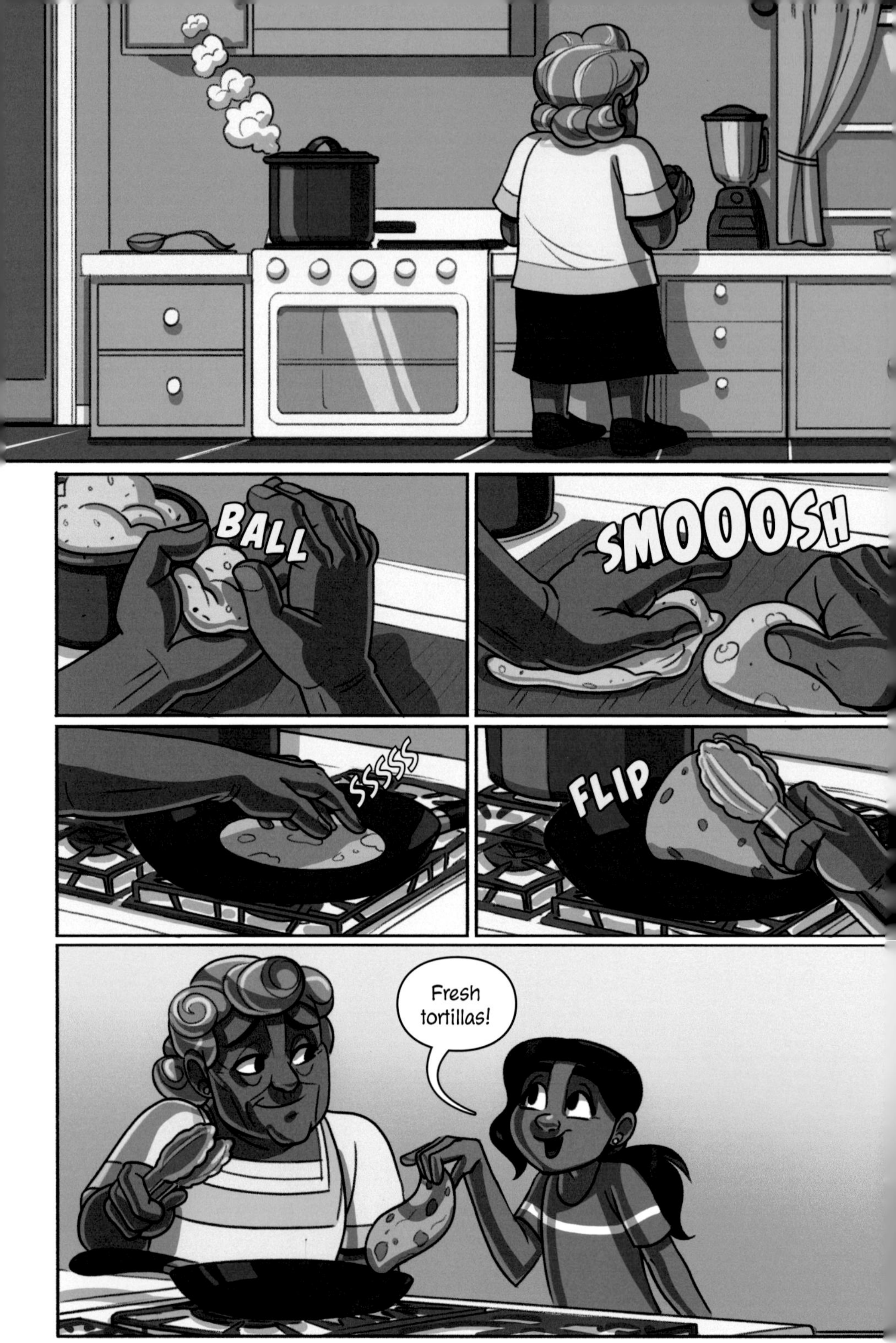
BALL
SMOOOSH
SSSSS
FLIP
Fresh tortillas!

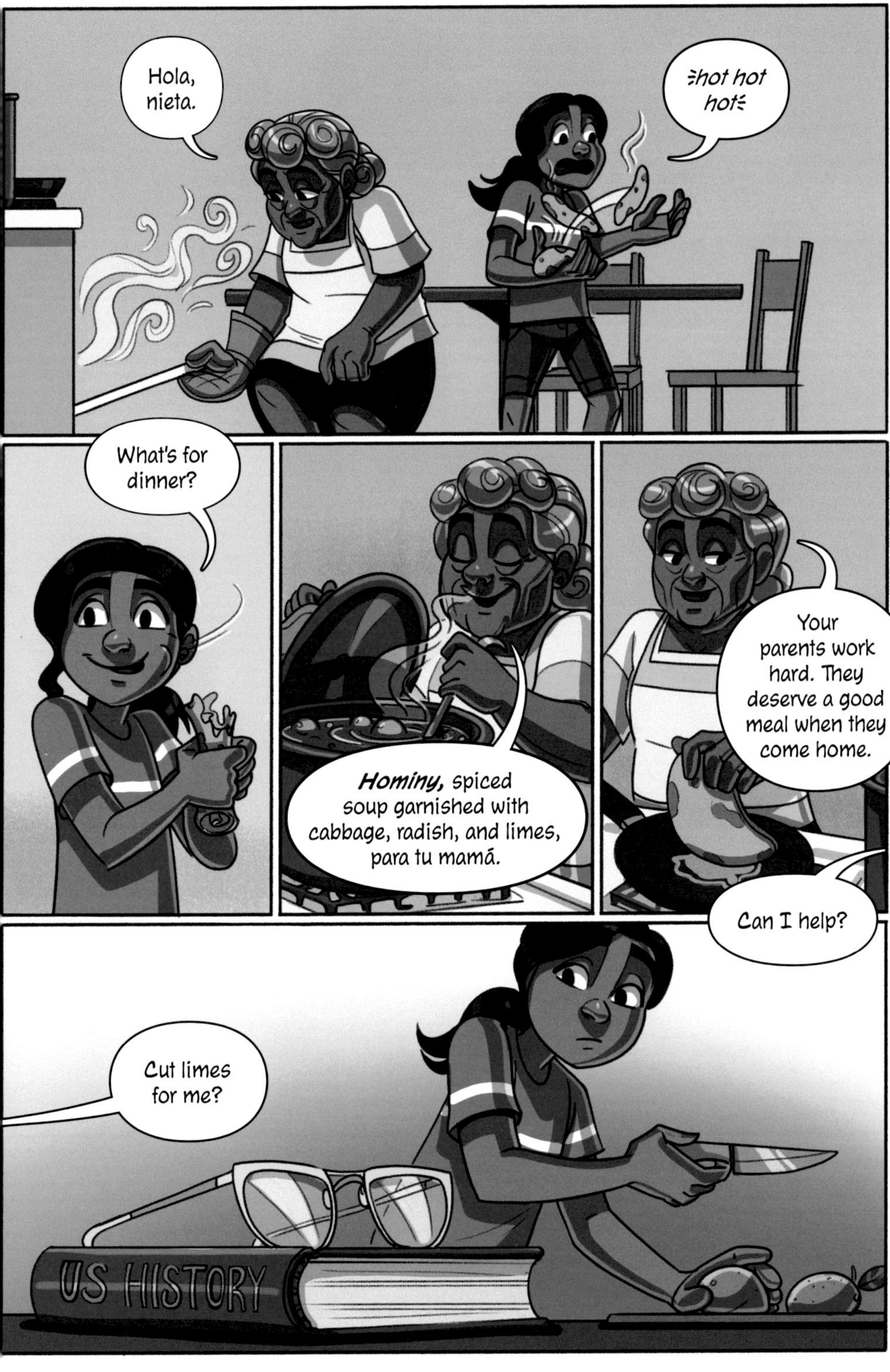
Hola, nieta.
hot hot hot
What's for dinner?
Hominy, spiced soup garnished with cabbage, radish, and limes, para tu mamá.
Your parents work hard. They deserve a good meal when they come home.
Can I help?
Cut limes for me?
US HISTORY

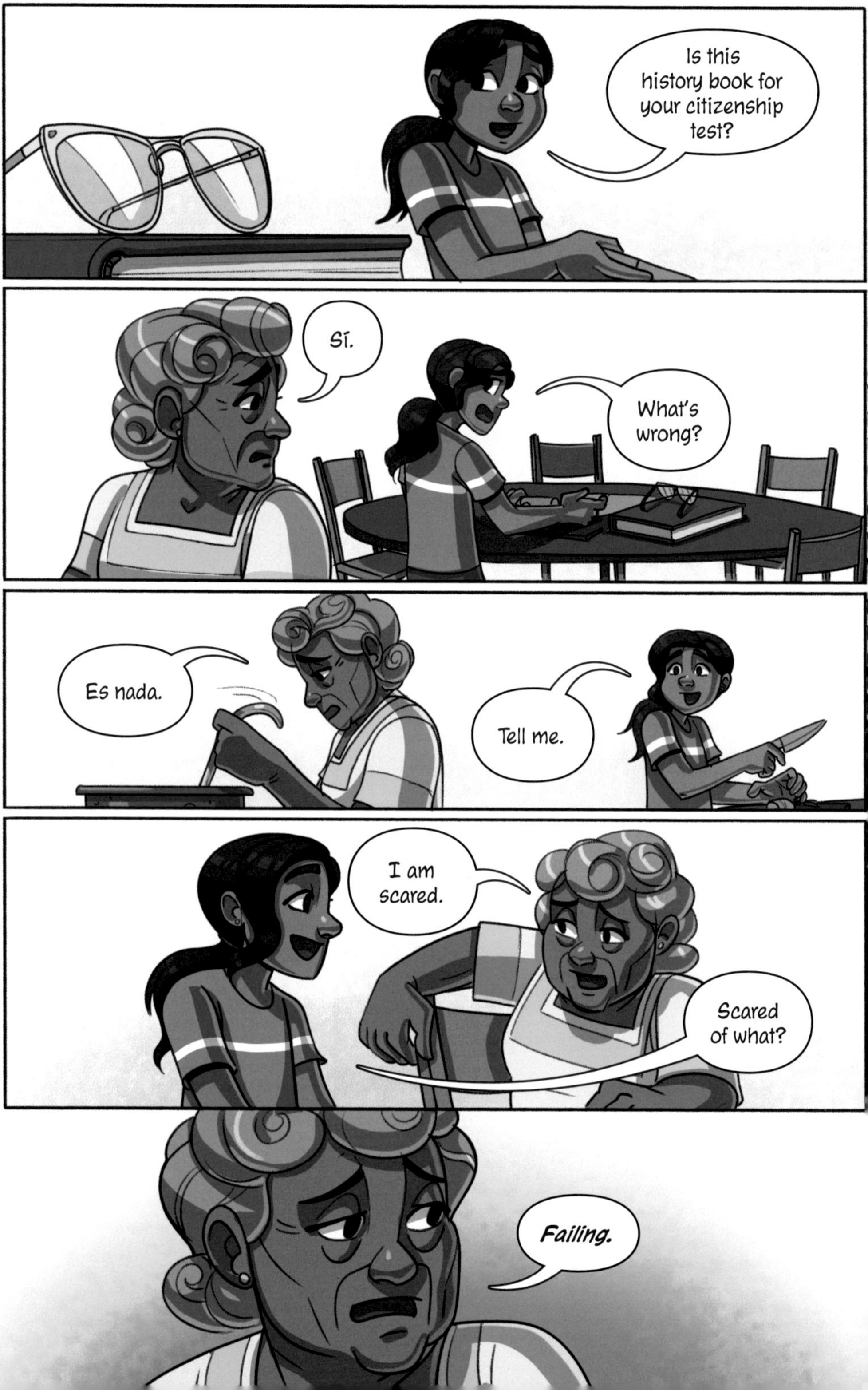
Is this history book for your citizenship test?
Sí.
What's wrong?
Es nada.
Tell me.
I am scared.
Scared of what?
Failing.

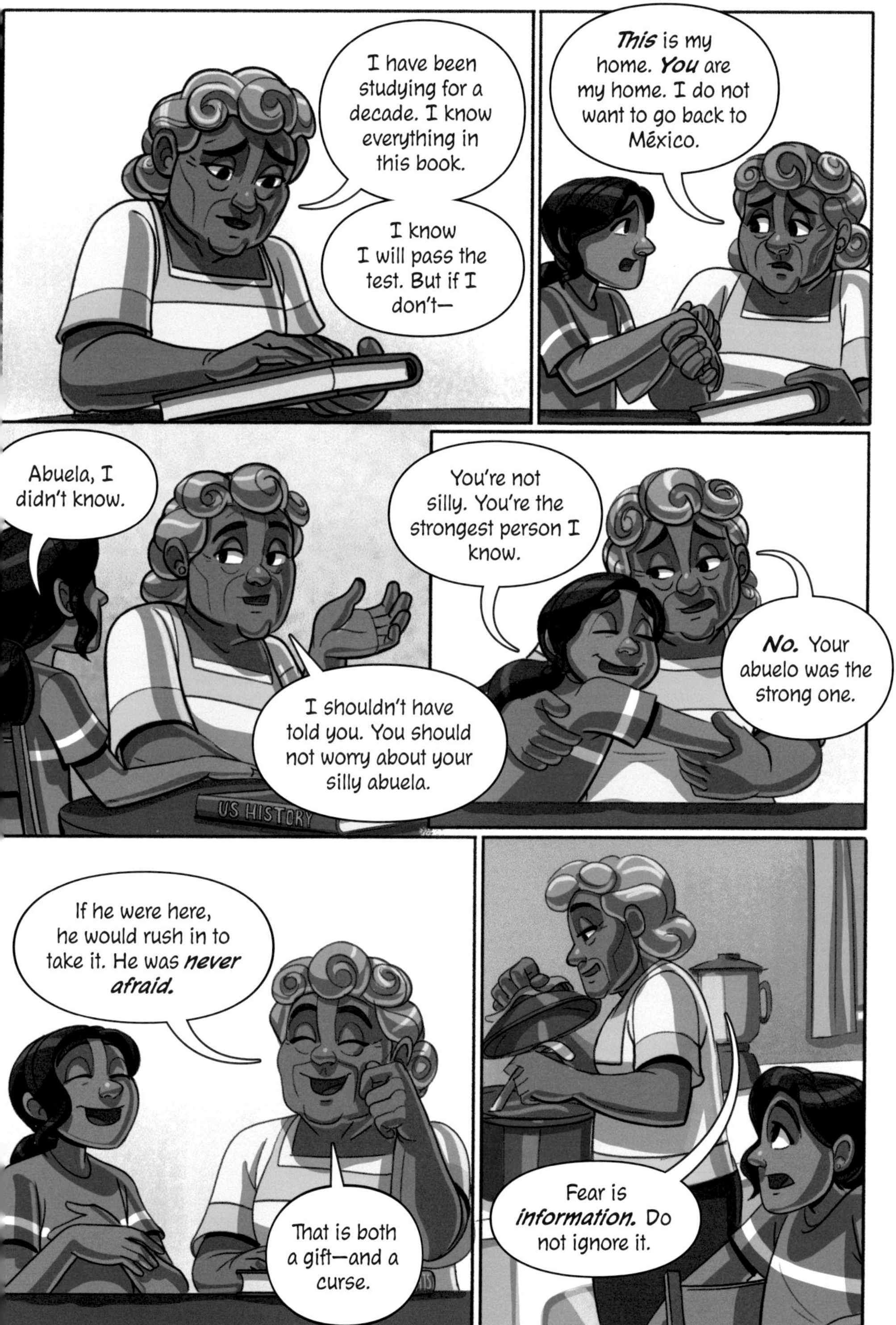
I have been studying for a decade. I know everything in this book.
I know I will pass the test. But if I don't—
This is my home. *You* are my home. I do not want to go back to México.
Abuela, I didn't know.
I shouldn't have told you. You should not worry about your silly abuela.
US HISTORY
You're not silly. You're the strongest person I know.
No. Your abuelo was the strong one.
If he were here, he would rush in to take it. He was *never afraid.*
That is both a gift—and a curse.
Fear is *information.* Do not ignore it.

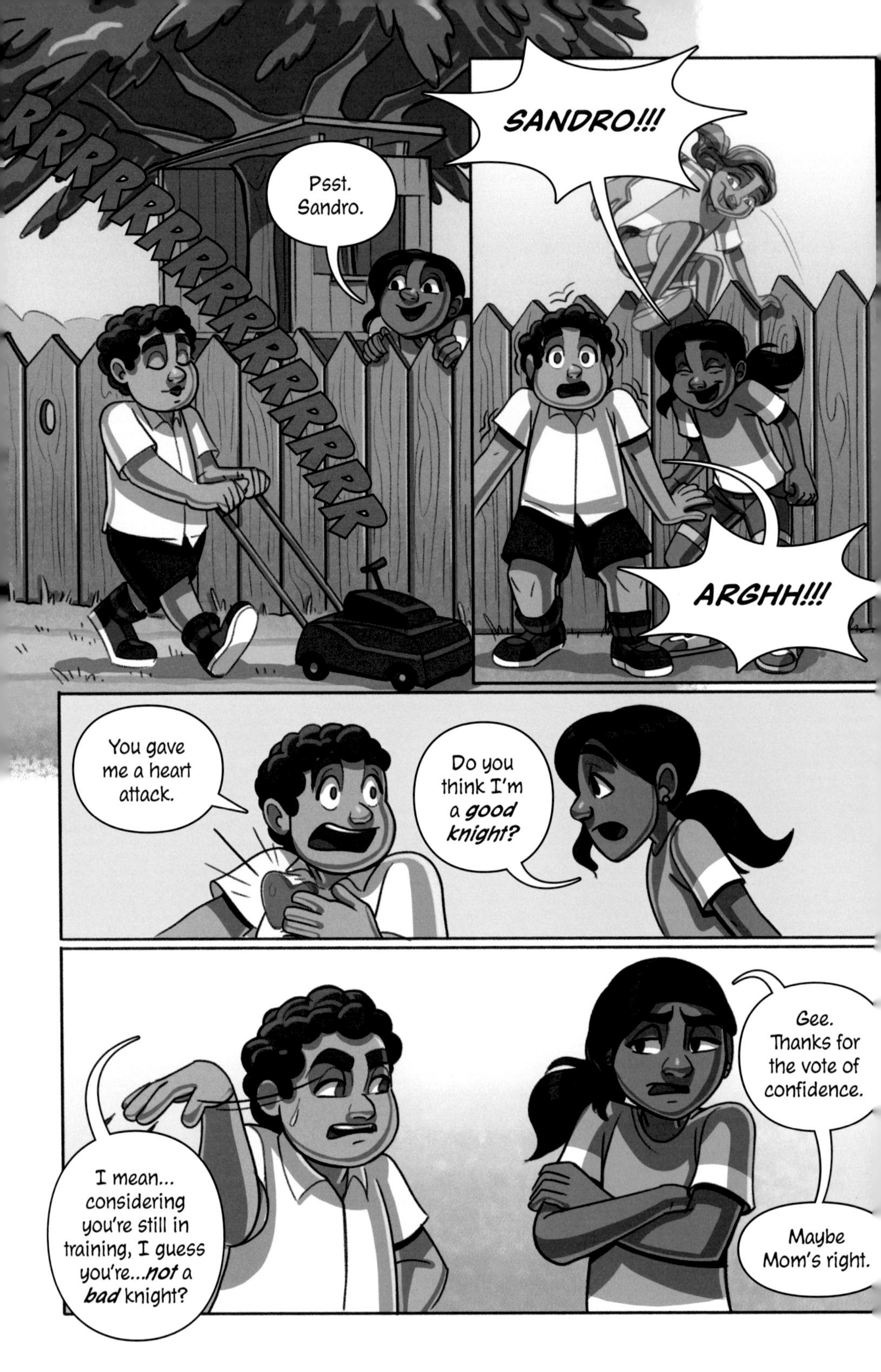

RRRRRRRRRRRRRRRRRRRRRRRRR
Psst. Sandro.
SANDRO!!!
ARGHH!!!
You gave me a heart attack.
Do you think I'm a ***good knight?***
Gee. Thanks for the vote of confidence.
I mean... considering you're still in training, I guess you're...***not*** a ***bad*** knight?
Maybe Mom's right.

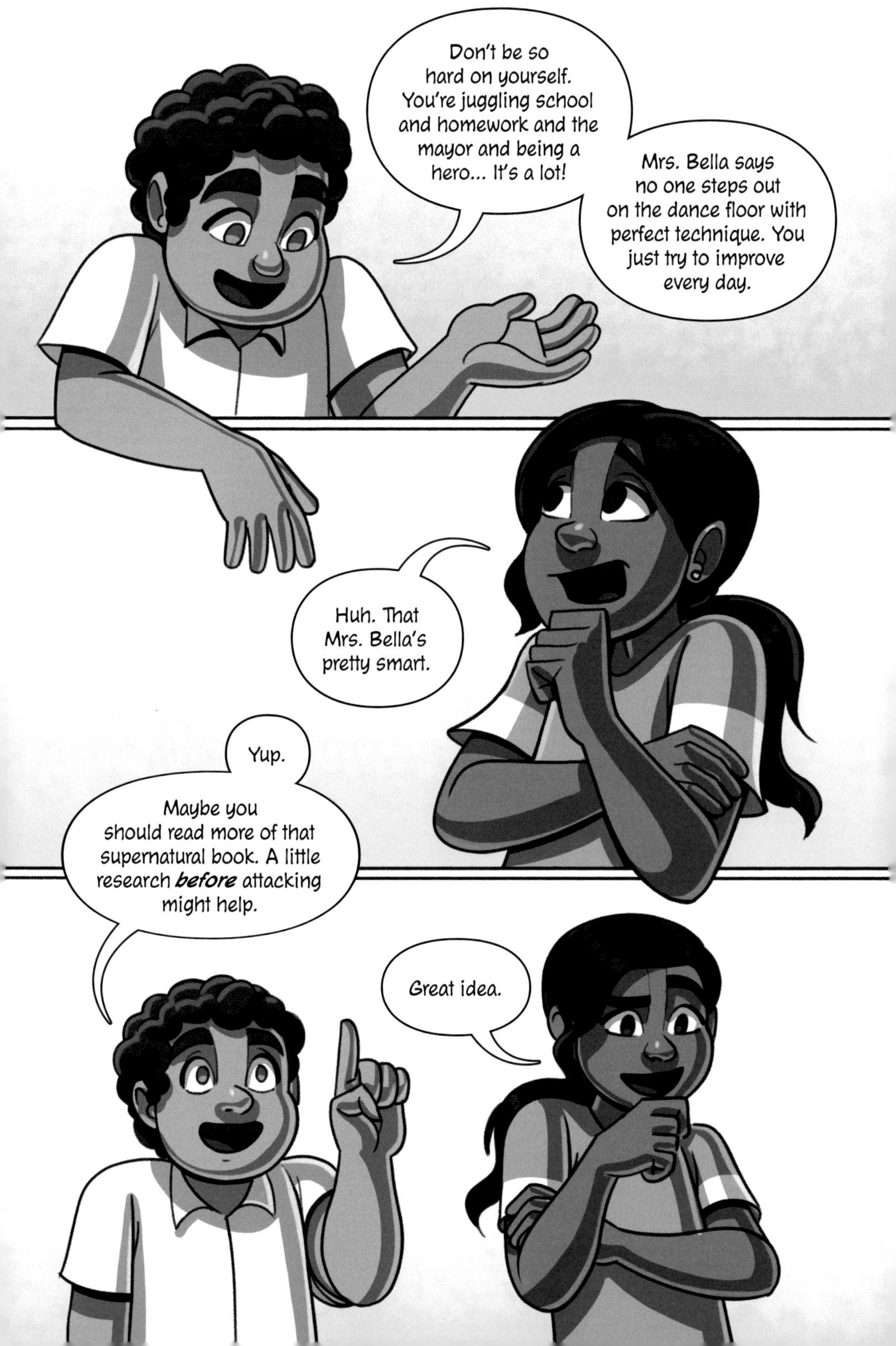
Don't be so hard on yourself. You're juggling school and homework and the mayor and being a hero... It's a lot!
Mrs. Bella says no one steps out on the dance floor with perfect technique. You just try to improve every day.
Huh. That Mrs. Bella's pretty smart.
Yup.
Maybe you should read more of that supernatural book. A little research ***before*** attacking might help.
Great idea.

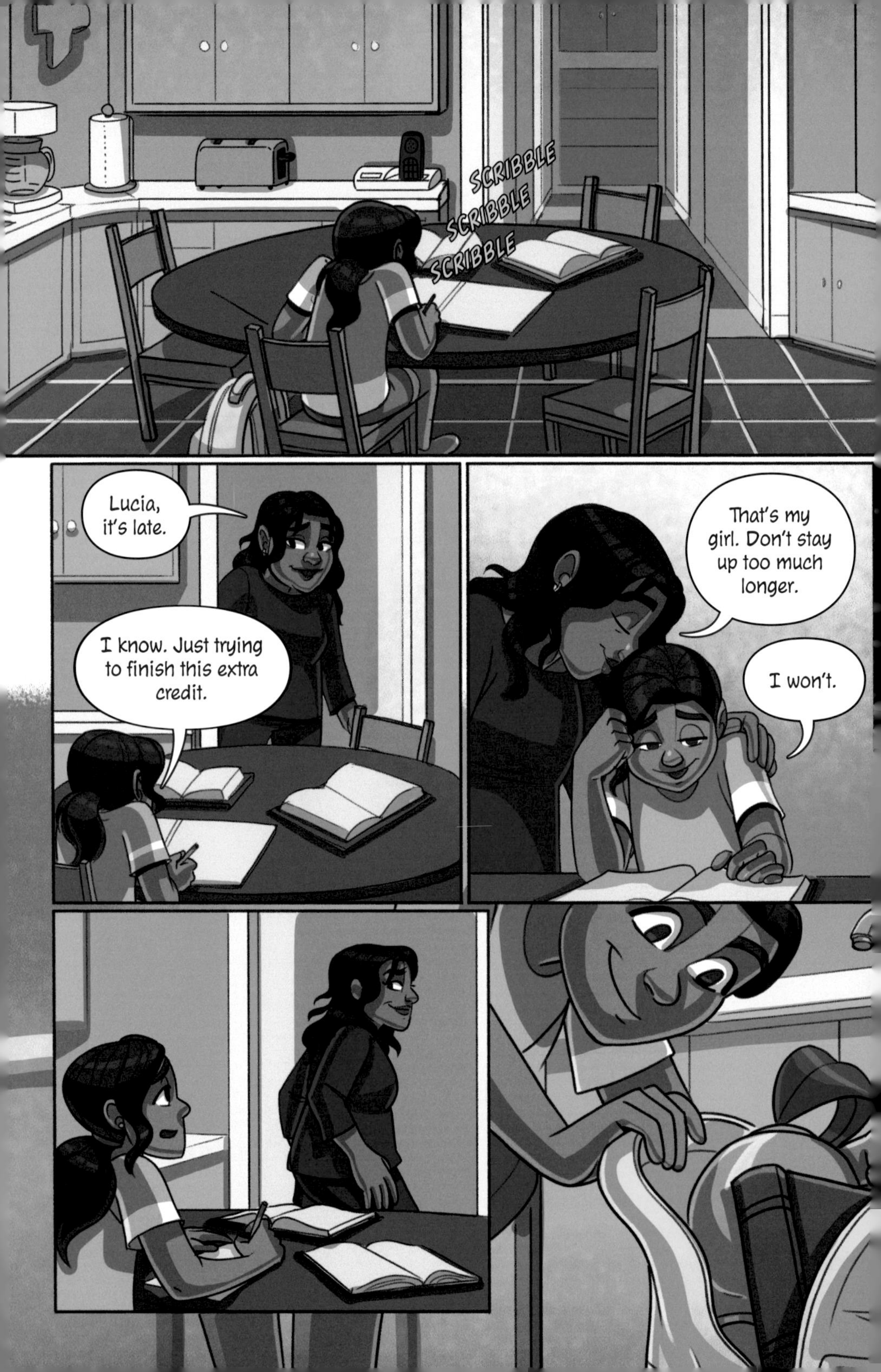
SCRIBBLE
SCRIBBLE
SCRIBBLE
Lucia, it's late.
I know. Just trying to finish this extra credit.
That's my girl. Don't stay up too much longer.
I won't.

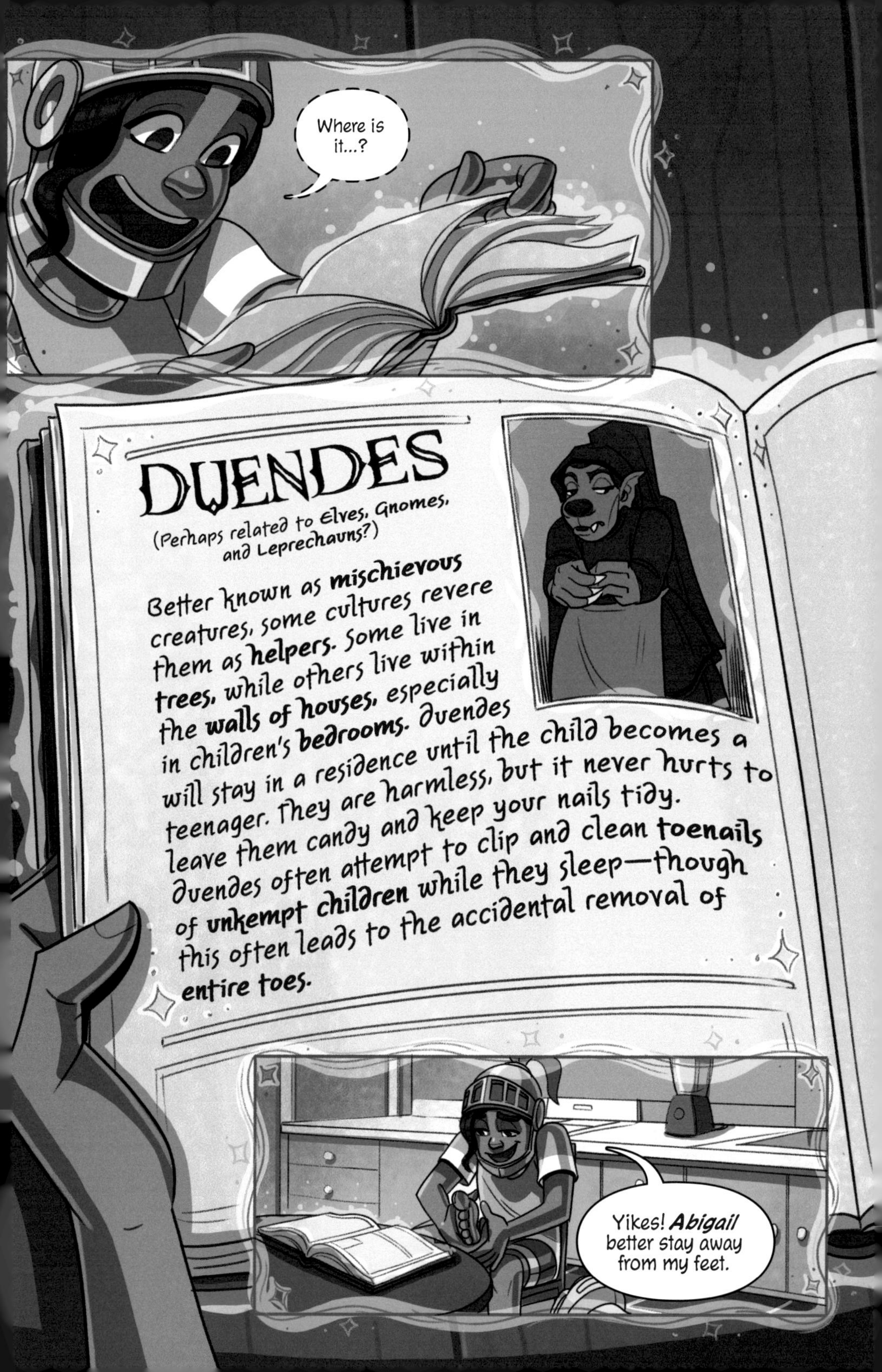
Where is it...?
DUENDES
(Perhaps related to Elves, Gnomes, and Leprechauns?)
Better known as mischievous creatures, some cultures revere them as helpers. Some live in trees, while others live within the walls of houses, especially in children's bedrooms. Duendes will stay in a residence until the child becomes a teenager. They are harmless, but it never hurts to leave them candy and keep your nails tidy. Duendes often attempt to clip and clean toenails of unkempt children while they sleep—though this often leads to the accidental removal of entire toes.
Yikes! Abigail better stay away from my feet.

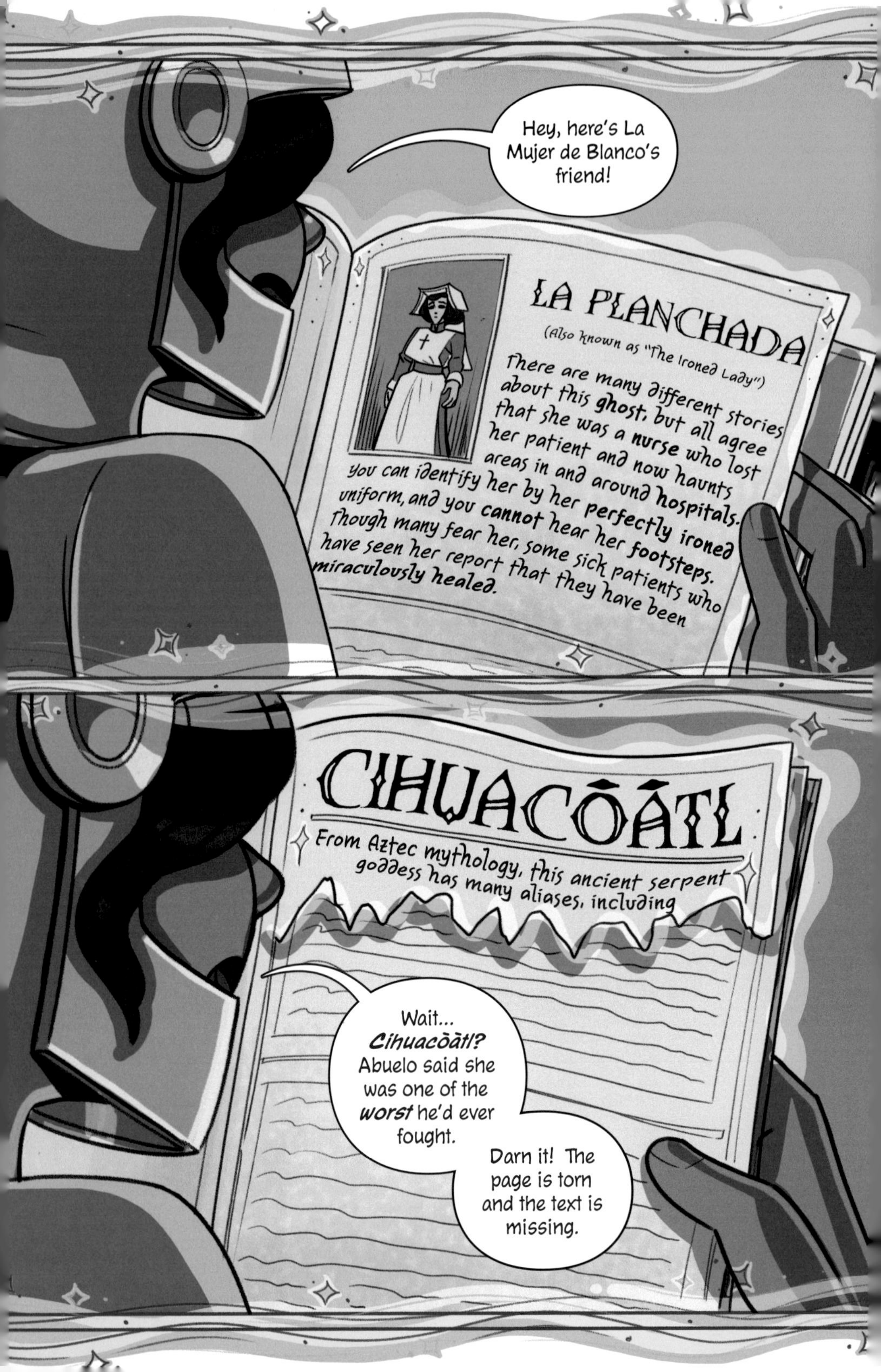
Hey, here's La Mujer de Blanco's friend!
LA PLANCHADA
(Also known as "The Ironed Lady")
There are many different stories about this ghost, but all agree that she was a nurse who lost her patient and now haunts areas in and around hospitals. You can identify her by her perfectly ironed uniform, and you cannot hear her footsteps. Though many fear her, some sick patients who have seen her report that they have been miraculously healed.
CIHUACŌĀTL
From Aztec mythology, this ancient serpent goddess has many aliases, including
Wait... Cihuacōātl? Abuelo said she was one of the worst he'd ever fought.
Darn it! The page is torn and the text is missing.

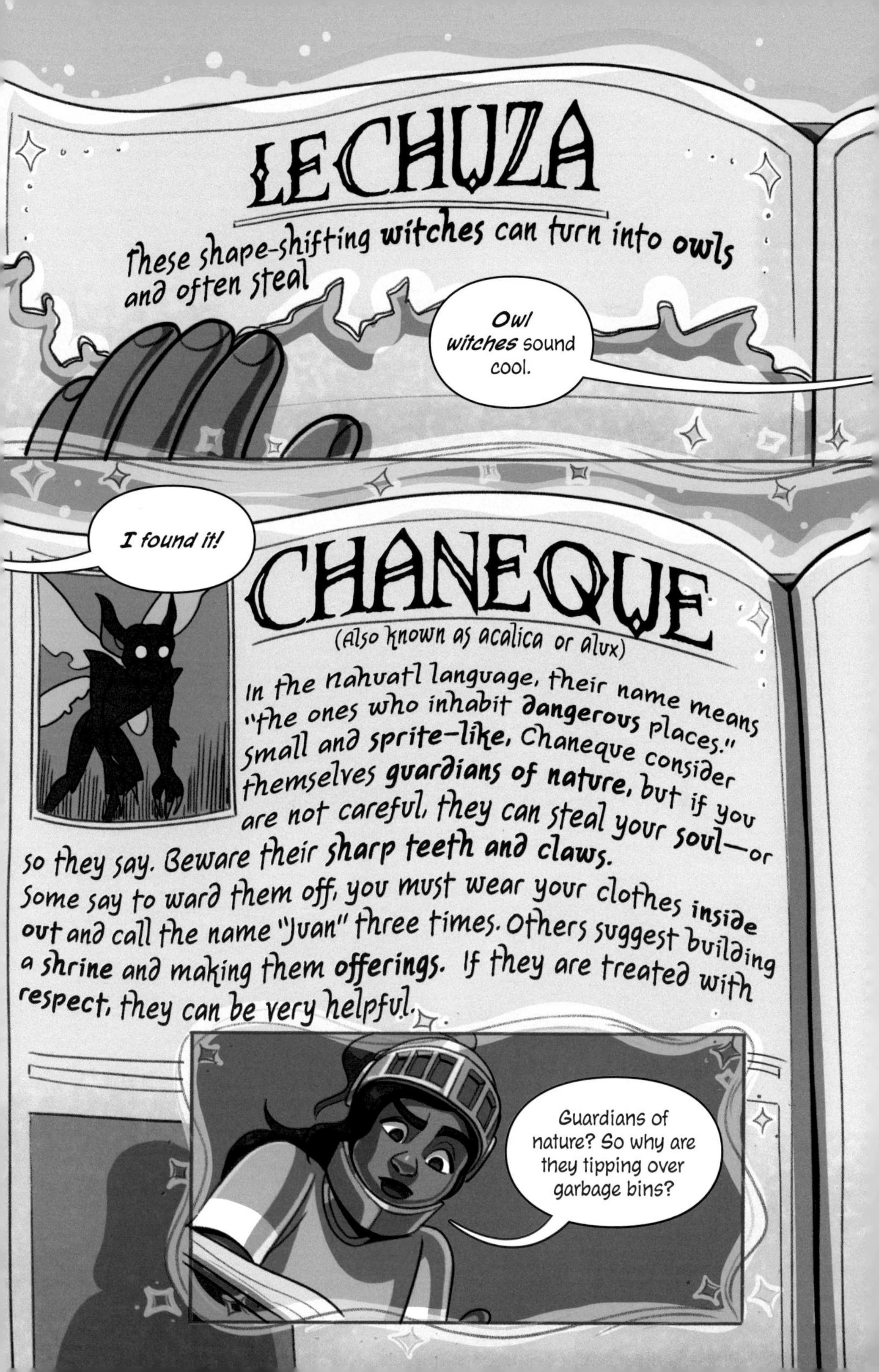
LECHUZA
These shape-shifting witches can turn into owls and often steal
Owl witches sound cool.
I found it!
CHANEQUE
(Also known as acalica or alux)
In the Nahuatl language, their name means "the ones who inhabit dangerous places." Small and sprite-like, Chaneque consider themselves guardians of nature, but if you are not careful, they can steal your soul—or so they say. Beware their sharp teeth and claws.
Some say to ward them off, you must wear your clothes inside out and call the name "Juan" three times. Others suggest building a shrine and making them offerings. If they are treated with respect, they can be very helpful.
Guardians of nature? So why are they tipping over garbage bins?

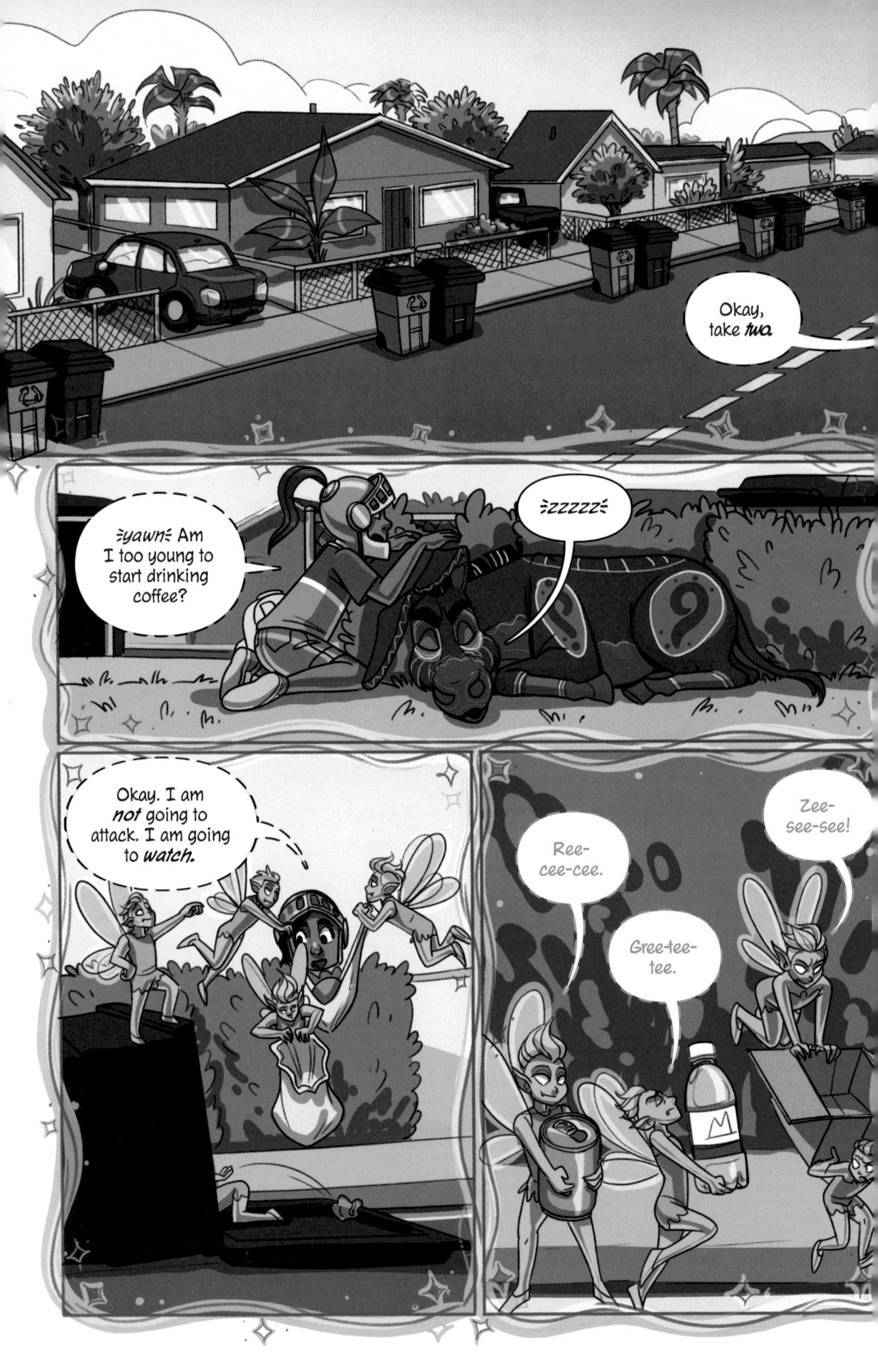

Okay, take two.
yawn Am I too young to start drinking coffee?
ZZZZZ
Okay. I am not going to attack. I am going to watch.
Ree-cee-cee.
Gree-tee-tee.
Zee-see-see!

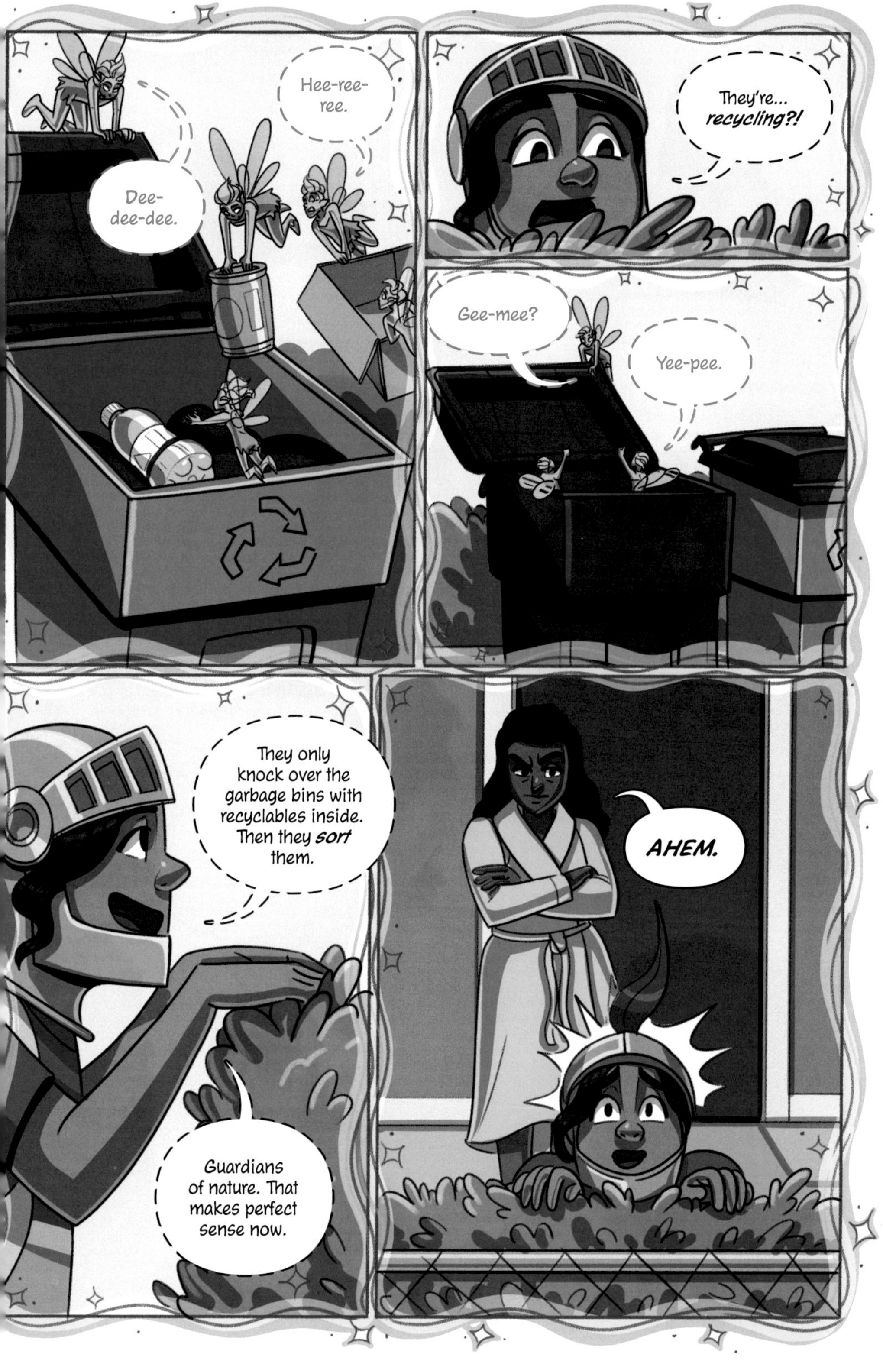
Hee-ree-ree.
Dee-dee-dee.
They're... *recycling?!*
Gee-mee?
Yee-pee.
They only knock over the garbage bins with recyclables inside. Then they *sort* them.
Guardians of nature. That makes perfect sense now.
AHEM.

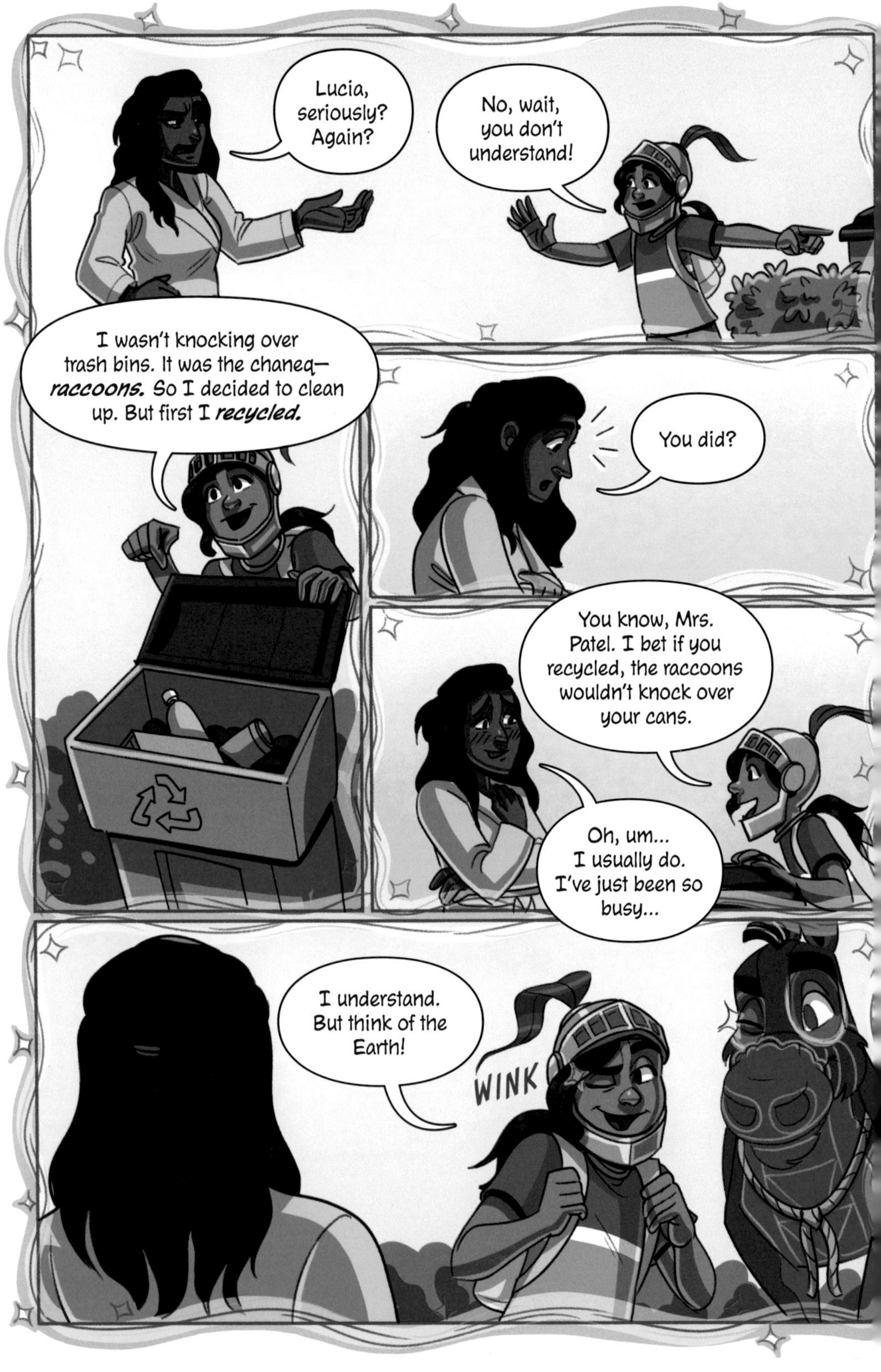
Lucia, seriously? Again?
No, wait, you don't understand!
I wasn't knocking over trash bins. It was the chaneq—*raccoons.* So I decided to clean up. But first I *recycled.*
You did?
You know, Mrs. Patel. I bet if you recycled, the raccoons wouldn't knock over your cans.
Oh, um... I usually do. I've just been so busy...
I understand. But think of the Earth!
WINK

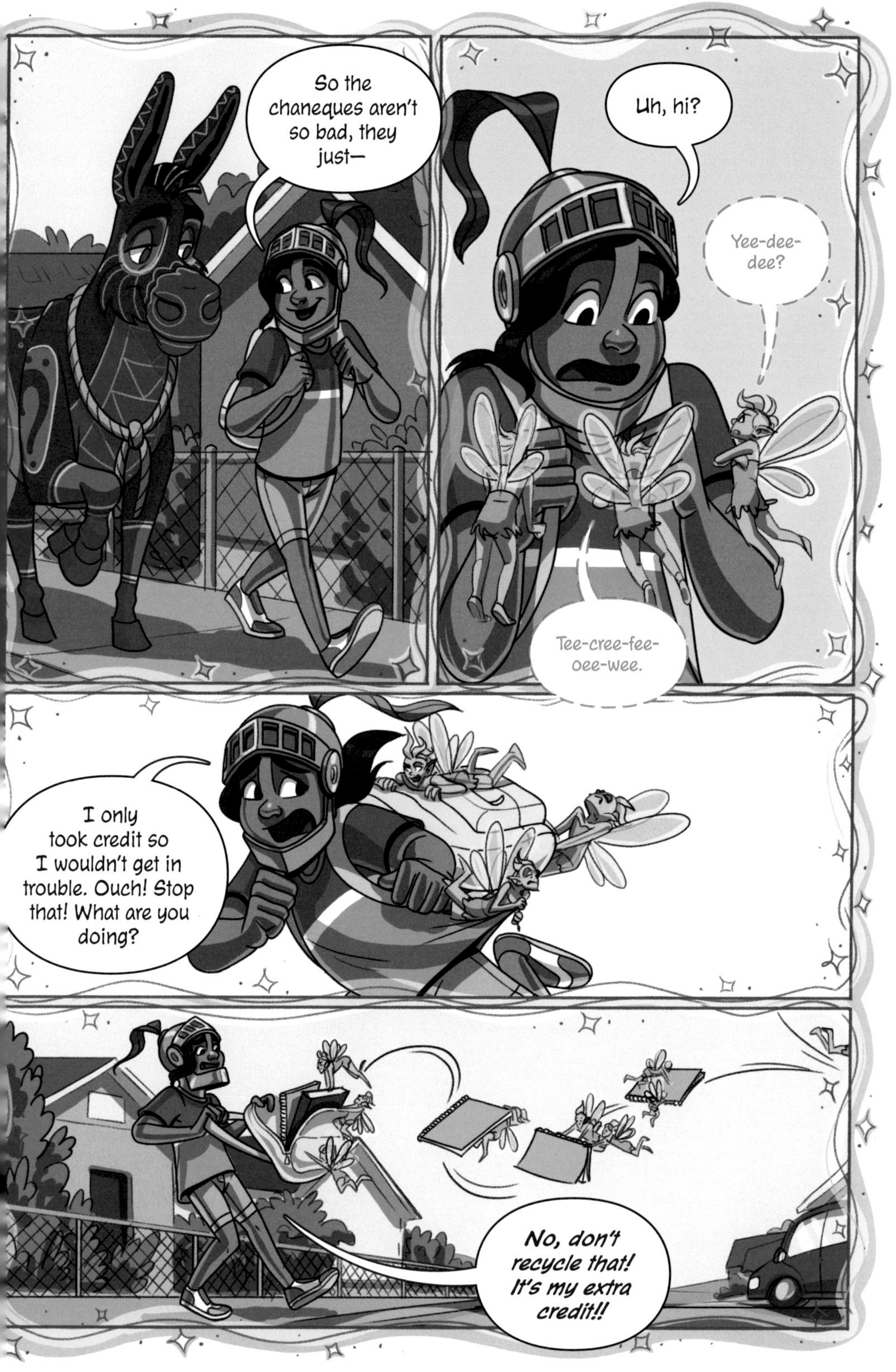
So the chaneques aren't so bad, they just—
Uh, hi?
Yee-dee-dee?
Tee-cree-fee-oee-wee.
I only took credit so I wouldn't get in trouble. Ouch! Stop that! What are you doing?
No, don't recycle that! It's my extra credit!!

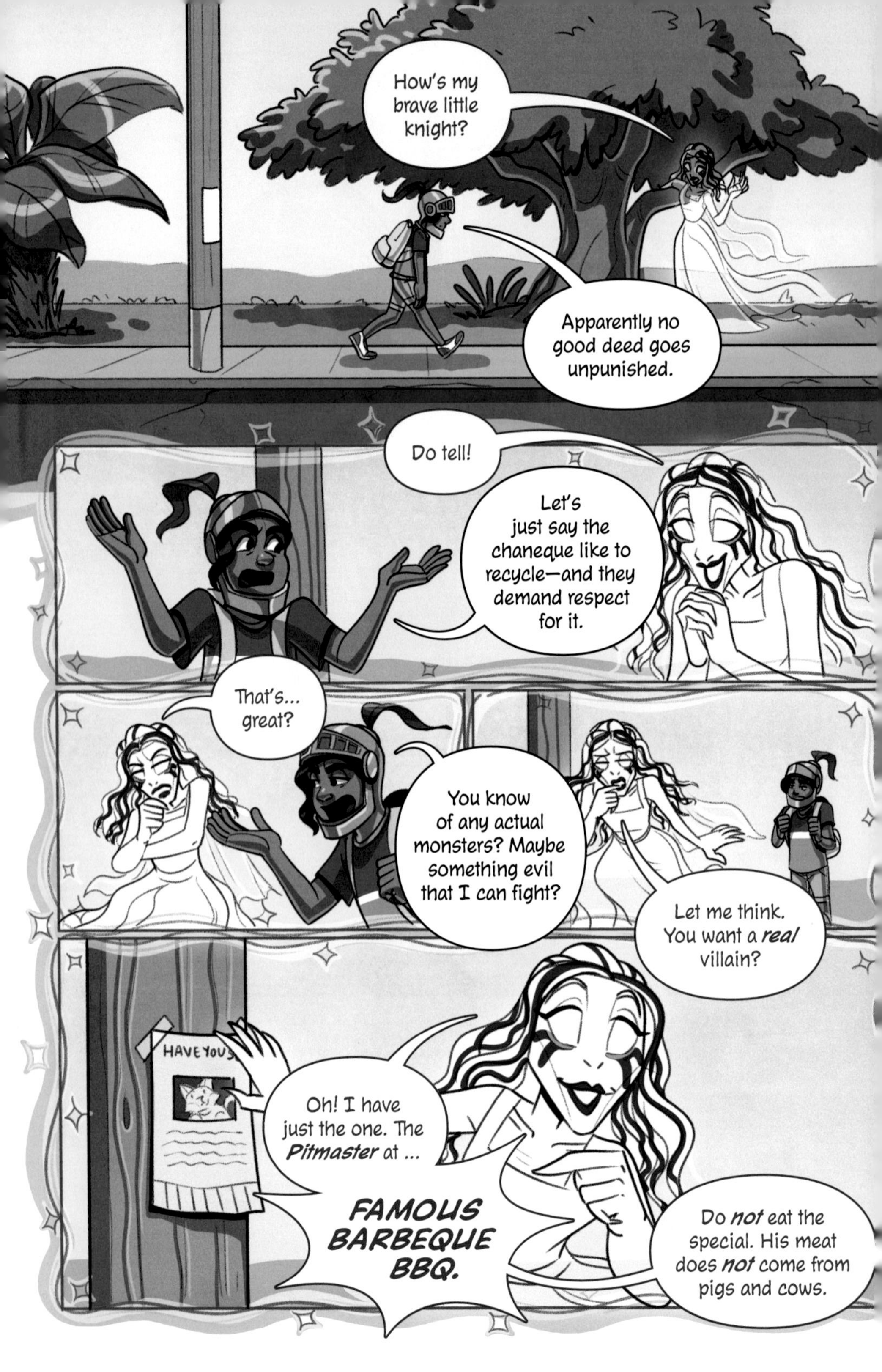
How's my brave little knight?
Apparently no good deed goes unpunished.
Do tell!
Let's just say the chaneque like to recycle—and they demand respect for it.
That's... great?
You know of any actual monsters? Maybe something evil that I can fight?
Let me think. You want a *real* villain?
HAVE YOU S
Oh! I have just the one. The *Pitmaster* at ...
FAMOUS BARBEQUE BBQ.
Do *not* eat the special. His meat does *not* come from pigs and cows.

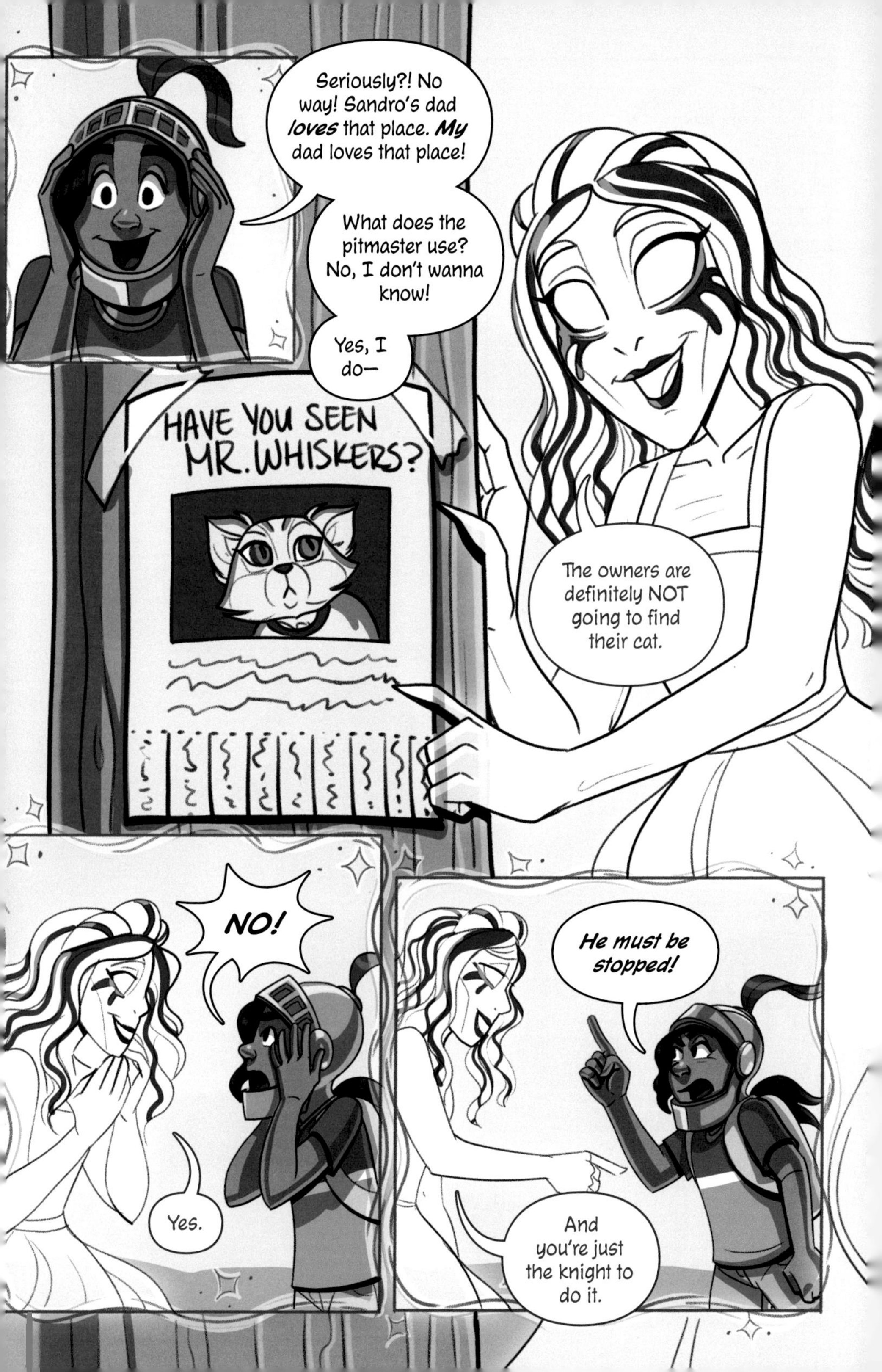
Seriously?! No way! Sandro's dad *loves* that place. ***My*** dad loves that place!
What does the pitmaster use? No, I don't wanna know!
Yes, I do—
HAVE YOU SEEN MR. WHISKERS?
The owners are definitely NOT going to find their cat.
NO!
Yes.
He must be stopped!
And you're just the knight to do it.

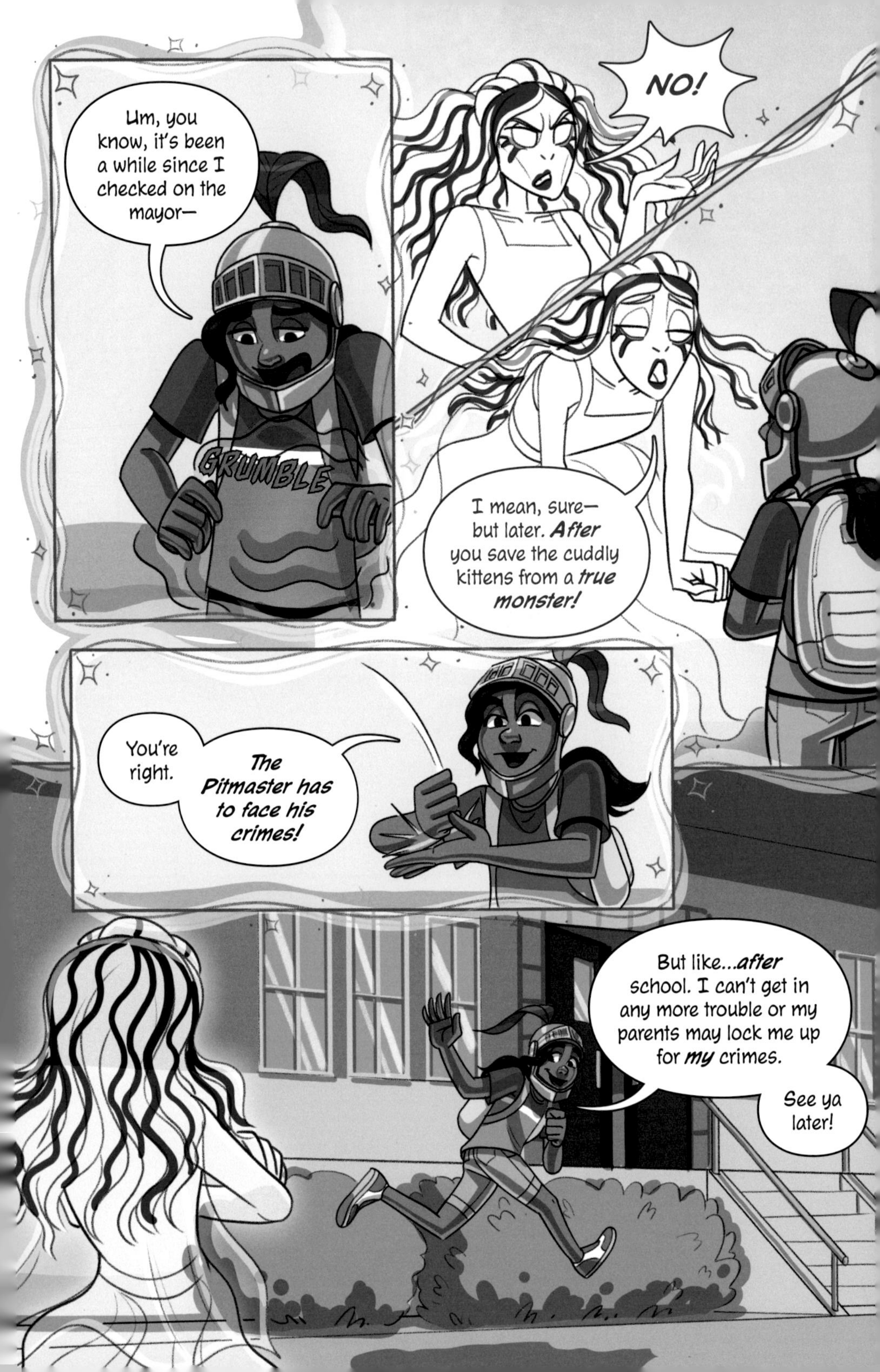
Um, you know, it's been a while since I checked on the mayor—
GRUMBLE
NO!
I mean, sure— but later. *After* you save the cuddly kittens from a *true monster!*
You're right.
The Pitmaster has to face his crimes!
But like...*after* school. I can't get in any more trouble or my parents may lock me up for *my* crimes.
See ya later!

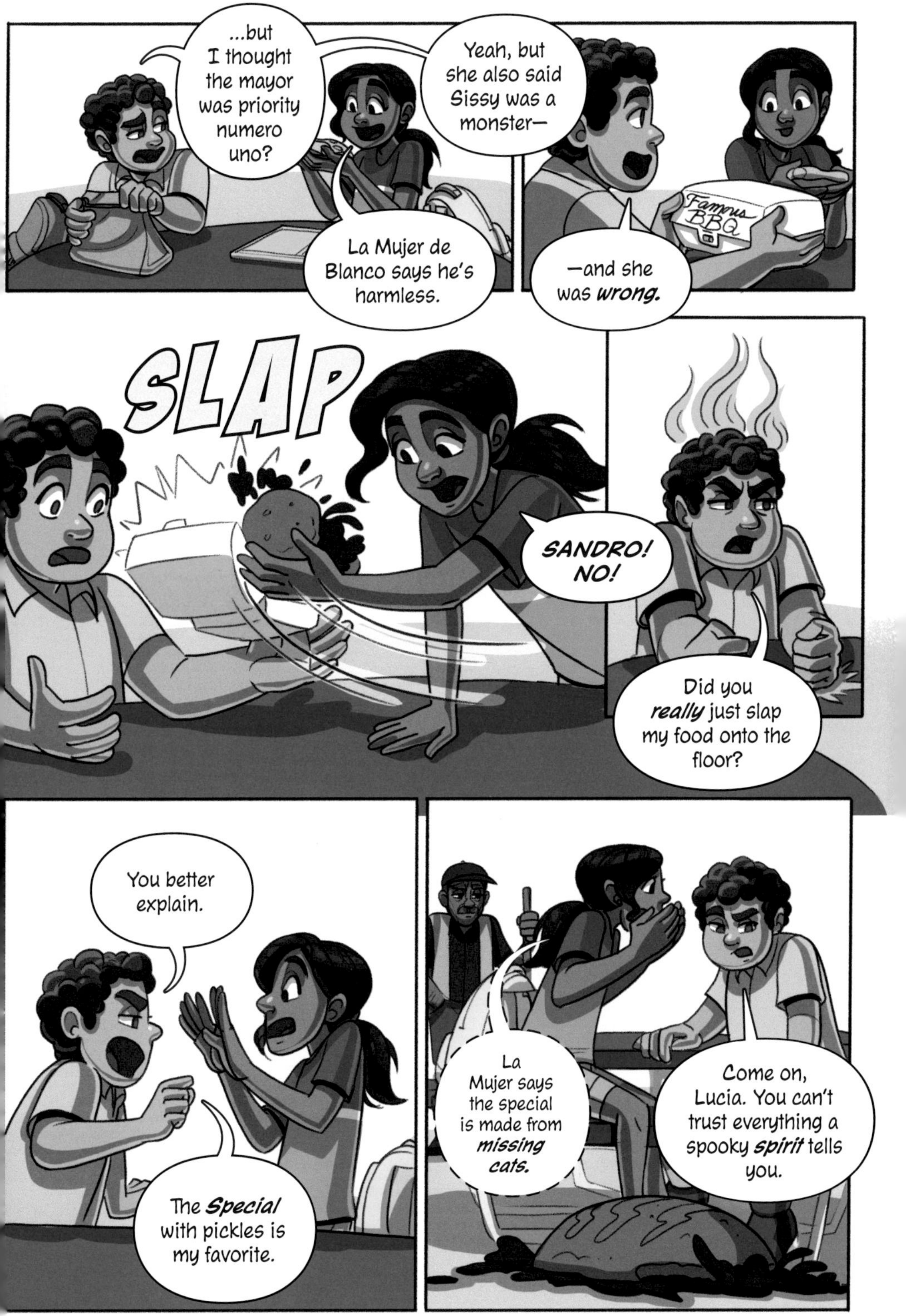
...but I thought the mayor was priority numero uno?
La Mujer de Blanco says he's harmless.
Yeah, but she also said Sissy was a monster—
—and she was *wrong.*
SLAP
SANDRO! NO!
Did you *really* just slap my food onto the floor?
You better explain.
The *Special* with pickles is my favorite.
La Mujer says the special is made from *missing cats.*
Come on, Lucia. You can't trust everything a spooky *spirit* tells you.
Famous BBQ

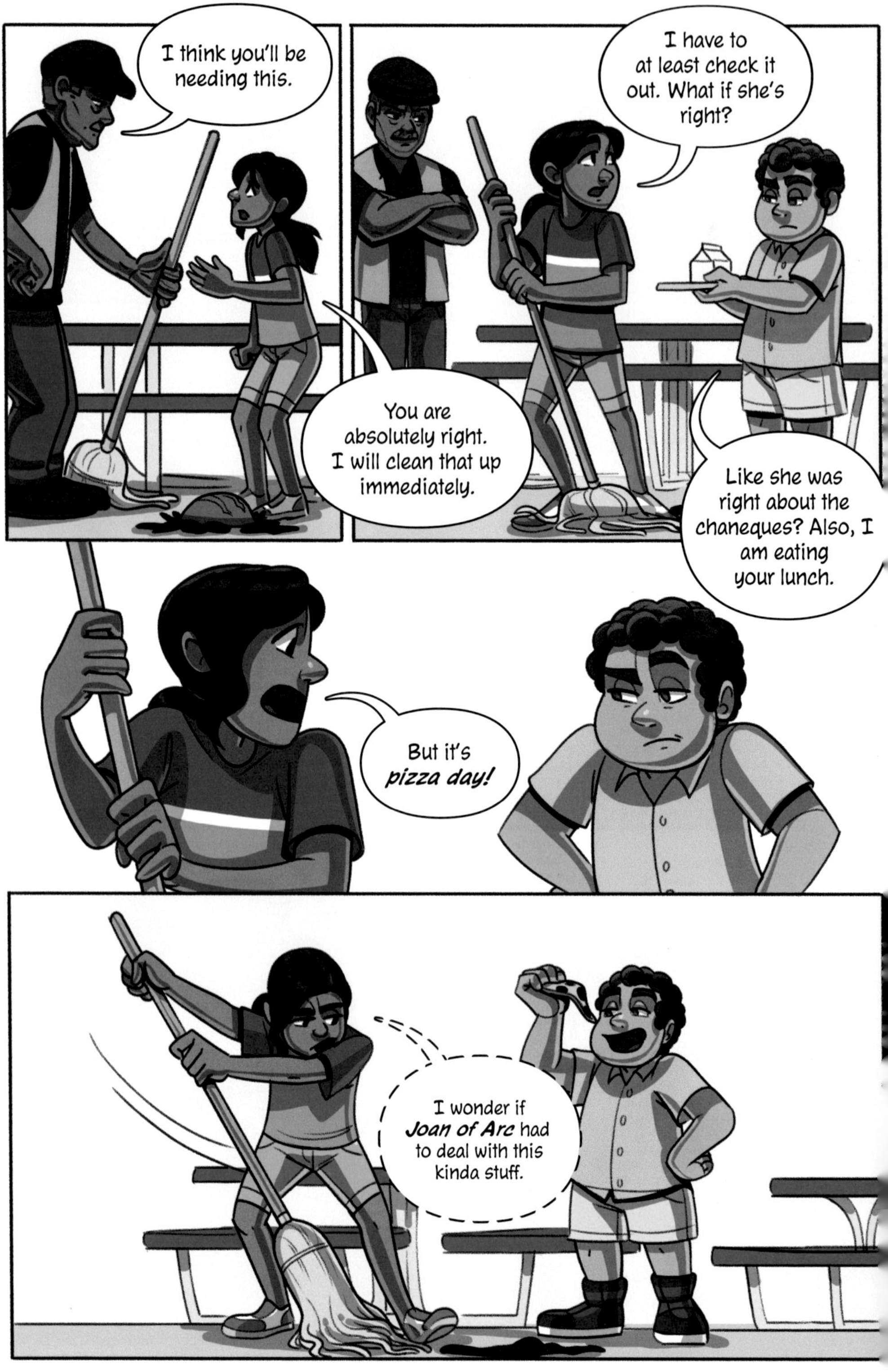
I think you'll be needing this.
You are absolutely right. I will clean that up immediately.
I have to at least check it out. What if she's right?
Like she was right about the chaneques? Also, I am eating your lunch.
But it's *pizza day!*
I wonder if *Joan of Arc* had to deal with this kinda stuff.

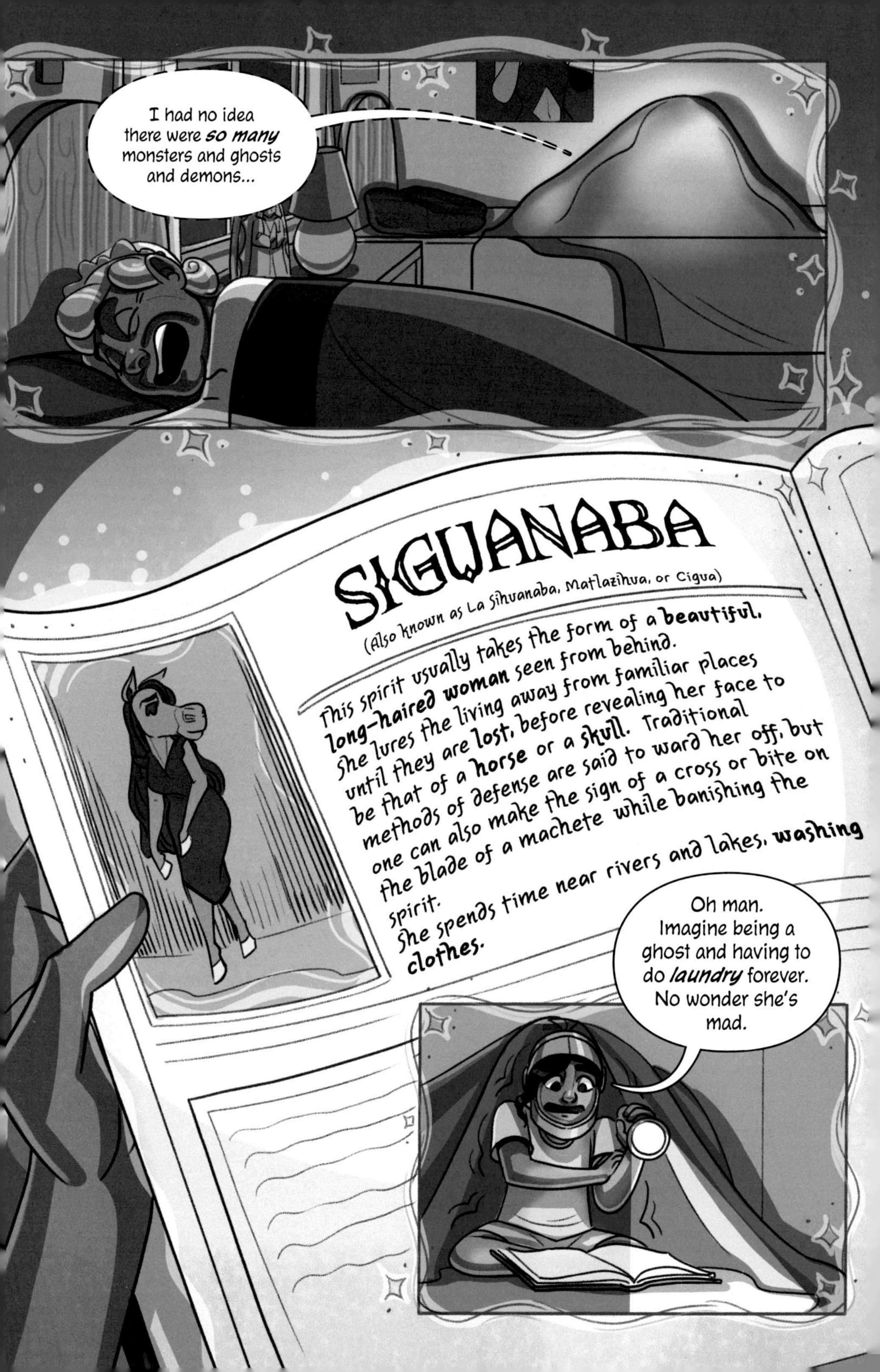

I had no idea there were *so many* monsters and ghosts and demons...
SIGUANABA
(Also known as La Sihuanaba, Matlazihua, or Cigua)
This spirit usually takes the form of a **beautiful, long-haired woman** seen from behind. She lures the living away from familiar places until they are **lost**, before revealing her face to be that of a **horse** or a **skull**. Traditional methods of defense are said to ward her off, but one can also make the sign of a cross or bite on the blade of a machete while banishing the spirit.
She spends time near rivers and lakes, **washing clothes.**
Oh man. Imagine being a ghost and having to do *laundry* forever. No wonder she's mad.

CHUPACABRA

(Also known as "Goat Sucker")

The size of a small bear, the reptile-like creature has large **eyes** and a row of **spines or quills** from its neck to the base of its **tail**. It often attacks **livestock** to drink their **blood**, especially cattle, sheep, and goats. When threatened, it is very **dangerous**.

"Goat sucker"?
Nasty!

Whoa. Is this really what the *mayor* is?

NAGUAL

(Also known as Nahual or Skinwalker)

Some say naguals are **shape-changing tricksters.** Others believe they are **shamans,** born with their abilities and able to change into a **variety of animals.** Still others believe naguals must make a **deal with a demon** to gain their powers. For some, the word "nagual" is the same as "**brujo**," a **wizard** who shape-shifts into an animal form at **night,** steals property, and causes disease in its victims. What is less known is that naguals can use their powers **for good** or **bad** based simply on their desires.

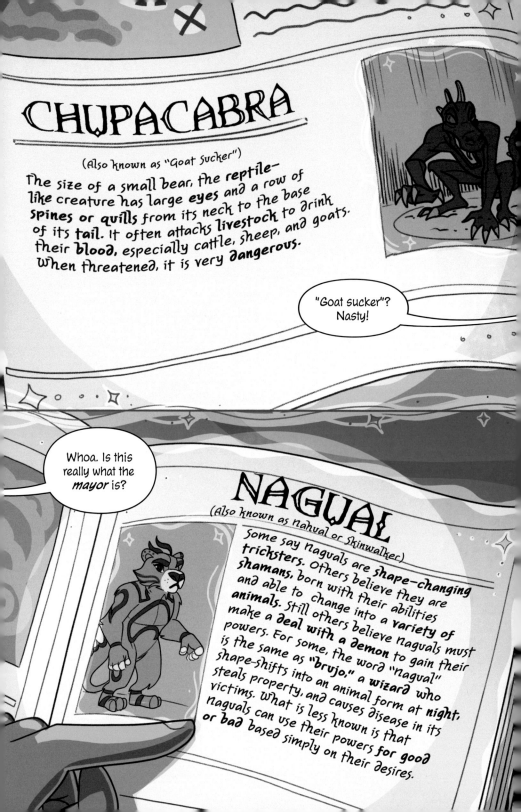

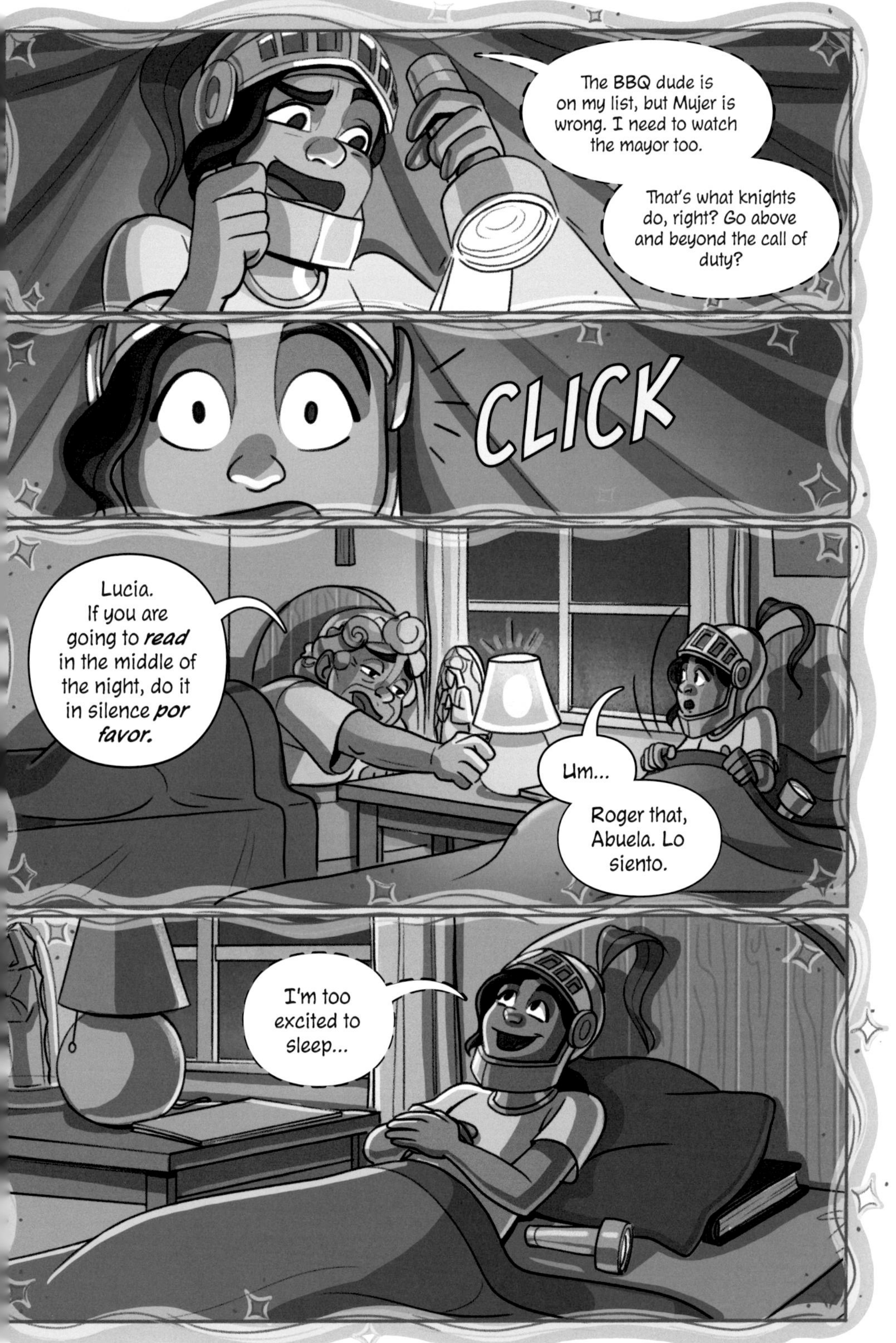
The BBQ dude is on my list, but Mujer is wrong. I need to watch the mayor too.
That's what knights do, right? Go above and beyond the call of duty?
CLICK
Lucia. If you are going to *read* in the middle of the night, do it in silence *por favor.*
Um...
Roger that, Abuela. Lo siento.
I'm too excited to sleep...

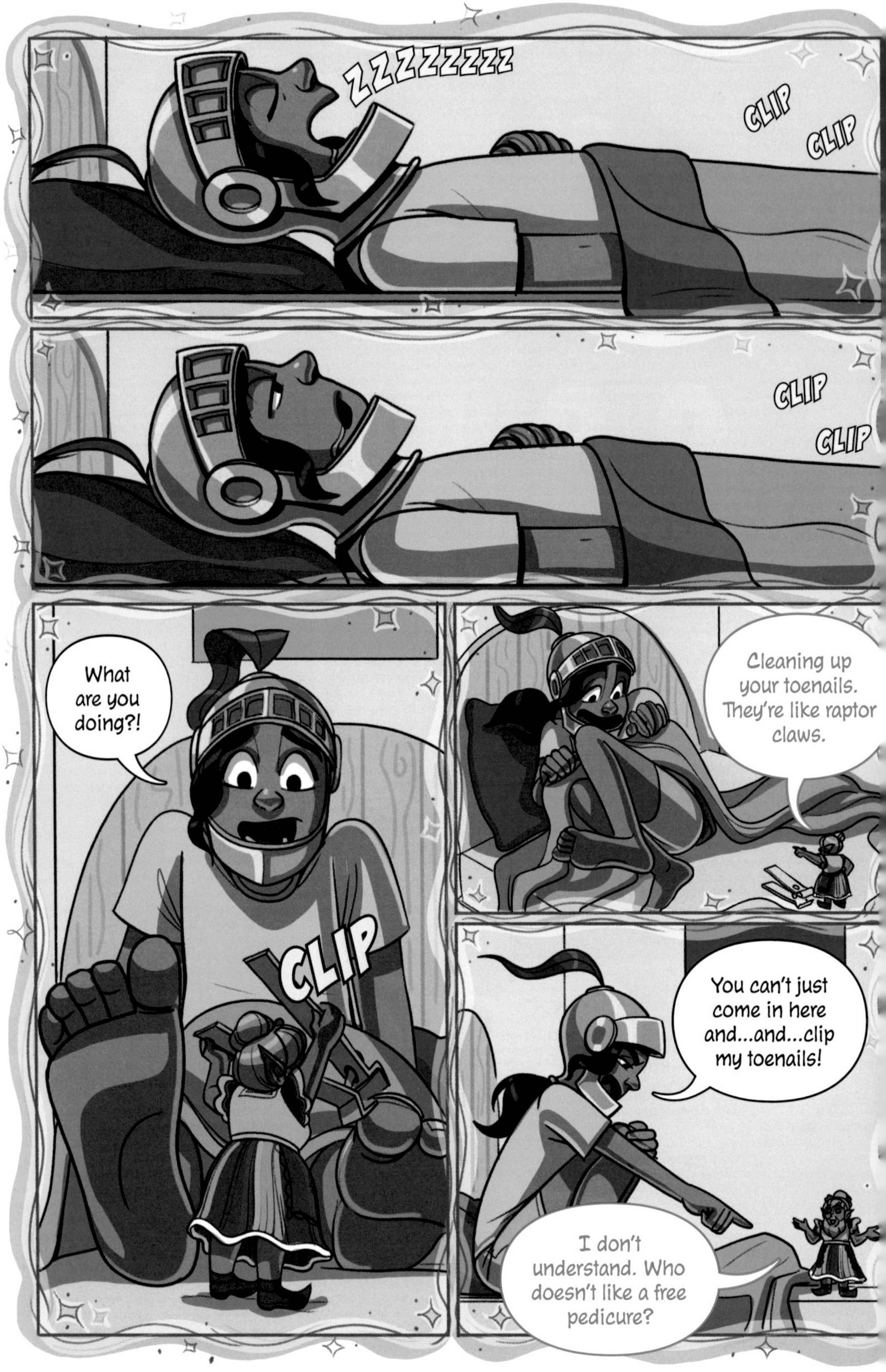
ZZZZZZZZ
CLIP
CLIP
CLIP
CLIP
What are you doing?!
CLIP
Cleaning up your toenails. They're like raptor claws.
You can't just come in here and...and...clip my toenails!
I don't understand. Who doesn't like a free pedicure?

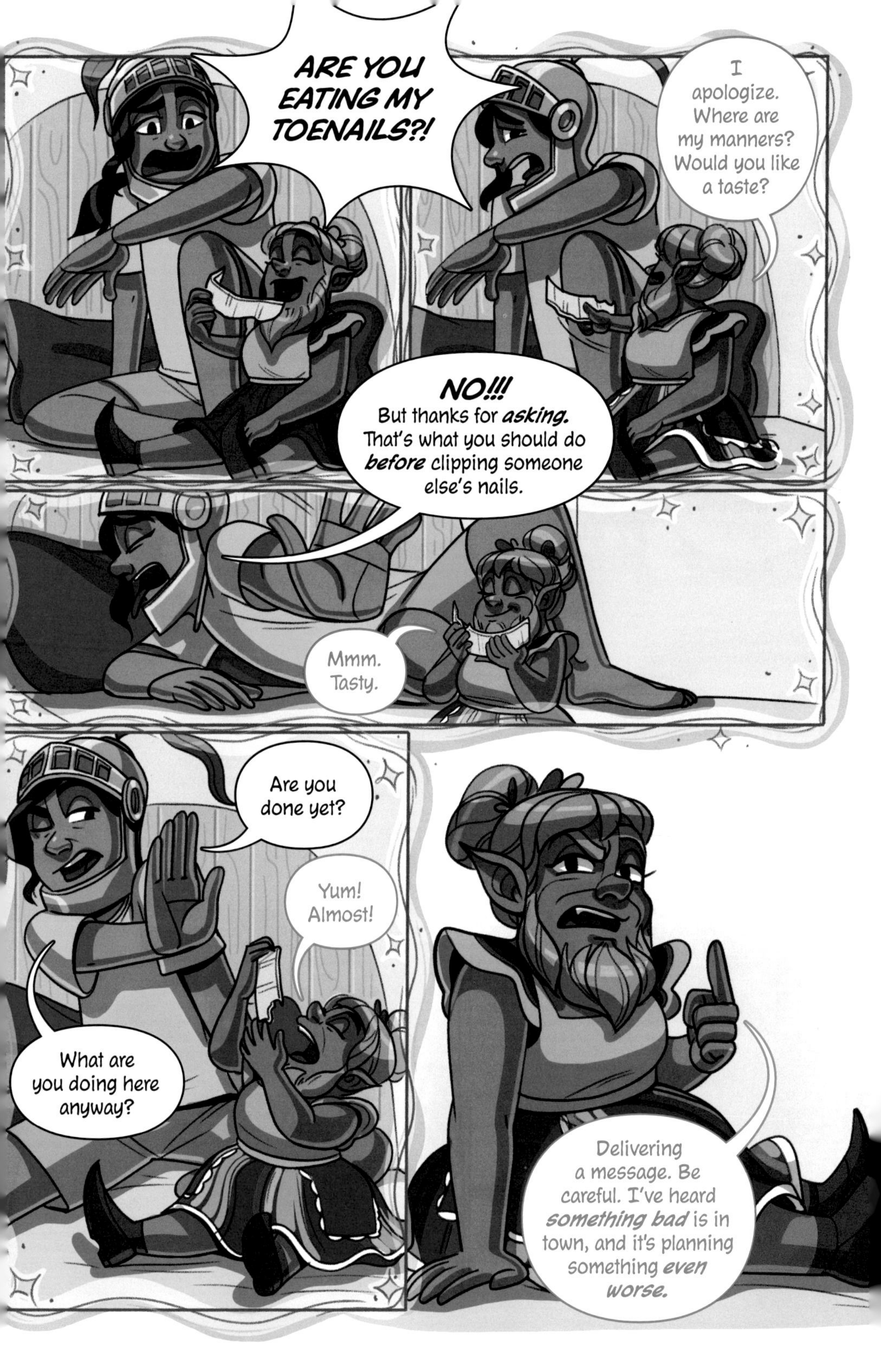
ARE YOU EATING MY TOENAILS?!
I apologize. Where are my manners? Would you like a taste?
NO!!! But thanks for *asking.* That's what you should do *before* clipping someone else's nails.
Mmm. Tasty.
Are you done yet?
Yum! Almost!
What are you doing here anyway?
Delivering a message. Be careful. I've heard *something bad* is in town, and it's planning something *even worse.*

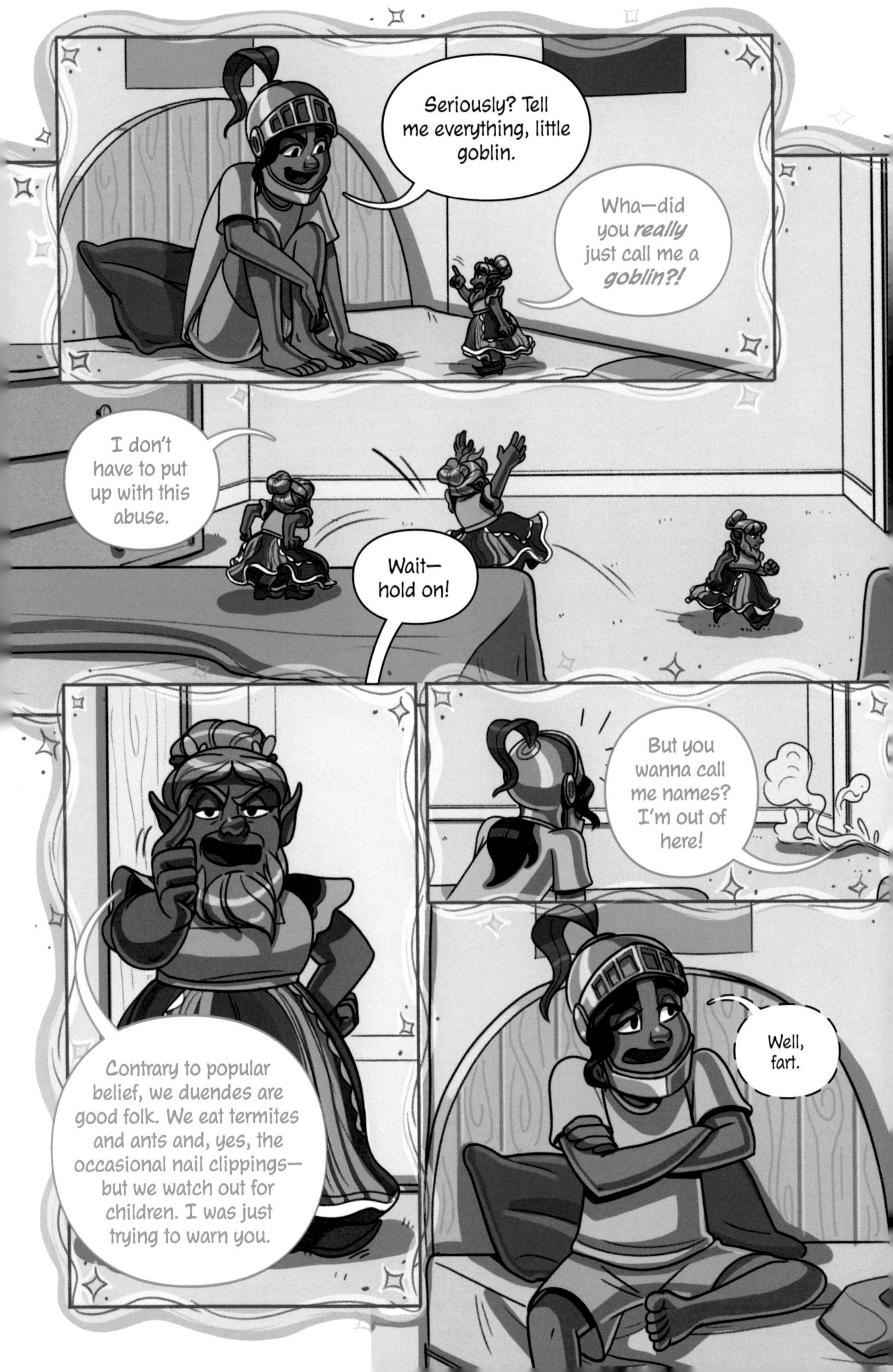
Seriously? Tell me everything, little goblin.
Wha—did you *really* just call me a *goblin?!*
I don't have to put up with this abuse.
Wait—hold on!
Contrary to popular belief, we duendes are good folk. We eat termites and ants and, yes, the occasional nail clippings—but we watch out for children. I was just trying to warn you.
But you wanna call me names? I'm out of here!
Well, fart.

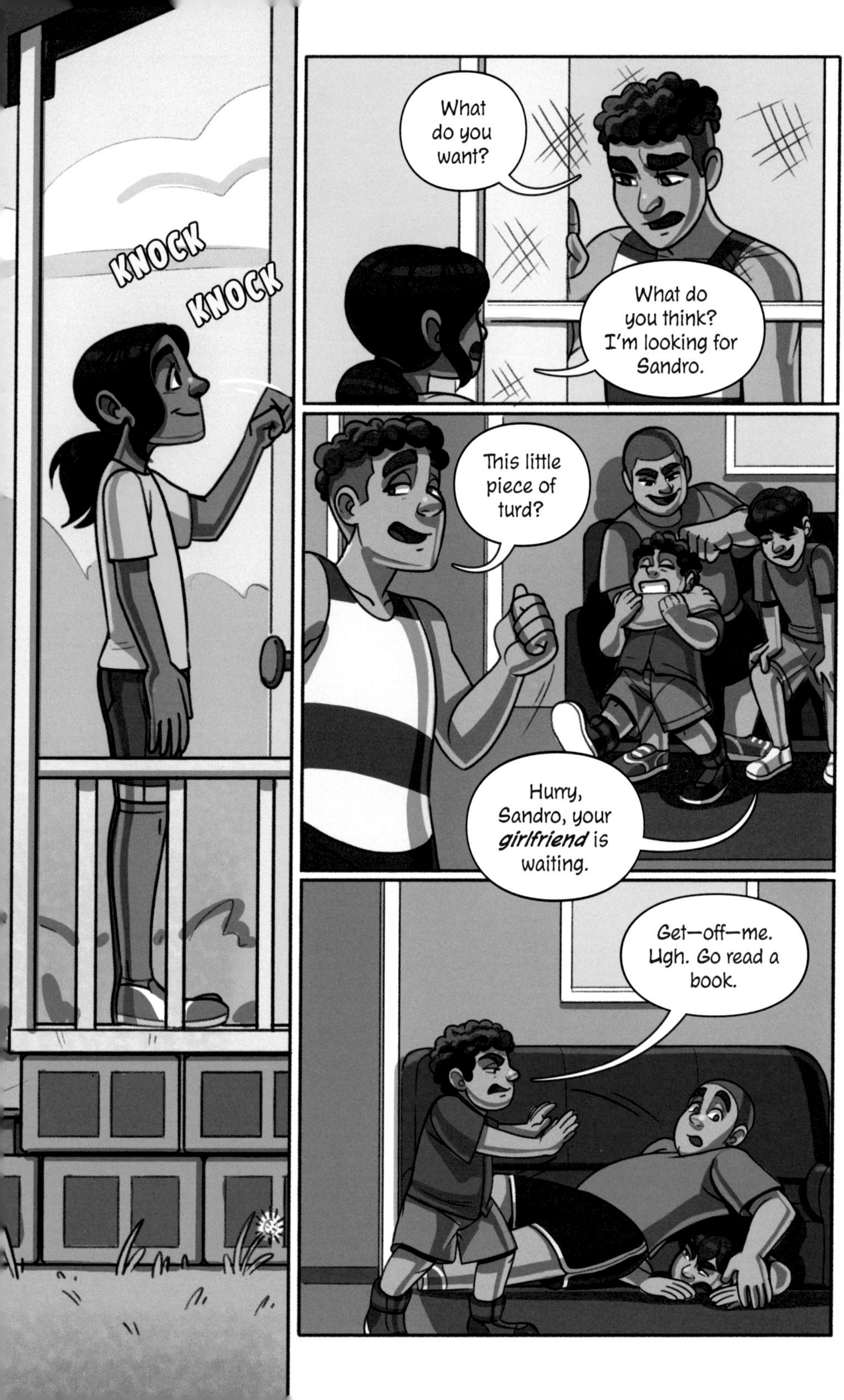
KNOCK
KNOCK
What do you want?
What do you think? I'm looking for Sandro.
This little piece of turd?
Hurry, Sandro, your *girlfriend* is waiting.
Get—off—me. Ugh. Go read a book.

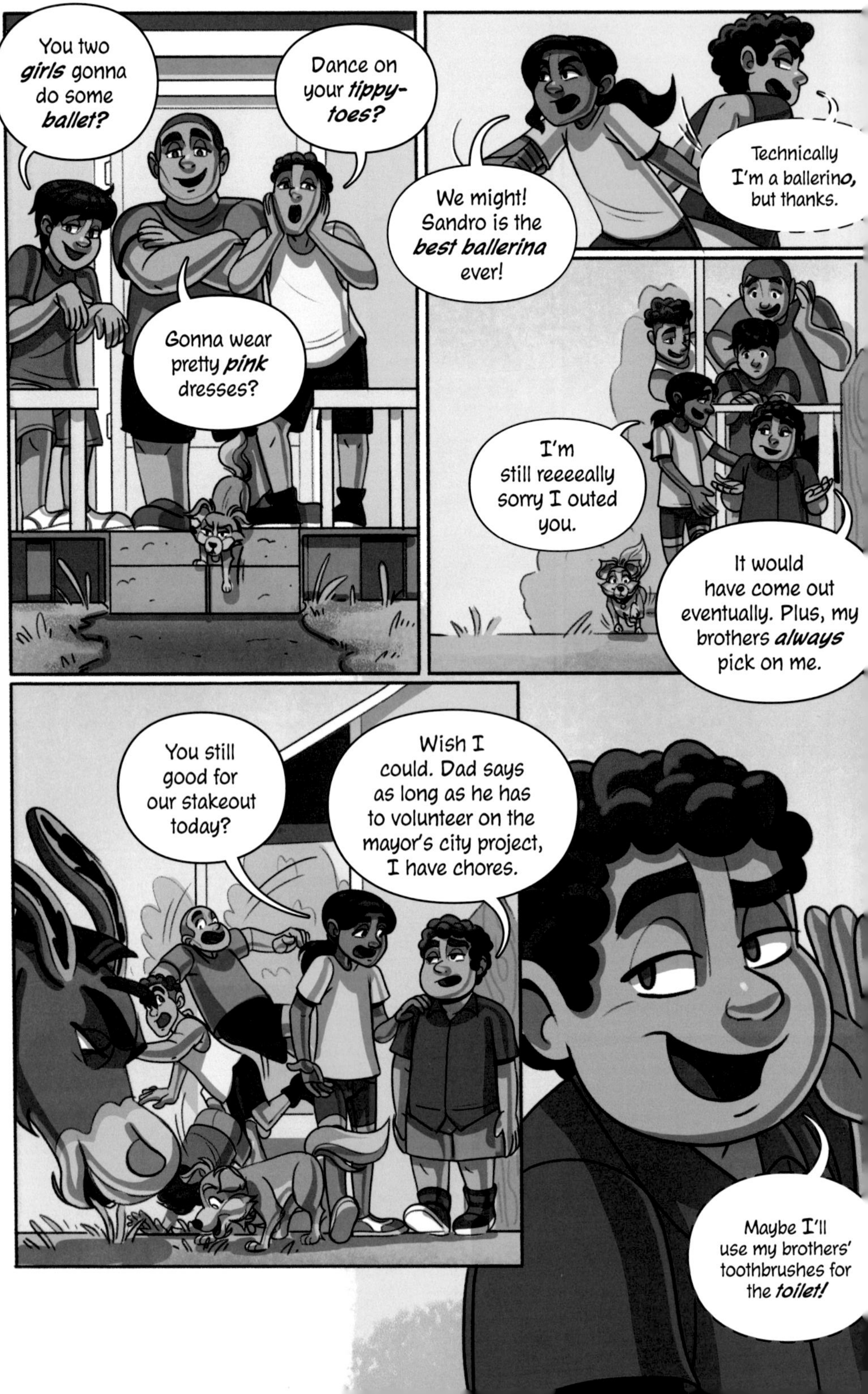
You two *girls* gonna do some *ballet?*
Dance on your *tippy-toes?*
Gonna wear pretty *pink* dresses?
We might! Sandro is the *best ballerina* ever!
Technically I'm a ballerino, but thanks.
I'm still reeeeally sorry I outed you.
It would have come out eventually. Plus, my brothers *always* pick on me.
You still good for our stakeout today?
Wish I could. Dad says as long as he has to volunteer on the mayor's city project, I have chores.
Maybe I'll use my brothers' toothbrushes for the *toilet!*

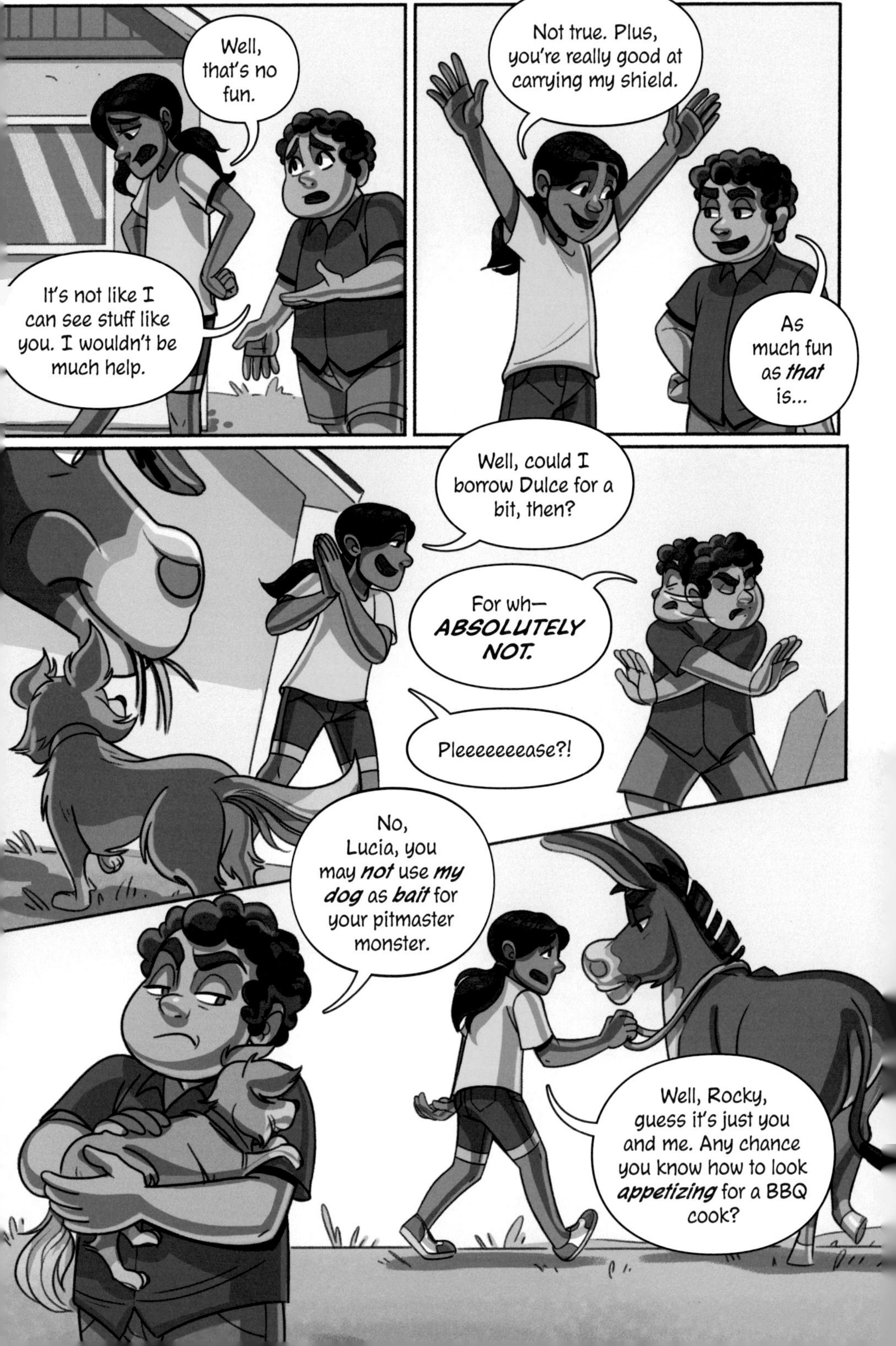
Well, that's no fun.
It's not like I can see stuff like you. I wouldn't be much help.
Not true. Plus, you're really good at carrying my shield.
As much fun as *that* is...
Well, could I borrow Dulce for a bit, then?
For wh— **ABSOLUTELY NOT.**
Pleeeeeeease?!
No, Lucia, you may ***not*** use ***my dog*** as ***bait*** for your pitmaster monster.
Well, Rocky, guess it's just you and me. Any chance you know how to look ***appetizing*** for a BBQ cook?

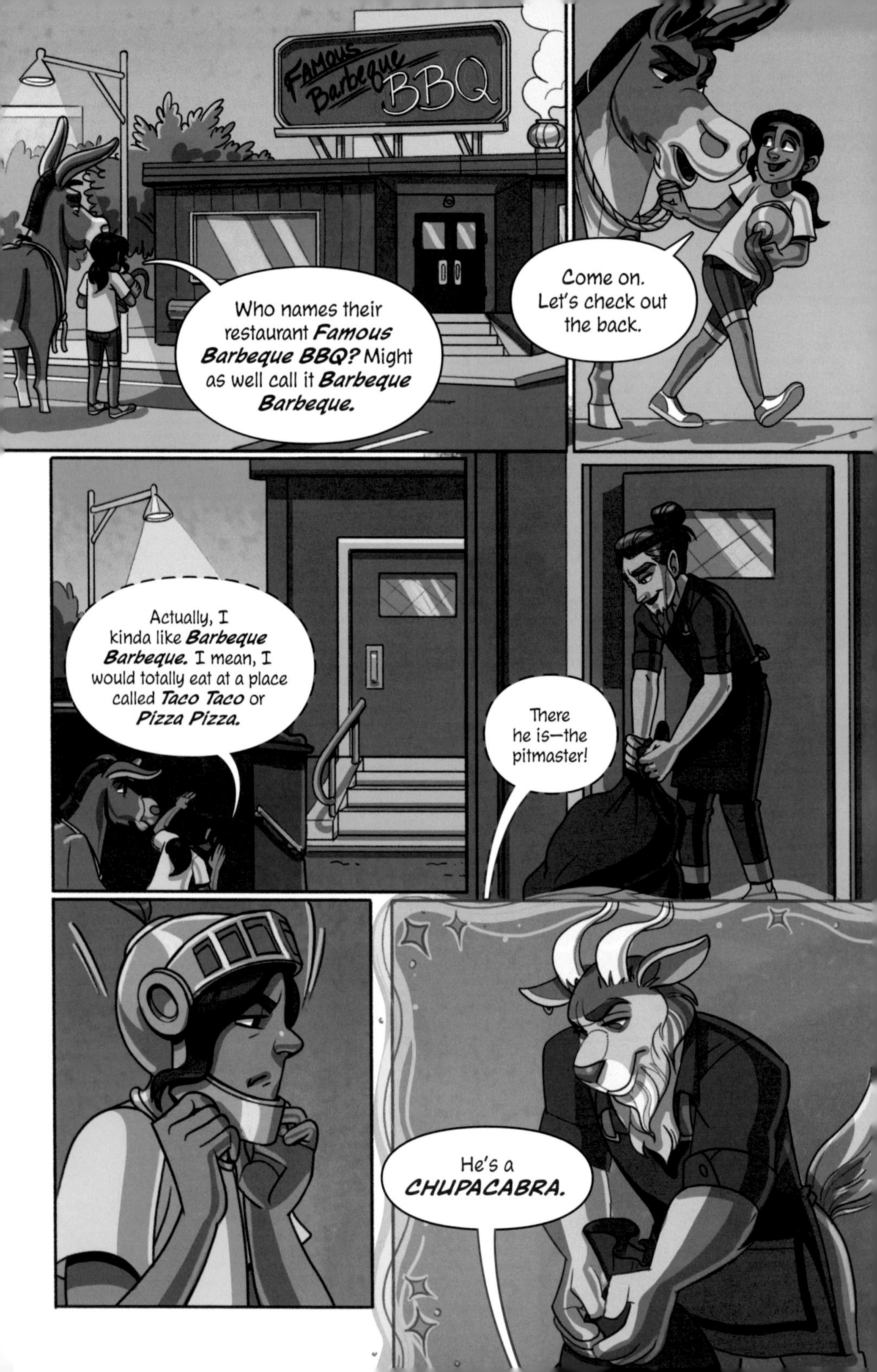
Famous Barbeque BBQ
Who names their restaurant Famous Barbeque BBQ? Might as well call it Barbeque Barbeque.
Come on. Let's check out the back.
Actually, I kinda like Barbeque Barbeque. I mean, I would totally eat at a place called Taco Taco or Pizza Pizza.
There he is—the pitmaster!
He's a CHUPACABRA.

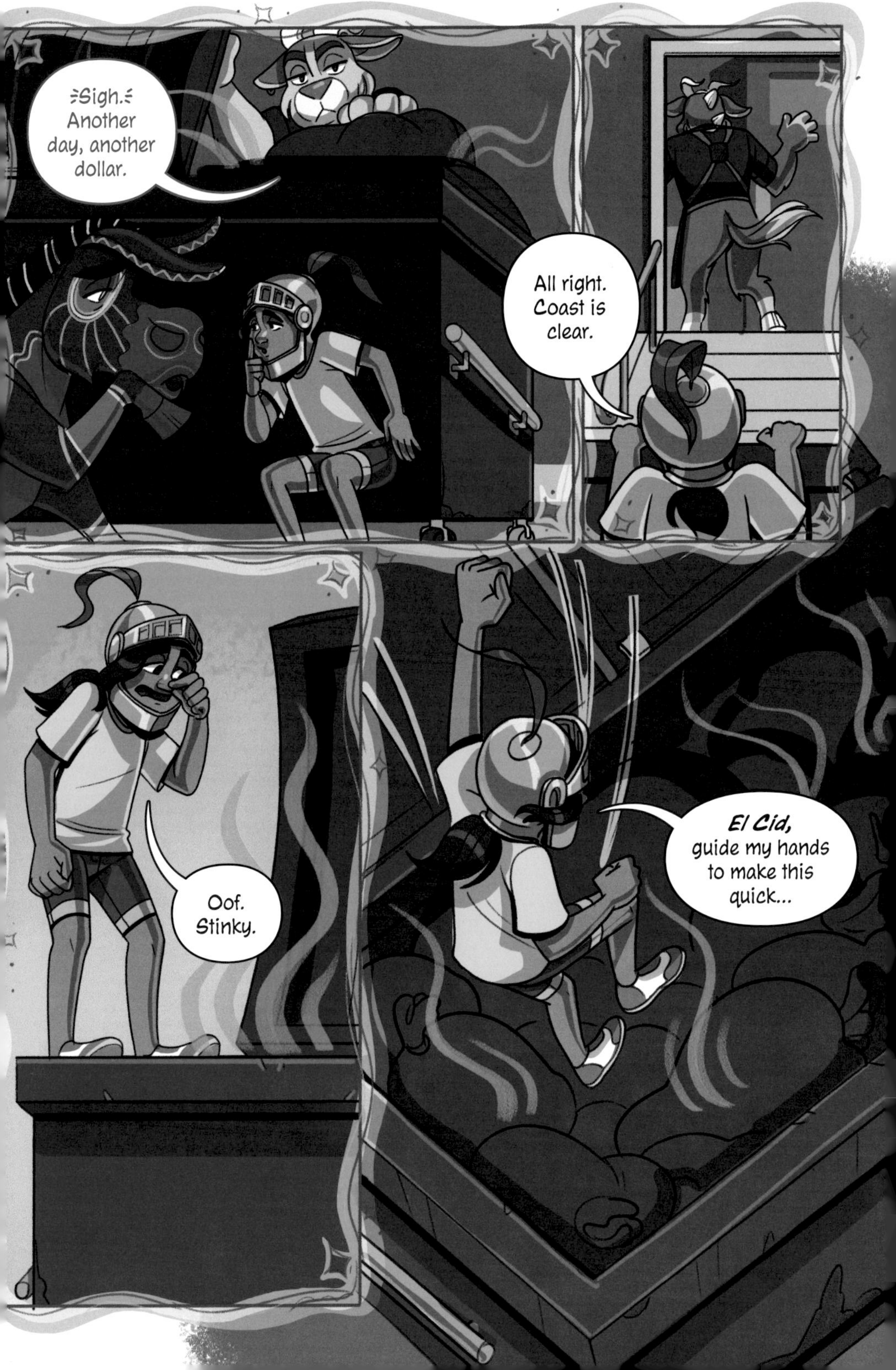

≈Sigh.≈ Another day, another dollar.
All right. Coast is clear.
Oof. Stinky.
El Cid, guide my hands to make this quick...

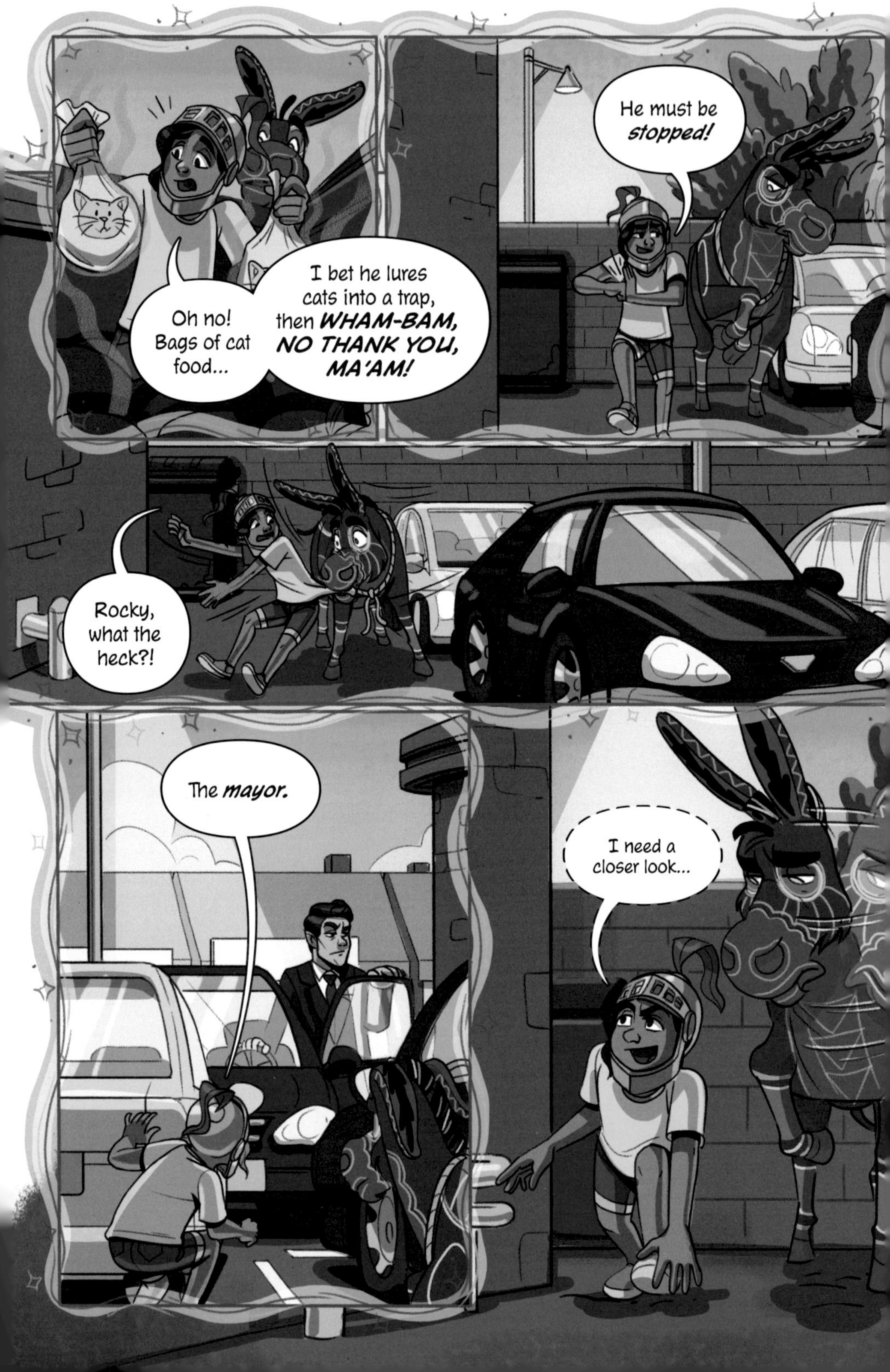
Oh no! Bags of cat food...
I bet he lures cats into a trap, then WHAM-BAM, NO THANK YOU, MA'AM!
He must be stopped!
Rocky, what the heck?!
The mayor.
I need a closer look...

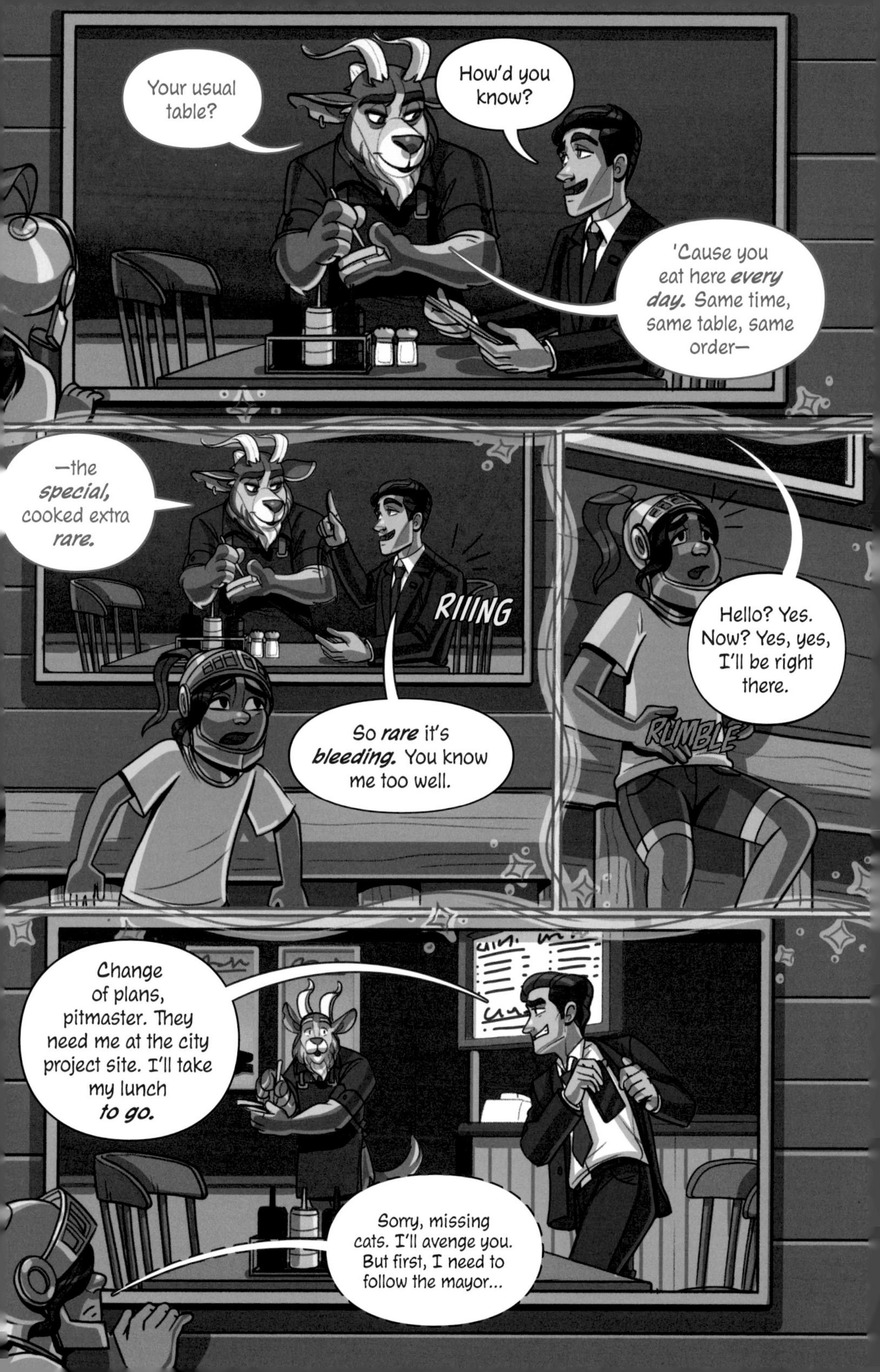

Your usual table?
How'd you know?
'Cause you eat here *every day.* Same time, same table, same order—
—the *special,* cooked extra *rare.*
RIIING
So *rare* it's *bleeding.* You know me too well.
Hello? Yes. Now? Yes, yes, I'll be right there.
RUMBLE
Change of plans, pitmaster. They need me at the city project site. I'll take my lunch *to go.*
Sorry, missing cats. I'll avenge you. But first, I need to follow the mayor...

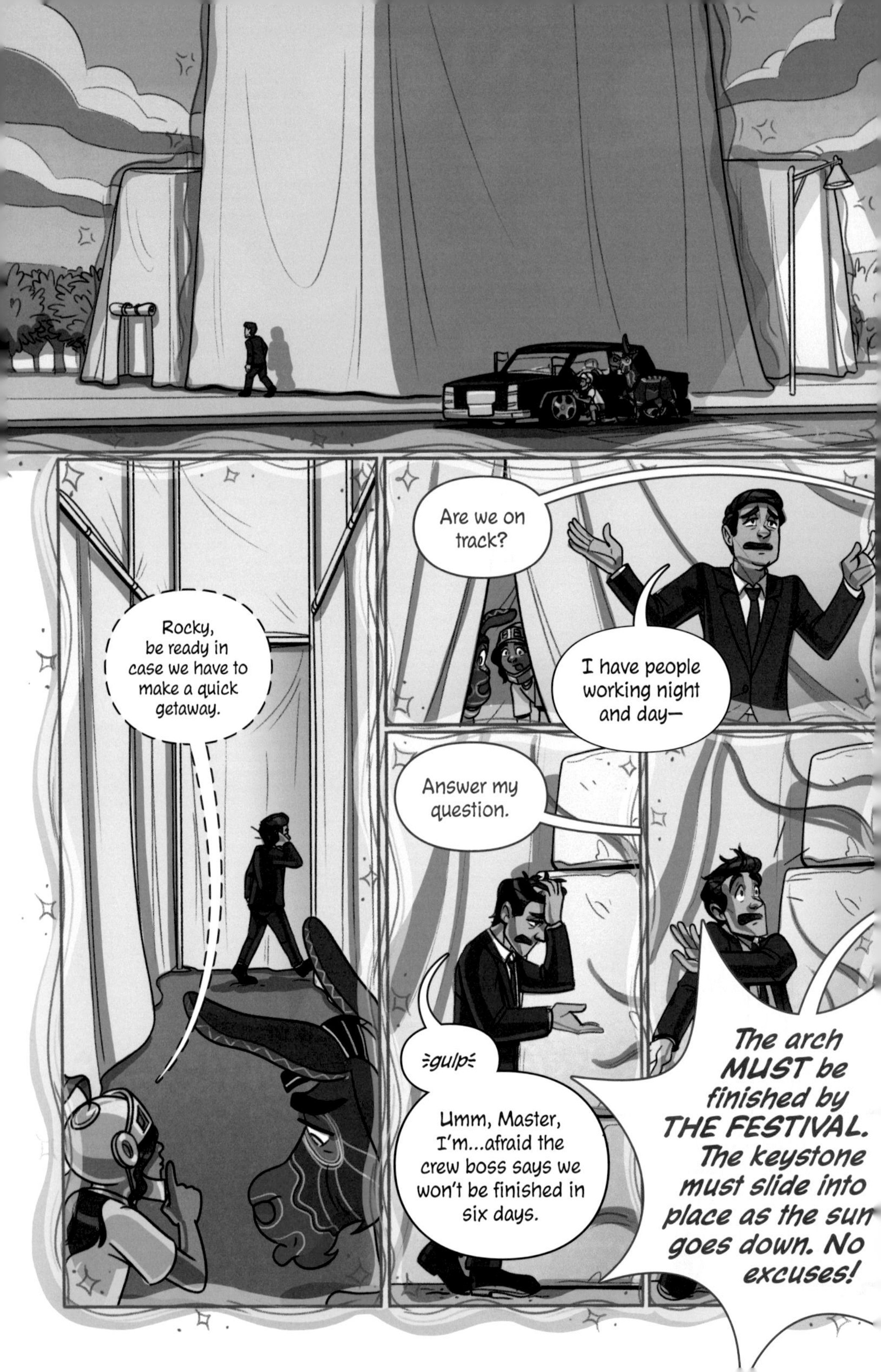
Rocky, be ready in case we have to make a quick getaway.
Are we on track?
I have people working night and day—
Answer my question.
=gulp=
Umm, Master, I'm...afraid the crew boss says we won't be finished in six days.
The arch MUST be finished by THE FESTIVAL. The keystone must slide into place as the sun goes down. No excuses!

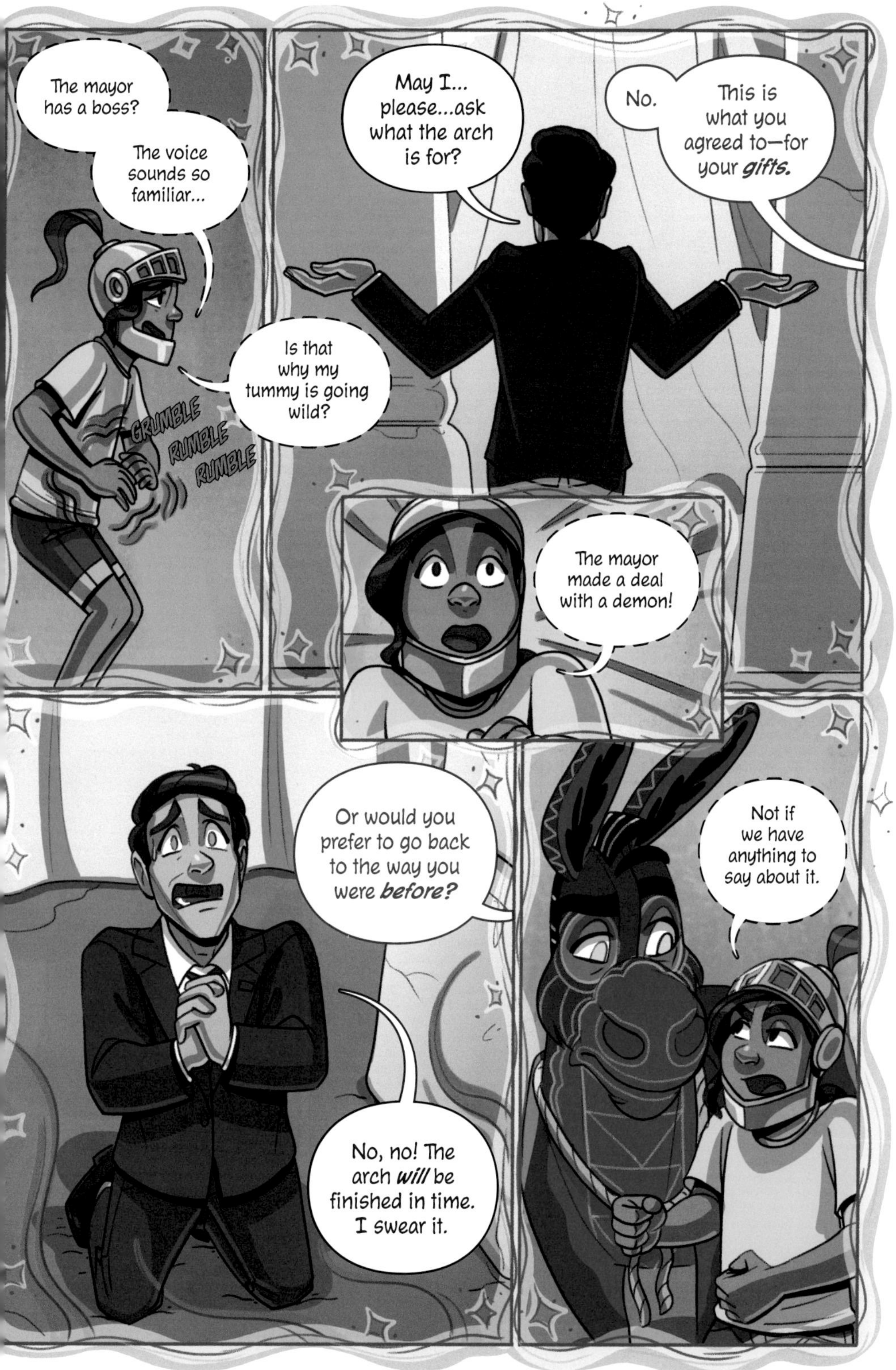
The mayor has a boss?
The voice sounds so familiar...
Is that why my tummy is going wild?
GRUMBLE RUMBLE RUMBLE
May I... please...ask what the arch is for?
No.
This is what you agreed to—for your *gifts.*
The mayor made a deal with a demon!
Or would you prefer to go back to the way you were *before?*
No, no! The arch *will* be finished in time. I swear it.
Not if we have anything to say about it.

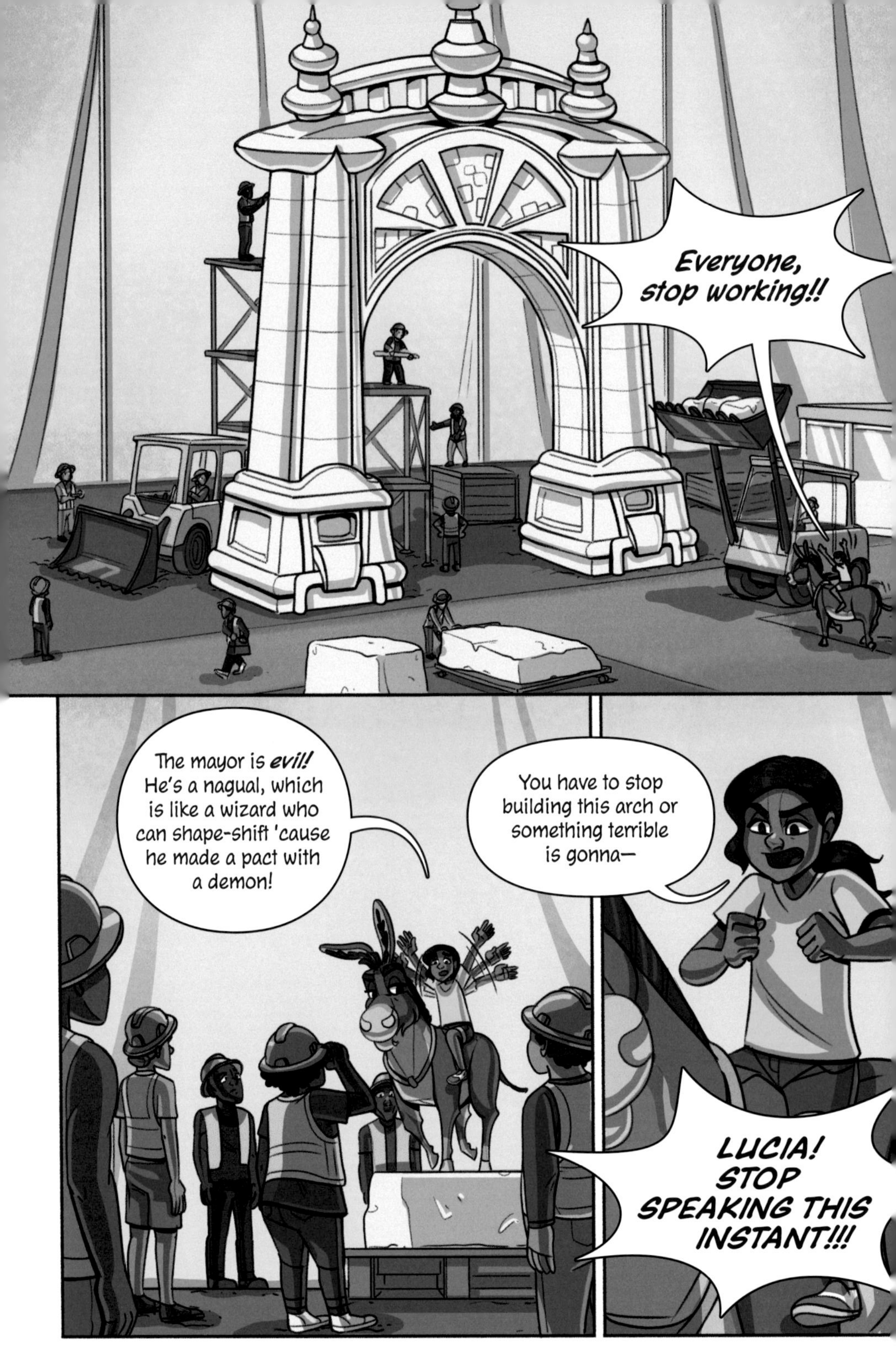
Everyone, stop working!!
The mayor is *evil!* He's a nagual, which is like a wizard who can shape-shift 'cause he made a pact with a demon!
You have to stop building this arch or something terrible is gonna—
LUCIA! STOP SPEAKING THIS INSTANT!!!

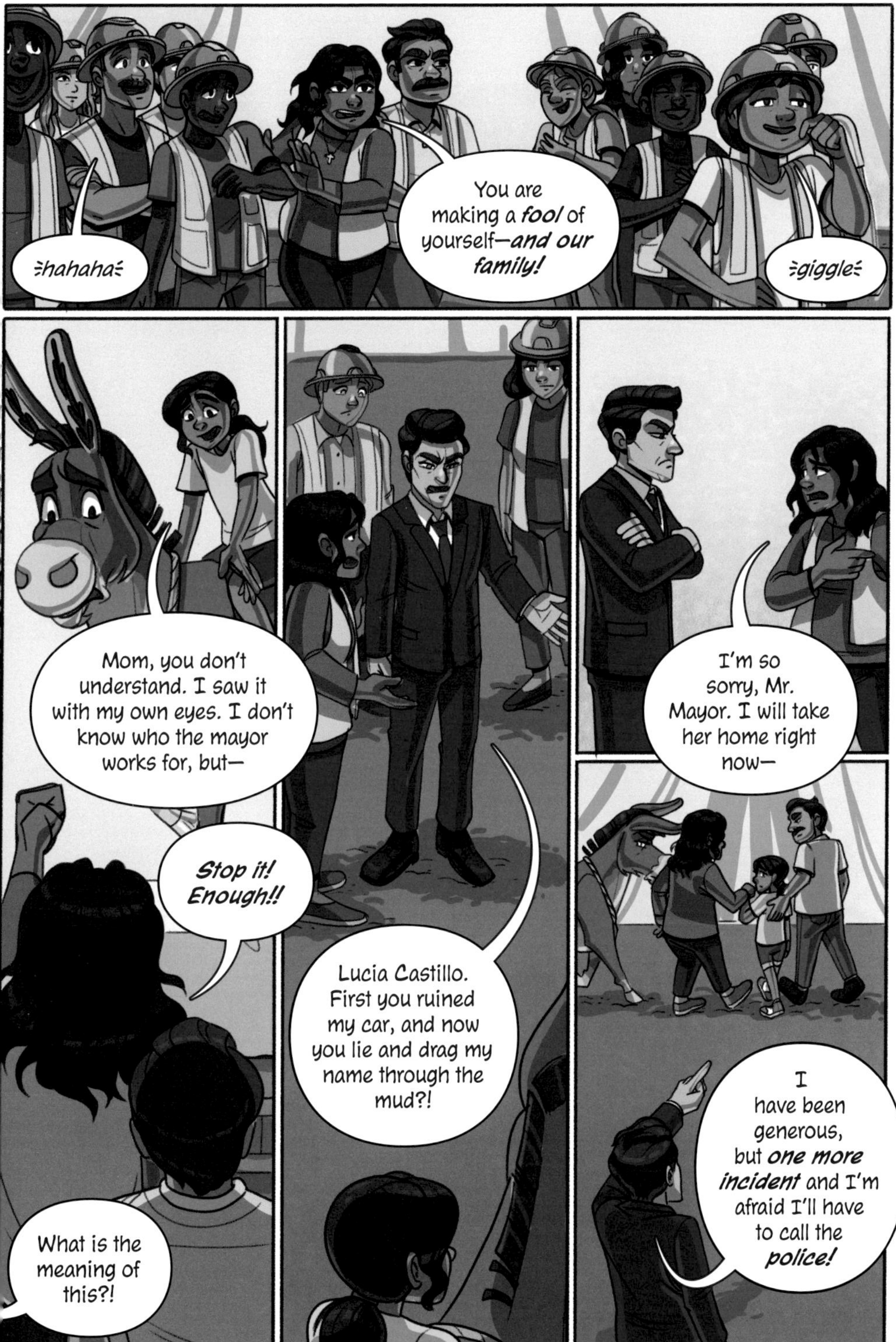

hahaha
You are making a *fool* of yourself—*and our family!*
giggle
Mom, you don't understand. I saw it with my own eyes. I don't know who the mayor works for, but—
Stop it! Enough!!
What is the meaning of this?!
Lucia Castillo. First you ruined my car, and now you lie and drag my name through the mud?!
I'm so sorry, Mr. Mayor. I will take her home right now—
I have been generous, but *one more incident* and I'm afraid I'll have to call the *police!*

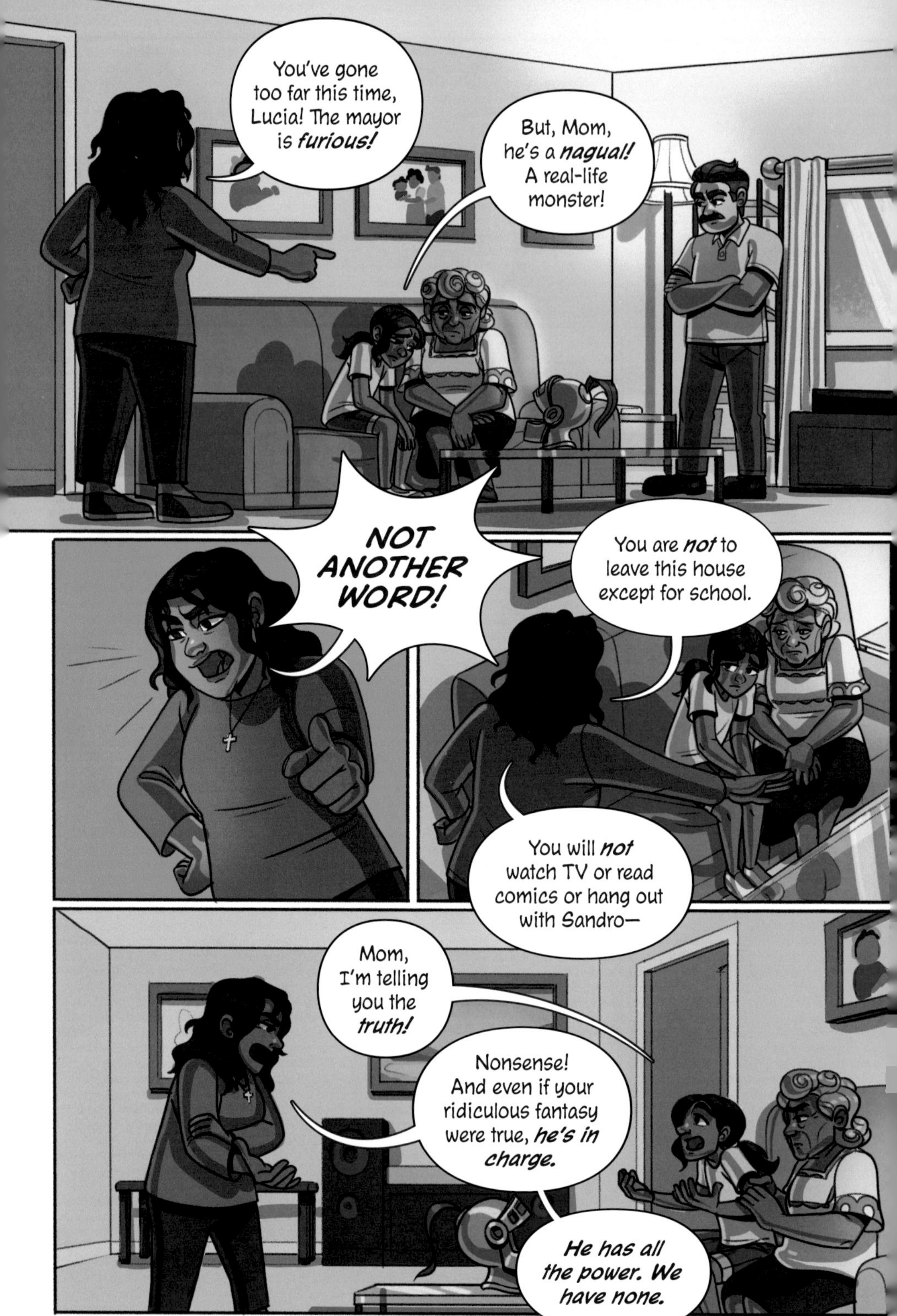
You've gone too far this time, Lucia! The mayor is *furious!*
But, Mom, he's a ***nagual!*** A real-life monster!
NOT ANOTHER WORD!
You are ***not*** to leave this house except for school.
You will ***not*** watch TV or read comics or hang out with Sandro—
Mom, I'm telling you the ***truth!***
Nonsense! And even if your ridiculous fantasy were true, ***he's in charge.***
He has all the power. We have none.

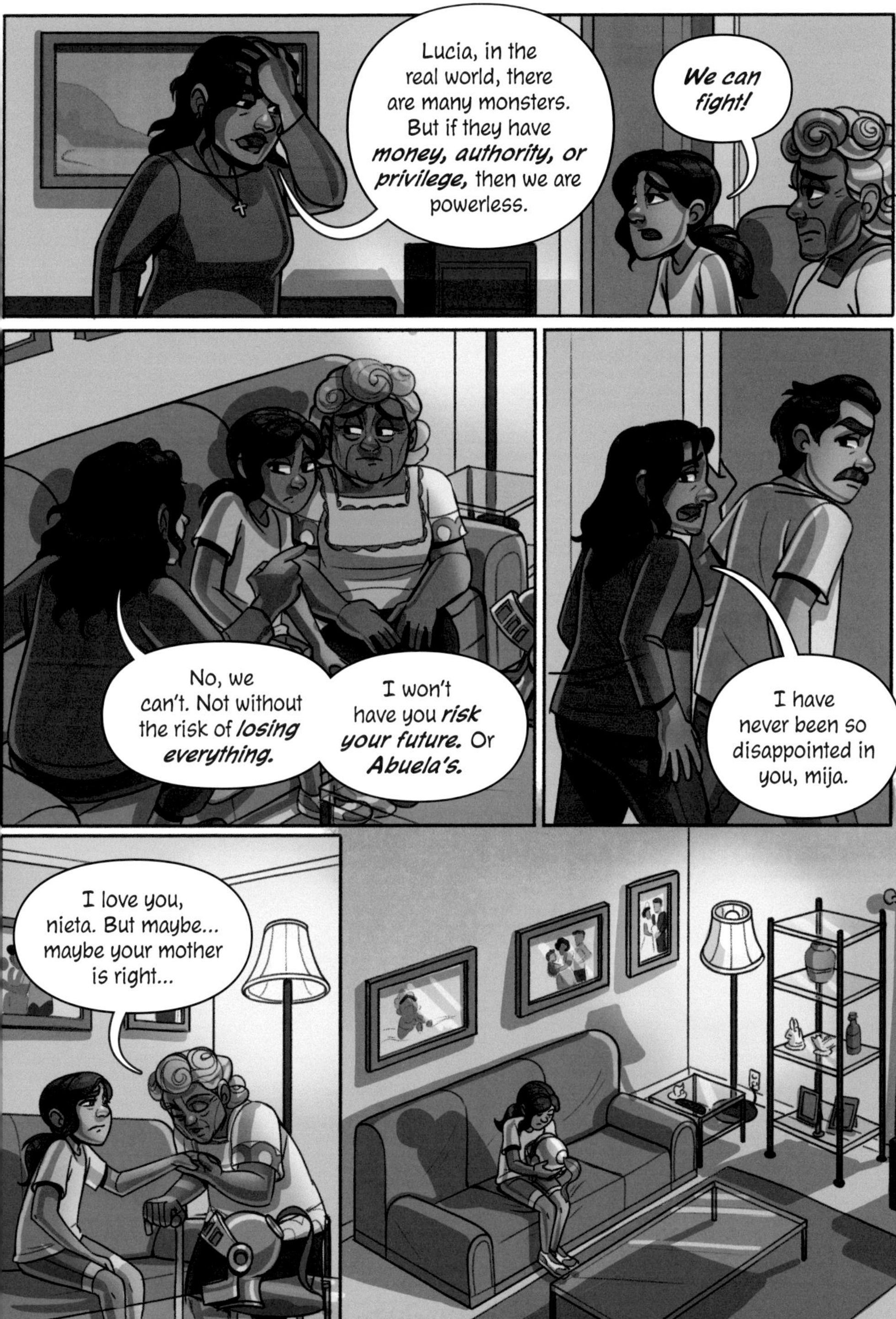
Lucia, in the real world, there are many monsters. But if they have money, authority, or privilege, then we are powerless.
We can fight!
No, we can't. Not without the risk of losing everything.
I won't have you risk your future. Or Abuela's.
I have never been so disappointed in you, mija.
I love you, nieta. But maybe... maybe your mother is right...

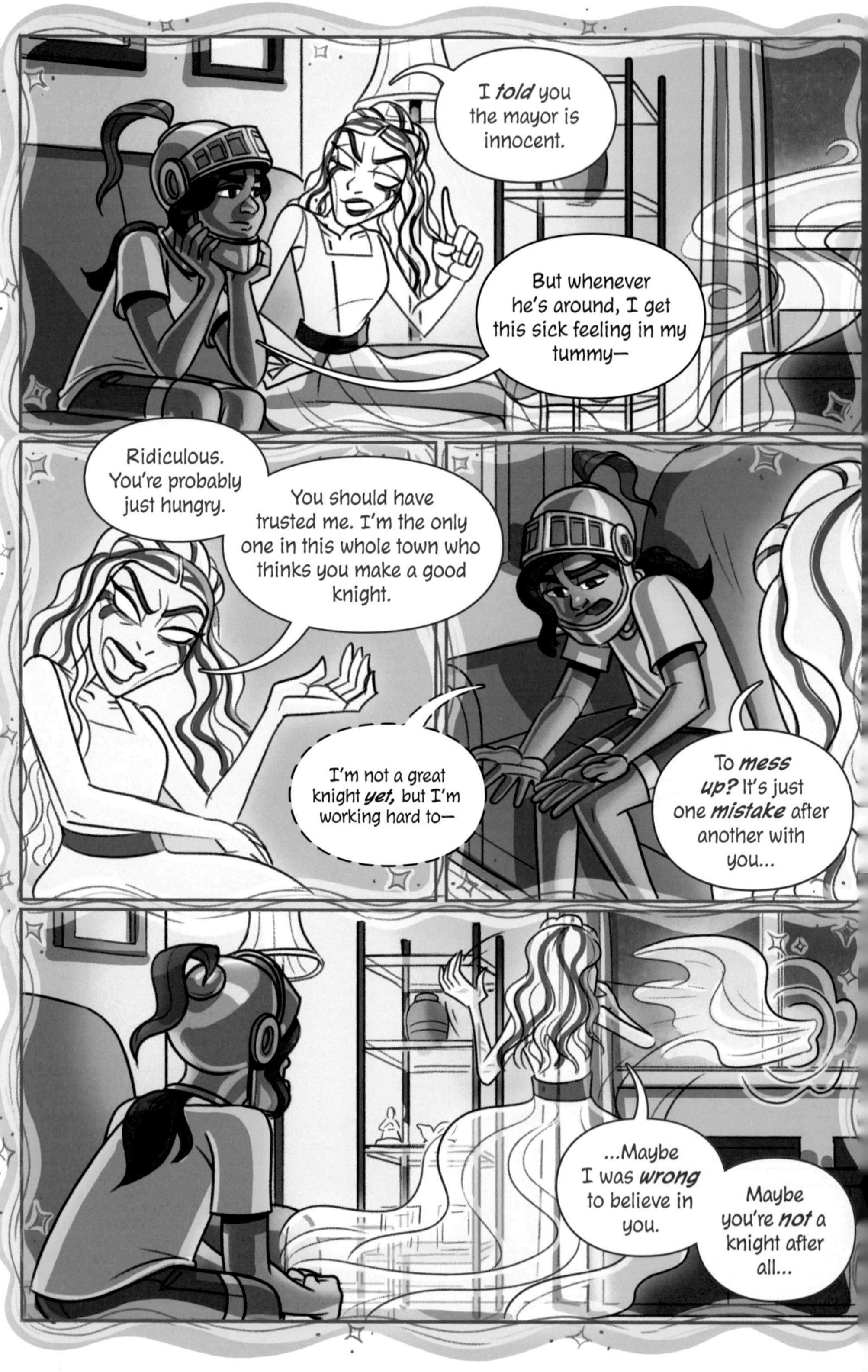
I *told* you the mayor is innocent.
But whenever he's around, I get this sick feeling in my tummy—
Ridiculous. You're probably just hungry.
You should have trusted me. I'm the only one in this whole town who thinks you make a good knight.
I'm not a great knight *yet,* but I'm working hard to—
To *mess up?* It's just one *mistake* after another with you...
...Maybe I was *wrong* to believe in you.
Maybe you're *not* a knight after all...

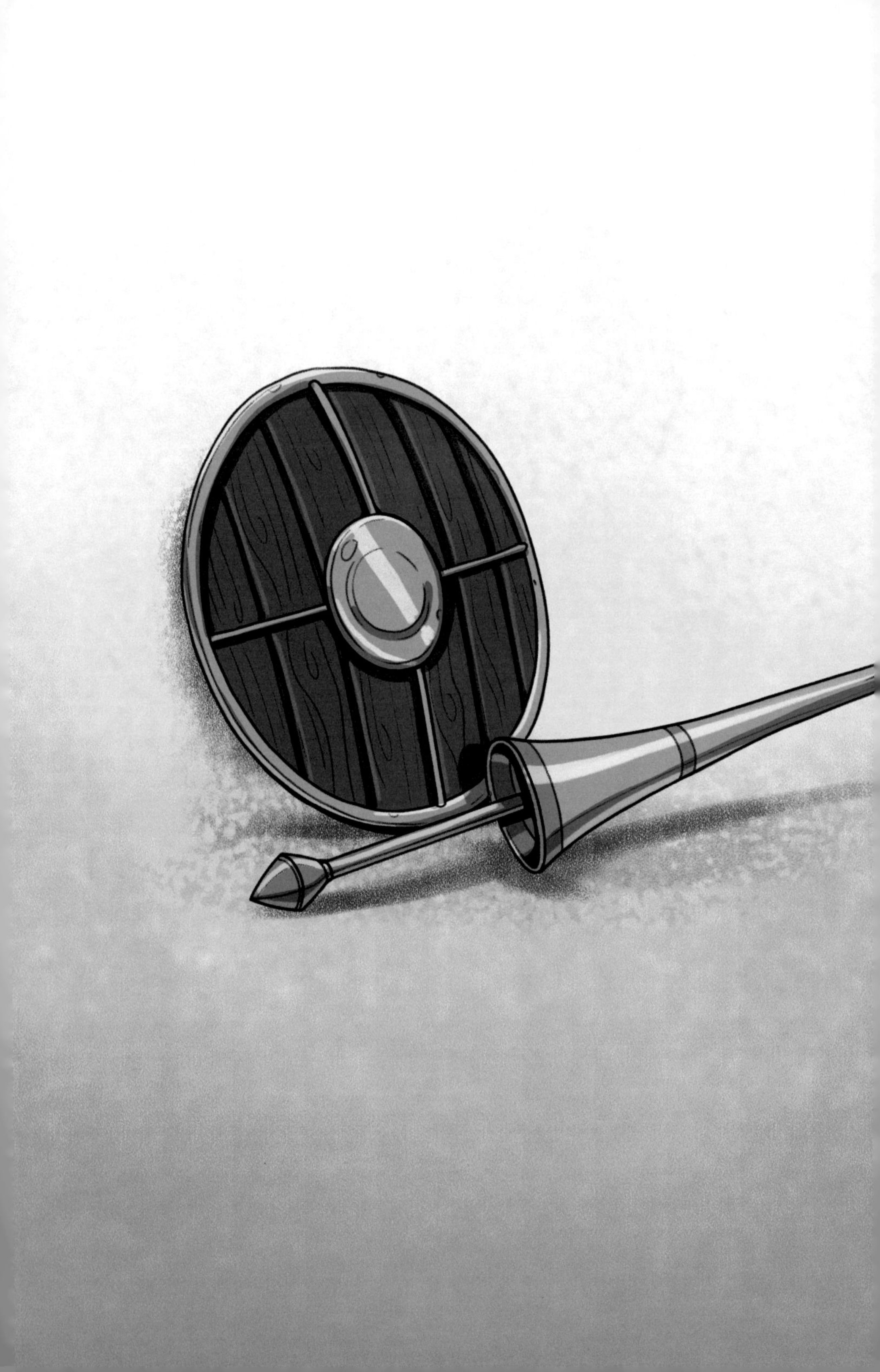

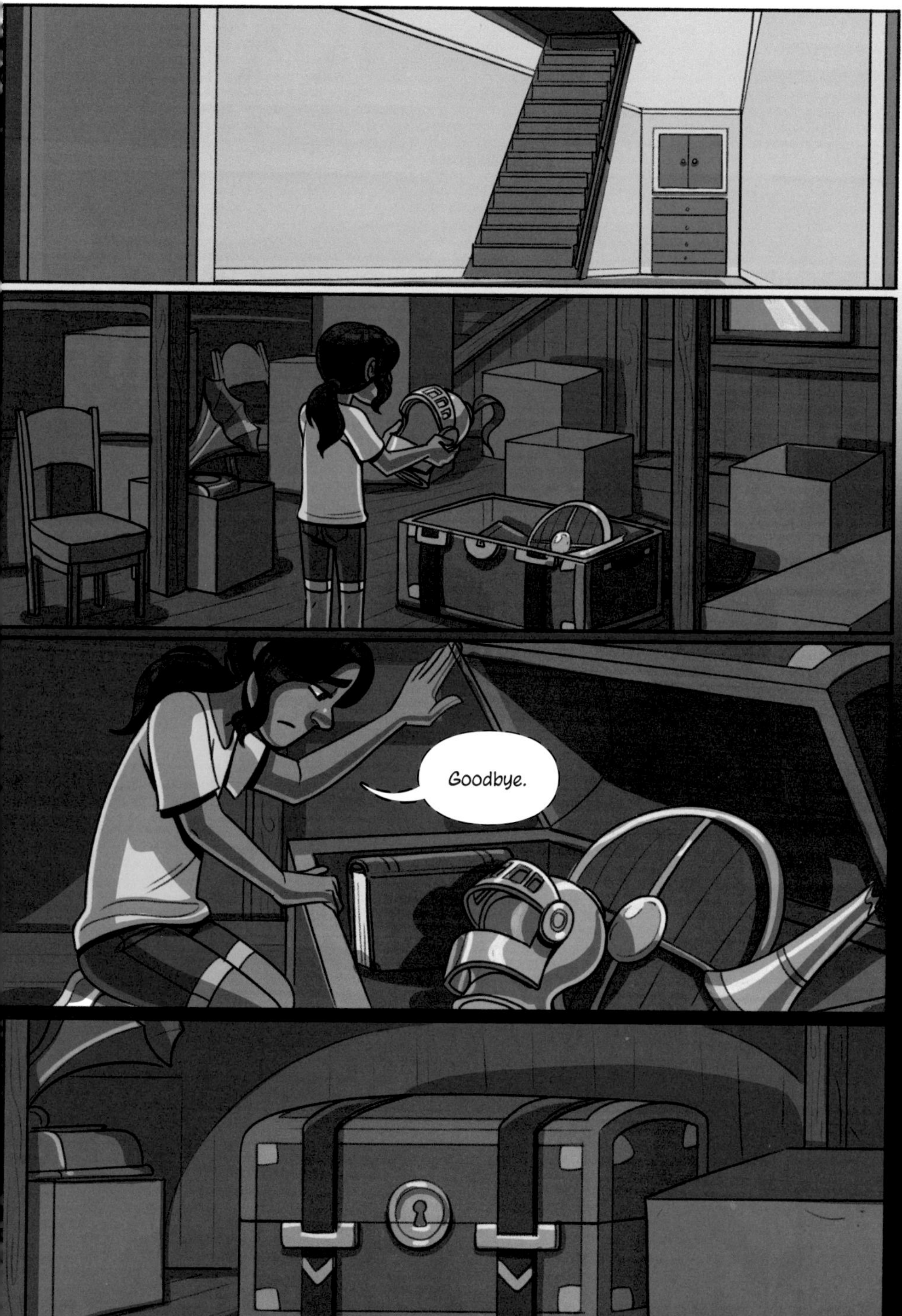
Goodbye.

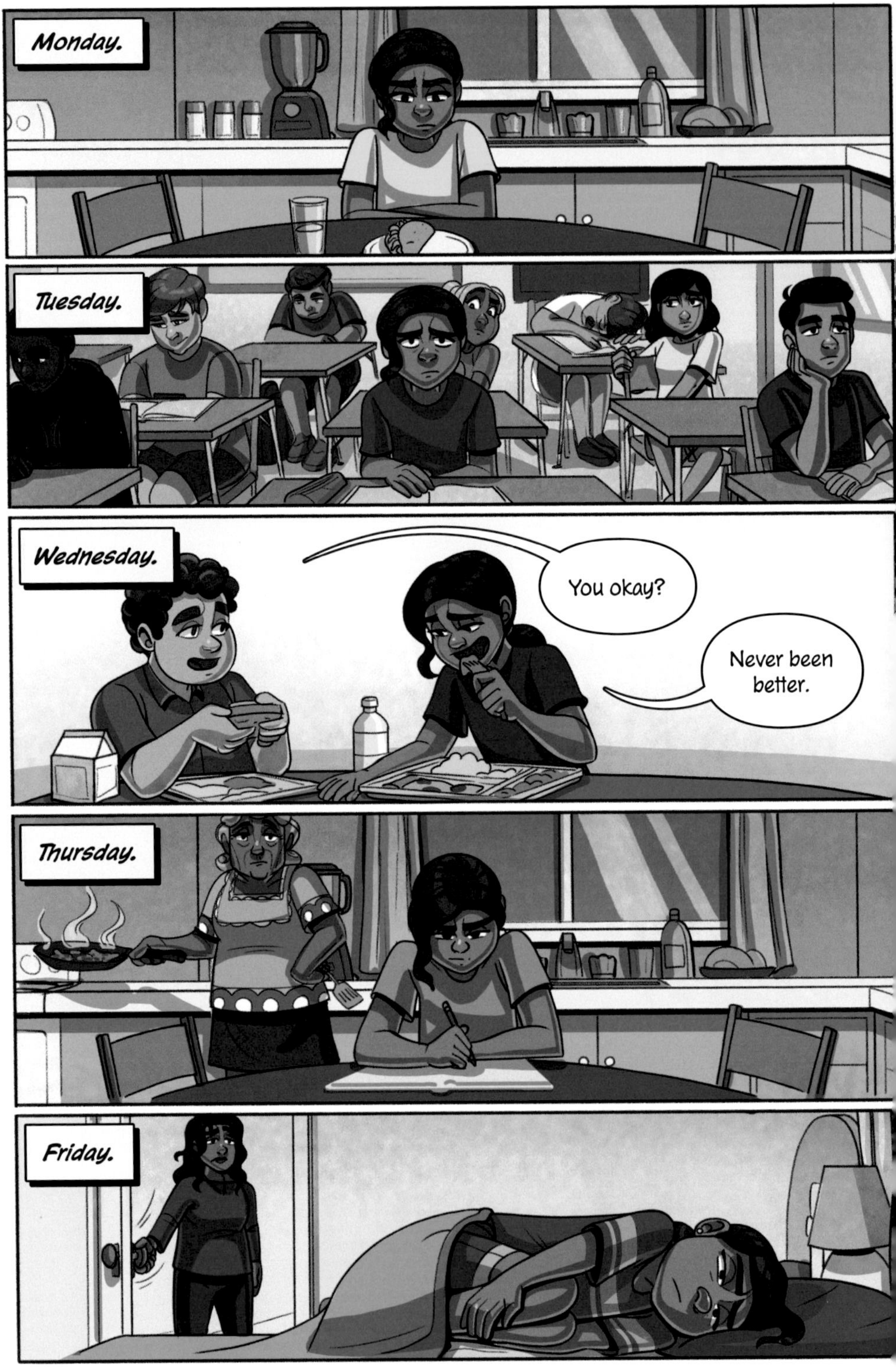
Monday.
Tuesday.
Wednesday.
You okay?
Never been better.
Thursday.
Friday.

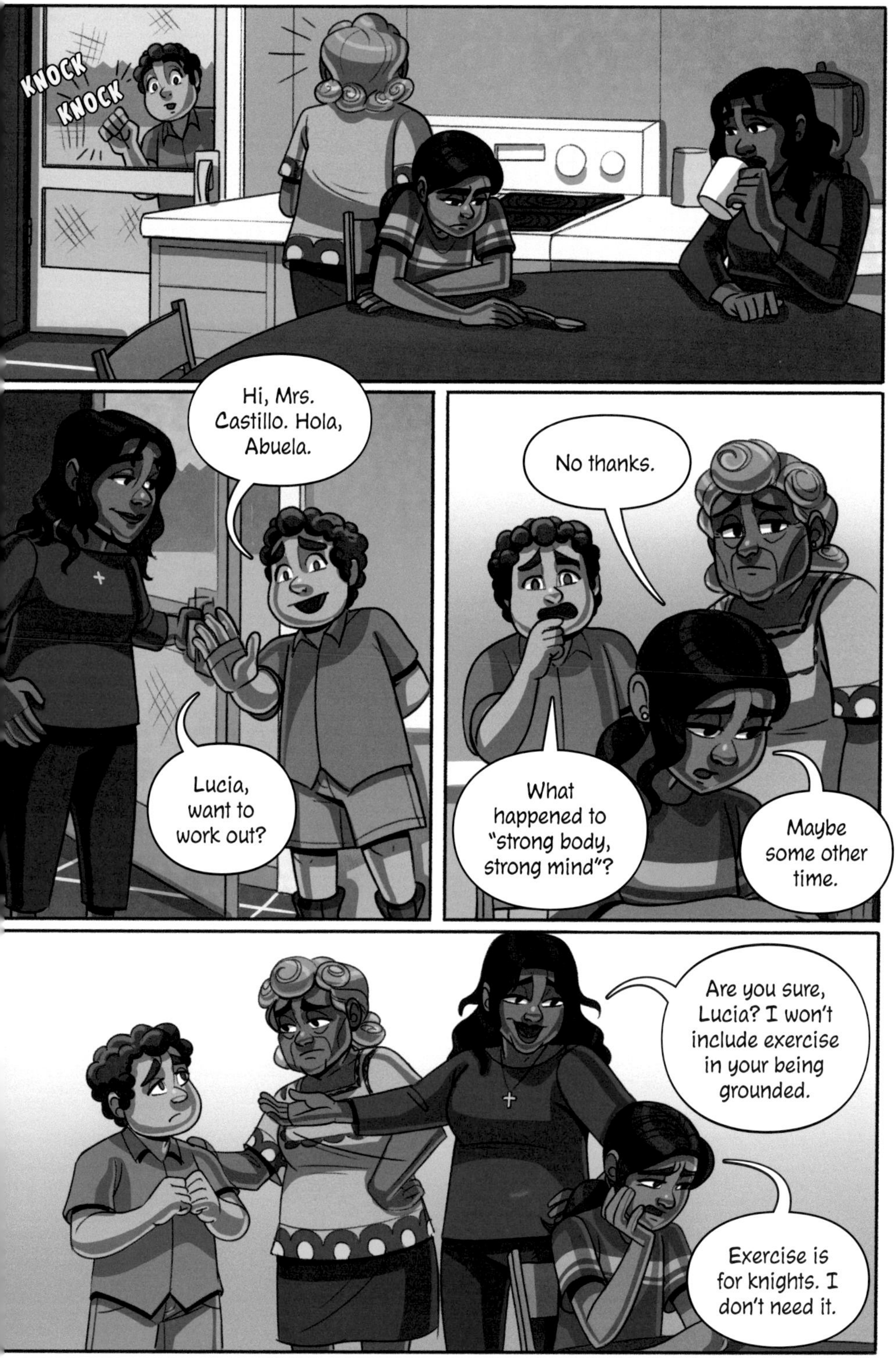
KNOCK KNOCK
Hi, Mrs. Castillo. Hola, Abuela.
Lucia, want to work out?
No thanks.
What happened to "strong body, strong mind"?
Maybe some other time.
Are you sure, Lucia? I won't include exercise in your being grounded.
Exercise is for knights. I don't need it.

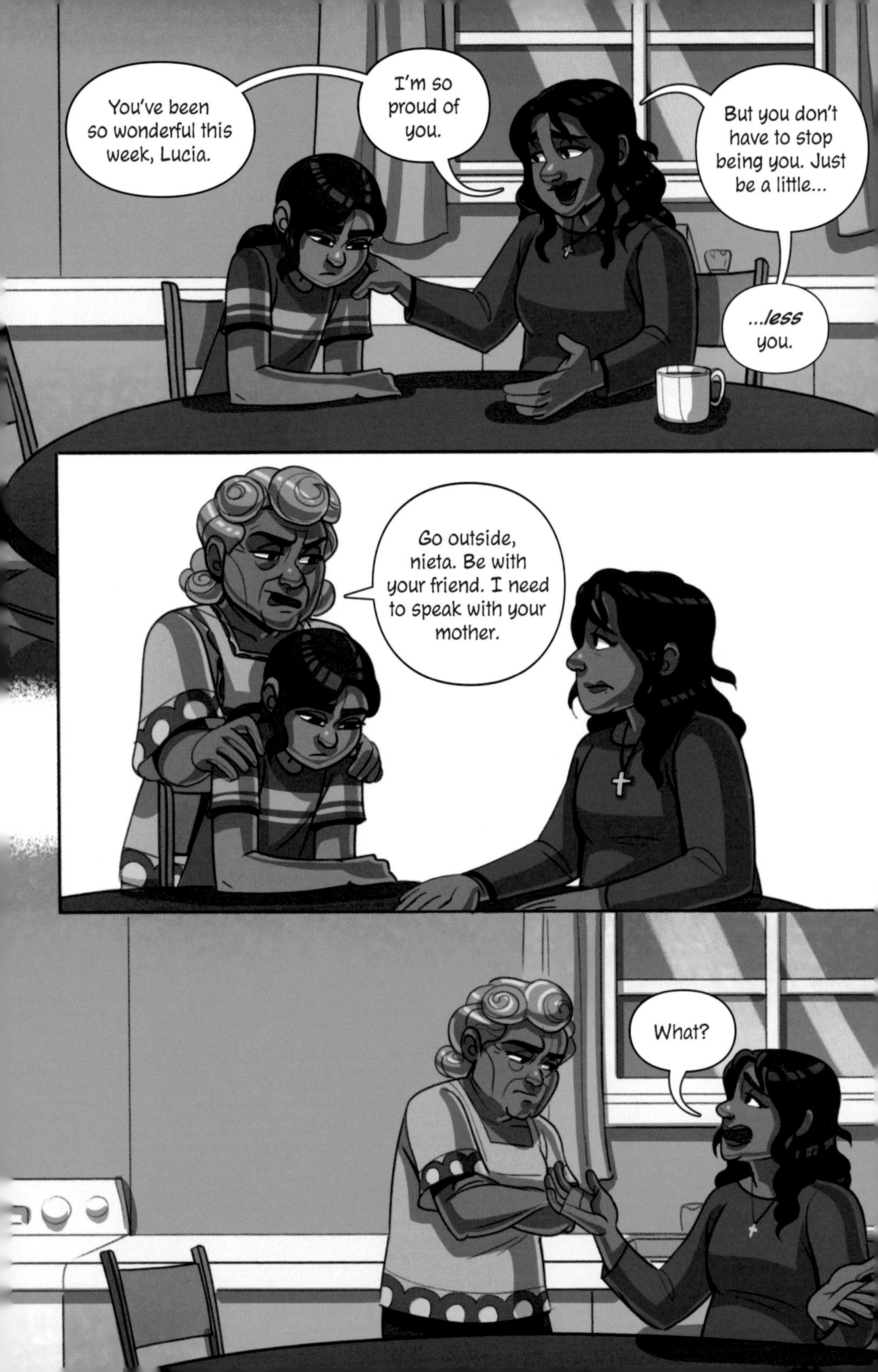
You've been so wonderful this week, Lucia.
I'm so proud of you.
But you don't have to stop being you. Just be a little...
...*less* you.
Go outside, nieta. Be with your friend. I need to speak with your mother.
What?

I thought I raised you better. Never tell a child to be less. Encourage them to be *more*.

Mamá, you don't understand—

Let's go to the tree house.

But it's sooo farrr...

KNIGHT'S CODE!

1. thou shalt help the helpless and defend the innocents!
2. thou shalt support and protect thy family and friends!
3. thou shalt guard the animals and keep the corn clean!
4. ... shalt be generous to those less fortunate!
5. ... shalt not lie, and remain faithful to thy pledged word.
6. thou shalt make war against the wicked without mercy
7. thou must always be the champion of right and good, against injustice and evil!
8) You must always trust (& listen) to your BEST Friend!

You can't give up on being a knight! It's your *dream*.

#2. Protect and support your *family*. And the only way I can do that is to *stop being me*.

But you can't *not* be you.

Wouldn't your family be happier if you weren't a ballerina?

Ballerin**o**. And yeah, probably...

...but it's not *their* life.

And one day, when they see *how good I am*, and *how happy it makes me*, and how I'm making the world a *better place* by *being me*— they'll get it.

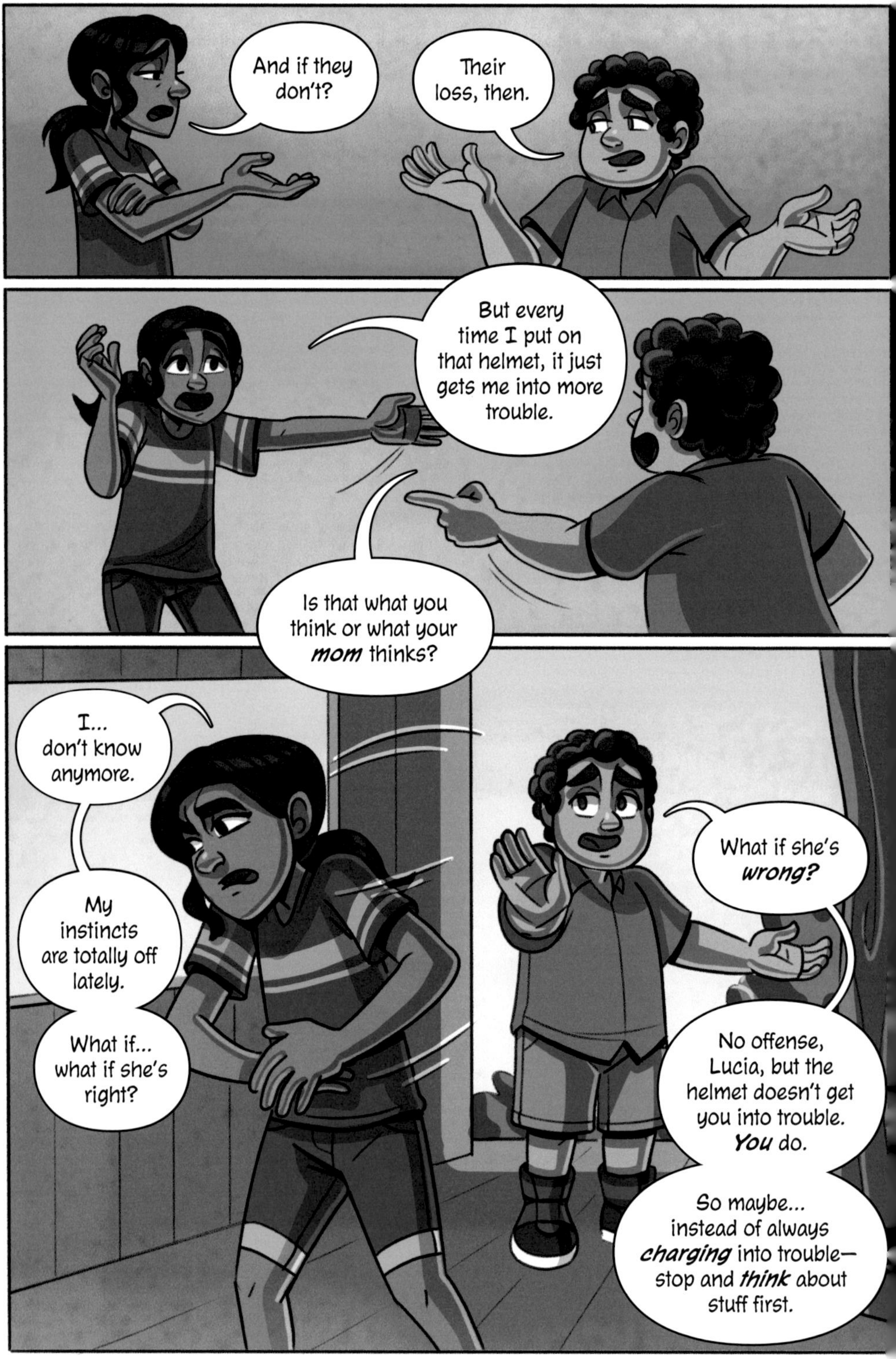
And if they don't?
Their loss, then.
But every time I put on that helmet, it just gets me into more trouble.
Is that what you think or what your *mom* thinks?
I... don't know anymore.
My instincts are totally off lately.
What if... what if she's right?
What if she's *wrong?*
No offense, Lucia, but the helmet doesn't get you into trouble. *You* do.
So maybe... instead of always *charging* into trouble—stop and *think* about stuff first.

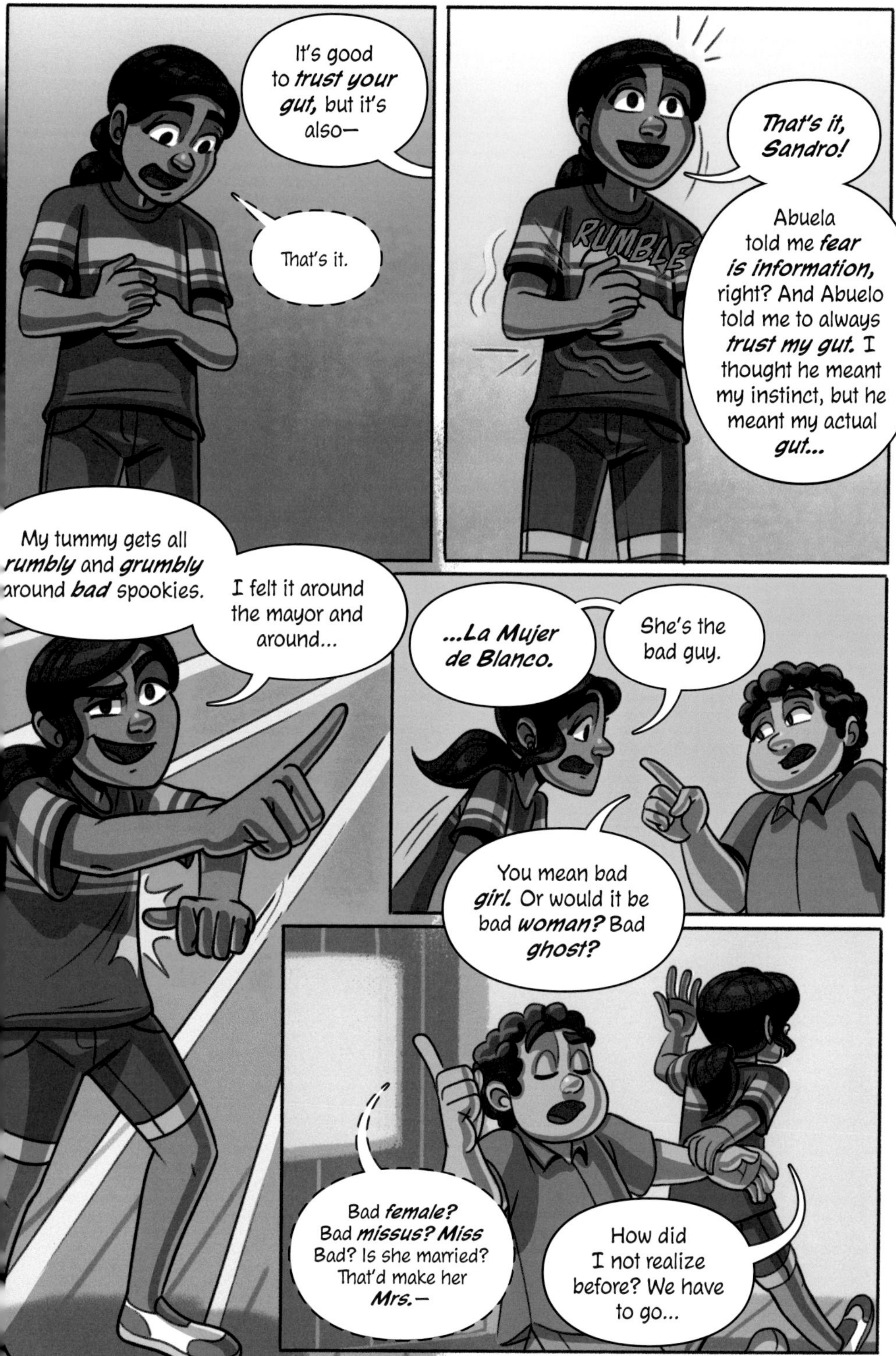
It's good to *trust your gut,* but it's also—
That's it.
That's it, Sandro!
Abuela told me *fear is information,* right? And Abuelo told me to always *trust my gut.* I thought he meant my instinct, but he meant my actual *gut...*
RUMBLE
My tummy gets all *rumbly* and *grumbly* around *bad* spookies.
I felt it around the mayor and around...
...La Mujer de Blanco.
She's the bad guy.
You mean bad *girl.* Or would it be bad *woman?* Bad *ghost?*
Bad *female?* Bad *missus? Miss* Bad? Is she married? That'd make her *Mrs.—*
How did I not realize before? We have to go...

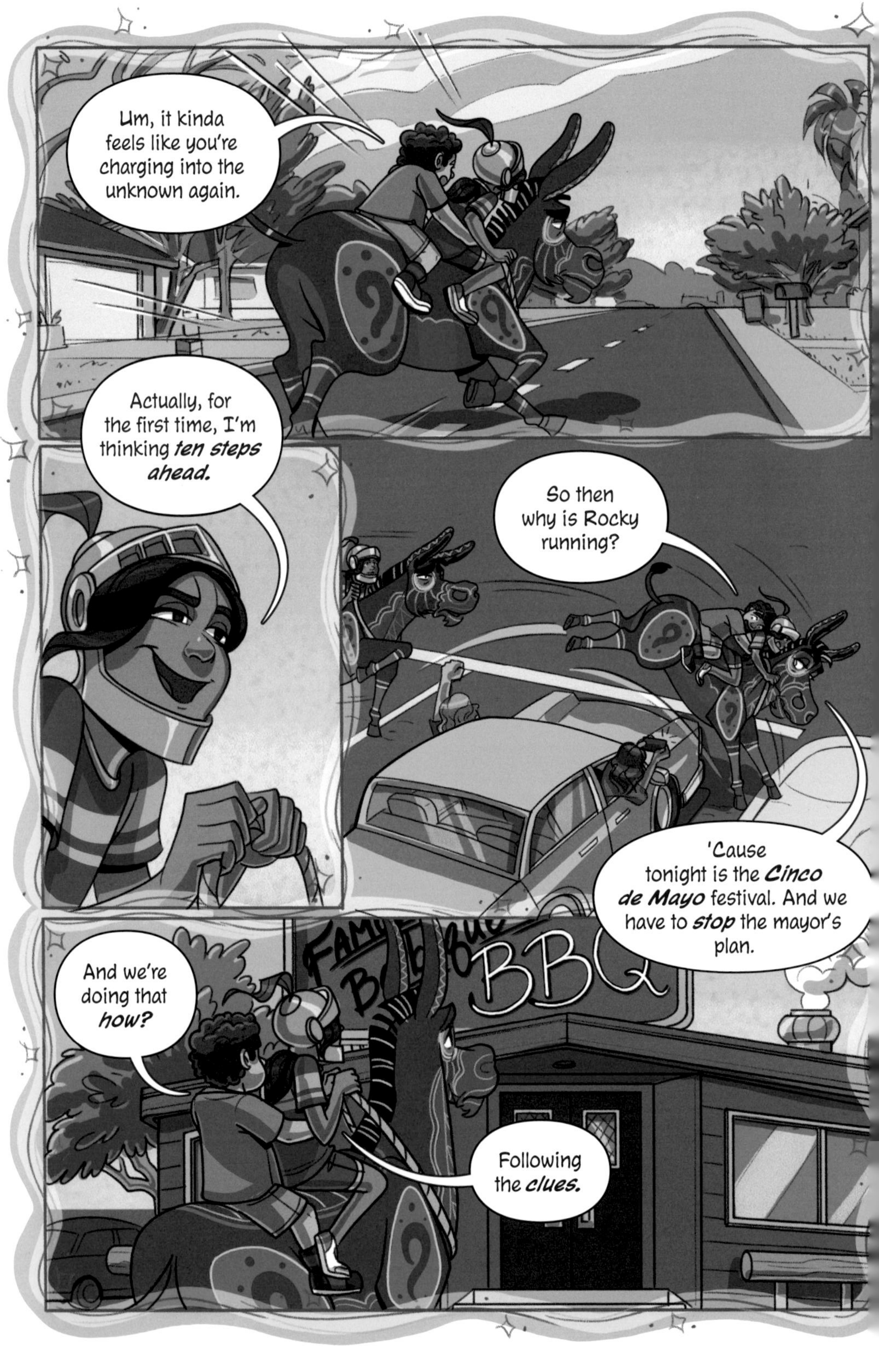
Um, it kinda feels like you're charging into the unknown again.
Actually, for the first time, I'm thinking *ten steps ahead.*
So then why is Rocky running?
'Cause tonight is the *Cinco de Mayo* festival. And we have to *stop* the mayor's plan.
BBQ
And we're doing that *how?*
Following the *clues.*

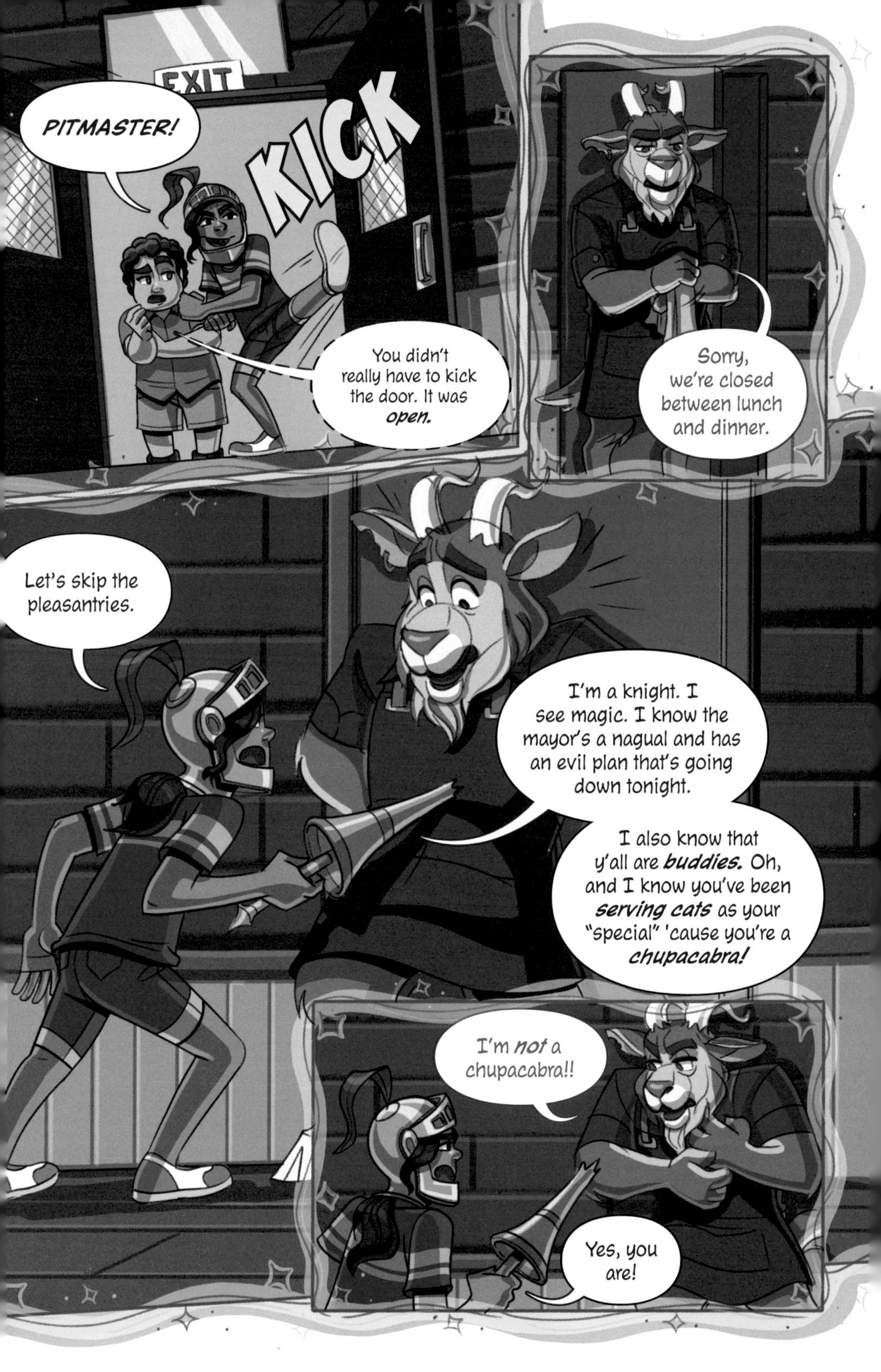

EXIT
PITMASTER!
KICK
You didn't really have to kick the door. It was *open.*
Sorry, we're closed between lunch and dinner.
Let's skip the pleasantries.
I'm a knight. I see magic. I know the mayor's a nagual and has an evil plan that's going down tonight.
I also know that y'all are *buddies.* Oh, and I know you've been *serving cats* as your "special" 'cause you're a *chupacabra!*
I'm *not* a chupacabra!!
Yes, you are!

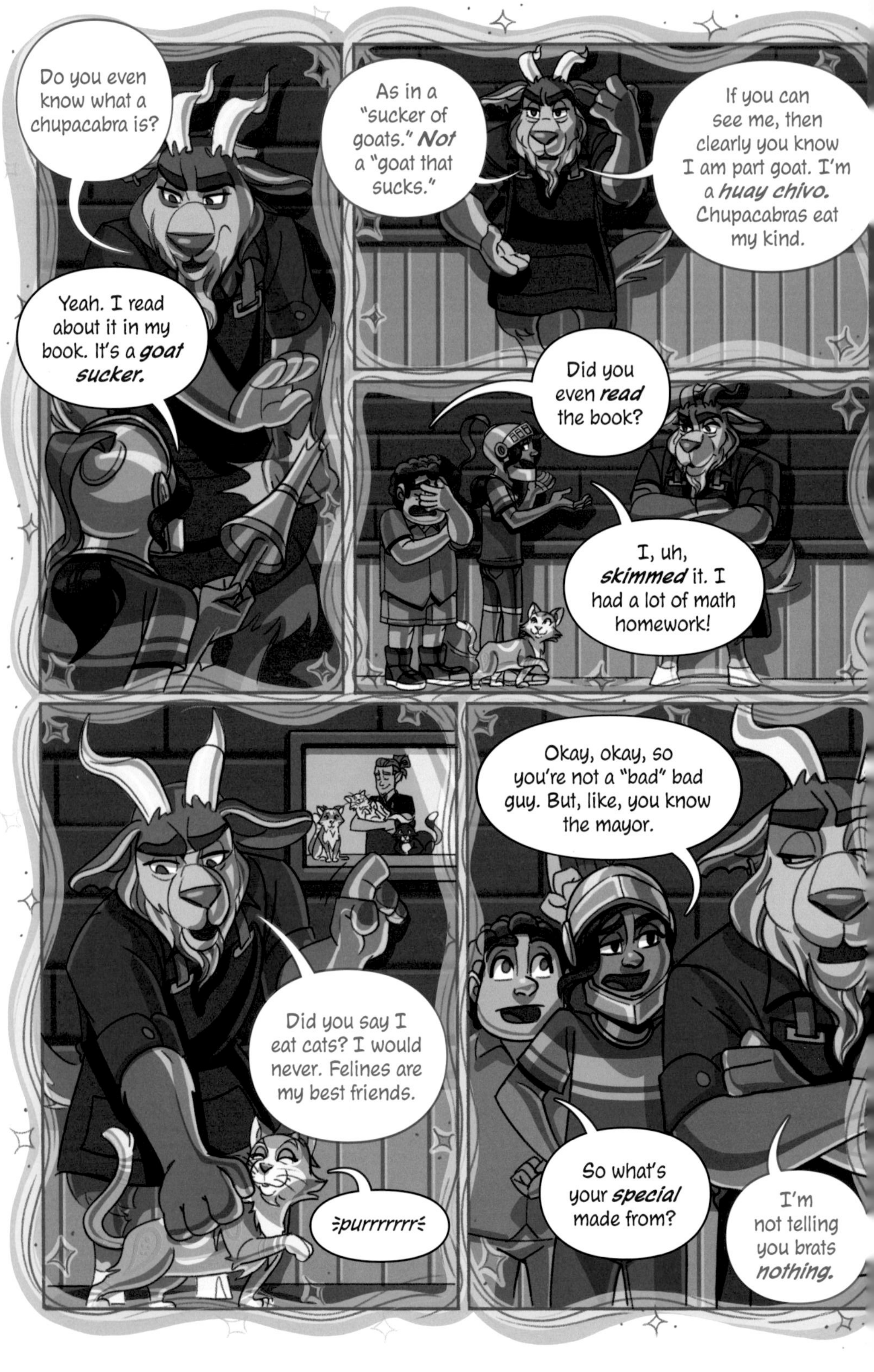
Do you even know what a chupacabra is?
Yeah. I read about it in my book. It's a *goat sucker.*
As in a "sucker of goats." *Not* a "goat that sucks."
If you can see me, then clearly you know I am part goat. I'm a *huay chivo.* Chupacabras eat my kind.
Did you even *read* the book?
I, uh, *skimmed* it. I had a lot of math homework!
Did you say I eat cats? I would never. Felines are my best friends.
purrrrrrr
Okay, okay, so you're not a "bad" bad guy. But, like, you know the mayor.
So what's your *special* made from?
I'm not telling you brats *nothing.*

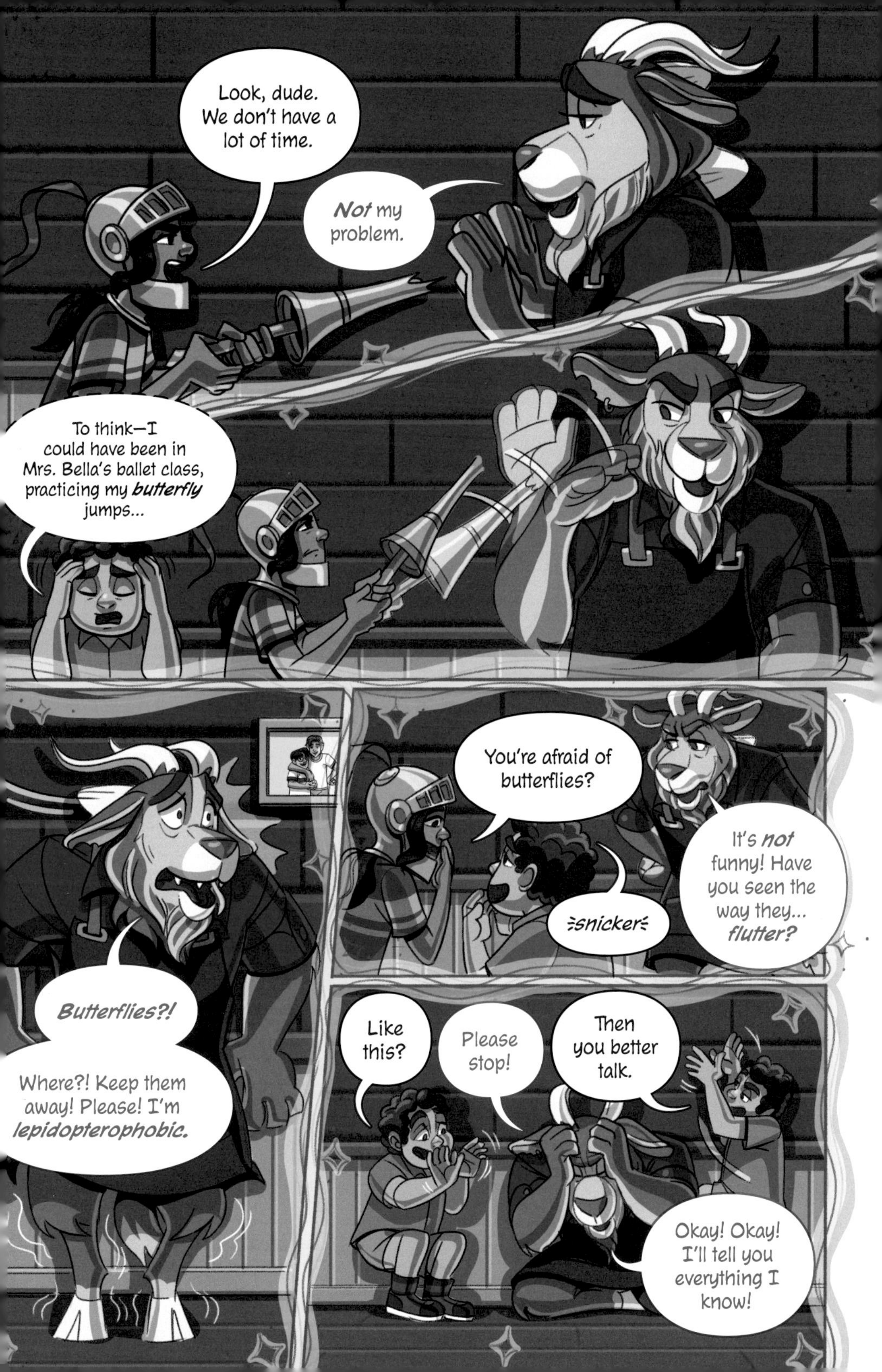
Look, dude. We don't have a lot of time.
Not my problem.
To think—I could have been in Mrs. Bella's ballet class, practicing my *butterfly* jumps...
Butterflies?!
Where?! Keep them away! Please! I'm *lepidopterophobic.*
You're afraid of butterflies?
snicker
It's *not* funny! Have you seen the way they... *flutter?*
Like this?
Please stop!
Then you better talk.
Okay! Okay! I'll tell you everything I know!

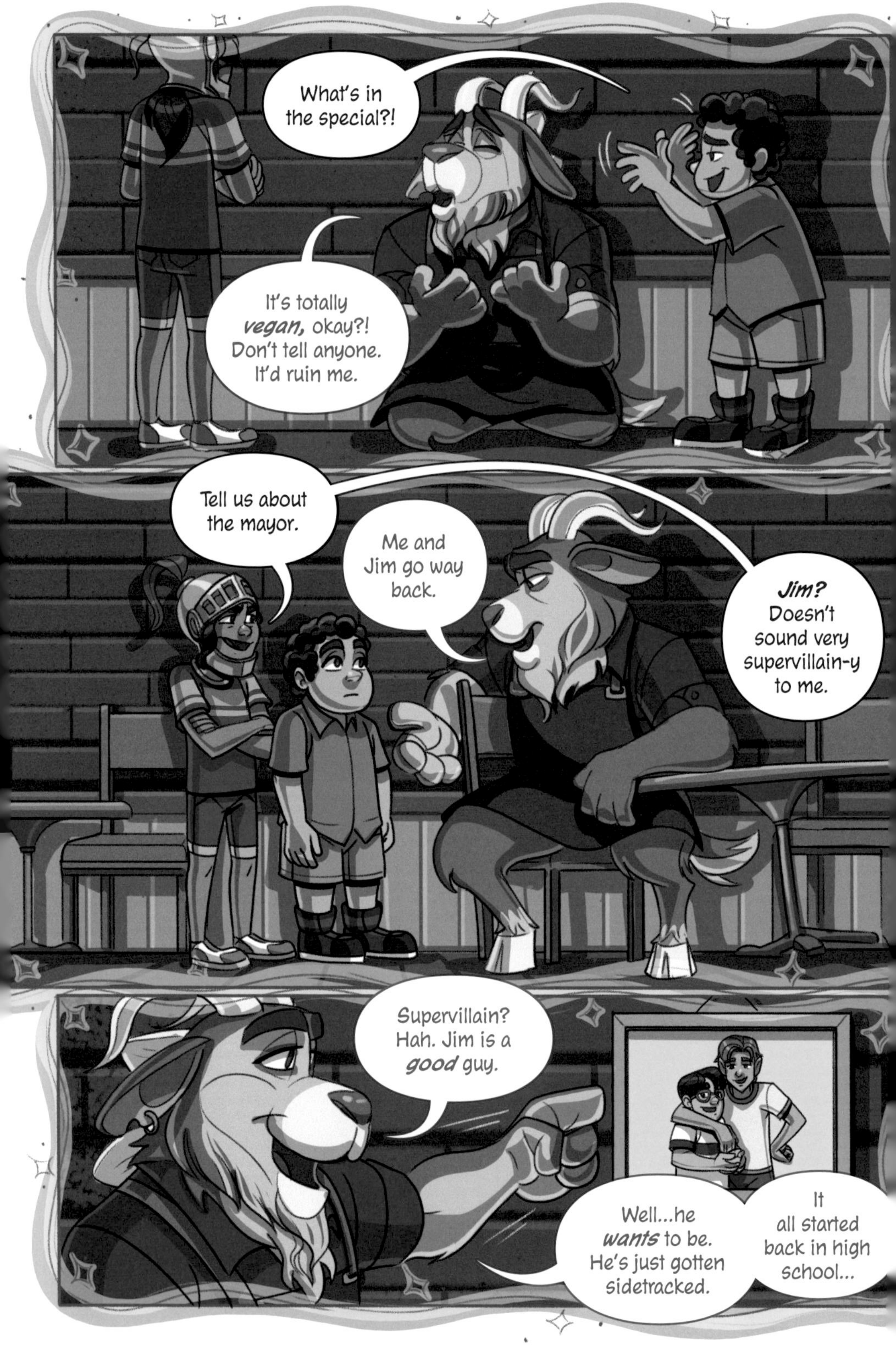
What's in the special?!
It's totally *vegan,* okay?! Don't tell anyone. It'd ruin me.
Tell us about the mayor.
Me and Jim go way back.
Jim? Doesn't sound very supervillain-y to me.
Supervillain? Hah. Jim is a *good* guy.
Well...he *wants* to be. He's just gotten sidetracked.
It all started back in high school...

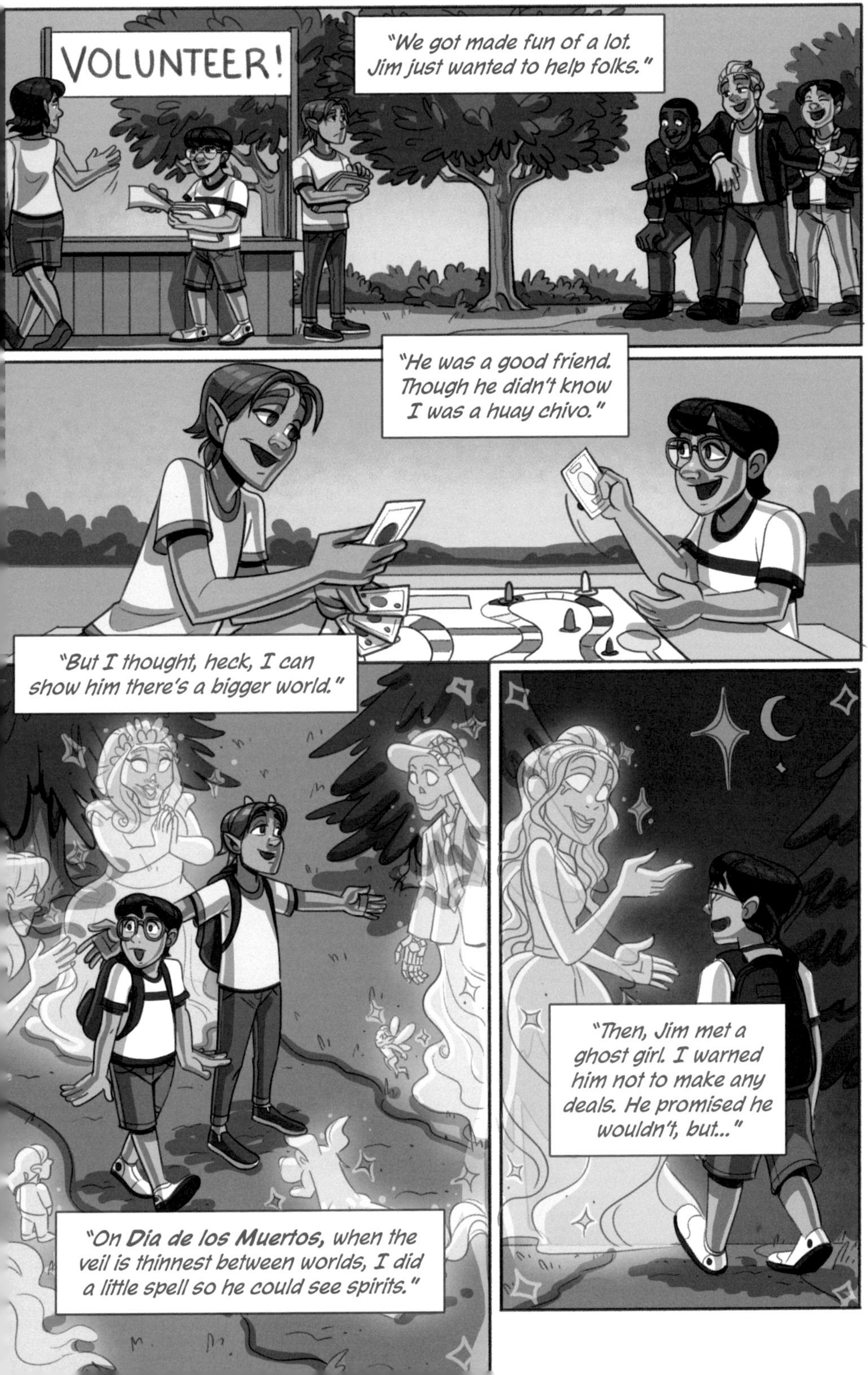
VOLUNTEER!
"We got made fun of a lot. Jim just wanted to help folks."
"He was a good friend. Though he didn't know I was a huay chivo."
"But I thought, heck, I can show him there's a bigger world."
"On *Dia de los Muertos,* when the veil is thinnest between worlds, I did a little spell so he could see spirits."
"Then, Jim met a ghost girl. I warned him not to make any deals. He promised he wouldn't, but..."

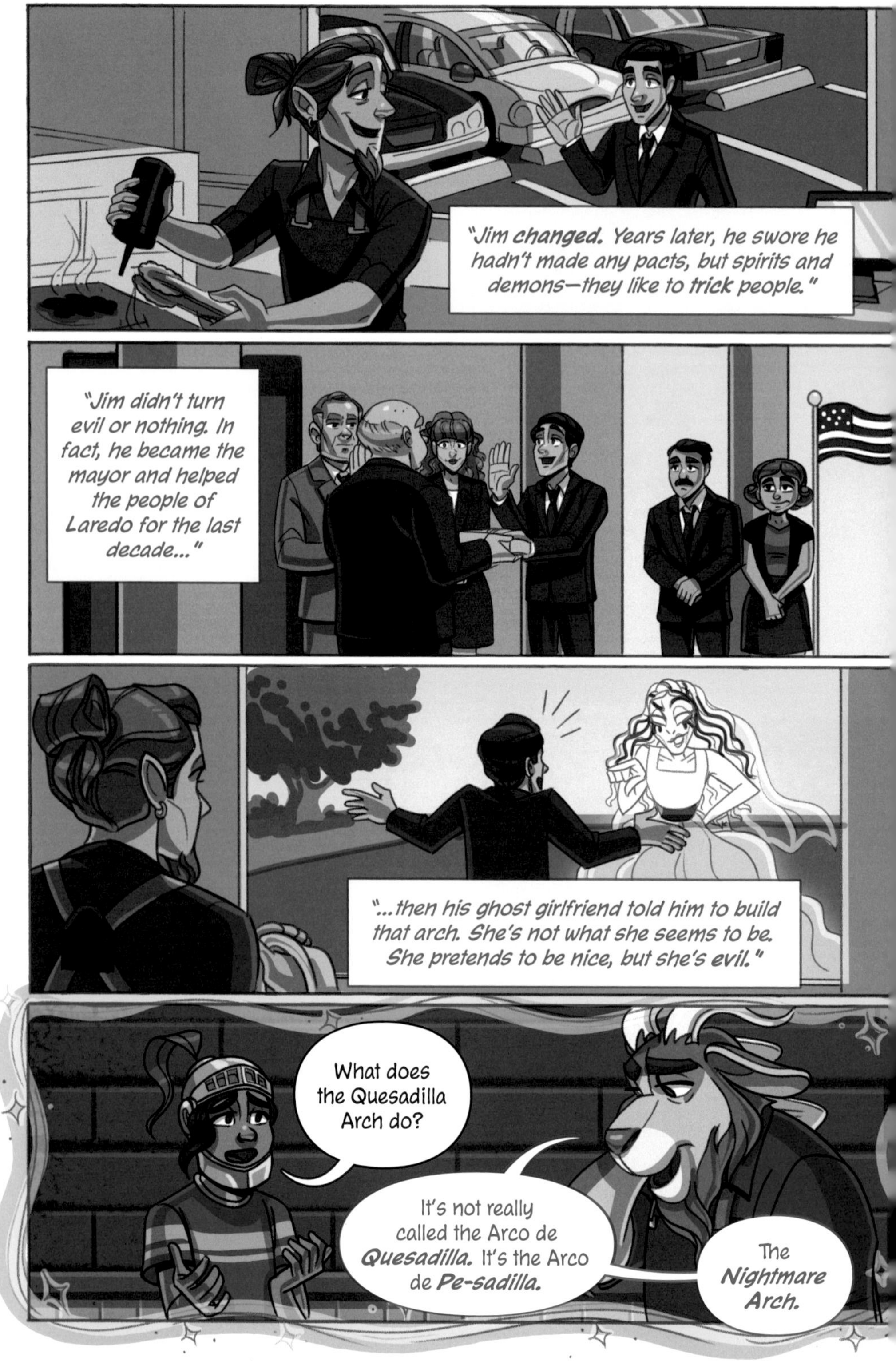
"Jim changed. Years later, he swore he hadn't made any pacts, but spirits and demons—they like to trick people."
"Jim didn't turn evil or nothing. In fact, he became the mayor and helped the people of Laredo for the last decade..."
"...then his ghost girlfriend told him to build that arch. She's not what she seems to be. She pretends to be nice, but she's evil."
What does the Quesadilla Arch do?
It's not really called the Arco de Quesadilla. It's the Arco de Pe-sadilla.
The Nightmare Arch.

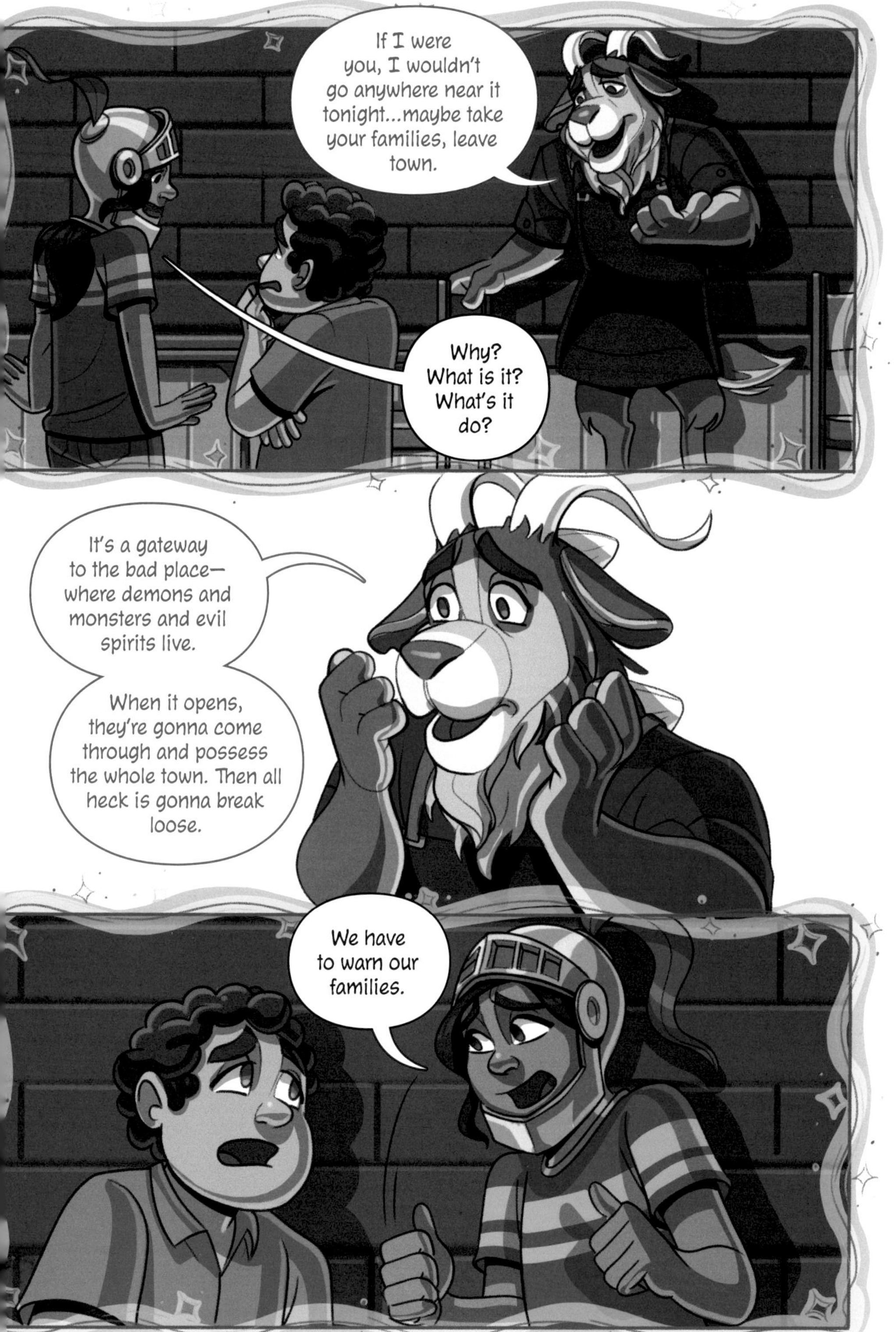

If I were you, I wouldn't go anywhere near it tonight...maybe take your families, leave town.
Why? What is it? What's it do?
It's a gateway to the bad place—where demons and monsters and evil spirits live.
When it opens, they're gonna come through and possess the whole town. Then all heck is gonna break loose.
We have to warn our families.

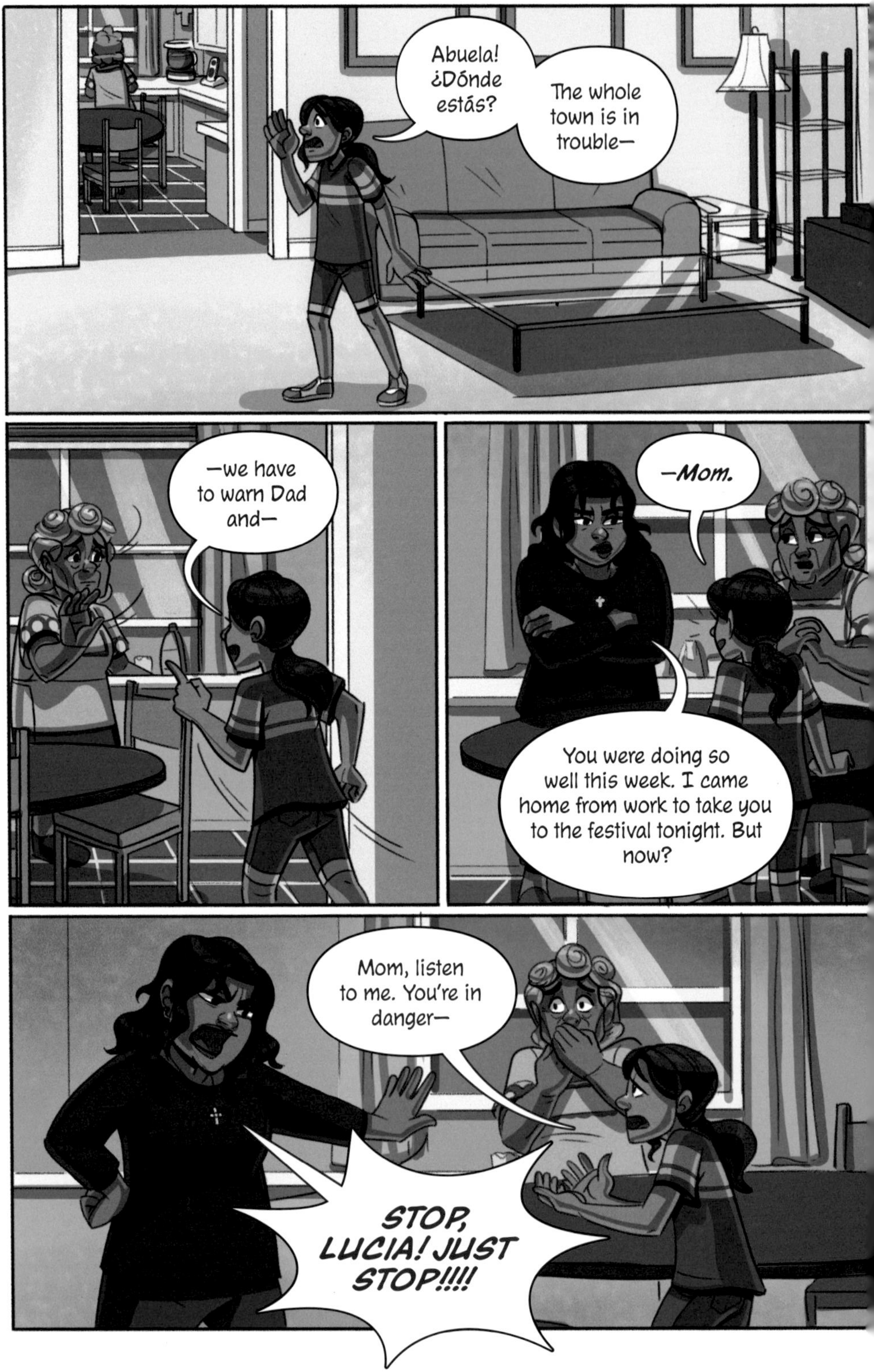
Abuela! ¿Dónde estás?
The whole town is in trouble—
—we have to warn Dad and—
—Mom.
You were doing so well this week. I came home from work to take you to the festival tonight. But now?
Mom, listen to me. You're in danger—
STOP, LUCIA! JUST STOP!!!!

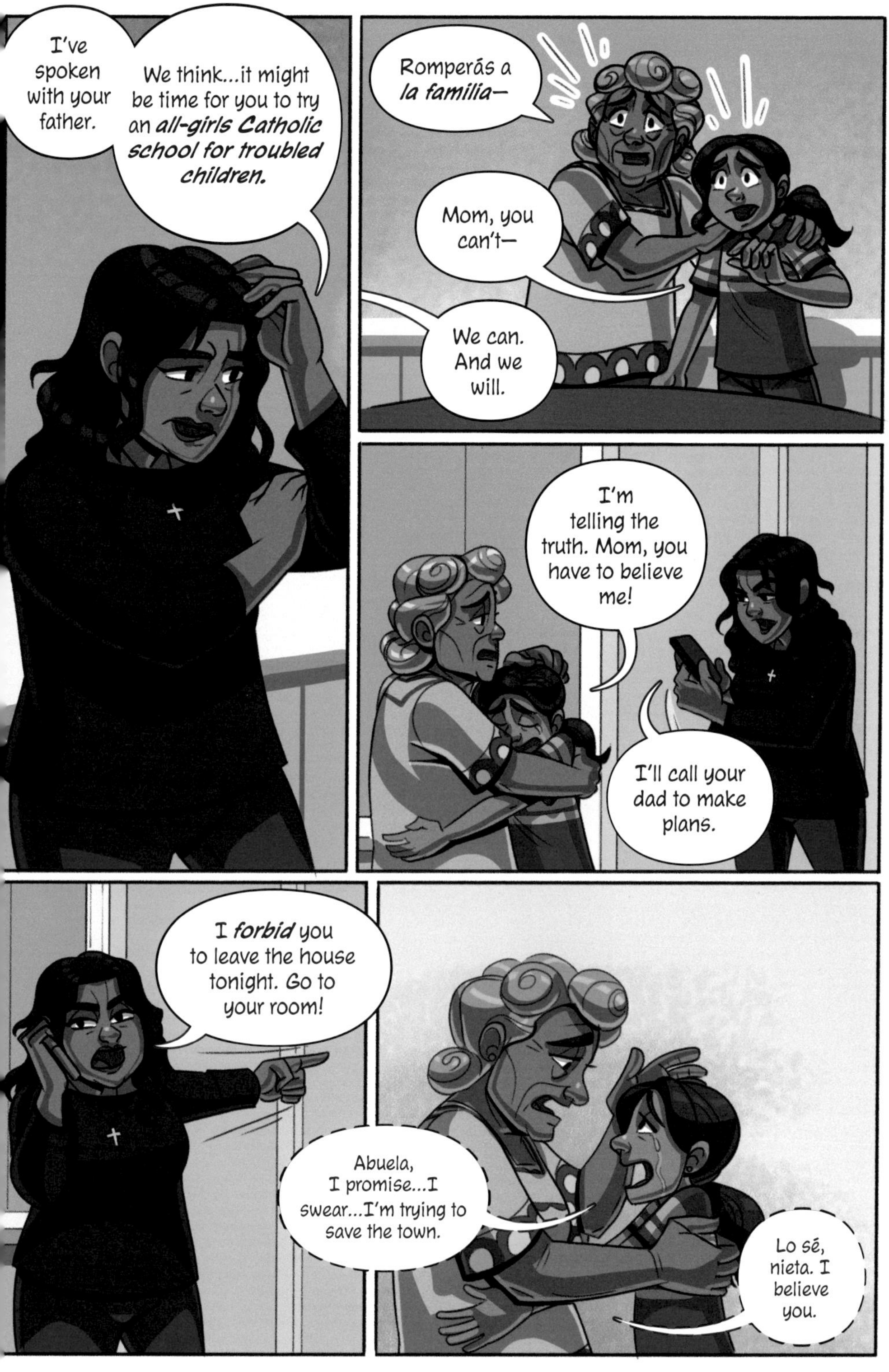
I've spoken with your father.
We think...it might be time for you to try an *all-girls Catholic school for troubled children.*
Romperás a *la familia*—
Mom, you can't—
We can. And we will.
I'm telling the truth. Mom, you have to believe me!
I'll call your dad to make plans.
I *forbid* you to leave the house tonight. Go to your room!
Abuela, I promise...I swear...I'm trying to save the town.
Lo sé, nieta. I believe you.

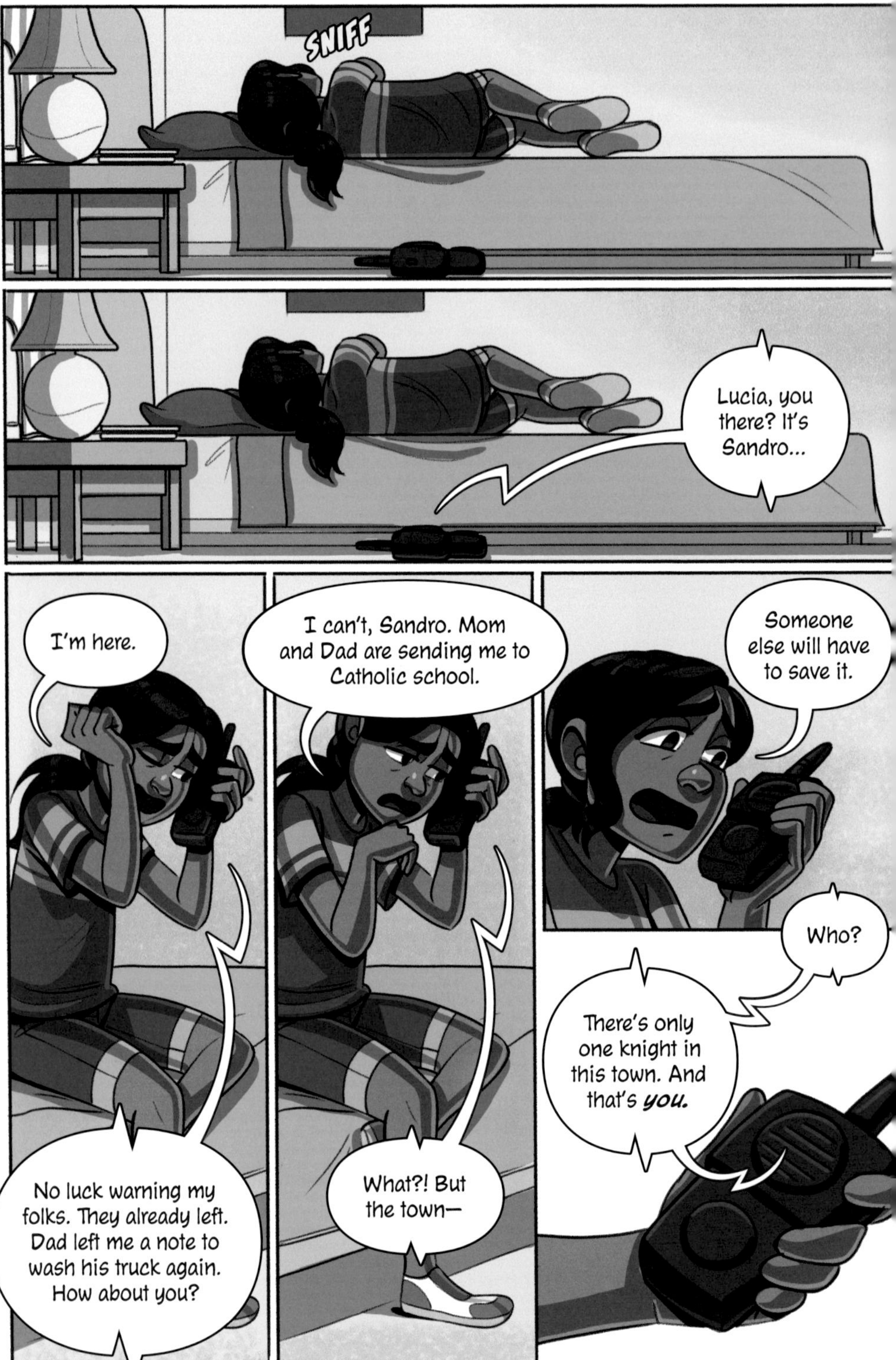
SNIFF
Lucia, you there? It's Sandro...
I'm here.
I can't, Sandro. Mom and Dad are sending me to Catholic school.
Someone else will have to save it.
No luck warning my folks. They already left. Dad left me a note to wash his truck again. How about you?
What?! But the town—
Who?
There's only one knight in this town. And that's *you.*

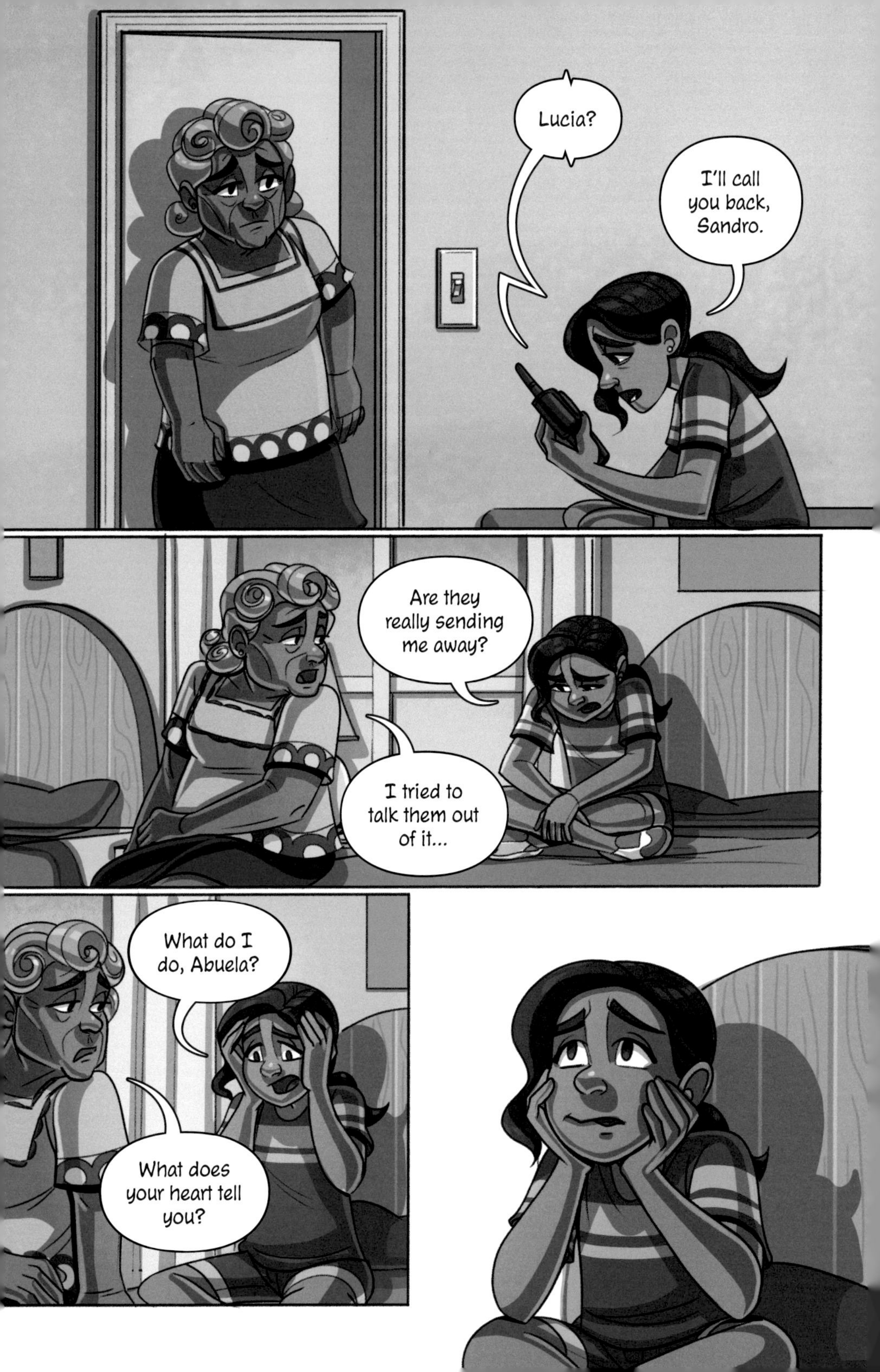
Lucia?
I'll call you back, Sandro.
Are they really sending me away?
I tried to talk them out of it...
What do I do, Abuela?
What does your heart tell you?

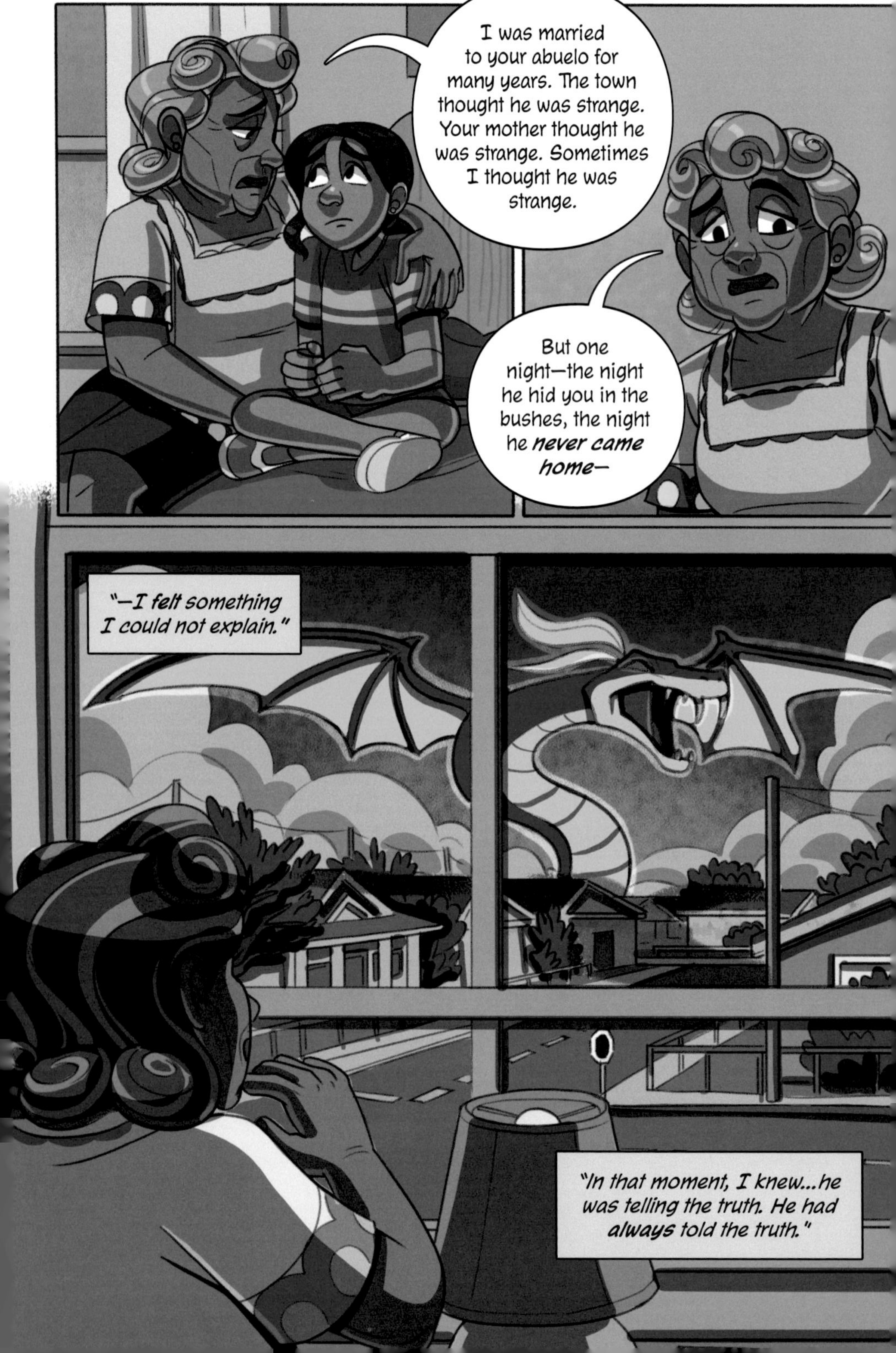

I was married to your abuelo for many years. The town thought he was strange. Your mother thought he was strange. Sometimes I thought he was strange.
But one night—the night he hid you in the bushes, the night he ***never came home***—
"—I *felt* something I could not explain."
"In that moment, I knew...he was telling the truth. He had ***always*** told the truth."

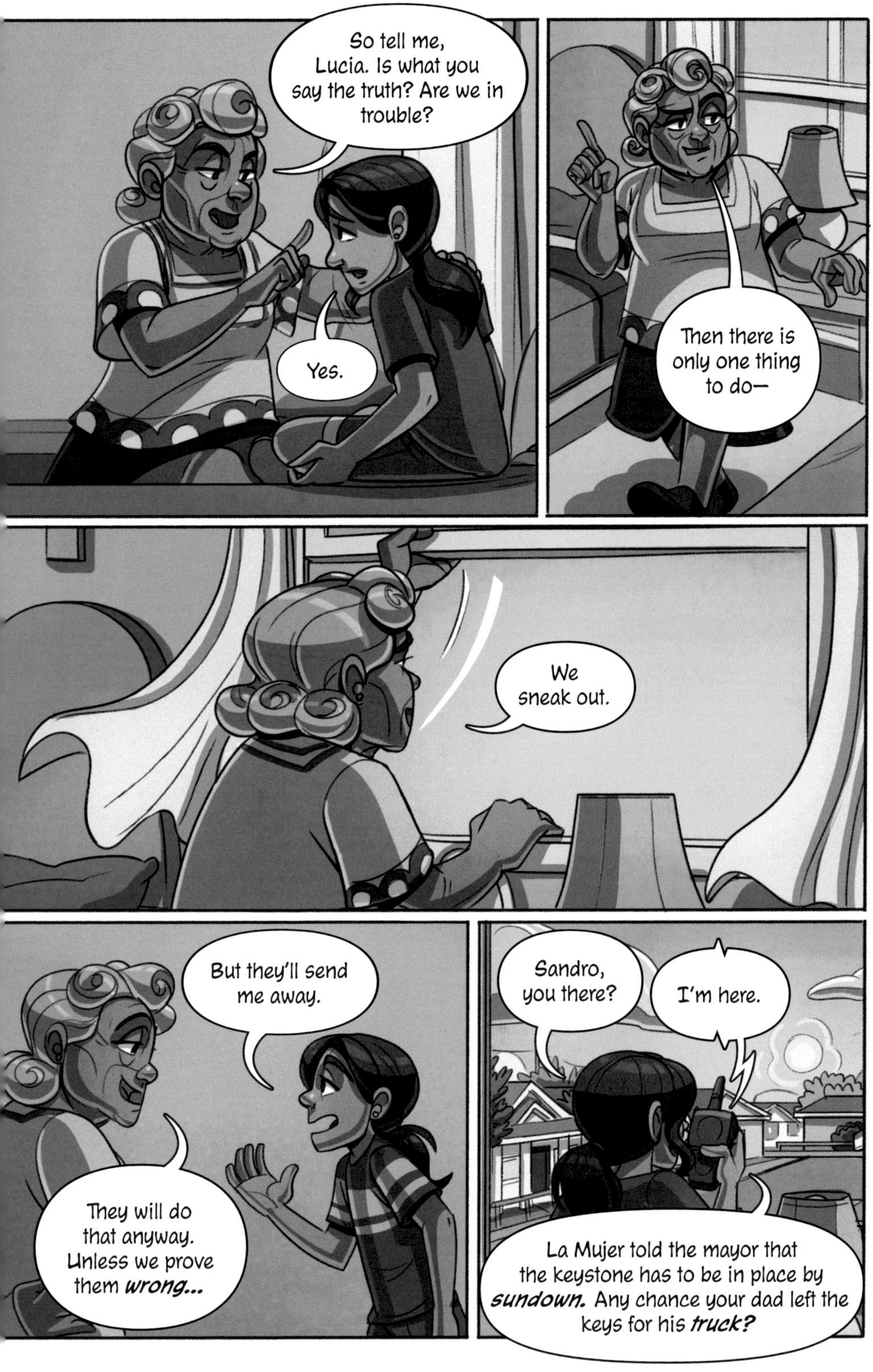
So tell me, Lucia. Is what you say the truth? Are we in trouble?
Yes.
Then there is only one thing to do—
We sneak out.
But they'll send me away.
They will do that anyway. Unless we prove them *wrong...*
Sandro, you there?
I'm here.
La Mujer told the mayor that the keystone has to be in place by *sundown.* Any chance your dad left the keys for his *truck?*

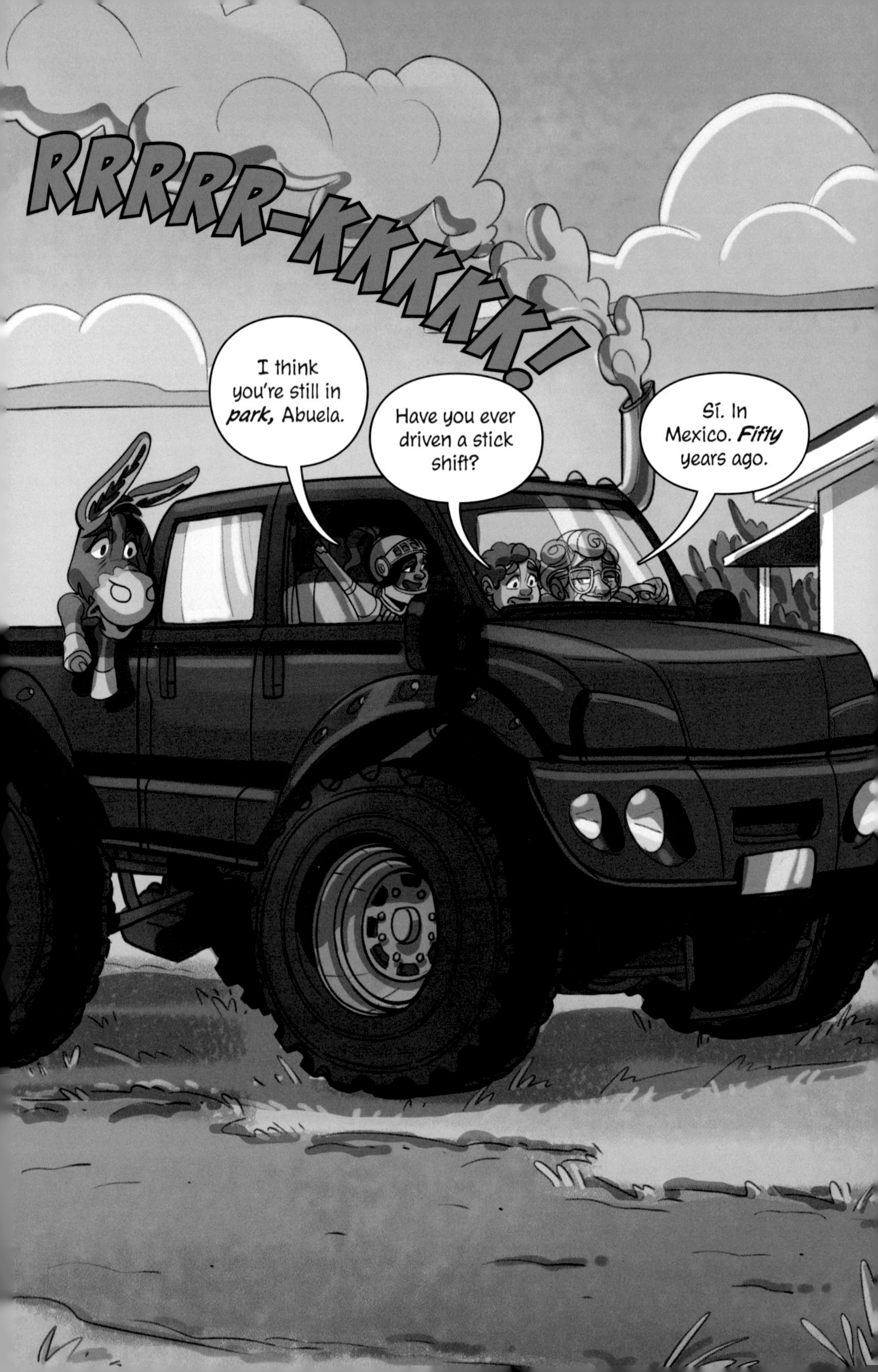

RRRRRR-KKKKKK!
I think you're still in *park,* Abuela.
Have you ever driven a stick shift?
Sí. In Mexico. *Fifty* years ago.

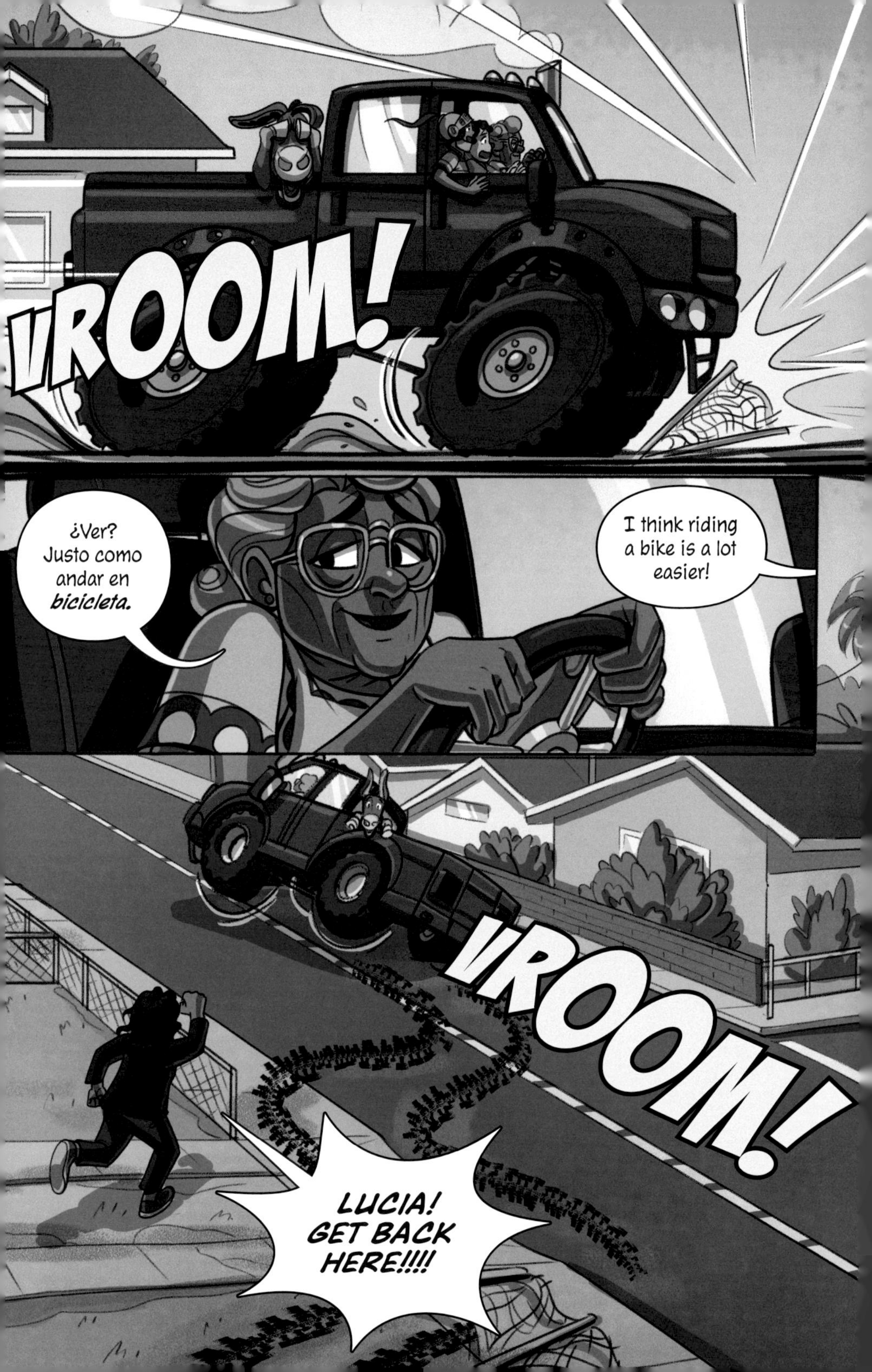
VROOM!
¿Ver? Justo como andar en *bicicleta.*
I think riding a bike is a lot easier!
VROOM!
LUCIA! GET BACK HERE!!!!

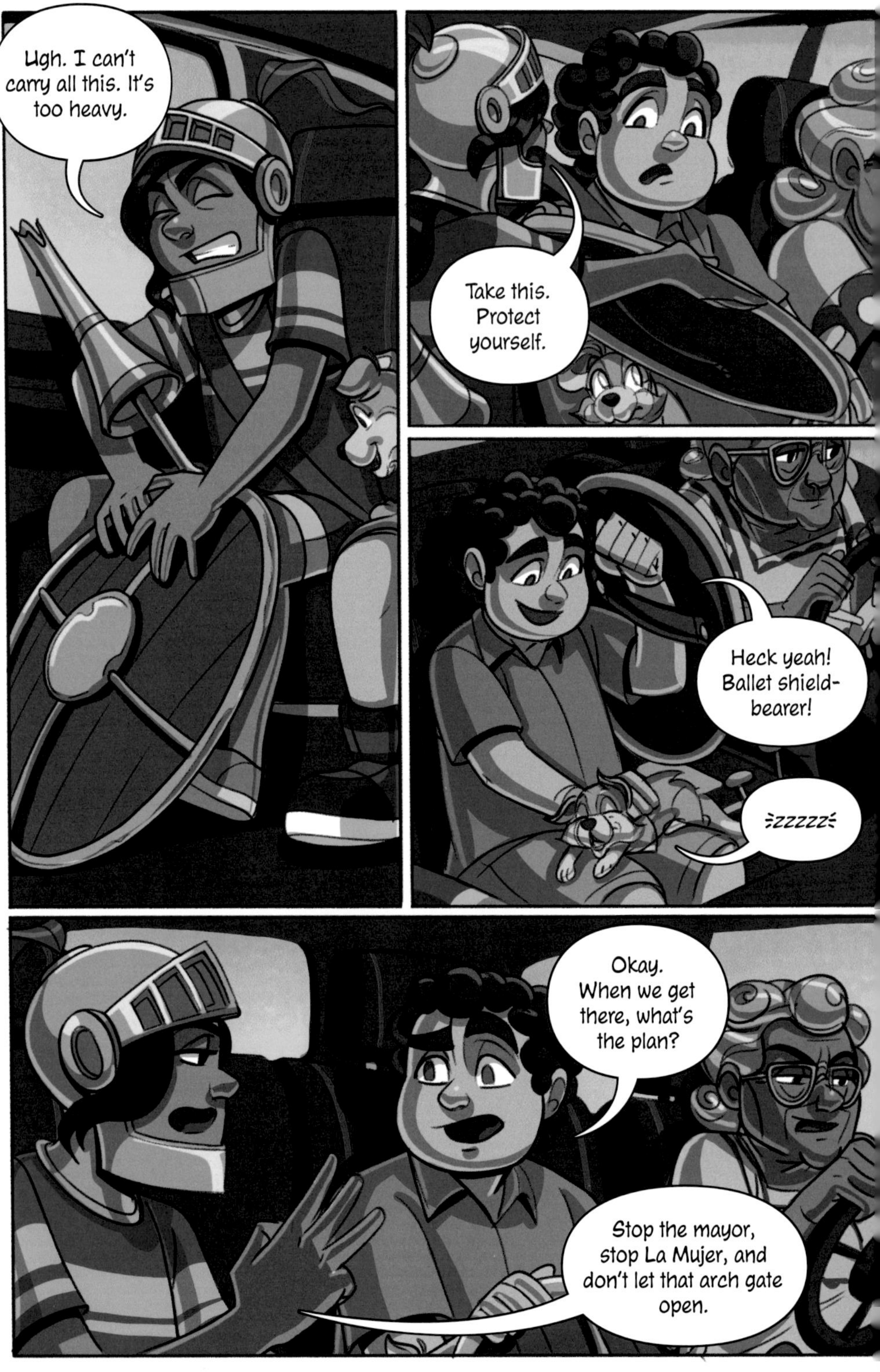

Ugh. I can't carry all this. It's too heavy.
Take this. Protect yourself.
Heck yeah! Ballet shield-bearer!
ZZZZZ
Okay. When we get there, what's the plan?
Stop the mayor, stop La Mujer, and don't let that arch gate open.

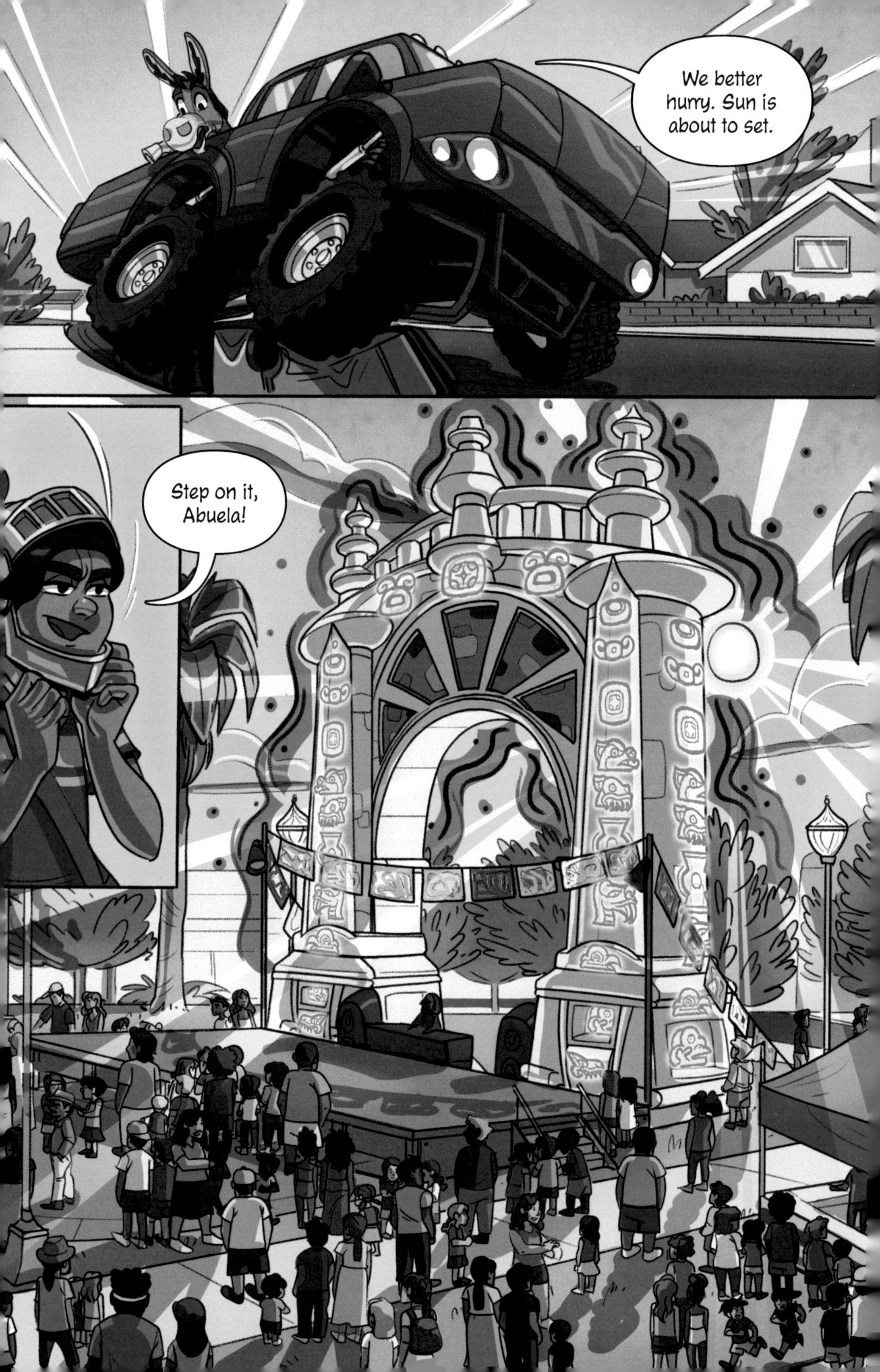
We better hurry. Sun is about to set.
Step on it, Abuela!

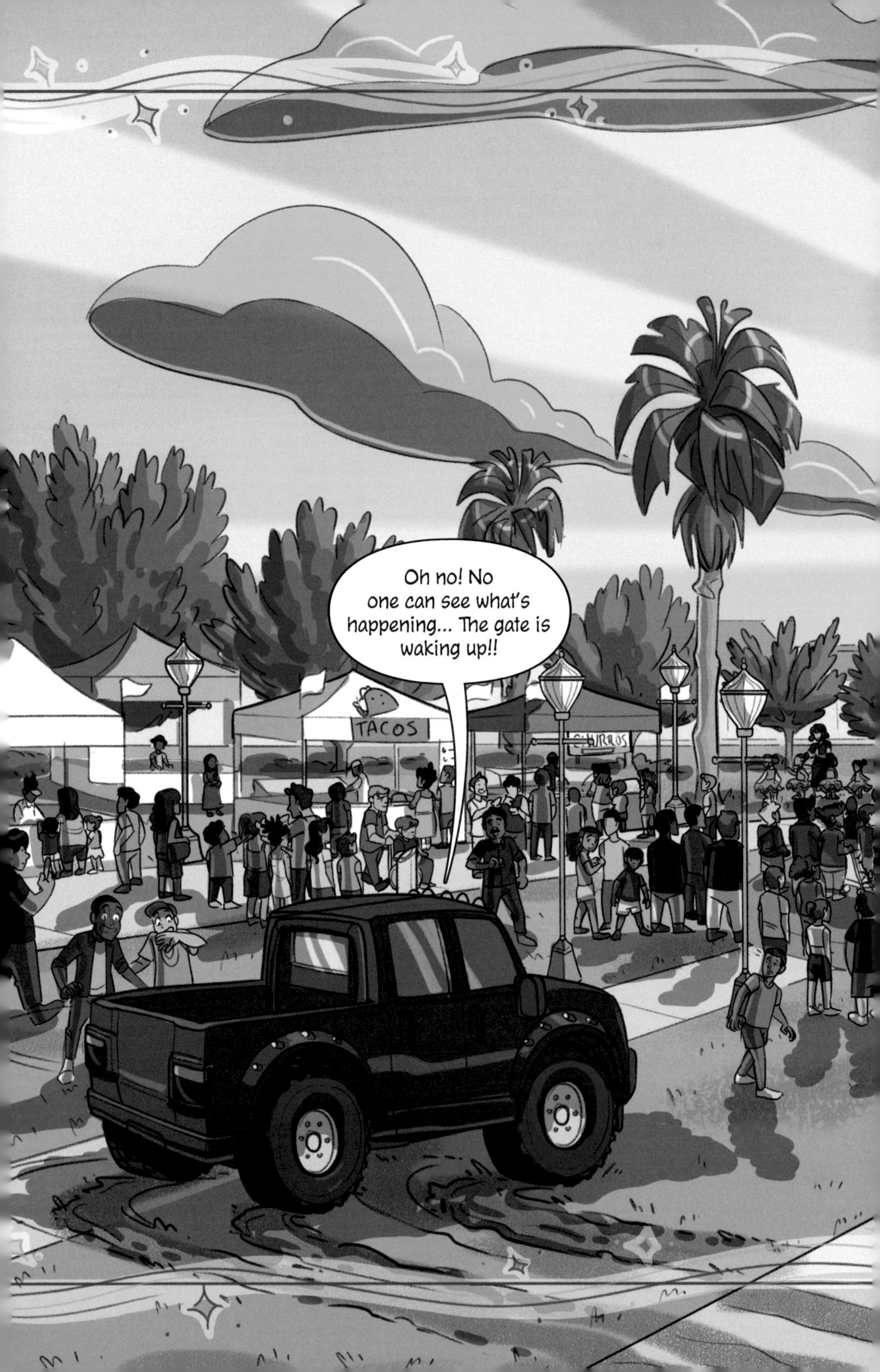
Oh no! No one can see what's happening... The gate is waking up!!
TACOS
CHURROS

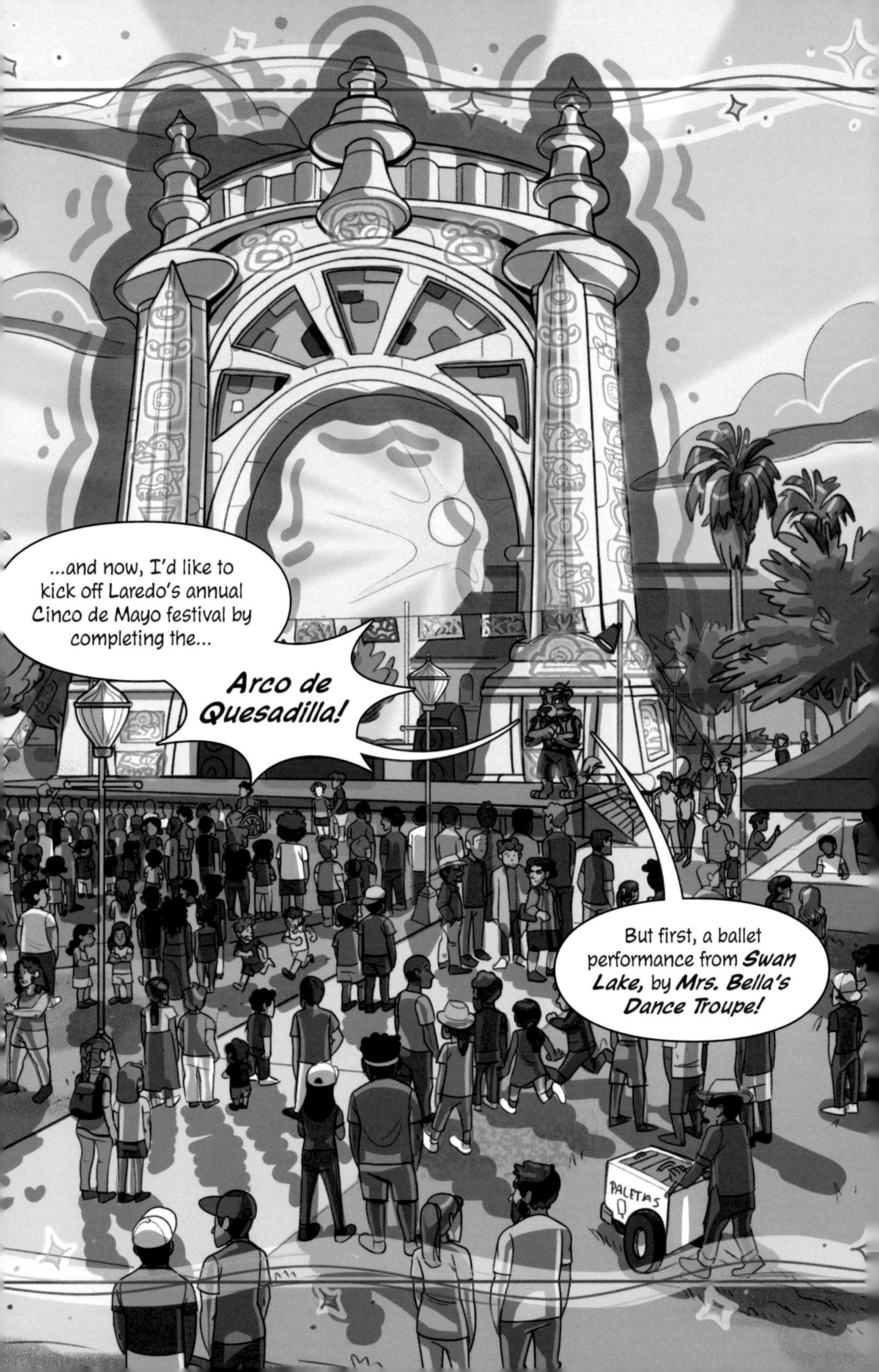
...and now, I'd like to kick off Laredo's annual Cinco de Mayo festival by completing the...
Arco de Quesadilla!
But first, a ballet performance from Swan Lake, by Mrs. Bella's Dance Troupe!
PALETAS

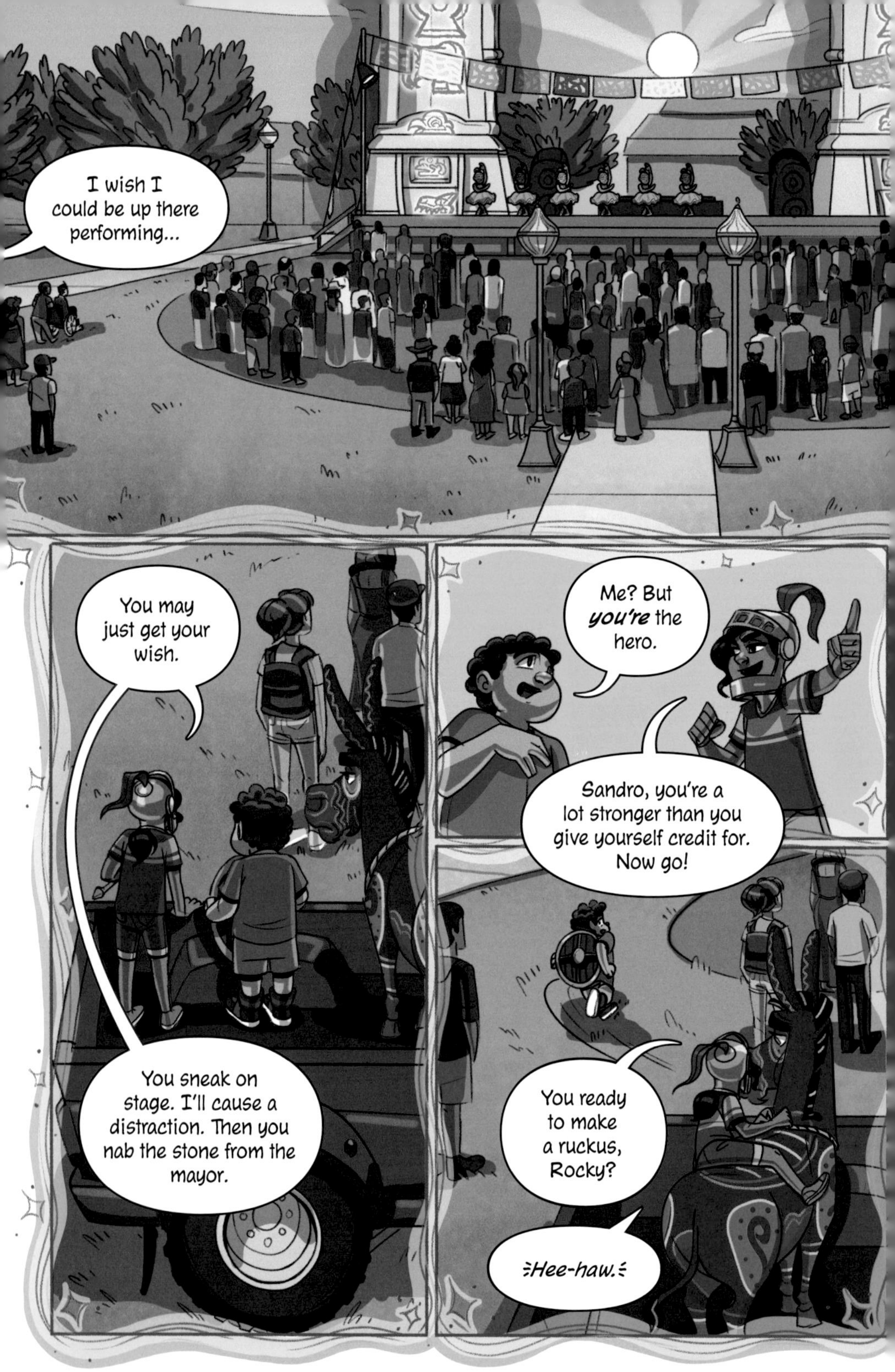
I wish I could be up there performing...
You may just get your wish.
You sneak on stage. I'll cause a distraction. Then you nab the stone from the mayor.
Me? But *you're* the hero.
Sandro, you're a lot stronger than you give yourself credit for. Now go!
You ready to make a ruckus, Rocky?
Hee-haw.

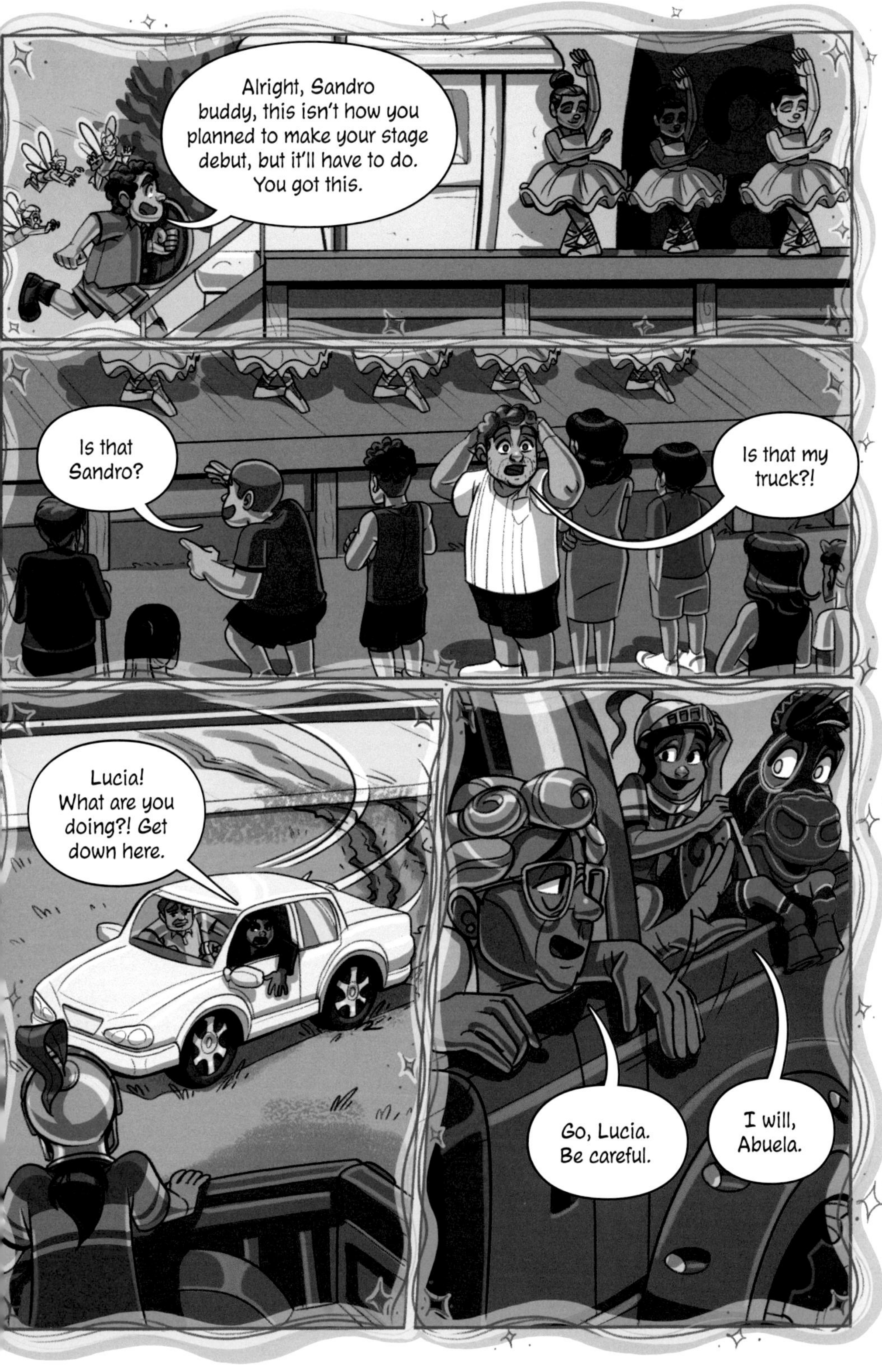
Alright, Sandro buddy, this isn't how you planned to make your stage debut, but it'll have to do. You got this.
Is that Sandro?
Is that my truck?!
Lucia! What are you doing?! Get down here.
Go, Lucia. Be careful.
I will, Abuela.

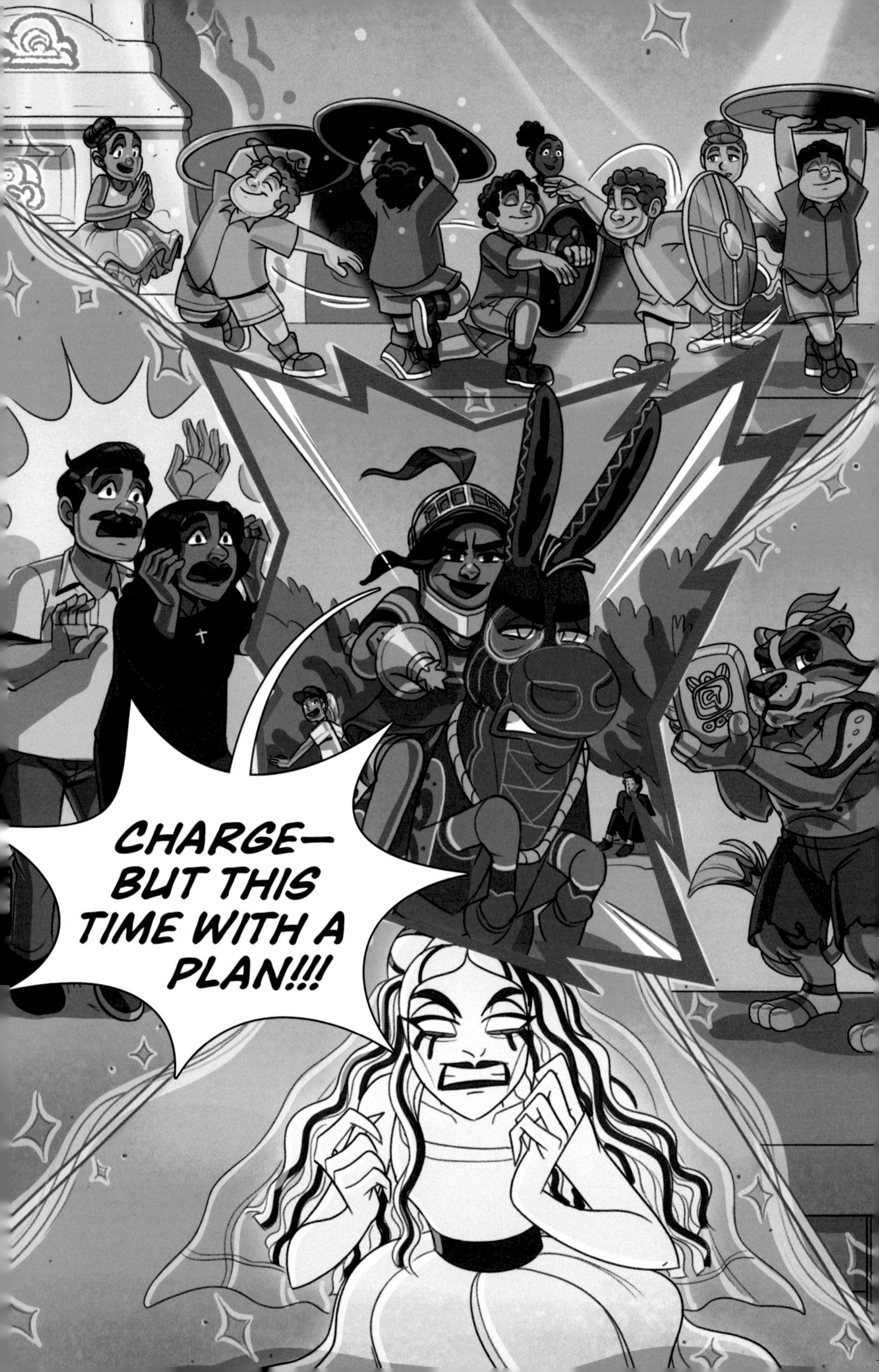
CHARGE—BUT THIS TIME WITH A PLAN!!!

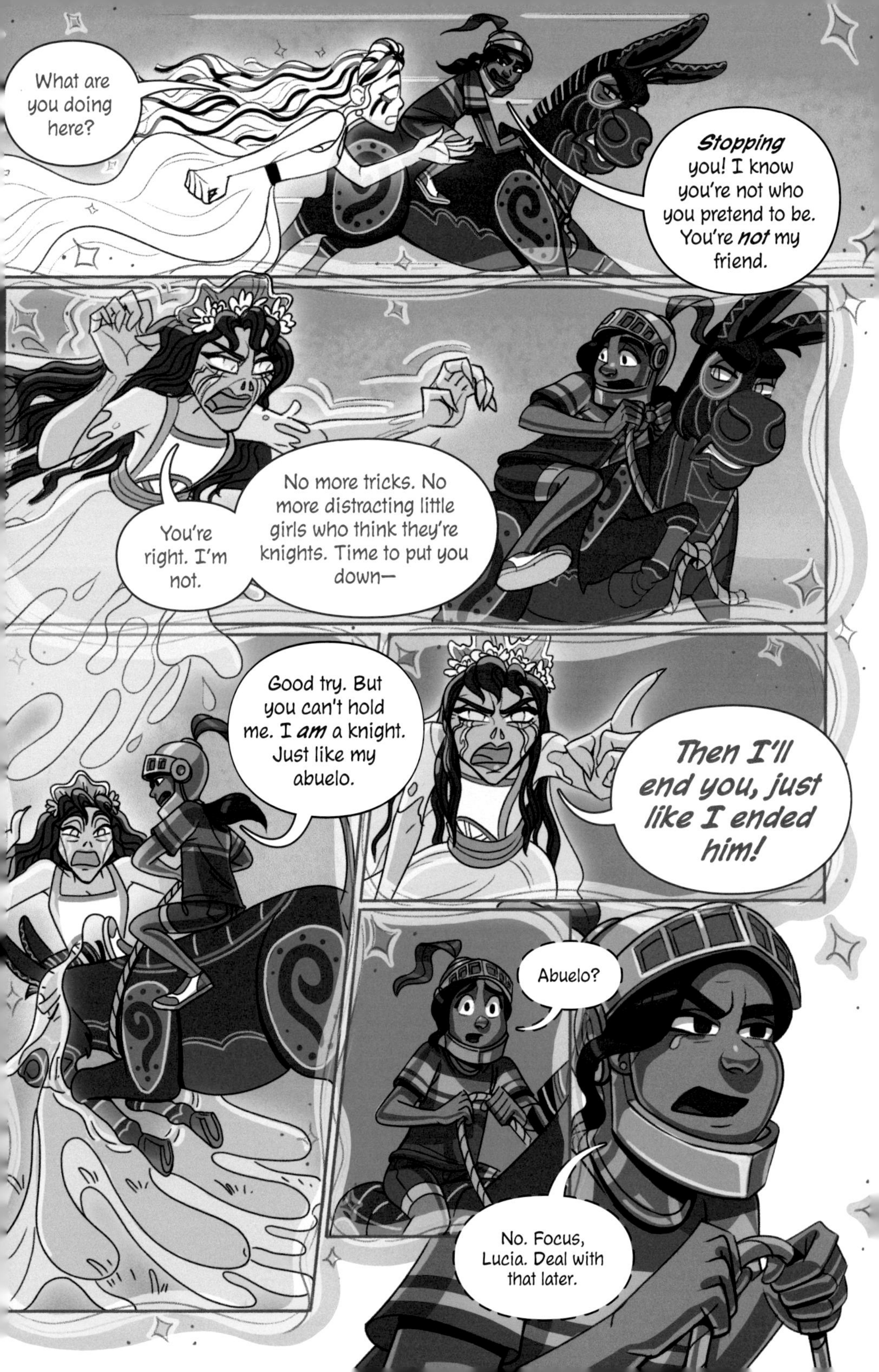
What are you doing here?
Stopping you! I know you're not who you pretend to be. You're not my friend.
You're right. I'm not.
No more tricks. No more distracting little girls who think they're knights. Time to put you down—
Good try. But you can't hold me. I am a knight. Just like my abuelo.
Then I'll end you, just like I ended him!
Abuelo?
No. Focus, Lucia. Deal with that later.

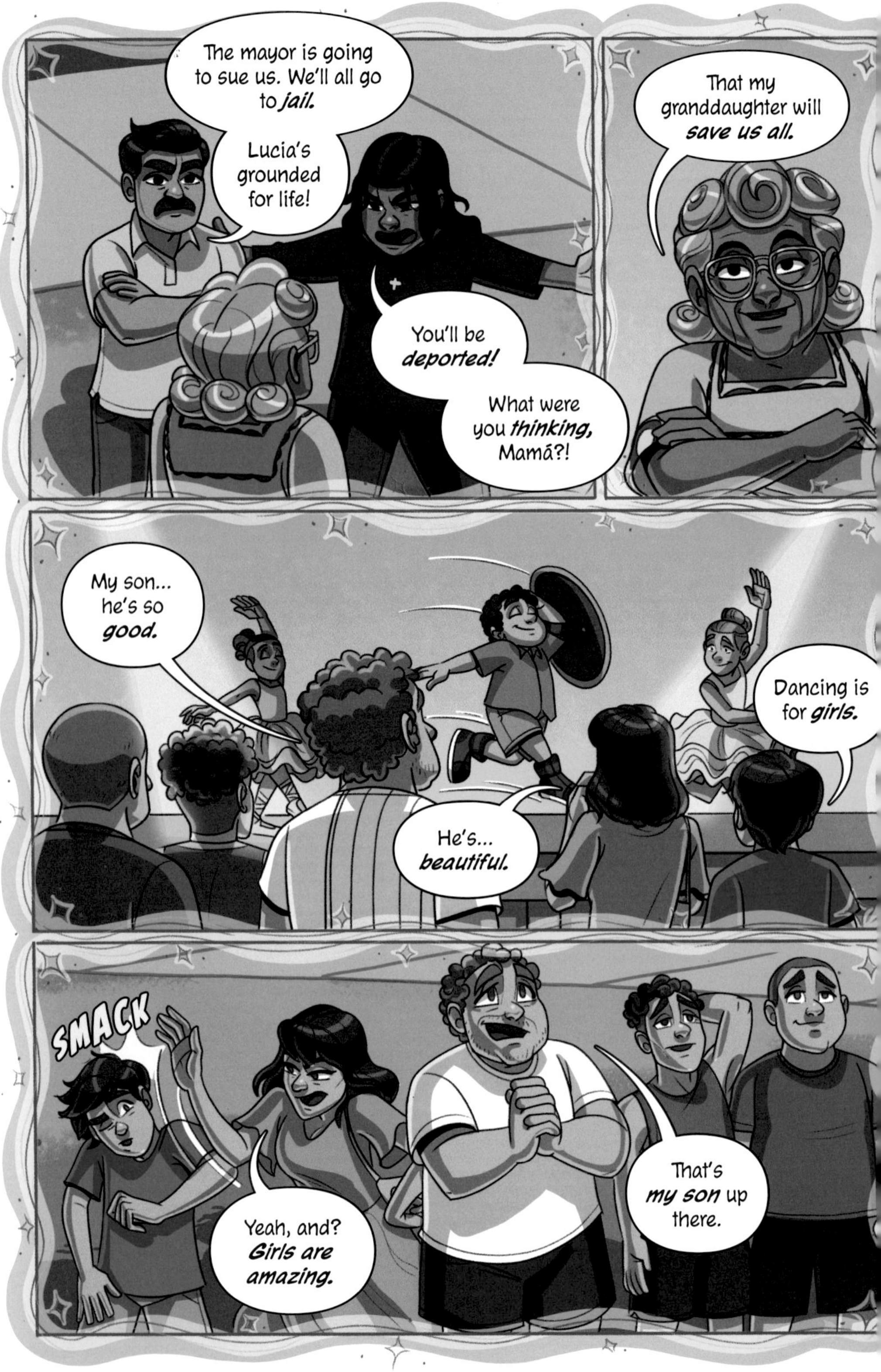
The mayor is going to sue us. We'll all go to *jail.*
Lucia's grounded for life!
You'll be *deported!*
What were you *thinking,* Mamá?!
That my granddaughter will *save us all.*
My son... he's so *good.*
Dancing is for *girls.*
He's... *beautiful.*
SMACK
Yeah, and? *Girls are amazing.*
That's *my son* up there.

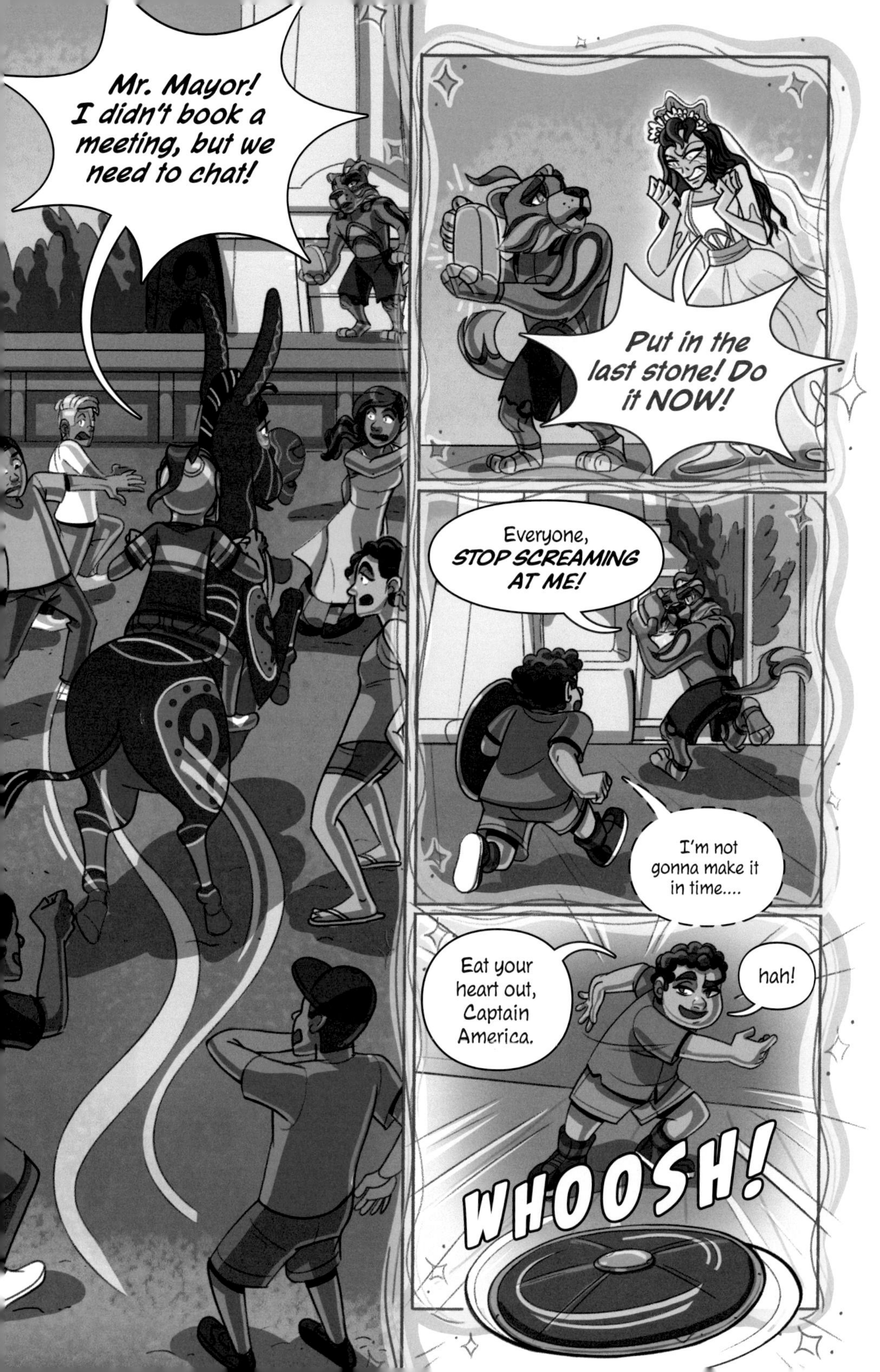
Mr. Mayor! I didn't book a meeting, but we need to chat!
Put in the last stone! Do it NOW!
Everyone, STOP SCREAMING AT ME!
I'm not gonna make it in time....
Eat your heart out, Captain America.
hah!
WHOOSH!

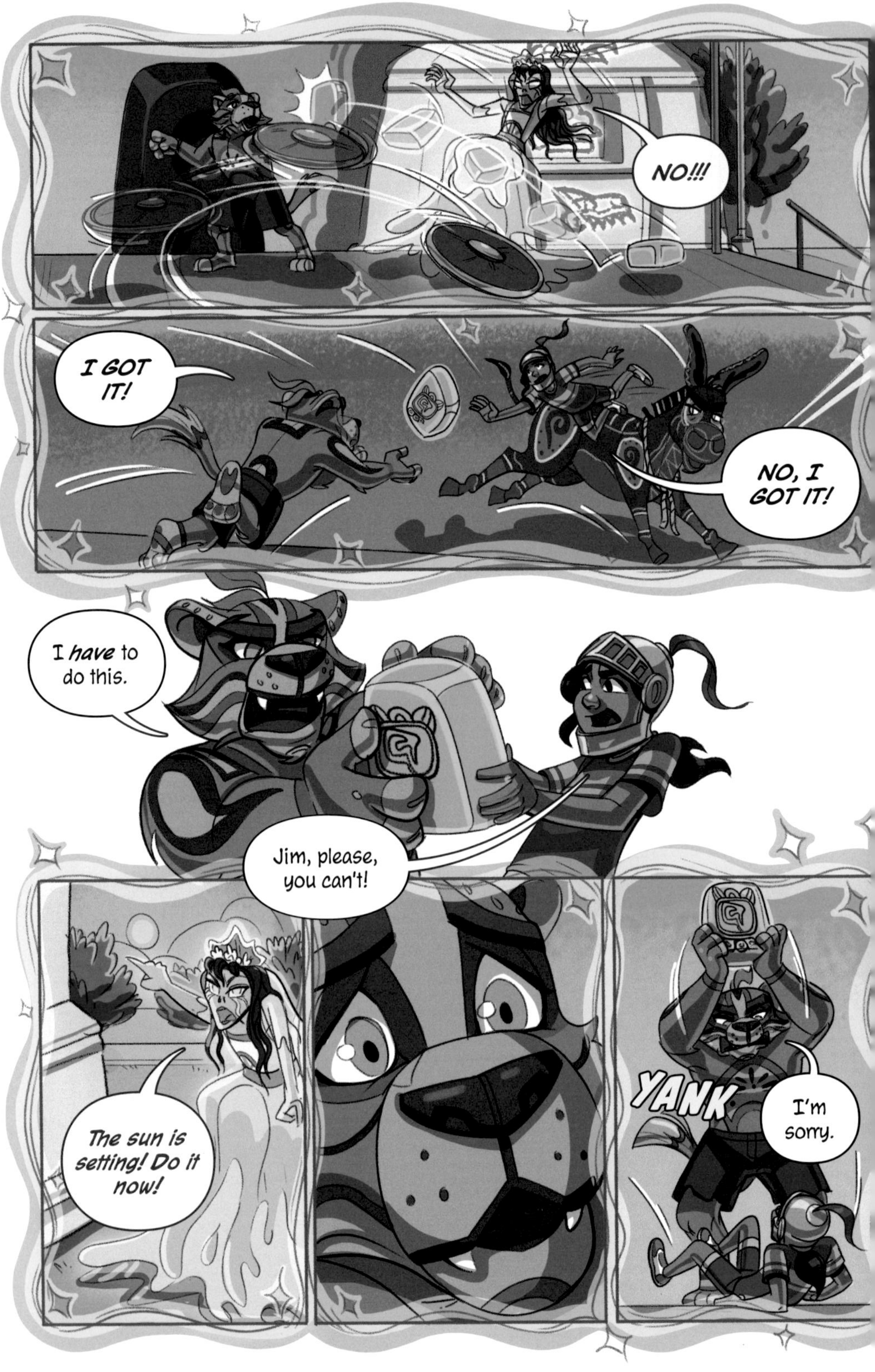
NO!!!
I GOT IT!
NO, I GOT IT!
I have to do this.
Jim, please, you can't!
The sun is setting! Do it now!
YANK
I'm sorry.

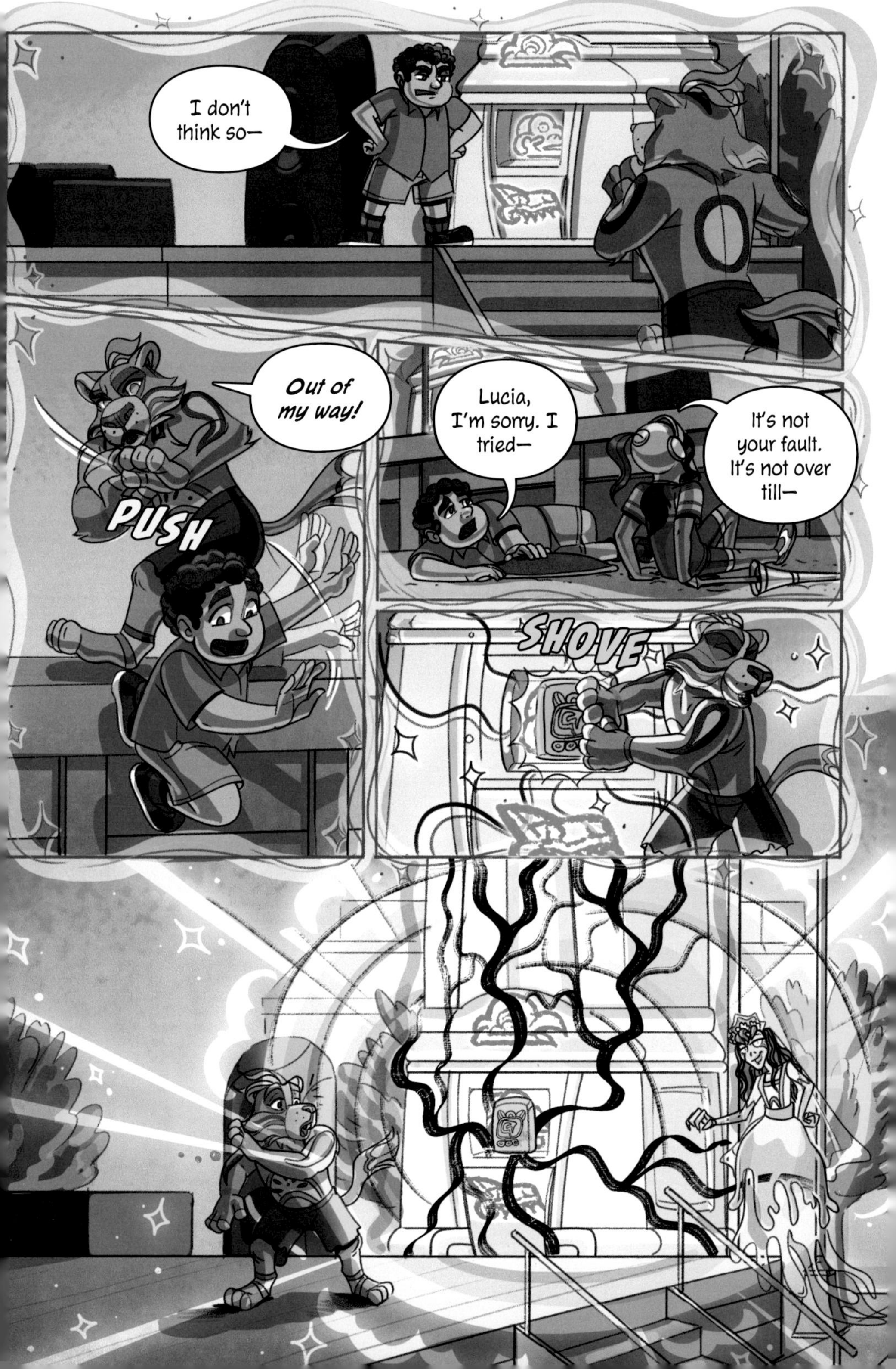
I don't think so—
Out of my way!
PUSH
Lucia, I'm sorry. I tried—
It's not your fault. It's not over till—
SHOVE

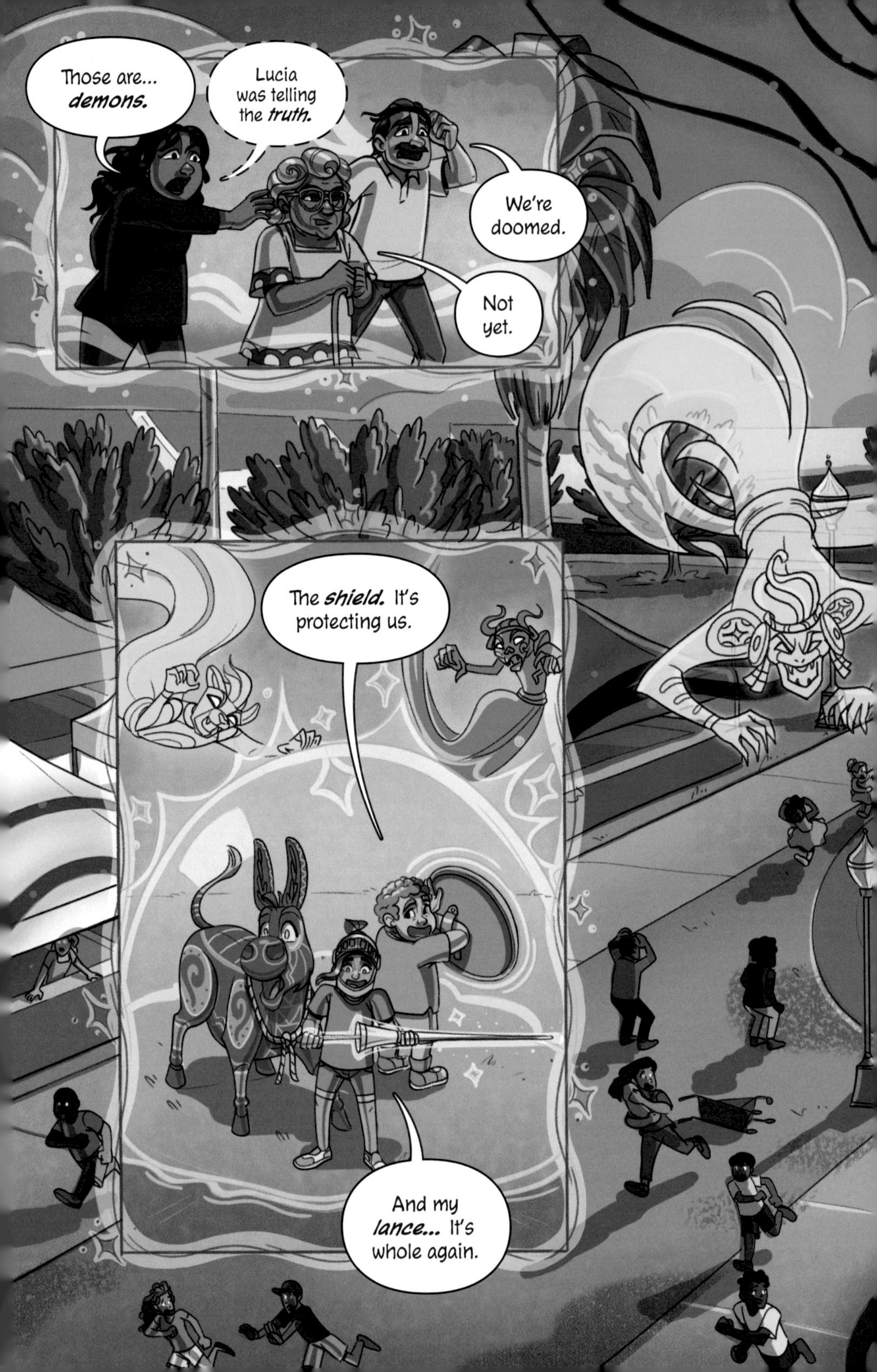
Those are... *demons.*
Lucia was telling the *truth.*
We're doomed.
Not yet.
The *shield.* It's protecting us.
And my *lance...* It's whole again.

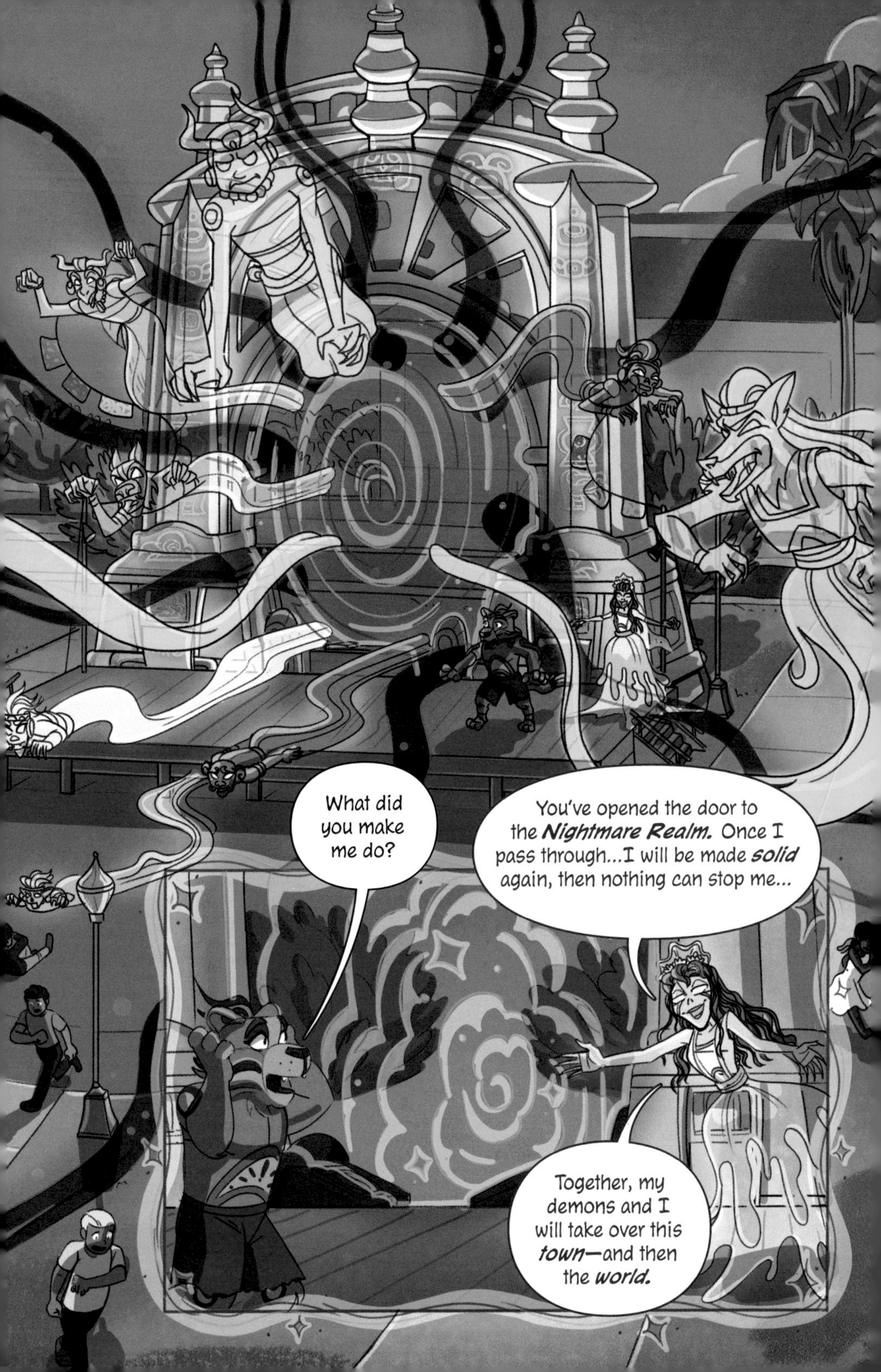

What did you make me do?
You've opened the door to the ***Nightmare Realm.*** Once I pass through...I will be made ***solid*** again, then nothing can stop me...
Together, my demons and I will take over this ***town***—and then the ***world.***

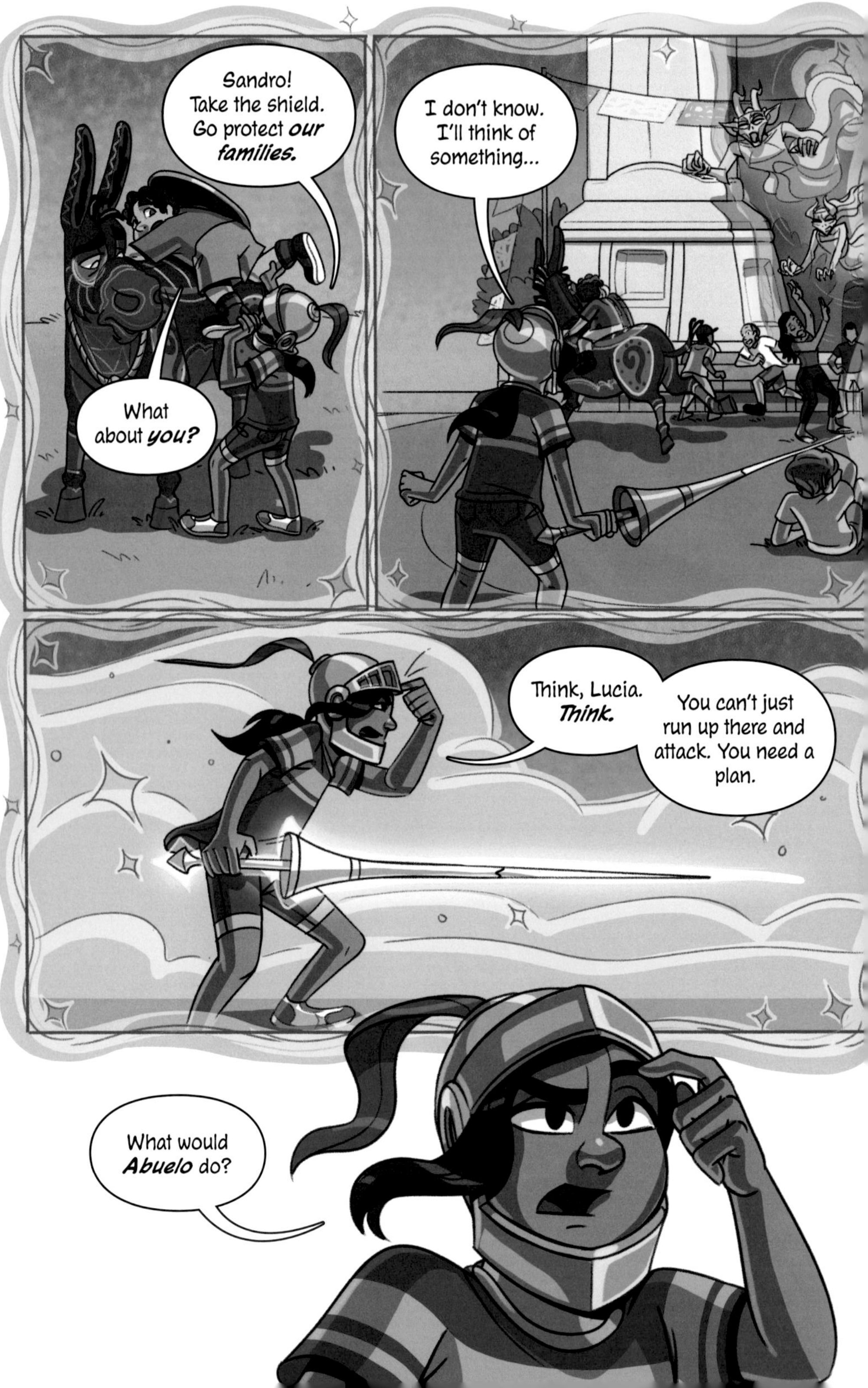
Sandro! Take the shield. Go protect *our families.*
What about *you?*
I don't know. I'll think of something...
Think, Lucia. *Think.*
You can't just run up there and attack. You need a plan.
What would *Abuelo* do?

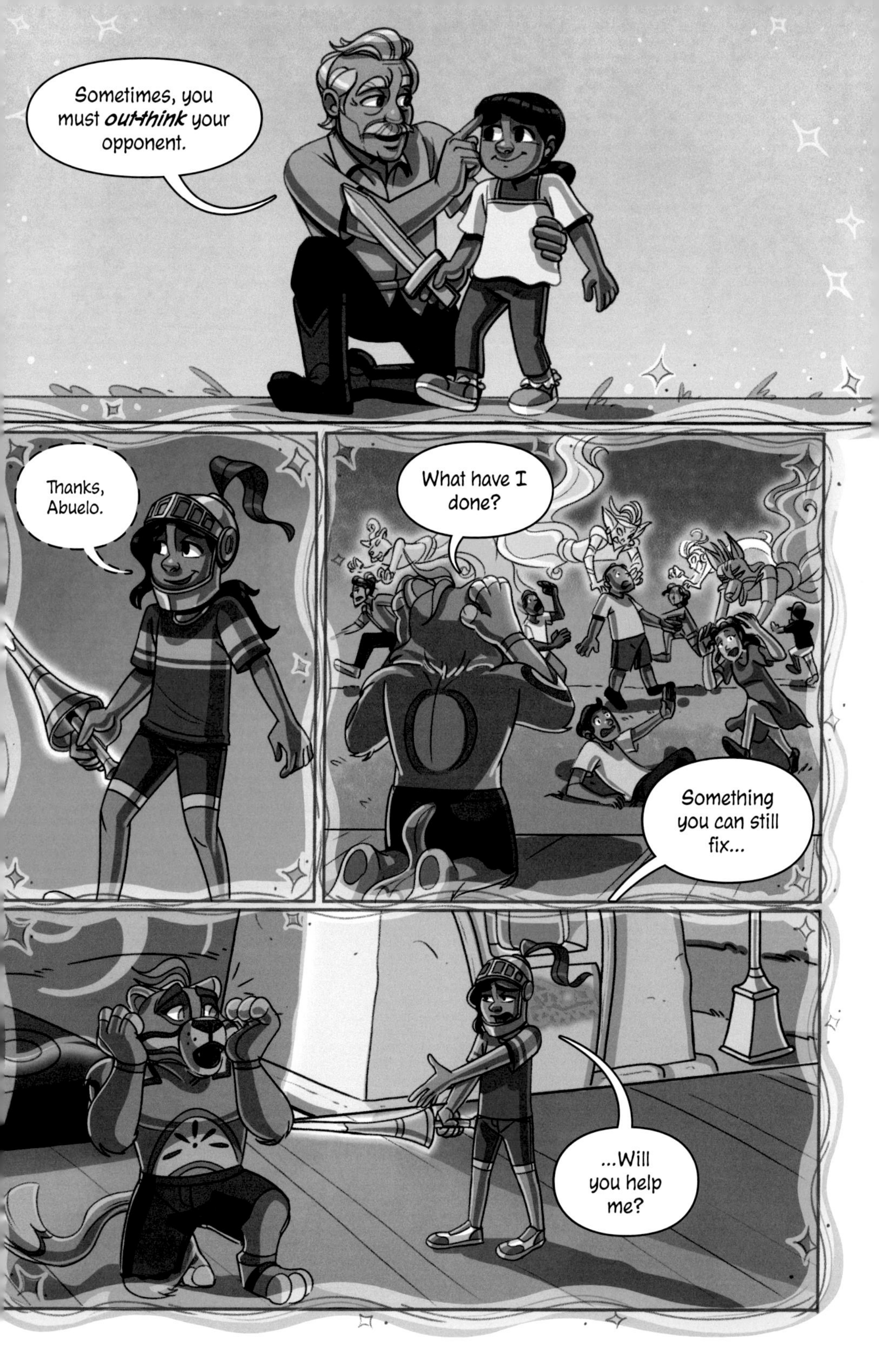
Sometimes, you must *out-think* your opponent.
Thanks, Abuelo.
What have I done?
Something you can still fix...
...Will you help me?

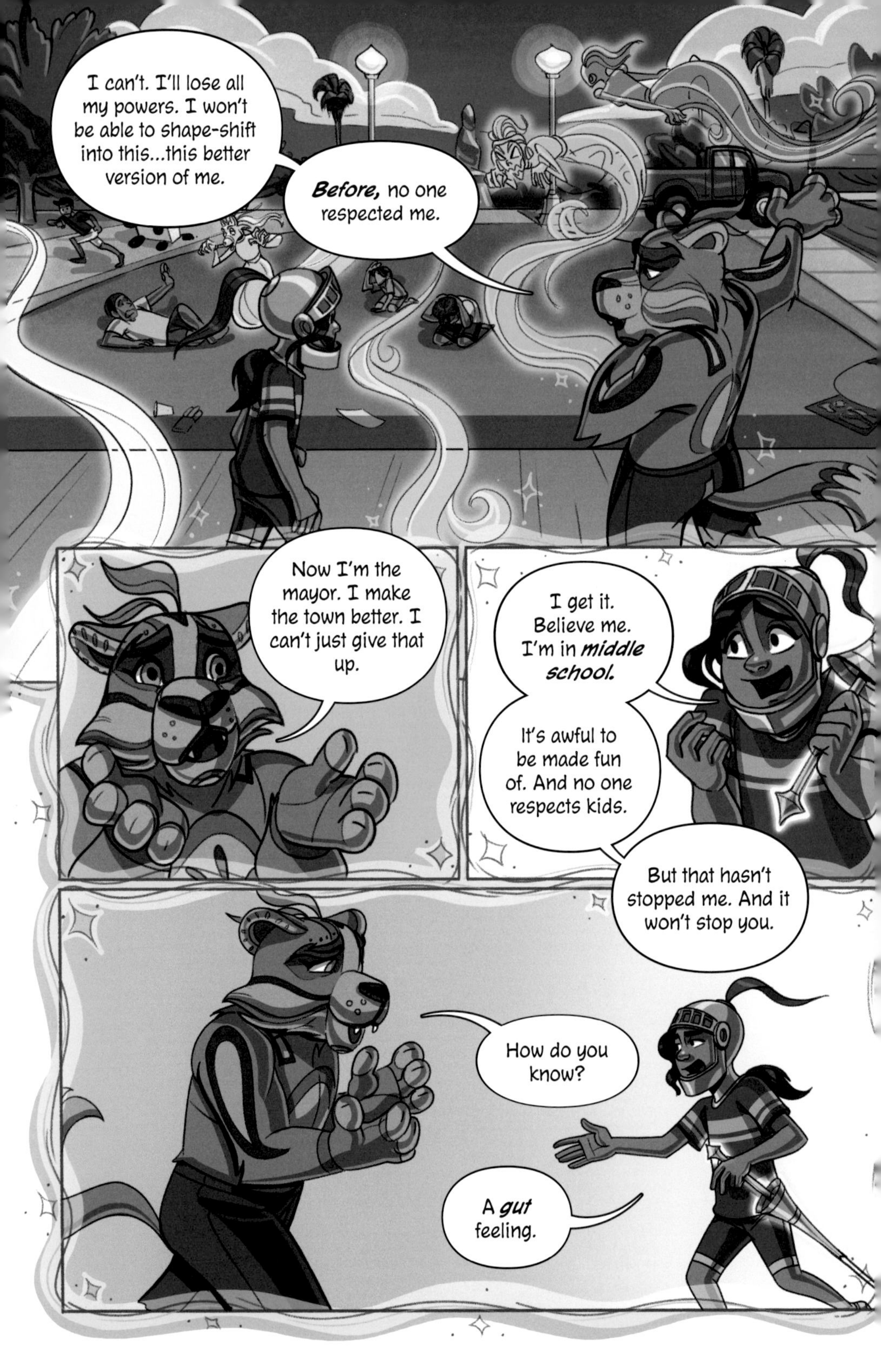

I can't. I'll lose all my powers. I won't be able to shape-shift into this...this better version of me.
Before, no one respected me.
Now I'm the mayor. I make the town better. I can't just give that up.
I get it. Believe me. I'm in *middle school.*
It's awful to be made fun of. And no one respects kids.
But that hasn't stopped me. And it won't stop you.
How do you know?
A *gut* feeling.

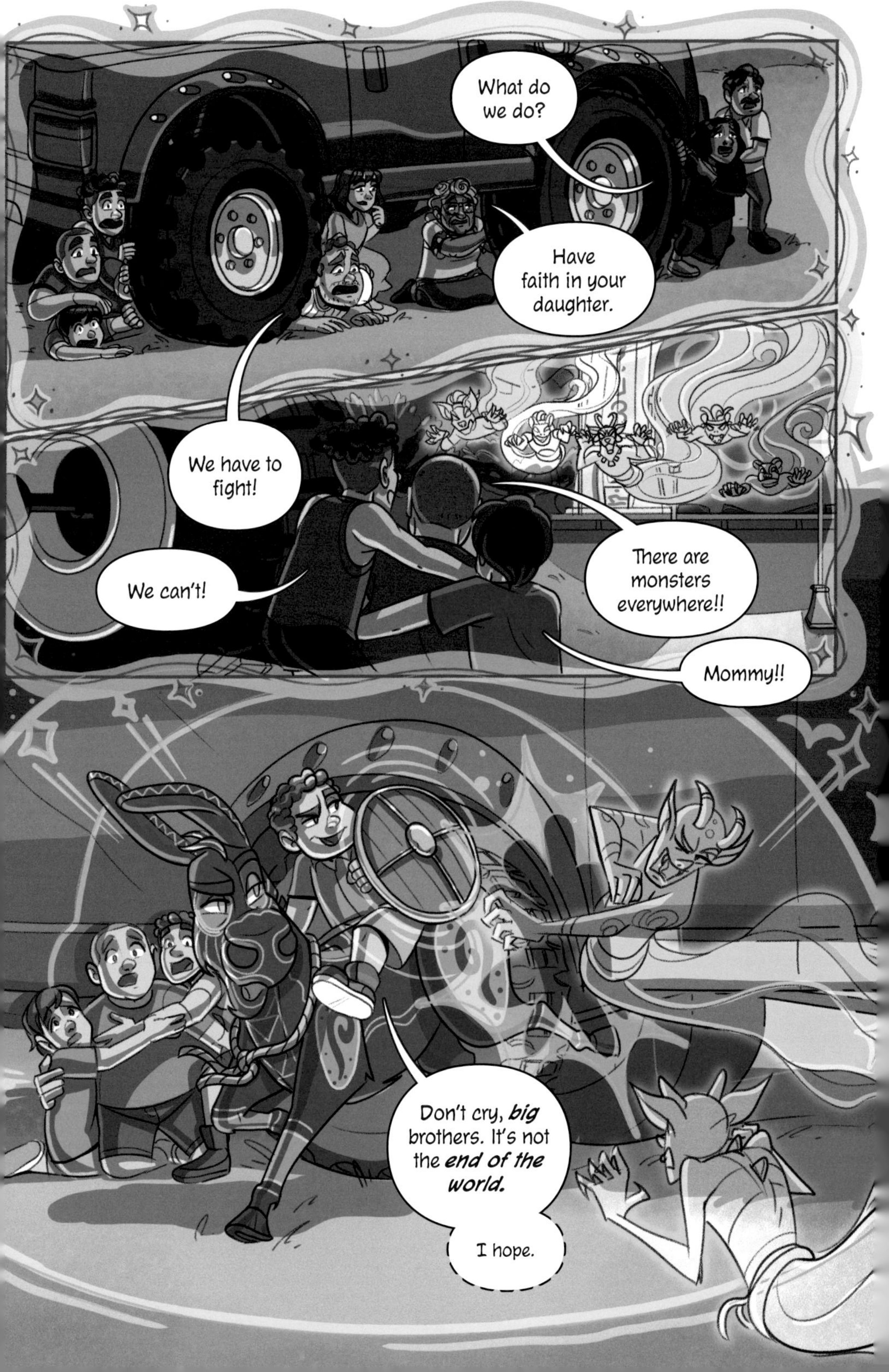
What do we do?
Have faith in your daughter.
We have to fight!
We can't!
There are monsters everywhere!!
Mommy!!
Don't cry, *big* brothers. It's not the *end of the world.*
I hope.

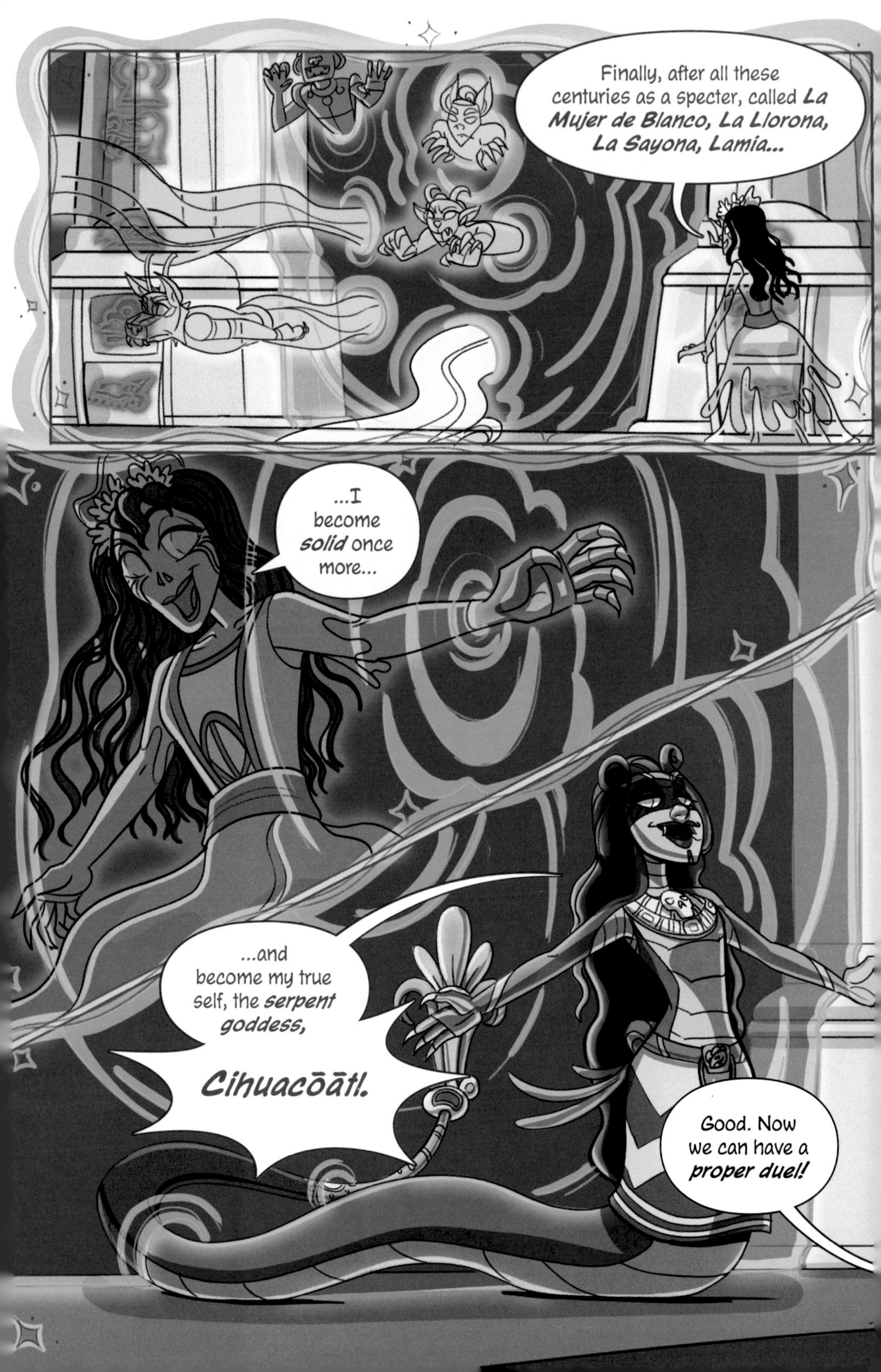
Finally, after all these centuries as a specter, called *La Mujer de Blanco, La Llorona, La Sayona, Lamia...*
...I become *solid* once more...
...and become my true self, the *serpent goddess,*
Cihuacōātl.
Good. Now we can have a *proper duel!*

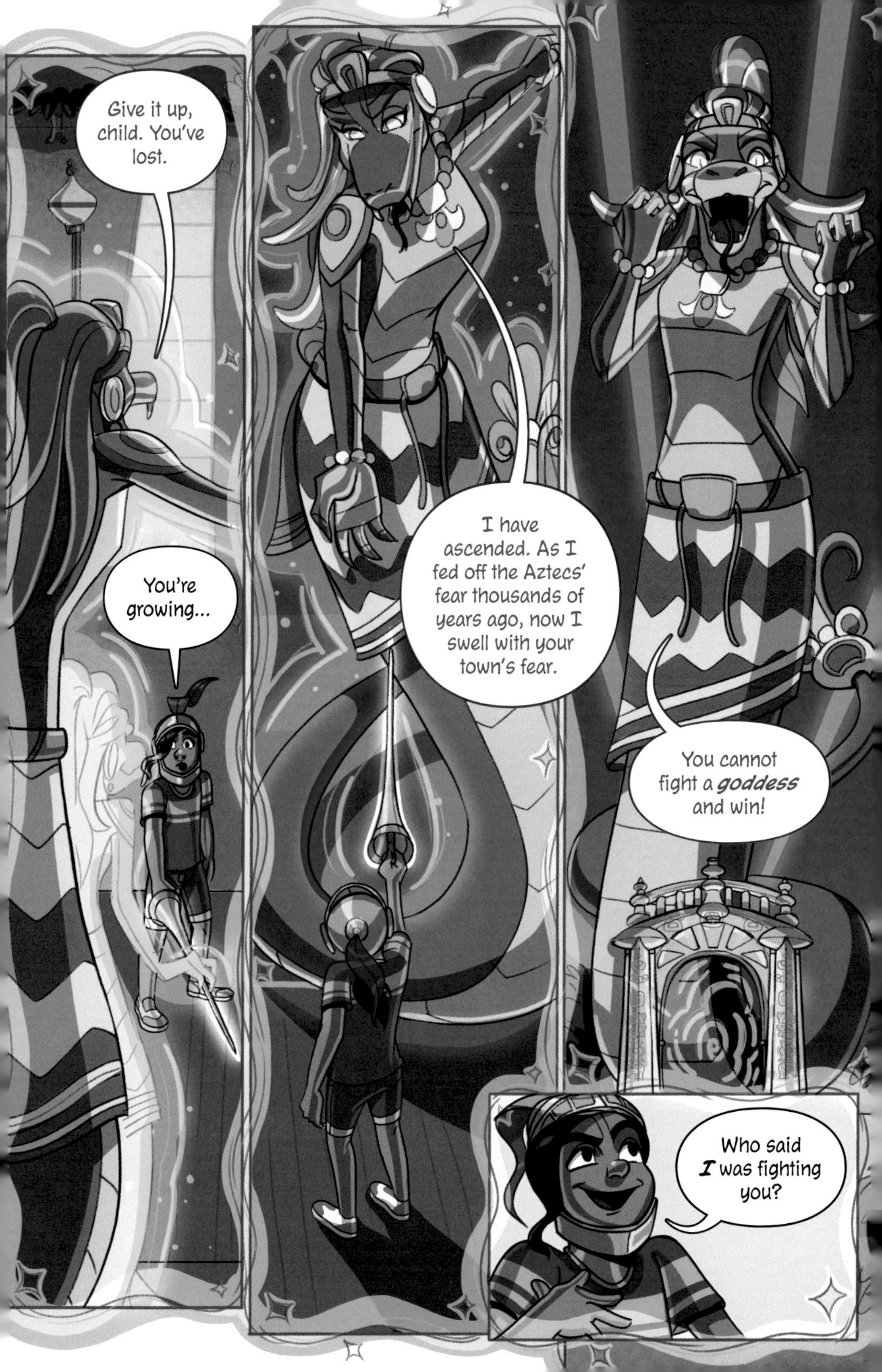
Give it up, child. You've lost.
You're growing...
I have ascended. As I fed off the Aztecs' fear thousands of years ago, now I swell with your town's fear.
You cannot fight a *goddess* and win!
Who said *I* was fighting you?

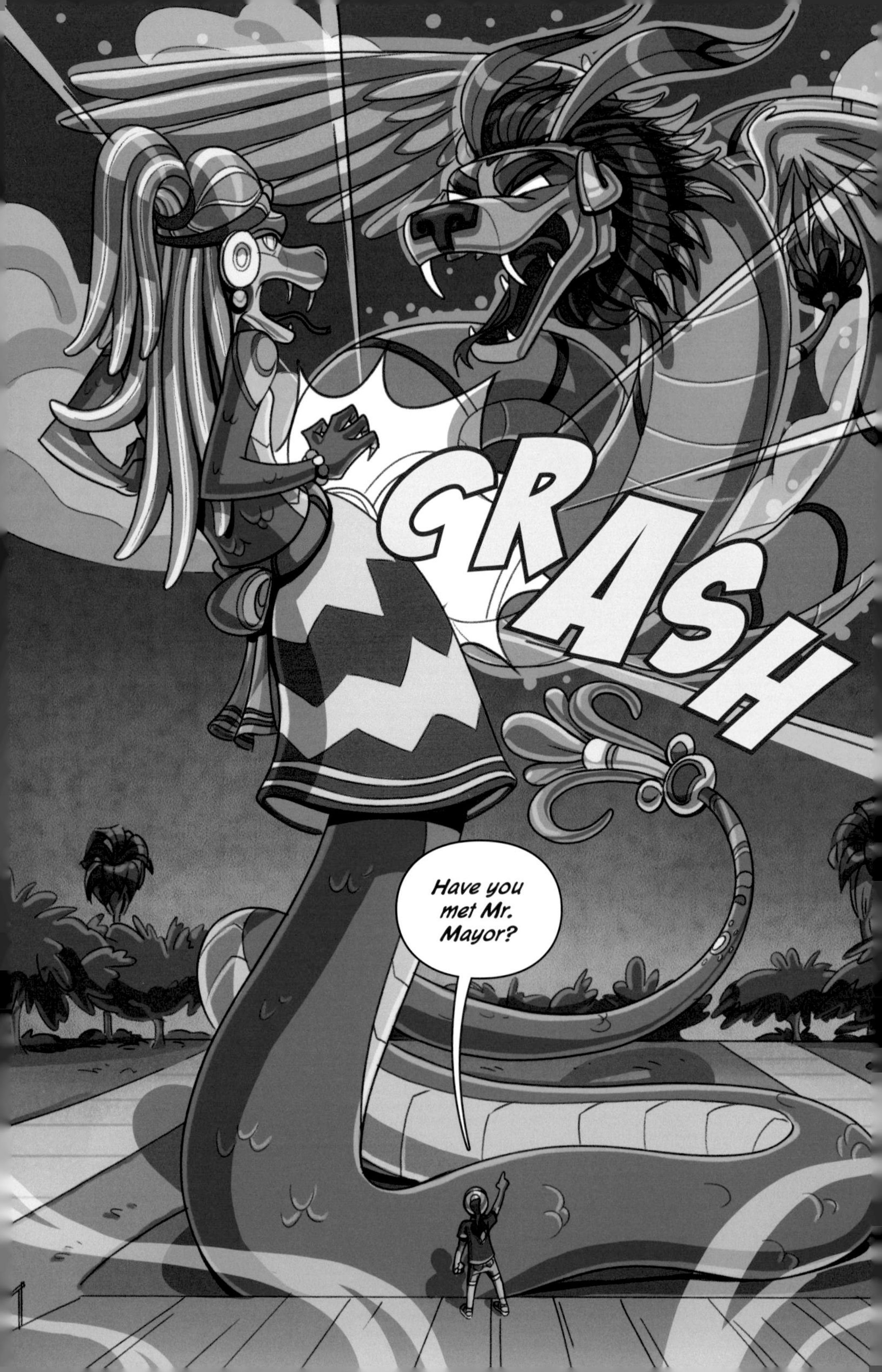
CRASH
Have you met Mr. Mayor?

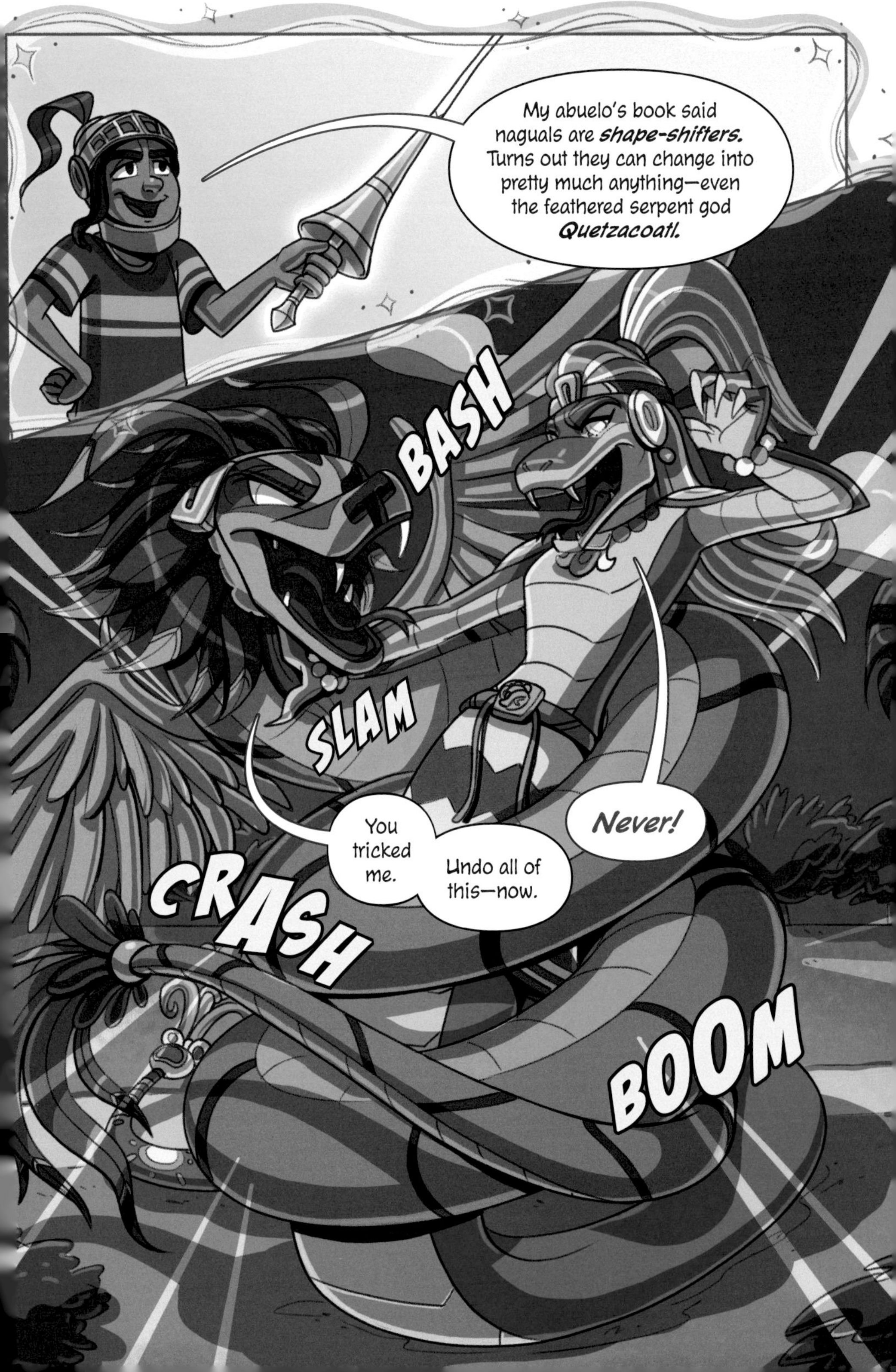
My abuelo's book said naguals are ***shape-shifters.*** Turns out they can change into pretty much anything—even the feathered serpent god ***Quetzacoatl.***
BASH
SLAM
You tricked me.
Undo all of this—now.
Never!
CRASH
BOOM

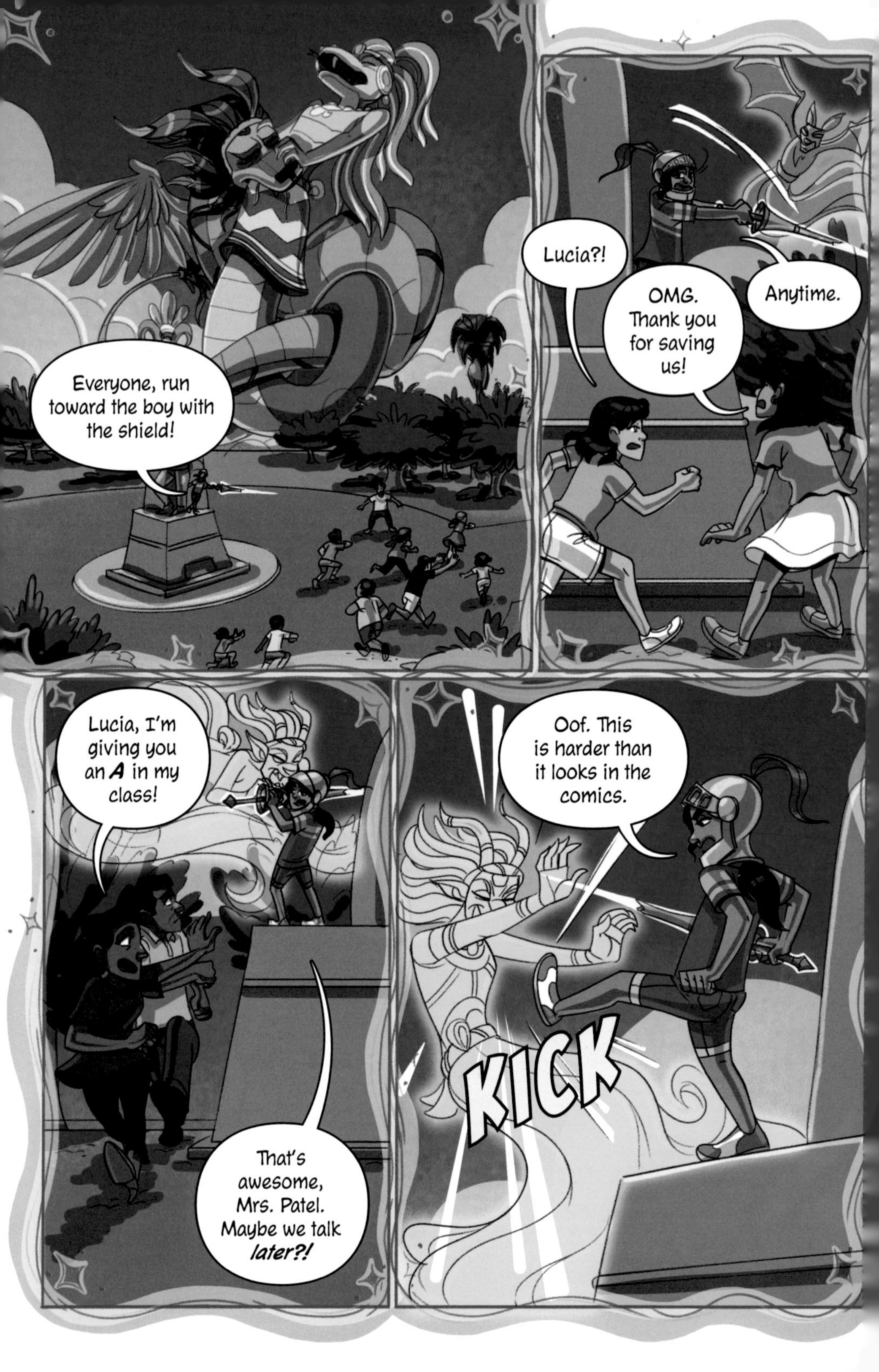
Everyone, run toward the boy with the shield!
Lucia?!
OMG. Thank you for saving us!
Anytime.
Lucia, I'm giving you an **A** in my class!
That's awesome, Mrs. Patel. Maybe we talk *later?!*
Oof. This is harder than it looks in the comics.
KICK

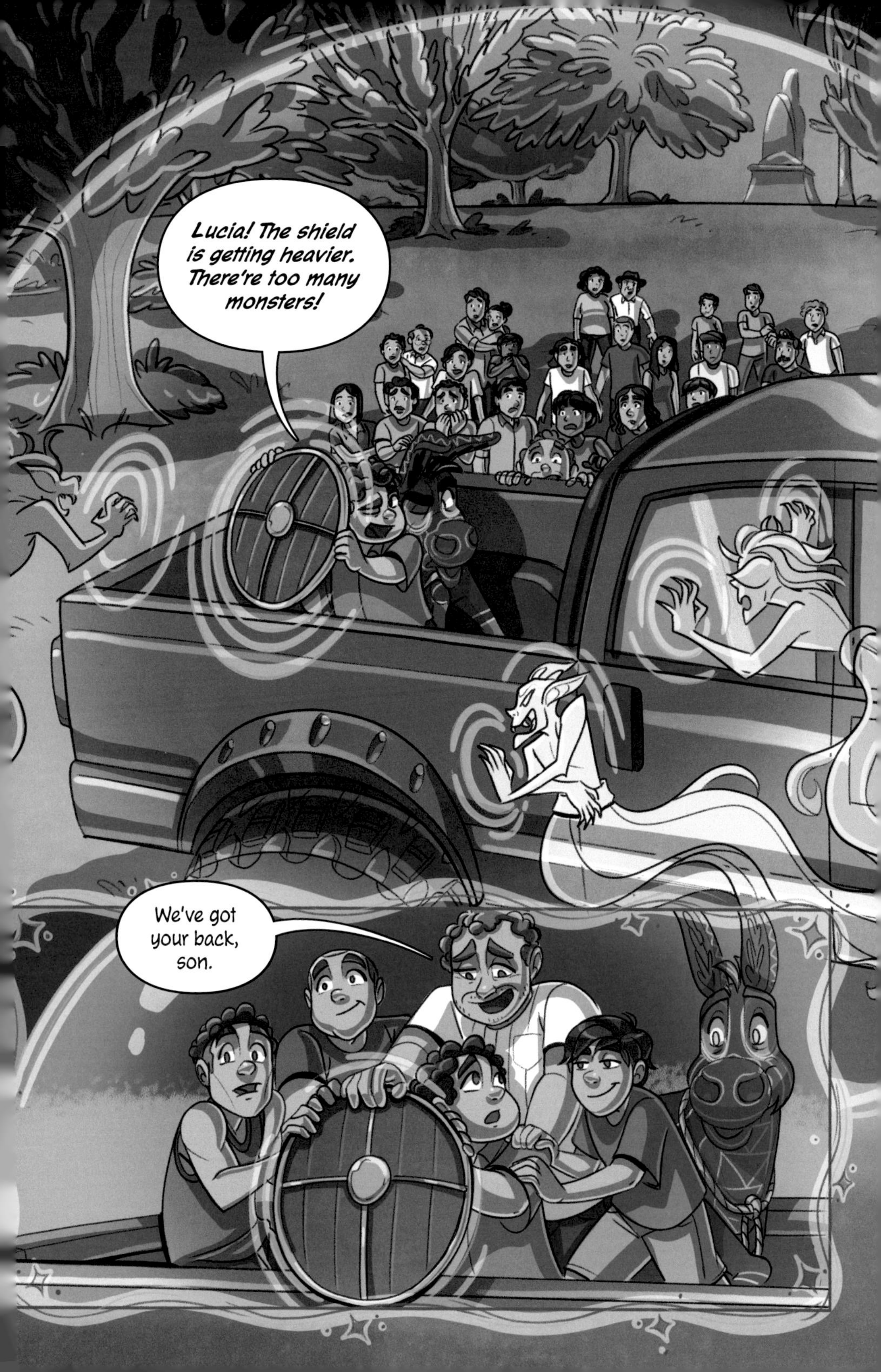
Lucia! The shield is getting heavier. There're too many monsters!
We've got your back, son.

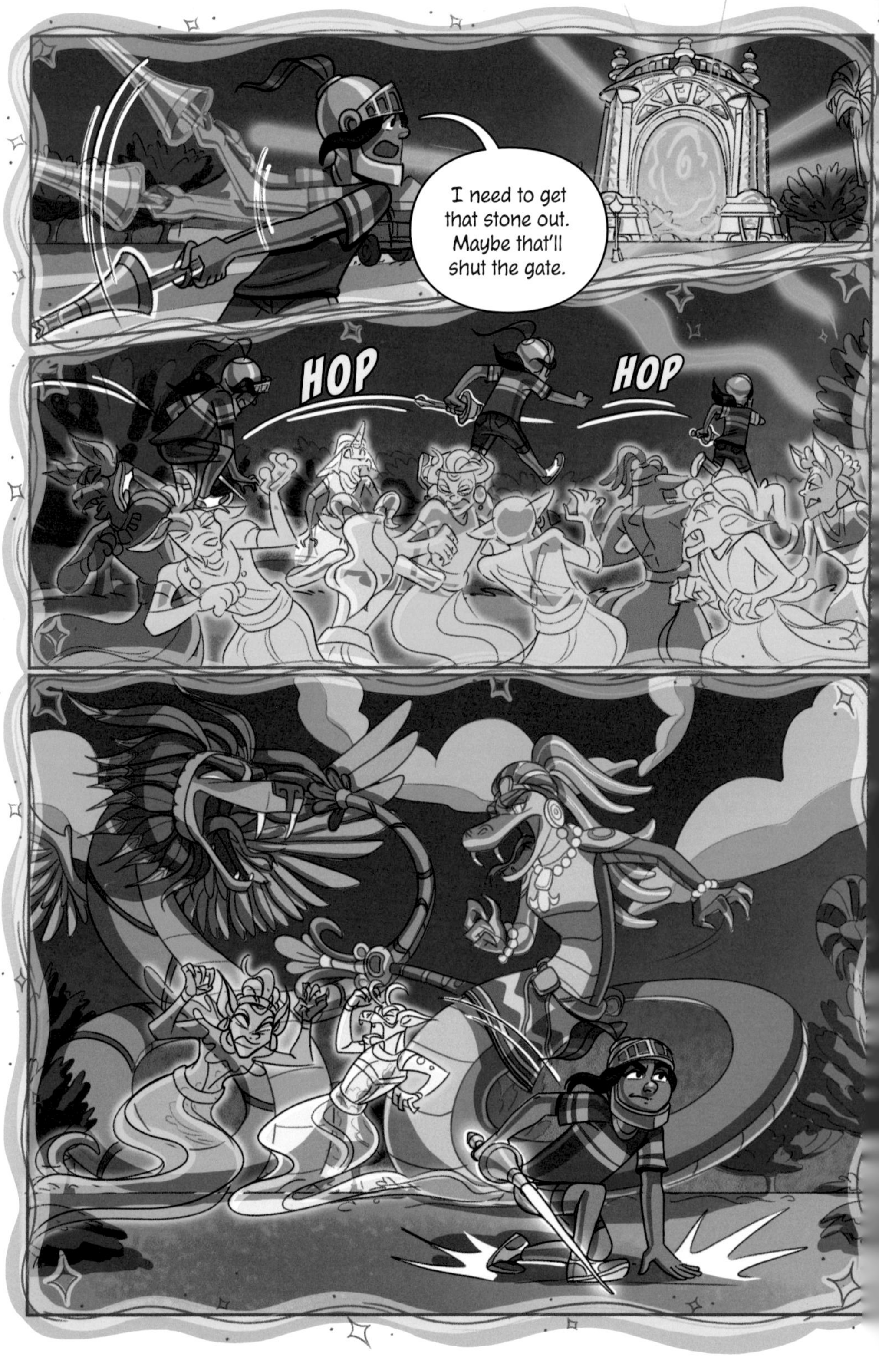
I need to get that stone out. Maybe that'll shut the gate.
HOP
HOP

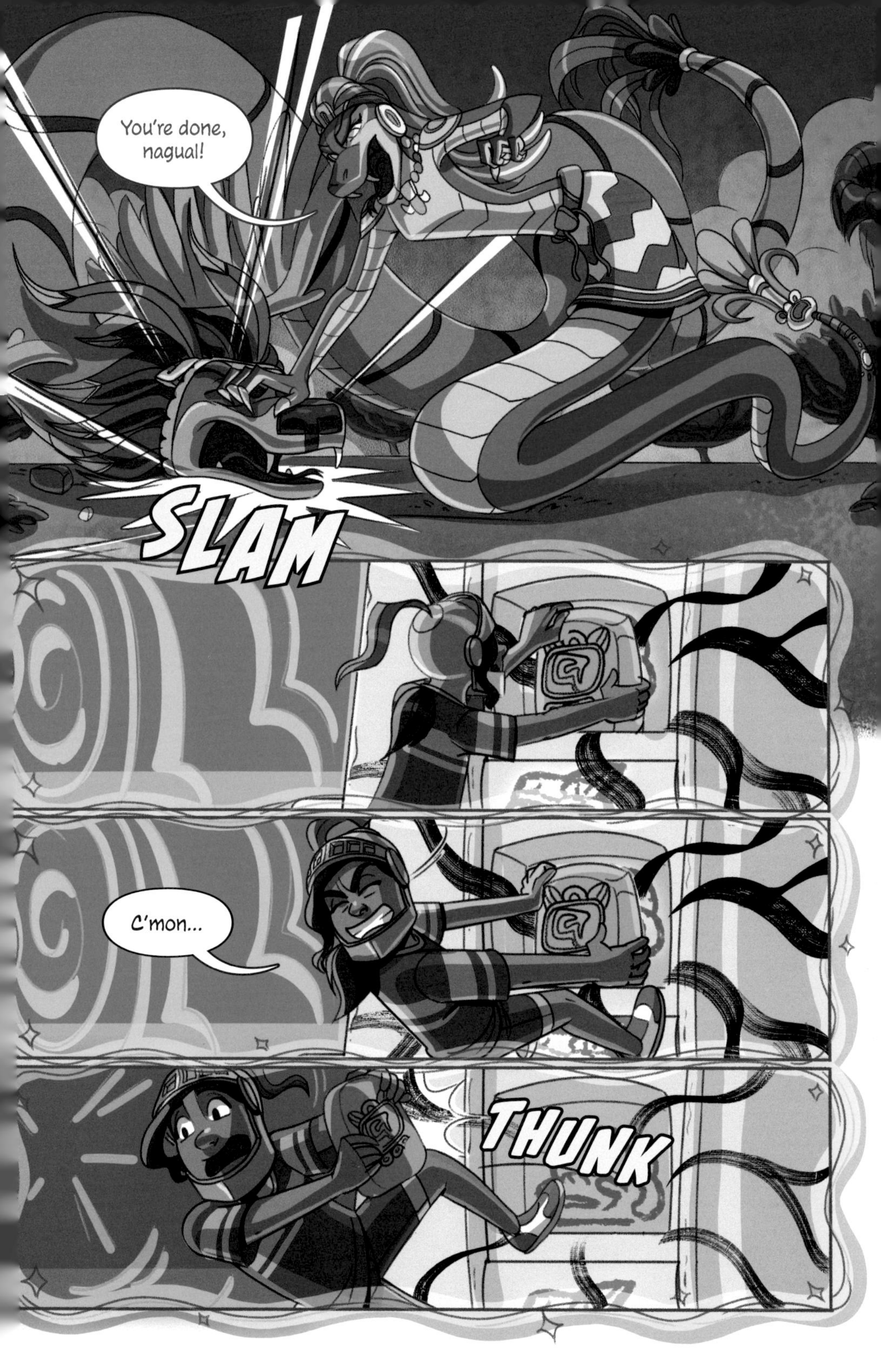
You're done, nagual!
SLAM
C'mon...
THUNK

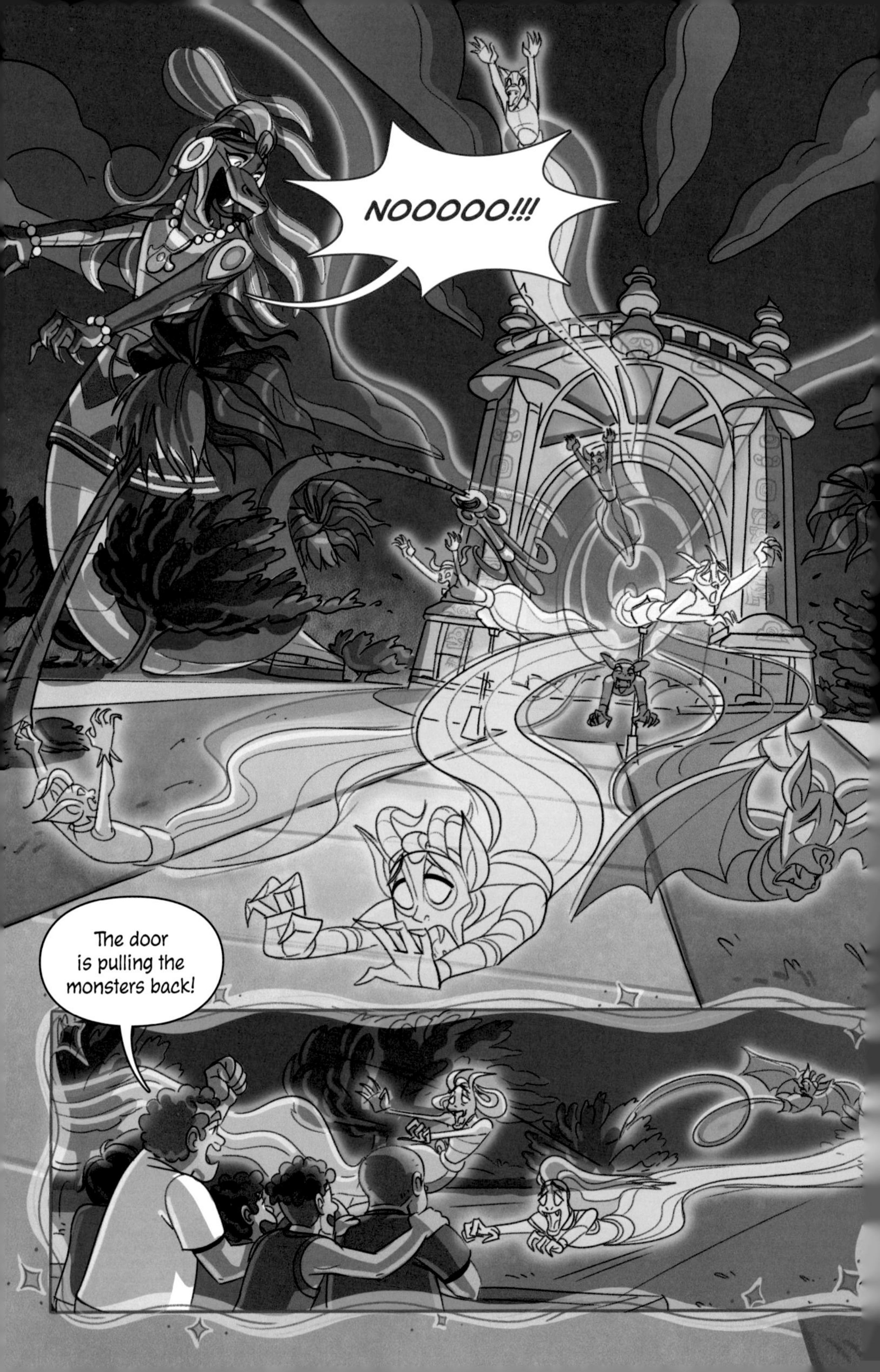
NOOOOO!!!
The door is pulling the monsters back!

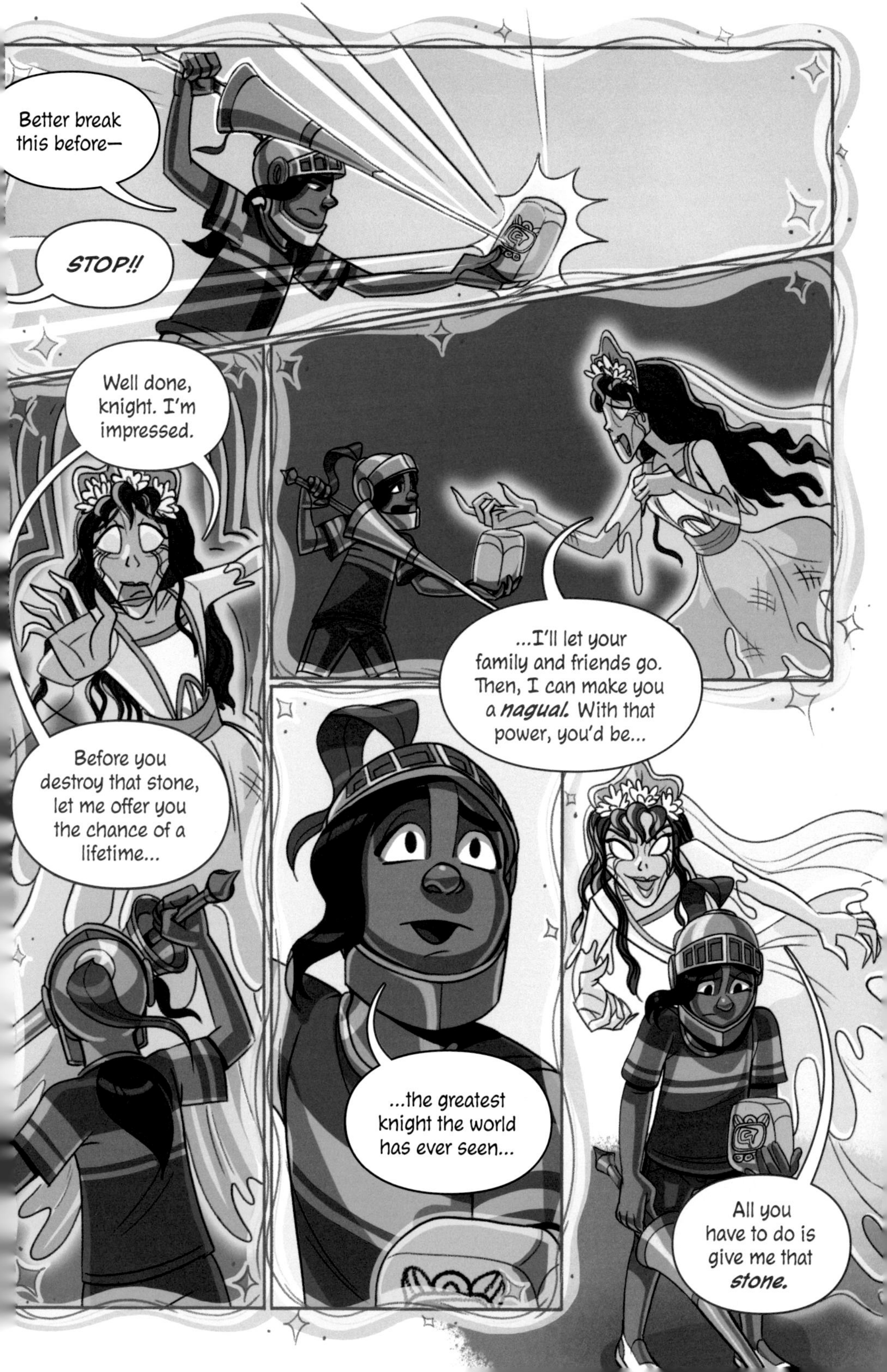
Better break this before—
STOP!!
Well done, knight. I'm impressed.
Before you destroy that stone, let me offer you the chance of a lifetime...
...I'll let your family and friends go. Then, I can make you a *nagual.* With that power, you'd be...
...the greatest knight the world has ever seen...
All you have to do is give me that *stone.*

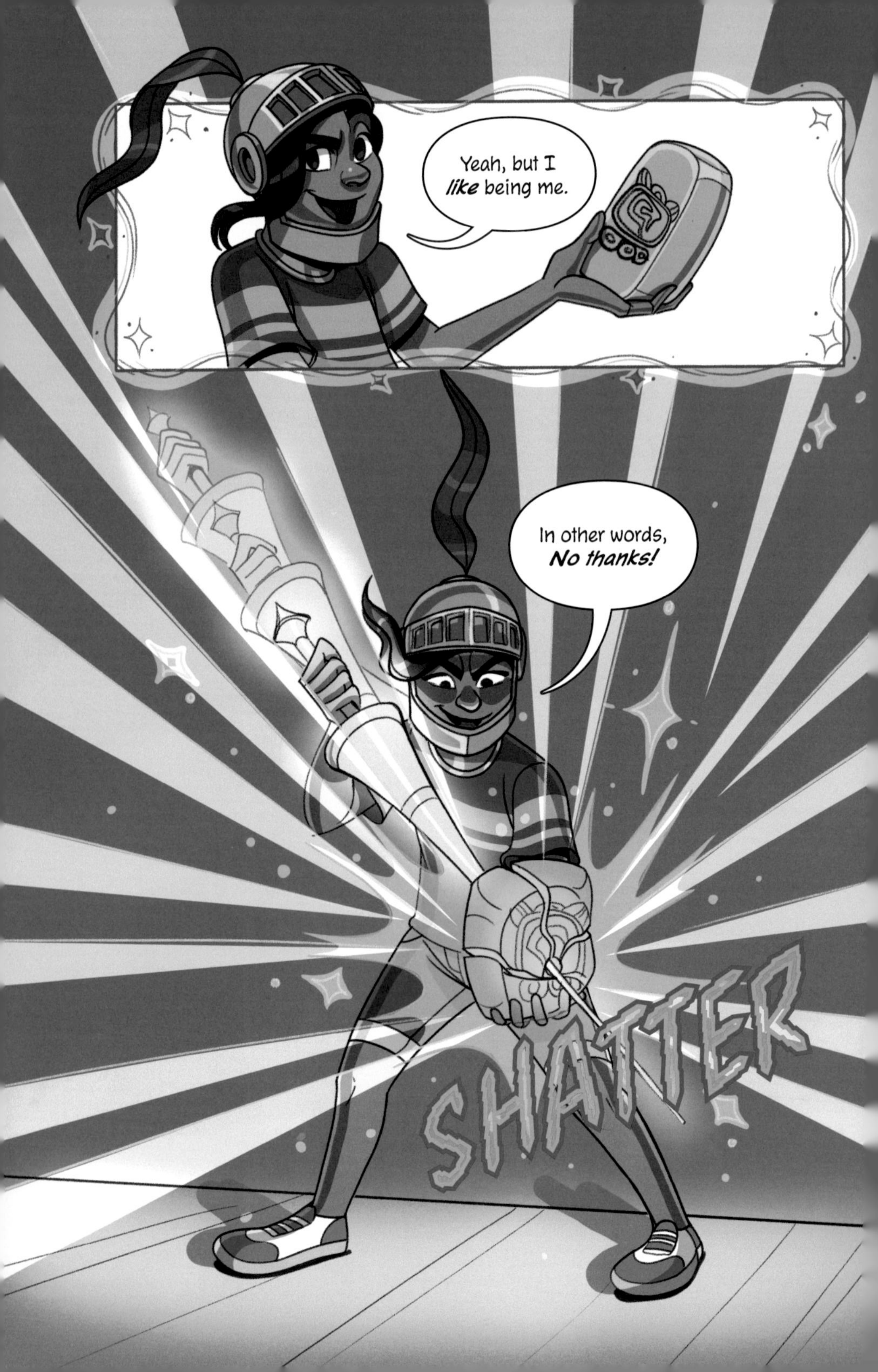
Yeah, but I *like* being me.
In other words, ***No thanks!***
SHATTER

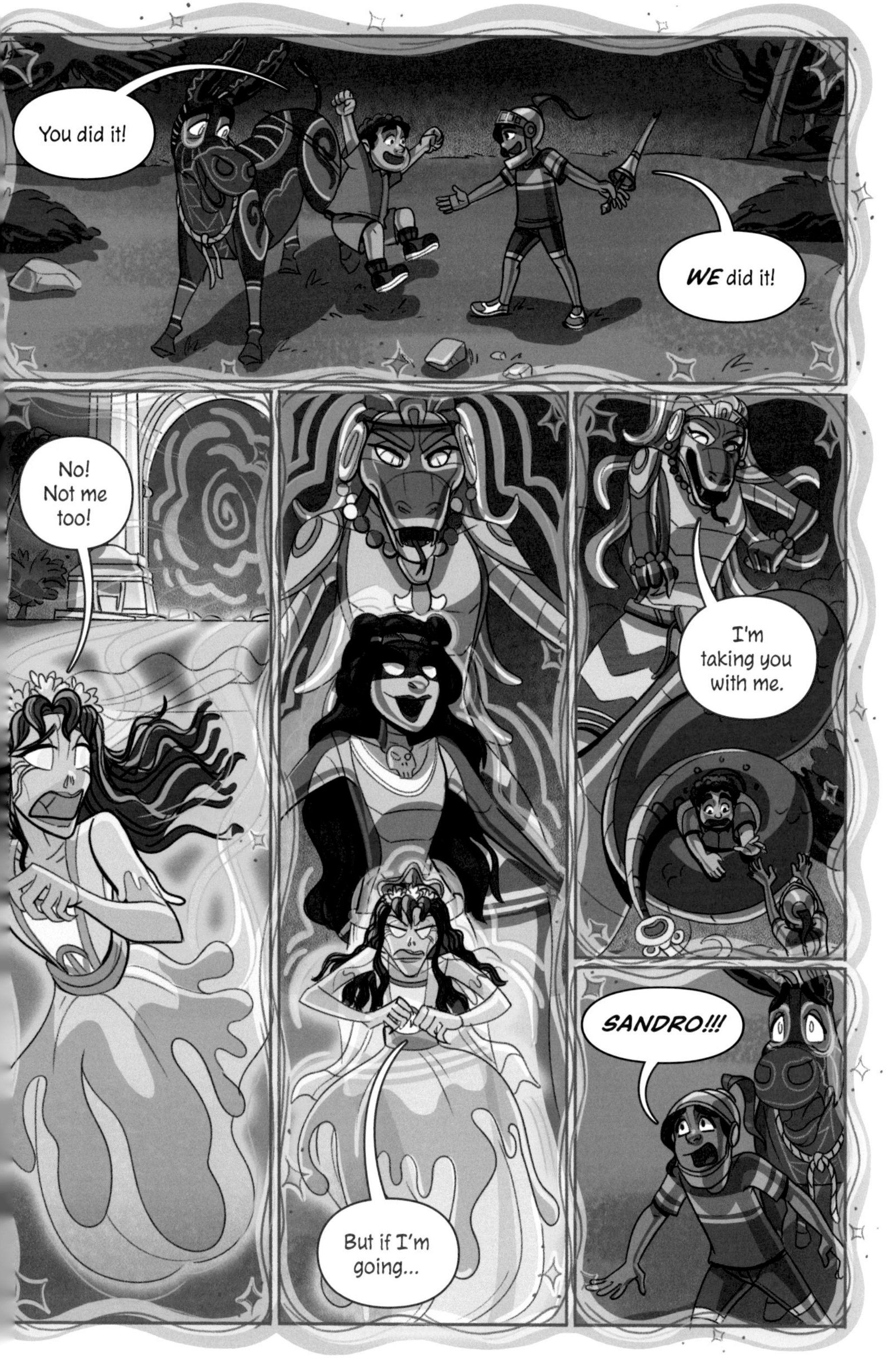
You did it!
WE did it!
No! Not me too!
But if I'm going...
I'm taking you with me.
SANDRO!!!

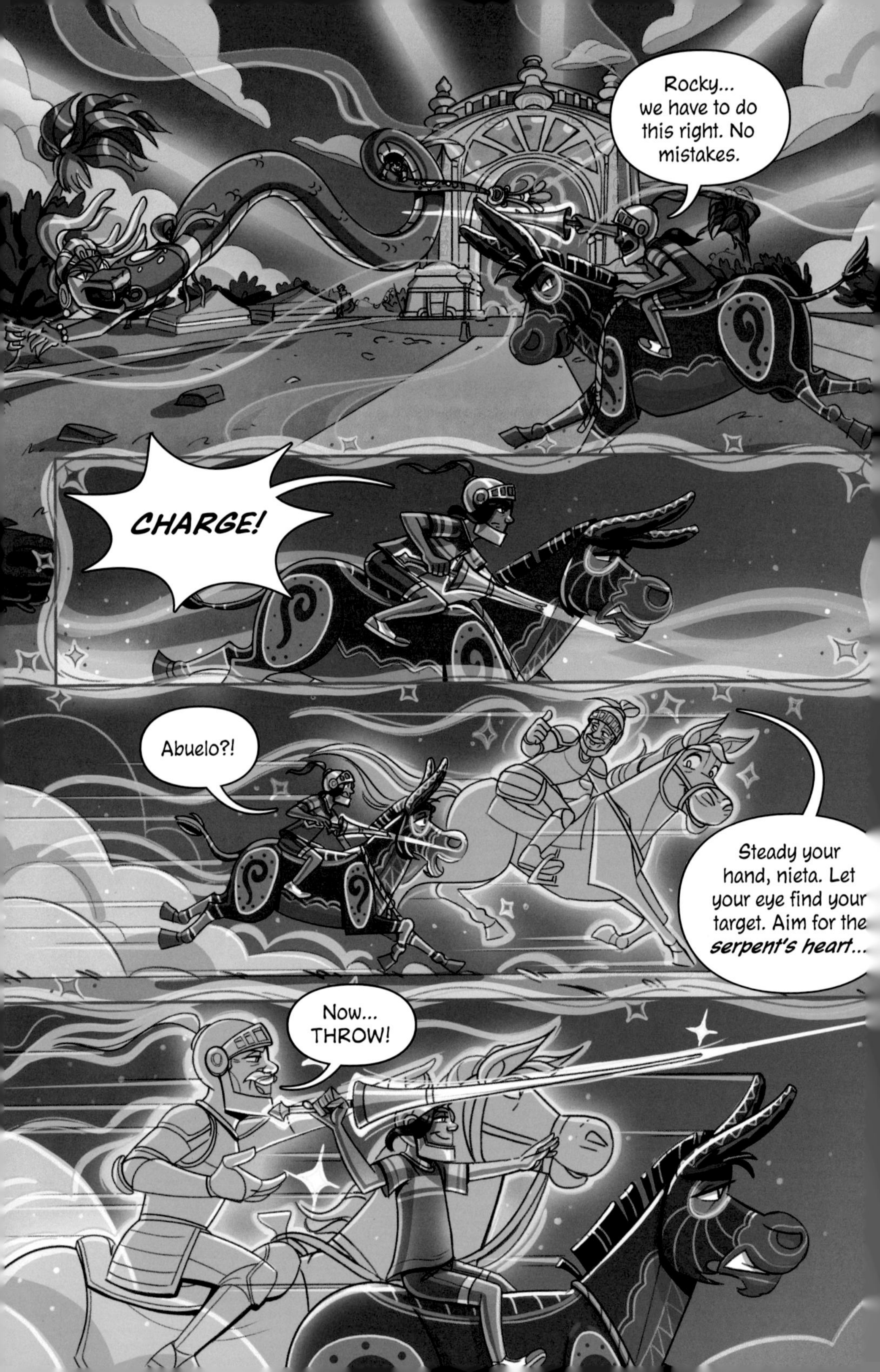
Rocky... we have to do this right. No mistakes.
CHARGE!
Abuelo?!
Steady your hand, nieta. Let your eye find your target. Aim for the *serpent's heart*...
Now... THROW!

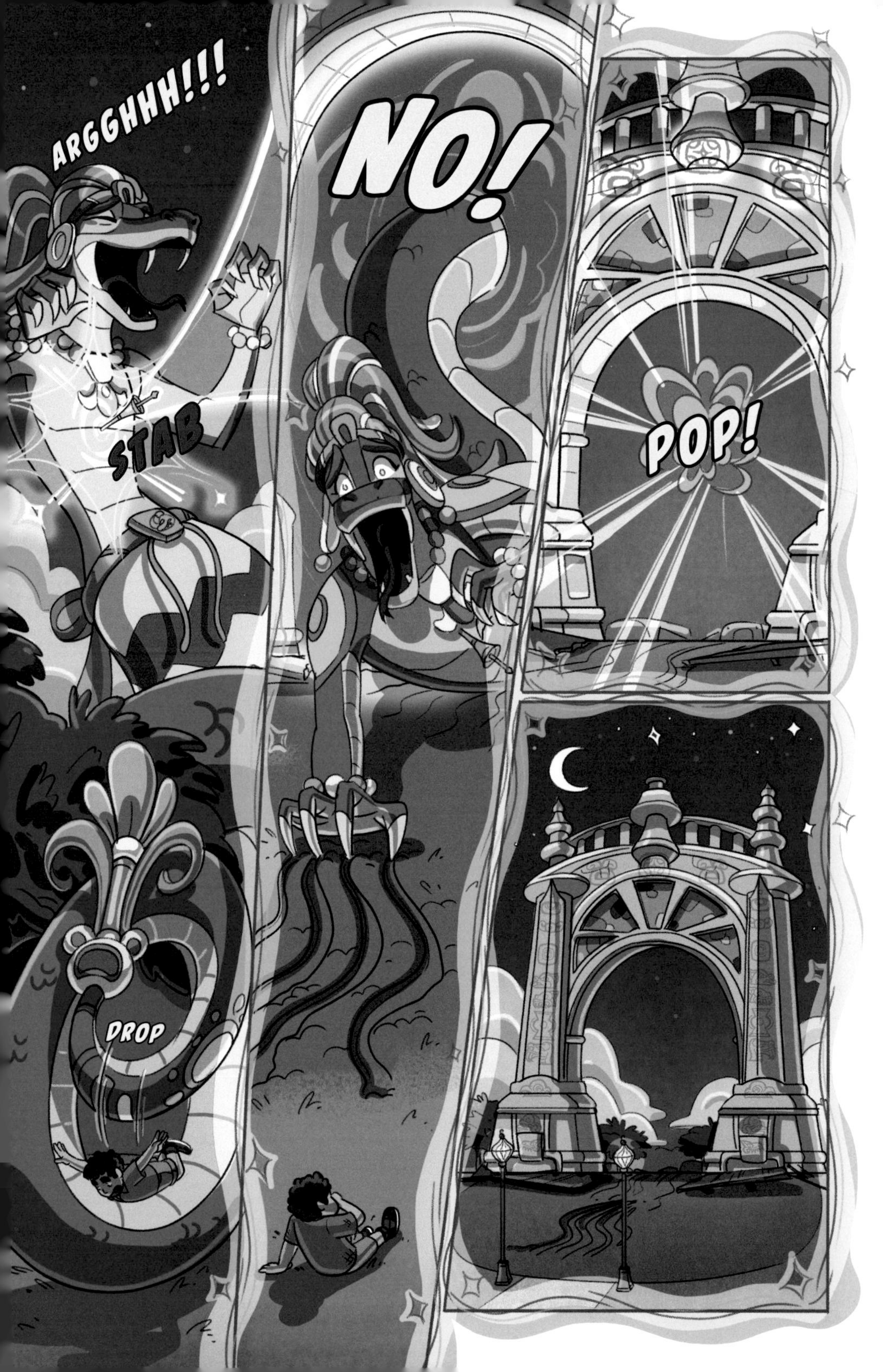
ARGGHHH!!!
STAB
DROP
NO!
POP!

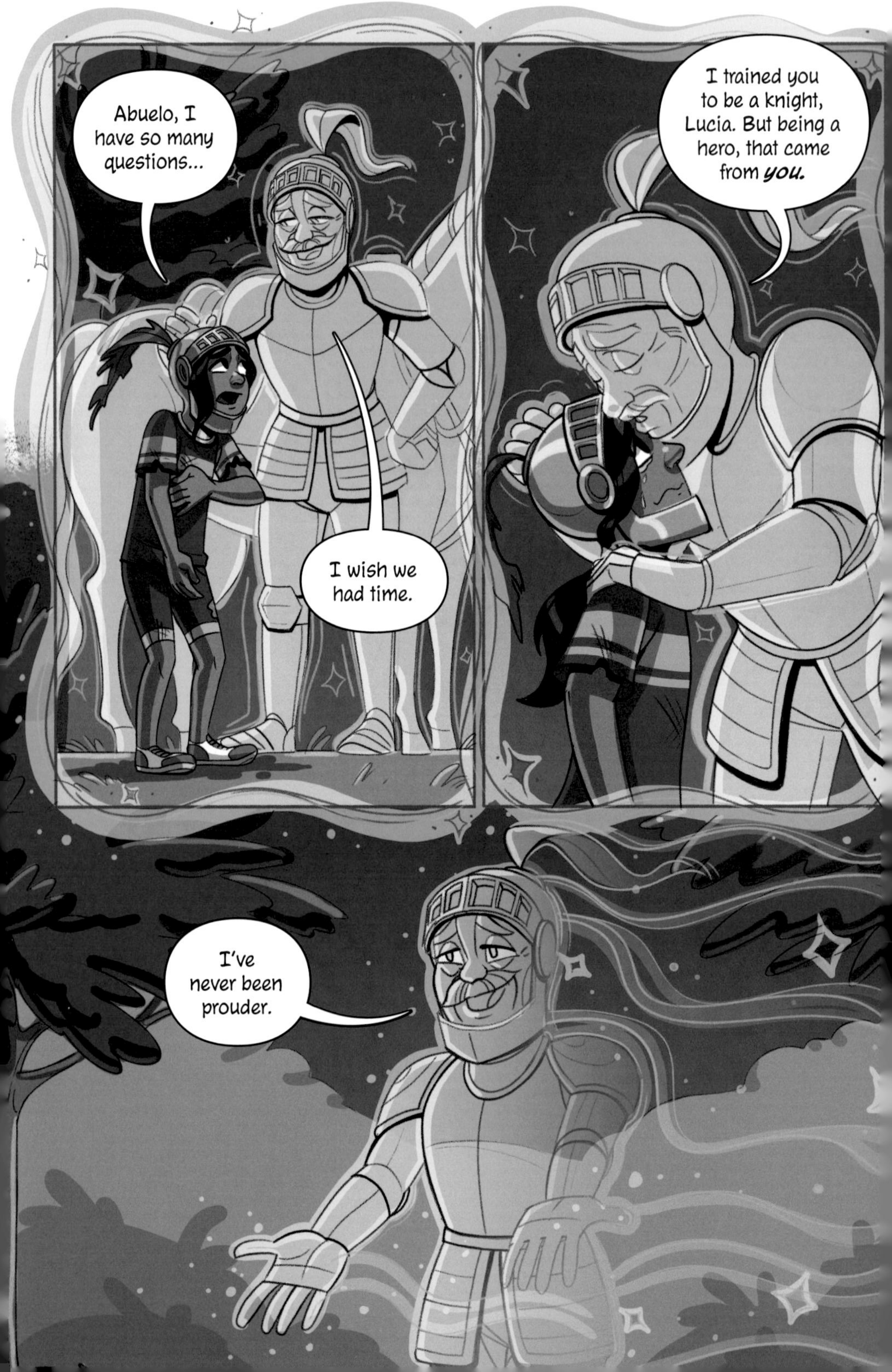
Abuelo, I have so many questions...
I wish we had time.
I trained you to be a knight, Lucia. But being a hero, that came from ***you.***
I've never been prouder.

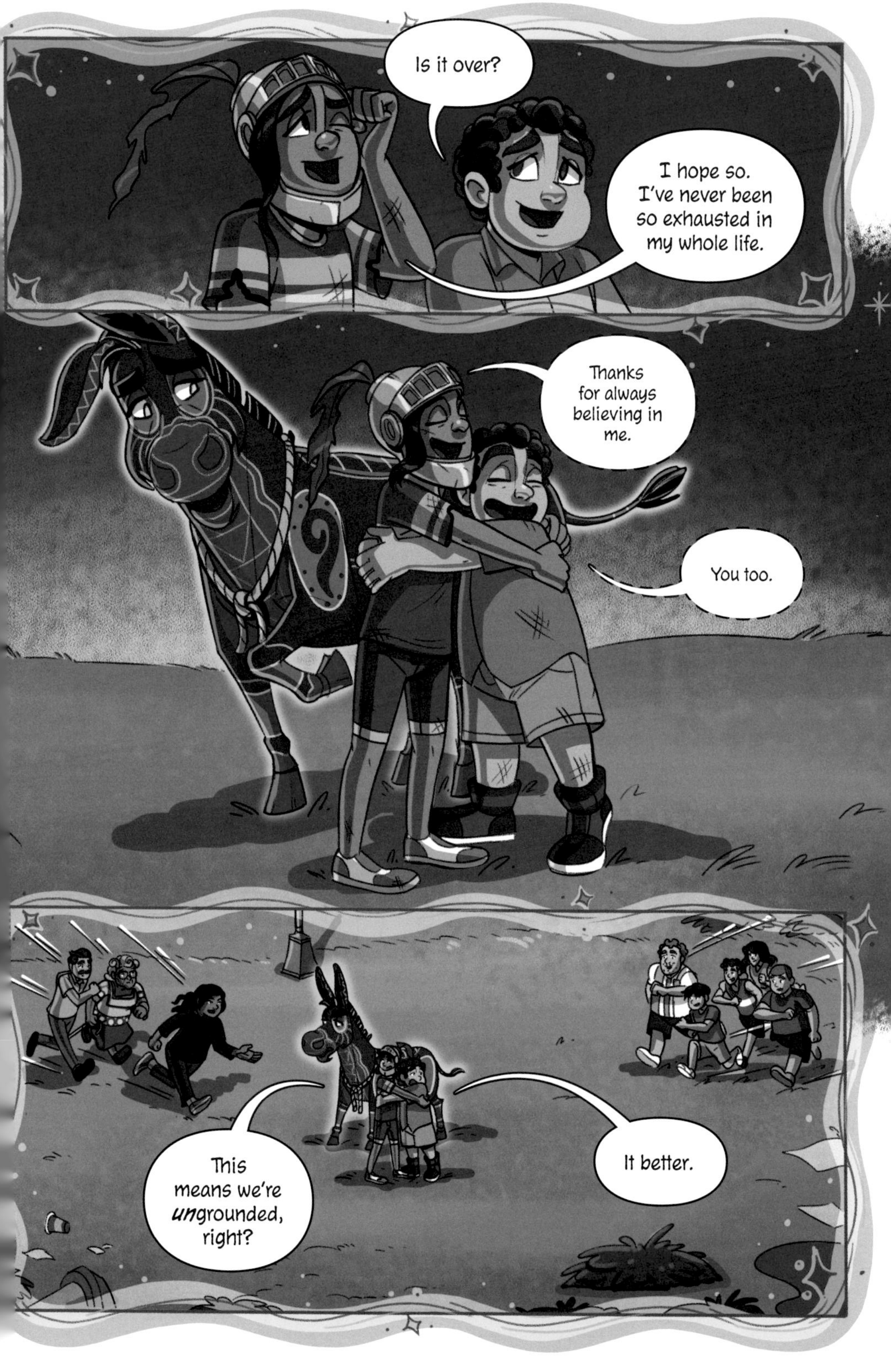
Is it over?
I hope so. I've never been so exhausted in my whole life.
Thanks for always believing in me.
You too.
This means we're *un*grounded, right?
It better.

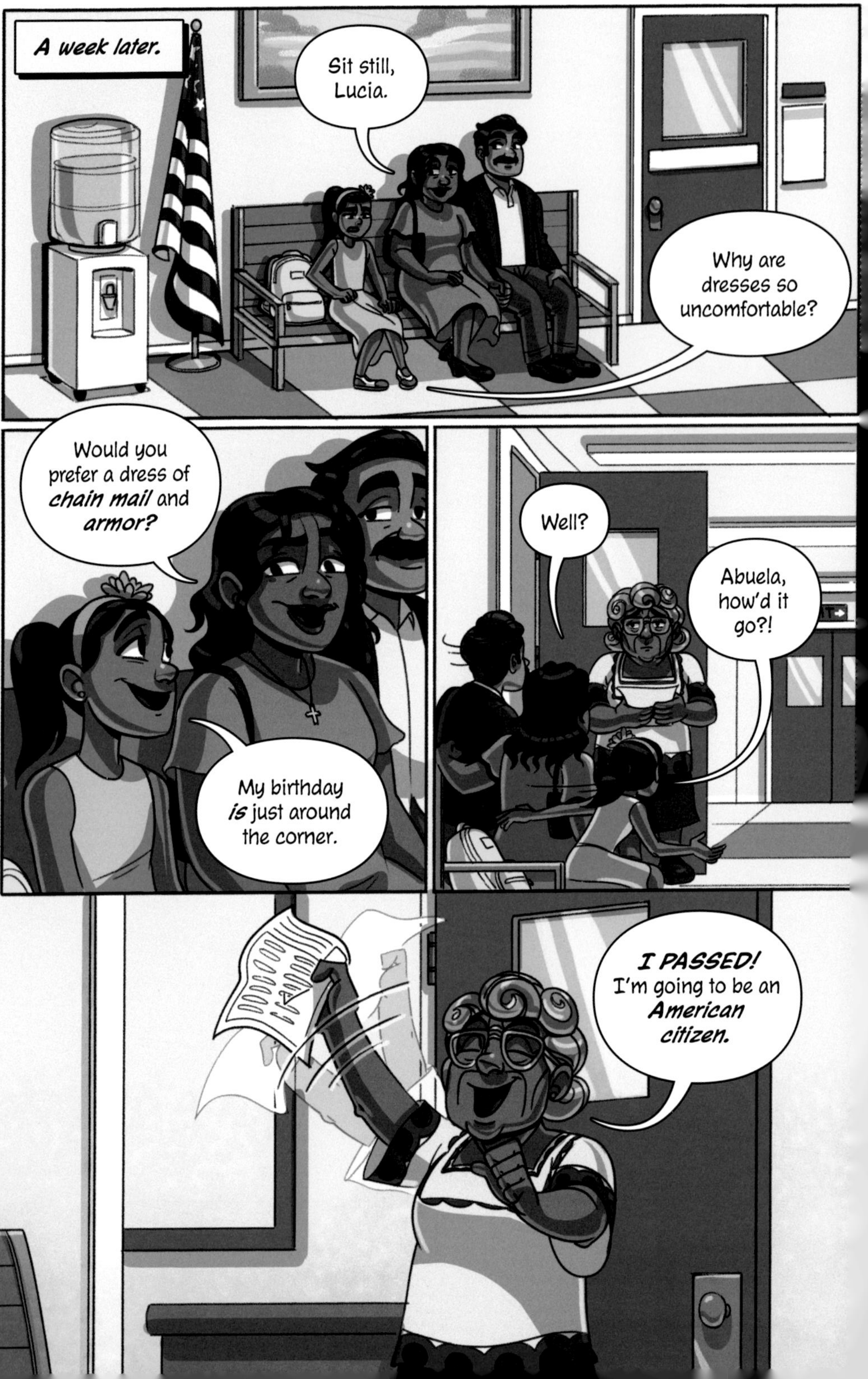
A week later.
Sit still, Lucia.
Why are dresses so uncomfortable?
Would you prefer a dress of *chain mail* and *armor?*
My birthday *is* just around the corner.
Well?
Abuela, how'd it go?!
I PASSED!
I'm going to be an ***American citizen.***

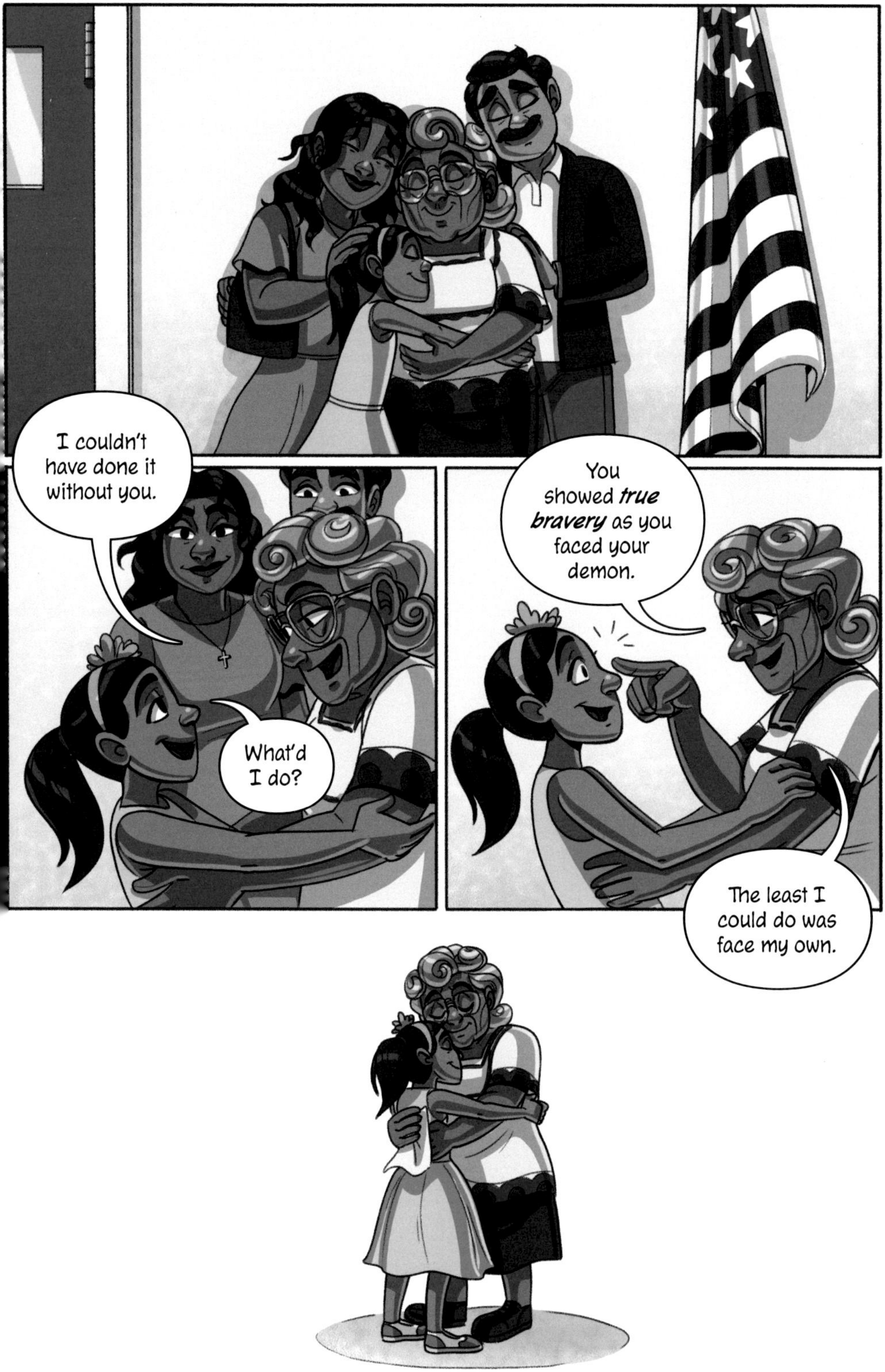

I couldn't have done it without you.
What'd I do?
You showed *true bravery* as you faced your demon.
The least I could do was face my own.

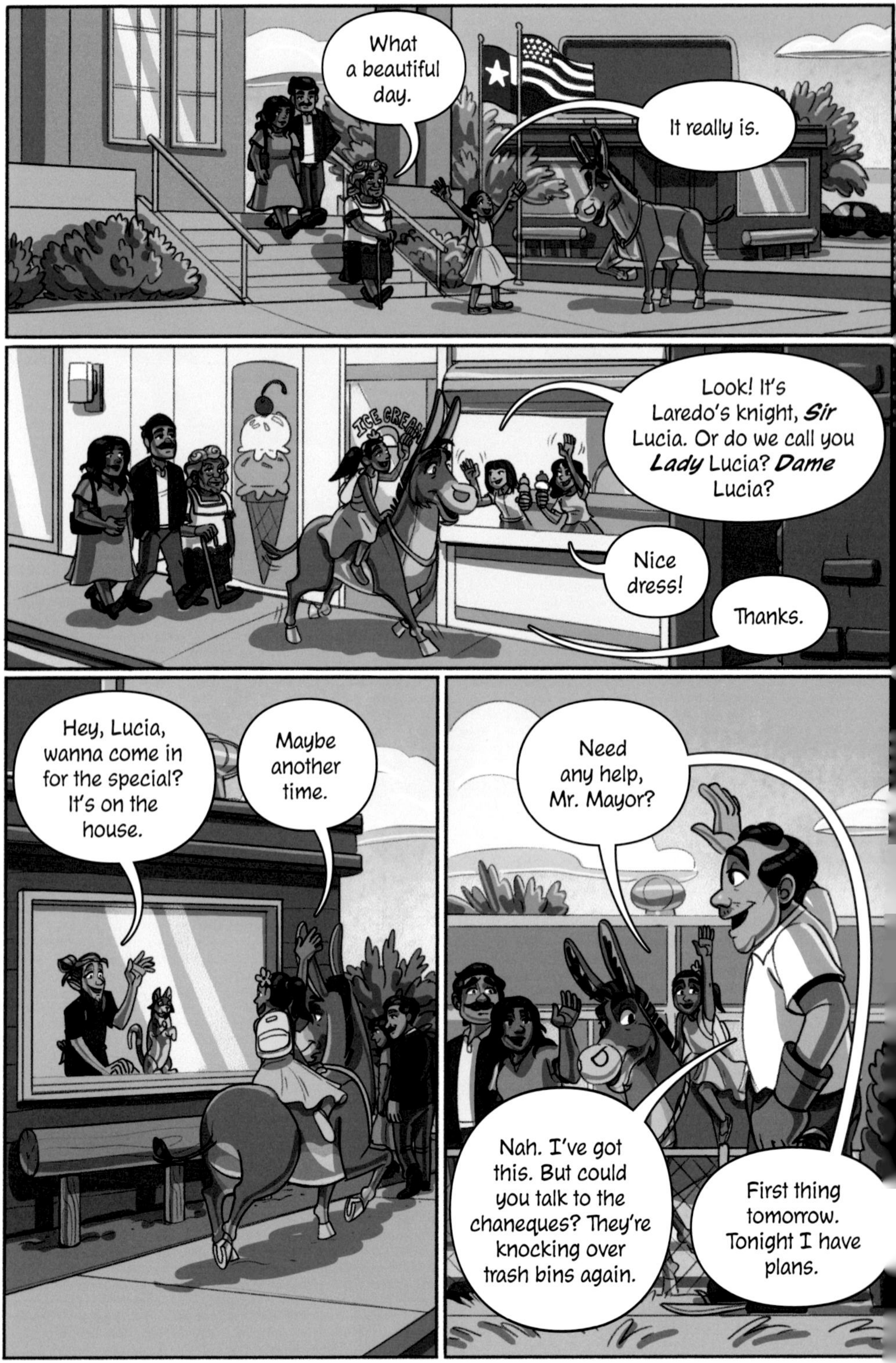
What a beautiful day.
It really is.
Look! It's Laredo's knight, *Sir* Lucia. Or do we call you *Lady* Lucia? *Dame* Lucia?
Nice dress!
Thanks.
Hey, Lucia, wanna come in for the special? It's on the house.
Maybe another time.
ICE CREAM
Need any help, Mr. Mayor?
Nah. I've got this. But could you talk to the chaneques? They're knocking over trash bins again.
First thing tomorrow. Tonight I have plans.

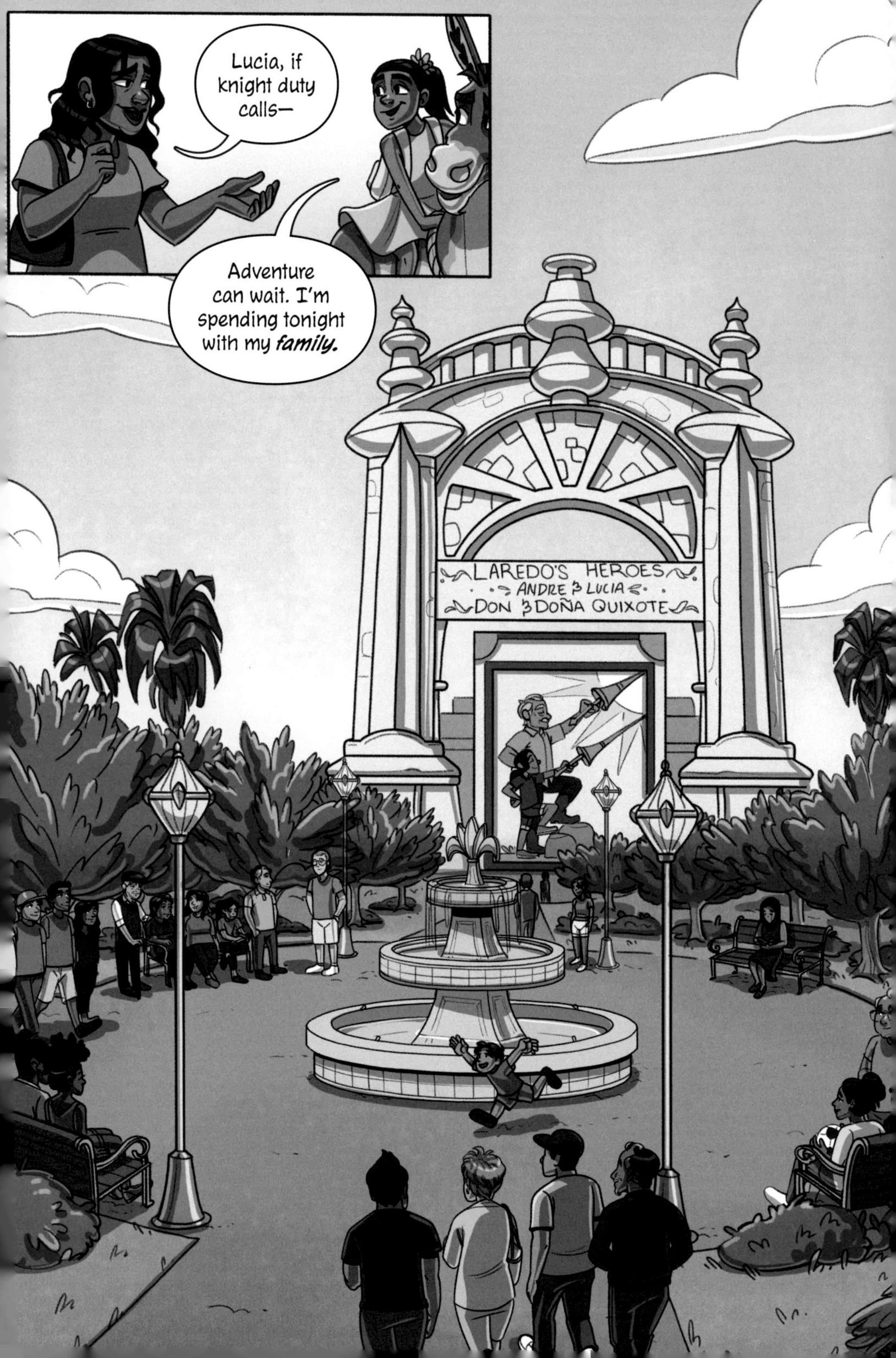
Lucia, if knight duty calls—
Adventure can wait. I'm spending tonight with my *family.*
LAREDO'S HEROES
ANDRE & LUCIA
DON & DOÑA QUIXOTE

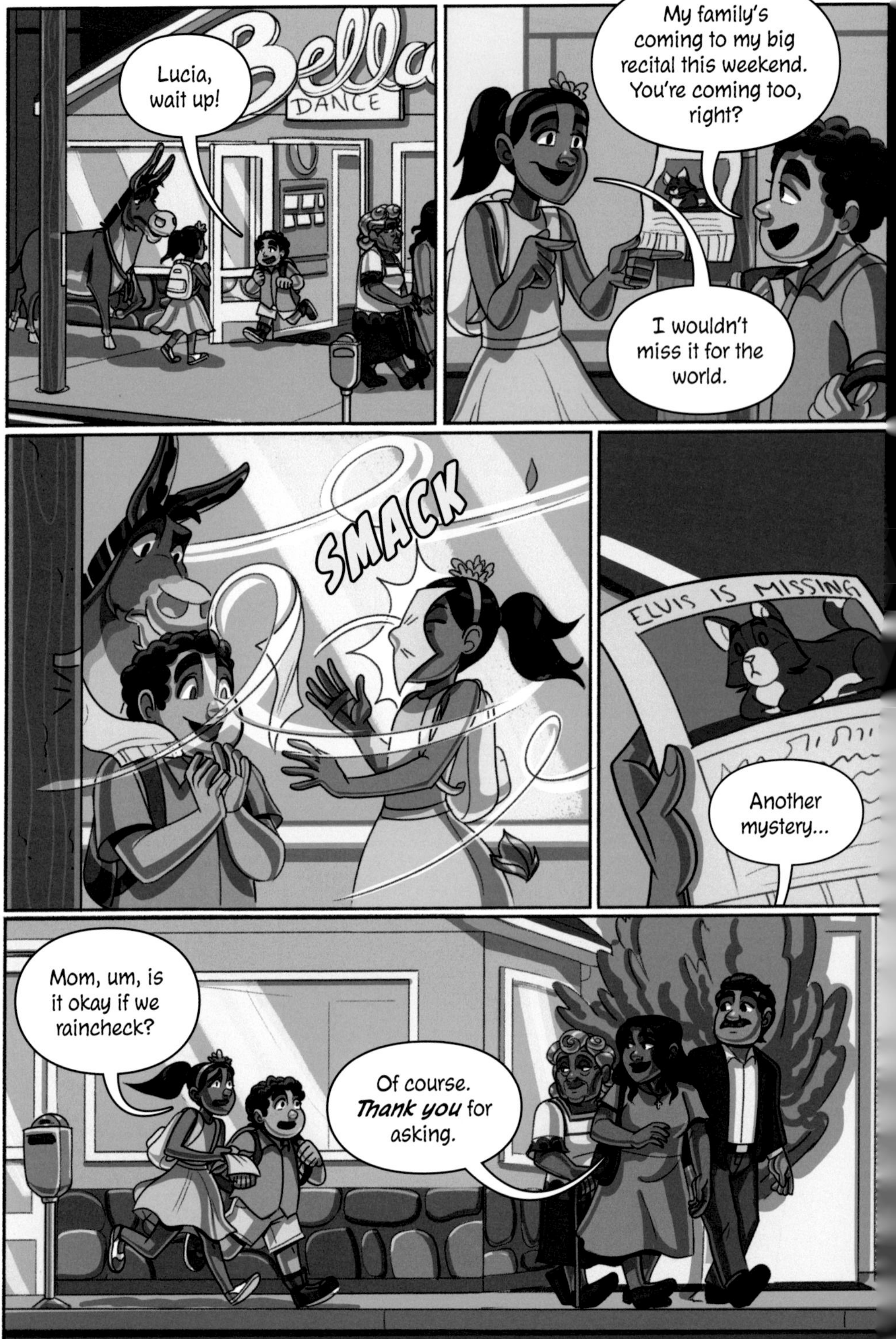
Bella
DANCE
Lucia, wait up!
My family's coming to my big recital this weekend. You're coming too, right?
I wouldn't miss it for the world.
SMACK
ELVIS IS MISSING
Another mystery...
Mom, um, is it okay if we raincheck?
Of course. *Thank you* for asking.

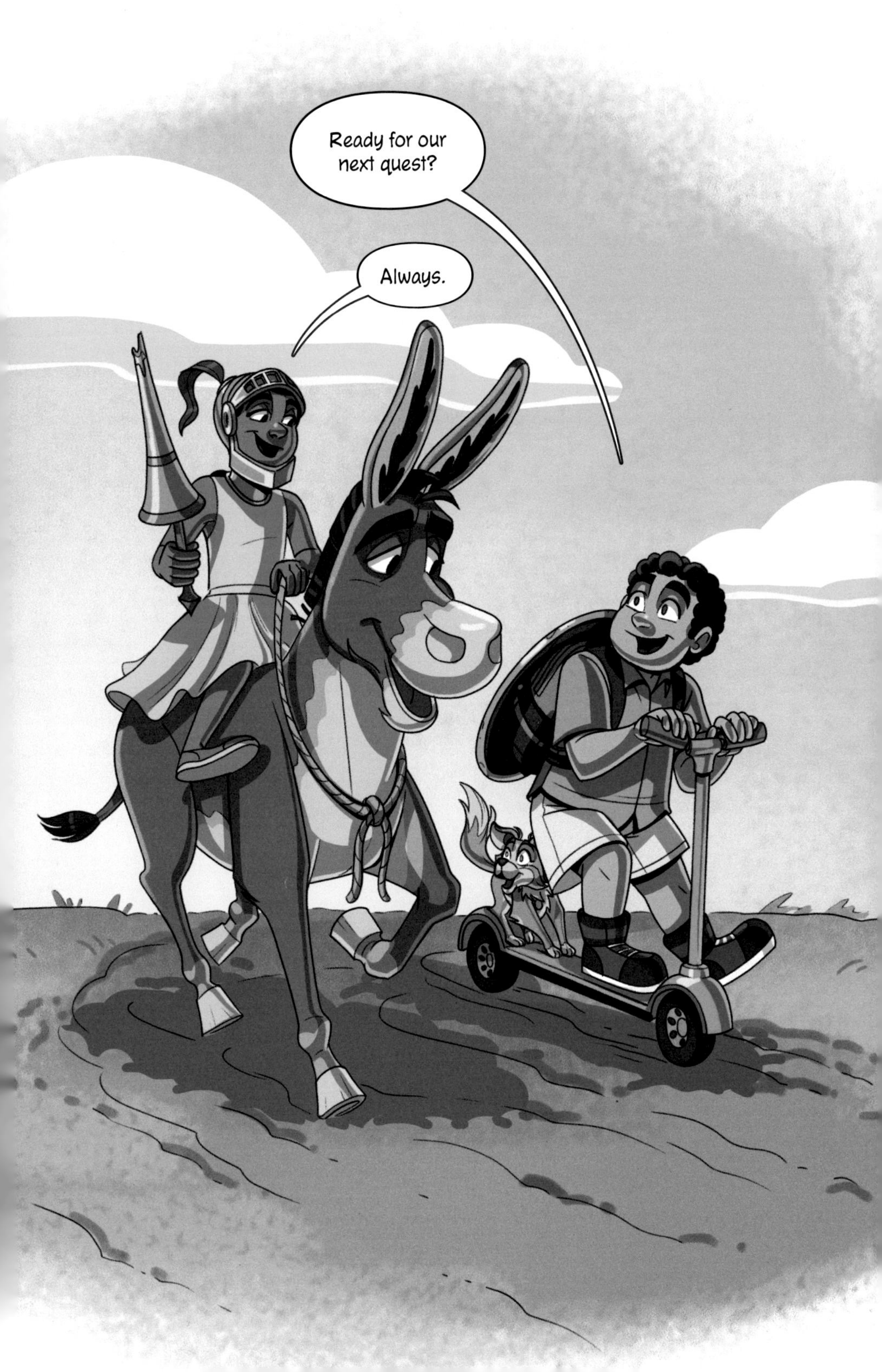
Ready for our next quest?
Always.

Author's Note

When I was a boy, I was obsessed with Saturday morning cartoon heroes. I loved *He-Man*, *Spider-Man and his Amazing Friends*, and *The Adventures of Don Coyote and Sancho Panda*, which made me laugh so hard my sides would hurt. I thought it was just a regular cartoon—until my abuela told me about its secret origin.

"Oh, mijo," Abuela said. "*Don Quixote* is not new. Your cartoon is based on the most important book of the Spanish Golden Age." I had no idea what she was talking about. So Abuela took me to the library. There was no internet back then, so we thumbed through the gold-trimmed pages of the D encyclopedia until Abuela found the entry. In it, I learned that the coyote and panda adventurers on my TV were, in fact, born four hundred years ago in a novel about a man who loses his mind after reading too many tales about being a heroic knight. My young mind was blown—and excited to learn about other retellings.

Now, as an adult and a writer, I find myself drawn to reimagining classic stories with a modern sensibility and fantastical graphic novel twists. Not only because I love revisiting my childhood favorites but because I find there's something really cool about leading readers to discover the secret origins of old stories told in a new light. And even better? I get to introduce readers to my favorite *monstruos, fantasmas, y cucuys*.

My secret origin is less exciting: I was born and raised in Texas in a world that frowned upon being Latinx. Growing up, I never saw Mexican heroes in TV, movies, and books. So as a writer, I want to create stories and characters that represent the best parts of me—including my own Hispanic heritage that I'm discovering later in life. After all, Abuela is still my hero and I've always strived to make her proud. And what better way to do so than writing a book all about a young hero and the grandmother whose love and support makes her strong? In a way, my own abuela is like Peter Parker's spider—she gave me my powers by always encouraging me to write and read. *Hrmph.* Maybe my secret origin is more exciting than I thought...but I guess that's up to you. ☺

Me and Abuela,
circa 1989, Abilene, Texas

—Rex Ogle (aka Rey Terciero)

Notes about the Original Story

The author of *Don Quixote*, Miguel de Cervantes Saavedra, was born around 1547 and passed away in 1616. Though much of his life was spent in poverty, he had a life full of rich experience. He worked in the household of a Catholic cardinal in Rome, enlisted in the Spanish navy, and was badly wounded in a battle but continued serving as a soldier until he was captured by pirates. After five years as a captive, he was eventually ransomed and returned to Spain where he worked as a tax collector while he wrote in his spare time.

His best known work was *El ingenioso hidalgo Don Quijote de la Mancha (The Ingenious Gentleman Don Quixote of La Mancha)*. Published in two parts in 1605 and 1615, some literary critics consider it to be the first modern novel in Western literature. While it's often labeled a comedy, others view it as social commentary on the world at the time. Either way, the book had a major influence on books that came later, as shown by direct references in Alexandre Dumas's *The Three Musketeers* and Mark Twain's *Adventures of Huckleberry Finn*.

Don Quixote and Sancho Panza by Cesare Augusto Detti

Henry Holt and Company, Publishers since 1866
Henry Holt® is a registered trademark of Macmillan Publishing Group, LLC
120 Broadway, New York, NY 10271 • mackids.com

Our books may be purchased in bulk for promotional, educational, or business use.
Please contact your local bookseller or the Macmillan Corporate
and Premium Sales Department at (800) 221-7945 ext. 5442
or by email at MacmillanSpecialMarkets@macmillan.com.

Library of Congress Control Number: 2022920578

First edition, 2023
Edited by Brian Geffen
Cover design by Sharismar Rodriguez and Marissa Asuncion
Interior book design by Marissa Asuncion and Cindy De La Cruz
Art direction by Sharismar Rodriguez
Production editing by Mia Moran
Color by Monica Magaña
Lettering by Joamette Gil
Printed in China by RR Donnelley Asia Printing Solutions Ltd.,
Dongguan City, Guangdong Province

ISBN 978-1-250-79547-2 (hardcover)
1 3 5 7 9 10 8 6 4 2

ISBN 978-1-250-79552-6 (paperback)
1 3 5 7 9 10 8 6 4 2

REY TERCIERO, also known as Rex Ogle, has written and edited hundreds of books and comics for children and young adults. He is a Latinx writer who has always been drawn to classic stories and enjoys retelling them for a contemporary audience. Born and raised (mostly) in Texas, Rey now lives in Los Angeles, where he writes full-time—that is, when he's not hiking with his dog, Toby, playing Mario Kart with friends, or reading.

MONICA M. MAGAÑA is an illustrator from Los Angeles who has worked in advertising, film, animation, and TTRPGs. She enjoys drawing fantastical characters, reading whimsical stories, and pushing for bold colors. With *Doña Quixote* being her first foray into publishing, she has found a new love in drawing comics. Monica now lives in Vancouver, British Columbia, with her husband, Jon, drawing, drinking as much tea as possible, checking her Animal Crossing island, and playing Dungeons & Dragons with friends.